The Founding of the Commonwealth

BOOKS BY ALAN DEAN FOSTER

Cachalot
Cat-A-Lyst
Cyber Way
Into the Out Of
Kingdoms of Light
The Man Who Used the Universe
Midworld
Nor Crystal Tears
Parallelities
To the Vanishing Point

The Adventures of Flinx

For Love of Mother-Not
The Tar-Aiym Krang
Orphan Star
The End of the Matter
Bloodhype
Flinx in Flux
Mid-Flinx
The Howling Stones
Reunion

The Spellsinger Sequence

Spellsinger
The Hour of the Gate
The Day of the Dissonance
The Moment of the Magician
The Path of the Perambulator
The Time of the Transference

Journeys of the Catechist

Carnivores of Light and Darkness
Into the Thinking Kingdoms
A Triumph of Souls

The Damned

A Call to Arms
The False Mirror
The Spoils of War

The Icerigger Trilogy

Icerigger
Mission to Moulokin
The Deluge Drivers

The Founding of the Commonwealth

Phylogenesis
Dirge
Diuturnity's Dawn

ALAN DEAN FOSTER

SFBC
SCIENCE
FICTION

Published by arrangement with
The Ballantine Publishing Group
A Division of Random House, Inc.
1540 Broadway
New York, New York 10036

Visit our website at *www.sfbc.com*
Visit Del Rey's website at *www.delreydigital.com*

ISBN 0-7394-2616-8

PRINTED IN THE UNITED STATES OF AMERICA

The Founding of the Commonwealth

Contents

PHYLOGENESIS

For Michael Goodwin and Robert Teague,
First citizens of the Commonwealth.

PROLOGUE

Things have a way of working out, if not always as planned. So it was with the Amalgamation that marked the establishment of the sociopolitical organization that came to be known as the Humanx Commonwealth. Contact having been established and maintained for some sixteen years, it was assumed by those advising both of the hesitant, uncertain species that procession to second-stage contact would take place within a predesignated time frame and would involve the implementation of carefully considered procedures, intricately designed programs, and closely scrutinized agendas.

That it did not happen this way was no fault of those charged with implementing the voluminously compiled and mutually agreed-upon contact strategy. All those involved, thranx and human alike, had done their work conscientiously and well. It was simply that, as history shows, there are times when events do not occur as planned. Physics included, the universe is not a perfectly predictable place. Action supercedes fabrication. Stars that are not supposed to go nova for a billion years do. Flowers that are expected to blossom die.

Anticipated ambassadors did not have the opportunity to exchange formal greetings. Innumerable carefully drawn covenants withered for lack of execution, made superfluous by unexpected realities. Formal protocols were rendered extraneous. Thus are the ways of virtuous diplomacy foully ambushed.

Chance chose a poet as its champion, while coarse circumstance on its behalf conscripted a murderer.

1

No one saw the attack coming. Probably someone, or several someones, ought to have been blamed. Certainly there was a convulsion of recriminations afterward. But since it is an unarguable fact that it is hard to apportion blame—or even to assign it—for something that is without precedent, nascent calls for castigation of those responsible withered for lack of suitable subjects. Those who felt, rightly or wrongly, that they bore a share of the responsibility for what happened punished themselves far more severely than any traditional queen's court or council of peers would have.

For more than a hundred years, ever since there had been contact between AAnn and thranx, animosity had festered between the two species. Given such a fertile ground and sufficiency of time, mutual enmity had evolved to take many forms. Manifesting themselves on a regular basis that varied greatly in degree, these were usually propagated by the AAnn. While a constant source of vexation to the ever-reasonable thranx, these provocations rarely exceeded the bounds of irritation. The AAnn would probe and threaten, advance and connive, until the thranx had had enough and were compelled to react. When forcefully confronted, the AAnn would invariably pull back, give ground, retreat. The spiral arm that was shared by both heat-loving, oxygen-breathing species was big enough and rich enough in stars so that direct conflict, unless actively sought, could be avoided.

Habitable worlds, however, were scarcer. Where one of these was involved positions hardened, accusations flew more sharply, meticulously worded phrases tended to bite rather than soothe. Even so, the swift exchange of space-minus communications was always sufficient to dampen a potentially explosive confrontation. Until Willow-Wane. Until Paszex.

* * *

Worvendapur bent his head and reached up with a truhand to clean his left eye. Out on the edge of the forest the wind tended to kick up dust. Lowering the transparent, protective shield over his face, he reflexively extended his antennae through the slots provided for that purpose and moved on, striding forward on all six legs. Occasionally he would arch his back and advance only on his four trulegs, not because he needed the additional manipulative capacity his versatile foothands could provide, but because it raised his body to its maximum standing height of slightly over a meter and a half and enabled him to see over the meter-high, lavender-tinted grass that comprised much of the surrounding vegetation.

Something quick and chittering scuttled through the sedge close to his right. Using the truhand and foothand on that side of his thorax, he drew the rifle that was slung across his back and aimed it at the source of the noise, tensing in readiness. The muzzle of the weapon came up sharply as half a dozen !ccoerk burst from the meadow. Letting out a whistle of fourth-degree relief, he let a digit slip from the trigger and reholstered the gun.

Their plump brown bodies shot through with purple streaks, the flock of feathered !ccoerk fluttered toward the satin-surfaced lake, cooing like plastic batons that had been charged with static electricity. Beneath a feathered, concave belly one trailed an egg sac nearly as big as herself. Idly, Worvendapur found himself wondering if the eggs were edible. While Willow-Wane had been settled for more than two hundred years, development had been slow and gradual, in the conservative, measured manner of the thranx. Colonization had also been largely confined to the continents of the northern hemisphere. The south was still a vast, mostly unknown wilderness, a raw if accommodating frontier where new discoveries were constantly being made and one never knew what small marvel might be encountered beneath the next hill.

Hence his rifle. While Willow-Wane was no Trix, a world that swarmed with dynamic, carnivorous life-forms, it was still home to an intimidating assortment of energetic native predators. A settler had to watch his steps, especially in the wild, uncivilized south.

Tall, flexible blue *sylux* fringed the shore of the lake, an impressive body of fresh water that dominated the landscape for a considerable distance to the north. Its tepid, prolific expanse separated the rain forest, beneath which the settlement had been established, from inhospitable desert that dropped southward from the equator. Founded forty years ago, the burgeoning, thriving colony hive of Paszex was already sponsoring outlying satellite communities. Worvendapur's family, the Ven, was prominent in one of these, the agri town of Pasjenji.

While rain forest drip was adequate to supply the settlement's present water needs, plans for future growth and expansion demanded a larger and more reliable supply. Rather than going to the trouble and expense of building a reservoir, the obvious suggestion had been made that the settlement tap the ample natural resource of the lake. As the possessor of a subspecialty in hydrology, Wor had been sent out to scout suitable treatment and pipeline sites. Ideally, he would find one as close to the lake as possible that was also geologically stable and capable of supporting the necessary engineering infrastructure, from pumping station to filtration plant to feeder lines.

He had been out in the field for more than a week now, taking and analyzing soundings, confirming aerial surveys, evaluating potential locations for the treatment plant and transmission routes for the water it would eventually supply. Like any thranx, he missed the conviviality of the hive, the press and sound and smell of his kind. Regrettably, another week of solitary stretched out before him. The local fauna helped to divert his thoughts from his isolation. He relished these always educational, sometimes engaging diversions, so long as one of them did not rise up and bite off his leg.

Seismic soundings could have been made from the air, or by a mechanical remote, but for something as critical to the community's future as a water facility it was felt that on-site inspection and evaluation by a specialist was required. Wor could hardly disagree. If it proved feasible, this same lake water would be used to slake the thirst of his own offspring. When the spouts opened inside the hive, he wanted their flow to come from a station that would not be subject to incessant breakdowns or microbial contamination.

Unlimbering his pack, he used all four hands to remove and set up the sounder. At the touch of a switch, its six slim, mechanical legs snapped into place. Setting the instrument down on the ground, he adjusted the controls until he was confident it was stationed in a precise and sturdy manner on the slightly boggy surface. Compared to many of the waterlogged sites he had already visited and evaluated, the present location looked promising. It would not do to situate a water treatment plant on sodden, potentially temperamental ground.

Activating the sounder, he stepped back and let his compound gaze wander to a formation of *gentre!!m* gliding past overhead. A widespread native species familiar from numerous encounters in the long-settled north, they were migrating to the southern rain forests to escape the onset of the northern wet season and its accompanying monsoon rains. Their translucent, membranous wings shimmered in the haze-heavy sunshine of midday. Long, flexible snouts inflated and collapsed as individuals called tumescently to one another.

The sounder beeped softly, signifying the completion of the survey. While he had watched the wildlife soar past to vanish beyond the far horizon of the lake, the sounder had taken a sonic scan of the immediate vicinity to a depth of more than a hundred meters. From a study of such scans as well as a mass of other accumulating data, Worvendapur and his colleagues would choose a site for the filtration and pumping station.

While there was no need for him to perform an in-depth analysis of the actual readings in the field, he was always curious to see the unit's findings. Even more so than the average thranx, he was intensely interested in what the earth beneath his feet was like because he might have to live in it someday. The initial readouts that flashed on the screen were promising and devoid of surprise. As it had proven to be in every previous reading, the ground on which he stood was composed primarily of sedimentary rock, with the occasional ancient igneous intrusion from a time when local tectonics were more active. Though the area, and for that matter the ground in which Paszex itself was located, was riddled with faults, they appeared to be long quiescent and of no especial concern.

He dipped his head lower. Having only a transparent, nictitating membrane in place of opaque eyelids, he could not squint, but his antennae dipped forward until the tips were almost brushing the screen. The sounder was reporting an anomaly, virtually beneath his feet. A very peculiar anomaly.

It was so peculiar that he considered returning to the aircar and reporting what he had found. But while reliable, sounders were not perfect. No instrument was. And neither were those individuals charged with their operation. If he called in his concern and it turned out to be baseless, he would come off looking more than a little foolish in the eyes of his peers. Thranx humor could be as sharp as a young dancer's ovipositors. Uncertain how best to proceed, he carried the sounder toward the lake, repositioned it, and ran a second scan. This time, instead of studying the wildlife, he waited impatiently for the compact device to complete its work.

The second scan, run from a different site, confirmed the readings of its predecessor. Worvendapur pondered long and hard. The unusual results he was getting could be due to a mechanical fault in the instrumentation, a consistent error in the analysis program, a simple imperfection in the readout system or screen itself, or any one of half a hundred other possible reasons—any one of which would make more sense than what he believed the instrument was telling him.

Breathing evenly through his spicules, he ran a detailed internal check on the sounder's systems. As near as he could tell without taking it apart, something he was not qualified to do, the device was working perfectly. He then examined himself, and decided that he was working perfectly as well. Very well then. He would leave it to a committee to debate and settle on an interpretation of his inexplicable findings. But he would not rely on one reading, or even two. Moving the sounder again, he set about making the third of several dozen soundings of the immediate area, unaware that he was not doing so in isolation.

His actions were being observed and subjected to the same kind of rigorous analysis that he was applying to the ground beneath his feet. The eyes that watched him were not compound, nor did they belong to representatives of the indigenous wildlife.

"What is he doing?" Clad in color-shifting, pattern-changing camouflage garb, the AAnn advance scout was virtually invisible where she stood crouching within the wall of weaving lakeside sylux. Together with her companion, she watched the blue-carapaced intruder shift his six-legged device, wait, then move it again.

"I enjoy no personal familiarity with thranx scientific mechanisms," the other scout confessed. "Perhaps he is taking weather readings."

The slightly larger of the two females gestured third-degree dissent and followed it with a hand movement indicating second-level impatience. "Why send a lone technician out here with a single small device to analyze the weather? Orbiters are far more efficient."

"That is so," her companion conceded testily. "I was simply trying to suggest possibilities in the absence of information."

The concealed reptilian visage peered through the gracefully swaying, dark blue stems. Their constant motion made detailed observation difficult. Furthermore, it was far too humid out here on the surface for her liking. While the thranx thrived in rain forest surroundings—the steamier the better—the AAnn were most comfortable breathing air that was starved of moisture.

"It takes readings of its surroundings. So *we* will take readings of it taking readings." Removing a small, tubular device from her belt, she activated it and aimed the shiny, reflective end at the thranx. It was a bit of a gamble, but so preoccupied was the settler with his own work that he did not notice the occasional brief, transitory light flashing from among the dense, oscillating stand of sylux.

The results confirmed the worst fears of both scouts.

"He is making subsurface sonic readings."

Her companion was properly alarmed. "That cannot be permitted!"

"Correction," her superior gestured. "The taking of readings can be allowed. What must be prevented is the reporting of those readings to his peers."

"Look!" Heedless of the fact that her sudden movement might reveal their position in spite of the camouflage gear, the other scout straightened and pointed.

The thranx was folding up his equipment. Turning, he started resolutely back through the grass, making a straight line for his waiting transportation. Keeping low, their suits shifting pattern and hue to match grass instead of sylux, the two scouts followed, steadily closing the distance between themselves and the visitor. As they stalked him, they debated how best to proceed.

"We should call this in," the smaller female decided.

"Cannot. By the time the seriousness of the situation is realized and a decision handed down, the intruder will be gone and it will be too late to halt the dissemination of the information he has gathered. A broken tooth must be filed down before it can spread infection."

"I dislike making a decision of such gravity without authority from above."

"So do I," her larger companion agreed, "but that is why you and I are here, and most everyone else is not."

The second scout straightened to her full height, her scaly tail switching nervously back and forth. "He is nearly to his vehicle."

"I can see that," hissed her colleague. "The time in which to debate how best to resolve this matter has passed." Powerful legs pumping, she broke into a sprint.

Worvendapur opened the storage compartment and carefully slid the folded sounder inside, making sure that the cover sealed tightly before turning and heading for the boarding ramp. He would call a meeting of his work group as soon as he returned to Paszex. The information contained in the sounder was of sufficient import to justify an emergency session. Even as he began mentally rehearsing his presentation, he fervently hoped that some mechanical glitch, some other explanation he had overlooked, was responsible for the controversial readings, and that he was not seeing what he thought the sounder was seeing.

In light of the potential explosiveness of that information he knew he ought to be more alert, but the peaceful, bucolic surroundings lulled him. Besides, in a minute or two he would be on his way back to the settlement, traveling at high speed just above the tops of the grass. There was nothing to worry about. Even when he glimpsed movement out of the side of one eye he felt no especial concern.

Then he saw the glint of light on something of artificial manufacture, and knew that what was approaching was at once larger and more lethal than anything he had encountered since commencing his survey.

Truhand and foothand reached down and back, all eight digits clutching at the rifle. Before it was halfway clear of its holster, a shaped sonic pulse struck the upper portion of Worvendapur's abdomen, stunning his nervous system and punching a hole in his blue-green exoskeleton. The force of the impact lifted him off the ground and threw him sideways against the idling aircar. Still trying to draw his weapon, he slammed off the gleaming, scored fuselage and collapsed to the ground.

As he finally managed to withdraw the rifle, a heavy sandaled foot came down on his truhand. Several of the delicate manipulative digits crumpled under the weight, but the wounded hydrologist was beyond feeling the pain. Despite the strong bracing of his chitinous internal structure, his insides were starting to leak out through the hole that had appeared just beneath his upper set of vestigial wing cases.

Consciousness and sight fading in tandem, he looked up to see a pair of homicidally alert eyes staring down at him. Then the piece of sky that framed the eyes shifted and he was able to discern the smooth outline of the skull, clad in camouflage suiting that was struggling to simulate a cloud. A second pair of eyes hovered nearby, glaring at him from behind a fluid mask of falsified brush. Words passed between the two figures. No linguist, Wor understood none of what they were saying in their clipped, sharp tones. He kept trying to reach his rifle with his foothand alone.

"What do we do now?" the smaller of the two assassins wondered aloud. "Take it in?"

"Of what use is a corpse?" Removing her foot from the thranx's crushed truhand, the scout nudged the gaping, bleeding abdominal wound with the tip of her weapon. The helpless researcher cried out softly beneath her. "The shot was a lethal one." Moving the muzzle forward, she placed it against the side of the blue-green, valentine-shaped head. Her expression did not change as she pulled the trigger. The skull jerked once, twin antennae twitched violently, and then the body lay still. As the two scouts deliberated how best to proceed, the bands of red and gold that shone from the compound eyes of their victim gradually began to take on the blank brown tint of lifelessness.

The scouts were stolid but apprehensive when they were called before the tripartite board of inquiry. Following the conclusion of the usual terse formalities, questions were put to the female pair by their superiors, to which answers were unhesitatingly given.

"We felt we had no choice," the senior scout explained yet again. "The thranx was about to depart."

"We had to act," added her comrade by way of support.

The senior officer present scratched at an itch behind his head. His neck scales were dulled with age, and he was long overdue to shed and replace his skin. But his eyes were still bright, his mind sharp.

"You did the only thing you could." He emphasized his conclusion with a gesture indicative of second-degree conviction. "If the field researcher had returned to his settlement with the information he had gathered, our solitude would immediately have been compromised. That revelation must be prevented until our presence here is militarily secure."

"Then we were correct in our assumptions about his activities?" the senior scout inquired.

A junior officer gesticulated assent. "The information contained in the alien field instrumentation you recovered was extracted. It was substantially as damaging as you feared."

"The situation is to be regretted," added the third presiding officer, "but had you not acted as you did it would be much worse. That was quick thinking of you to place the body in the aircar, program it to retrace its course, and self-destruct after it had traveled a specified distance." He looked at his colleagues. "With luck, the locals will make the assumption that their researcher died as the result of a mechanical failure on the part of his equipment."

The senior officer gestured affirmatively. "These thranx are simple settlers. They are not sophisticated visitors from Hivehom. Our report will reflect these considerations." Slitted eyes met those of the two scouts who continued to stand stiffly at attention, their tails held motionless and straight out behind them. "It is fortunate you were in a position to effect this nullification. Appropriate commendations will be forthcoming."

The two scouts, who had entered the inquiry desiring simply to avoid condemnation for having precipitated the fatal confrontation, were silently overjoyed.

The hopes of their superiors, however, and of their superiors' superiors, were not to be fulfilled. Contrary to their overly sanguine predictions, the local thranx proved not to be as unresponsive as would have been wished. Puzzled by the circumstances in which the competent, well-liked hydrologist had perished, a pair of auditors was sent out from Paszex with orders to retrace the path of the deceased. When *they* failed to return, a larger search party was empowered. Following its equally inexplicable disappearance, the settlers requested and not long thereafter received an official commission of inquiry from the long-established northern government.

Covering the same conspicuously murderous ground as the thranx who had gone before them, they rediscovered what the by now long-demised Worvendapur had threatened to expose. In the ensuing violent confrontation, most of the heavily armed force was wiped out. But this time, the AAnn could not kill them all. Their retreat and flight covered by their rapidly falling comrades, a small contingent of thranx succeeded in reaching the settlement to report not only what they had found, but what had taken place subsequent to their discovery.

With serious escalation now appearing to be the only choice left to them, the AAnn proceeded to track the survivors in hopes of taking them out before they could file a formal report with the authorities in the northern hemisphere. Though the AAnn moved quickly, efficiently, and in strength, the thranx managed to hold Paszex and slip revelation of their situation past their assailants' attempts to impose a communications blackout on the settlement. At the same time, the AAnn noble in command was compelled to request that his position be bolstered by reinforcements from offworld.

Paszex was nearly taken by the time the first military transport arrived from the north. Startled by the strength of the attacking AAnn, the relieving thranx promptly called for reinforcements of their own. Analysis of sounding data revealed the presence of not merely an outpost, but an entire complex of AAnn settlements located beneath the innocent surface of the extensive lake. Excavating, quarrying, building, the AAnn had made a comprehensive and expensive effort to establish a permanent presence on Willow-Wane before the thranx became aware of their intent. The subsurface lines the late, lamented Worvendapur had detected and recorded on his instrumentation had been tunnels, not geologic faults.

Eventually, the AAnn were driven out of and away from Paszex. But their underground installation proved too extensive and well fortified to be taken. Diplomatic, if not military, attrition led to the AAnn being granted a portion of their claim to Willow-Wane, allowing them to maintain and expand the settlement in an area not seriously coveted by the thranx but forbidding them to establish any others. This compact was wildly unpopular on Willow-Wane itself, but larger factors were at work. Better to concede the existence of a single settlement, however far-ranging and illegal, than to risk war over a world already extensively settled and developed.

So the intruding AAnn were tolerated, the least of their specious claims accepted. Such are the workings of broad-scale diplomacy, in which assorted small murders are ingenuously subsumed into what professional diplomats euphemistically refer to as the "overall picture." In its inert and hypocritical shadow, the pain of those who have lost friends and relations is conveniently overlooked.

Revenge was not a prominent passion among the thranx, but there were more than a few feelings of loss and betrayal among the survivors of Paszex. Among these were what remained of the family Ven. Comprising a sizable portion of the settlement's population, they had nearly been wiped out in the first assault. The survivors struggled to carry on the family name, but ever thereafter not many were to be found who could boast of the patronymic Ven among the hive Da and the clan Pur. Acutely conscious of their loss and their responsibility to keep the family line from dying out, these few became more insular than was normal among their kind. Their offspring were inevitably inculcated in these same aberrant traits, and in turn passed them on to the next generation.

To one in particular.

It had been a long day, and the members of the Grand Council had retired, as was their custom, to the hot, steamy quiet of the contemplation burrow deep beneath the council chamber, there to relax and relieve the stress of governance. Solitude was not sought, and conversation turned to more pleasant, less weighty matters.

Except among two. Though aged by any standard, they were among the youngest members of the council. Together they discussed two recent events of import that appeared to have no connection. It was in fact a connection they were drawing.

"The AAnn grow bolder than usual."

"Yes," declared the male. "A terrible shame about Paszex." As he spoke he inhaled perfumed steam from the herbal wrap that covered half his breathing spicules. "Nothing to be done about it. You cannot bring back the dead, nor can one in good conscience vote to embark on an all-out war in memory of the already deceased."

"The AAnn always count upon us to be reasonable and logical in such matters. May their scales rot and their eggs shrivel."

"Sirri!!ch, why not? We always are. But you are right. The incursion onto Willow-Wane was unprecedented for its size. But we can do nothing about it."

"I know," agreed the senior female. Her ovipositors lay flat against the back of her abdomen, no longer capable of laying eggs. "I am concerned about preventing a recurrence elsewhere in the future. We must strengthen ourselves."

The male tri-eint gestured second-degree ambivalence. "What more can we do than what we have done? The AAnn dare not make a blatant attack. They know it would invite an overwhelming response."

"Today that is true. Tomorrow . . ." Her antennae fluttered significantly. "Every day the AAnn work to strengthen and enlarge their forces.

What is needed is something to keep them off guard, to divert them."
Amid the steam, her gleaming compound eyes glittered softly. "Something perhaps not as predictable as the thranx."

The male was intrigued. He shifted his position on the resting bench.
"You are not hypothesizing. You have something specific in mind."

"You know of the alien outpost on the high plateau?"

"The bipeds? The hu'mans?"

"*Humans*," she replied, correcting his pronunciation. Human words had no bite and were difficult to enunciate. Their speech was soft, like their fleshy exteriors. "I have just read a report. Progress there is good. So good that preparations are being made to take the next step in deepening and developing relations."

"With the humans?" The tone in the tri-eint's voice was palpable and was accompanied by suitable gestures of disgust. "Why would we want to enhance relations with such unpleasant creatures?"

"You do not deny their intelligence?" The female was challenging him.

"Their morality and manners, perhaps, but their intelligence, no—not based on the secret reports I have seen." Sliding off the bench, he reached back to remove the herbal wrap.

"They have a conspicuous military capability."

"Which they are hardly about to put at the service of such as ourselves." Antennae twitched. "I have seen those reports as well. The great majority of the human population finds our appearance abhorrent. I must say that the feeling is mutual. Mutual dislike is a shaky pedestal on which to raise an alliance."

"Such things take time," she chided him as she used a foothand to rub scented polish across her exoskeleton. Combined with the steam that permeated the chamber, it imparted to the purplish blue chitin a semimetallic sheen. "And education."

The male councilor barked his antipathy. "You cannot educate without contact. Admittedly, from what little is released to us the project here goes well enough. But it is modest in size and scope, and does nothing to deal with the revulsion most humans seem to experience in our presence."

"That is so." Nictitating membranes flushed condensation from individual lenses. "But there is another project, larger in scope and more pointed."

Her counterpart looked up, uncertain. "I have not heard of another."

"It is being kept quiet until it has matured sufficiently for mutual revelation. Only a few know of it. A very few. It is considered absolutely crucial to the development of relations between our two species. Above all, the AAnn must not learn of it. As it is, they consider the humans a threat to their expansionist intentions. The thought of a human-thranx axis might drive them to do something . . . ill considered."

"What human-thranx axis? We hardly have relations with the bipeds."

"There is work afoot to change that," she assured him.

The male chirped skeptically. "Proper, formal relations between our two species I can envision. But a permanent alliance?" He executed the strongest possible gesture of negativity. "It will never happen. Neither side wants it."

"There are visionaries, admittedly few in number for now, who believe otherwise. Hence this second, most secret project." Her declaration of seriousness was leavened with just the barest hint of amusement. "You will never believe where it is." Moving close so that the other eints in the relaxation chamber could not possibly overhear, she touched antennae with him while whispering into the hearing organs on his b-thorax.

She was right. He didn't.

2

The thranx do not bury their dead: the deceased are lovingly recycled. Like so many components of thranx culture, this was a tradition that reached back to their primitive origins, when hives were ruled by pretech, egg-laying queens, and anything edible was deemed worthy of consumption, including the remains of a demised fellow citizen. Protein was protein, while nourishment and survival continued to take precedence over emerging notions of culture and civilization. The manner in which the traditional recycling was carried out was more decorous now, but the underlying canon remained the same.

Farewell giving was far more elaborate and formalized than it had been in the times before talking, however, though the one whose praises were presently being sung would doubtless have dubbed them overwrought. For a poet famous on not just Willow-Wane but all the thranx worlds, Wuuzelansem had been even more than conventionally modest.

Desvendapur remembered the last time he had sat with the master. Wuuzelansem's color had deepened from the healthy aquamarine of the young beyond the blue-green of maturity until in old age his exoskeleton had turned almost indigo. His head had swayed uncontrollably from side to side, the result of a nonfatal but incurable disease of the nervous system, and he but rarely rose up on only four legs, needing all six all the time to keep him from falling. But though they might flash less frequently with the fires of inspiration, the eyes still gleamed like burnished gold.

They had gone out into the rain forest, the great poet and his master class, to sit beneath a yellow-boled *cim!bu* tree that was a favorite of the teacher's. Possessed of its own broad, dense canopy of yellow-gold, pink-striped leaves, this was the time of year of the cim!bu's flowering. Nectar-rich blossoms of enormous length saturated the air with their perfume, their dangling chimelike stamens thick with pollen. No insects hummed busily about those blooms; no flying creatures lapped at the dripping nectar. Attendants looked after the pollination of the cim!bu. They had to. It was an alien, a foreigner, an exotic outsider that was native to Hivehom, not Willow-Wane. A decorative transplant propagated by settlers. It thrived in the depths of the native forest, even though surrounded by strangers.

Beneath the cim!bu and the rest of the dense vegetation, Yeyll throve. The third-largest city on Willow-Wane, it was a hive of homes, factories, training institutes, recreational facilities, and larvae-nurturing chambers. Technologically advanced they had become, but when possible the thranx still preferred to dwell underground. Yeyll wore the preserved rain forest in which Wuuzelansem and his students strolled on its crown, like a hat. Though it exuded the scent of wildness, in reality it had been as thoroughly domesticated as any park.

There were benches beneath the cim!bu. Several of the students took advantage of them as they listened to the poet declaim on the sensuousness of certain lubricious pentameters, resting their bodies lengthwise along one of the narrow, rustic wooden platforms and taking the weight off their legs. Des preferred to remain standing, absorbing the lesson with one part of his mind while the other contemplated the lushness of the forest. The morning had dawned hot and humid: perfect weather. As he scanned the surface of a nearby tree, his antennae probed the bark, searching out the tiny vibrations of the creatures that lived both on and beneath its surface. Some were native insects, ancient relatives of his kind. They paid no attention to the declamations of the revered Wuuzelansem or the responses of his students, being interested only in eating and procreating and not in poetry.

"What do *you* think, Desvendapur?"

"What?" Dimly, it registered on his brain that his name had been invoked, together with the attached verbal baggage of a question. Turning from the tree, he saw that everyone was looking at him—including the master. Another student might have been caught off guard, or left at a loss for words. Not Des. He was never at a loss for words. He was simply sparing with them. Contrary to what others might believe, he *had* been listening.

"I think that much of what passes for poetry these days is offal that rarely, if ever, rises to the exalted level of tendentious mediocrity." Warming to the subject, he raised his voice, emphasizing his words with rapid, overexpansive movements of his truhands. "Instead of composing we have composting. Competitions are won by facile reciters of rote who may be craftsmen but are not artists. It's not all their fault. The world is too relaxed, life too predictable. Great poetry is born of crisis and calamity, not long hours whiled away in front of popular entertainments or the convivial company of friends." And just in case his audience felt that he was utilizing the opportunity to answer the query in order to grandstand before the master, he concluded with a choice, especially coarse, expletive.

No one spoke, and fixed thranx countenances were capable of little in the way of facial expression, but rapid hand movements showed that his response had elicited reactions ranging from resentment to resignation. Desvendapur was known to be habitually outrageous, a quality that would have been more readily tolerated had he been a better poet. His lack of demonstrated accomplishment mitigated against acceptance by his peers.

Oh, there were occasional bursts of rhetorical brilliance, but they were as scattered as the *quereequi* puff-lions in the trees. They manifested themselves just often enough to keep him from being kicked out of the master classes. In many ways he was the despair of the senior instructors, who saw in him a promising, even singular talent that never quite managed to rise above an all-consuming and very unthranxlike preoccupation with morbid hopelessness. Still, he flashed just enough ability just often enough to keep him in the program.

Even those instructors bored with his disgraceful outbursts were reluctant to dismiss him, knowing as they did his family history. He was the last of the Ven save two, the progenitors and inheritors of his family having been wiped out in the first AAnn attack on Paszex more than eighty years earlier. This harsh hereditary baggage had traveled with him all the way north to Yeyll. Unlike the wrong word or an inept stanza, it was something he would never be able to redraft.

"Ven, Ven? I don't know that family," acquaintances would murmur. "Does it hail from near Hokanuck?"

"No, it hails from the afterlife," Desvendapur would muse miserably. It would have been better for him if he had come from offworld. At least then it would have been easier to keep his family history private. On Willow-Wane, where everyone knew the tragic history of Paszex, he could indulge in no such covertness.

Wuuzelansem did not appear upset by his comments. It was not the first time his most obstreperous student had expressed such sentiments. "You condemn, you criticize, you castigate, but what do you offer in return? Crude, angry platitudes of your own. Specious sensitivity, false fury, biased frenzy. 'The jarzarel soars and glides, dips to kiss the ground, and stumbles, perspiring passion: contact in a vacuum.' "

Softly modulated clicks of approval rose from the assembled at this

typically florid display of words and whistles from the master. Desvendapur stood his physical and intellectual ground. Wuuzelansem made it
seem so easy, the right words and sounds spilling prolifically from his
jaws, the precisely correct movements of his hands and body accompanying and emphasizing them where others had to struggle for hours, days,
weeks just to compose an original stanza or two. The war was particularly
acute within Des, who never seemed quite able to find the terminology to
frame the emotions that welled up from deep inside him. A simmering
volcano, he emitted much steam and heat, without ever really erupting
creatively. Artistically, something vital was missing. Aesthetically, there
was a void.

He accepted the lyrical rebuke stolidly, but the way in which his
antennae curled reflexively back over his head revealed how deeply he
had been stung. It wasn't the first time, and he did not expect it to be the
last. In this he was correct. Poetry could be a savage business, and the
master's reputation did not extend to coddling his students.

Looking back, Des was not surprised that he had survived the rigors
of the curriculum. But despite being utterly convinced of his own brilliance, he was nonetheless surprised when he was graduated. He had
expected dismissal with less than full ordination. Instead, he found himself armed with private blessings and official certification. Graduation
had led to a boring but just barely tolerable position with a private company in the wholesale food distribution business, where he spent much
time composing attractive jingles lauding the beauty and healthfulness of
the concern's produce and products. While it provided for the maintenance of his physical upkeep (he certainly ate well), his emotional and
artistic well-being languished. Day after day of waxing lyrical about the
multifarious glories of fruits and vegetables left him feeling like he was
ready to explode. He never did, with the result that one vast, overriding
fear dominated his waking thoughts.

Would he ever?

Dozens of invited guests were arrayed in the traditional circle in the
garden where the dead poet was to be recycled. Notables and dignitaries,
former students both famous and obscure, representatives of clan and
family, all listened politely to the respectful speeches and ennobling
refrains extolling the virtues of the deceased that droned out on the
steamy morning breeze. The ceremony had already gone on too long.
Much longer than the humble Wuuzelansem would have liked. Had he
been able to, Des reflected amusedly, the master would long since have
excused himself from his own sepulture.

Wandering through the crowd as the sonorous liturgy wound down,
he was surprised to espy Broudwelunced and Niowinhomek, two former

colleagues. Both had gone on to successful careers, Broud in government and Nio with the military, which was always in need of energetic, invigorating poets. He wavered, his habitual penchant for privacy finally giving way to the inherent thranx proclivity for the company of others. Wandering over, he was privately pleased to find that they both recognized him immediately.

"Des!" Niowinhomek bent forward and practically wrapped her antennae around his. The shock of familiarity was more refreshing than Des would have cared to admit.

"A shame, this." Broud gestured with a foothand in the direction of the dais. "He will be missed."

" 'Rolling toward land, the wave pounds on the beach and contemplates its fate. Evaporation become destruction.' " Nio was quoting from the master's fourth collection, Des knew. His friends might have been surprised to know that the brooding, apparently indifferent Desvendapur could recite by rote everything Wuuzelansem had ever composed, including the extensive, famously uncompleted *Jor!k!k* fragments. But he was not in the mood.

"But what of you, Des?" As he spoke, Broud's truhands bobbed in a manner designed to indicate friendliness that bordered on affection. Why this should be so Des could not imagine. While attending class he had been no more considerate of his fellow students' feelings than anyone else's. It puzzled and even unnerved him a little.

"Not mated, are you?" Nio observed. "I have plans to be, within the six-month."

"No," Desvendapur replied. "I am not mated." Who would want to mate with him? he mused. An unremarkable poet languishing in an undistinguished job leading a life of untrammeled conventionality. One whose manner was anything but conducive to the ordinary pleasures of existence. Not that he was lacking in procreational drive. His urge to mate was as strong as that of any other male. But with his attitude and temperament he would be lucky to spur a female's ovipositors to so much as twitch in his direction.

"I don't think it's such a shame," he went on. "He had a notable career, he left behind a few stanzas that may well outlast him, and now he no longer is faced with the daily agony of having always to be brilliant. The desperate quest for originality is a stone that crushes every artist. It was good to see you both again." Dropping his foothands to the ground to return to a six-legged stance, he started to turn to go. The initial delight he had felt at once again encountering old friends was already wearing off.

"Wait!" Niowinhomek restrained him with a dip and weave of both antennae—though why she should want to he could not imagine. Most females found his presence irksome. Even his pheromones were deficient, he was convinced. Searching for a source of conversation that might hold him, she remembered something recently discussed at work. "What do you think about the rumors?"

Turning back, he gestured to indicate a lack of comprehension. Suddenly he wanted to get away, to flee, from memories as much as from former friends. "What rumors?"

"The stories from the Geswixt," she persisted. "The hearsay."

"*Chrrk*, that!" Broud chimed in with an exclamatory stridulation. "You're talking about the new project, aren't you?"

"New project?" Only indifferently interested, Des's irritation nevertheless deepened. "What 'new project'?"

"You haven't heard." Nio's antennae whipped and weaved, suggesting restrained excitement. "No, living this far from Geswixt I see that it is possible you would not have." Stepping closer, she lowered her voice. Des almost backed away. What sort of nonsense was this?

"You cannot get near the place," she whispered, her four mouthparts moving supplely against one another. "The whole area is fenced off."

"That's right." With a truhand and opposing foothand Broud confirmed her avowal. "With as little fanfare and announcement as possible, an entire district has been closed to casual travel. It is said that there are even regular aerial patrols in the area to seal off the airspace all the way out to orbital."

Mildly intrigued in spite of himself, Des was moved to comment. "Sounds to me like somebody wants to hide something."

Using four hands and all sixteen digits, Nio insinuated agreement. "A new biochemical facility doing radical research. That's the official explanation. But some of us have been hearing other stories. Stories that, in the fourteen years they've been being propagated, have become harder and harder to dismiss."

"I take it they don't have anything to do with biochemical research." Des desperately wanted to leave, to flee surroundings that had become suddenly oppressive.

Broud implied concord, but left it to his companion to continue with the explanation. "Maybe a little, but if so and if the stories are true, then such research is peripheral to the central purpose of the Geswixt facility."

"Which is to do what?" Des inquired impatiently.

She glanced briefly at Broudwelunced before replying. "To watch over the aliens and nurture a growing relationship with them."

"Aliens?" Des was taken aback. This was not what he had expected. "What sort of aliens? The Quillp?" Refusing to ally themselves with either thranx or AAnn, that race of tall, elegant, but enigmatic creatures had long been known to the thranx. And there were others. But they were well and widely familiar to the general populace. Why should any of them be part of some mysterious, secretive 'project'?

But then what did he, bard to fruits and vegetables, know of covert government undertakings?

"Not the Quillp," Nio was telling him. "Something even stranger." She edged closer, so that their antennae threatened to touch. "The intelligent mammals."

This time, Des had to pause before replying.

"You mean the humans? That's an absurd notion. That project was shifted in its entirety to Hivehom years ago, where the government could monitor it more closely. There are no humans left on Willow-Wane. No wonder it's the basis for rumor and speculation only."

Nio was clearly pleased at having taken the notoriously unflappable Desvendapur aback. "Bipedal, bisexual, tailless, alien mammals," she added for good measure. "Humans. The rumor has it that not only are they still around, they're being allowed to set up a colony right here on Willow-Wane. That's why the Council is keeping it quiet. That's why they were moved from the original project site to the isolated country around Geswixt."

He responded with a low whistle of incredulity. Mammals were small, furry creatures that flourished in deep rain forest. They were soft, fleshy, sometimes slimy things that wore their skeletons on the inside of their bodies. The idea that some might have developed intelligence was hardly to be credited. And bipedal? A biped without a tail to balance itself would be inherently unstable, a biomechanical impossibility. One might as well expect the delicate *hizhoz* to fly in space. But the humans were real enough. Reports on them appeared periodically. Formal contact was proceeding at a measured, studied pace, allowing each species ample time to get used to the existence of the fundamentally different other.

All such contact was still ceremonial and restricted, officially limited to one project facility on Hivehom and a humanoid counterpart on Centaurus Five. The idea that a race as bizarre as the humans might be granted permission to establish permanent habitation on a thranx world was outlandish. There were at least three different antihuman groups that would oppose such a development, perhaps violently. He said as much to his friends.

Nio refused to be dissuaded. "Nevertheless, that is what the rumors claim."

"Which is why they are rumors, and why stories imaginative travelers tell so often differ from the truth." For the second time he started to turn away. "It was pleasant to speak with you both."

"Des," Nio began, "I . . . we both have thought about you often, and wondered if . . . well, if there is ever anything either of us can do for you, if you ever need any help of any kind . . ."

He stopped, turning so suddenly that her antennae flicked back over her head, out of potential harm's way. It was an ancient reflex, one she was unable to arrest.

Preparing to leave, he had been struck by a thought pregnant with possibility. Bipedal, tailless, intelligent mammals were an oxymoron, but no one could deny that the humans existed. Tentative, restricted contacts between humankind and the thranx had been taking place for a number of years now. There were not supposed to be any humans on his world. Not since the project begun on Willow-Wane had been shifted to Hivehom. But what if it were true? What if such outrageous, fantastic creatures were engaged in building not a simple research station, but an actual colony right here, on one of the thranx's own colony worlds?

It was what the AAnn had sought to do by force, in their repeated attacks on the Paszex region. It was extraordinary to think that the Grand Council might actually have granted equivalent permission to another species, and to one so alien. What possibilities might such an unprecedented situation present? What wonders, however inherently appalling, did it conceal? What promise would such an outlandish discovery hold?

The promise, just possibly, of the inspiration his muse and life had thus far been lacking? The thought simultaneously terrified and intrigued him.

"Broud," he said sharply, "you work for the government."

"Yes." The other young male wondered what had happened to transform his former colleague's manner so dramatically. "I am a third-level soother for a communications processing division."

"Near this Geswixt. Excellent." Desvendapur's thoughts were churning. "You just offered me help. I accept." Now it was his turn to lean forward, as the members of the commemorative funeral crowd began to disperse. "I am experiencing a sudden desire to change my living circumstances and go to work on a different part of the planet. You will recommend me to your superiors, in your best High Thranx, for work in the Geswixt area."

"You ascribe to me powers I don't possess," his age-counterpart stammered, truhands fluttering to indicate his distress. "Firstly, I don't live as near this Geswixt as you seem to think. Neither does Nio." He glanced at the female for support, and she gestured encouragingly. "Rumors may alert and influence, but they weigh little and travel without effort. Also, as I told you, I am only a third-level soother. Any recommendations I might make will be treated by my superiors with less than immediate attention." Antennae dipped curiously forward. "Why do you want to uproot your life, shift tunnels, and move nearer Geswixt?"

"Uproot my life? I am unmated, and you know how little family remains to me."

His friends gesticulated uncomfortably. Broud was beginning to wish Des had never come over to talk with them. His behavior was uncouth, his manner unrefined, and his motives obscure. They should have ignored him. But Nio had insisted. Now it was too late. To simply turn away and leave would have been an unforgivable breach of courtesy.

"As for the reason, I should think that's obvious," Des continued. "I want to be nearer to these bizarre aliens—if there is any basis to these rumors and if there actually are any still living on Willow-Wane."

Nio was watching him uneasily. "What for, Des?"

"So I can compose about them." His eyes gleamed, the light reflecting gold from intricately interlocking lenses. "Wuuzelansem did. He was a frequent contributor to the original project, composing for as well as about humans. I personally attended at least three performances during which they were mentioned." His antennae twitched at the remembrance. "Difficult as it may be to believe, he always claimed that despite the absence of appropriate cultural referents, they appreciated his poetry."

"What if there are no humans near Geswixt?" Broud felt compelled to point out. "What if the rumors of this implausible, unlikely, alien colony in the making are just that and nothing more? You will have embarked upon a radical change to your life for nothing."

Des turned to look at his colleague. "Then I will meditate on my impulsiveness and try to salvage illumination from the depths of quandary. Either way it will be an improvement over my present circumstances." He gestured with a truhand in the direction of the nearest tunnel entrance to the city below. "There is nothing for me here. Comfort, shelter, familiar surroundings, daily work, ritual compliments, intimacy with familiars. Nothing more."

Nio was openly shocked. Desvendapur was even more maladjusted than she had ever supposed. "Those things are what all thranx desire."

Des whistled sharply and clacked his mouthparts together in a particularly offensive manner. "They are the enemies of poetry. My mind embraces all, but with them my aesthetic is eternally at war."

"Poetry should reassure, and comfort, and soothe," Broud was moved to protest.

"Poetry should explode. Stanzas should burn. Word sounds should cut like knives."

Broud drew himself up on all four trulegs. "I see that we suffer from a serious difference of philosophy. I believe that my job as a poet is to make people feel better, about both themselves and their surroundings."

"And mine is to make them uncomfortable. What better source of inspiration than beings so grotesque they are scarcely to be believed? What rationale could the government possibly have for allowing them to set up a colony here?" He gestured emphatically with both truhands. "A small, official contact station to which access is severely restricted is one thing—but an actual colony of the creatures? If this is true, no wonder it is being carried out in secret. The hives would never stand for it."

Nio gestured uncertainly. The crowd was continuing to thin around them, the park emptying as attendees vanished down a handful of subsurface accessways. "If colonization is actually being carried out, there could be other reasons for the government wanting to keep things quiet. We are not privy to the rationale that underlies the Grand Council's inner decisions."

Des indicated understanding with a flip of his antennae. "What other reasons? They're afraid that hasty exposure of these aliens' intentions might enrage the populace, especially with the AAnn's repeated attempts to establish and enlarge their presence here by force. It would make sense to keep a second alien presence among us quiet for as long as possible." He stridulated wistfulness. "I have heard recordings of their voices. They can communicate, these mammals, but only with difficulty."

"I know nothing about them," Broud protested. "Remember, at this point their continued presence on Willow-Wane is only a rumor. Officially, they were all moved to Hivehom years ago. To find out if the rumor has any basis in fact you would have to speak with someone directly connected to this new project. If there *is* a new project."

Des pondered furiously. "That should be possible. Surely these colonizing humans, if they exist, must be supervised and attended by specialists of our own kind, if only to see that their activities remain unknown to the population at large. Aliens can be isolated, but not their supervisors. Every thranx needs the camaraderie of the hive."

Nio whistled amusement. "Why, Des, you hypocrite."

"Not at all," he shot back. "I need the hive around me as much as anyone. But not at all times, and not when I'm in search of inspiration." He looked up and past her, to the north. "I need to do something wonderful, something unique, something extraordinary, Nio. Not for me is the comfortable, easy life we usually aspire to. Something inside me pushes me to do more."

"Really?" Broud had had just about enough of their pretentious and probably unbalanced colleague. "What?"

Eyes full of reflected sunlight focused on his. "If I could explain it away, my friend, I would be assembling appliances and not words. I would be like a worker and not a poet."

Broud shifted uncomfortably. Without actually coming out and saying so, or directly denigrating Broud's profession, the other male had made him feel a bit like a lowly line worker himself. Des did not give him time to ponder the actuality of any deeper meaning hidden in his comment, however.

"Can you help me, Broud? *Will* you help me?"

Caught between Desvendapur's unwavering stare and Nio's curious one, Broud felt trapped into assenting. "As I've said, there is little I can do."

"Little is what I have here. Your help is more than I could hope for."

All four trulegs shifted beneath Broud's abdomen. "If it will make you happy . . ." he clicked lamely.

"I'm not sure that anything will make me happy, Broud. There are times when I would welcome death as an end to all this purposeless striving and futile activity in search of newness. But in lieu of an incipient demise—yes, it would make me less miserable."

"Then I'll see what I can do for you. I do not know how close I can get you to this mythical colony site. It is possible that I am already the nearest artist within our classification, and as you know, a little poetry goes a long way."

"Do the best you can." Advancing almost threateningly, Des dipped his antennae to entwine them tightly with the other male's. "After inspiration, hope is the best any poet can wish for."

"Just how close to these creatures are you hoping to get?" Nio asked him.

Desvendapur's tone, his whistles and clicks, were charged with excitement. "As close as possible. As close as you and I are now. I want to see them, to look upon their deformities, to smell their alien odor, if they have one. I want to peer into their eyes, run my truhands over their soft, pulpy skin, listen to the internal rumblings of their bodies. I will incorporate my reactions in a dramatic narrative suitable for distribution across all the thranx worlds!"

"What if, assuming any are present, they're simply too hideous, too alien to study at close range?" she challenged him. "I've seen the pictures of them, too, and while it is nice to think that we might have some new intelligent friends in this part of the Arm, I'm not sure I would want to spend any time in their actual company. That may be a matter best left to contact specialists." One foothand contorted in a gesture of mild distaste. "It is said that they have a vile odor."

"If specialists can sustain contact and survive, so can I. Believe me, Nio, there is little in reality that can exceed the warped imaginings of my mind."

"I have no doubt of that," Broud muttered. Already he was regretting his compliance, his offer to assist his colleague in his inexplicable efforts to get close to the aliens. Of course, it was very likely that there were no humans on Willow-Wane and that Desvendapur would be wasting time and energy looking for them. The thought made him feel better.

"If it exists, this is not only a secretive but highly sensitive government undertaking." Nio put a truhand on Des's thorax, just below the neck and above the first pair of breathing spicules. "You're not going to do anything antisocial, are you? I would hate for you to end up as a negative mention on the daily tidings."

"I don't care about that." She found his degree of indifference alarming. "But I will be careful, because if I break a law it will keep me from accomplishing what I hope to achieve. My own inner, personal goals—not the rules of society—will keep me honest."

"You need help." Broud's head was bobbing steadily, an indication of how seriously he viewed his colleague's intentions. "Urgent therapy."

"Perhaps the effort alone will be enough to divert me into the tunnel of satisfaction. Perhaps the presence of humans is in fact no more than rumor. In either event, the change will relieve me of my boredom and help to alleviate my depression."

Broud was heartened by this assessment, if not entirely put at ease. "I will research possible openings near Geswixt. As soon as I have found the closest, I will recommend you for the position. It might be a lesser post than the one you enjoy now."

"That does not matter," Des assured him. "I will compose poetry for sanitation workers charged with disposing of hazardous wastes. I will sweep tunnels."

"Machines do that," Nio reminded him.

"Then I will write poetry for the machines. Whatever is necessary." Seeing the way in which they held themselves, he was compelled to comment further. "I can tell that you both think I'm crazy. Let me assure you that I am in possession of all my mental faculties and am perfectly sane. What I am is relentlessly driven."

"As a fellow poet, I know how small the difference is," Broud commented dryly. "You walk a thin line in this matter, Desvendapur. Have a care you don't fall off."

3

The image in the center of the room was notably unstable, flickering between two and three dimensions, the colors shifting more than the broadcast parameters ought to have allowed. But it was an old tridee projector, the best the backcountry establishment could afford. Nobody complained. Here in the depths of the Amistad rain forest, even the smallest comfort was appreciated.

Nor were the men and women whose blurred gazes occasionally turned to the image sufficiently sophisticated to complain about such details. Most appreciated the noise that emanated from the image more than the visuals. They were too engrossed in other matters to pay much attention to the broadcast, their serious interests lying in copious alcohol, swift-acting narcotics, cheap sex, expensive promises, and each other.

At the bar—a traditional affair of battered cocobolo wood, hard unupholstered seats, bottles of luminescent metal and glass and plastic, foul-mouthed conversation and unrealized dreams, overhead lighting, and a complaisant mixologist—the dented but still functional multiarmed automated blender was the only concession to modernity. A couple sat at one end, negotiating a price for services that had nothing to do with the surrounding rain forest and everything to do with the most basic mammalian needs. One man lay on the floor, snoring loudly in his own spittle, ignored by those around him.

Two others had turned in their seats to watch the tridee. Near them a third sat hunched over his drink, a pale green liquid concoction that whispered to him in soft, reassuring tones. The liquorish voice was not metaphorical: The drink actually spoke, its reassuring recording embedded in the fizzing molecules within the glass. As the level was lowered by consumption, new sentences manifested themselves for the benefit of the drinker, like the layers of a drunken onion.

"Fat Buddha, would you look at that!" Shifting on his seat, whose aged and poorly maintained internal gyros struggled to keep the boisterous tridee-watching imbiber they supported from crashing to the floor, the speaker pointed at the image hovering in the center of the room. His clothes were thick with decomposing rain forest and he needed a shave.

"Man, I never seen anything so ugly!" agreed his companion. Turning slightly in his chair, he jabbed a finger hard into the side of his neighbor. "Hey, Cheelo, take a look at this, man!"

The false promises of his voluble drink lingering in his ears, the third drinker turned reluctantly to gaze at the tridee. The image presented therein, in unstable three dimensions, only barely impacted on his liquor-sedated consciousness.

His tormentor, an ostensible friend, poked him again. "Are they gruesome lookin', or what?" An unpleasant frown creased the man's dark face. "Hey, Cheelo—you getting any of this?"

"Look at his eyes," the heavyset drinker urged his companion. "He's right on the edge. Push him again and I bet you five credits he passes out. His chair ain't strong enough to hold him."

The words stung worse than the liquor. Cheelo Montoya sat a little straighter in his seat. It took a sustained effort, but he forced himself. "I ain't—I'm not going to pass out." He struggled to focus on the tridee image. "Yeah, I see 'em. So they're ugly. So what?" He looked sharply at his "friend." "You just have to look at 'em, not sleep with 'em."

This observation struck the two other men as uproariously funny. When the coughing and hooting had died down, the larger man wagged a fat finger at the diminutive Montoya.

"Sometimes I can't never figure you, Cheelo. Sometimes I think you're as stupid and ignorant as the rest of these sorry-ass poachers and *grampeiros* around here, and then you'll go and surprise me by saying something almost intelligent."

"Thanks," Montoya muttered dryly. He nodded in the direction of the tridee image. Feeling the familiar, irresistible glaze spreading over his eyes like heavy honey, he determinedly blinked it back. "What are they, anyway?"

The other men exchanged a look, and the one nearest Montoya replied. "You mean you don't know, man?"

"No," Cheelo mumbled. "I don't know. So shoot me."

"Waste of a bullet," the heavyset drinker husked, but too softly for Montoya to overhear.

"They're bugs, man. *Bugs.*" The speaker waved his arms wildly in front of Montoya, though the visual emphasis was unnecessary. "Giant, gross, filthy, stinking, alien bugs! And they're here! Right here on Earth, or at least at the two official contact locations."

Leaning back against the bar, the heavyset drinker gazed dully at the tridee. "Actually, I hear they smell kind of nice."

Visibly outraged, his lanky friend whirled on him. "What? Smell nice? They're *bugs,* man! Bugs don't smell nice. Especially alien ones." His tone fell threateningly, bursting with false courage. "I wish I had a size fifty shoe, so I could step on 'em and squish every one of 'em." Glancing down at the floor, he promptly slid off his seat and landed feet first on a large tropical roach. The insect tried to dodge, failed, and crunched audibly beneath the pair of heavily scored jungle boots. "*That's* how you treat bugs, man. I don't care if they do make speeches and build starships."

The bartender leaned slightly forward to peer over the bar. A look of mild distaste soured his expression as he evaluated the fresh black smear on the floor. "Did you have to do that, Andre?"

"Oh, right," the bug smasher replied sarcastically. "Like it seriously impacts the elegant décor of your fine establishment."

The eyebrows of the beefy individual behind the bar rose. He did not blink. "If you don't like it here anymore, there's always Maria's down the street."

The heavyset drinker choked melodramatically. "Maria's? This dive is Ambergris Cay compared to that hole. Hey, hey—" He prodded his friend. "—I bet if you paid enough you could get one of Maria's whores to sleep with a bug." He chuckled at his own debased humor. "They'll sleep with any*body.* Why not any*thing*?"

"Ay—they build starships?" Swaying slightly, Montoya struggled to focus on the tridee image.

"That's what they say." The man next to him resumed his explication. "First the lizards, now bugs. Me, I think we should keep to the solar system and forget about the rest of it."

"They're not lizards." His marginally more erudite associate did not hesitate to correct his drinking companion. "The AAnn are lizardlike. Just like the thranx are insectile, but not insects."

"Ahhhhh, go plug yourself, Morales. They're *bugs.*" The other man's conviction was not to be denied, nor was he about to let awkward facts interfere with his ripening xenophobia. "If it was up to me, I'd call the nearest exterminator. Let 'em infest their own planet, but stay the hell away from ours. Keep Earth pure. We already got enough bugs of our own." He downed a long, corrosive swallow of biting blue brew, wiped his lips with the back of a hairy hand that was too conversant with manual labor, and remembered the smaller man on his other side.

"What about you, Cheelo?" Andre nodded at the tridee. "What do you think we should do about 'em? Let 'em hang around us or dust the lot of 'em? Me, I'd rather hang out with the lizards. Least they got the right number of legs. Cheelo? Hey, Montoya, you in there?"

"What?" Swaying on his seat, the smaller man's response was barely audible.

"I said, what would you do about the bugs, man?"

"Forget it," Morales said. He had turned away from the media image on the tridee and back to the bar. "You expecting a considered opinion on alien contact from *him*?" He tapped his glass, calling for a refill. "Might as well ask for his opinion on how to retire the world debt. He doesn't have an opinion on anything, and he's not going to do anything about anything." Small, porcine blue eyes glanced contemptuously in Montoya's direction. "Ever."

The words penetrated the dark, sweet mist that was slowly creeping through Cheelo's consciousness. "I am too going to do something." He coughed, hard, and the man seated next to him hastily backed out of the line of fire. "You'll see. One of these days I'll do something. Something *big*."

"Yeah, sure you will." The drinker next to him guffawed. "Like what, *qué*? C'mon, Cheelo, tell us what big thing you're gonna do."

There was no reply from the other seat because it was now vacant, its occupant having slid slowly out of the chair and down to the floor like a lump of diseased gelatin. Overwhelmed, the seat's internal gyros whirred back to vertical.

Peering over the barrier, the bartender grunted as he gestured to the other pair. "I don't give a good goddamn if he does something big, so long as he doesn't do it in my place." Reaching into a front pocket of his shirt, he removed a handful of small white pills and passed two of them to the heavyset man. "Take him outside and let him do his big thing there. If you're his friends, don't dump him in the street." He glanced at the ceiling. "Coming down pretty hard tonight, and you know it won't let up again till sunrise. Try and get these down him. It'll detox some of the alky radicals so maybe when he comes around he won't feel like his brain's trying to punch its way out of his skull. Poor bastard." Having done his duty, he turned back to his liquids and potions and other customers.

Thus co-opted, the two speakers reluctantly hauled Montoya's limp corpus outside. Tropical rain was plunging vertically into the earth, shattering the night with unrelenting moisture. Beyond the dark row of tumbledown buildings that marked the other side of the town's single street, rioting vegetation climbed a dark slope, the beginnings of the wild and empty Amistad.

Making ample show of his distaste, the heavyset man forced the pills into Montoya's mouth and roughly massaged his throat before rising.

"He get 'em?" the other drinker wondered. His gaze turned upward, to the deluge that formed a wet wall just beyond the dripping rim of the porch overhang.

"Who the hell cares?" Straightening, his companion nudged the limp form with one booted foot. "Let's toss him out in the rain. Either it'll sober him up or he'll drown. Either way he'll be better off."

Together, they lifted the pliant form off the prefab plastic sidewalk sheeting and, on the count of two, heaved it far out into the downpour. It wasn't difficult. Montoya was not a big man and did not weigh very much. Chuckling to themselves, they returned to the warmth of the bar, the heavyset man glancing backward toward the street and shaking his head.

"Never done anything, never will."

There was mud seeping into his open mouth, and the rain was falling hard enough to hurt. Montoya tried to rise, failed, and collapsed face first back into the muck that was running down the imported plastic avenue. Standing up being out of the question, he rolled over onto his side. The tepid rain coursed down his face in miniature cascades.

"Will too do something," he muttered. "Something big. Someday."

Got to get out of this place, he heard himself screaming. Got to get away from here. Miners too tough to skrag; merchants too heavily armed to intimidate. Need money to get to someplace decent, someplace worthwhile. Santo Domingo, maybe. Or Belmopan. Yeah, that was the place. Plenty of tourists with wide eyes and fat credit accounts.

Something was crawling across his stomach. Sitting up quickly, he saw a giant centipede making its many-legged way across his body. Uttering the forlorn cry of a lost child, he slapped and swung at himself until the enormous but harmless arthropod had been knocked aside. It was a harbinger, but he had no way of knowing that.

Then he turned once again face down to the street and began to retch violently.

4

As time passed and contact was not resumed, Desvendapur could not keep from wondering if his friends had indicated their willingness to help him in his endeavor only to shut him up, and had forgotten all about his request as soon as they had returned to the comfort and familiarity of their own homes. But though it took a while to make things happen, the reluctant Broud eventually proved to be as good as his word.

There came a day when Des received a formal notification from the sub-bureau in charge of poets for his region, informing him that he had been assigned the post of fifth-degree soother to Honydrop. Hastily, he looked it up on his *scri!ber*. It was a tiny hive situated outside the main current of Willow-Wane life whose inhabitants worked at gathering and processing a few fields of imported, cultivated berries. Located high on a mountainous plateau, it suffered from weather sufficiently harsh to discourage most thranx from wanting to visit, much less immigrate. He would need protective clothing, a rarity among his kind, and a stolid disposition to endure the unforgiving climate. Furthermore, accepting the transfer would drop him two levels in status. He did not care. Nothing else was important.

What mattered was that the Honydrop hive was situated less than a day's journey from Geswixt.

There was no information to be had on a hypothetical, unacknowledged, and highly improbable human colony, of course. His personal scri!ber was a compact device capable of accessing every information storage dump on the planet, and he had long since given up hope of finding even the most oblique reference to such a development in its innards, no matter how clever or rigorous a search he assigned to it. There was plenty of information on the humans—more than he could hope to digest in a lifetime—and some on the progress of the mature project on Hive-hom. But there was nothing about a continued presence on Willow-Wane of bipedal, intelligent mammals. Despite his most probing efforts, it all remained nothing more than rumor.

Reaching Honydrop involved no less than four transfers, from a major tube line to, at the last, a place on one of the infrequent independently powered supply vehicles that served the isolated mountain communities of the plateau. He had never imagined so hostile an environment could exist on a world as long settled and developed as Willow-Wane.

Outside the transparent protective dome of the cargo craft in which he was riding, trees grew not only at absurd distances from one another, wasting the space and soil that lay between, but stood independent of mutual contact. No familiar vines or creepers draped in graceful arcs from one bole to its neighbor. No colorful blossoms added color to trunks that were drab and dark brown. The tiny leaves they sported seemed too insignificant to gather sufficient sunlight to keep the growths alive.

Still, many grew tall and straight. It was exactly the sort of landscape in which one might expect to encounter alien visitors. But the only movement came from animals that, while exotic to his lowland eyes, were quickly recognized by the transport's crew and were well documented in the biological history of the planet.

A glance at the cargo craft's instrument panel showed that the temperature outside was much nearer freezing than he had ever hoped to experience other than theoretically. He made sure his cumbersome leg wrappings were securely belted and that the thermal cloak that slipped over his abdomen was sealed tight. This left his head and thorax unavoidably exposed. A thranx had to be able to see and to breathe. Knowing that he would tend to lose the majority of his body heat through his soft under-abdomen, he felt as confident as one could be in his special apparel.

The two drivers were similarly clad, though in contrast to his their suits displayed evidence of long wear and hard use. They ignored the single passenger seated behind them as they concentrated on their driving and on the softly glowing readouts that hovered above the instrument panel. The vehicle sped along over a crude path pocked with muddy patches and small boulders. These did not impact on its progress because the bulky cargo craft traveled on a cushion of air that carried it along well above such potentially irritating natural obstructions. Outlying communities like Honydrop and Geswixt were too small and isolated to rate a loop on the network of magnetic repulsion lines that bound together Willow-Wane's larger hives. They had to be supplied by suborbital fliers or individual vehicles like the one on which he managed to secure transport.

One of the drivers, an older female with one prosthetic antenna, swiveled her head completely around to look back at him. "Cold yet?" He gestured in the negative. "You will be." Her mandibles clicked curtly as she turned back to her controls.

The paucity of vegetation compared to what he was used to was more than a little unnerving. It suggested an environment hostile beyond anything he had ever experienced. Yet, thranx lived up here, even at this daunting altitude and in these horrific conditions. Thranx, and if the Willow-Wane Project was more than just rumor, something else—something the tri-eints who made the decisions that affected all thranx wanted to keep from the eyes of their fellow citizens.

Other than an orbiting station, they couldn't have chosen a better place, Des mused as the cargo vehicle sped along below the granitic ramparts of the high mountains that framed the plateau. This was not terrain where thranx would casually wander or vacation. The AAnn would find the thinner air and infinitely colder temperatures equally uninviting. Glancing out the dome, he saw that the upper slopes of the peaks whose gaze they were passing beneath were clad in white. He knew what *rilth* was, of course. But that did not mean he had any desire to see it up close or to touch it. His body shivered slightly at the thought. There were certain kinds of inspiration he could do without.

Hardship, however, was not among them. Even if there was no colony, or if there was some other kind of clandestine government project involving subject matter that did not include bipedal intelligent mammals, the harsh surroundings had already suggested more than a few couplets and compositions to him. Any poet worthy of the designation was an open spigot. He could no more turn off the thoughts and words that cascaded through his head or the relevant twitches and tics that convulsed his arms and upper body than he could cease breathing.

There was little to see when they arrived. Unlike more established thranx communities in more salubrious climes, Honydrop was situated almost entirely below ground. Normally the surface would be covered with vehicular docking alcoves, a forest of power air intakes and exhausts, bulk storage facilities, and parks—lots of parks. But except for places where the brush and some of the peculiar local trees had been cut down, the terrain the cargo carrier embraced late that afternoon had been left in a more or less natural condition.

He had been expecting too much. Honydrop, after all, was only a very small community on the fringe of what was still the ongoing settlement of Willow-Wane. Three hundred and sixty-odd years was a long time in the settlement of a continent, but with an entire world to develop and civilize, there was still space to accommodate little-visited, empty places. The vast plateau on which Honydrop, Geswixt, and a few other minuscule outposts had been established was one locale where frontier still prevailed.

The transport slipped smoothly into a weather-battered shelter. Immediately, double doors labored to close behind it. To Des's surprise, the two drivers did not wait for the interior temperature to be raised to a comfortable level. They cracked the dome soon after shutting down the vehicle's engines.

The blast of cold air that struck the poet made him gasp. Shocked spicules caused his entire thorax to contract in reaction. Using all four hands he hurried to tighten the unfamiliar, constricting clothing around his unacclimated limbs and abdomen.

At least the interior of the warehouse reflected traditional thranx values. Everything was organized and in its place, although he had expected to see more in the way of supplies. An isolated community like Honydrop would require more support than a hive of similar size set in an equitable climate. Perhaps there were other storage facilities elsewhere. Disembarking from the cargo carrier, he took further stock of his surroundings. Power suits and mechanical assistants at the ready, a stevedore crew appeared. Working in tandem with the drivers, they began to unload the big bulk carrier. Des waited impatiently for his baggage, buried unceremoniously among the rest of the cargo.

A foothand prodded him from behind. Turning clumsily in the cold-weather gear, he saw a middle-term male staring back at him. Seeing that the local was encumbered by even more clothing than himself made Desvendapur feel a little bit better. The people who lived up here were not superthranx, inured to temperatures that would stiffen the antennae of any normal individual. They were subject to the same climatic vagaries as he.

"Greetings. You are the soother who has been assigned from the lowlands?"

"I am," Des replied simply.

"Wellbeing to you." The salutation was curt, the touch of antenna to antenna brief. "I am Ouwetvosen. I'll take you to your quarters." Pivoting on four trulegs, he turned to lead the way. When Des hesitated, his host added, "Don't worry about your things: They will be brought. Honydrop is not a big enough place in which to lose anything. When can you be ready to recite?"

Apparently, traditional protocol and courtesy were as alien to his new home as was the climate. A bit dazed, Des followed his guide. "I've only just arrived. I thought—I thought I might accustom myself to my new surroundings first."

"Shouldn't take you long," Ouwetvosen declared bluffly. "The people here are starved for therapeutic entertainment. Recordings and projections are all very well in their way, but they're not the same as a live performance."

"You don't have to tell me." Des followed his host into a lift. When the doors closed, the temperature within approached something closer to normal. His body relaxed. It was as if he had stepped into a larval nursery. Aware that Ouwetvosen was watching him closely, he straightened his antennae and shifted from six legs back onto four.

"Chilled?"

"I'm fine," Des lied.

His guide's attitude seemed to soften slightly. "It takes some getting used to. Be thankful you're not an agricultural worker. You don't have to spend time on the outside if you don't want to. Myself, I'm a fourth-level administrator. I don't go to the surface unless somebody orders me."

Desvendapur felt emboldened. "It can't be that bad." He indicated his cold-weather gear. "Equipped like this, I think I could stand it for a workday."

The administrator eyed him thoughtfully. "After a while, you probably could. That's how the agri folk dress. Except when the rilth is precipitating out of the atmosphere, of course. Then they require full environmental suits." His mandibles clicked sharply. "One might as well be working in space."

Des had not made it to the administrator's sarcasm. "You are subject to falling rilth? Here, at Honydrop? I saw some compacted on the high peaks, of course—but it actually *falls* here?"

"Toward the end of the wet season, yes. It does sometimes grow cold enough to freeze precipitation and make it fall to the ground. You can walk on it—if you dare. I've seen experienced, long-term agri workers do it barefoot. Not for more than a few moments," he added quickly.

Des tried to imagine walking barefoot in rilth, the icy frozen moisture burning the underside of his unprotected foot-claws, numbing nerves and crawling up his legs. Who would voluntarily subject themselves to such hell? That kind of cold would penetrate right through the chitin of a person's protective exoskeleton to threaten the moist, warm fluids and muscles and nerve endings within. Did he dare?

"One question, Ouwetvosen: Why did they name a hive situated in country like this, in a climate like this, Honydrop?"

His host glanced back at him and gestured with a truhand. "Someone had a sense of humor. What kind of sense, I'd just as soon not say."

Desvendapur's private quarters turned out to be of modest dimensions and were equipped with comfortable appointments. Once settled within, he prepared to address the matter of the individual climate control. His mouthparts parted contemplatively, then hesitated. It was his state of mind that was chilled, not his body. Here below the surface, within the Honydrop hive, the temperature was set at thranx norm and the internal humidity was raised to the appropriate 90 percent. Stop thinking about conditions on the surface, he admonished himself, and the rest of your body will follow your mind's lead.

Already he had composed and discarded a good ten minutes' worth of material. Inspired by what he had seen, it had been full of portentous references to the searing cold and barren mountains. Reviewing the stanzas, he realized that these were not what the locals would want to hear about. They wanted to be soothed, to be transported by his words and sounds and hand gestures; not reminded of the harshness of their surroundings. So he threw out everything he had contrived and began anew.

His inaugural recitation was well attended. Anything fresh was a novelty in Honydrop, and that included a recently arrived therapist like himself. Having full confidence in his abilities, he did not force his performance, and it went "soothly." Following his well-thought-out coda, more than a few females and males walked to the center of the small community amphitheater to congratulate him and to chat amiably. After the stark, tense journey up from the lowlands, it felt good to be back among a swarm, the warmth and smell of many unclothed thranx pressing close around him. He accepted their thanks and comments readily, grateful for the attention. Veiled promises of possible mating opportunities were appreciatively noted.

Reassured and exhausted, he retired to his quarters at the appropriate hour, reviewing in his mind all that he had seen and experienced since arriving. The isolation, the ruggedness of his surroundings, should make for inspired composing. In a few days he felt he would be mentally secure enough to join the agricultural workers on one of their daily forays to the berry fields, to watch them at work and experience more of this exotic, little-visited corner of Willow-Wane.

He knew he would be watched while his work was being evaluated. It would not do to inquire too quickly into rumors about a nearby mysterious project, or to ask frequently about clandestine government operations in the area. Honydrop was located a respectable distance away from and on the opposite side of a high, sharp mountain ridge from Geswixt, the hive that would be the support base for any eccentric outworld operations. Somehow he would have to find a way to pay the place a visit without arousing any suspicions. Honydrop was a typical agricultural community, albeit a markedly isolated one. Its inhabitants went about their business free of immoderate surveillance. Geswixt could be different.

If it wasn't, then he had come all this way and gone to all this trouble—not to mention sacrificing two levels in status—for nothing.

As the weeks passed he found himself settling in among his fellow workers. They were a hardy lot, the thranx of Honydrop. They appreciated every word of his poetry, every mannered gesture, dip of head, and spiral of antennae. Even the less inspired of his workmanlike refrains drew praise. His success, he felt, was due more to the ardor he emanated while performing than to any brilliance of invention. As a soother, he was inescapably impassioned. This additional emotional warmth was gratefully embraced by the citizens. Unsolicited commendations piled up in his record. There was talk of recommending him for an embedded shoulder star.

At any time, he could have requested a transfer to a larger, more rewarding venue. Promotion within his calling also beckoned. He made no effort to procure either.

What he did do was strive to make friends with anyone engaged in transportation, be it the operator of one of the loaders that gathered the plump fruit from the scattered fields, the drivers of internal individual transports, or the occasional visiting cargo pilot. A check of maps showed that it would be futile to attempt to walk overland to Geswixt or anywhere in its vicinity. Without a full environment suit he would never get across the intervening ridge, and there was no viable reason why a poet should need to requisition that kind of extreme-weather gear. It left him no choice but to try and hitch a ride some day.

The difficulty was that despite their geographic proximity, there was little interchange between Honydrop and Geswixt. The produce harvested by Honydrop hive went directly out of the mountains and down to processing plants in the nearest city. Nothing was shipped from Honydrop to Geswixt, and all necessary supplies came straight up from the lowlands. For all the formal intercourse that took place between the two hives they might as well have been on opposite sides of the planet.

He was sitting in one of the two community parks, surrounded by supplementary humidity, dense tropical growth, and edible fungi, basking in the artificial light that filtered hazily down from the ceiling, when he was approached by Heulmilsuwir. A logistics operator who, like many, admired his work, she had become a good if casual friend.

"Sweet tidings to you, Desvendapur."

He set his scri!ber aside, mildly irritated at having been interrupted in midcomposition. "Good day, Heul. Are you on off-time?"

"For a little while." She settled herself on the bench next to his, strad-dling it with her abdomen, her trulegs splayed out to either side. "You're still working, even here?"

"The curse of creativity." He made a soft, humorous gesture to take the edge off his tone. "Even a soother needs soothing. I find that in all of Honydrop, this place does that for me."

"Only this place?" Reaching out with a truhand, she stroked his slick, blue-green thorax just below the breathing spicules.

Idly, he mused on the slenderness of her ovipositors, curled up over her lower abdomen. "There are others," he conceded with grudging warmth.

They made inconsequential but diverting chatter for a while. Then her tone changed. "Am I wrong, or in the intervals when we were talking days ago did you mention that you would like to visit Geswixt?"

He fought to suppress his initial reaction. While his face was inflexi-ble, his limbs were not. He felt he largely succeeded in hiding from this female what he was feeling. "A change of scenery, however transitory, is always a welcome diversion."

She indicated disagreement and clicked her mandibles sharply for emphasis. "Not if it means going outside. Personally, I can't imagine why anyone would want to go to the trouble of visiting Geswixt. Everything I've heard about the place suggests that it's a grim, spare little mining sta-tion, with nothing in the way of amenities." She gestured with a truhand. "Less so even than Honydrop."

"What do they mine there?" he asked absently. "What kind of ore?"

She gestured uncertainty. "I do not know. I think I remember hearing something about an ongoing dig for nonferrous materials, but I don't believe they've actually hit an ore body yet. They're still searching."

"And tunneling a lot, I imagine. A mine would mean many tunnels. A great deal of earth and rock would have to be moved."

She eyed him curiously. "Why, yes, I suppose so." Light flashed off the multifarious golden mirrors that were her eyes. "Anyway, if you really want to go there and have a look around, I've found someone who might take you."

His hearts pounded a little faster. "That is interesting. Would I know this person?"

"Perhaps. Her name is Melnibicon. She's a driver." When Des indi-cated his ignorance, Heulmilsuwir elaborated. "We've met a number of times, in the course of checking her manifests. It seems that there is a need for a certain medicine in Geswixt. A small quantity of a little-used enzymatic catalyst. Rather than wait to have it shipped from Ciccikalk, our department is sending some over the mountains to Geswixt. A quick courtesy run. Melnibicon is taking it. Since her transport will be pretty much empty except for a single package of medication, I thought she might have room for a passenger."

"You asked her on my behalf?" Had he not made a conscious effort to suppress it, Desvendapur might have been moved to affection.

"I knew you were interested, and I have enjoyed your recitals so much—and your company."

"I thought travel was prohibited between Honydrop and Geswixt." He watched closely for any reaction.

"Restricted. Not prohibited. Otherwise, clearing the requisite bureaucratic strictures would prevent Melnibicon from making the trip. Officially, casual travel is not supposed to take place. But now and again, people do make the journey." Leaning forward, she reached into a beautifully embroidered, hand-woven abdominal pouch and handed him an embossed plastic rectangle.

"This is where you will find her. She's leaving mid-midday so she can make it back before dark. It is better to do these things on the cusp of the moment. Too much planning can lead to exposure. Are you going to meet with her and try to do this?"

Gathering all four trulegs beneath him, he slid off the bench. "I don't know," he lied. "I'll have to think about it. If I am found out, it could mean trouble for me."

"I won't tell." The logistics officer flexed her ovipositors coquettishly. "You will get there, have your little look around and visit, and be back before anyone in a position to object realizes that you've gone. Where is the harm in that?"

No harm indeed. Eventualities cascaded through his mind like logs swept before a spring monsoon. "I will be back tonight," he declared flatly.

"Of course you will." She abandoned her own bench to stand alongside him. "And I will be waiting to greet you, to hear all about your furtive visit to exotic Geswixt." She gestured amusement.

He started to leave, composing the necessary preparations in his mind. Then he hesitated and looked over at her. "Heul, why this interest in me? Why the persistence on my behalf?"

"You're a poet, Des. You conform so differently." With that she was gone, scampering off in the direction of one of the south tunnels. He watched her depart, then headed for his modest quarters. There were several small items he wanted to be sure and take along with him—just in case.

If he was lucky, the opportunity might arise not to come back.

* * *

Melnibicon was an older, taciturn thranx whose ovipositors had long since lost their resilience and collapsed against her wing cases. After assuring herself that Desvendapur had come alone and had not been followed, she directed him into the back of the cargo lifter's cramped cockpit. No one saw him board, the rest of the warehouse facility's crew being fully occupied with tasks of their own.

Granted clearance, the lifter trundled out through the weather-tight double doors onto a small, spotless landing area. Des was jolted when the craft took off straight up, rising to a height of several hundred feet before leveling off and accelerating eastward.

"Sorry about that." Melnibicon grunted a terse apology as she kept a careful watch on her instrumentation, occasionally glancing up to take in the daunting view forward. "I'm used to hauling cargo and produce, not sightseers."

"It's all right." Settling himself onto the narrow, empty bench alongside her, he studied the view outside. Rugged peaks and jagged ridges saddled with rilth separated the fertile but cold valley beneath which Honydrop lay from the higher vale that was home to Geswixt. Once again, he saw that attempting to cross between the two on foot in anything less than full environmental gear would have brought a quick death to the hardiest thranx. In contrast, the lifter would make the trip in less than an hour.

He felt some sort of thanks was in order. "This is very good of you."

A reply that was more grunt than whistle assailed his ears. "This job is boring enough. A little risk is worth it for a little company. Talk to me, poet. Tell me about yourself, and the world beyond this cold hell. How goes life in Ciccikalk?"

"Why ask me? You have pictures, images."

"That's not the same as hearing it from someone who's recently been places. Use flowery language, poet. I like being soothed in High Thranx."

He complied as best he was able, resorting to improvisation when knowledge and experience failed, and all the while doing his best not to look outside. Doing so reminded him of the cold death that awaited below.

In spite of his nervousness he found that the time passed quickly. When Melnibicon indicated that they had crossed the ridge and were descending into Geswixt, he forced aside his unease and pressed his face and antennae to the port.

The view was less than instructive. Not having any idea what to expect, he was still disappointed. The panorama was less than inspiring. Certainly it dispensed no revelations.

Below them, a long, narrow valley stretched from the impossibly inhospitable high mountains that lay to the north off in the direction of the distant sea. A fast-flowing river ran down the center of the valley. Unlike the country above and around Honydrop, the land showed no signs of cultivation. Only the rubble-free disc of the landing platform indicated the presence in the valley of intelligent inhabitants. They were flying over one of the most remote regions on Willow-Wane. Geswixt, like Honydrop and every other thranx hive built in a less than ideal climatic zone, would of course be located entirely underground.

What did you expect? he admonished himself as the lifter hummed through a pass between two rilth-clad crags. Hordes of humans dashing about in all directions, or genuflecting at the approach of every craft making an arrival? The absence of any visible indication that the bipedal mammals were present was hardly conclusive proof of their absence.

Neither, however, was it encouraging.

After an uneventful descent, Melnibicon set the lifter down gently on the landing disc and taxied forward until they were once more within a sheltering enclosure and surrounded by other vehicles. The assortment of battered, weather-scoured craft parked in the Geswixt terminal betrayed no hidden uses. The terminal looked exactly like the one in Honydrop, only larger. Cargo was being unloaded from one aircar while a small lifter was being filled with an assortment of crates and barrels from a pair of container transports. There was no evidence of unusual activity or exceptional security.

If it was after all nothing but rumor, he thought disappointedly, then he had wasted not just an afternoon but the past several seasons of his life on a quixotic, futile quest.

The muted hum of the lifter's engine died. Slipping free of the pilot's bench and gear, Melnibicon turned to look back at him. "Welcome to Geswixt. Is it what you expected?"

He gestured noncommittally. "I haven't seen anything yet."

She generated the high-pitched whistle that was thranx laughter. "Have a look around. I need to make delivery of that medication. They're waiting for it, so it shouldn't take long. Then I am going to take a little break for myself, chat with some fliers I know here." She spoke to the lifter and it replied with the correct time. "Be back in four time-parts. I'd rather not fly through these mountains after dark, even if the lifter does most of the flying itself. Just because the route is preprogrammed doesn't mean I don't want to be able to see where we are going."

Disembarking, he found himself alone in the spacious terminal. With no specific destination in mind, he wandered from craft to craft, observing handlers at work and asking what he hoped were innocuously phrased questions that would give the impression he knew about something that might or might not actually exist. The replies he received varied from the bemused to the straightforwardly indeterminate. In this manner he passed most of the remainder of the afternoon, at the end of which period he was no more enlightened than he had been prior to leaving Honydrop.

One young male in particular was having a difficult time shifting a stack of six-sided containers from an off-loading platform onto the back of a small transport vehicle. The machinery he was using to perform the work was balky and uncooperative. It was a rare example of thranx patience wearing thin. Having nothing else to do and already resigned to returning to Honydrop devoid of the edification he sought, Des wandered over and offered his help. If there was nothing here to stimulate his mind, at least he could exercise his body.

The youth accepted the stranger's offer gratefully. With the two of them working in tandem the process of shifting the containers accelerated noticeably. The open back of the little vehicle began to fill.

"What is in these?" Only mildly interested, Desvendapur glanced down at the container cradled in his four arms. The information embossed on the side of the gray repository was less than descriptive.

"Food," the other male informed him. "Ingredients. I am a food-preparation assistant, third level." There was no false pride in his voice. "Graduated at the top of my classification several years ago. That is how I secured this position."

"You make it sound like it's something special." Never known for his tact, Desvendapur was not about to open a new wing case now. He passed another container to the waiting male. "This is Geswixt, not Ciccikalk." In what had become a rote comment, he fished automatically. "Of course, if the humans were here, it would be different."

"Here?" The hardworking preparator whistled amusedly. "Why would there be any humans here, in Geswixt?"

"Why indeed? An absurd notion." A practiced Des displayed neither discouragement nor excitement.

His new acquaintance barely paused to catch his breath. "It really is. They are all up-valley, in their own quarters." He indicated the rapidly growing stack of containers. "This is food for them. I'm learning how to prepare sustenance not for our kind, but for humans."

5

Having by now more or less come to the depressing conclusion that the presence of humans in Geswixt was a myth, Desvendapur made the fastest mental adjustment of his life. With admirable lack of hesitation, he responded, "Yes, I know."

"You know?" The preparator hesitated uncertainly. "How do you know that?"

"By the markings on the containers," the poet replied without hesitation, supple prevarication being close kin to the white heat of creation. The only difference was that he was creating for the sake of convenience and not for posterity.

His new acquaintance clicked dubiously. "Every shipment is coded. How do you come to know the codes?"

Self-immersed in semantic mud and unable to see a way clear to extricating himself, Des blithely burrowed in deeper. "Because I'm here to cross-check you. I am also in food preparation, just assigned here as a general kitchen assistant." He tapped the repository he was cradling with all four digits of one truhand. "How are your skills? Current? Up-to-date? Tell me what this contains."

Distracted, the preparator glanced at the embossing. "Powdered milk. A natural mammalian bodily extract that is used as an ingredient in many meals."

"Very good!" Des complimented him slavishly even as he wondered what 'powdered milk' might be. "This one's trickier." He singled out a cylinder with a larger embossed identification area than its predecessor. "How about this?"

The younger male hesitated only briefly. "Soya patties, various nut extracts, dehydrated fish, assorted fruits and vegetables. I don't know all the individual names yet."

"Go on, try," Des urged him. "I'm going to catch you out yet before we're finished here."

"Nothing was said to me about another assistant being assigned to my section," the preparator murmured, still uncertain.

"That's what I thought." Des moved to stack the container without letting the other have a look at its index. "This one is too alien for you."

"No content listing is too alien for me. At least, I don't think it is." Antennae gyrated pridefully. "I complete all my assignments and receive notable ratings."

They continued in this fashion until the last of the containers had been transferred and its contents elucidated. "Where are your quarters?"

"They have not been designated yet." Des continued to improvise, a skill at which poet-soothers excelled. "I came up early. I'm not supposed to present myself until next day next."

The preparator considered. "There is not much to see here in Geswixt proper. Why don't you come with me? You can share my room until you have been assigned."

"Many thanks, Ulunegjeprok."

His new friend glanced around. "Where is your personal gear?"

"It missed the transport because I decided to come up early," Des explained. "Don't worry about me. It will work its way through the system in a couple of days."

"You can borrow some of mine if you need anything. I see you've already got cold-climate gear." He indicated the special protective attire that covered most of Desvendapur's body. "I need to see if there is any other cargo here for the kitchen. If not, we can leave in half a time-part."

"I will meet you right here," Des assured him.

Leaving the preparator, the poet rushed from one part of the terminal to the next in search of Melnibicon. When he found her, she was conversing amiably with a pair of older thranx. Fighting to conceal his excitement, he drew her aside.

"What's going on?" She eyed him warily. "Your spicules are dilated."

"I have . . . met someone," he hastened to explain. "An old friend. He has invited me to stay with him for a while."

"What's that? You can't do that." The senior flier looked around uncomfortably. "I took a chance just in bringing you over here for the afternoon. I can't leave you here. Your absence will be questioned."

"I'll take care of it. I will not involve you in any way, Melnibicon."

She took a step back from him, fending him off with both foothands.

"Blood parasites, you won't! I am already involved. You came *with* me, soother, and you are coming back with me."

"It is only for a day or two," he pleaded with her. "I won't be missed."

"What about your regular daily recitals, your rounds?"

"Tell anyone who asks that I'm not feeling well, that I am suffering from an internal upset and am self-medicating myself. Have Heul activate the privacy lock on my quarters."

"So you would involve her in your subterfuge as well. I will not be a party to this, Desvendapur. If you want to spend time here, place an application through the proper channels."

"It will not be approved," he argued. "You know it won't. Geswixt is a restricted destination."

"Exactly why you're coming back with me." She started to turn away. "Now if you will excuse me, *soother,* I am not finished talking with my friends."

He stood motionless, thoughts churning and anger rising as she persisted in ignoring him. It was impolite of him to remain standing there, but she remained adamant. Since she did not acknowledge his presence, her friends did not feel compelled to, either. Hiding his mounting frustration and his fury, he turned and started back across the broad, flat surface of the terminal. He would meet his new friend Ulu at the designated pickup point and at the appointed time, but first he had to make a stop at the lifter that had brought him here from Honydrop.

Walking gave him time to ponder what he was about to do. Though his mind was clear, his intentions firm, a part of him remained hesitant. What he contemplated was unlike him, unlike anything he had ever done before. But wasn't that the source of true artistic inspiration: the naked plunge, the embarkation into regions never before visited, the effort to break free of convention and restraint? He argued with himself all the way back to the lifter, while he was on it, and after he left it behind. But having set his mind, he solidified his decision as he approached the meeting place. He took considerable pride in not looking back over his shoulder, not even when he boarded the small truck and drove off in the company of chattering Ulunegjeprok.

Melnibicon would look for him, he knew. She would ask who had seen him. He doubted she would receive much in the way of response. Everyone in the terminal was busy, intent on his or her own business. No one would have noticed one more thranx striding purposefully through their field of vision. Eventually she would give up, cursing all the while, and reboard the lifter for the return flight to Honydrop. It was not her fault if he missed the departure. Upon her return she would report him as absent, accept whatever chiding was due for taking an unauthorized passenger to Geswixt, and go on about her business.

It troubled Desvendapur, but not to the point of preventing him from engaging in conversation with Ulu. They spoke about alien foodstuffs and their sometimes eccentric preparation, Des giving the impression he knew a great deal while in reality he was utterly ignorant on the subject. But the more Ulu talked, the more Des 'tested' and 'checked' him, the greater grew the poet's rapidly burgeoning store of knowledge. By the time they reached the checkpoint, he felt he could have carried on a limited conversation on the subject. Certainly he now knew more about it than any nonspecialist.

It was rare to see a hive tunnel blocked or guarded. Desvendapur supposed that access to military installations was similarly restricted, as was that leading to sensitive scientific installations, but this was the first time in his life he had actually encountered an armed guard. One of the pair recognized Ulunegjeprok immediately. Des tensed when the no-nonsense sentry turned his attention to the truck's passenger. But it was late in the day and the guard was tired. When Ulu cheerily explained that his passenger was another newly arrived worker assigned to his own section, the body-armored thranx accepted the explanation readily. There was no reason not to. Why would anyone not ordered to do so want to willingly place himself in close proximity to a bunch of soft-bodied, pinch-featured, antenna-less, malodorous mammals? The truck was waved through.

They entered a much longer tunnel, featureless except for periodic electronic checkpoints. Their progress was being monitored, Des realized. The amount of security was daunting. How long he would be able to continue to brazen his way through he did not know. Long enough to gain inspiration for a small volume of stanzas, he hoped. Phrases, at last, that would be underlain with real meaning and significance. After what he had gone through to get this far, he had better accomplish at least that much.

Would Melnibicon notice that the lifter's navigation system had been accessed? Would it occur to her to recheck a preprogrammed course that the craft had followed faultlessly many times before? If she did, then he would have only hours of freedom in which to seek inspiration. If she did not, and relaxed on board as she had on the flight over, then he might have a day or two in which to interact with the aliens and the storm of exotic sights and sounds they hopefully represented before Security caught up with him. As for Melnibicon, her hastily reprogrammed lifter would set her down automatically among the rilthy peaks, whereupon if he had done his work properly the flight instrumentation would then freeze up and compel her to call for rescue.

It never occurred to him while he had been entering his irate, hasty adjustments that the disoriented craft might simply run into the side of a mountain.

For a service tunnel, the corridor they were speeding down seemed to go on forever. Locked into the passageway's guide strip, Ulunegjeprok abandoned the controls to let the truck do its own driving. He would return to manual when necessary.

"So, where did you study?" he inquired innocently of his newly arrived counterfeit colleague.

Nothing if not voluble, Des spun an elaborate story woven around what he knew of Hivehom. Since Ulu was a native of Willow-Wane and had never been offworld, he could hardly catch Des in any mistakes. By the time the truck finally began to slow as they approached another floor-to-ceiling barrier, the poet had half convinced himself of his own skill at food preparation.

He held his breath, but the facility on the other side of the seal was disappointingly ordinary. Certainly there was nothing to indicate the presence of aliens. He was reluctant to press Ulu for details lest he appear too eager. Besides, the less he opened his mouthparts, the better. Silence was the best way of hiding ignorance.

Turning down a subsidiary corridor, Ulunegjeprok eventually parked the truck in a vacant unloading slot. Wordlessly, acting as though he knew exactly what he was doing and that he belonged, Des proceeded to help him unload. The kitchen facilities were extensive, spotless, and more or less familiar, though he did espy several devices whose purpose was foreign to him. That did not necessarily mean they were intended for the preparation of mammalian food, he reminded himself. He was a poet, not a cook, and the only food preparation equipment he was familiar with was the individual kind that he had made use of personally.

Encountering and finding himself introduced to a couple of Ulu's coworkers, he was delighted to discover that he could pass himself off as a colleague with a certain aplomb. They in turn were able to present him to still others, with the result that by nightfall he was an accepted member of the staff. Thus accredited through personal contact, his presence was not further remarked upon. He even assisted in the preparation of the night-time meal, noting that for this purpose the staff responsible for the preparation of the alien food had the extensive facility entirely to themselves.

To his surprise he discovered among the courses a number that were familiar to him. He did not comment on this revelation lest he expose his ignorance. But it was fascinating to learn that the humans could eat thranx food.

"Not all of it, of course," Ulu remarked in the course of their work, "but then you know that already. Fortunately, they don't ask us to assist in the treatment of meat."

"Meat?" Desvendapur was not sure he had heard the preparator correctly.

"That's right, joke about it," Ulu whistled. "I cannot imagine it myself. They warned us when we were taking the special courses, but still, the idea of intelligent creatures consuming the flesh of others of their own immediate family was more than a little terrifying. Didn't you find it so?"

"Oh, absolutely." Desvendapur was quick to improvise. "Meat eaters! The proclivity seems utterly incompatible with true intelligence."

"I have not seen them do it myself. I do remember asking, early on in the first seminar, why they did not just do all their own food preparation, but as you know the idea is to encourage them to become as comfortable as possible here. That means learning to eat food that we prepare." He whistled a soft chuckle. "What the media would not give to know that the only contact project isn't on Hivehom." Light flashed from his compound eyes as he looked over at Des, who was whitened up to his foothands in something called flour. "Wouldn't it be funny if you were a correspondent who had slipped in here under cover, and not a preparator assistant?"

Desvendapur laughed in what he fervently hoped was an unforced manner. "What an amusing notion, Ulu! Naturally, I am as sworn to secrecy as everyone else who has been chosen to work with the aliens."

"Naturally." Ulunegjeprok was forming the flour into loaves. Watching and learning something new and useful every minute, Des imitated him with rapidly accelerating skill. Alien food formed the basis for a nice quatrain or two, but where were the aliens themselves? Where? Would he have the opportunity not simply to prepare their food but to see them eat? To observe their flexible mouthparts in motion and see the long pink tongue thing that resided, like some symbiotic slug, within their mouths? That would provide inspiration for more than a few stanzas! Horror was always an efficacious stimulus.

He did not get his wish. The food was taken from them for final treatment and delivery, leaving the prep staff alone in the kitchen to clean up before retiring. Desvendapur followed Ulu to his quarters, memorizing sights and routes, learning something new and useful with every step.

"I have to present myself and my credentials in the morning, so I will be late to work," he told Ulu as they were preparing to retire. "Meanwhile, thank you for all that you have done, and for your hospitality tonight."

"Glad to be of help," the preparator replied guilelessly. "All kitchen assistance gratefully welcomed. You're good at your work."

"I had excellent instruction." By now Desvendapur had come to believe it himself. As of this moment he was not only an amateur poet, but a professional food preparator, one specializing in alien cuisine, who was and always had been a denizen of large, professional kitchens.

The death of Melnibicon, when he learned of it the following morning, threatened to shatter his resolve as much as his confidence. He had never intended for her to die, only to be delayed a day or so while he penetrated the secrets of Geswixt. But he was forced to set aside the overwhelming sense of guilt as he considered the ramifications of the corollary knowledge that in addition to her passing, the crash of the lifter had also resulted in the death of one Desvendapur, poet and soother, whom she had illegally transported to Geswixt for an afternoon. It seemed that neither body had been recoverable from the incinerated crash site.

He had become an instant nonperson. Desvendapur the soother no longer existed. His family and clan would grieve. So might Heul, for a short while. Then all would go on with their lives. As for himself, he had a chance to begin a new one—as a simple, hardworking, lowly food preparator for humans.

But first he needed a place to sleep, not to mention an identity.

There were a number of empty living cubicles. Settling on one located as far from the nearest inhabited space as possible, he moved himself in. The dearth of personal possessions within might puzzle a visitor, but he did not expect to have much in the way of company. His personal credit having perished along with his former identity, he would have to establish a new one with the fiscal facilities in Geswixt.

Altering a personal identity chit was a serious crime, but such ethical considerations no longer weighed heavily on Des. Not after having committed, however inadvertently, a killing. Artists died for their art, he rationalized. Melnibicon had died for his. He would compose a suitable, grand memorial to her in dance verse. It would be more honor than someone like herself was due or would normally rate. She should be grateful. Certainly her clan and family would be. Meanwhile, he had more important things to do than mourn the passing of someone who was, after all, practically a complete stranger, and an individual of indisputably little importance.

With the aid of the electronics in the cubicle it turned out to be surprisingly easy to forge a new identity. It helped that he was not attempting to have his new self classified as a specialist in military weaponry, or a communications expert, or a financial facilitator. Who would want to assume a false identity as a bottom-level food preparator? With a few delicate cybernetic twitches, his name became Desvenbapur, a change sufficiently significant to render him wholly separate and apart from the dead poet, but not radical enough to make a mess of his original identity chit. He waited tensely while the hive network processed his work. Because he had a position, because he was there, because he could now rely on the confirmation of others to support his new self, it was accepted, showing a credit balance of zero. Because he had been acknowledged by the system, no one thought to question his presence. With each succeeding day, Desvenbapur the assistant food preparator became a more familiar and well-liked figure around the complex. With each succeeding week, applying himself intensely to a job classification for which he was seriously overqualified, he grew more and more adept at its practice.

A day came when a newly arrived sanitation tech appeared, luggage in tow, to claim his previously unassigned cubicle. Finding someone already living within, both thranx referred the situation to the official in charge of housing. Preoccupied with more serious matters, she acknowledged that it was clear some degree of oversight had been at work. With Ulunegjeprok and other coworkers vouching for the amiable Des, she simply reassigned the newcomer to a different vacant cubicle, at which point the shelter the poet had earlier appropriated was officially entered into the hive records as his.

With an official residence, an accepted line of credit into which seasonal income was placed—as soon as the hive financial officer was informed by Des's friends that he was not being paid, the oversight was hastily corrected—and an occupation, Desvendapur's reinvention as Desvenbapur was complete. The chance of exposure still existed, but with each succeeding day it became less and less likely. Finding himself gifted with another highly efficient and willing assistant who seemed to have materialized out of nowhere, the food division supervisor was more than happy to have the additional, to all intents and purposes legitimate, help. Des's name began to creep, by default, into the official records of daily life at the complex. Desvenbapur the food preparator came into conclusive existence through the inherited process of bureaucratic osmosis.

He learned that anyone associating in any capacity, however distant, with the visiting humans was encouraged to learn more about them. Des was quick to take advantage of these free educational facilities. His off-duty hours were spent poring over the history of thranx-human contact, the official records of the ongoing project on Hivehom, and the hesitant but ongoing attempts to broaden contact between the two radically different, cautious species. There was nothing in the official records about another project at Geswixt. As far as publicly available history went, the complex did not exist.

He was afraid to be promoted, but commendations came his way in spite of his efforts to avoid them. The alternative was to work less diligently, to slack off on the job, but that might attract even more attention, and of an unwanted sort. So while striving to endear himself to his coworkers, he struggled to do that work which was assigned to him and little more, seeking safety in anonymity.

Already more knowledgeable about human food intake than all but the biochemists and other specialists, Desvendapur absorbed what knowledge was available about everything from the bipeds' appearance to their tastes in art and amusement to their mating habits. That a great deal was marked *unknown* did not surprise him. Though improving, contact between the species was still tentative and infrequent, proceeding officially only at the single recognized project site on Hivehom.

The reason for the clandestine complex at Geswixt was obvious: Both sides wanted to speed the pace of contact, to increase the opportunities for an exchange of views, and to stimulate learning. But it had to be done in such a way as not to alarm the general populace. Even after some fourteen years, each side was still far from confident they could trust the other. The thranx had more experience than they wished with duplicitous, deceitful intelligences, among whom the AAnn stood foremost. Sure, these soft-skinned mammals seemed sociable enough, but what if it were all a ruse, a ploy, an attempt to lull the hives into a fatal relaxation of their guard? No one wanted to see another Paszex happen on Hivehom, or anywhere else.

Among the humans there existed an equal if not greater number of concerns. With insects constituting a hereditary racial antagonist, the idea of becoming close friends with their giant, albeit distant alien cousins, the thranx, was difficult for many to stomach. Objections and concerns emerged less often intellectually than they did viscerally.

So each species continued to feel the other out, to study and to learn, and as they did so to keep a wary eye on the activities of the AAnn as well as the other known intelligences. The covert complex north of Geswixt was an attempt by the thranx to broaden and accelerate those contacts.

Though he experienced a delicious shudder of instinctive revulsion every time he called forth in his cubicle a three-dimensional projection of a human, Desvendapur relieved the nausea by composing a new set of sonnets, complete with appropriate accompanying choreography. These files he encrypted and secured with great care lest someone stumble upon them accidentally and wonder at the extraordinary aesthetic skills of a simple food preparator. The lines he devised were facile, the inventions clever, but they lacked the fire he sought. Where was the explosion of brilliance that would gain his work universal recognition? How was he to fabricate lyrical phrases so glorious that they would leave listeners stunned?

In his off hours he threw himself into a study of the humans' principal language, after first dismissing as a hidden joke the revelation that they still practiced dozens of different tongues. That was an absurd notion, even for creatures as alien as humans. Different dialects could exist, to be sure, but different languages? Dozens of them? How could a civilization arise out of such a counterproductive babble? Deciding that the first linguists to make contact were having a little fun at the expense of those who came after, he ignored the assertion as he concentrated on the language of contact.

Recordings of their speech yielded a brutal, guttural mode of communication that made Low Thranx sound like a clear stream running over water-polished stones. It was not unpronounceable, but it was unwieldy. And where were the whistles and clicks that gave civilized speech so much of its color and variety? Not to mention the modulated stridulations that humans seemed utterly incapable of duplicating. Though it was difficult to countenance, the records indicated that some human linguists had succeeded in mastering portions of both High and Low Thranx. Furthermore, they had the ability, like the AAnn, to take in air through their mouths instead of through designated, specialized breathing orifices as did the thranx and others. Like the AAnn, their air intakes were located on their faces, resulting in a severe crowding of important sensory organs in the same place. And there were only two air intakes. The thranx had eight, four on each side of the thorax. Given such a deprived physiological architecture, Des thought it something of a minor miracle that the humans were able to take in enough air to supply their blood with sufficient oxygen.

With no one to practice on, he learned by means of repeating human phrases in the solitude of his cubicle. As he studied, he composed, waiting for the time when blinding inspiration would strike. What would help, what he wished for more than anything else, was to meet an actual alien. He knew their food, or at least the thranx food they could digest. Now he wanted to know them.

He had been at the complex for more than a year, long enough to experience the first feelings of despair, when the opportunity finally came.

6

Golfito wasn't much of a city. Located in a fine natural harbor, it existed only to service the cruise ships and other tourist vessels that stopped to give their passengers a quick taste of the Corcovado rain forest. After making a wild flurry of purchases and embedding tridee cues into their home units like crazy, they reboarded the giant, luxurious hydrofoils and zeps and floated or flew onward, heading for more glamorous destinations to the north, the south, or across the isthmus. In their wake they left memories of foolish behavior, hasty sexual assignations with Golfito's enterprising exotics, and much-appreciated credits.

Montoya had tried his best to attach himself to some of the thousands of credits that spilled from the bulging credcards of the laughing, wide-eyed visitors, but despite his most strenuous efforts he never seemed quite able to cement any valuable contacts. He was always a little too slow, a step behind, left fumbling for the right word or phrase, like the fisherman who never manages to pick the right lure to attract the fish that surround him on all sides.

But if he had failed to cash in on the bounty offered up by the regular loads of visitors, he had succeeded in making a few potentially useful contacts among the less reputable denizens of Golfito's waterfront and rain forest suburbs. Among these sometimes agreeable, sometimes surly specimens was one who dangled promises in front of the struggling immigrant like sugarcease before a diabetic.

Surprisingly, the ever-hopeful but always realistic Montoya had received word that one of those promises might actually be on the verge of being fulfilled.

Ehrenhardt's place hugged one of the steep rain forest-covered hillsides that rose above the town. As he rode the silent electric lift up to the gated enclosure, Montoya gazed down at the exquisite blue of the bay and the dark Pacific beyond. Monkeys, jaguars, quetzals, and all manner of exotic creatures inhabited the carefully preserved lands on both sides of the city. They interested him only to the extent of their cash value. Not that he would dare to compete with one of the known poacher consortiums. He knew better. Try, and he'd end up a skin at the bottom of somebody else's trophy case.

A lanky Indian with a prominent sidearm and expressionless eyes met him at the top. Beckoning for the intimidated guest to follow, he escorted Cheelo out onto the porch that overlooked the sultry panorama below. Rudolf Ehrenhardt did not rise, but he did offer Montoya a drink from the iced pitcher sitting on the lovingly polished purpleheart table before him. He did not, however, gesture for his visitor to take a seat, and so Montoya remained standing, drink awkwardly in hand.

"Cheelo, my friend." The fixer squinted behind his polarizing glasses, eyes completely hidden. It was like conversing with a machine, Montoya thought. "You really should invest in some nose work."

Montoya flinched inwardly. It was not his fault that over the course of a difficult life that distinctive protuberance had been broken and reset more times than he cared to remember. "If I could afford it, Mr. Ehrenhardt, sir, I'd certainly consider it."

The older man nodded approvingly. It was a good reply. "What if I were to tell you that the opportunity to afford that, and many other good things, has finally arrived for you?"

His guest put the already empty glass back down on the table. He had been unable to identify any of the contents beyond wonderful. "Ay, you know me, sir. I'll do whatever is necessary."

Ehrenhardt chuckled, enjoying himself, drawing out the suspense even though he was quite aware that his guest was in an agony of expectation. A harpy eagle soared past below, skimming the treetops in search of somnolent monkeys. Somewhere an indolent pet macaw screamed.

"You've always told me that you wanted to do something big."

"Just the opportunity, Mr. Ehrenhardt, sir. All I want is for someone to give me a chance. That's all I've ever wanted."

The fixer smiled condescendingly. "There is an opening in Monterrey that has come about through . . . let us say *attrition*." Ehrenhardt did not add the word *natural* before attrition, and Montoya did not question him as to the reason for the omission. "I have been asked to recommend someone suitable to take over the franchise. It is exceptionally lucrative, but it requires the attention of someone with drive, intelligence, and desire. Also someone who knows the meaning of loyalty, of when to speak and when to keep his mouth shut."

"You know me, Mr. Ehrenhardt, sir." Cheelo drew himself up to his full, if unprepossessing, height.

"No, I do not know you." The older man was staring hard, hard into Montoya's eyes. "But I am learning more each time we meet. I placed your name before the involved parties, and I am happy to say it has been accepted. Conditionally, of course."

"Thank you, sir! Thank you!" At last, Montoya thought. The chance to fulfill all his dreams! He would show them all. Everyone who had ever mocked him, looked down on him, spit on his intentions. Here at last was the opportunity to prove himself to all of them, to each and every one of the sarcastic, heartless bastards. In particular, there was a worthless little town up in the Amistad . . .

Something Ehrenhardt had said made him hesitate. "Conditionally, sir? Conditional on what?"

"Well, my ambitious friend, surely you know that such opportunities do not come along every day, and those special things that do not come along every day are not for free. A franchise is what it is because it must be paid for. A minimal sum, provided as a guarantor of the prospective franchisee's good faith."

Montoya swallowed and maintained his self-control. "How much?" So nervous was he that he forgot to say *sir*.

Either Ehrenhardt did not notice or chose magnanimously to ignore the oversight. Smiling, he pushed a piece of embossed plastic across the table in the direction of his apprehensive guest. Montoya picked it up.

He breathed a little easier. The amount was daunting, but not impossible. The date . . .

"I have until this day of the indicated month to raise the required fee?"

Ehrenhardt nodded paternally. "If it is not forthcoming by then, the franchise must by mutual agreement of the parties involved be awarded to another. That is the way of things. Tell me: Can you be in compliance?"

"Yes, sir! I know that I can do it." The time allowed was generous. But he had none to waste, to linger on the beaches and ogle the ladies in the bars and restaurants.

"That is what I told the others." The smile faded. "I know the extent of your financial condition, Cheelo. It is not one to inspire confidence."

He did his best to shrug off the criticism. "That's because I enjoy myself, sir. I spend credit as I acquire it. But if you know my status, then you know that it is not always so insignificant."

To Montoya's relief, the fixer's smile returned. "Another good answer. Keep giving the right answers, Cheelo, and come up with the necessary fee by the indicated date, and you will have your chance to do something big. Take advantage of this opportunity, work hard, and you can become a wealthy and important person, just like myself. I need not tell you that such a chance comes along but rarely in a man's lifetime. For most, it never comes at all."

"I won't fail it, sir—or you."

Ehrenhardt waved diffidently. "This has nothing to do with me, Cheelo. It has everything to do with you. Remember that." He sipped contemplatively at the pale liquid maintained at just above the freezing point by the thermotic tumbler. Somewhere within the rambling white stucco building that idiot macaw refused to shut up. It was making Montoya nervous. "Tell me, Cheelo—what do you think of these aliens that are so much in the news these days?"

"Aliens, Mr. Ehrenhardt?"

"These insectile creatures who persist in trying to further relations with us. What do you think is their real purpose?"

"I really don't know, sir. I don't think much about such things."

"You should." Adjusting his dark glasses, the fixer gazed out across the bay to the open ocean beyond. "This is a surprisingly crowded corner of the galaxy, Cheelo. It behooves every one of us to consider what is taking place here. We can no longer go about our business here on Earth indifferent to what happens on other worlds, as we could in the days before the invention of the drive. Take these reptilian AAnn, for example. The thranx insist they are incorrigible, aggressive expansionists. The AAnn deny it. Whom are we humans to believe?"

"Ay—I really couldn't say, sir."

"No, of course you couldn't." Ehrenhardt sighed deeply. "And it's wrong of me to expect it of someone like yourself. But living here, I am inescapably surrounded by those of limited vision." Rising abruptly, he took the startled Montoya's hand and grasped it with a firmness that belied his age.

"Deliver the fee by the indicated date and the franchise is yours, Cheelo. The franchise, and the prestige and everything else that goes with it. One thing more: The credit transfer must be made in front of me. I am required by those others involved in the business to witness it in person. There are many traditionalists among us who do not trust long-distance electronics. So I *will* see you before the indicated date?" Montoya nodded, and the hand moved to the jittery younger man's shoulder. "Then you can do your 'big things.' " He sat back down. The interview was at an end.

Cheelo rode the lift back down to the city in a haze of euphoria. His chance at last! By all the gods of his forefathers and all the gonads of those who had ever kicked, beaten, or insulted him, he would raise the necessary money somehow. It shouldn't be too hard. He had ample experience in such matters.

But he could not do it in Golfito. Because of the prevalence of the tourist ships and zeps there were simply too many police about. They were alert to the activities of denizens such as himself. He was too well known to them. He would have to go to work elsewhere.

He knew just the place.

7

Ulunegjeprok's voice was flat, betraying no hint of the excitement he felt. "Instead of preparing foodstuff basics for humans," he asked his friend and fellow worker, "how would you like to deliver some?"

Desvendapur did not look up from where he was cleaning a large quantity of pale pink *vekind* root. "Do not joke with me, Ulu. What are you talking about?"

"Hamet and Quovin, the senior biochemists in charge of final checkout and delivery, are both down sick. It has fallen to Shemon to carry out the transfer of this week's produce. I spoke to her earlier. She has never done this before and is apprehensive about doing it alone."

"Why?" Des wondered. "You know the procedure as well as I. It is not complicated."

"It isn't procedure that concerns her. She has never dealt with the humans in person, only via communicator, and she is not sure how she will react. So she asked for subsidiary personnel to accompany her." His antennae straightened. "I volunteered. Knowing of your interest in the aliens, I also volunteered you." He extended a foothand. "I hope you are not disappointed in me. If you want to withdraw your services for this afternoon . . ."

"Withdraw?" Desvendapur could hardly believe his good fortune. At last, after all he had suffered—physically, mentally, and emotionally—he was going to encounter the bipeds in person instead of via research team projections and odorless images. Already mellifluous phrases and biting stanzas were bubbling in his brain. "This afternoon? How soon?"

Ulunegjeprok whistled amusedly. "Clean your eyes. We have several time-parts yet."

Des did his best to concentrate on his work, but everything he managed to accomplish subsequent to his friend's revelation he did by rote. His mind was spinning. He would take a scri!ber with him so that he could compose on the spot, to ensure that nothing was lost and every advantage taken from the forthcoming confrontation. There was no telling how long his superiors' illnesses or Shemon's aversion would last. It might be some time before the opportunity arose again.

"What are you doing?" As he labored at his own station, Ulu eyed his weaving, bobbing coworker curiously.

"Composing poetry."

"You? Poetry?" Ulunegjeprok whistled long and hard. "You're an assistant food service preparator. What makes you think you can compose poetry?"

"It is just a hobby. Something to occupy my recreational time."

"Good thing Hamet and Quovin are both out sick and Shemon is busy inventorying the week's consignment. They wouldn't look upon this as recreational time. Well, as long as you're making the effort, I'll give it a try. For friendship's sake, even though it will be painful. Go on, I'm braced—recite something."

"No, never mind." Aware that in his excitement he was skirting potentially dangerous territory, Desvendapur turned back to his work, stripping the thorny casing from oblong *cazzi!!s* fruit. "I'm not very good at it."

"That goes without saying, but I would still like to hear something." Ulu would not be put off.

Cornered, Des complied, trilling and clicking as inconsequential and unsophisticated a brace of stanzas as he could manage, a feeble collage of words and sounds guaranteed to get him whistled down at any semiprofessional gathering of qualified soothers.

Ulu's reaction was wonderfully predictable. "That was awful. You had better stick to making *hequenl* buns. You're good at that."

"Thank you," Des told him, and he meant it.

Systems idling, the small transport truck in the warehousing chamber hovered an arm's length off the floor. Des and Ulu saw to the transfer of assorted crates and containers while the venerable Shemon accounted for each one as it was loaded. It was evident from her attitude as well as her words that she did not want to be doing this, that she dearly wished the absent Hamet or Quovin were present instead, and that the sooner they had concluded the delivery and returned, the better she would like it.

There was barely enough room in the vehicle's enclosed cab for three. As she adjusted the guide controls and the truck started silently forward down a well-lit corridor, Desvendapur checked to make certain his scri!bers were nestled snugly in the abdominal pouch slung over his left side. He had brought two, in case one should fail.

"Why do you need us to come along anyway?" Ulu was asking her. At these words, Des wanted to reach out and smother him. "Are these creatures so physically feeble that they cannot unload their own supplies?"

"The ones that are present are engaged in more important tasks. They are scientists and researchers, not manual laborers. Easier for us to do such work." She looked over at him. "Why? Do you want to go back?"

Desvendapur hardly dared to breathe.

"No. I was just wondering," the unimaginative Ulu concluded.

The corridor was blocked by another guard station. Here they were waved through without an identification check, the contents of the transport being sufficient to establish their legitimacy and purpose. As the vehicle accelerated, Des looked for any sign of a change, for anything exotic or alien, and saw nothing. They might as well still be traveling through the thranx portion of the complex.

Eventually they pulled into a storage chamber scarcely different from the one they had left. Easing the truck into a receiving dock, Shemon shut off the power to the engine and slipped off the driver's bench. Ulu and Des followed her around to the back of the conveyance.

Under her direction, they began unloading the foodstuffs they had brought. Save for small robot handlers and cleaners, the chamber remained empty. He tried not to panic. Where were the humans? Where were the aliens he had sacrificed his career, more than a year of his life, and the life of another to see? Unable to stand it any longer, he asked as much.

Shemon gestured indifferently. It was evident that she was well pleased with the turn of events. "Who knows? It is not necessary for them to be here for the unloading."

"But don't they have to acknowledge receipt? Don't they need to check the delivery to make sure everything's here?" Desvendapur was moving as slowly as he possibly could without appearing to be deliberately inhibiting the unloading process.

"What for? They have been notified that the weekly delivery was on its way. If anything is missing, or out of the ordinary, our department will be notified and the omission corrected." Her relief was palpable. "At least *we* won't have to deal with it personally."

But that was precisely what Des wanted, needed to do: to deal with things personally. Despite his best efforts to bring about an inconspicuous slowdown, the quantity of cargo in the back of the transport was diminishing at an alarming rate. At this pace they would be done and gone within half a time-part. He invented and discarded dozens of scenarios. He could fake an injury, but Shemon and Ulu would only load him into the rear of the transport and hurry him back to the infirmary in the thranx sector. He could try overpowering the two of them, but while Shemon might prove a less than challenging adversary, Ulunegjeprok was young and fit and might be difficult to surprise. Besides, Des was a poet, not a soldier. And while such a hostile action might gain him a few time-parts of independence, the reverberations of such a gesture would undoubtedly result in his expulsion from the Geswixt hive and the loss of any further opportunity to encounter the aliens.

There was nothing he could do. He was trapped in a web of inexorably contracting time. His abdomen twitched, reminding him that his thoughts did not operate independent of his body.

Revelation congealed like a ripe pudding. Perhaps that was enough.

Passing a self-hovering cylindrical container twice his size to the waiting Ulu, he glanced in Shemon's direction. "I have to relieve myself."

She did not even look up from the readout on which she was tallying inventory. Truhand and foothand pointed. "Over there, through that second door. Don't you recognize the markings?"

Desvendapur looked in the indicated direction. "Those are indicators for a human facility."

"It is a joint facility, or so the instruction manual claims. But you didn't see my instructions; you only saw yours, so I suppose your ignorance is understandable. Be quick, and do not linger." There was unease in her voice. "I want to leave this place as soon as possible."

He gestured assent leavened with understanding as he hurried off in the indicated direction, all six legs working. The doorway yielded to his touch and granted entry, whereupon he found himself confronted with as exotic a panoply of devices as if he had stepped into the cockpit of a starship—although their functions were far more down to earth, in more ways than one.

In addition to the familiar sonic cleanser and slitted receptacles in the floor, there were a number of what appeared to be hollow seats attached to a far wall. He would have liked to inspect them more closely, but he was here to try to encounter aliens, not their artifacts. Desperately he searched the waste chamber for another exit, only to find none.

Refusing to give up and return to the unloading dock, he eased the door to the service chamber open and peered out, folding his antennae flat back against his smooth skull to create as small a profile as possible. Shemon was focused on her readout while Ulu was preoccupied with the remainder of the unloading. Waiting until his coworker was busy in the back of the vehicle, Desvendapur bolted to his right, hugging the wall of the storage chamber while hunting desperately for another way out. He had to try three sealed portals before he found one that was not locked.

Entering and closing the door behind him, he noted that it was of human design, being narrower and higher than that intended solely for thranx. Ahead lay a ramp leading upward. Advancing with determination, he took in a plethora of alien artifacts around him: contact switches of human design in a raised box; a railing of some kind attached to the wall head-high, too elevated to be useful to a thranx; a transparent door behind which was mounted equipment whose pattern and purpose he did not recognize; and more. Though the ramp was oddly ribbed instead of pebbled as was normal, it still provided excellent purchase for his anxious feet.

A second, larger door loomed in front of him. From its center bulged a recognizable activation panel dotted with unfamiliar controls. Touching the wrong one, or the wrong sequence, might set off an alarm, but at this point he didn't care. Even if that proved to be the ultimate result of his intrusion, at least there was an outside chance aliens might respond to the alert. Without hesitating, he pressed two of the four digits of his left truhand against a green translucency. From his studies he knew that humans were as fond of the color green as were the thranx.

The door buzzed softly and swung back. Without waiting for it to open all the way, he dashed through as soon as the opening was large enough to allow his abdomen to pass. There was a temperature curtain ahead, and he hurried right through it as well. Then he came to a stop, stunned physically as well as mentally. He was outside. On the surface.

In the mountains.

His feet sank into drifted rilth, and incredible iciness raced up his legs like fire. The shock was magnified by the fact that he was not wearing cold-weather gear, but only a couple of carrying pouches. There was no need for special protective attire in the hive below. Looking around, he saw whiteness everywhere—the whiteness of newly fallen rilth.

Turning, he took a step back toward the portal. The intense cold was already numbing his nerves, making it difficult to feel his legs. It struck him forcefully that no one knew he was out here. Ulu and Shemon would not begin to wonder at his continued absence for another several minutes at least. When they did, they would start by searching for him in the unloading area. By the time anyone thought to look for him outside, he would be dead, his respiration stilled, his limbs frozen solid.

He tried to take another step, but even with all six legs working, the cold had reduced his pace to a bare shuffle. Fresh rilth, frozen white precipitation, began to sift down around him, spilling from a leaden sky. I'm going to die out here, he thought. The irony was unspeakable. His death would provide excellent fodder for some bard in search of inspiration. The tragic demise of the poet aspirant. No, he corrected himself. Of a stupid assistant food preparator. Even his motives would be misascribed.

"Hey over there! Are you all right?"

He found that he could still turn his head, though the effort made the muscles in his neck shriek. The salutation had come from a figure a full head taller than himself—from a biped, a human.

From his studies Des knew that humans rarely went without protective attire, even when indoors and out of the weather. This one was clad in a single pouch of loose gray clothing that covered it from neck to ankle. The leggings fit neatly into short gray boots of some synthetic material. Astonishingly, its head and hands were unprotected, directly exposed to the falling rilth. Though it evinced no sign of an integrated heating unit, it moved freely and easily through the accumulated rilth that came up to just below the tops of its footwear.

Though it was far from the circumstances under which Desvendapur had first hoped to try out his store of meticulously memorized human phrases, he was not shy about responding. The vocal modulations sounded unnaturally harsh to his ears, and he hoped he was not overemphasizing the guttural nature of the mammalian speech.

Evidently he was not, because the human responded immediately, hurrying toward him. It was astonishing to observe it lifting first one foot and then the other, plunging one uncaringly downward into the rilth, raising the other, and bringing it forward. How it managed to stand upright, much less advance on only two limbs, and without a counterbalancing tail like the AAnn or the Quillp, was something to behold.

"What are you doing out here like this?" Up close, the biped's odor even in the clear outside mountain air was all but overpowering. Desvendapur's antennae flinched away. Performed in front of another thranx, the reaction would have constituted a grave insult. Either the human was unaware of its meaning or did not care. "You guys hate the cold."

"You—" Desvendapur continued to hesitate over the words even though it was clear that the human understood him. "—You don't mind it?"

"It's not bad out today, and I'm dressed for it." With a soft, fleshy hand that boasted five flexible digits the human began brushing accumulated rilth from the errant thranx's head and thorax.

"But your face, and your hands—they're exposed."

The creature had only two opposing mouthparts instead of the usual four. These parted to reveal teeth as white as the falling rilth. Des did not have teeth, but he knew what they were. He struggled to recall the library information that dealt with the utterly alien aspect of human facial expressions. While the bipeds could and did gesture with their limbs, they preferred to use their obscenely flexible faces to convey meaning and emotion. In this ability they exceeded even the AAnn, whose visages were also flexible but because of the scaly nature of their skin, far more stiff and restricted.

As the human continued to brush rilth from the thranx's numbed body, seemingly oblivious to the dangerous damp coldness melting against its hands, Des marveled at the exposed flesh. Why the rippling pink stuff simply did not slough off the internal skeleton was another of nature's marvels. There was nothing to protect it: no exoskeleton, no scales, not even any fur except for a small amount that covered the top of the skull. The creature was as barren of natural cover as the muscles that were barely concealed within. The poet shuddered, and not entirely from the cold. Here was the stuff of nightmares indeed—and of shocking inspiration. Animals could exist so, but something sapient? He found it hard to believe the evidence of his eyes.

"We've got to get you inside. Hang on."

If Des had wondered at the biped's ability to ambulate on only two limbs without toppling sideways at every third or fourth step, he was positively stunned when it bent at the middle lower joints, reached beneath his abdomen, and lifted. He felt himself rising, the lethal cold of the drifted rilth sliding away from his exposed feet, the heat of the creature reaching out even through its protective clothing. Then he was being carried. That the biped, heavily burdened with its load, did not immediately fall over backward was scarce to be believed.

Not only did it not collapse or lose its balance, it carried Des all the way back through the temperature curtain. Warm moist air enveloped them like a blanket. Feeling began to return to Desvendapur's limbs, and the creeping stiffness started to recede.

"Can you stand by yourself?"

"Yes, I think so."

Once they were through the main door the human set him down, keeping a steadying hand on his thorax. Despite the absence of a supportive exoskeleton, the digits were surprisingly strong. The sensation was one no library spool could convey.

"Thank you." He gazed up into the single-lensed human eyes, trying to fathom their depths.

"What the hell were you doing outside like that? If I hadn't come along you'd be in a bad way."

"I would not be in a bad way. I would be dead. I intend to compose a sequence of heroic couplets about the experience. The sensation of the cold alone should be worth several inspiring stanzas."

"Oh, you're a poet?" Absently, the human checked a numerical readout attached to his wrist. Desvendapur had decided the creature was a male due to the presence of certain secondary sexual characteristics and the absence of others, though given the thickness of the voluminous protective clothing it was difficult to be absolutely certain.

"No," Des hastily corrected himself. "That is, I am an assistant food preparator. Composition is a hobby, nothing more." To try to change the subject he added, "If you have sampled thranx fare, I have probably worked on the initial stages of its preparation."

"I'm sure that I have. We eat your stuff all the time. No way we could import enough to keep everybody fed and still maintain our privacy here. Willow-Wane fruits and vegetables and grains are a welcome change from concentrates and rehydrates. What's your name?"

"Desvenbapur." He whistled internally as the human gamely assayed a comical but passable imitation of the requisite clicks and whistles that comprised the poet's cognomen. "And you?"

"Niles Hendriksen. I'm part of the construction team working with your people to expand our facility here."

Expand, Des thought. Then the human presence on Willow-Wane likely *did* consist of more than just a small scientific station. Still, that did not make it a colony. He needed to learn more. But how? Already the human was exhibiting signs of impatience. It wanted to resume its own schedule, Des suspected. Furthermore, perspiration was pouring down its exposed face. Even deprived of every last piece of attire, Desvendapur knew, it would find the heat and humidity within the unloading area acutely uncomfortable.

"I would like to see you again, Niles. Just to talk."

The human's smile was not as wide this time. "You know that's not allowed, Desvenbapur. We're breaking a couple of pages of stipulations and restrictions right now by just standing here conversing. But I'll be damned if I was going to walk on by and let you freeze to death." He started to back up, still without falling down. "Maybe we'll see each other again. Why don't you apply to come work in our sector?"

"There is such a position?" Des hardly dared to hope.

"I think so. There are always a couple of thranx working with our own food people. But I think they must be master preparators, not assistants. Still, with the installation expanding and all, maybe they can use some lower-level help." With that he turned and headed back up the ramp, closing the door at the top behind him.

Thoughts churning, Desvendapur made his way back to the central dock and the waiting truck. A distraught Ulu and an angry Shemon were waiting for him, having long since completed the unloading.

"Where were you?" Shemon inquired immediately.

"I needed to relieve myself. I told you." Desvendapur met her gaze evenly, his antennae held defiantly erect.

"You're lying. Ulu went to check on you. You were not in the facility."

"I was having digestive convulsions so I took a walk, thinking that it might ease the discomfort."

She was having none of it. Her antennae dipped forward. "What more appropriate place to deal with intestinal convulsions than the hygienic facility you were already inside?"

"I wasn't thinking straight. I am sorry if I caused you to worry."

Ulunegjeprok stepped forward and spoke up in his coworker's defense. "There is no need to torment him. Look at his eyes. Can't you see that he is not feeling well?" He reached out to lay a reassuring hand on Des's thorax.

Desvendapur quickly stepped back. His friend gestured surprise, and Des hastened to concoct an explanation. "I am sorry, Ulu. It's nothing personal, but I do not want to be touched just now. I am afraid it might irritate my insides, and they do not need any more stimulation." The real reason was that his chitin was still chilled from his sojourn on the surface, a phenomenon that would not be so easily explained away as his extended absence.

"Yes, I can see that." His colleague gestured concern. "You should report to the infirmary immediately upon our return."

"I intend to," a relieved Des replied.

Little was said on the return journey down the access tunnel. Desvendapur kept, physically and verbally, largely to himself. Believing him ill, neither Ulu nor the still silently fuming Shemon intruded on his personal privacy.

Once back in the complex, the poet excused himself. He went not to the infirmary but to the preparation area. There he searched until he found a suitable bin of spoiled *hime* root and ripely decomposing *coprul* leaves. From this he fashioned a suitably noxious meal and forced himself to eat every last leaf and stem. Within half a time-part he was able to present himself outside the complex's medical facilities with a genuine, full-blown case of severe gastrointestinal upset, for which he was tenderly treated.

By the next day he was feeling much better. He could hardly wait for his work shift to end, whereupon he retired to his cubicle, set a flagon of thin !eld by the side of his resting bench, lowered the lights, activated his scri!ber, and in the carefully crafted privacy of his quarters, prepared to compose. And then a strange thing happened.

Nothing happened.

When he struggled to find the words and sounds to describe his encounter with the human, nothing suitable manifested itself. Oh, there were sounds and phrases at his disposal: an ocean of suitable components wanting only inspiration to lock them tightly together. He assembled several stanzas—and erased them. Attempting to mime the sound of the human voice while utilizing thranx terminology, he constructed an edifice of hoarse clicks—and tore it apart.

What was wrong? The words were there, the sounds— but something was missing. The consecution lacked fire, the framework elegance. Everything had happened so fast he had only been able to react, when what he really needed was time to absorb, to study, to contemplate. Concentrating on survival, he had not had time to open himself to inspiration.

The only explanation, the only solution, was obvious. More input was needed. More of everything. More contact, more conversation, more drama—though next time, not of the life-threatening variety. He remembered the words of the human Niles. But how could he apply for a professional position in the human sector that might not even exist? Or if it did, how could he ingratiate himself with the necessary authority without revealing information he was not supposed to know?

He would find a way. He was good with invention, with words. Not inspired, perhaps. Not yet. But he did not need to be inspired to proceed. He needed only to be clever.

Would the human speak of their encounter to his own superiors or coworkers? And if he did, would word of the unauthorized contact reach the thranx authorities who administered the indigenous half of the complex? Desvendapur waited many days before he was convinced that the human had kept the details of the confrontation and rescue to himself. Either that, or his coworkers did not feel the incident worthy of mention to their hosts. Only when Des felt halfway confident that news of the occasion had not been disseminated did he risk probing possibilities.

"I do not understand." Rulag, Des's immediate superior, was gazing at the readout on her screen. "It says here that you are to report for service to the human sector tomorrow morning at sunrise. You have been assigned to the inner detail."

Somehow Desvendapur managed to contain himself. This was what he had been waiting for. "I have repeatedly applied for any opening in food preparation in the human sector, in the hopes that they might expand our presence there."

"You know very well that they have been doing so, albeit slowly and carefully. But that's not what puzzles me." With two digits of a truhand she indicated the readout, which was positioned out of Des's line of sight. "It says here that you are to bring all your belongings with you. Apparently you are not only to work in the human sector; you are also to reside there." She looked up at him. "To my knowledge, all thranx who work with the bipeds have their quarters here, on the border of Geswixt proper."

He shifted edgily on all four feet. "Obviously there has been a change in policy. Or perhaps it is part of some new experiment."

Her interest as she studied him was genuine. "This doesn't bother you? You are prepared to go and live among the humans?"

"I will be with others of my own kind." He genuflected confidence. "Surely I'm not the only one to be so assigned. The humans would not request only a lowly assistant food preparator to come live and work among them."

"No, there have been others. You are right about that. Only you from our division, but I have talked with other level-nine supervisors. One from meteorology has been similarly assigned, another from engineering—you will have company." She gestured brusque negativity. "*I* couldn't do it."

"You don't have a sufficiently open or exploratory nature," Desvendapur replied gently. It was not a criticism.

"Yes I do, but only where innovative food preparation is concerned." Rising from the desk, she dipped her antennae toward him. "I will miss you, Desvenbapur. Not particularly on a personal basis, but in the kitchen. You are a good worker. In fact, I don't believe I have ever seen such dedication in so prosaic a classification. It is almost as if you have the capability to achieve much more."

"As you say, I like to work hard," he replied evasively, refusing to bite on the bait of the compliment. "At first light, you said?"

"Yes." She turned away. "Report to the transition chamber, dock six. I am told there are three others who are going at the same time, so your first encounter with the humans will not be a solitary one."

He had already had a first encounter, but that was and would always remain a private matter. "It will not take me long to gather my things."

"No, from all that I've been told you are not an accumulator. I suppose that under the circumstances that's all for the best. Farewell, Desvenbapur. I hope you find your stay among these creatures enlightening, or at least not too frightening."

She would not have understood if he had told her that he hoped to be frightened—also amazed, overwhelmed, terrified, awed, and subject to every other strong emotion possible. It was only from such extremes of feeling that true art arose. But he could not tell her that. He could not tell anyone. What emotions he experienced, as first assistant food preparator Desvenbapur, were only supposed to arise from intimate contact with vegetables.

8

He was the first of the four adventurous ones to present himself at the designated assembly point. The others arrived soon after. The meteorologist was there, as was a senior structural engineer. The third member of the group was a young female sanitation worker who went by the dulcet patronymic of Jhywinhuran. Forcing himself to ignore the more interesting conversation of the two high-level researchers, he gravitated toward the only one of the group with whom he might naturally be expected to bond.

He would much rather have discussed their situation and prospects with the two scientists, but joining in an ongoing discussion with two such cerebral heavyweights was just the sort of misstep that could call his carefully constructed false identity into question. As it turned out, he was only mildly disappointed. Jhywinhuran was lively, personable, far more attractive than either of the two senior techs, and did not rank his job classification. It did not take much of an effort on his part to settle readily onto the bench alongside hers.

"This is so exciting!" Light from overhead sparkled in her eyes. He observed that the red bands that streaked the predominant gold of her multiple lenses shaded delicately to pink. "Ever since the existence of the bipeds was acknowledged by the government I've dreamed of working closely with them. That's why I applied for a position here. But I never imagined I would ever have the opportunity of actually living among them as well."

"Why?"

She gestured uncertainty. "Why what?"

"Why do you want to work and live among them?" Beneath them, the transport shifted slightly as it backed out of the loading bay and moved toward a tunnel whose terminus he knew from a previous visit.

"I've always liked new things," she replied. "Anything new. When I heard about this, it seemed like the newest thing there could be."

He looked away from her, scrutinizing the tunnel ahead. "You sound like you should be an artist."

"Oh, no!" She seemed shocked at the notion. "For that you need a constructive imagination. Mine is purely deductive. I have no aesthetic discipline at all. But I'm very good at what I do."

"You must be," he told her, "or you would not have been chosen for this transfer."

"I know." She stridulated personal pride. "I'm proud of my skills, even if my position is a lowly one."

"Not at all," he chided her. "Mine is lower still. In essence we are both laborers in the same discipline: biology. I work one end, and you the other."

To make the mild witticism work he was forced to employ a couple of whistles in High Thranx. It took her several moments for comprehension to dawn, but when it did her gesture of amusement was highly appreciative. As always, he knew that he would have to be careful not to reveal too much of his erudition. Assistant food preparators rarely made use of High Thranx, which was not a dialect but a second language whose use was largely reserved for the learned.

The journey through the tunnel seemed to go on forever. Certainly he did not remember it taking half so long on his previous visit. When questioned, the transport driver could only say that he was taking them to the destination decreed on his manifest. What would happen to them after they arrived at their destination he did not know.

After what felt like an interminable junket the transport pulled into a dock unlike any Des had seen before. All thranx facilities were spotless, but this one gleamed as if it was scoured down every other time-part. Security was noticeably prominent. The travelers were escorted off the transport, equal attention being paid to scientists and support workers. Ushered into a clean room, their bodies and personal luggage were minutely inspected, scanned, probed, and analyzed. Desvendapur would have been uneasy had he not observed that Jhy was even more nervous. Was she too the manufacturer and possessor of a false identity?

No, that was absurd, he told himself. As ever, he needed to be wary of slipping into paranoia. The four of them were going to be working in close quarters with humans. What more natural than that they should be profoundly screened?

Still, the procedures being followed struck him as excessive. After all, he had experienced close contact with one of the bipeds without any prescreening whatsoever, to the detriment of neither. But that contact had been unofficial.

He had anticipated the inspection and review would last a few time-parts at most. It occupied the better part of three days, during which time the four assignees were kept isolated not only from humans but from all other thranx except those immediately involved in their examination. At the end of that period they were directed to board another transport. Des noted that it was not independently powered, but instead was mounted on magnetic repulsion strips. That suggested a high-speed journey, and a much longer one than he had expected.

He was moved to query the official marching alongside him. She had a silver star and two subsidiary bursts embedded in the chitin of her right upper shoulder. "Where are we going? Why the rapid transport?" He gestured with a truhand. "The human sector is right over there somewhere."

"The Geswixt sector is," the escort agreed. "But you four have not been assigned to Geswixt. You're going to the project."

"The project!" Striding along just behind the poet, Jhywinhuran was listening intently. "The project on Hivehom. They didn't tell us."

"No point in keeping it a secret now. I envy you," the escort murmured. "You will have the opportunity to meet and interact with the famous first-contact supervisor, the Eint Ryozenzuzex. Quite an honor."

"I've never been offworld." Desvendapur's mind was spinning. Space-plus travel itself—the experience of journeying between different star systems—should provide marvelous fodder for composition. And then there was the opportunity to live and work with members of the original project, set up soon after the first tentative thranx-human contact was established.

"Neither have I." The escort gestured appropriately as they reached the portal that provided entrance to the transport. "Nor is it likely I will ever be. But I am grateful for the opportunity to work here and contribute to interspecies understanding."

"How many humans have you met?" Des asked as he stepped into the waiting vehicle. "How many have you dealt with?"

"None." The escort stood stiffly to one side as they boarded, all four arms upraised in salute. "I am with Security. Our job is to keep the wandering curious away from the humans, not to interact with them. But there is still the satisfaction of contributing. Sweet traveling to you."

Anticipation surged through Desvendapur as he settled his abdomen over a vacant bench, straddling it expectantly. Very soon thereafter, the transport began to move, picking up speed as it rose above the strip and raced toward an unknown destination. No, not entirely unknown, he told himself. There would be a ship waiting, a shuttle to lift them into orbit. There they would board a starship for the journey through space-plus to Hivehom, the thranx homeworld and the location of the project.

For someone who had hoped only to meet another human or two in their own environment, events were moving along encouragingly indeed.

There were no signs to identify the station where they eventually disembarked, and no crowds to query. Insignia and attitude indicated that they had arrived at a military as opposed to a commercial facility, a supposition that further inspection and scrutiny confirmed.

Everything was going so well that Desvendapur was unprepared when the processor standing on the other side of the railing looked up from his readout to declare calmly but firmly, "Desvenbapur? There's no Desvenbapur in this file."

The poet's blood went colder than it had on the day he had stumbled inadvertently outside the Geswixt hive and into the accumulated rilth above. The new identity he had worked so long and hard to construct seemed to evaporate like a puff of perfumed *pleorin*, leaving him standing exposed and revealed to every set of compound eyes in the facility. But no one was looking in his direction; no one was staring at him accusingly. Yet.

"There must be a mistake. I made a proper application and have been passed on through to this point without any difficulty." He struggled to keep his antennae from twitching, fought to conceal the fear that was raging through him.

The processor was not impressed. He was a senior, his chitin shading heavily to purple, but he was still alert and in full possession of his faculties. He replied without looking up from the readout.

"That is why a hive has multiple layers of security. What slips past one can be caught by another."

There was nothing Desvendapur could do but stand and wait. Having passed on to the next station, a puzzled Jhy walked back to see what was taking so long. When Des explained, she became irate.

"What nonsense is this? Of course this male belongs. He is one of four assigned to this duty. No—*honored* by this duty."

"Really, Jhy." He did his best to quiet her, looking around uneasily. Drawn to the commotion, the two scientists who had already been cleared had paused at the top of the landing to look back. The one thing Des did not seek in his present incarnation was attention. "I'm sure it will sort itself out."

She gazed at him out of eyes that were a flaxen composite of shattered mirrors. "You shouldn't let him treat you like this, Des. You are special now. All four of us are." She eyed the processor sternly. "Regardless of our individual job classifications."

The elderly drone remained unperturbed. "Procedures must be followed. Otherwise you do not have a hive: you have anarchy. If he is not in the file, then it admits of an irregularity. Irregularities must be resolved."

"I am sure this one will be." The poet made short, swooping, soothing gestures with both truhands. "It has to be some sort of administrative error."

"No." The processor was adamant. "There is no Desvenbapur registered here." A truhand reached toward a communicator. "I will have to summon a superior—and Security."

Tussling with a couple of warriors with oversized mandibles would not get him a cubicle on the waiting starship, Des knew. There was nothing he could do but stand and wait. Wait, he feared, for the inevitable—for that which he had succeeded in putting off for more than a year.

"I do not understand." If Desvendapur was distressed, Jhywinhuran was openly baffled. "He has been working at Geswixt hive for some time. That is a security-sensitive area, and there has been no difficulty. Why should there be a confusion now? It's not as if he is laboring for military intelligence or energy research. He works in food processing."

"It does not matter," declared the processor with finality. "A security breach is a security breach, no matter what the status of the . . ." He halted in midapprobation. "Food preparation?"

"Eighth-level assistant," Desvendapur supplied quickly.

The processor clicked sharply, his mandibles grinding together just so. "The file lists you as a food *synthesizer*. That is a much more illustrious designation."

"I completely agree," Des told him, "but it is not one that applies to me. I am only an assistant preparator." Leaning forward, he tried to steal a glimpse of the readout, and failed. It was attuned only to the eyes of the processor.

Digits moved and the readout changed. Desvendapur reminded himself to breathe.

"*Aht,* here it is." The drone's tone did not change. "Desvenbapur. Assistant food preparator, level eight. You may proceed to the next checkpoint."

"That's it?" The challenge emerged of its own accord. "After all that?"

"After all what?" The processor eyed him curiously. "It was a simple filing error. I was doing my job."

He would have to learn to accept such things in stride, a relieved

Desvendapur told himself. His identity had not been compromised—only momentarily misplaced. With Jhy leading the way, he advanced to the next station, ready now for whatever challenge it might present.

He need not have concerned himself. At each successive checkpoint his presence was acknowledged and his legitimacy confirmed. If he had been at all worried about the integrity of his newly wrought identity, two days of processing did much to lay his concerns to rest.

They were housed together until the following morning, when they were due to lift off via atmospheric shuttle. Waiting in high orbit was the space-plus transport *Zenruloim*. No one had officially told them they were going to Hivehom, and no one had to: That was where the project was located.

He tried to prepare himself mentally for the voyage ahead. His first journey offworld should be good for a folio at least. Then would come the descent to an entirely new planet, the ancestral homeworld of the thranx. Finally there would be, at long last, extended and intimate contact with the extraordinary bipedal mammals called humans. His sleeping chamber was comfortable enough, but he hardly slept at all.

Morning brought with it an excitement that was as difficult to contain as it was to quantify. He was pleased to note that the two scientists, far from being intellectually or emotionally above such simple emotions, were as visibly excited as food preparator and sanitation worker.

They boarded the shuttle via a long access ramp. At no time were they exposed to the outside, but that was perfectly natural. Very little of a hive beyond parks and recreational sites was located on the surface. The atmospheric shuttle itself was of modest dimensions, long and low. Brief prelift instruction was given; no one materialized to offer good-byes or farewells; and before he really had time to inspect his surroundings, Desvendapur found himself airborne and thundering toward orbit.

Offworld. There were no ports on the government transport, but by utilizing the seat controls he was able to call up a three-dimensional projection of the external view in any direction. He saw Willow-Wane receding below him and the firmament of stars and worlds and other species—primitive and intelligent, familiar and alien—drawing infinitesimally closer. Within him fresh inspiration simmered but did not boil. That would come with consistent contact, he felt. When he was surrounded by alien bipeds, by humans dwelling in their own facilities, that was when the river of enlightenment would wash over him to cleanse him of the puerile, classical heritage of traditional thranx rhythmic narrative.

He had studied hard, had prepared for this his whole life. What it was permitted to know, he had absorbed, from available records and reports. He knew how humans lived, but that was not the same as living with and among them. He knew how they were supposed to smell, but that was not the same as smelling them. He knew how they moved, how their peculiarly restricted speech patterns sounded, how they viewed the universe out of undersized single-lensed eyes, how their digestive systems worked to process not only normal food but dead animal products as well. All these things he knew, but studying them in recordings and reading about them in second- and third-hand reports was not the same thing as experiencing them for himself.

Furthermore, almost all of it was knowledge that had been gained under controlled conditions. From the standpoint of an artist as opposed to a scientist, he valued his single, brief, dangerous encounter with the lone human in the rilth above Geswixt more than all the recorded lore he had assimilated. How he was going to duplicate and expand upon that under the controlled conditions of the project he did not know. He only knew that it was necessary, even vital, to the maturation of his art. Somehow he would make it happen.

But first they had to get there.

When the *Zen* made the jump from normal space to space-plus he was sufficiently disoriented to contrive the sounds for what he believed to be a modestly successful tripartite stanza. Realizing that it undoubtedly duplicated, in spirit if not in actual phraseology, a hundred similar initial deep-space experiences, he promptly discarded the entire minor opus. He had not come this far, had not lied and invented and lowered himself and abandoned the patrimony of his hive, to grind out pale imitations of the work of others who had gone before him. He sought the unique, the new, the distinctive. That would not be found in duplicating the obvious experiences of predecessors.

As the journey through distorted space-time progressed he came to know his fellow travelers better. Though he focused his attentions on Jhywinhuran and the two scientists who had also been assigned to the project, he did not neglect the other passengers or those members of the crew who found time to spend with an inquisitive lower-level passenger. He partook of everything. A true artist disdained nothing, never knowing from where true inspiration might arise. So he acquired and stored away information on topics as diverse as hydrological engineering and starship maintenance, not neglecting the area of food preparation, in which he could boast some expertise.

They were two eight-days out and he was sleeping soundly in his private cubicle when he heard the noise. It was a muffled creaking, repeated at regular intervals. Since the components of a thranx vessel fit together seamlessly, it was difficult to imagine what might be causing noise sufficient to wake him. As he regained consciousness, lying in the dark on the low sleeping bench, he listened intently to the soft, unsettling sounds. He did not have to open his eyes because they were always open. He had only to struggle to pull together the constituent bits and pieces of his consciousness.

The subtle shushing was produced by the movement of clothing against the body of its wearer. But it was not the slick rush of thranx protective attire against smooth, hard chitin. The noise that had awakened him was more subtle, almost as if cloth were being dragged across water.

Looking up, he saw the shape looming over him. In the twilight that filled the cubicle it was enormous and unarguably human. From his studies Des knew that specific bipeds varied considerably in size, as opposed to other sapient species like the thranx or the AAnn whose individual physical dimensions were relatively consistent. This one was at least twice as big as the solitary male he had encountered in the exposed air of Geswixt. An enormous waterfall of tangled black fur sprouted from its face and head to hang down over the upper portion of its chest and shoulders. Its eyes were black and protruding. Its immense five-digited hands, of which the creature had only two, gripped a shiny length of projection-studded metal that was vaguely ominous in outline. The creature wore a heavy jacket of some dun-colored material and matching pants, and its single pair of feet were shod in calf-high black boots fashioned from some muted, reflective material.

Towering above his bed, it glared down at him, showing the even, white teeth that served the same function as normal mandibles. Its entire aspect was quietly intimidating. No empathetic "Are you all right?" greeted the awakening of the single sleeper. From head to foot the massive figure was the perfect embodiment of alien nightmare.

Despite the insulation, he could hear some commotion outside the door to his cubicle. There were high-pitched whistles that passed for screams, followed by the muted whisper of running feet and loud, anxious conversation. Querulous mandibular clicks filtered into his quarters from the corridor outside as if it had been invaded and was being assaulted by a horde of migrating carnivorous *metractia* from Trix.

Raising his upper body off the sleeping bench he whispered in the direction of the cubicle's scri!ber. The aural pickup winked to life. "Projective intrusion noted. Presumed unscheduled emotional stability test acknowledged. Returning to sleep." When no further vocals were forthcoming from the sleepy occupant of the room, the scri!ber winked off, having duly made note of Desvendapur's terse report.

Glancing to his right, he saw that the forbidding figure had vanished. The projection really had been well done, he mused as he drifted back toward unconsciousness. Had he been confronted with it the previous year he undoubtedly would have joined the others who had been assailed with the same nocturnal visitation in scrambling in panic for the corridor outside his cubicle. But he was not the same individual he had been then. He knew more now—a great deal more. That acquired knowledge was reflected in the calm with which he had confronted the figure, and in his ability to return readily to a state of uninvolved repose.

Following the daybreak meal the four fellow travelers were called away from the other passengers to a private, secured conspectus session in a spacious meeting chamber. Warm earth tones dominated the décor, and the walls exuded the familiar fragrance of rammed earth and decomposing vegetation. The two senior researchers who debriefed them were especially intrigued with Desvendapur's laconic reaction to the finely rendered three-dimensional imaging of the previous night.

"You did not panic when confronted with the human visualization," the elder, a female, declared almost accusingly. "To greater and lesser extent, your colleagues did."

Des was aware that this time not only Jhy but the two scientists were watching him curiously. Had he stepped too boldly outside his carefully constructed identity? Should he, too, have run out into the hall whistling in fear and panic? But he had been awakened from a sound sleep and had reacted, not as a false persona, but as himself, bringing into play all the knowledge he had acquired in the past year. He could only hope that it would not mark him so singularly as to prompt a probe from which this time he might not emerge unscathed.

Realizing that the longer he delayed responding the greater the likelihood of suspicion germinating in the minds of his interrogators, he replied succinctly, "I saw no immediate reason for alarm."

A slightly younger male questioner spoke up sharply. Desvendapur wondered if in addition to being recorded, this encounter was also being broadcast to and studied by an unknown number of other suspicious professionals.

"An armed alien of considerable size and menacing aspect appears without warning in your sleeping quarters in the middle of the night, waking you from a deep rest, and instead of panicking you immediately recognize the intrusion as specious, react accordingly, and go back to sleep. How many thranx do you think would react in such a fashion?" Awaiting his response, every antenna in the chamber was inclined in his direction. He hoped he was not emitting a strong odor of concern.

"Probably very few."

"Probably not more than a handful." The female's tone was sharp, incisive but without overtones of anger. "An assistant food preparator from Willow-Wane would not generally be accounted a member of that group."

Subdued light glinted off the curve of the male's eyes. "How did you recognize so quickly that the intruder was a projection, and therefore posed no threat to you?"

"From his clothing." This time Des replied promptly and without hesitation.

The interrogators exchanged a glance and passing antenna contact. "Every effort was made to ensure the verisimilitude of the human's appearance. What was wrong with its clothing?"

"There was nothing wrong with it. At least," the poet hastened to add, "nothing that I, based on my own private studies of humans and their habits and accouterments, could see."

"Then why did you react so calmly?" the male pressed him. "What about the appearance of the simulacrum's attire told you that it could not be real?"

"There was too much of it." Des felt safe in indicating mild amusement. "Humans thrive in a climate of considerably less heat and one-third the humidity that thranx enjoy. They can *endure* what we consider optimum living conditions, but they are not comfortable in them. And what we would regard as an excessive but tolerable climate could prove fatal to even well-adapted humans." Feeling more confident, he shifted easily on the resting bench.

"The temperature in my quarters was, if anything, set slightly warmer and moister than usual to accommodate my personal sleeping preferences. The bipedal figure wore not less than two layers of *heavy* human clothing. According to my studies, no human—no matter how well acclimated to Willow-Wane or Hivehom or any thranx world—would voluntarily wear a fourth as much apparel. Its system could not tolerate it for more than a time-part or so without suffering serious overheating. Yet the figure that woke me from my sleep did not appear even slightly inconvenienced by the microclimate in my room. The characteristic cooling condensation known as sweat was not present on its skin at all." He looked from his interrogators to his colleagues. "That's how I knew it couldn't be a real human."

The examiners looked briefly to their scri!bers before the female replied. With a truhand she indicated not suspicion or accusation, but admiration. "You are observant beyond your station, Desvenbapur. It is no wonder you were chosen to participate in as significant an undertaking as this."

He hastened to demur. "I have always tried to learn everything possible about any task I was involved with, whether it concerned food preparation or anything else. The simulacrum *could* have fooled me. It just happened that I was studying that section provided to us that deals with human physiology only last eight-day, and remembered it right away. It was at the front of my memory."

"A fine memory," she complimented him. "I would let you prepare my food anytime." Indicating that their involvement in the meeting was concluded, she and her companion rose and left the room. Their place was taken by four new officials, one of whom had two full stars inset into her right shoulder.

Desvendapur leaned toward Jhy and whispered. "I wonder what we have done to deserve the attention of so much rank."

"I don't know." She was grooming an antenna, bending it forward and down with her left truhand and running the sensory organ delicately through her mandibles. "You certainly elevated yourself in the project's estimation with your actions last night."

"I was lucky." Using a surreptitious foothand, he stroked her upper abdomen. Her ovipositors reacted with a slight quiver. "Easy enough to be nonchalant in the presence of a projected simulacrum. Next time I will probably be the one who runs screaming."

"Somehow I don't think so." She would have said more, but the first of the newly arrived ranking elders was speaking to them.

"You four will be joining and participating in what many eints have dubbed the most important social experiment in thranx history. As you know from your studies, ever since contact was first made we have found these bipedal mammals to be at once fascinating and frightening, refreshing and appalling, useful and dangerous. They are an aggressive, inventive species that exhibits a disturbing tendency to act before thinking. More often than you might expect, this produces results that are not to their benefit. Yet they will plunge blindly on, sometimes even when they are aware that what they are doing is detrimental to their own cause. It has been theorized that they have too much energy for their own good.

"Based on our initial contacts with them they are, I am pleased to report, not fond of our old friends the AAnn. But neither are they openly antagonistic toward them. Their attitude toward *us* is characterized by an unreasonable, irrational fear of the innumerable small arthropods that inhabit their own world, against which they have been waging a war not merely for dominance but for survival since they acquired the first stirrings of sapience. Our physical appearance was therefore something of a shock to them, from which only the most intelligent and responsive of their kind have managed to recover. Progress in advancing relations has therefore been much slower than either government would like. Yet to rush matters risks alienating the more conservative among our own kind while simultaneously activating the latent xenophobia that is regrettably endemic among the vast majority of humans.

"Overall, their present attitude toward us might best be characterized as a suspicious ambivalence. It is hoped that this will correct itself with time. In the interim, various proposals have been put forth, by both sides, for different means of accelerating the process of contact."

"The project," the meteorologist pointed out.

"Yes." It was the two-star who responded. "Everyone who wants to be or needs to be—human as well as thranx—is familiar with the project and its estimable goals." Her great golden eyes lingered individually on each of the four designates. "What is not known except among the highest representatives of both governments is that a similar project has been established elsewhere."

"The need for secrecy is absolute," a third supervisor commented tersely. "As suspicious and mistrustful as the humans are of us, it is believed they would react in a manner most unfriendly to the revelation that not simply a contact post, but the beginnings of a real colony were being established in their midst."

Desvendapur was not sure he had heard correctly. The thranx had begun establishing colonies on habitable worlds generations ago, but to the best of his knowledge they had never tried to situate one on a world already inhabited by another intelligent species. The idea of establishing a full-blown hive on a human-occupied world was more than daring. Many would call it foolhardy.

Yet he sensed this was not a test, as the simulacrum of the previous night had been. The supervisors were as serious as a pregnant female about to lay.

"Which world?" the engineer asked. "Centaurus Five, or one of the other Centaurian spheres?"

"None of those." The two-star was speaking again. If possible, her manner was more serious than before. "It is to this colony that you have been assigned. It is there that you will be working, often in closer quarters with humans than any thranx anywhere else. Nothing of this kind has ever been attempted before. You will be part of a pioneering interspecies social experiment." Lifting a scri!ber, she flicked a control on the panel. A fully featured three-dimensional globe appeared in the air between supervisors and incipient colonists.

"The great majority of humans are unaware of it, and if everything goes according to plan they will remain so for quite some time, but there is even as we speak an expanding thranx presence here, growing and thriving with the help of a few dedicated, farseeing humans."

As she spoke the global image rotated before them, the view zooming in and out at the whim of the controller. It was a beautiful world, Desvendapur thought, swimming beneath its sea of thin white clouds. Not as beautiful as Hivehom, or even Willow-Wane, but except for the prevalence of large oceans, an inviting planet nonetheless. He wondered which of the human-colonized worlds they were seeing, wondered what the name of their destination might be.

The one supervisor who had not spoken yet now stood back on all four trulegs and proceeded to enlighten, elucidate, and explain.

"Burrowers, fellow hive pioneers, future colonists, here is your destination. I extend to you all an early welcome— to Earth." Turning, he gesticulated somberness mixed with humor. "After all, if the humans can be allowed to have a colony on Hivehom, why should we not have reciprocal privileges on their homeworld?"

9

They looked like a prosperous couple. Too staid to be romantic, walking side by side without touching or holding hands, they had probably gone for a stroll in the tropical downpour so they would be able to tell their friends back home that they had done it. Anyone with any sense would have stayed inside a nice dry hotel until the clouds closed back up. That was what the permanent residents of San José were doing. That was what the great majority of tourists were doing.

But not these two. Since they were wearing matching electrostatic repulsion rain gear, only their hands were getting wet, and these only when they emerged from large, accommodating pockets. The tepid water struck the invisible protective fields and slid off, leaving the strollers and the expensive clothing they wore underneath comfortable and dry.

Montoya followed them at a discreet distance. There were a few others out walking or running through the heavy rain. In the hilly downtown historical district there were always people making deliveries or pickups. There were plenty of other tourists out and about besides the couple he had targeted, but they were sensibly holed up in gift shops, restaurants, or hotel lobbies, waiting for the storm to piss itself out.

Hold-ups were not Cheelo's preferred mode of personal enrichment. He disliked confrontations. Like narcotics, mugging was a bad habit that could all too easily become addictive. He'd seen it happen to acquaintances. He would have seen it happen to friends, if he'd had any. Given a choice, he would have preferred to rifle a hotel room or two, or pick a plump pocket, or lift a purse. No such opportunity had presented itself for days. Now he was growing anxious.

One more good score, just one more, and he would have all the good-faith money he needed to present to Ehrenhardt to secure the franchise.

Well ahead of the deadline that had been set, too. Ehrenhardt and his people would be suitably impressed—which was Montoya's intention.

This would not be the first time he had mugged. Unlike a number of younger compatriots he derived no thrill from it, got no adrenaline rush from seeing the look of fear on the faces of his intended victims. With him it was all business, in the tradition of professional highwaymen going back to archaic times. To fulfill his dream he needed a few hundred credits more. These negligent travelers would provide it.

He continued to track the couple, pausing when they paused, turning to peer into a store window whenever they chanced to look in his direction. For the most part he remained invisible, another tourist like themselves out for a lazy afternoon's stroll in the rain. Only unlike them, he was unable to afford expensive water-repulsion rain gear. Already he was damp and uncomfortable beneath his old-fashioned maroon slicker.

In a sense he *was* a tourist, having come up from Golfito specifically to make the money necessary to buy the franchise. He had learned early in life that it was better to keep one's place of business separate from one's current home. Avoiding the authorities was difficult enough without living in the same city as the ones who would be most interested in finding him. Besides, there were far more opportunities to accumulate the requisite credit in bustling San José than in the smaller, sleepier city on the coast.

He tensed slightly, preparing his thoughts and muscles, and began to walk a little faster, closing the gap between himself and the perambulating couple. They had turned down one of the city's quaint alleys, a narrow street with scoured cobblestone sidewalks.

He was reaching inside his coat when they unexpectedly stepped into a store specializing in the distinctive woodwork for which the city was famed. Forced to continue on past, he glanced surreptitiously at the paduk and cocobolo handicrafts on display in the window. The next store was closed. Beyond, a serviceway barely wide enough to admit one person at a time split the line of old buildings as it penetrated to the heart of the block. Ducking inside, he found some shelter from the rain.

He waited there, biding his time, occasionally leaning out to look back up the hill. The sodden stones were deserted. Rain staccatoed off the pavement, fleeing in small distinct rivulets into the nearest storm drain. If the couple chose to retrace their steps instead of extending their excursion, he would have no choice but to continue following them, like a caiman marking the progress of a tentative tapir grazing along a riverbank.

Before long he heard the subdued murmur of casual chatter: three voices—those of the couple and that of the store owner. Then footsteps, splashing in the rain, growing louder instead of more distant. Reaching into his coat, his fingers closed around the grip of the tiny pistol.

Timing his appearance, he stepped right out in front of them, trying to make himself look larger than he was. The stunned expressions on their faces showed that his surprise was complete.

Quickly now, he told himself. Before they have time to think or time to react. He extended his other hand, palm upward.

"Wallet!" he snapped curtly. When the man, who was despite his age large and fit looking, hesitated, Cheelo barked as threateningly as he could, "Now—or I'll skrag you and take it anyway!"

"Martin, give it to him!" the wife pleaded. "Everything's insured." Ah, traveler's insurance, Cheelo mused. The casual thief's best friend.

"Slowly—so I can see it as you bring it out." He couched the warning in his most intimidating manner.

Glaring down at him, the well-dressed pedestrian removed a soft plastic pouch from beneath his coat and handed it over. Cheelo took possession gingerly, never taking his eyes off the man. Slipping the prize into his own inner shirt pocket, he turned his attention to the woman. Above and below them, the narrow street remained deserted. A couple of vehicles hummed past on the main avenue above, their occupants oblivious to the pitiful drama that was being played out beyond their windows.

"Purse," he ordered her. "And jewelry."

Trembling fingers passed over the handbag of woven metal, then reluctantly followed it with a ring and two bracelets. Nervously eying the front of the store from which they had recently emerged, he gestured imperatively at her left hand. "Come on, come on—the rest of it."

The woman covered the remaining exposed ring with her other hand. Her expression and tone were imploring. "Please—it's my wedding ring. I've given you everything else." He knew the droplets that were starting to run down her cheeks were tears because her face was protected from the rain by the wide brim of her stylish water-repelling hat.

He hesitated. Enough time had been spent standing out in the street. He had wallet, purse, and jewelry. The woman's anguish *seemed* genuine. He had seen enough of it faked by those attempting to protect expensive but impersonal possessions. Wearing the same expression he had presented when he had first stepped out of the alley, he started to turn away from them.

"Sure, why not? Look, I'm sorry about this, but I've got a big deal pending—the opportunity of a lifetime—and I just need a few more credits to . . ."

That was when the husband jumped him.

It was a stupid move, a foolish move, the kind propounded by middle-aged men who think a little regular exercise and a lifetime of watching action tridees equips them with the wherewithal to handle sinewy professionals. He was a lot bigger than Cheelo, which made him bold, and a lot stronger, which made him overconfident. In fact, he superseded Cheelo in every aspect of fighting ability except the most important one: desperation.

As the man's large hand, fingers aligned in a karate chop, came down on Cheelo's flinching arm, the impact caused his finger to contract on the trigger. The compact weapon spat a small, silent blue flash. Instantly, the delivered charge interrupted the flow of electrical impulses running through the millions of neurons in the man's body. A shocked look on his face, he collapsed onto the sidewalk, falling over sideways so that his shoulders and then his head struck the pavement. The skull took a visible bounce. Hovering over him, pistol in hand, Cheelo was no less shocked than the woman, who immediately dropped to her asinine husband's side. His eyes were wide open.

When it had gone off, the muzzle of the pistol had been aimed right at his chest. His heart had momentarily been paralyzed. That was not necessarily a lethal proposition—except that the man's heart had not been an especially sound one to begin with. The problem was not that it had stopped; the problem was that it did not start beating again. Cheelo had seen death before, though it had not been propitiated by his own hands. He saw it now, in the gaping frozen face that was filling with rain where it lay upturned to the sky on the cobblestone sidewalk.

Heedless of her own circumstance, the woman began screaming. Cheelo raised the pistol, then lowered it. He had not meant to shoot the poor dumb grandstanding bastard. He had certainly not meant to kill him. He doubted the admission would carry sufficient weight with the authorities. Clutching the purse close to his chest beneath the raincoat, he turned and ran, shoving the weapon back into his pocket. Behind him, the woman's screams were swallowed up by the gray torrent that fortuitously continued to spill from the clouds. He was more grateful than ever for the rain. For a little while at least, it would keep the shopkeeper from hearing her wails.

Breathing hard, he threw himself onto the first public transport that presented itself. Surrounded by preoccupied, indifferent *ticos* and *ticas*, he pulled the collar of his raincoat higher around his neck and head and strove to make himself as inconspicuous as possible. *Now* what the hell was he supposed to do? Self-defense made a bad defense for a known brigand. At the very least he would be sentenced to a selective mindwipe, the extent of which would depend on how tolerant a court he found himself in. The truth machine could possibly support his claim that he had not intended to kill, but his state of mind at the time might appear as a gray area on the device's readout.

It didn't matter. He had no intention of being incarcerated or of letting the authorities erase any part of him.

He did not go back to the cheap hotel room that was his address when he stayed in San José. Instead, he transferred to public transport traveling in the opposite direction. By the time he reached the airport the rain was diminishing, the sky becoming merely sentimental instead of sorrowful.

The nearest shuttleport where he could secure offworld transport was in Chiapas. Even if he could somehow make it that far without being picked up, he couldn't be sure his efforts of the past month had accumulated enough credit to purchase passage. Not that it mattered. The first thing the local authorities would do would be to run a report on the incident, complete to a police molder's rendering of the attacker based on the woman's eyewitness account. As soon as he stepped off a down shuttle on, say, one of the Centaurus colonies, a grim-faced welcoming committee would be there to greet him. Besides, he had no intention of traveling offworld. Not when he had important business on this one.

What he needed was to get as far away as possible as quickly as possible, but not so far that he couldn't get back to see Ehrenhardt before the deadline that had been set for payment. At least for the moment, returning to Golfito was out of the question. Ehrenhardt would not take kindly to a personal visit from a man wanted by authorities for murder. As a known antisoc, his home and businesses would be watched.

Paying with credit from his personal account, Cheelo locked himself in a shower room at the airport while he renegotiated the unfortunate husband's credcard. In minutes, using the room's public terminal, he had succeeded in draining the credit and switching it into his own account. Colorless and untraceable, it would provide him with a means of flight. He was grimly gratified to see that with the addition of the latest sum, even after the purchase of a ticket to somewhere else, enough remained for him to pay Ehrenhardt what was required. The transaction would simply have to be delayed for a while. There was no reason to panic. He had plenty of time.

The woman would remember what he had been wearing. With considerable reluctance, he discarded the raincoat, shoving the crumpled bundle of fabric into a disposal chute where, hopefully, it would be compacted and then incinerated. Underneath, he wore attire that was simple but clean and untattered. Adopting as best he could the air and attitude of a small businessman, he approached one of the automated ticket dispensers and logged in.

"Where is it you wish to go today, sir?" The device's synthesized voice was brisk and feminine. He tried not to be too obvious as he looked sideways, backward, down, anywhere but directly into the visual pickup.

Frequently, he passed a hand over his face as if wiping rain from his eyes. He kept his voice at the lower limits of audibility as he shoved his illegally recharged credcard into the accept slot.

"As far as this will take me on the next flight out and still leave twenty thousand in the account. No, make that twenty-two thousand." If his estimate was off he could always cancel the request and make a new one.

"Could you be a little more specific, sir? Random, spontaneous vacationing is a joyous adventure, but it would be helpful to me if you could at least pick a direction."

"South," he mumbled without thinking. His choices were simple. West or east would send him out over one of two oceans. North would find him very, very cold.

The dispenser hummed softly. Seconds later a small plastic strip emerged from a slot. Cheelo stood ready to bolt if the device's internal alarms went off, but his credcard popped out normally alongside the ticket a moment later. Taking the strip, he placed it on his card, to which it promptly adhered.

"Thank you for your patronage, sir," the dispenser told him. He turned to go, then halted and spoke without looking anywhere in the direction of the unit's visual pickup.

"Where am I going?"

"Lima, sir. Via suborbital, gate twenty-two. Enjoy your flight."

He did not offer thanks as he strode purposefully in the direction of the requisite concourse. A glance at a monitor showed that he would have to hurry if he was to make the departure. His expression set; he was inwardly pleased. The last thing he wanted to do was to have to linger in the vicinity of the airport.

No one challenged him as he approached the gate. The ticket processor did not eat his card, passing it through to him on the other side of the entryway. The man and woman seated next to him ignored him as they chattered inconsequentially.

Even so, he did not allow himself to react until the plane was in the air, gaining altitude to climb above the tropical weather while accelerating rapidly to supersonic speed. He had to try to relax. He had a couple of hours before the next crisis, when the time would come to disembark. It was futile to agonize. If the police traced him to the flight, they would be waiting for him when he stepped off the plane. There would be nowhere to run. He would be promptly put on a return flight and extradited back to San José.

As he leaned back in the seat he remembered the face of the lurching husband, the sharp pain of his big hand coming down on Cheelo's arm. He did not even recall pulling the trigger. Then the man collapsing, his life imploding like a mud wall under assault from a rain forest downpour. His wife falling to her knees next to him, disbelief seizing control of her throat and vocal cords. He shuddered slightly. Though he had administered his share of beatings, he had never killed anyone before. He still felt the same. The pistol had done the killing, not him. The man had set if off himself, as a consequence of his own idiotic actions. Why couldn't he have just stood there for another lousy couple of minutes? Why couldn't he have played out his role of victim? A lot of good his insurance did him now.

Lima. Cheelo had never been to Lima, had in fact never been south of Balboa. Whenever he accumulated a little credit he usually went to Cancun or Kingston for a while, until he was broke again. He tried to recall what little he knew of planetary topography. Lima was near the Andes, but was it in them? He was dressed for the subtropical clime of San José, not high mountains.

Well, he would find out when they landed. Assuming the ticket dispenser had abided by his instructions and that his transfer of credit from the dead man's account was not compromised, he would have the additional wherewithal beyond the franchise price to purchase clothes as well as food and shelter. And transport. He could not afford to linger long in Lima, or in any big city boasting competent police technology. He began to feel a little better about his randomly selected choice of destination. Mountains were a good place to hide. He knew nothing of the region, but he would learn quickly. As soon as he landed he would purchase a guidebook or two and have them transferred into his card where he could peruse the information at leisure.

Somehow, he would manage to lose himself. He had done it before, though not under the impetus of such urgency. A new identity, a new look, and he would be safe. He was thirty-five years old and for twenty of that had lived off his wits and illicit activities. He was not about to let himself in for even a partial mindwiping. Hell, no! Not when the answer to all his dreams lay virtually within his grasp.

Just let me get off the plane and out into the city, he thought tightly. Just that one moment of freedom and from then on I'll be able to make my way in silence and safety.

He was shaking when the plane slowed to a stop at the disembarkation gate. When one of the flight attendants remarked on his evident distress he managed to reply in a calm and unaffected voice that he was just a little cold, and he even thanked her for her solicitude. Shuffling off the aircraft, he kept his gaze fixed resolutely straight ahead. As the passenger load thinned around him—businessmen striding toward connection gates or baggage pickup, families reunited joyfully—he kept walking without any real destination in mind. When he was halfway through the terminal and it was apparent that no officials were waiting to intercept and detain him, he lengthened his stride.

Public transport into the city was readily available in various familiar forms. Avoiding both the cheaper bulk carriers and the more expensive private vehicles with drivers, he chose an automatic. It answered his questions as readily as any human escort and without propounding inquiries of its own.

Once downtown he immediately felt better about his situation. New clothing, a meal, the purchase of a guidebook, and a dose of depilatory to remove his attractive but too distinctive beard improved his outlook considerably. All he had to do was to disappear for a while. It was much too soon after the incident to search out a surgery where he could have his appearance permanently altered. When the furor over the killing had been pushed off the front page of police screens he could return to Golfito and conclude the transaction with Ehrenhardt.

Lima was not in the Andes, he discovered, and at this time of year it was subject to heavy fog, a development that delighted him. The less visible he was at all times, the better. But, like any large metropolitan center, the city boasted an unobtrusive yet sophisticated police center and an appropriate number of active response sites. Enough stolen credit remained in his account to get him out of the city and away from public scanners without impacting on the twenty thousand he needed to keep for Ehrenhardt. The only question was where to go. It would have to be someplace where the police presence was slight to nonexistent, someplace where he could walk without having to worry about keeping his face turned away from pole-mounted scanners.

The guidebook suggested several possibilities. To the north lay a largely uninhabited region of rolling hills and flat plains. But the area was thick with important archeological sites that were periodically swarmed with tourists. That wouldn't do. The mountains were a suitably forgotten fastness, except that the habitable valleys were full of neat vegetable farms and ranches that echoed to the hoofbeats of alpaca, llama, and cattle genetically engineered to thrive at altitude. The higher elevations were sufficiently inhospitable to discourage settlement. Similarly, the low temperatures and thin air were more than enough to discourage him.

More promising was the strip of southern coastal desert. Behind the beaches, with their resorts and desalinization plants, few people lived who did not work in one of the numerous mines gouged from the arid landscape. There was still room for a person to lose himself, but not enough room—not for the kind of near-total disappearance Cheelo had in mind.

That left the enormous Reserva Amazonia. The most biologically diverse stretch of rain forest wilderness left on the planet, it had seen its last indigenous inhabitants resettled elsewhere more than a hundred years earlier. Since then it had been abandoned to its great profusion of plants and wildlife, save only for scheduled incursions by tourists and scientists. The dense canopy would hide him from prying overhead eyes, and the presence of so many other forms of life would mask his heat signature from patrolling remotes.

According to the information he read on his card, the most primitive and isolated part of the park lay at and encompassed the eastern foothills of the Andes. There, where cloud forest met lowland rain forest, there had never been a need to remove and resettle traditional inhabitants because there had never been any. The region was as inhospitable to man as it was lush, a place where some of the rarest creatures left in the wild roamed free. Yet even there, isolated tourist facilities could be found that catered to the most adventurous, to those seeking a true wilderness experience.

Having spent some time in the rain forest himself, plucking tourists instead of tropical fruit, he enjoyed a certain familiarity with such country. The miserable months he had spent drunk and diseased in Amistad came back to him in a rush. It wouldn't be very comfortable—he would be hot and sweaty all the time, and there would be bugs—but the same conditions that would make it unpleasant for him would also discourage extended examination by officers of the law. If stopped and challenged, he could pass himself off as just another tourist. If anyone thought to probe further, he could vanish into the immense forest while they were running a background check on him.

He was unable to outfit himself to his satisfaction in Lima, but Cuzco boasted a number of shops where he was able to obtain his modest requirements. The lightweight, rip-proof pack he purchased filled rapidly with a good supply of basic emergency concentrates and vitamins, a permanent water filter and purifier, insect-proof bedroll and tent, fuel-cell cooker, and mapping ware for his card. The live clerk assured him that his new clothes would repel everything from army ants to a rainy season downpour.

Thus equipped, he booked passage on a slow lift to Sintuya, the only community permitted within the boundaries of the southwestern portion of the Reserva. It existed solely to serve the needs of tourists and researchers. Since he could hardly pass himself off as the latter, he assumed the identity of the former. At the same time, he had as little intercourse with his fellow sightseers as possible, though he made a conscious effort to be polite rather than taciturn. Anything to render himself as bland and forgettable as possible.

The flight over the Andes from Cuzco was spectacular, an unfolding panorama of ancient Inca terraces—now groomed and tended by machines—irrigated ranches, and tiny, quaint Quechua alpine communities that made a good living from crafts and tourism. Then the peaks gave way to mist-swathed cloud forest. The slow lifter descended, following the steep eastern slopes, occasionally blowing mist and cloud aside to give those aboard a glimpse of the thick vegetation beneath. Once, a family of spectacled bears ambled into momentary view, and recorders whispered as the travelers imaged the moment for replay back home in London and Cairo, Delhi and Surabaya.

Cheelo Montoya took no pictures, though he made a show of oohing and aahing over the scenery as energetically as those around him. A tourist who failed to tour would stand out in the minds of his fellow travelers, something he intended to avoid. The absence of a recorder did not have to be explained. Not everyone spent their vacation gazing fixedly into a color imager.

Sintuya proved to be even smaller than he had expected. A few restaurants served meals of exotic rain forest produce, everything from starfruit mousse to caiman fritters. Aware that it might be the last meal he would enjoy for some time that he would not have to prepare himself, he splurged on a ragout made with agouti, yuca, assorted vegetables, and blanched Brazil nuts. A couple of hostels, a flurry of handicraft and gift shops, the usual traveler's aid stations, and an outlying scientific complex comprised the rest of the town. Though the air-conditioned, dehumidified hostels beckoned, he resolutely ignored their civilized blandishments. Except for the purchase of one meal, he would leave no record behind of his presence in the remote community.

Idling away the rest of the day among the town's minor amusements, he waited until well after nightfall to steal a boat. It was a small, silent tour lifter that could carry up to four persons. There were half a dozen of the sleek little craft bobbing at the dock. He set all of them free, shepherding the others out into the middle of the current and watching as they drifted off downstream. Theft might be suspected in the disappearance of one boat. The flight of all six would be interpreted as a consequence of bad luck, vandalism, or a youthful prank gone awry. When only five of the errant craft were recovered it would be assumed that the other had sunk or that it would be found washed up in some overgrown bend of the river or stream mouth.

The silent engine whisked him upstream at high speed, the boat's built-in sensors automatically avoiding any obstacles in its path. An aircar would have offered greater speed and more flexibility, but unless he wanted to skim along above the canopy it would have been as useless as an ancient ground-bound vehicle. Also, it would have run out of power in a few days. The boat's energy cell ought to last for a couple of weeks, at least. By keeping to the main river and hugging close to its lush, overgrown banks, he ought to be able to make his way deep into the Reserva without much risk of detection. Once he turned up a tributary, there was no reason to suppose anyone would come looking for him at all. Runaway boats did not head themselves up the current.

He would find a suitable site, perhaps an old abandoned tourist blind, and settle in until his supplies began to run low. Supplementing his stores with living off the land, he should be able to exist quite tolerably, if not entirely comfortably, for a number of months. By that time the urgency attending the death of one unfortunate traveler in distant San José would have faded, and he would still have several weeks in which to make his meeting with Ehrenhardt. Emerging from the rain forest, he would solidify his credit balance, arrange to have his physical appearance altered, and start afresh as master of a lucrative, semilegal franchise. He would finally, at last, be someone important. He would finally have done something *big*.

Setting the boat on automatic after programming it to follow the course he had predetermined, he settled back within his bedroll and watched the stars slide past in a pristine, uncontaminated sky. A typical criminal would have sought refuge in the depths of one of the great cities. That was where the authorities would be looking for him now—running scans, posting electronic flyers, querying informants. He was reasonably certain he had escaped San José unnoticed, was more confident his arrival in Lima would pass unremarked upon, and was sure he had transited Cuzco without being scanned. Let them hunt for him in Golfito, ransack his tiny one-room apartment. Out here, in the depths of the great wild park, there was nothing and no one to take notice of him. Even the rangers who monitored the Reserva were concentrated in the areas of highest tourist density. He had deliberately chosen a section famed for the ferocity of its insect life. In return for physical anonymity he would gladly sacrifice some skin and blood.

Feeling pretty good about himself and his resourcefulness, he rolled over and let the near-silent hum of the boat's engine lullaby him to sleep.

10

The world outside the port matched precisely the projection Desvendapur and the others had been studying for days: an impressive globe of cloud and earth all but submerged by a disproportionate volume of water. It seemed impossible that intelligent life could have arisen and matured on such a scattering of isolated landmasses, but such was indisputably the case. Then the time for study was over, and a senior official was delivering their last briefing.

"Because of the need for secrecy, transport to the surface must be carried out clandestinely." The large male gestured for emphasis. "Since we and our human associates established the colony a routine has been devised whereby this can be accomplished with some degree of safety and assurance. That isn't to say that some risk is not involved." He eyed each of them in turn. The four new colonists-to-be waved truhands and twitched antennae to indicate that they understood the gravity of the situation.

"If by some chance the drop is intercepted, you four know nothing. You are workers on your way to the official contact site at a place called Lombok." To Desvendapur it sounded as if the official's spicules must be underwater and that he was in the first stage of drowning, but in spite of linguistic difficulties he managed to pronounce the human word clearly. "If questioned, you may describe your respective specialties. There is nothing in them to indicate that you are bound for a covert colony as opposed to the officially recognized site.

"Collect your personal gear and report to the disembarkation chamber in two time-parts." He gestured a mixture of caution and admiration. "You are to be part of a great experiment. In twenty or so years, when it is time to reveal the existence of the colony, it is expected that humans will be sufficiently used to our presence among them so that they will not only accept it but be amused at their own initial uncertainty. It will also show that we are capable of sharing one of their worlds as opposed to one of our own without adversely impacting their society or environment. There are other important social questions that the colony will answer, but it is not necessary to go into the details now. You will be thoroughly briefed about your sojourn among these creatures by those living and working on-site."

The meteorologist gesticulated a question. "What about you? Have you spent much time among them?"

"Some," the official admitted.

"How do you find them? Our own contact to this point has so far been limited."

"Frustrating. Friendly but hesitant. Impulsive to the point of nonsapience. Vastly amusing. Threatening. Liquid of movement, clumsy of hand. You will see for yourselves. They are a bumbling, stumbling, wondrous medley of contradictions. And I am speaking of the best of their kind, those within their government who have helped to establish the colony project by deceiving their own people. The general human population, which this experiment is designed to help win over, is a surging, unpredictable, cacophonous sea of barely controlled chaos. One moves among humans the way one would among an arsenal on the cusp of detonation. Each individual is a bomb waiting to go off. Collectively, they make one want to flee their presence as rapidly as possible. Personally, I do not like them. But it has been decreed by the Grand Council that we are to try and make them our allies. Myself, I would prefer the Quillp." He moved forward.

"But I am bound by my instructions. I admit that they are undeniably clever and intelligent. It is claimed that in spite of individual dislikes we must work to make them our friends, and us theirs, lest the AAnn or some other equally unpleasant species gain the low ground with them. That will be part and parcel of your work. You are all specialists, some in advanced fields of research, others in support, but each of you is an ambassador. Never, never, forget that."

They were dismissed to return to their quarters to collect their belongings and their thoughts. Des did not know what was racing through the minds of his three companions, but as for himself he could hardly contain his excitement. This was what he had worked for for so long. This was what he had lied and deceived and falsified to attain: inspiration wild and fresh, of a kind that was denied to every other poet on all the thranx worlds.

A sudden thought clouded the dream. What if there was already a poet within the secret colony? Surely it would boast among its complement an official soother or two. He decided he could not worry about that. If they existed they would be occupied with official duties, with performing for their fellow colonists. He labored under no such obligation. When not carrying out his rote, lowly duties in the kitchen he would be free to compose, locking his inventions away from prying eyes in the secure section of his scri!ber. They would be revealed only when he was back on Willow-Wane, only when it was time to retire Desvenbapur the assistant food preparator and resurrect Desvendapur the poet.

In time, he cautioned himself. In good time. Stimulation and enlightenment first, then revelation.

To all outward appearances there was nothing to distinguish the thranx shuttle from the dozens that had preceded it. A sleek multiwinged shape designed for atmospheric as well as orbital travel, it emerged from the side of the *Zenruloim* like a *vlereq* voiding its egg. There was nothing in its external configuration to suggest to observant eyes either in orbit or on the planet below that there was more to it than what was immediately visible.

Receiving final clearance from planetary authorities, it drifted away from the starship on secondary thrusters before engaging its main engine at a safe distance. Braking against orbit, it began to fall not only behind but below its parent craft.

Along with that of his companions, Desvendapur's attention was fixed on the screen before him as they drifted clear of the queen vessel's gravity field. It showed a portion of the cloud-bedecked globe filling the field of view. They fell past a human orbiting station, a massive assemblage of rotating interlocking discs that swarmed with smaller craft. A pair of starships were docked at one end. To the poet's untrained eye they appeared to be about equal in size and mass to the *Zenruloim*. It was an impressive sight, but hardly an overawing one. Certain aspects of human design were quite similar to those of the thranx while others were radically, even incomprehensibly, different. It seemed impossible that the laws of physics could be bent to identical ends by engineering that differed so startlingly.

Then the shuttle was below and beyond the busy station. An intensely blue ocean loomed below. From his studies Des knew there were three such primary bodies of water on the human homeworld, the least of which was larger than the most extensive sea on either Willow-Wane or Hivehom. Though he knew there was no reason to worry, the sight chilled him more than he would have cared to admit. With its breathing spicules located on its thorax, a thranx could stand upright with its head and all its principal sensory organs held well above water—and it would quietly drown. A hard exoskeleton and slim legs made swimming difficult.

Humans, he had learned, not only swam efficiently but were naturally buoyant. Put representatives of both species side by side and a human would turn on its back and float whereas a thranx would, after suitable panicky thrashing, sink to the bottom of whatever body of water it had been unfortunate enough to stumble into. Conversely, no human could match an active thranx, with eight limbs at its disposal, for stability. Nor were the bipeds as dexterous, their two hands and ten manipulative digits unable to equal the finesse of the thranx four and sixteen.

When they wished to be, however, humans could be much louder. Whether this was a particularly useful trait was the subject of debate.

As the shuttle entered atmosphere, weight began to return, dragging Des's abdomen down against the thickly padded flight bench he straddled. The view on the screen shifted wildly between impenetrable ramparts of cloud and flickering glimpses of surface. The colors of the latter varied considerably, as did those of any world that supported indigenous life. He heard Jhywinhuran calling out to ask how he was doing, and he replied absently. His attention was wholly focused on the alien world that was rushing up toward them.

Calm and collected flight commands echoed over the chamber speakers. Then there was a sharp lurch as the secondary shuttle that was mounted within the belly of the larger dropped away. Its plunge toward the surface was precipitous, masked and electronically warped to avoid detection by planetary instrumentation. It helped that they were descending over a swath of unbroken rain forest that boasted one of the lowest population densities anywhere on the planet.

At the low altitude at which separation occurred and given the velocity and angle of the drop, there was absolutely no room for error. Too conservative an approach and the shuttle would overshoot its target, appearing unannounced and uninvited above a populated area. Too extreme, and it would be unable to brake in time, resulting in tragedy as well as accusation. But the pilots of the tiny craft had performed the requisite difficult maneuvers before. The g-forces that piled up against Des and his companions pressed their antennae back against their skulls and kept them pinned to the flight benches. It did not worry him. They had been briefed to expect it, and in the cramped confines of the downsized sub-shuttle there was nowhere for them to walk anyway.

Oversized braking thrusters rocked the craft, and his mandibles clamped tightly together. The viewscreen darkened as they dove into heavy weather. It rained frequently in the region chosen for the site of the

secret colony—a warm, wet reminder of home. Familiar with such conditions, the rain forest downpour posed no unexpected difficulties for the
pilots.

Through dark gray cloud and mist he had a glimpse of a vast, unbroken forest full of unfamiliar shapes. Then he felt impact and a jarring,
wrenching slide as the shuttle disappeared into a heavily camouflaged
opening. The noise level within the chamber rose appallingly as the shuttle slowed, finally coming to a halt within a sealed corridor. As his
respiration returned to normal and he began to release himself from the
landing harness, Desvendapur saw small service vehicles, mechanicals,
and several heavily laden six-legged figures advancing swiftly and efficiently toward the craft.

He and his companions emerged into a landing chamber that except
for its exceptionally compact dimensions was little different from one
they might have encountered on Willow-Wane. The same equipment, the
identical facilities, were much in evidence although greatly reduced in
mass. A single young female was waiting with transportation and greetings to welcome them when they disembarked. Assured that their belongings would follow, they climbed onto a stripped-down surface transport
and were promptly whisked away from the shuttle chamber.

Nothing unfamiliar assailed their senses. Strong, lightweight composites had been sprayed on the walls of the excavation to form a solid
seal against intrusion from outside. Familiar fixtures and markings indicated the location of side corridors, specific facilities, water, and utility
conduits. It looked exactly like the hive facilities they had just left. To all
outward intents and appearances, they might as readily be back on
Willow-Wane.

He had a horrible thought. What if this and they were part of some
extraordinary, extreme social experiment? What if they had indeed traveled through space-plus, but only to make a looping curve back to
Willow-Wane, or to journey on to Hivehom itself? What if they were
gullible volunteers in an experiment to see how humans and thranx would
get along in close quarters—in a physical and mental environment faked
to resemble the humans' homeworld? The view out starship and shuttle
windows could be simulated. What if they had simply landed on a thranx
world? It was impossible to tell. Everything was the same; nothing was
different.

Except for the air.

It stank of exoticism, of alien vegetation and musk. Even purified and
cleansed before being drawn into the colony it was still ripe with the fragrance of the utterly foreign. Of course, an atmosphere could be falsified
as easily as images. All manner of smells and stinks could be artificially

introduced into a closed environment. If so, he thought, someone was doing a superb job.

Because of his unique personal circumstances he was inherently more distrustful than any of his companions. Aware of this he chose not to reveal his suspicions. He hoped they would be proved wrong.

If the gravity differed from that of Willow-Wane, the difference was negligible. He didn't know whether to be uneasy or delighted at the realization. The transport turned down a second corridor and began to slow. That was when many, if not all, of his suspicions were laid to rest.

A trio of specialists were strolling down one side of the tunnel, chatting amiably among themselves, their antennae bobbing and weaving animatedly. They wore no special attire, nothing to mark their surroundings as unusual. Two humans were walking and talking with them, gesturing with their forelimbs. Compared to the lone human Desvendapur had encountered on the surface of Willow-Wane, these two wore virtually nothing. Their fleshy, multihued epidermi were blatantly exposed for all to see. Recalling his studies, Des decided that both were male. It was neither their presence nor their lack of clothing that particularly intrigued the poet, however. It was their nonthranx companions.

The pair of small quadrupeds that gamboled around both human and thranx legs were covered with a bristly substance that he managed to identify as fur before the transport hummed on past. One had covering that differed significantly from that of its counterpart. It was also considerably larger, though neither would have come up to the underside of the poet's abdomen. They had long faces, intelligent eyes, and jaws that resembled those of the AAnn more than they did those of their human associates.

He fought to recall the details of human society. As he remembered it, the bipeds not only consumed the butchered flesh of other creatures, they kept representatives of certain species in their own homes, as if the company of their own kind was insufficient to sate their need for companionship. In this regard, certain subspecies were more privileged than others. Among the latter were dogs, of which the two furry quadrupeds accompanying the strollers appeared to be legitimate representatives. What was especially fascinating was that despite their lack of sapience, the dogs appeared to be paying as much attention to the three thranx as to the two humans.

To the best of his admittedly restricted knowledge, no such creatures had been imported to Willow-Wane. They did not occupy space reserved for humans on Hivehom. Support facilities were designed to provide for humans, not their domesticated animal companions. It was costly enough to properly care for the bipeds. On the human homeworld no such restrictions would apply. The presence of the dogs had not entirely erased his concerns, but they had made it much easier for him to be convinced. The domesticated furry quadrupeds had appeared far too comfortable in the company of the three thranx to have been recently imported to a project site.

The transport slowed to a stop, settling to the floor with a whine. They were met by a pair of females wearing a type of insignia Desvenda-pur had never seen before. While the two scientists were whisked off to a separate destination, Des and Jhy were given a quick tour of the facilities where they would be working before being escorted to their new quarters. The two of them made arrangements to meet and share the nightfall meal along with the rest of the day's experiences.

Waiting for his belongings to arrive, the poet inspected the double cubicle that would serve as his new home for an indeterminate period. Nothing was unfamiliar; little differed from the living chamber he had occupied at Geswixt. Everything appeared to be of thranx manufacture. Given the professed secretive nature of the nascent colony, he would have expected nothing else. The bipeds who were surreptitiously helping the thranx to establish a foothold on their own homeworld could hardly place an order with one of their local manufacturers for a load of thorax massagers.

He halted. Something rising from the equipment stand at the foot of the sleeping bench caught his eye. As he turned toward it, an odor as pleasant as it was subtle tickled his antennae. The small, carefully arranged cluster of flowers was unlike anything he had ever seen, with spreading white petals that shaded to deep purple at the base of the sta-mens. Bending close, he dipped his antennae forward to sample the essence of the bouquet. The stems rested in a fluted afterthought of tinted glass. If it had been grown on Willow-Wane or Hivehom, there was a group of botanists who deserved whatever compensation they had been allotted. But it did not smell of either of those thranx worlds. The ampu-tated blossoms reeked of the here and now.

He looked forward to learning his way around the kitchen facility, but that pleasure was denied him until tomorrow. No one was expected to step off a shuttle after completing an interstellar journey and get right to work. If it was all part of a script to convince them they were on Earth when in fact they had never left home, it showed an attention to detail he could only admire. But with each passing time-part he became more and more convinced of the reality of the interstellar trek, and that they had truly arrived at a furtive colony-to-be hidden on the most hallowed of all human worlds.

He had hoped to encounter some of the bipeds, but the nightfall meal was attended only by fellow thranx. A number smelled strongly of *outside*, and of a moist, pungent, alien outside at that. He consoled himself with the knowledge that he would probably have the opportunity to interact with humans tomorrow or the next day. Had he not seen two of them walking casually in the company of three of his own kind on the way in? He had been patient this long; he could wait a while longer.

But as the days went by without even a glimpse of a human, he found himself growing uneasy. He had not traveled all this way, had not forged a false identity, to toil at the preparation of food for the rest of his life. Though he had mastered the limited demands of his new vocation, he was anxious to shed it and resume the mantle of full-time poet. In order to do that it was necessary for him to immerse himself in his chosen source of new inspiration. But that source remained as elusive as ever.

Where were the humans? Save for the pair he had passed on the day he and his fellow assignees arrived, the bipeds had been conspicuous by their absence. It was absurd to think that he might have less contact with the bipeds on their own world than on his. Yet for all the contact, inspirational or casual, that he had experienced so far he might as well have stayed on Willow-Wane. His frustration gave rise to several robust, acidic stanzas, but while well crafted and original they did not burn with the fervor of discovery he so desperately sought.

Any attempt to probe further would require great caution on his part. An assistant food preparator who was both persistent and inquisitive about subjects that were far removed from his official duties might well draw unwanted attention to himself. Any queries would have to be carefully framed and delivered in an offhand, almost indifferent manner. His coworkers in food preparation were notable for their lack of enlightenment.

Jhywinhuran was only marginally more helpful. Despite his intentions to keep his distance, he found himself drawn to her. Though her hive ranking was no lower than his, it was clear that she regarded him as her intellectual superior and looked up to him in matters outside their respective specialties. It was not a matter of flattery for ulterior motives or extraneous personal ends. Her attention and admiration were genuine. In her presence he relaxed far more than he intended. Constantly on guard, ever alert to the possibility of discovery, he luxuriated in the companionship of another of his kind who was openly fond of him no matter how mysterious his origins or how unforthcoming he was when certain subjects were broached.

In response to his query she informed him that she had actually seen humans on two occasions, but at a distance. There had been no personal contact. There was no reason for it to occur at her level. No doubt the rogue humans had to consort with their thranx friends on matters that reached beyond the boundaries of the colony. In matters of Jhywinhuran's field of sanitation, outside advice and help would be necessary unless the incipient colony was designed to act as a completely closed system. That was possible, but only up to a point. That it was not the case was clear from the limited interaction that had taken place between human and thranx specialists on the two occasions that Jhy had observed.

But there was no reason for humans to come into the kitchens. Desvendapur and his coworkers needed no assistance in preparing the basics of the colony's meals. That there was another feeding station he already knew from contact between the two. It was no consolation to him to learn that his counterparts in the other facility had no more interaction with humans than he did.

He had to find some way to reach out to them, to immerse himself in the strange culture of these creatures and their world. While personally satisfying, advancement in his adopted specialty promised nothing in the way of additional contact while exposing him to additional personal scrutiny he did not want. Given the extremely sensitive nature of the secret installation, like everyone else in the subterranean colony his movements were restricted. He was allowed to wander freely within the food service area and to roam the communal recreational and social inter-course areas, but everything else was strictly off-limits. This included the heavily camouflaged shuttle bay and all hive departments with access to the outside, of which there were very few.

The location of these exits, the majority of which had been estab-lished for categorical emergency purposes only, were well known. Keep-ing them secret would only have obviated their purpose. No thranx, however curious, would brazenly defy restrictions by attempting to make unauthorized use of any such egress. Not only would it violate strict hive procedure, there was no reason to do so. Within the colony all was com-fortable and familiar. Outside—outside lay an unknown alien world swarming with exotic fauna and dominated by an unstable intelligence. Who would *want* to go outside? Any sensible thranx who expressed a desire to do so would immediately find himself branded as unbalanced, marginally mad, or outright insane.

As a poet, Desvendapur qualified on multiple counts.

If he had spent all his time dwelling on his frustrations, he might well have ended up in the hospital. Aware of the dangers, he forced himself to concentrate on his work. It was much worse at night, when he had noth-ing to occupy his hands or mind, when he was free to meander both phys-ically and mentally. Unable to fathom a reason for the agitation that sometimes bubbled to the surface of Desvendapur's personality, Jhywinhuran did her best to comfort him. He responded as best he was able, but there were times when she could do nothing. How could she understand the nature of the creative fury that seethed within him, a raging torrent dammed and held back by stricture and circumstance?

It was a state of affairs that could not go on, he knew. Sooner or later his mounting frustration would overwhelm his good judgment and common sense. He would do something stupid and end up exposing himself. Then he would be removed from his duties, taken into custody, and shipped offworld for treatment and, inevitably, castigation. If his link to the death of the transport pilot Melnibicon was discovered, he would be subjected to worse than that. Any chance for a notable creative career, of course, would be permanently dashed.

How to inquire about matters outside his area of expertise without appearing too curious? After careful consideration of possible alternatives, he decided that a bold approach to one person offered fewer risks than dozens of furtive queries put to many different individuals.

He settled on a junior transport operator named Termilkulis who periodically delivered supplies to the kitchen facility. Cultivating friendship, slipping the active and efficient young male leftover delicacies from food storage, Des gradually drew him out until the operator felt completely comfortable in the assistant food preparator's company.

It was early one morning, after preparations for the morning meal had been concluded and the results turned over to the division masters for final tinkering, that he encountered Termilkulis concluding a delivery. Remarking that he was about to take time for a rest, Desvendapur was gratified when the operator responded agreeably to the suggestion that they do so together. They retired to a back corner of the facility, near the narrow unloading dock, and assumed resting stances on all four trulegs and both foothands.

Following an indeterminate number of minutes spent in lazy contemplation of the morning that were interrupted only by inconsequential remarks, Des ventured casually, "It seems strange to me that, finding ourselves on the human homeworld, we do not see more of the natives."

"Well, I don't imagine that you would, working in the department that you do." Wholly at ease, Termilkulis's antennae drooped listlessly over his forehead.

Desvendapur indicated assent, careful to keep his gestures moderated and brief. "I suppose that's true. What about you?" he asked with apparent indifference. "How many have you seen?"

The transport operator did not appear to find the question in any way out of the ordinary. "One or two."

"But I would think that in the course of making deliveries throughout the colony you would surely have the opportunity to see many of the bipeds."

"Not really. You know, for a while after I was first assigned here I wondered about the same thing myself." The poet tensed, but it was evident from the operator's attitude that the food preparator had not triggered any latent suspicion in the young driver. "So I inquired about the seeming discrepancy, and what I was told made perfect sense."

"Did it?" responded Desvendapur casually. "Did it really?"

Termilkulis turned toward him. "This is a thranx colony, a thranx hive. Only a few humans, working for an enlightened but covert division of their government, know of its existence. It is designed to show that we can live among them, in sizable numbers, without adversely impacting their civilization. When the time comes, when the xenosociologists on both sides think it is all right, our existence will be revealed and will hopefully have a salutary effect on the bipeds' opinion of us.

"But there is no reason for more than a very few of them to visit the hive. This is a thranx colony. As such, it is populated by thranx." A foot-hand rose to gesture. "By such as you and me."

It made damning, frustrating sense, Desvendapur knew. Why should any hive, even one located on the human homeworld, require the presence of humans? While the respective projects on Willow-Wane and Hivehom had been designed from the start to explore the ramifications of intimate human-thranx interaction, this colony was different. It was surreptitious, officially unacknowledged by both governments. It was designed to show that thranx could thrive on a human-dominated world. Open interaction here would come later, when both species had become acclimatized to the presence of the other, when humans did not find thranx abhorrent and vice versa.

This much he could understand. He also found many aspects of humankind distasteful. The difference between him and his fellow thranx was that for him, abhorrence was an excellent source of inspiration.

But how to immerse himself in that and its related emotional states if he was denied interaction with its progenitors, in all their billions? He would gladly settle for contact with a dozen or so, but it appeared that even that was to be denied him. He could not wait indefinitely for something to happen, for circumstances to change. His term of service was finite. More than that, he was too impatient to wait around and react. Fatalistic resignation was not a component of his character.

What to do? If he happened to see another human in the distance, walking the fringe of a sector off-limits to him, he could ignore restraint and brazenly confront the visitor. That might work—for a minute or two, until Security forestalled extensive interaction by hauling him away. Too much risk for too little potential reward. Or he could try to isolate a visiting biped, keep it to himself for a while, but even the suggestion of the use of force within the colony would find him shipped offworld faster than he could pack his meager belongings. With his access to vehicular transport, Termilkulis might be of real help—until he became aware of his new friend's intentions. That would doubtless result in immediate termination of their relationship and the reporting of the food preparator's eccentric behavior to hive authority.

No, whatever he did, Desvendapur decided quietly, he would have to do it on his own. His choices were decidedly limited. Or at least, the sensible, rational ones were. There remained the option of the insensible and the irrational. These were not available to the average thranx. Had there been anything average about Desvendapur, he would not even have been contemplating them.

The solution was as obvious as it was insane. If he could not find humans to interact with within the hive, then he would have to find a way to encounter them without.

11

As had quickly become his routine, Cheelo was awakened by the gothic choir of howler monkeys greeting the return of the sun. Lying on his back beneath the thin tropical blanket, he gazed up through the dense, feather-weight material of the tent. This close to the Earth's waist, the sun rose and set with equal alacrity. "Lingering twilight" was terminology that belonged to the temperate zone and had no place in the equatorial rain forest.

Yawning, he reached up to scratch an itch—and sat up fast, yelping. Looking down, he saw a rushing river of red-tinged brown flowing across his stomach from left to right. The river entered through a hole in the left side of his tent and exited through a gap of correspondingly tiny dimensions on his right. It went over, around, or through anything and everything in its path. It might have gone through him as well if he had not been tucked into the tough, inedible blanket.

He had gone to sleep without activating the electronic insect repeller in his backpack.

The army ants had eaten through his tent because it was in their path. Able to surmount his sleeping form, they had chosen to go over him. This was fortunate, though he did not think so until later, when he had time to reflect on the closeness of his call. At the moment he was standing and screaming, slapping at the soldier ant that had sunk its mandibles deep into the flesh of his right thumb. Had he known more of army ants and their ways he would have reacted in a more circumspect fashion.

Detecting the release of alarm pheromones from their smashed colleague, a subsection of the living brown stream detached and attacked. Flailing wildly as if afflicted with some aberrant disorder of the nervous system, Cheelo hopped and stumbled out of the tent and the trees, across the open, intervening beach, and into the river. Even submerged, the ants hung on tenaciously. Since it was not the dry season and ample customary prey was available, the resident piranhas ignored this violent intrusion into their world. The four-meter long black caiman on the far bank did not, slipping silently into the water, its dragon's tail cleaving the rippling, mirrored surface as it sinuously advanced to investigate. By the time it arrived, a fully awake and much chastened Montoya had slogged back onto the beach. Disappointed, the caiman sank back beneath the surface, its intended quarry as ignorant as ever of its majestic, carnivorous presence.

Muttering a steady stream of gutter curses, Cheelo made his way back to his tent. Reaching inside, he checked his pack carefully before picking it up. A pouch within yielded ointment to treat the red welts left behind by the jaws of the soldiers. A pair of tweezers were necessary to remove the mandibles and attached heads of those ants that had refused to release their grip, even after having been drowned and dismembered.

There was not much he could do then except wait for the column to finish moving through. Fortunately, all of his foodstuffs and concentrates were vacuum sealed. This was critical not only to prevent spoilage in the dank depths of the rain forest but to keep edibles from detection by marauding scavengers no matter what their size.

It was late afternoon before the rear guard moved through the hole in his tent and out the other side. After carrying out a visual inspection to ensure that no stragglers remained, he broke down the shelter and its contents and placed them once more in the boat. Normally before loading his gear he would have first checked everything for those dangerous lovers of dark places who inhabited the rain forest: scorpions, spiders, kissing bugs, and their ilk. Subsequent to the column's passage he knew that would not be necessary. As efficiently as if they had intentionally been making amends, the ants would have scoured clean his tent and belongings. In the wake of their passage, nothing lived.

He vowed that from now on he would be more careful in his choice of campsites. In the rain forest no locality was perfect, however. Bushes concealed dangers of their own; trees were home to voracious insects of other species; and sleeping in the boat, where he could not erect his tent, would expose him to predation by mosquitoes and worse, such as disgusting parasites like the human botfly. Despite his unfortunate experience, he continued to favor open ground within the forest itself for sleeping. He carried a patch kit for the tent, and the holes the insectile multitude had gnawed could be repaired.

Perversely, he was grateful for the presence of everything that stung, bit, chewed, or parasitized. All contributed to conditions the average tourist found uninviting. The worse the climate, the more rapacious the fauna, the less likelihood there was of him running into a tour supervised by a querulous escort. Despite the area's isolation, a guide or even a tourist equipped with a communicator could quickly call a skimmer full of rangers down on him. With the unfortunate encounter in distant San José still a recent item on police call sheets throughout the hemisphere, that was a confrontation Cheelo desired devoutly to avoid. By the time he was ready to return to Golfito, the furor surrounding his unfortunate encounter ought to have died down.

So far he had been successful. What was proving more difficult than evading the attention of the authorities was living off the land. He had succeeded in catching plenty of fish: The river was awash with them, and they bit at the first hint of bait. But he discovered that there were far fewer edible fruits and nuts than he had hoped to find, and he had been beaten to most of those by the park's thirteen species of monkey or dozens of parrots and macaws before he could so much as find a ripening tree. The fish were plentiful and tasty and kept him sated, but after a couple of weeks, even a steady diet of piranha and catfish grew boring.

The craving for variety in both taste and nutrients forced him to draw down his stock of concentrates to a point where he began to grow uneasy. Having worked so hard to isolate himself, he was extremely reluctant to make his way to Maldonado, the nearest town, to replenish his supplies. He did find some yuca root that he cleaned and fried. That restored his confidence in his back-country abilities, learned if not polished during his youth in Gatun and its own tropical environs. He knew he was being too hard on himself. Nothing could really prepare one for living beyond the limits of civilization, in the greatest surviving rain forest on Earth, in the place known as the lungs of the planet.

When he found the grove of fruit trees, planted long ago by vanished villagers and now gone wild, he was euphoric. Not yet decimated by monkeys, the fruit was a welcome and refreshing addition to his food stores. His success cheered him mentally as well as physically. That evening he caught a thirty-kilo catfish on his compact line and streamer, enough meat to fill the preserver compartment in his pack to bursting.

Cruising upriver, he lay back in the boat and let the onboard navigator take control. It would keep him from running into the banks, or any floating logs or embedded snags. Beneath him, the electric motor hummed almost silently, its batteries recharged by the amorphous solar cells that lined the sides and top of the boat. For a fugitive, he was exceptionally relaxed.

Until the boat struck something unseen.

A cry of distress, a pained yelp, came from near the bow. Sitting up quickly, Cheelo looked over the side just in time to see the injured pup floating on the surface. Blood streamed from the side of its head and flank. Preoccupied with chasing fish in the murky water, it had failed to react to the boat's presence in time. Now it limped along the surface, yipping piteously.

Swarming to its aid, the rest of the pack instantly focused on the assumed attacker. Nearly two meters long and weighing in at more than thirty kilos, the adult river wolves swarmed the boat, barking angrily.

"Ay, it was an accident!" Cheelo found himself yelling as he scrambled frantically to unholster his pistol. "The kid ran into me!"

The dozen or so giant otters did not understand him. Even if they had, it was conceivable they would not have been swayed in their course of action. Two leaped into the boat and began nipping at his feet, taking bite-sized bits out of his jungle boots. Their canines were as long as his thumb. Jaws powerful enough to crunch bone snapped at his calves while bright black eyes glared furiously.

It took an eternity to free the gun, but he couldn't use it lest he risk holing the boat. Instead, he fired over the heads of his attackers. Barking and squeaking in panic, they dove back over the side, but not before one practically ran up his leg to take a bloody chunk out of his left biceps. By the time the cursing, fulminating fugitive could bring the weapon to bear, the otters had vanished into the depths of the river.

Setting the pistol aside, he grumbled aloud as he sought to bind up the wound. With all the poisonous insects, lethal snakes, giant crocodilians, burrowing parasites, and voracious rodents in the rain forest, leave it to him to be grievously assaulted by otters. Dousing the open wound with disinfectant, he sprayed sealer over the injury and wrapped it in a thin layer of transparent artificial skin. The tape immediately contracted and began to bond with his own flesh. Once healing had concluded beneath, the artificial epidermis would dry, crack, and flake off, leaving the restored flesh exposed. Finishing up the first aid, he restowed the emergency kit and cleared some vegetation from the autobailer so it could more efficiently remove from the bottom of the boat the water the otters had brought in with them.

That was when one of them, apparently deciding that the intruder had not been punished enough, jumped out of the water and onto his back.

As its teeth and claws tore into his shoulders, a screaming, cursing Cheelo flailed wildly at his back in an attempt to pull it off. Twisting violently, locked together, man and otter overbalanced the narrow craft and tumbled into the river. As he fell, the flailing fingers of Cheelo's free hand contacted his backpack and instinctively grabbed hold. The safety strap connecting it to the side of the boat gave way beneath his weight and followed him into the water. Automatically righted by its internal gyro, the swift craft promptly resumed its course upstream—carrying with it Cheelo Montoya's tent, sleep sack, and all of his supplies that were not contained in the pack.

Perhaps the impact dislodged the river wolf as well as discouraging it. Or possibly it had finally slaked its need for revenge. Regardless of the reason, the meter-and-a-half-long otter released its bloody grasp on Cheelo's shoulders and swam off, occasionally popping its head out of the water to look back long enough to sputter a few final insulting chirps and barks at the intruding human. Treading water, Cheelo had no time to respond to the insults of his fellow mammal. Clutching tightly to the backpack with one hand and his pistol with the other, he struck out for the shore opposite the one favored by the otter clan, occasionally glancing upstream to track his boat as it blithely powered on out of sight minus its absent passenger.

He shouldn't have been such a lazy sailor, he reflected in dismay. With its autonav activated the craft would continue to make steady progress until halted by impassable rapids or some other obstacle it had not been designed to cope with. Then it would stop and wait for instructions from its absent owner.

Thoroughly drenched, he hauled himself out on the nearest beach. Smooth-shelled turtles watched him from a nearby log, butterflies fluttering about their snouts in search of extruded salts. Wading birds accelerated their stride to give him additional room. Checking his pants for worms, candiru, and other potentially dangerous hangers-on, he contemplated his options.

Recharging by day, the boat would not run out of power. Programmed to proceed upstream, it would not pause for rest or sleep. It was gone, and along with it much that he had brought to sustain him in the rain forest. By great good fortune he had shoved the compact fishing kit into the backpack after the last time he had used it. That was helpful, but still left him with little choice. No longer could he gambol carelessly through the forest. In order to make his critical appointment with Ehrenhardt, he had to find his way to a town, an isolated farm, even a tourist encampment, and he had to start now. Anyplace would do so long as it was not home to official authority. A convincing liar, he felt that he could successfully pass himself off to a group of adventurous tourists as a kindred spirit. It would take very little to render wholly believable the story of falling out of a boat set on autonav and not being able to catch back up to it.

With luck he would find assistance in returning to civilization. There he could access his credcard and without further ado, book the sequence of flights necessary to take him back to Golfito. Because he was on foot he would have to move a little faster now, that was all. He still had ample time to make the deadline.

But first he had to find those hypothetical charitable tourists, and avoid the attention of park rangers while doing so.

Two days later he felt he was closer to the nearest town but no nearer fellow sightseers. So preoccupied was he with searching for food to supplement the small stock of concentrates that remained in his pack that he almost overlooked the probe. Disguised as a split-tailed eagle, the drone came gliding down the river at treetop level. It was not the smoothness of its flight that caught Cheelo's attention and caused him to duck deeper into the woods, but the fact that the too-perfect raptor did not flap its wings—not even once. Superb glider that it was, even a large eagle needed the intercession of an occasional wingbeat to keep it aloft.

Tracking its progress from behind the buttress roots of a rain forest hardwood, he watched as the drone circled a spot on the far bank, descended to a height of several meters, and proceeded to hover. Eagles could hover, he knew, but only on strong, warm updrafts. There was no updraft a couple of meters above the riverbank, certainly not one forceful enough to support even a medium-sized hawk, much less the eagle. The cameras that were its eyes were doubtless taking pictures and relaying them back to one of the distant ranger stations that ringed the perimeter of the immense Reserva. Monitoring the health of the forest and its fauna without disturbing any of the inhabitants was a task best carried out by such disguised mechanicals.

Surely they couldn't be looking for him, he thought. Even if the authorities had somehow managed to track him and trace his flight from San José to Lima, there was next to nothing to lead them to the middle of the rain forest. He thanked whatever deities looked after such as him that he had grabbed his pack while falling out of the boat: It contained all his identification. Then it occurred to him that they might not be looking for him, Cheelo Montoya, wanted for murder, but for the missing occupant of a runaway boat. Proceeding mindlessly on its way upriver, it was not unreasonable to assume that the intruding craft had caught the attention of one of the Reserva's robotic monitors. Rangers and administrators could be expected to wonder at the presence of an unoccupied craft, packed with supplies, cruising blithely northward devoid of passengers. It would be percipient for them to assume that a small disaster might have occurred and to go looking for the owner of the wayward craft.

That was fine, except that he did not want to be rescued. It was his intention in coming to the Reserva to get himself good and lost. He did not want to be found, no matter how well-intentioned his would-be saviors were. Despite his reluctance to abandon the only landmark he knew, he had no choice but to move away from the main river and deeper into the forest. Searchers, human or mechanical, would assume that stranded travelers would keep to the shoreline and the beaches where they could easily be spotted. He had taken care to acquire a boat that could not be traced, so if scanned it would not lead back to him. With luck, it would sink and break up before inquisitive rangers could haul it ashore and check its contents.

Meanwhile he plunged deeper into the forest, knowing that it would conceal him like a hot, green blanket. The profusion of life in the canopy and on the ground would make it next to impossible to isolate his heat signature from the air, even if a properly equipped drone knew exactly where to search. He made slow but steady progress. Unlike thicket or jungle, virgin rain forest permitted relatively easy hiking. Large trees grew well apart, and the canopy harvested the sunlight before it could hit the ground, restricting the density of the undergrowth.

Not only was the solid overstory reassuring, it was also beautiful—diverse with epiphytes and flowers. Monkeys rattled their way through the arboreal highways, and the bell-like warbling of the oropendula punctuated his footsteps. He was careful to shuffle his feet as he walked. Making as much noise and vibration as possible would keep the local serpents out of his path. Avoiding the authorities would not help him if he accidentally stepped on a bushmaster or fer-de-lance.

After making a careful check for ants, he settled down between the buttress roots of a sprawling tree and prepared to spend the night. His tent was still on the boat, but his pack yielded a light, strong emergency blanket. One root curved sideways and out, creating a swooping overhang that when combined with the blanket served to protect him from the evening rain. It was a good thing he had not come in the wet season, he mused. Without his boat he would be helpless, trapped by flooded rivers and lakes, unable to cross ground churned to mud. That he was going to get wet despite the lightweight raincoat he could extract from the pack was a fact he could not avoid: He was, after all, deliberately lost in Earth's greatest rain forest. But he would not drown and, so long as he could fish, he would not starve. He did not care to think what he would have done had the folding fishing kit been lost along with the boat.

He had no difficulty the following morning pulling several small fish from a sizable pond. Using his belt knife, he gutted and filleted them. His camp stove was on the wayward boat, and making a fire was out of the question. Even if he could find sufficiently dry wood in the waterlogged forest, it would most likely be too soft to burn for long, or already so rotted it would fall apart in his hands. Nor could he risk giving away his location by producing smoke.

As he ate the fish raw he wished for a few limes or lemons. They were not available, so the tang of ceviche would have to wait until he found himself once more in a town. But the fish would give him strength. With the small remaining stock of supplements contained in the pack's emergency kit, he ought to be able to keep going for some time. At least, he thought with a grim smile, he would not be slowed down by the weight of supplies.

Settling the pack on his shoulders and back, he struck off into the trees, keeping to the highest ground that presented itself. His feet stayed warm and dry, as the surrounding mud and muck was repelled by the permanent static charge in his jungle boots. He was glad that when he had made his purchases he had not stinted on appropriate clothing. It would have been nice, however, to have the tent.

On the other hand, he might have grabbed something besides the pack when tumbling out of the boat. He did not care to think about what his situation might be like without it. He would have had no choice but to risk rescue by the Reserva rangers and to hope that no one connected his face to the one that was by now no doubt splashed across police wanted files all across the planet.

The repeller in the pack kept the swarms of ravenous insects at bay. He could see them, could hear them humming and clicking and chittering as they flew and crawled all around, unable to enter the restricted sphere of electronic dislocation that had at its core a warm, pulsating, blood-filled figure. They wanted to nibble on his flesh and drink his blood. Mosquitoes and flies, beetles and ants, all gave way as the precisely modulated stridulations of the repeller urged them aside like a drifting iceberg parting the sea. Without the compact device, he knew, his skin would by now have taken on the reddened, uneven contours of a strenuously abused golf ball.

The birds kept him company, and the monkeys. While easy to hear, the latter were difficult to see. The natives who had once inhabited this region had been fond of monkey, but the thought of consuming a simian was not one that appealed to Cheelo. Anyway, he had only a single-bladed knife and could not have used a bow and arrow had heaven provided them.

The following morning a skimmer flashed by overhead, traveling slowly at treetop level. Alerted to its approach by the startled screeches of a family of squirrel monkeys, he had taken shelter beneath a dense cluster of dieffenbachia. Thick, spatulate leaves shielded him completely from above. Peeping out as the skimmer thrummed past, he saw that it was camouflaged visually as well as aurally. If not for the panic that had arisen among the monkeys he would never have noticed it until it was right on top of him. Despite the cover provided by the trees, he might have been spotted.

The forest is my friend, he thought, waiting beneath the concealing leaves until he was sure the patrolling vehicle was gone. When he resumed his march, his confidence was shaken by unexpected uncertainty.

Come to think of it, why would Reserva rangers need to camouflage their patrol craft? True, the soft whine a skimmer generated might disturb the native fauna, but it was hardly loud enough to be flagrantly unsettling. Masking the sound of an engine was an expensive procedure that hardly seemed justified by the limited disruption it might cause.

He could understand disguising drone probes as eagles and other birds. They could move more freely among the forest creatures, taking surveys and monitoring their health. But it seemed a waste of money to camouflage a skimmer. Its size and unfamiliar shape would instantly identify it to the creatures of the forest as an unknown and possibly hostile intruder. His confusion deepened.

If the skimmer was not disguised to conceal it from the denizens of the rain forest, then from whom? Wouldn't it be more likely that an official Reserva vehicle would be boldly emblazoned with identifying marks and colors? A scientific expedition might opt for anonymity, but not for expensive camouflage. In the event of an emergency, they would want to make certain their craft could be spotted from the air by a search party. The same would be true for a tourist vehicle.

That left open to speculation the possibility that there were others in the rain forest who did not wish their presence advertised. Biochemical companies, for one, extracted enormously valuable and useful derivatives from rain forest plants. Most of these took the form of legal, government-approved, exhaustively tested products. A few did not. Their scarcity and novelty value enhanced their price.

If botanical pirates were active in this part of the forest, they might—once he had the chance to explain himself—accept him as a kindred spirit and take him in. That would obviate his need to find his way into a town, thereby risking exposure to the local authorities. On the other hand, such illicit organizations did not usually take kindly to the appearance of uninvited outsiders, no matter what their social standing. Depending on the frame of mind of the people in charge of such a hypothetical illegal operation, they might as readily decide to punch a hole in his chest and dump him in the nearest river for the caimans and the piranhas to clean up as invite him to share their camp.

He would have to tread carefully. He might already have tripped hidden sensors, resulting in the appearance of the patrolling skimmer. If he had strayed inside some undefined perimeter, the possibility of automated traps could not be discounted. From now on he would have to pay even more attention than usual to where he put his feet. But, he reminded himself, any assault by the authorities on a clandestine rain forest operation would come from the air. He would be cautious anyway. He did not know what he was dealing with, and until he did, he would continue to treat his immediate surroundings with heightened suspicion.

Another skimmer flew over later that day, forcing him to take shelter a second time. He knew it was a different vehicle from its size and silhouette. It only reinforced his conviction that it was someone other than the local authorities who was searching for him. If it was the police and they suspected a fugitive was afoot in the area, they would have called for him to surrender himself. If it was the as-yet-unidentified owner of the wayward boat who was being sought, they would have advertised the opportunity for rescue rather than gone to expensive lengths to conceal its presence.

That left him with his suspicions of a criminal operation hidden somewhere in the depths of the rain forest, its operators as eager as he to avoid the attention of the authorities. They would be people who might as readily kill him as welcome him, even if he invoked Ehrenhardt's name. The choices thus presented were not easy ones. He decided that until he knew more he would maintain his privacy. Meanwhile let them search for him. He had avoided the authorities all the way from San José to the Reserva. No manufacturers of illicit pharmaceuticals were going to find him if he did not want to be found.

Whoever they were, he reflected as he stepped over a fallen log lush with fungi, they had money. Camouflaging a skimmer's appearance was one thing, but muting its engine called for expensive technological expertise. This remote corner of the vast rain forest was not being guarded by a handful of amateurs working out of a few thatched huts. The presence of not one but two such costly disguised skimmers hinted at a level of sophistication outside his experience.

Maybe he could do more than merely survive here, he thought. Maybe there was a chance to make some contacts—big, important contacts. If the opportunity presented itself to fall in with a group of well-connected felons, he would take it. Or he might learn all he could about them and then turn in their operation to the nearest authorities, using his knowledge to bargain for the dropping of the charges that would have arisen from the incident in San José. That had been an accident, after all. No one could claim premeditation. Either way, he had options. What he needed now was to supplement them with knowledge, as much as he could gather without being discovered.

It struck him that the drone that had been disguised as an eagle might be owned and maintained not by the Reserva authority but by these same people. Monitoring a buffer area outside their immediate zone of operations, it could watch for patrolling rangers and unwitting tourists without drawing attention to itself. He whistled softly to himself, impressed by the implications. Everything he had seen so far suggested the existence of an illegitimate operation on an imposing scale. That was assuming he was right in his assumptions and that it was not the local authorities who were conducting the flyovers.

For a moment he worried that the electronic repeller might give him away. Then he relaxed, secure in the knowledge that if it was going to, it already would have. Its output must be infinitesimal, he decided. Anyone close enough to pick it up would be able to see and identify its owner. Even so, he considered turning it off. The continued presence of the active insect multitude that had helped to keep this portion of the Reserva pristine for hundreds of years forestalled him. He was uncomfortable enough already. He would not add to his discomfort by exposing his flesh to the attentions of a million marauding mandibles, stingers, and probing proboscises. Aside from the potential for loss of blood and the acquisition of disease, he flat-out hated and always had despised bugs.

Trying to make as little noise as possible as he advanced, he kept his eyes alert for the glint of metal and plastic and composite, and his ears attuned to the harmonic discord of the surrounding forest. If the monkeys failed to warn him next time, the birds might do so. He was not alone here; he had allies, however unconventional. He had escaped confinement and mindwipe by never letting down his guard and by trusting no one. Early in his life he had chosen to swap companionship for freedom. It was a philosophy that had served him well, and he saw no reason to tamper with it now.

Overhead, a pair of scarlet macaws were screeching with pleasure as they attacked a cluster of ripe figs. A pair of the juicy green fruits fell to earth not far from where Cheelo was standing. Bending, he picked them up and, after checking for ants, shoved them in a pocket. Later, when his stomach was feeling more adventurous, he might try a bite. Raising a hand, he saluted his rain forest confederates with a grin before moving on.

It did not matter who was looking for him, he decided with satisfaction. Police or traffickers, rangers or poachers—he would avoid them all until he and he alone decided it was time for Cheelo Montoya to leave the Reserva. They kept the rain forest at arm's length: He embraced it. The trees and the animals and the insects were his friends, his shield. All he had to do was find out what was going on here, in this empty, isolated place, and figure out the best way to profit from that knowledge before he left.

While taking care, of course, to make sure that his friends and his shield did not poison, infect, dismember, eviscerate, or otherwise impede him.

12

Sustenance would not be a problem, at least not in the short term. Desvendapur had readier access to food than anyone else in the colony, far more than he would be able to carry. Besides, it was his intention to live as much as possible off the alien land. Just as the bipeds had been able to derive nourishment from many of the native foodstuffs available on Willow-Wane, so the residents of the hidden colony on the human homeworld found that their digestive systems could tolerate a significant variety of the local plant products. This greatly facilitated settlement and the perpetuation of secrecy, since suspiciously large quantities of food did not have to be brought down from orbit.

Certain vital minerals and vitamins not found in terrestrial vegetation, or available only in insufficient quantity or incorrect proportion, were supplied to the colonists in the form of supplements, and it was these that Desvendapur was careful to stockpile for his pending enterprise. As a food preparator he was as familiar as the senior botanists and biochemists with those local growths that provided the bulk of the colony's provender. Once outside, he would know exactly what to look for in its raw form and how best to prepare it. Provided he could get outside, of course.

He spent a good deal of his leisure time surreptitiously studying and evaluating potential egresses. There was only one main exit to the surface: The shuttle dock where he had first arrived. On those occasions when it was necessary for them to pay a visit, the colony's human friends and facilitators entered via the same portal.

There were in addition a number of artfully concealed emergency exits, to be used only in the event of disaster. Their design and construction was familiar to him. Every hive boasted similar "shoot" tunnels equipped with automatic, individually powered lifts to the surface. Utilizing one in the accustomed manner was out of the question, as its activation would set off all manner of alarms.

At least he would not have to deal with guards, armed or otherwise. The forest that grew above the colony was undisturbed and empty save for those remote monitors that had been designed jointly by humans and thranx to keep watch for unforeseen intruders. Since the establishment of the colony there had been none. This portion of the planet was not only vast and untouched, it was guarded by the humans themselves against unauthorized entry. The monitors were a calculated afterthought, a precaution whose presence was very likely unnecessary. Nevertheless, they existed, and he would have to deal with them.

But no one guarded the exits. There was no reason, no need for sentinels. Bold and audacious as the colonists were, no thranx in its right mind would think of taking a solo, unsanctioned jaunt on the actual surface, exposed to thousands of exotic alien life-forms. Additionally, it could get uncomfortably cool outside, especially at night. There was also hostile fauna with which the colonists were utterly unfamiliar, and they wanted to keep it that way.

All except Desvendapur. Hostility was fertilization for tragedy, and tragedy was the foundation for many a noble epic. As for the climate, he would cope. Of all the places on Earth, the colony had been established in the one most copacetic to his kind. If he could not persevere on the surface above the colony, it was highly unlikely he would be able to do so anywhere else on the world.

It took him some time and much careful calibrating to forge the necessary internal directives. Anyone who chanced across them would discover that he had been temporarily transferred to the colony's other food preparation facility. Anyone who happened to check personnel records would note that he was still hard at work in the colony. With his work location temporarily blurred, no one should miss him at either location. He would be free to wander, to absorb and learn, to discover and explore. When he was finished he would return to his old station, there being a good likelihood of his never having been missed. He would resume work while devoting the majority of his time to the tailoring of his rough notes.

When they were revised to his satisfaction he would submit them to the appropriate sources on Willow-Wane for criticism and publication. That they would cement his celebrity he had no doubt. Then he would gladly submit to the public revelation and exposure of his true self, in the process reclaiming his identity. If this connected him with the death of the transport driver Melnibicon, he would deal with the consequent ramifications as required. What happened after that did not matter. His fame would be assured. The honor and renown he would bring to his much-reduced family, to his clan and his birth hive, would blaze forth no matter what his eventual disposition at the hands of the authorities. There was even a good chance he would escape punishment. Great art traditionally excused a multitude of sins, as well it should. He did not dwell long on the morality of this conviction.

But his compositions would have to be exceptional indeed.

It was with growing confidence that he made ready. The thrill of preparing to do something as illicit as it was extraordinary inspired him to fire off half a dozen scrolls filled with screaming hot stanzas. Reviewing them, he decided that they represented his best work to date. And they only anticipated the sights he expected to see, the experiences he proposed to have. He could foresee that any creative difficulties that might develop were not going to arise from insufficient inspiration, but from a need to channel and guide a surfeit of illumination.

And then, falling upon him as heavily and abruptly as a collapsing tunnel, the chosen day was at hand. He bade temporary farewell to Jhywinhuran and his friends and coworkers within the food preparation section, assuring them that he would return from his temporary reassignment to their quadrant of the colony within a single moon cycle. Returning to his quarters, he made certain that everything was in order and that, should anyone come calling and enter uninvited, they would find a chamber in a state reflecting the continued residence of its occupant. He had arranged everything just so, even to programming his favorite relaxation music and visuals to power up at appropriate times of the day.

There was only so much he could do. If someone should post a watch on his living quarters they would quickly discover that the cubicle was not in use. But why would anyone do that? As jointly devised by humans and thranx, colony security was designed to keep a lookout for wandering strangers on the surface. It was intended to keep outsiders sealed out, not residents locked in.

The supplies he had so patiently and laboriously accumulated were packed within a waterproof commodities sack appropriated from food preparation. Anyone observing him in transit would think he was making a delivery. The fact that he would be traveling outside the usual food freighting routes was unlikely to give rise to a great deal of comment. It was not as if he were transporting a bomb.

Strapping the sack onto his back, he used a reflective surface to make sure that it was properly balanced against the long, narrow sweep of his abdomen. The fact that he had not been mated and still retained his vestigial wing cases helped, since the additional layer of hard chitin served to shoulder some of the weight. Slipping a carry pouch over his thorax found him heavily burdened, but not intolerably so. Taking a last look around the comfortable chamber that had been his home ever since he had touched down on the world of the bipeds, he walked out, closing and securing the entrance behind him with his personal code.

He had deliberately chosen the hour of early morning when hive shifts were in flux. With half the colony's workers retiring and the other half rising to their assignments, there was a lot of traffic in the corridors. Everyone walked who could. The fewer vehicles the colony utilized, the less the chance that an accumulation of stray vibrations might be picked up by unknowing travelers on the surface above. Given the isolation of the colony's site within the immense protected rain forest, that was extremely unlikely, but every precaution that could be taken to ensure secrecy had been fully implemented.

No one confronted him or greeted him as he made his way westward through the hive. General anonymity was one of the benefits of working in food preparation, and he had deliberately done nothing since his arrival to cultivate conviviality or friendship among his fellow thranx outside his department. Jhywinhuran was the one exception. He tried not to think of how she might react to the revelation of his true identity. Seeing her perfect vee-shaped face, her golden eyes that seemed to glow within, the elegantly sensuous sweep of her ovipositors and the gleam of soft light off her brilliant blue-green exoskeleton made him uncomfortable. He forced the images from his mind. A poet on the hunt was not permitted to indulge in the balm of soothing reminiscence.

As he traveled farther from the centers of operation and into zones designed for general maintenance he encountered fewer and fewer residents. Machines held sway here, muffled and muted to emit as little in the way of vibration and telltale impulses as possible. Every technological blanket available had been thrown over the colony to screen it from prying eyes.

But in addition to basic foodstuffs imported from orbit and water from the colony's own wells, there was one other component vital to the continued health of the facility: air.

Filtered and purified, the alien atmosphere was drawn into the hive by means of a series of all-but-silent vacuum pumps. Narrow of diameter, camouflaged to look like tree stumps, they dotted the floor of the rain forest above, inconspicuous and immobile. When he entered via a servicing and maintenance hatch the one he had singled out, Desvendapur struggled against the pull from below. If he lost his grip, if he fell helplessly, arms and legs flailing, he would find himself trapped at the bottom of the shaft. If he was lucky, someone would detect the reduction in the flow of air and come to see what was causing the obstruction. If not, he would lie there until his food ran out and until—despite the presence of biological inhibitors—he began to rot.

Bracing all four legs, both foothands, and both truhands against the sides of the vertical cylindrical shaft, he stepped through the opening, using his truhands to carefully close the service hatch behind him. Even with eight limbs to brace himself against the dark composite walls, it was a struggle to ascend against the powerful downdraft. The untreated atmosphere being sucked down into the hive was ripe with a pervasion of exotic odors that threatened to overwhelm him. He persisted in his ascent. As expected, the air was cooler than he would have preferred, but adequately impregnated with moisture. He might get cold, but he would not dry out.

Once, he slipped, a rear leg losing its grip, threatening to send him hurling down the shaft. His other legs stiffened to take up the slack, and he quickly reasserted his stance, resuming the full brace. The supply sack strapped to the back of his abdomen now felt as if it were filled not with food and medication and survival gear but with bars of unrefined metal. The place where his thorax met his upper abdomen rubbed painfully together with each upward step, threatening to crack and expose his semi-open circulatory system. If that happened and the break was serious, he could easily bleed to death before he reached the surface.

Though always in view, the upper terminus of the shaft seemed impossibly far away. He elected not to look at it lest the distance he still had to climb discourage him. From the trembling in his legs he knew that he had already passed the point of no return. The top of the shaft was closer than the service hatch through which he had entered. Since it required almost the same energy to rise as to retreat, he clasped his mandibles tightly together and continued his ascent. His thorax pulsed with his hard breathing.

The higher he rose, the stronger became the alien stench from outside. Just when he thought his legs could no longer support him, his head slammed into something unyielding. The pain that raced down his unprotected antennae was intense. Only the shock kept him from losing his grip on the walls of the shaft entirely and plunging to the bottom. If that happened at this height he would not have to worry about rescue. Drawn inward by the suction from below, alien air entering through screened, eye-sized gaps blasted his face and exposed eyes. Ignoring the dust and grit, he reached up with both truhands to feel along the inner edge of the rim. There should be a single latch. In the near darkness he could see very little, and he was constantly having to look down to protect his eyes from the barrage of minuscule debris that threatened to rip the shielding nictitating membranes.

If he failed to locate the latch, or if it refused to open, he would have no choice but to try and work his way all the way back down the shaft to the service hatch. Given how his legs were shaking, he doubted very seriously if he would be able to make it.

He had studied the design of the air shafts closely, but perusing a schematic in the comfort of his quarters was very different from hunting for a tiny component part, trembling and exhausted, while braced only by his legs at the top of a lethally high duct full of incoming air that seemed determined to break his grip and send him hurtling downward. The delicate digits of his left truhand skimmed the place where the upper rim met the top of the shaft. They encountered an immovable obstruction. Raising his head, Desvendapur fought to see clearly in the poor light and softly moaning air. It was the latch. It *had* to be. Using all four digits, he pressed and twisted according to the schematic he had memorized.

The latch did not respond.

Regulating his breathing as best he could, he tried again. The latch might as well have been welded shut. Refusing to concede, unable to do anything else, he readied himself for a third attempt. But he needed more leverage—or more strength.

Sending his last surge of energy and determination into his lower body, he released his grip on the shaft walls with his upper limbs. Braced now only by his four trulegs, he grasped the latch with all sixteen digits of his foothands and truhands while pressing and twisting. Something unyielding complained. The latch gave.

He was not sure whether his legs lost their brace before he pulled himself out or at the same time. All he knew was that he was hanging on with his upper limbs for what seemed like an eternity before he was able to finally kick, pull, and drag himself out of the shaft. He lay on the ground, breathing hard, his vision unfocused, alongside what looked like the stump of a dead diderocarpus. The last thing he had done before collapsing was to close the top of the shaft. It had snapped shut, automatically resealing.

He was committed now. He could not reopen the shaft and regain access to the hive from outside. He was trapped on the surface of an alien world, the world of the bipeds. Right where he wanted to be.

It had not been difficult to learn where the few fixed monitors were located, or when the mobile scanners passed over their respective sections of the site. Colony-based security was necessarily limited lest it attract the attention of the local human authorities. Of necessity, the majority of it was left to those renegade humans who had assisted in the establishment of the colony, and even they had to keep a low profile.

Those few who had infiltrated the park authority were the most useful, but even they could not linger in the colony's vicinity. It would be difficult to explain the attraction of a patch of rain forest that, literally on the surface, was no different from the thousands of square kilometers surrounding it. So while he remained attuned and alert to the possibility, he believed that any chance of imminent discovery remained slight.

His excitement at having made it this far was muted by his exhaustion. Every joint in his exoskeleton ached. He lay on his lower abdomen, his legs folded beneath him, slowly regaining his strength. Gradually it returned, and with it, the ability to marvel at his outlandish surroundings.

The trees were all the wrong color: gray or grayish-green where they should have been dark brown. Leaves tended to be broad and spatulate, which was normal, but with their veins all too visible. It was a relief to observe distant ancestor types crawling and flying through the forest. The screech of primitive mammals, the predecessors of the dominant planetary species, pierced the sodden air. Any less humidity and Desvendapur would have been distinctly uncomfortable, but the near-normal moisture content helped to mitigate the cool temperature. He might feel a slight chill now and then, especially at night, but otherwise he anticipated no difficulty surviving.

Having devoted himself in his spare time to the study of the biology of the surface in the immediate vicinity of the colony, he was able to locate not one but several edible plants. None of them were palatable to humans, whose ability to consume and digest plant matter was notably inferior to that of the thranx. Rising, he hefted his pack and started off into the woods, choosing an easterly heading. He ignored the edible vegetation. At the moment he was not hungry, and there would be plenty to choose from in the course of his journey. Nor did he wish to leave behind any evidence of his passing.

With that in mind he was careful to step only in very wet or very dry places so as not to leave footprints, to avoid the breaking off of leaves or branches, and to disturb as little of the forest litter as possible, even though there were other large animals in the forest and any such damage would likely be ascribed to them. Even a human specialist would find it hard to tell whether a branch had been snapped off by a thranx or a tapir.

As he traveled farther from the site of the colony and deeper into the untouched terrestrial rain forest his elation increased. This was what he had come for, what he had struggled so long to achieve—exposure to something utterly new and different. Already, long lines of continuous verse were scampering unbidden through his brain so voluminously that he had to halt from time to time to recite them into his scri!ber. Every tree, every flower and insect, peeping amphibian or raucous bird, inspired him to compose. He could no more stop himself from doing so than he could halt his breathing. It slowed his progress but raised his spirits.

A fruiting tree was ablaze with cacophonous color, not from flowers but from the flock of scarlet macaws busily gorging themselves in its upper branches. Pausing below, Desvendapur assembled an entire sonnet, complete to rhythm and accompanying stridulation. Following a creative lull of many cycles, the explosion of artistry left him giddy. And this was only the first morning of the first day! What inspirational wonders awaited him in the cycles to come? He resolved to maintain his freedom for as long as possible, or at least until the last of his strategic supplements gave out.

It did indeed grow decidedly chilly when the sun set, but the personal covering and tubular shelter he had brought with him proved sufficient to ward off the cold. A human would have spent the night sweating in the nocturnal heat and humidity, but the comfort level of a thranx demanded more of both. Within the solitary six-legged sightseer, excitement and elation battled exhaustion. To Desvendapur's benefit, exhaustion won. He slept soundly and well into morning.

Rising, he repacked his gear and resumed his march eastward. Surrounded by a profusion of exotic edibles, he did not hesitate to try one after another, but only if he was certain of his identification. Many terrestrial growths contained toxins to discourage the attention of predacious herbivores. Some of these were deadly to humans but harmless to thranx, and vice versa. Strong botanical alkaloids that would have sickened or disabled a biped, for example, the thranx considered piquant and spicy.

Ambling along between the trees, the poet ate as he walked. Truhands reached out to pluck leaves from surrounding bushes or hanging branches. Many things a human would have considered fair game the vegetarian thranx ignored, including the abundance of insects. For Desvendapur to have consumed a plump, protein-rich grub would have been akin to a biped eating a baby monkey.

Water was everywhere, eliminating the need for him to carry a supply. Obstacles that would have given a human pause proved no impediment to a six-legged thranx. His only fear was that there might not be room enough in his scri!ber to hold all of the endless stream of invention that poured from his mandibles.

Carefully picking his way through a jumble of small fallen trees that had been washed up in one place by the annual wet-season flood, he felt something strike his middle left leg forcefully. Looking down, he was intrigued to see the three-meter long bundle of lethal curves known to the

humans as a fer-de-lance drawing warily away from him. With a soft hiss
it turned to slink off into the rotting litter. Its method of locomotion
greatly intrigued him. Nothing half so large lived on Willow-Wane that
was capable of rapid movement over land without legs. He observed its
departure with interest. A glance at the limb that had absorbed the impact
revealed a pair of shallow dimples in the faintly metallic blue-green chitin
where the elapid's fangs had struck. When they had failed to penetrate,
the aggressive and slightly bewildered snake had turned to slink off into
the darkness of the forest understory.

Having paid close attention to his studies, Desvendapur had been
able to identify the snake instantly. Had it bit the soft, unprotected leg of
a human, pain and paralysis would have rapidly ensued and—without the
prompt application of the appropriate antivenin—death. Unless struck in
the eye, the soft underside of the abdomen, or between joints, an armored
adult thranx ran no such risk.

Not every threat manifested by the wild rain forest could be so easily
dismissed. Knowing this, Desvendapur was alert to its many dangers. A
large constrictor like a boa or an anaconda could kill a thranx as readily as
an unwary human. So could a startled spectacled bear or an angry
caiman. By virtue of his hard exoskeleton the poet was, however, virtually immune to the attentions of the omnipresent hordes of biting, sting-
ing, blood-sucking insects.

Despite the wonderful excess of exotic tastes freely available on the
trees and bushes growing all around him, he was careful not to over-
indulge. It would be foolish to survive the forest only to succumb to a
self-inflicted stomach upset. There would be plenty of time later to try
everything.

The narrow, shallow rain forest streams were a source of constant
wonder and delight, but the first sizable tributary he encountered gave
him pause. It was less than five meters across, no more than half a meter
deep, and devoid of visible current. Any human child could have plunged
in and crossed it easily. Not so Desvendapur or any other thranx. No matter how hard they thrashed and kicked, even with all eight limbs they
were feeble swimmers. Their bodies had simply not been designed with
buoyancy in mind. And while members of both sapient species could
keep their heads above water while they swam, humans breathed through
double openings set in the center of their faces. A thranx utilized eight
breathing spicules, four to each side, located on the thorax. Following
immersion, these invariably found themselves situated below the surface.

Turning upstream, the poet kept alert for a place to cross. A large
fallen mahogany tree trapped among rocks provided a bridge. It was

shakier than he would have liked, but in the absence of alternatives he felt he had no choice but to trust it. He wanted to put as much distance as possible between himself and the colony as rapidly as he could.

The log held steady beneath his weight, and with all six legs securing his footing he was able to accomplish the potentially lethal transit without difficulty. Besides, there was nothing like tempting death to stimulate the creative muse within. Composing as he walked, the scri!ber held comfortably in one truhand, he plunged gleefully into the dense rain forest on the far shore.

In this manner he passed a number of days, camping in a different place every night, sampling the local vegetation, composing relentlessly, crossing intervening streams with an abandon that began to border on recklessness. He was drunk with delight at the sights he encountered, knowing that few if any of his kind had ever seen half as much of the world of the bipeds as he was seeing now. Via recordings, yes, but that was not the same as and could not compare with trudging through the deliciously decomposing muck of the rain forest floor, catching the flash of light from a flitting morpho or dragonfly, listening to the squawk and screech of birds arguing with tree-dwelling simians, or pausing to ingest and sample the taste of yet another exotic leaf or flower.

It was worth everything he had gone through to get here, he told himself with satisfaction. It was worth anything the authorities might do to him if he was caught. He had composed more and better in the past few days than in his entire previous lifetime. For a true artist, that made any and all consequences worthwhile.

He marveled at the miniature jewels comprising the family Dendrobatidae, the poison arrow frogs. When he encountered a sloth lumbering lugubriously between trees, he sat for hours watching it. Reaching a stream whose bottom was clearly visible through the transparent water, he chose to wade it instead of hunting for a bridge or a way around. The meter-deep water covered his legs and submerged his abdomen, coming right up to the base of his thorax. All four trulegs were underwater, a condition designed to make any sensible, right-thinking thranx exceedingly nervous. What if he stepped into a hole and went under? What if the appearance of the streambed was deceptively deeper than it appeared, or gave way beneath his feet?

Holding his breath, he deliberately lowered himself until the stream rose to his mandibles. With his spicules submerged, only his head remained above water. He could still see with his eyes, hear with his ears, taste with his antennae, but he could not breathe. He held the unnatural position for as long as his lungs would allow before finally straightening.

Water trickled off his exoskeleton as he emerged onto the far bank. The experience had been empowering as well as exhilarating.

Raising the overworked scri!ber to his mandibles, he poured a stream of florid composition into the integrated pickup. As he walked and dictated, he strode into a patch of low swamp seething with voracious, newly hatched leeches. They swarmed onto his legs and promptly dropped off, unable to penetrate his exoskeleton. Those that persisted he picked off and flung aside. They tried to cling to his digits but were unable to secure a grip on the hard, smooth surface.

There were sizable native predators on Willow-Wane, and in prehistoric times primitive social thranx on Hivehom had suffered predation at the claws of rampaging *colowact* or the ferocious burrowing *bejajek*. Large meat-eaters tended to make a good deal of noise prior to attacking, however. So it was with more than a little surprise that Desvendapur, who thought himself by now comparatively well attuned to the movements and the rhythms of the terrestrial forest, stepped through a clump of deep green calathia and found himself confronting a round, speculative face deep of eye and carnivorous of aspect.

More than a little surprised itself, but equally intrigued, the jaguar inclined its head upward and sniffed curiously. Recognizing the quadruped from his studies, the poet halted where he was standing. One foothand reached up and back to remove the kitchen cutting tool he had appropriated from the food preparation section. It was the nearest thing to a weapon Desvendapur had been able to expropriate and bring along. Food preparators did not have access to stunners or projectile devices. Not that it mattered. Even if he had been allowed open and free access to the colony's stores he doubted if such appliances were extant. Even the rogue humans who had assisted in helping the colony to get started might balk at the unregulated importation of alien weaponry.

Taking care not to make any sudden movements that might agitate the big carnivore, Des transferred the cutting tool from his foothand to a truhand. The foothand was stronger, but the truhand was more dexterous and agile. Also, it could reach high enough to protect his face. Thranx and jaguar stared, each one utterly foreign to the other.

When the big cat took a deliberate step forward, the poet fought down the urge to turn and run. Thranx were not noted for their sprinting ability, and he didn't doubt for a moment that the terrestrial predator could overtake him with little effort. Approaching, the jaguar lowered its head and commenced a thorough olfactory inspection of this unprecedented prowler, beginning at the excessive number of limbs and working its way upward. The scent it was inhaling was not unpleasant, but neither did it correlate with anything in the jaguar's experience. Ears inclined sharply forward, it worked its way along the length of the thranx's body.

Was this peculiar creature alive? Was it something good to eat? A thick pink tongue emerged to take a lick of Desvendapur's hind left leg. Finding this foray inconclusive, the jaguar employed the only sampling means left at its disposal. Opening massive jaws, it placed them around the poet's leg just above the middle joint and bit down.

Desvendapur winced at the pain and lashed out with the cutting tool. It was not the resultant shallow incision that caused the jaguar to leap up and backward, however, but the reflex stridulation generated by the wing cases on the thranx's back. Sharp, piercing, and unprecedented in the big cat's experience, the reflexive distress cry hurt its sensitive ears. With the alien vibration ringing in its head, it landed on all fours, whirled, and disappeared into the forest.

Breathing hard, Desvendapur hung onto the cutting tool with one truhand while he used the truhand and foothand on his other side to explore the injury. Though oozing blood and body fluids, the wound was not deep. Unpacking his improvised medical kit, he disinfected and then patched the hole, filling it with quick-drying synthetic chitin. Fortunately, the jaguar had not bit down with its full strength, or it might have cracked the limb. That would have posed serious problems indeed, though less so for a six-legged thranx than for a two-legged human. He could have rigged a splint, but it was just as well that the attack had not been more serious.

He could not really call it an attack, he decided. The bite had been more in the nature of a tasting. But for purposes of dramatic composition, he would remember and render it otherwise. Exaggeration was as much a tool of the poet as accent and cadence. Like everything else he had experienced since escaping the hive, the encounter with the big cat would be turned to creative profit. Unlike nearly everything else, it was one experience he had no desire to repeat.

The next large predator might decide to see if the eight-limbed alien was edible by taking a bite out of his head instead of a leg.

13

Increasingly confident of his ability to elude the attentions of whoever was probing this portion of the rain forest, Cheelo finished the last of his supper and prepared to retire for the night. The enormous branch that protruded from the lower portion of the trunk of the diderocarpus would not have been easy for a city dweller to reach, but in his time Cheelo had been forced to do more than his share of scrambling over, around, and through obstacles to avoid the attentions of security guards, alerted authorities, and violated merchants. The modest ascent caused him no difficulty.

In minutes he had his pack snugged deep in a crook formed by two tributary branches and his thin emergency blanket spread out on a flattened portion of the largest. Safer than usual from those forest inhabitants who chose to do their marauding after dark, he settled down to a meal of fruit supplemented with vitamin pills and dehydrates. The latter responded gratifyingly to his experienced ministrations and the application of a little water.

The sun did not so much set as silently evaporate behind the clouds and trees, so he could not watch it drop below a vaporous horizon. But seated silently in his temporary aerie he was able to observe the performance of parrots and macaws, of monkeys and lizards, and to hear the ever-present thrum of hyperactive insects. For company he had a brace of black-and-yellow frogs, each of which was no bigger than his thumb. The rain forest was an unending, round-the-clock carnival in which one never knew what act was going to present itself next.

That did not mean he retained his composure when the meter-and-a-half tall bug wandered out of the woods in the direction of his tree.

At first he thought he was hallucinating, a not-uncommon occurrence in the deep tropics. As opposed to the giant insect, however, everything else looked, smelled, felt, and sounded unceremoniously real. Hallucinations usually involved more than one element of perception. Excluding the outlandish apparition, nothing—not even the clouds, not even the explosion of green growth—appeared abnormal.

As it came closer he saw that while it was insectlike, it was not an insect. It had eight limbs instead of the compulsory six, but neither did that make it a spider. Other details marked it as significantly different. Each of the upper four limbs terminated not in hooks or claws, but in four manipulative digits of equal length. Cheelo could not avoid thinking of them as fingers. Not while one delicately gripped a device of some kind and another casually held a stick.

As he stared, the blue-green, hard-shelled specter halted. It looked down at the device it was carrying, up and around at its immediate surroundings, and again at the device before reaching back to place it in a pocket or slot in the sack slung across its body. The sack was fashioned from a synthetic material Cheelo did not recognize. Unable to reach the pouch with the smaller limb that had held the device up for inspection, the creature was forced to transfer the object to a second set of arms in order to complete the transfer.

Raising itself up onto its four hind limbs, it looked around before resuming its approach. Unless it deviated from its present course, it would pass directly beneath the branch on which Cheelo had chosen to make his bed. Flattening himself out, he fumbled apprehensively for the pistol in his backpack. He could see nothing like a weapon hanging from or attached to the bug or its gear.

That was when he recognized the creature from a hazy remembrance of an old media report. As he recalled, it was his mind that had been hazy at the time, not the report. He had been very, very drunk; he recalled the moment as one of the low points in his life, of which he had suffered many. If he remembered correctly, this creature was a representative of one of the several intelligent, space-traversing species mankind had encountered subsequent to the development of the posigravity, or KK-drive, that had made other-than-light travel possible. He tried to remember the species' name: cranks or drinks or—thranx. That was it. Never one to care about or much keep up with planetary, much less extrasolar, news, he had overheard and filed the information in that corner of his mind where he stored data that was unlikely to immediately impact his personal social and financial standing.

Explorers might contact and encounter a dozen new species or a hundred: It meant nothing to him if he was unable to somehow profit from it. Nor was he alone in his reaction. Convinced that all matter, existence, and the universe revolved around each of them individually, the bulk of humanity paid little attention to that which did not affect their lives directly. The far-reaching, far-ranging vision that the species possessed as a whole tended to dissolve into its billions of self-serving individual components when redacted to the petty concerns of one person at a time.

Well, he was damn well concerned now. Tense and wary, he observed the alien's approach, marveling at the fluid yet jerky motion of the four hind limbs that propelled it forward. What the hell was one of these bug-like thranx things doing here, in the empty reaches of Earth's largest rain forest preserve? Shouldn't it be quarantined on an orbiting station, or at the very least confined to a well-established diplomatic site like Geneva or Lombok?

Anxiously scanning the trees behind the creature revealed no other signs of movement. Though it would be premature to make the assumption, as far as his senses could tell him, the alien was alone. As he stared, it stopped again to take stock of its surroundings. The valentine-shaped head, about the size of his own, turned almost a hundred and eighty degrees to look back the way it had come. In striking contrast to the blue-green exoskeleton, the oversized compound eyes were a muted gold marked by latitudinal streaks of red. Like an extra pair of fingers, the two antennae would incline first one way, then another, and sometimes in opposite directions, as they investigated their immediate surroundings.

Individuals of a different and more advanced intellectual bent would have reacted to the intrusion with curiosity and interest. A nervous, edgy Cheelo just wanted the stiff-legged monstrosity to go away. He had spent too much time in the company of cockroaches, had been stung too often by scorpions, had been bitten too many times in his life by spiders and ants and aggressive tropical beetles, to want this gigantic if distant relation to tarry in his vicinity. Even though he knew it was intelligent and not an insect in the accepted terrestrial sense, he just wanted it to go away. If it did not, if it caused him the slightest bit of trouble, if it reacted in any way, shape, or form that might be construed as hostile—his fingers were firm and unyielding on the butt and trigger of the compact pistol.

That killing the intruder might precipitate some kind of interstellar diplomatic incident never crossed his mind. Interstellar diplomacy and interspecies relations had no immediate impact on the lifestyle of one Cheelo Montoya and therefore did not concern him. If there was trouble of that kind it was up to the government to sort out. All that concerned him was *his* freedom of movement, *his* health, and the fluctuating status of *his* bank account. He did not see how the shooting of one overlarge, out-of-place, alien bug would adversely affect any of that.

Hopefully, he would not have to deal with any such exotic ramifications. Preferably, the extraordinary creature would keep right on walking—through the forest, under his branch, and off in a westerly direction, intent on pursuits or destinations that would remain forever a blissful mystery to the uninterested Cheelo. As it drew nearer still he noted the size of the second, larger sack strapped to the alien's back and wondered what it contained besides small lumpy devices of unknown purpose. It was preparing to pass beneath his bough now, and he edged a little farther back, the tough bark scraping against his legs, belly, and chest.

Dislodged by his actions, one of the fruits he had scavenged tumbled backward, off the branch, and plunged to the ground directly in front of the extraterrestrial visitor. It halted immediately, gazing down at the green orb where it had landed among the leaf litter. Cheelo held his breath. There was no reason for the creature to look up. In the fecund rain forest, fruit fell from the canopy all the time.

But it did look up—directly at him. Though it had no pupils on which he could focus, he could not escape the feeling that it was staring directly at him. It was an unnerving sensation, an unsettling feeling, as if all the bugs he had ever stomped, sprayed, squashed, or swatted had been rolled up together into one measureless, accusatory, all-encompassing insectoid stare. Even though he knew it was his own memories and guilt that were gazing back up at him, the realization did nothing to alleviate the unease in his mind or the pounding of his heart. Bringing up the hand that held the pistol, he started to point it at the silent specter standing beneath the branch. While he knew nothing about alien physiology or vulnerability, he was willing to chance that it could not take a burst to the skull at close range. He lowered the muzzle so that it was pointed right between the two bulging, reflective eyes. His finger started to tighten on the trigger.

The accent was soft to the point of being incomprehensible, but slight and wispy as it was, there was no mistaking the conjoined syllables of Universal Terranglo.

"Hello," the big bug said. "I hope you will not expose me."

Expose me? Had he expected the outrageous apparition to say anything at all, that was not what Cheelo would have predicted. "Greetings, man," perhaps, or maybe "Can you tell me how to contact the nearest authorities?" not "I hope you will not expose me." It had also, he noted, not reacted either visibly or verbally to the presence of the lethal weapon that the nervous human was pointing directly at its head. Cheelo hesitated.

Could the soft voice and gentle words be a ploy to relax him and put him off his guard before it attacked and sucked out his innards? Simply by looking at it he could not tell if it could climb. Was it trying to lure him down to the ground where it could set upon him with all eight limbs? It was shorter and looked like it weighed less, but knowing as he did nothing about the species he had no idea how strong it might be. Crabs were smaller than humans, too, but they had jointed chitinous limbs that could effortlessly amputate a man's fingers.

"Can you talk?" it inquired in a manner that could only be described as curiously polite. "I spent a great deal of time studying recordings of your language until I thought myself fluent. Of course, mimicry is not the same as competency."

"Yeah." Cheelo found himself responding reflexively. "Yeah, I can talk." As for competency, the thranx's Terranglo was more cultivated than his own. Montoya's speech reflected its origin in small villages and mean streets, not fancy recordings or educational programming. "You're a thranx, aren't you?"

"I am thranx." The creature gestured elaborately with its set of small upper limbs and their eight digits. "I am individually, in the sounding of your speech, called Desvenbapur."

Cheelo nodded absently. Was there any harm in telling this alien his name? Was there anything to be lost or gained by it? If they were going to continue this conversation—and the bug showed no signs of being in a hurry to move on—it would need to call him something. He gave a mental shrug. Whatever else the thranx might represent, he doubted it worked for the local police.

"Cheelo Montoya."

He smiled at the thranx's initial attempts to pronounce his name. Maybe its speech wasn't all that cultivated after all. It was, however, sufficiently inquisitive to cause Cheelo to tense all over again.

"What are you doing out here in this empty place?" Desvendapur inquired innocently. It took a step backward, away from the branch and the tree. "Are you a ranger on patrol?"

At the mention of the word *ranger* Cheelo started to bring the pistol up again—only to relax, not a little confused, when he saw that the alien suddenly appeared to be more nervous than he was himself. It was looking around with rapid, twitchy movements and had drawn its forelimbs up against its—well, whatever passed for its chest. Being utterly ignorant of alien gesture and motivation, Cheelo could only interpret what he was seeing based on that which he knew, and it looked to him as if the creature was ready to bolt.

"No," he responded cautiously. "I'm not a ranger. I'm not an official of any kind. I'm . . . a tourist. An amateur naturalist, studying the forest."

Sure enough, the two withdrawn forelimbs resumed their previous relaxed position and the searching, rotating, head twisting ceased as the creature focused once more solely on the man in the tree. "You must be a confident one. This is supposed to be an exceptionally remote, uninhabited area."

"That's right." Cheelo nodded agreeably, then found himself frowning. He had drawn the pistol aside, but he did not put it down. "How do you know that? And what are *you* doing here, anyway?"

Desvendapur hesitated. Unable to interpret human gesture or the extraordinary range of expression their flexible faces were capable of producing, he had no way of determining the biped's true intent. As such, he had to rely entirely on his knowledge of their language. For a thranx, used to employing and translating gesture as organically as sound, the absence of interpretable gesticulation was akin to hearing only every other word of a conversation. He would have to fill in the gaps by inference, as best he could.

As near as he could tell based on what he thought he knew, the human struck him as curious rather than hostile, though the poet could not help but wonder about the function of the small device it had previously been pointing at him. That it was no longer doing so was a relief. But how to respond to the coarse, guttural inquiry? Of course, if he had simply stumbled into the lair of a wandering naturalist, then there was nothing to fear. He doubted that the human counterpart to a thranx researcher would be much of a threat. Students of science, regardless of species, tended to be reflective rather than violent.

That did not mean it would hesitate, if provoked, to give him away. He could do nothing, could not determine on a course of further action, until he knew what means of communication the human maintained with the outside world. At least, he decided, it had not immediately drawn forth a communicator of some kind to announce the encounter. As a naturalist, it might well be as curious about Desvendapur as the poet was about him.

In any event, benefits from the confrontation were already manifesting themselves. A rush of suggestive stanzas raced through Desvendapur's freshly stimulated brain. Reaching back with a foothand, he searched for his scri!ber.

The sudden movement alarmed the suspicious biped. "Hey, what are you doing there?" Again, the small pointed device the mammal was holding made an appearance on the rim of the bough.

Maybe it's got a gun, Cheelo found himself thinking nervously. And if it did, would he be able to recognize an alien weapon if it was pointed in his direction? Maybe he should just shoot it, right now. But what if it was not alone? What if it was a member of some larger exploration party? What if it was working in concert with people, with human scientists? Painfully aware of his ignorance, he realized that until he knew more it would be prudent to react cautiously. He had not survived worse than the rain forest and come as close to realizing his lifelong dream as he had by acting impetuously. Observe, analyze, think, plan, then act: the ancient lessons of the street.

Besides, the stiff-legged alien didn't look particularly fast, and it gave no indication of wanting to run away. He could always shoot it later.

Not wanting to upset the biped further, Desvendapur brought the scri!ber out very slowly. "This is a harmless recording device."

"I don't give a shit what it is." Cheelo gestured with the pistol. "Don't point it at me." He did not want his picture taken, either.

"As you wish." Exhilarated by the tension and the unexpectedness of the contact, Desvendapur proceeded to deliver a stream of clicks, whistles, and sibilant syllables to the scri!ber, together with breathless suggestions for appropriate accompanying gestures. Throughout the euphonious discursive, the human continued to gaze down at him from its perch up in the tree. Such a primitive stare! the poet thought. So straightforward and unvarying, heightened by the directness of a single lens. Human eyes were very vulnerable, Desvendapur knew. A thranx could lose part of an eye, dozens of individual lenses, and still be able to see, albeit with a reduced field of vision and focus. Should a human lose its lens, the ocular function of the entire orb would be largely lost. The realization transformed part of his discomfiture into sympathy.

When he was finished he attached the scri!ber to the pouch hanging from his thorax, where it could be accessed quickly. The human responded by lowering the unidentified mechanism it had been clutching so tightly in one hand.

"You still haven't answered my questions. I told you who I am and what I'm doing here. I'm still waiting to hear your story."

Desvendapur knew he would have to summon all the creative inventiveness at his command. It was vital to prevent the human from notifying the authorities. If that happened, not only would the poet's presence be revealed to the outside world, so would that of the colony. He could hardly explain that he had found his way to the forest preserve from the official, highly restricted contact sites halfway around the planet. Officially, few thranx had even set foot on the human homeworld.

The biped claimed to be an amateur naturalist. But unless he was concealing his equipment, he appeared to Des to be traveling exceptionally light even for a casually interested nonprofessional. For that matter, why was he even bothering to have this conversation? Any human encountering an unannounced alien could be expected to immediately contact a higher authority. Instead, this Cheelo individual seemed content, at least for the moment, to perform his own interrogation. Something was not as it seemed, but Desvendapur knew it was far too early for him to render judgments. He needed more information—a great deal more. After all, what did he know of human scientific procedures? Perhaps this self-proclaimed naturalist's gear was stored or buried nearby.

Irrespective of the actual explanation, the delay was greatly to the poet's liking. The longer the encounter lasted before it was terminated due to contact with the planetary authorities, the greater the opportunities to set down new and exciting poesy.

"I am a food preparations specialist." He spoke slowly to make certain he was being understood.

He was being understood, all right. Utterly ignorant of thranx dining deportment, Cheelo did not much like the sound of "food preparations specialist."

"Who do you prepare food for?" He looked past the bug, scrutinizing the rain forest from which it had emerged. "Not just yourself, surely? There must be more of you."

"There are," Desvendapur explained creatively, "but they are, *crrrk,* carrying out limited studies of their own far, far from here. I am on a solitary expedition of my own."

"To do what?" Suspicious to a fault, Cheelo kept searching the woods for any hints of closing ambush. "Gather herbs and spices?" He lowered his gaze. "Or maybe you'd like to catch me off guard so you could kill and eat *me*?"

Utterly unanticipated, the sickening speculative accusation caught Desvendapur completely off guard. He had thought that his surreptitious research and studies adequately prepared him for just this kind of contact, but he was wrong. Unwilled and unbidden, an image formed in his mind: the human, stripped of clothing and nude, its pulpy, fleshy pink form stretched out over a fire; raw animal fat dripping from its scorched limbs, oozing into the flames and sizzling; the smell of carbonizing meat . . .

Reeling, he promptly regurgitated the undigested portion of the day's meal that had been quietly fermenting in his upper stomach. He had turned away not out of embarrassment but to avoid retching into the space between himself and the human. That would have constituted a serious breach of manners, though without further knowledge of human habits he was unsure how the biped would have reacted to it.

As it was, the lone male's tone rose in volume. Based on his studies, a retching Desvendapur thought it sounded slightly alarmed.

"Ay—what're you doing? Are you all right?" It looked like the alien was throwing up, but for all Cheelo knew it might have been seeding the ground with its spores, planting more of its kind deep in the rain forest soil. As the creature explained when it finally recovered its equilibrium, Cheelo's initial assumption had been the correct one.

"I am apologizing." As it spoke, the bug was cleaning its four opposing mandibles with the back of a leaf it plucked from a nearby plant. "Your insinuation conjured up a most unpleasant picture. Thranx do not eat"—his voice quavered—"do not eat . . . other creatures."

"Ay—vegetarians, eh?" Cheelo grunted. "Okay, so you're a cook or something. That still doesn't explain what you're doing out here all by your lonesome."

Desvendapur plunged ahead. He had nothing to lose now, less so by revealing himself to this representative of another species. "I am also an amateur poet. I was transmuting my impressions of my alien surroundings into art."

"No shit? You don't say?"

Desvendapur was unsure if he had heard correctly. "Yes I do say," he responded hopefully.

A poet. That sounded about as unthreatening as anything Cheelo could imagine. "So when you were speaking into that recording device of yours, you were composing poetry?"

"A portion of it. Much of the artistry lies in the delivery. You humans use gesture as a supplement to language. For thranx, how we move is as important a part of communication as what we say and how we say it."

Cheelo nodded slowly. "I can see that. If I had four arms, waving them around would probably be twice as important to me, too." While he still did not trust the alien, neither did it appear as threatening as it had at first appearance. Nevertheless, a giant bug was still a giant bug, even if taxonomically it wasn't a bug at all. He kept the pistol drawn as he rose from his crouch and scrambled down the trunk of the tree.

Desvendapur watched in awe. While adept at traversing rocky slopes or narrow ledges, a thranx had difficulty with verticalities. A certain sinuosity of self was required that their inflexible exoskeletons did not permit. To thranx eyes, the actions of a climbing human were as fluid as those of a snake.

Leaping the last meter to the ground, Cheelo found himself confronting the outlandish visitor. Inclined back on its four hind legs with thorax, neck, and head stretched as high as possible, the creature's face came about to Cheelo's chest. He estimated its weight at fifty kilos or so, perhaps slightly less. When erected, the twin feathery antennae added another thirty centimeters to its height.

"So," Cheelo continued, "this expedition of yours? It's authorized by the authorities? I thought all aliens were restricted to contact on orbiting stations, with only a few high-ranking diplomatic types allowed to actually set foot on Earth."

Desvendapur falsified rapidly. "A special waiver was granted to my group. They are being supervised by representatives of your own kind."

Years of practice had given him the ability to lie with great facility and skill.

"Then you'll be rejoining them soon?"

How best to answer so as neither to make the biped suspicious nor activate its defensive instincts? "No. They will be continuing their work for," he fumbled for the appropriate human time referents, "another of your months."

"Uh-huh." The human's head bobbed up and down several times. From his studies Desvendapur recognized the gesture as a "nod," an indication of general concurrence. It was one the thranx could easily mimic. Though he normally would have used his truhands to suggest agreement, the poet duplicated the motion in so natural and relaxed a fashion that the biped did not think to question its unlikely origin.

For a self-proclaimed naturalist, Desvendapur reflected, the human's queries seemed to troll far from the realms of science.

"So this special group of yours is here kind of secretly, so it can do its work without alerting the media or even the locals?"

For a second time Desvendapur "nodded," finding the movement natural if overly simplistic, as were the majority of human gestures.

Cheelo was more than merely relieved. For a disquieting time he had been forced to deal with the prospect of dozens of reporters swarming the site of the first thranx expedition to pastoral Earth. Wandering media types might well have trailed an adventurer like this Desvenbapur, anyway. That was all Cheelo needed—half a dozen tridee pickups shoved in his face as their manipulators asked the rain forest hiker for comments. Following broadcast, one of the automated fugitive matchers that monitored the media would set off alarms in half the police centers in this part of the world, and that would be the end of his freedom and anonymity, not to mention any chance of delivering his fee to the waiting Ehrenhardt in time to secure the precious franchise.

But if he was reading the situation correctly, then this small group of thranx this Desvenbapur was talking about were as anxious to keep their presence hidden from the rest of the world as was he. He and this cook-poet were symbiotes in secrecy. Unless . . .

"Okay, I accept that you are what you claim to be. But what are you doing out here by yourself?" He gestured expansively without stopping to wonder if the sweeping movement of his arm would be interpreted correctly, or indeed if it would mean anything at all to the alien. "This is one of the most isolated, primitive places on the planet. There are dangerous animals here."

"I know." With its inflexible face the thranx could not smile, but its upper limbs moved expressively. "I have met several of them. As you can see, I am still unharmed."

"Defended yourself, huh?" Cheelo squinted as he tried to identify the purpose of the visible bulges in the creature's backpack. Amiably as they were conversing, he still did not trust the alien as far as he could throw it.

"Not really. Some I avoided, while others proved not as dangerous to me as I believe they are to your kind." With the middle digits of his left truhand Desvendapur tapped the center of his thorax. "Unlike you, my people wear their supportive skeletons on the outside. We are more resistant to punctures and cuts. However, because of the nature of our respective circulatory systems, if epidermally compromised, we bleed more easily."

"Then you're not armed?" Cheelo tried to peer deep into the alien's eyes but was unsure where to focus.

"I did not say that. Should it prove needful, I can protect myself." The biped was being agreeable, but it would not do to let it know how helpless Desvendapur really was. Capabilities unrevealed are capabilities held in reserve.

"Glad to hear it." Cheelo was mildly disappointed. Not that the alien had acted in any way hostile.

"Actually," it continued in its soft, melodious rendering of Terranglo, "I am lying. I am actually part of a large complement of warriors scouting sites for the invasion."

Cheelo's expression dropped, and he started to bring up the hand holding the pistol. Then he hesitated. The bug was emitting a vibrant, high-pitched whistle, and the feathers of its antennae were quivering.

"Chinga—that was a joke, wasn't it? A goddamn up-front right-out-there joke! Bugs with a sense of humor. Who woulda thought it?" Carefully, he holstered the pistol, though he kept the safety off.

"You see, despite your unavoidably hideous appearance we have many things in common." The valentine-shaped head inclined slightly to one side, momentarily giving the alien the appearance of a querulous canine. "You will not reveal my presence here to the local authorities? To do so would be to put an end to my gathering of raw material for my artistry—and to the work of my fellow expedition members as well."

"Naw, I won't give you away. Tell you what—I won't mention your presence here, and you don't mention mine to your coworkers when you rejoin them."

"I am pleased with the arrangement, but why do you wish your presence here to remain unknown? Surely secrecy is not a necessary component to the work of a naturalist?"

Cheelo did not think as fast as the poet, but he managed to improvise a reply before Desvendapur could grow uneasy.

Lowering his voice, he moved a little nearer. As the lanky bipedal form loomed over him, Des took a step backward, then forced himself to halt. Was this not, after all, what he had come for? The decreasing distance that separated them would have been easier to deal with if the human had not smelled so bad. The climate of the humid rain forest served to magnify the pungency of its body odor, which unavoidably reeked of previously ingested flesh.

"To tell you the truth, I'm sort of here illegally myself. Access to this part of the Reserva is restricted. Not everyone can get a permit to do work in the Manu. And I needed to be here." Oh, how I needed to be here, he thought. "So I just kind of slipped in, quietly and on my own. It's not hard to do, if you know how to go about it. The Manu is big, and ranger outposts hereabouts are isolated and lightly staffed." He drew himself up proudly.

"Not many people would think of exploring this region on their own, much less actually try to do so. You might say that I'm an exceptional person."

"Yes, I can sense that." Were humans, too, vulnerable to praise and flattery? It was another similitude, but this time one that Desvendapur chose not to expound upon. Such knowledge could prove valuable in the days ahead.

"Well, this has been fascinating, really fascinating, but I have to get on with my work, and I'm sure you feel the same about your own." Demonstrating astonishing balance, the biped pivoted and turned to leave. In so doing, Desvendapur saw the wrenching, intense inspiration he had worked so long and hard to access disappearing with it.

By taking several steps forward, he induced the human to turn back once again. Rather abruptly, the poet came to a decision. "Your pardon." He fought down the churning in his stomachs that was induced by proximity to the creature. "But if you would not object, I would just as soon adapt my route so that it coincides with yours."

14

Words had never been Cheelo Montoya's forte. Needing some to cope with an unexpected moment deep in the rain forest was no exception. He found himself fumbling for an appropriate response.

The last thing he wanted was company. The more alone he was, the better his chances of avoiding the attention of local authorities. He saw no advantage to having his tracks shadowed by a curious artist, be it human or alien.

Unable to think of an all-inclusive reply, he stalled. "Why would you want to tag along with me?"

"I am—I have been interested in your kind ever since I learned of the inaugural project that was set up on Willow-Wane to try and facilitate communication and understanding between our species. Long ago I resolved to thrust myself, with only my studies and my wits, into direct confrontation with your kind, seeking in it a source of inspiration as new to me as it was forbidden to my brethren."

Cheelo could not help but respond with a short, derisive snort. "If it's inspiration you're looking for, you won't find it in my company."

"Allow me to be the judge of that."

Formal sort of bug, Cheelo found himself thinking. He wondered if they were all like this. "I travel alone." He indicated the surrounding rain forest. "Isn't this enough alien inspiration for you? A whole new world to explore?"

"It is wonderful," Desvendapur agreed, "but better I see it through your eyes, peculiar as they are, than only through mine. Don't you see? In your company I experience everything twice: as I apperceive it, and as you do."

"Well, you're going to have to damn well apperceive it by your lone-some. I don't like company." For the second time he turned away.

"If you do not allow me to travel with you, I will expose you to the local human authorities," the poet declared rapidly.

This time Cheelo grinned wolfishly. "No you won't. Because you're not supposed to be here, either. Your little research expedition is poking its antennae way, way outside established perimeters for alien visitors. Even I know that much. You don't belong here. In fact, I ought to be the one threatening to expose you!"

Desvendapur deliberated. "Then why don't you?"

"You already know. Because to do so would mean revealing my own unauthorized presence here. I don't belong, and neither do you. So neither guy can risk exposing the other. But that doesn't mean I have to let you follow me around."

"I would rather have your cooperation." The thranx's antennae were never entirely still, Cheelo noticed. "But if necessary, I will follow and observe you and your interactions with the environment at a distance."

"No you won't." The lanky human patted his holster. "Because if you do, I'll splatter your bug guts all over the forest."

The valentine-shaped head dipped slightly to allow compound eyes to focus on the weapon. "That is a very belligerent attitude for a professed naturalist to take."

"We all have our little character flaws." Cheelo's lips were set in a thin, tight line.

The human's expression had no effect on the contemplative Desvendapur, but his words did. Did he realize how deep the truth of his observation ran? The poet suspected the biped did not.

"You won't shoot me. If I do not report in according to a prearranged schedule, my hive companions will come looking for me. When they see how I died, they will come looking for *you*."

"I'll take my chances." Cheelo's fingers twitched in the vicinity of the holster. "If your compadres can identify your remains after the caimans and the piranhas have finished with them, then they're better forensic pathologists than any I've ever heard about."

Desvendapur did not have to ask for elucidation. From his studies he was familiar with both varieties of local predators. "What makes you think your native carnivores will find my body palatable? They will ignore me. My corpse will drift until it is found. Then those who will come looking for me will react in a relentless and savage fashion."

They would do no such thing, he knew. Their only concern would be to remove the body lest it be found by other humans, thereby giving rise to awkward inquiries. But the biped did not know that. All he knew of the thranx, Desvendapur suspected, was what the poet chose to tell him.

Man and thranx regarded one another speculatively, each as ignorant as to the true motives of the other as they were to those of their respective kind. Neither had any training in interspecies contact. Operating from mutual nescience, they were making it up as they went along.

"All right." Cheelo's fingers reluctantly drifted away from the gun. "So maybe I won't shoot you. But that still doesn't mean I want you following me."

"Why not? If you choose, I will not intrude on your solitude. You may continue to conduct your research as if I was not there. I only wish to observe, and record, and compose."

My *research*, Cheelo thought. All he was doing was researching a way to keep one step ahead of the police. He did not see how an eight-limbed insectile alien could assist in that end.

Yet despite his otherwordly origins, the hard-shelled poet seemed to know a great deal about their surroundings. It had spoken of studying the area. If not an advantage, maybe it at least wouldn't be a burden. Come to think of it, if the police did manage to track him down, Cheelo could always claim—after first blowing the bug's head off, of course, so it couldn't contradict his story—that he had uncovered an illicit alien outpost. If he could not get rid of it, either by threat or inducement, he would have to find a way to turn the creature's persistence into an advantage. That was something Cheelo Montoya had always been good at.

"You're right, as far as it goes," he snapped. "I can't keep you from following me, and even though I'm not sure I believe all your chatter about your buggy friends coming looking for revenge, I'm not going to risk it by killing you. Not right away, anyhow. Just stay out of my way and do your recording, or composing, or whatever the hell it is that you're doing, quietly."

"I will become a veritable nonentity," a pleased and much relieved Desvendapur assured him.

Too bad you couldn't become a real one, Cheelo mused. Maybe the alien would drown in a river or break a couple of legs and fall behind. Then no one could be blamed for the consequences. Given the right place and time, he might even be able to hurry the process along. If not, well, hadn't the bug said that he only had a month to do his work? Before then Cheelo would be ready to quit the forest himself in order to make the journey back to Golfito.

How fast was a thranx? How durable? After a day or two of trying to follow and keep up with the agile, hardened thief, the many-limbed poet might decide that it was a good idea to seek inspiration from less wearisome sources. Cheelo would lead him a chase, all right!

"Come on, then." Turning, he gestured with a hand—and paused. Head back, expression reflecting uncertainty, he found himself sniffing the air. To Desvendapur, who sensed odors through his antennae, it was a fascinating display worthy of several original and elaborately bizarre stanzas.

"What is it? What are you doing?"

"Smelling. Can't you see that?" Noting the absence on the alien's face, or for that matter anywhere else on its body, of anything resembling nostrils, Cheelo added tersely, "No, I suppose you can't. I'm sampling the air for odors. For one particular odor, actually."

The feathers that lined Desvendapur's antennae flexed to allow as much air as possible to pass between them. "What particular odor?"

Turning, Cheelo found himself inexorably drawn to the exotic exoskeletoned alien. There was no longer any doubt as to the source of the subtle, suggestive aroma. "Yours."

The thranx regarded the tall biped warily. "And what does mine remind you of?"

As Cheelo sniffed, Desvendapur watched the pair of openings in the middle of the human's face expand and contract obscenely. "Roses. Or maybe gardenia. I'm not sure. Could be frangipani. Or bougainvillea."

"What are these things?" None of the names the human was reciting were familiar to Des from his studies.

"Flowers. You smell like flowers. It's a strong fragrance, but not overpowering. It's not . . . it's not what I expected."

Desvendapur remained on guard. "Is this a good thing?"

"Yes." The human smiled, though his attitude suggested that the expression was dragged forth involuntarily. "It's a good thing. If I seem surprised, it's because I am. Bugs aren't supposed to smell like flowers. They never smell like flowers. They stink."

"I am not a 'bug,' which I believe is a generic colloquial human term for insects. Thranx and terrestrial insects are an example of convergent evolution. Yes, there are many similarities, but there are significant differences as well. Carbon-based life forms that have evolved on planets with similar gravity and within stable atmospheric and temperature parameters frequently display many recognizable characteristics of form. But do not mistake body shape for species relationship."

Cheelo's gaze narrowed slightly. "You know, for a cook's helper, or whatever the hell it is exactly that you do, you seem awfully smart."

Desvendapur could not give himself away with a startled expression, and the human was untutored in the subtle meanings of thranx hand movements. "The position I occupy requires more intelligence than you might suspect. All members of my expedition were chosen from the elite within their respective categories of expertise."

"Yeah, right." Cheelo was unconvinced. He had known the alien for only a short while, but unless the nature of thranxkind differed greatly from that of humans (a possibility that could not be discounted), he almost felt as if the bug was hiding something.

He sniffed again. Orchids this time—or was it hibiscus? The distinctive scent seemed to change with each successive sampling, as if the alien's shiny blue-green body was emitting not one but a complex, everchanging bouquet of fragrances. He was surprised it was not being swarmed by rain forest nectar eaters, from hummingbirds to bees. But while it exuded a strong natural perfume, it did not look very much like a cluster of blossoms. Also, birds and bees were more sensitive to odors than any human. It was likely that they could detect subtle alien overtones to the thranx's body scent that his cruder sense of smell missed completely.

What other surprises did the bug have in store? "What about me?" he asked curiously. "How do I smell to you? You *can* smell, can't you?"

Desvendapur dipped his antennae forward, but not before compacting their sensitive feathering to shutter his perception of the biped's odor as much as possible. "I can. You are . . . pungent."

" 'Pungent,' " Cheelo repeated. "Sure, okay." Turning, he climbed back up into the tree to get his pack. Desvendapur observed the process with fascination, composing avidly as he watched. Not even the most gymnastic of thranx could match the flexibility of the human's body and limbs. Nor would they want to, he reflected. His reaction was similar to what a human would feel watching an octopus unscrew the lid of a sealed jar to get at food left inside.

Cheelo started to toss his pack down, considered, and then called out, "Here, make yourself useful. Catch this." He held the tough, lightweight material out over the branch.

It was not a significant drop, but Desvendapur knew nothing of the bag's contents. Still, based on what he knew of human physiology he did not think it could be dangerously heavy. Obediently advancing until he was beneath the branch, he extended both foothands, taking care to ensure that his smaller, more delicate truhands were folded tight against his body and out of the way.

"Ready? Catch." Cheelo let the pack fall.

The thranx caught it easily in both outstretched foothands, then used all four manipulative limbs to place it gently on the ground. Satisfied, Cheelo rolled up his blanket and tossed it over next, then climbed down to join his implausible companion. Desvendapur watched silently as the human bundled his equipment together, straightened, and slipped the pack-and-strap arrangement onto his back. It was difficult to understand how and why the additional weight did not cause the biped to fall over backward. Though smaller and lighter, with a minimum of four legs and a maximum of six to support its slim body, an adult thranx could carry more than even a very large human. This knowledge led him to make an offer that was in the nature of a painless gamble.

"Want me to carry that for you? It has to hurt your upper body, trying to support it that way."

Cheelo eyed the shorter creature in surprise. "What's the matter? Aren't you packing enough gear of your own?"

"I can manage the extra mass easily. If we are going to travel together we should each make use of the other's natural strengths. I could not climb into that tree without help, as you did, but I can carry a good deal of weight. Your pack would not inconvenience me."

Cheelo found himself grinning. "That's real nice of you." He started to reach up and around to slide the pack off his back. Abruptly, his smile faded. "No, on second thought, I think I'll hang onto my own stuff for a while longer. But thanks for the offer."

Desvendapur automatically gestured an appropriate response. The rapid hand and finger movements meant nothing to the human. "As you wish."

It might have been an honest offer, Cheelo thought as he turned and strode off into the trees. But what did he know of alien motivation? Suppose the thranx was operating from ulterior motives. At an opportune moment it might decide to take off with a nice, prepacked grab bag full of terrestrial souvenirs, graciously supplied by one trusting, half-witted Cheelo Montoya. He knew next to nothing about the big bugs, including how fast they could run. It had confessed to being a poor climber, but it didn't look clumsy or lumbering. He was willing to bet that when it utilized all six legs it could move over the ground at a respectable clip.

The thought of allowing someone else to haul his gear through the hot, steamy rain forest was a tempting one. His back and legs were wholly in favor of the notion, but his brain vetoed it outright. Surviving alone in the vast rain forest was hard enough. Trying to do so without blanket, electronic insect repeller, food supplements, water purifier, and other gear might prove well nigh impossible. So he would suffer on. Time enough to figure out if he could trust something with eight limbs, twin antennae, and eyes like shattered mirrors.

It sure did smell good, though.

That night he had the opportunity to see how a thranx not only ate, but slept. As it sipped liquids from a narrow-spouted utensil and chewed compacted food with its four opposing mandibles, he wondered what it thought of his own dining habits. The fact that it kept its distance could be considered significant. Cheelo took some of the fish he had caught the previous day out of his pack. The thranx studied the process of consuming with obvious interest, chattering and whistling into its recording device without pause.

Finally Cheelo could stand it no longer. "I'm just having supper. No big deal. Where's the poetry in that?"

"There is verse in everything you do, because it is all exotic to me. Presently I am much taken with the contrast between your exceedingly civilized behavior and your lingering barbarism."

"Excuse me?" Breaking off a small fillet, Cheelo scaled it with his fingernails before shoving it into his mouth and biting off a piece. He chewed slowly.

"You utilize the tools and knowledge of a contemporary civilization to eat the flesh of another creature."

"Yeah, that's right. Are you guys all vegetarians?" He held out the pungent fistful. "This is just a fish."

"A water-dwelling animal. It has a heart, lungs, nervous system. A brain."

Cheelo squinted through the gathering darkness. "What are you trying to tell me? That a fish thinks?"

"If it has a brain, it thinks."

"Not much it don't." He chuckled and bit off another chunk.

"Thought is an absolute, not a matter of degree. It is a question of morality."

The human gestured back the way they had come. "How'd you like to go find your creative inspiration elsewhere? So now I'm immoral?"

"Not by your own standards. I would not presume to judge a member of another species by standards that were developed to apply to my kind."

"Smart boy." Cheelo hesitated with the remaining fish halfway to his mouth. "What kind of poetic inspiration are you getting out of me eating a fish, anyhow?"

"Crude. Powerful. Alien." The thranx continued chattering into its scri!ber.

"Shocking?" Cheelo inquired thoughtfully.

"I would hope so. I did not come all this way and go through a great deal of trouble to find inspiration of a cloying, puerile kind. I came in search of something radical and extreme, something dangerous and unsafe. Ugly, even."

"All that from a guy eating a fish," Cheelo murmured. "I'm not much on poetry myself, but I wouldn't mind hearing some of what you've written. As your source of inspiration, I think I have that right."

"I would be glad to perform it for you, but I am afraid much of the subtlety and nuance will be lost. You don't have the necessary cultural references to understand, and there are concepts that simply cannot, given its innate restrictions, be rendered in your language."

"Is that so?" Taking a long swig from his purifier, Cheelo leaned back against a tree, knees apart, and gestured commandingly at the oversized arthropod. "Try me."

"Try you?" Confusion impregnated the thranx's response.

"Let me hear what you've done," Cheelo clarified impatiently.

"Very well. I dislike performing without proper rehearsal, but since you are not going to understand very much of it anyway, I suppose that doesn't matter. I cannot translate into your language and properly follow through, but I hope that you will get some sense of what I am trying to accomplish."

"Wait. Wait a minute." Rummaging through his pack, Cheelo produced a compact flashlight. A glance at the canopy showed that they were reasonably well hidden from above. No low-flying scanner blocked out the few visible stars, and clouds would conceal their presence from anything higher. Flicking the light to life, he placed it on the ground so that its soft beam illuminated the thranx. In the darkness the alien's stiff limbs, bobbing antennae, and reflective compound eyes were components of an atavistic nightmare shape—but it was hard to be afraid of something that exuded the aroma of a Paris perfume boutique.

"I am afraid that the title of my latest exposition is not translatable."

"That's okay." Cheelo waved grandly. "I'll think of it as 'Human Eating Fish.' " Scarfing down the rest of his supper, he leaned back and began licking grease and bits of white flake from his fingers. Suppressing his distaste, Desvendapur began.

In the tropical night, surrounded by the sounds of the rain forest's emerging nocturnal inhabitants, words mingled with whistles sharp and soft, with clicks that varied in volume and intensity from that of tiny tappings to a rhythmic booming that might have been generated by muffled drums. Accompanying this stately carillon were intricate dancelike gestures, weavings in the air executed by four limbs and sixteen digits. Antennae twisted and curled, dipped and bobbed, as the insectile alien body swayed and contorted.

At first the sight was somewhat frightening, but as Cheelo grew more comfortable with the thranx's appearance he found himself starting to think of it not as a giant bug but as a sensitive visitor from a distant star system. The scent of fresh flowers that emanated from the hard-shelled body certainly played a large part in effecting his change in perception—not to mention attitude. As for the performance, even though Desvendapur was right and Cheelo understood little of what was being imparted, it was undeniably *art* of a complex, sophisticated order. Poetic, even. While he understood nothing of what the creature was saying, the confluence of sound and movement conveyed a grace and elegance the likes of which he had never encountered before.

Growing up poor and forever on the fringe of society, Cheelo Montoya had never had much of an opportunity to sample anything other than the crudest kinds of art: violent tridee recordings, raucous popular music, unsophisticated pornography, cheap stims, and low-level hallucinogens. He was aware that what he was hearing and witnessing now, alien though its origins might be, comprised creation of a much higher order. At first amusedly contemptuous, the longer and more intricate the thranx's interweavings of movement and sound became, the quieter and more solemn Cheelo's expression grew. When a quietly triumphant Desvendapur finally concluded the performance, the sun had set completely.

"Well," he prompted when no response was forthcoming from the silent, seated human, "what did you think? Did you get anything out of it, or was it all nothing more than alien mumblings and twitches?"

Cheelo swallowed—hard. Something crawled over his left hand without biting, and he ignored it. In the nearly complete darkness the light from the flashlight was stark on the thranx's blue-green exterior.

"I . . . I didn't understand a goddamn word of it, and I think it was one of the most beautiful things I've ever seen."

Desvendapur was taken aback. It was not the reaction he had anticipated. A polite gesture of courtesy, perhaps, or a mumbled word of mild appreciation—but not praise. Not from a human.

"But you say you didn't understand." Taking a chance, presuming on an acquaintance that was still untested, he moved forward, out of the throw of the flashlight and into proximate darkness.

The human did not shy away. The scent of fresh-picked posies was very close now. In the shadow of night his absurdly tiny but nevertheless sharp eyes searched those of the thranx. "Not your speech, no. Not a word of it. But the sounds you made, like music, and the way all four of your hands and the rest of your body moved together with it—that was wonderful." He shook his head from side to side, and Desvendapur struggled to interpret the meaning of it.

"I don't know anything about it, of course," Cheelo continued, "but it seems to me that you're very good at your hobby. People—humans—would pay to watch it."

"You really think so? As I said earlier, I am only an amateur."

"I know they would. I may not know much, but I know that. I . . . would pay. And if you could figure out a way to translate your speech into Terranglo without sacrificing anything of the performance . . . Well, it would *have* to contribute to understanding and good relations between our species. Doesn't anyone do performances like that at the project on your world—what's it called?"

"Willow-Wane," Desvendapur murmured softly. "I suppose they must, but I do not really know. I don't know any more about what goes on within the project than what the Grand Council chooses to disseminate. They might have soothers there, or they might not."

"Is that what it's called? Soothing?" In the poor light, Cheelo nodded thoughtfully. "Listen, I know I'm not much of an audience—not knowledgeable or anything like that—and I can't exactly return the favor with constructive criticism, but anytime you want to practice a new piece or a part of one, I'd be real pleased to look at and listen to it."

"You *did* actually enjoy it, didn't you?" Desvendapur stared at the biped.

"Damn right I did. Tell you what. Tomorrow night I'll eat something different, just to give you fresh inspiration. Maybe I'll try and kill an agouti or something."

Desvendapur gagged, and his antennae flinched reflexively. "Please do not cannibalize a living creature on my behalf."

"I thought you wanted radical, extreme stimulation."

"My mind does. My digestive system is a different matter."

Cheelo crossed his legs and grinned. "Okay. We'll build up the inspiration gradually." Leaning over and reaching into his pack, he extracted a stimstick and unwrapped the vacuum tip. On contact with the air, it flashed alight.

Desvendapur watched the human place one end of the burning shaft between its lips and inhale. This was more than he could have hoped for. Every moment spent in the biped's company was a source of unprecedented enlightenment. What whimsical pleasure the creature gained from placing combusting organic matter in its mouth the thranx could not imagine, but the inscrutable activity proved to be the source of not one but two complete, condensed compositions before the evening bored its way into night and they were compelled to retire.

15

It was not the howlers that woke Cheelo the following morning. A sharp, cawing call caused him to roll over and sit up, the lightweight blanket falling away from his neck and chest and down to his hips. The bird that was pecking at some fallen, rotting fruit nearby was grotesque in the extreme. Outsized red eyes peered from a narrow, blue-skinned face that was lined and surmounted by a crest of stiff, yellow-black feathers. His rising startled the creature and it flew, awkwardly and with undisguised effort, into a nearby tree. The size of a small turkey, it rocked on a branch while contemplating the odd duo resting on the ground below.

As he rubbed at his eyes and climbed to his feet, Cheelo tried to remember names from the guideware he had bought in Cuzco and installed in his card. The bird was big enough to be a raptor, but its short beak and small claws, not to mention its awkwardness in the air, marked it as belonging to some other family. Still blinking away sleep, he opened his pack and took out the card. A few adjustments called forth the guidebook and the section on birds.

The clumsy flier with the prehistoric mien was a hoatzin. If there ever was a bird that looked like a dinosaur, he thought, here it was. His attention shifted from the red-eyed forest dweller to the far more alien figure slumbering nearby.

Having found a suitable fallen log, the thranx had straddled it. Three legs hung on one side, three on the other, with the first set of arms tucked neatly up against the insectoid's chest, if that's what the forward-facing portion of its anatomy could be called. Since it had no opaque eyelids, but only a very thin, transparent membrane that sometimes slid down to protect those golden orbs, it was impossible to tell by looking at it whether it was awake or asleep. The absence of any movement or reaction as Cheelo cautiously approached, coupled with the steady bellows-like pumping of its thorax, was enough to convince him it continued to occupy whatever unimaginable region such creatures visited when they turned off their consciousness for the night.

What kind of dreams did aliens dream? he wondered. For the first time, he found himself within touching distance of the creature. Up close, the ambrosial fragrance of its body odor was even stronger. Bending over, he was able to see himself reflected dozens of times in the multiple lenses of one golden eye. A line of small openings in the blue-green chitin of the thorax pulsed rhythmically, showing where the creature siphoned air. The sensitive, feathery antennae described twin limp, forward-facing arcs on the otherwise smooth curve of the skull.

Reaching out, he ran fingertips along the glistening exoskeleton of one wing case. It was hard, smooth, and slightly cool to the touch, like plastic or some highly polished building material. Letting his hand drift downward he felt of a leg, unable to escape the feeling that he was exploring a machine and not a living creature. That perception vanished the instant the thranx woke up.

Startled by the unexpected human touch, Desvendapur let out a shrill stridulation and kicked out reflexively with all six legs. One caught Cheelo in the thigh and sent him stumbling backward. Scrambling frantically, shocked into wakefulness, the poet slid off the makeshift bed and promptly fell over on his side onto the moist, leaf-strewn earth. He recovered quickly to stand facing the human across the log.

"What are you doing?"

"Take it easy," Cheelo admonished his otherworldly companion. "Nothing weird."

"How can I be sure of that? Humans are noted for their peculiar habits." As he spoke, Desvendapur was checking the length of his body. Everything appeared to be undamaged and where it belonged.

The human snorted derisively. "Look, it was hard enough for me just to touch you."

"Then why did you?" Desvendapur shot back accusingly.

"To make sure that I could. Don't worry—I won't be doing it again." Cheelo rubbed his fingers together, as if trying to remove dirt or grease from beneath the nails. "It was like rubbing a piece of old furniture."

The poet walked over to his pack and checked the seal. It was undisturbed, but he could not be absolutely sure until he checked the contents. "Better than making contact with flesh that flexes beneath one's fingers." His antennae quivered. "All that soft, pulpy meat held in check only by a thin layer of flexible epidermis, full of blood and muscle, just waiting to be exposed to the air. It's indecent. I cannot imagine what nature was thinking when she designed such animal forms and then built them from the inside out."

"You're the one who's inside out." Walking back to where he had laid his own gear, Cheelo crouched and pondered breakfast. "Walking around with your skeleton on the outside."

"And it is not bad enough that all your support is internal," Desvendapur continued, "you come in a bewildering variety of colors. There is no harmony, no consistency at all. Our color deepens naturally as we age, a reflection of the natural progression of time. Yours only changes when diseased, some of which you induce voluntarily. And it shrivels." Truhands were in continual motion as the thranx spoke. Cheelo had no idea what the bug was saying with its eloquent limbs, but he could make inferences from the tenor of its comments.

"Because of these flaws, which are the unavoidable consequence of defective genetics, I feel an instinctive sympathy for you."

"Gee, thanks." As he prepared his simple morning meal Cheelo wondered if the bug could detect sarcasm and decided it probably could not. "Not that it means anything, or matters, but why?"

This time a truhand and a foothand on the same side of the smooth body gestured in tandem. "Your epidermis is so incredibly fragile, so easily cut or compromised, that it is outright wondrous you have survived as a species. One would think that mere incidental contact with the world around you would result in the incurring of an unavoidable succession of incapacitating wounds."

"Our outside's tougher than it looks." By way of demonstration, Cheelo pinched up a fold of skin on the back of his hand. Simultaneously fascinated and repelled, Desvendapur could not turn away from the incredible sight. It was at once ghastly and captivating to behold. Grossly descriptive, the burgeoning verses that hurtled through his mind skittered on the very edge of possible censorship.

"Here." Walking toward the thranx, Cheelo rolled up one sleeve and held his naked arm out to the alien. "Try it yourself."

"No." The boldness that had brought Desvendapur this far wavered at the sight of the exposed, almost transparent skin, with its components of deeply tanned muscle, tendon, and blood clearly visible beneath. Mushy and resilient, the soft mammalian flesh would deform beneath his fingers, he knew. Envisioning this threatened to bring up what remained unprocessed of his previous meal.

Steeling himself, he forced a halt to his mental flight. If it was safe, unthreatening inspiration he wanted, he should have stayed on Willow-Wane, ascended through the customary methods of promotion, and accepted a conventional academic post. Instead, he was here, on the homeworld of the humans, illegal and alone. Raising a truhand, he reached out.

All four of the delicate manipulative digits came together. They were of equal length and shorter than a human thumb. Making contact with the exposed flesh, Desvendapur felt the heat rising from within. No wonder humans had to eat so much, he thought. Without a proper exoskeleton to provide insulation, they must lose enormous quantities of energy in the form of heat to the surrounding air. How they spent as much time in water as they did without instantly freezing was one of those exotic physiological mysteries best left to the xenobiologists.

When the skin and flesh of the human's arm compacted and rose between his fingers, he nearly gagged. The compression did not seem to hurt or harm the biped at all, though surely if pressure was increased it would ultimately do so. Utilized for extraordinarily delicate manipulation, a truhand was incapable of exerting that kind of force. A foothand could do so, but the poet had no desire to put the hypothesis to the test.

When the human deliberately moved his arm slightly, the flesh and skin in the thranx's grasp flexed with the motion but did not tear. Cheelo grinned, enjoying the alien's discomfort. When it released its grip, he rolled his sleeve back down.

"See? No harm done. We're *flexible*. It's a much better physical design."

"That is an assertion very much open to debate." Dipping his head, Desvendapur searched the surrounding ground until he found a small rock with an edge. Holding it in one truhand, he extended a foothand and, to Cheelo's surprise, deliberately drew the sharp edge of the stone across the upper portion of the smaller limb. A pale white line appeared in its wake. "Try this on your 'better design.' " He chucked the rock.

Cheelo caught it reflexively. The ragged, splintered stone edge was sharp enough to slice easily through skin, leaving exposed flesh raw and bleeding. Tight lipped, he let the stone fall from his fingers. He didn't like being shown up, never had, whether it was by some street punk or a sassy well-dressed citizen or a visiting alien.

"Okay, shell-butt. So you made a point. It doesn't make you any less ugly. You smell nice, sure, and I guess you're sort of smart, but to me you're still nothing but a big, bloated, overgrown bug with brains. My people have been stepping on your kind since we could walk."

Open hostility! Where virtually any other thranx would have been dismayed and appalled by the grimy human's response, Desvendapur was elated. Such primal social interaction was all but unheard-of among the thranx, whose close-quarter, underground society was necessarily founded upon an elaborate hierarchy of courtesy and manners. Here was inspiration indeed! Drawing forth his scri!ber, he directed a rapid-fire stream of clicks, whistles, and wordings at its pickup.

Cheelo frowned. "What are you jabbering about now?"

"I am just trying to capture the moment. Outright anger is rare among my kind. Please, sustain that tone of voice and those urgent syllables."

"Sustain . . . ? What the hell do you think I am, some kind of archetype for you to capture in verse?" His voice rose. "D'you think I was put here just for your stinking benefit, to give you something to compose about?"

"Wonderful, marvelous!" the thranx breathed in his whispery Terranglo. "Don't stop!"

Cheelo folded his arms over his chest and set his jaw. Seeing that the human had finished, or at least terminated his current rant, a disappointed Desvendapur paused the scri!ber. Might there be some way he could induce the biped to resume? Proceeding against nature, in direct contravention of everything he had been brought up to believe in and act upon, he unhesitatingly hostiled back. The larval adolescent within him rebelled violently at his tone, but there was no one else around to overhear or to be shocked.

"I am not your tiny, primitive insect pest. Try stepping on me, and you'll slide off. Or I will throw you into the nearest river."

Cheelo's gaze narrowed. "You and what bug army? If there's any throwing to be done, I'll do it."

"Come on, then." Astonished at his audacity, his mind storming with inspired verse that burned and crackled, Desvendapur turned to face the taller, heavier human head-on. He adopted a defensive posture; truhands folded back, stronger foothands extended, eight digits splayed in grasping position, antennae erect and alert. The thranx might be excessively polite, but they were not helpless. "Let's see you try."

The pistol weighed heavily as Cheelo Montoya mulled the challenge. He was bigger and heavier than the bug, but out-limbed eight to four. Since all its musculature was internal, hidden beneath the chitinous exoskeleton, he could not get an idea of its strength from looking at it. He knew that small insects like ants and fleas could lift many times their own weight, but that did not mean such physical ability would scale up proportionately to something the size of a thranx. In their brief time together he had not seen it throw any logs around or push trees out of its way.

Slowly, he slid the pack off his back. A small stream flowed through the woods nearby. It was no river, but it did spread out to form a sizable pool. For purposes of demonstration it would have to do.

As Cheelo approached, the thranx began weaving slowly from side to side, up and down, forcing the human to deal with a moving target. When he tried to circle around and get behind it, it pivoted on its four legs to keep facing him. Experimentally, he struck out with his right hand, grabbing for one of the extended foothands. It drew back, and the other foothand came down sharply on his wrist. The blow stung more sharply than he expected, and he reflexively jerked his arm back.

"Come on." Desvendapur chided the human even as he tried to store as many new stanzas in his head as possible. This was extraordinary! The possibility that the confrontation might end in injury did not enter his mind. "I thought you were going to throw me in the river."

Cheelo continued to circle the alien, searching for an opening. With eight limbs blocking his reach, he saw that it wasn't going to be easy. "You're quick, I'll give you that. You can block a grab, and probably a punch—but what can you do about this?"

Arms outstretched, he rushed forward. When the thranx tried to feint, Cheelo swerved in response. He'd survived too many breathless fights in too many dark alleys and deserted buildings to be easily fooled. As his arms wrapped around the alien's lower thorax, he tucked his head low and out of reach.

Perfume exploded in his face. His upper body blocked the weaker truhands from extending and getting a grip, while the foothands clutched at his back and tried to pull him off. They were insistent, but not strong enough. Bending his knees, he lifted the alien off the damp ground and started walking toward the stream.

He'd taken two steps when all four feet slammed into his belly, knocking the air out of him. Losing his grip, he stumbled backward, tripped, and sat down hard on his backside, curled over and clutching at his stomach. When he released the thranx, it fell on its side. All four legs churning, it scrambled back onto its feet and came toward him. This time all four hands were extended.

He waited until they grabbed his shirt. Reaching up, he wrapped his fingers around the foothands, the unyielding chitin smooth and slick beneath his fingers. Bringing up his right foot, he planted it in the middle of the alien's abdomen and rolled backward, pushing with his leg as he did so. The thranx went flying over his head to land hard on its back.

Rolling, breathing hard, he staggered to his feet. Lying on its back and kicking with all eight limbs, the alien's resemblance to an upturned crab or spider was unnerving. Finally succeeding in getting a couple of legs under its body, it pushed, straightened, and once more stood confronting him. A truhand reached up to groom flexible antennae. It did not look like it was hurt, but it was hard to tell. Rigid chitin did not bruise in the manner of soft flesh.

"Had—had enough?" Cheelo gasped, bending over and bracing one hand against his right thigh.

Though quite familiar from training with the techniques of hand-to-hand combat, Desvendapur was unfamiliar with the consequences. Execution and practice in a polite, scholastic setting was one thing; being thrown around on hard, unyielding, alien ground was quite something else. He was sore from head to foot. But if the transliteration of the extraordinary experience from reality to exposition did not win him a major prize in composition, then he truly might as well give up trying to be an innovative poet and remain a food preparator for the rest of his life. The experience was exhilarating, rousing, and yes, inspiring.

"A time-part fraction, if you will. Please. I have to get this down!" Removing the scri!ber from its padded pouch, the poet once again spewed a stream of elegantly embellished alien rhetoric into its pickup.

"Sure," Cheelo responded graciously. "Take your time." Approaching cautiously, he gave the device a curious once-over before bending to wrap both arms quickly and tightly around the alien body and lifting it for a second time off the ground—but this time from behind.

Flailing arms and legs could not reach him. The thranx was not flexible enough to reach behind its back. The head, however, could swivel almost a hundred and eighty degrees. The face was expressionless as always, but the rapid movement of mandibles coupled with the anxious writhings of all eight limbs succeeded in conveying the creature's distress.

"Kick me in the gut *now*, why don't you?" Cheelo was not a big man, and the bug was as much of a load as he could handle, but he was determined to fulfill his earlier threat. Bending slightly backward to manage the weight, he staggered toward the stream.

Despite his helpless position in the human's grasp, Desvendapur continued to compose until they stood at the water's edge. The stream meandered rather than flowed into a pool and was no more than a meter or so deep.

"You have proven your point," he declared as he slipped the scri!ber back into its pouch. "I accept that you can throw me into this unpretentious river. Now you may put me down."

"Put you down?" Cheelo echoed stiffly. "Sure, I'll put you down." Swinging both arms, he flung the thranx forward. All eight legs kicking in surprise and alarm, it landed noisily in the water—in the center of the pool.

It resurfaced immediately, flailing violently. A grinning Cheelo watched from shore. At any moment, the creature would come staggering out onto dry land, dripping water and weeds, its dignity more bruised than its body. It would glare up at him but acknowledge the human as its physical superior. He wondered if it would drip-dry or shake like a dog.

His smug expression faded to uncertainty. The fluttering of blue-green limbs was slowing. It was almost as if the alien was in some kind of trouble. But how could it be in difficulty, with its head and neck well above water? And if it was hurting, why didn't it cry out, in its own singular combination of clicks and whistles and words if not in Terranglo?

It could not cry out, he realized, because its lungs were filling with water. Even as he met its resilient, reflective gaze, it was drowning before his eyes. The thorax, he remembered. The damn things breathe through holes in their thorax—and all eight of those vital openings were submerged beneath the surface of the pond.

Leaping forward, he plunged into the water. At its deepest point, the pond came up to his neck. No wonder the alien was having trouble. Unlike many of its smaller terrestrial cousins, it had negative buoyancy. It might not sink like a stone, he reflected, but sink it obviously would.

He half carried, half dragged it out of the pool. Once safely back on land he stepped back and watched as it convulsed in great heaves, exuding water through a spasming thorax that expanded and contracted like a blue-green bellows. When the last drop had been expunged from the anguished lungs, it stumbled sideways until it found support against the buttress roots of a nearby strangler fig. The bulbous, red-streaked, golden eyes turned to face him.

"That lethal a demonstration was not necessary. I would not have done the same to you." A hacking cough convulsed the aquamarine-hued body, emerging from the sides of the thorax and not the alien's mouth.

"You couldn't do the same to me," Cheelo could not resist sneering.

"Don't be so sure. My kind learn quickly." A truhand gestured at the human's lower limbs. "That was a clever trick, that earlier move with the leg. I think I could do it. After all, I have four or six to your two. It would not work on me a second time."

Cheelo shrugged. He'd gone *mano a mano* with his share of street punks and thugs, though never before with an alien. Maybe he was the first, he thought. "Doesn't matter. I know more than one trick." He stared unblinkingly at the contentious thranx. "Maybe next time I won't pull you out." An edgy, mildly contemptuous snicker born of hard life on the streets emerged from his lips as he nodded at the still convulsing body. "Eight limbs and you bugs still can't swim?"

"Regrettably, no. We tend to sink. Not immediately, but all too soon. And no thranx can kick hard enough to hold its entire upper body out of the water. So we drown. Thank you for pulling me out."

"I'm beginning to wonder if that was such a good idea." As he mumbled the rest of a reply, Cheelo saw that the alien neither drip-dried nor shook. Instead, it inclined its head downward and used its mandibles to squeegee water from its body and limbs. Its large supply pack lay on the ground nearby, but the thorax pouch had gone into the pond with it. He wondered if it was watertight. It contained everything the insectoid had composed since their fractious first encounter.

"Look," he proposed condescendingly, "if you want to write about me, or compose, or whatever the hell it is that you're doing, go ahead. Just don't provoke me for the sake of your art, okay? You want to tag along, fine, but keep out of my way. I can be—I have a temper, and I've been known to lose control of myself on occasion, see? Next time I might not be able to get to you in time—or want to. Or I might hit hard enough to break one of your limbs."

The head paused in its grooming to look up at him. "That I do not think you can do. You would be more likely to damage your own appendage. You may be more flexible, but I am physically tougher."

"Says who? Maybe we should just . . ." Hearing his own words, Cheelo calmed himself. "This is stupid shit, what's going on here. It doesn't matter who's stronger, or tougher, or whatever. What am I—in a competition here with another species? So, educate me: If I'm ever in a life-or-death struggle with a thranx, what do I aim for?"

"Why would I tell you that?"

Why indeed? Cheelo mused. Not that the information was vital. The aliens might have particularly vulnerable points that were not obvious, but he could see that in a fight it would be best to strike at anything soft and unprotected by chitinous body armor. The eyes, for example, or the soft under-abdomen. A tug on one of those feathery antennae would probably make an attacker let go, too. Not that he was anticipating a fight, but it was always better to be prepared for one. That was how it was on the streets of Gatun and Balboa and San José. Why should it be any different in the jungle?

All he knew about the thranx was the little, the very little, he had picked up while absently listening to media. This one, this Desvenbapur, might be friendly, might be harmless, might be merely suspicious and sarcastic, or it might be some kind of giant arthropod alien schizo, agreeable one moment and eager to cut his throat and suck out his organs the next. Hope for the former and plan for the latter had always been Cheelo's motto. Proof of its efficacy was that he was still alive and, except for a few scars and a couple of missing teeth, reasonably intact.

"Okay. You've got a tough outside, and you smell good. Those I'll grant you." His mouth split in a nasty grin. "But you're still ugly."

"Ugly?" The vee-shaped head cocked sideways as compound eyes studied the human. "What a profound observation coming from a representative of a species whose bodies are raised up out of jelly. Not only do you all wobble when you walk, you can practically see through the thinner patches of your skin. You look at the world out of a single lens which, if damaged, practically renders that organ blind. Your sense of smell is primitive and relies on olfactory organs set in the middle of your face, where they have to strain to detect even a hint of a scent." By way of illustrating the superiority of thranx design, feathery antennae wagged back and forth.

"You have only four limbs instead of a much more sensible eight, and those four are restricted in their function." Foothands rose from the ground in a demonstration of how the second set of thranx appendages could be utilized either as feet or hands. "Your skin is exceedingly vulnerable to even the slightest cut or puncture, you can't make any music worthy of the designation by rubbing any of your limbs together, and you're not even properly symmetrical."

"Who's not symmetrical?" Using the fingers of his right hand, Cheelo pointed to the appropriate portions of his anatomy. "Two eyes, two ears, two arms and legs. Where's the asymmetry in that?"

"Look at your hands." Desvendapur nodded in their direction. "Are the number of digits divisible by two? No. There should be six fingers—or four, like mine. Additionally, you need to look deeper."

"Deeper?" Shifting his pack higher on his shoulders, Cheelo frowned uncomprehendingly.

"Within your pitiful self. How many hearts do you have? One, shoved off to one side. The same is true for all other major human organs, except your lungs, of which you have, by what mysterious quirk of nature I cannot fathom, the proper division." A foothand ran down the front of the poet's thorax to his abdomen. "Two hearts, two livers, two stomachs, and so forth. A proper body design for an advanced species, symmetrical and serene. Whereas yours is a mess of internal nonsense, with lonely, vulnerable organs struggling for space and pushed all out of proper position."

Out-argued, not to mention a bit overwhelmed, Cheelo could only mumble, "So you're saying that you guys have two of everything inside you?"

Finding the equivalent, appropriate human gesture amenable, Desvendapur nodded. "Not only is such an arrangement aesthetically pleasing, it makes us more durable. Thranx can lose any major organ secure in the knowledge that another just like it will keep them alive. Humans have no such luxury. You must live every day of your existence in fear of organ failure."

"If you've got two or more of everything," Cheelo replied thoughtfully as he started off into the forest with the thranx following close behind, "and your bodies run smaller than ours, then everything that's inside must also be smaller—heart, lungs, everything. Our organs are bigger."

"Better to have backup than size," Desvendapur argued.

They ambled along in that fashion, debating the merits of their respective anatomies, until Cheelo's train of thought was interrupted by a germinating uncertainty. "For a cook, or cook's assistant, or whatever it is you are, you sure know a lot about humans."

Though the biped could not interpret his reflexive gestures, Desvendapur instinctively tried to mute them nonetheless. "Those of us who were assigned to this information-gathering expedition were well prepared."

"Ay, you told me that." Still dubious, Cheelo was watching the bug closely. Its body language might be throwing off all kinds of suggestive signals, but he wouldn't know it. The thranx's complex hand and head movements held less meaning for him than the antics of the monkeys in the canopy overhead. Fellow primates he could relate to: a pontificating alien bug he could not.

The thranx had the advantage. It had been prepared for contact with humans, whereas he knew next to nothing about the eight-limbed aliens. But he was learning. Cheelo Montoya was nothing if not a fast learner.

"Also," his otherworldly companion added by way of a delayed afterthought, "you stink."

"I can see why they put you in food preparation instead of the diplomatic corps." However, Cheelo had no comeback for the thranx's latest imputation. While it continued to exude an ever-changing panoply of aromatic perfumes, he pushed on through the brush, grime-soaked and sweaty, reeking of mammalian ooze.

As for appearance, he had to admit that the more often the bug strayed into his range of vision, the less alien and more pleasing to the eye it became. There was much to admire in the graceful flow of multiple limbs; the glint of light shining off smooth blue-green chitin that was one moment the color of dark tsavorite, the next that of Paraiba tourmaline; the delicate rustling of twin antennae; and the splintering of sunshine by the bulging, gold-tinted compound eyes. While not the dreamed-of exotic dancer from Rio or Panama City, neither did it make him anymore want to raise a leg and stomp it.

With a bit of a shock, he realized that in appearance it was not so very different from its distant, terrestrial cousins. Did mere intelligence, then, count for so much in altering one's perception? If ants could talk, would people still find them so disagreeable?

People would if they persisted in trying to eat a person out of house and home, he decided. It's not a bug, he kept telling himself. It's not a spider. It's a recently contacted alien species, intelligent and sensitive. He had some success convincing himself of that—but only some. Ancient, atavistic sentiments died hard. Easier to think of the thranx as an equal and not something to be stepped on when he kept his eyes closed. You couldn't do that very often in the rain forest. There was too much to trip over or step into.

Perfunctory insults aside, he found himself wondering what the alien really thought about him.

16

The court of the Emperor MUUNIINAA III was designed to impress and overawe, from its profusion of bejeweled robotics and whisper-silent electronic attendants to the luxuriousness of its furnishings. The fact that everything in the throne room was functional as well as decorative was wholly indicative of the AAnn mind-set. While the AAnn were fond of ceremony, it was never allowed to get in the way of operational efficiency. This extended from the lowliest sand monitor to the highest levels of government.

The Emperor, of course, had not possessed absolute powers since ancient times. It was an elective position, as were those of lord and baron and the lesser nobles who ruled beneath them. It was simply that the AAnn could not let go of tradition, so they adapted it to fit a contemporary, star traversing cluster of systems and worlds. Though it rang of history and ancient regimes, it was in reality about as feudal in nature as the programming of the latest massive parallel quantum computers that navigated the ships that darted and plunged through space-plus.

So while Lord Huudra Ap and Baron Keekil YN wore the ceremonial robes of high office, each noble's elegant attire and gem-studded investitures powered individual defensive screens and a full suite of communications gear to keep them in constant touch with both immediate underlings and detached constituencies. Standing with bowed heads and lowered tails as the Emperor retired from the chamber to deal with the mountainous and decidedly unglamorous paperwork of office, they exchanged a glance that signified a mutual need to talk.

Other groups broke away from the assembly to chat informally or to discuss matters of serious import. For Huudra and Keekil it was a matter of both.

Heads bobbed in greeting, and finely manicured claws were courteously sheathed. In addition to their repertoire of other skills, both nobles were masters of manners. Together with several other nobles, they formed one of the dozen or so organized cliques that dominated the politics of the assembly. The matter that Keekil wished to discuss with Huudra, however, had nothing to do with imminent business of state. It was more a matter for mutual speculation that both had made a specialty of theirs. Aware that everyone from the opposition parties to the emperor himself relied on them for the most current information on the matter, they had made it their business to keep in constant communication with those far-flung representatives of the Empire who were in a position to be knowledgeable.

It was in this spirit of curiosity and need that Huudra greeted his friend and ally, whom he would not hesitate to undermine to advance his own status and position. Keekil hissed a warm greeting, quite aware of what his associate was thinking. He was thinking the same thing. There was no animosity involved. It was the natural order of things. Such constant competition strengthened the assembly, and by inference, the Empire.

"It is all sso very peculiar." Keekil favored blue in his robes, in all its most sallow permutations. Even the communicator that hovered patiently several centimeters to the left of his mouth was plated in gleaming pale blue metal. "Thiss business of the thranx attempting to make alliess of the mammalss."

Huudra excused himself long enough to answer a priority call and suggest several alternatives to a disagreeable situation to the technocrat on the other end. "Apologiess, honored Keekil. Then you think the inssectiles are sserious about it?"

The baron gestured assent, adding a supportive hiss. "Yess, I do. The quesstion iss, are these humanss?"

Overhead, hoverators hummed back and forth, scanning for intruders, petitioners, and possible assassins. The temperature in the room was high, the humidity a tolerable 6 percent. Both nobles' personal communicator suites hummed for attention. For the moment, they were ignored.

"My own ressearchess indicate an inherent reluctance on the part of the human population, both on their homeworld and their coloniess. More than that, they sseem to have a vissceral fear of the thranx sshape." He hissed his amusement. "Can you imagine it? Deciding intersstellar politicss on the basiss of sshape? They are an immature sspeciess!"

"There iss nothing immature about their technology," Keekil reminded his aristocratic colleague. "Their weaponry iss the equal of the besst of the Empire's—or of the thranx. Their communicationss are ssuperb. Their sshipss . . ." The baron gesticulated admiration mixed with paranoia, a difficult gesture for any but the most accomplished orator to execute eloquently. "Their sshipss are elegant."

Huudra drew back his upper lip to reveal even, sharp teeth set in a long jaw. "I have sseen ssome of the preliminary reportss. There iss ssome dissagreement as to whether they are better than ourss."

"If they do indeed exceed the capabilitiess of ourss, then they are better as well than anything flown by the thranx." Irritated, Keekil waved a ringed hand across his waist. The persistent hum of communications demanding response promptly died.

"That would be reasson enough to sseek them as alliess." Huudra scratched at a loose scale on the side of his neck. Sparkling in the bright artificial light of the throne room, it fell to the floor and was promptly vacuumed away by an unobtrusive remote cleaner built to resemble a four-legged *kerpk*. "Our interesstss would be better sserved by convincing them to become confederatess of the Empire."

"You know our envoyss have had little ssuccess in perssuading the humanss of the many advantagess that would lie in aligning themsselvess with our interesstss." Raising a hand, Keekil had to wait less than a minute for a drifting sustainer to place a filled drinking utensil between his fingers.

"Yess." Huudra was not thirsty. Idly, he wondered if Keekil's drink might be poisoned. It was a natural thought, as was the corollary that the baron would not be so readily consuming the contents of the container if they had not been thoroughly tested by an independent machine prior to arrival. "These mammalss value their independence."

"That will have to change. I am persuaded by our pssych sspecialisstss that the humanss *can* be convinced. We already know that they are resisstant to pressure. Nor have rational argumentss ssucceeded in sswaying them."

Huudra indicated his irritation. He ranked Keekil, but not by enough to intimidate the other noble. "Then what are we to do?"

"Have patience, I am told. The most convinced human iss one that hass convinced itsself. Wait for them to entreat *uss*. When that happenss, it will make for a sstronger alliance between uss, as well as one in which we remain the dominant component." The baron sipped at his refreshment. "There iss only one problem: otherss who have the ssame hope."

"The benighted, dirt-loving insectiles." Huudra added a general curse notable for its grace of understatement.

"Truth. They have had only the most modesst ssuccess thuss far in overcoming the humanss' natural antipathy toward them. For that matter, a great many thranx find the appearance, habitss, and activitiess of humanss detestable. Thiss mutual abhorrence iss of coursse greatly to our benefit."

"Then nothing hass changed." Huudra prepared to depart. The administration of his own fief awaited, and decisions waited on no AAnn.

"That iss not entirely true, honored friend, if certain reportss are to be believed."

Huudra hesitated. "What reportss? I have heard nothing to indicate that the relationsship between human and thranx hass changed. Certainly not for the better."

Keekil gestured apology mixed with slyness. "Perhapss that iss becausse my ssources are more penetrating than yourss." He was unable to resist the dig.

Huundra scowled. "I will grant you the ssmall triumph of esspionage—if you have ssomething worth hearing."

"There iss ssomething very ssecret afoot. Information sspeakss to a great rissk the thranx are taking, in concert with a few sselect human aliess."

The lord of the Southern Fief spat his disbelief. "The thranx do not gamble. They are cautiouss, calculating, and predictable. They do not take 'risskss,' esspecially on matterss of ssuch importance."

Keekil refused to be put off. "Nevertheless, the report iss there, for any who care to read it. It claimss that the inssectiless have embarked on a rissky coursse of action that, if ssuccessful, would greatly accelerate the improvement of their relationss with the humanss."

Huudra's instinctive inclination led him to shrug off this outrageous claim. The thranx did not gamble, and any attempt to rush humans into a decision, as experience had already shown, usually had the opposite effect. The insectiles knew this as well as the AAnn, and whatever else the eight-limbed might be, they were not stupid.

"I would deign to perusse ssuch a report," he replied absently, thus presenting a formal request to see the analysis in question. "I do not dissmiss it out of hand. I ssimply find it difficult to countenance."

"As do I." Finishing the last of his drink, Keekil held the utensil high over his head. A cleaner swooped down to pluck it painlessly from his fingers. "Yet to ignore it sshould the information it containss mature to fruition could prove perilouss."

It was a diplomatic way of saying that their titles, not to mention their tails, might be at stake. Buried as he was in administrative work, Huudra knew he could not ignore any report that commented upon human-thranx relations, no matter how seemingly ludicrous. Not when he and Keekil had been charged with keeping the emperor's council informed of the matter. He hissed soft resignation.

"I will read it through, of coursse. Tell me, honored colleague: Sshould the leasst of it prove to have a basiss in fact, iss there anything we can do about it?" The thought of frustrating the aims of the pedantic but indomitable thranx raised his spirits.

Keekil blinked slyly. "Jusst possibly, honored associate. Jusst possibly. The thranx are not the only sspeciess capable of ssubtle interference in the affairss of other sspeciess of ssignificance. It iss amazing how with a little imagination and careful planning, one ssecret can be turned againsst another."

Caucusing quietly, they exited the room as the rest of the assembly trickled out behind them. The more Huudra heard of Keekil's intentions, the greater his professional admiration for his colleague. In the shifting sands where cunning slithered, none traveled more subtlely than the AAnn.

17

Cheelo knew he probably should have seen the anaconda. What such a big snake was doing in so small a stream he could not imagine, but the serpent's motivation was not important. What mattered was that it was there, that it had been aroused by their passage, and that it struck.

Not him, but his unwary companion.

When the snake hit, the thranx emitted a loud, startled stridulation, the wing cases on its back vibrating like cellos. The blunt, reptilian head grabbed a middle leg, biting down hard, the small, sharp teeth gaining an immediate purchase without completely penetrating the chitin. Coil after coil emerged from beneath the cola-colored, tannin-stained water to wrap around the thranx's rear legs and abdomen. It struggled, antennae and upper limbs flailing wildly, but it could no more break that steel-cable grasp than its vestigial wings could carry it aloft.

The mass of writhing alien limbs and constrictor coils went down in a heap. A loud, distinct crack split the humid, still air and the alien screamed a sharp, high-pitched whistle. Cheelo stood off to one side, wary and watching.

Doesn't look like a very superior body now, he found himself thinking.

The alien was going to die. That much was clear. Whether the anaconda was capable of swallowing it was another matter, but it would quickly suffocate the thranx no matter how many lungs it had. The huge constrictor would continue to tighten its grip until its prey could no longer exhale. Cheelo wondered if the brilliant compound eyes would dim in death.

"Do something!" the alien was gasping. "Get it . . . off. Help me!"

Did he want to do that? Montoya mused. He had lived a long time without knowledge of or the company of aliens of any kind. He could certainly continue to exist in that same fashion. If he got too close, the snake might decide to forsake its present cumbersome, hard-shelled prey for something softer and more familiar. Why take the chance? He owed this garrulous representative of a race from a distant world absolutely nothing. *It* had intruded on *his* privacy, and he had graciously consented to allow it to accompany him. That did not imply in any way that he took any kind of responsibility for it. Besides, he had an appointment to keep.

If they happened to stumble across its indigestible, extruded remains, no searchers, human or thranx, could connect Cheelo Montoya to the fatality. More likely than not, the bug's own people would come to the conclusion that their wayward associate had received exactly what he deserved for wandering off on his own. Its death meant nothing to Cheelo, meant less to him than the passing of a bird or monkey. Besides, if their situation was reversed, there was no reason to assume that the alien would do anything for him.

"Ah, *shit,*" he muttered as he reached into his pocket holster for the compact pistol.

Edging closer to the combatants, one of whom was tiring rapidly, he tried to draw a bead on the snake's blunt, shovel-shaped skull. Initially impossible, it became easier to aim as the thranx's struggles steadily weakened. Sensing the imminence of its prey's demise, the serpent began to relax. Though he wasn't sure he had a clean shot, Cheelo's finger tightened on the trigger. It wouldn't do any good to wait until the snake stopped moving completely, because by then the thranx would be dead.

When the full charge struck, the constrictor's head jerked sharply. The tiny anacondan eyes made it hard to tell how effective the shot had been. Risking contact, Cheelo put the pistol as close to the snake's skull as he could and fired a second time. This time the resultant spasmodic twitch was purely reflexive.

Pocketing his weapon, he began struggling with the weighty mass. It took more than a few minutes to unwind several hundred pounds of solid, limp serpent from the thranx's body. "How're you doing?" he queried the alien. "Talk to me, bug. Let me know I'm not wasting my time here."

"You're not." The Terranglo was more heavily accented than usual as the injured thranx strained to mouth the humanoid phrases. "I am alive, but I'm afraid that one of my legs is broken."

"Ay, I heard it snap." With a grunt, Cheelo heaved a center length of snake aside. "You hurting?"

"Of course I am hurting!" Freed from the imprisoning coils, a shaken Desvendapur turned to look back at the human who had saved him. "Do you think I'm made of metal?"

"No, I think you're made of crab shell and bug guts. Pardon me for asking."

Aware that his artless declaration of fact might have been misinterpreted by his savior, a grateful Desvendapur hastened to soothe any misconceptions. "I meant no scorn. It is just that I would think it obvious to anyone that a broken leg would be found to be painful."

"I don't know bullcrap about your internal makeup, or how your nervous system works." Under Cheelo's strong fingers, a last span of solid muscle sloughed away from the thranx's upper abdomen.

"Then listen and learn: We feel pain as surely as do you."

"But not in the same places, or to the same degree." Kneeling, Cheelo examined the section of leg where the anaconda's jaws remained locked, even in death, on the chitin of one foreleg. "If you did, this would have you screaming in pain." He glanced up, meeting compound eyes, and with both hands wrenched sharply on the snake's neck. "That hurt?"

"Only slightly. Few nerves run through our outer covering. We are not as tactilely sensitive as you."

"I'm not sure if that's a good thing or bad. In this case, though, it's for sure good. Stay there."

With a truhand and a foothand Desvendapur gestured down at himself. "I have a broken leg. Where would I go?"

"Beats me. A while ago you were boasting about having four or six legs as opposed to my lousy, inadequate two and how much better the arrangement was for getting you around."

Sliding his pack off his back he searched inside until he found the multitool. Returning to the alien's side, he deployed a pliers configuration to remove the great constrictor's teeth, one by one, from the thranx's foreleg. Only when the last tooth had been forcibly extracted did the dead snake's head finally slide away from its would-be prey.

Though he was ready to apply disinfectant and appropriate followups, Cheelo saw that the wound was beyond his simple knowledge of first aid. The chitin was bleeding profusely. A double line of small holes showed where the snake's teeth had sought and found a grip.

"Can we do anything with this?" he asked curiously.

"With time and the proper dietary supplements, yes." Looking back and down, Desvendapur examined the wounds. "Though they testify to impressive jaw strength, the punctures are fortunately not too deep."

"What about applying a sterile covering or spray?"

"The necessary materials for sealing the wounds are in my pack. Once treated, the internal perforations will heal on their own." His abdomen shifted. "The break is another matter."

Cheelo sighed. Why he didn't just offer a final salute and farewell and return to the solitary depths of the rain forest on his own he didn't know. Perhaps it was because it was beginning to occur to him that there might, just might, be a way to realize some profit from his unexpected encounter. Experience had taught him that there was always money to be made from the new and the different, and if the alien wasn't new and different, why then, nothing qualified.

"Let's have a look."

It was the lower portion of the middle right limb that had been snapped. Blood poured from the split more freely than it would have from any human. Under Desvendapur's direction, Cheelo applied sealants and dressings from the thranx's kit to freeze and close the wound, binding it shut with a pastelike composite that would set the fracture firmly. Derived from a synthetic chitin, it would become as much a part of the alien's body as his natural limbs.

It did not set instantaneously, however. They would need to move slowly for several days. Additionally, the broken limb required supplementary support. Demonstrating a dexterity that surprised the poet, Cheelo fashioned a makeshift double splint from available wood, securing it to the mended limb with multiple twists of tough vine.

"That should do you." He stepped back to admire his handiwork.

"It will suffice very well," the thranx agreed. "But then, it's only natural that someone who spends his time working alone in vast tracts of jungle should have mastered such necessary survival skills."

"That's right." Cheelo did not go on to explain that the jungle whose survival skills he had mastered consisted of dark streets and back alleys, shadowy business enterprises and their glowering associates. On reflection, it was not surprising how many of the abilities that allowed someone like himself to survive the threats and dangers of the urban jungle were applicable to survival in the natural world as well.

In lieu of a suitable couch, Desvendapur settled himself across a broken stump padded with thriving fungi, resting as much of his abdomen as possible on the wooden brace. "Now that immediate problems have been dealt with, I was wondering if you could answer a question or two for me?" His human companion was not surprised to see that the alien's scri!ber was out and activated.

More in an endless succession of queries about humankind, Cheelo grumbled silently. For someone who had developed a healthy dislike of questions, he found himself answering an awful lot of them lately.

"Okay, as long as we don't waste the rest of the day playing Who's Got the Answer. I'm working on a schedule. What do you want to know this time? How our 'hives' are organized? What our hobbies are? Why we keep other animals as pets? Details of our mating habits?" His face broke into a wide smirk. "Ay, yeah—let's talk about mating habits. Only this time, for every one of your questions I answer, I get to ask one of my own."

"For the moment I would prefer not to delve into matters so intimate, though in a way my first question might be considered even more personal." The thranx was staring at him. Leastwise, Cheelo thought it was staring at him. Given the amorphousness of those multiple compound lenses, it was hard to tell.

"Like what, for instance?" The human was still grinning. It pleased him to think that his directness might have unsettled the alien.

"Like, for instance, why have you been lying to me?"

Cheelo tensed. There was no reason for him to do so, not with the only other intelligent creature for kilometers around an alien—and one that was reduced to hobbling on a busted wheel to boot. His reaction was pure reflex.

"Lying to you? *Who's* been lying to you? Not me. What makes you say that?" He was watching the insectoid closely. "What are you—telepathic or something?"

"I am nothing of the kind. There is no such thing as telepathy. At least, its existence has not yet been formally verified. I don't need to be able to read your mind, Cheelo-person, to know that you have been lying."

"You've got some nerve, bug. I save your life and fix up your leg real good, and the first thing you can think of to say to me afterward isn't 'Thank you very much, man, for saving my life,' it's 'Why have you been lying to me?' "

"Thranx are very forthright—and you are being deliberately evasive."

Cheelo shrugged diffidently. "I got nothing to hide. So if I'm lying, give me an example. Catch me out with one." Sneering, he leaned forward and made beckoning motions with both hands. "Come on, big-eyes. Hand me back one of my own lies."

"Very well. You are not a naturalist."

Cheelo looked up sharply. Why was he wasting his time on this nonsense? "You're new to this planet, I'm the first native you've spent any time with, and already you can tell when a human is telling the truth or not? Sorry, but I don't think you're that smart."

"It is merely a matter of analyzing causal observations made during the time we have spent together." Desvendapur was neither intimidated nor angered by the human's attitude. "We have shared each other's company for a number of days now. In all that time I have not seen you perform a single act of scrutiny that might justify your presumed appellation. You have examined nothing, identified nothing, collected nothing. You have utterly ignored the 'natural' world around you except when it threatened to impede your progress or complicate your movements.

"While I am willing, indeed am forced, to assume the existence of significant differences in our cultures, science is not nearly so variable. Body shape, size, and perceptive abilities may vary, but certain things remain constant throughout the galaxy.

"One is that all science is based on observation. In the time I have spent in your company, you have made none. Not one. Nor have you taken notes, or made visual recordings, or done anything else to indicate that you are in the profession of gathering and analyzing information."

"See these? These are my cameras!" Using forked fingers, Cheelo indicated his eyes. "And these are my scri!bers—my recorders." He pointed to his ears. "I've got a good memory, and I remember everything I see."

Desvendapur gestured comprehension, then remembered to follow it with a head nod so that the human would understand. "Do you? Yesterday a flock of most interesting avians flew past overhead, visible through a fortuitous gap in the forest canopy. Both of us remarked on their appearance. Can you tell me what color they were?"

Cheelo fought to remember. "Blue!" he announced finally. "They were bright blue, with touches of yellow." He smirked triumphantly at the multilimbed alien. "How's that for an example of a naturalist's memory at work?"

"More than sufficient to diminish his standing, if he were thranx. They were green, not blue, and their beaks were red."

"Not true!" Cheelo objected strenuously. "Blue with yellow, and you can't prove otherwise!"

"But I can." Holding out his scri!ber, Desvendapur gestured with the instrument. "I do not only record my compositions; where possible I also record their sources of inspiration. Would you like to see the flock in question? I can play it back for you, together with my notes for the stanzas I composed to accompany the flight."

Caught. Cheelo snarled at the compact alien instrument. "Okay, so I *can't* remember everything. So what? That proves nothing."

"It proves that you are either the most extraordinary naturalist of your species, or the most indifferent. Any thranx claiming to hold such a position would carry instruments designed to take measurements, carry out analyses, and make records. I have not seen you utilize a single such device." A truhand indicated the human's pack. "Show them to me. Show me one. Now."

Yet again, Cheelo found himself wondering why he was tolerating this aggravating alien's company. Use the pistol, dump the body in the river, and be done with it, he thought. Still, he could not escape the feeling that there was money to be made here, and that the quantity would be greatly augmented if the subject of potential recompense was preserved in an animate as opposed to a defunct condition.

Besides, what was the thranx going to do? Report him to the nearest branch of the Global Association for the Advancement of Science? If he and his absent multilimbed companions were carrying out their observations under the umbrella of a special scientific dispensation, he could hardly go shooting off his mandibles about the status of a human who claimed to be doing essentially the same thing.

"Well, hoorah for you. You've found me out. So what? It means nothing."

"On the contrary, it means a great deal." The thranx was staring at him now, Cheelo was sure of it. "It means that if you are not a naturalist, as you have claimed, then you are something else." Painfully, using foot-and truhand, he manually repositioned his injured leg.

"The question then becomes, What are you?"

18

Electric with the realization that the colony was in the forefront of developing human-thranx relations, the terrestrial hive was an exhilarating place to work. The knowledge that it was also illicit, an operation whose very existence was unknown to all but a few enlightened members of the human government and scientific establishment, only added to the excitement. Rising to work every shift, one never knew when the operation might be discovered. Having been as thoroughly briefed on humankind and its peculiarities and distinctive foibles as was possible before their journey to the colony, every assigned thranx had been made fully aware of the inherent irrationality built into each individual human. If anything went wrong and they were subject to unforeseen exposure, there was no telling how the great mass of seething humanity might react to the presence of an unauthorized alien colony in its midst. Consequently, even as they went about their commonplace, everyday tasks, the colonists had to be ever vigilant and prepared for anything.

As weeks and months passed without discovery, a modest sense of security invariably settled over the colony. If even the apprehensive rogue humans who had cooperated and conspired in the secret establishment of the hive could relax, then certainly their thranx associates could do no less.

So it was that Jhywinhuran's thoughts were far from such matters as she busied herself at the end of the day's work, running a final check and chemical disbursement before signing off her station to her shift replacement. Instead of concentrating on the admittedly rote toil at hand, her mind strayed to remembrances of the time spent in the company of a particularly distinctive male. Somewhat to her chagrin, her thoughts had been repeatedly drawn in that direction for several days now.

Why she should have found an assistant food preparator so fascinating she could not quite explain. Certainly her attraction had nothing to do with his vocation, which was even more prosaic and mundane than her own. Within the bustling colony there were many unmated males who found her attractive, stridulating softly in her presence in an attempt to attract more than polite attention. Some she spent time with, chatting and disporting, but always her thoughts returned to a certain singular food preparator.

What it was about him that she found so distinctive proved elusive, no matter how often she tried to define it. Something in his manner, perhaps, or in the way he modulated communication: not only his vocalizations but the attendant clicks and whistles that were as much a part of thranx speech as strings of individual words. Maybe it was the way that when he became excited, exquisitely inflected snippets of High Thranx slipped into his conversation; something not to be expected from an assistant food preparator. There were other distinctions: the way he spoke of the alien world above, the animation that overwhelmed his gesturing when they attended a less-than-proficient performance by one of the colony's official soothers, the indifference with which he acknowledged both praise and criticism of his own work.

There was something not quite right about the food preparator Desvenbapur, something simultaneously irresistibly enticing and edgily off-putting. Try as she might, she could not get him out of her mind. She considered visiting a senior matriarch for counseling but decided that her condition had not yet advanced from the merely affected to the obsessive. Until that line was crossed she would deal with the situation herself.

One way to do so would be to go and visit the object of her anxiety. As in any hive, the colonists had been assigned not only labor but living quarters and sectors. While with certain specific exceptions the length and breadth of the hive was open to all who dwelled within and no permit or permission was required to wander beyond those sections that had been individually apportioned subsequent to arrival, it was infrequently done. There was no reason to explore beyond one's assigned territory. Everything a colonist needed could be found within an individually prescribed zone. It was a system that was traditional and efficient and that contributed mightily to the efficiency of every hive, whether on Hivehom, Willow-Wane, or the alien world known to its dominant inhabitants as Earth.

Humans, by contrast, the colonists had been told, were far less orderly. Superficially well organized, they tended to scatter and move about with considerably less regard for the effective organization of the whole. Life in their hives frequently bordered on the anarchic. Somehow, out of confusion and turmoil, they had succeeded in raising a civilization.

She determined to resolve the contradictions that were boiling within her. The very next off-period, she identified the location of the hive's subsidiary food preparation facility and headed in its direction, following the directions provided by her scri!ber. As she entered unfamiliar parts of the colony she paused from time to time to converse with thranx never before encountered, and they with her. No one questioned her presence. While out of the ordinary, there was nothing unlawful about it.

She spent some time talking with sanitation workers who supervised the hive's other waste terminus. The colony had been designed with at least two of everything in mind. If a critical component broke down, there was no hailing a neighboring hive for repairs or replacements. The nearest supplies lay parsecs away, and support could not be provided as soon as it might be needed. Between their incompatible technology and the restrictions placed on their movements, the hive's allied humans could provide only limited help. Of necessity, the colony had to be as self-sufficient as possible.

Despite diversions both enjoyable and educational, she eventually found herself in the auxiliary kitchen area. From there it was a simple matter to obtain permission to visit food preparation. What she saw there was a duplicate of the station where Desvenbapur had worked previously, identical down to the individual appliances and utensils manipulated by its work force. At present they were engaged in cleaning and treating a variety of native plants, rendering them suitable for thranx consumption. Without the ability to digest terrestrial vegetation, the rapid growth of the colony would have been greatly reduced.

She chatted amiably and casually with members of the staff, who were curious as to the presence in their midst of an unfamiliar representative of the sanitation division. No, an assistant preparator named Desvenbapur was not currently a member of their team. In fact, none of them had ever heard of him. Perhaps he worked exclusively on the night shift.

She knew she ought to make the journey back to her cubicle so she could get some rest before she had to report for the new day's work. She was being foolish, letting an incidental interest grow into a dangerous fixation. Hadn't Desvenbapur told her that he would be too busy establishing himself in a new zone and a new routine to welcome casual social contact? Hadn't he told her that as soon as he was settled in and comfortable with his work in the new sector that he would return to visit her? He had specifically asked her to terminate contact until such time as he felt ready to take pleasure from it again. Despite that, here she was, forcing the issue, trying to initiate intercourse he had requested she avoid. What was the matter with her?

She started to leave, to return to her own sector. Certainly if he had any reciprocal feelings for her he would be in touch as soon as he felt at ease with his new surroundings. It might well be counterproductive, even damaging, to their relationship for her to pursue the matter so vigorously. Did they *have* a relationship? She knew that *she* desired one, and she thought that he did as well. A demonstration of excessive inquisitiveness on her part might spoil everything.

She considered her options. There was a way to at least partially satisfy her interest without much risk of damaging relations. Locating a private information terminal, she plugged her scri!ber in and ran a search. Relief was palpable when his name appeared on the roster of workers assigned to this zone, food preparation division.

That should have been enough to satisfy her. Instead, adding to her distress and confusion, it only made her that much more anxious to see him again. She stood before the terminal until a polite whistle roused her to the realization that two other hive members were standing behind her, waiting to make use of it themselves. Restless and preoccupied, she wandered off.

She would wait until the night shift, she resolved. Not to speak with Desvenbapur, but to assure herself that all was well with him. This she could do by speaking briefly with others who worked in his department. Even deprived of sleep, she was confident she could perform her duties tomorrow adequately, if not commendably.

She passed the remaining portion of the day shift exploring the immediate vicinity, finding it, as expected, a veritable duplicate of her own. As shifts began their switch, she made her way back to the kitchen area and lingered in its vicinity, randomly querying those arriving to begin work. None knew of an assistant food preparator who went by the name of Desvenbapur.

By the time the last worker had arrived she found herself growing concerned. What if the transfer had not worked out and he was ill? A check of medical records for the entire colony took only an instant. It did not show a Desvenbapur listed as being among the unwell.

This was senseless, she told herself. Obviously, today was an off-period, a rest time for her friend. He would return to work tomorrow. And she could not wait around and eschew her own labor simply to assure herself that he was all right.

But why hadn't she been able to find at least one coworker who recognized his name? He had been assigned to this sector long enough to

have established, if not intimate friendships, at least casual acquaintances. From what she knew and had seen of his work, an assistant food
preparator did not function in a vacuum.

Perplexed, she waited until the terminal was free to again call up the
rostering for food preparation in this zone. There was his name on the list,
bold and unmistakable. Not being assigned herself to the kitchen division, she could not access individual shift assignments. But she *could*
locate anyone's place of habitation. This she proceeded to do.

There it was: Desvenbapur, habitat level three, cell quadrant six,
cubicle eighty-two. She contemplated the readout for a long moment,
wavering. Then, antennae set determinedly forward, she strode off along
the appropriate corridor.

It did not take long to locate the living quarters in question. A pass
with her scri!ber over the door ident revealed the occupant to be one
Desvenbapur, assistant food preparator. Proof enough of his residence—
but not of his health. Still, she hesitated. Request admittance, and she
risked jeopardizing their consanguinity. Depart now, and she would preserve it, but without having achieved any personal satisfaction after having come all this way and spent all this time.

Perhaps she had acquired some of her friend's intermittent hints of
irrationality. Perhaps she was simply stubborn. In any event, she resolved
to wait for him.

The following day shift passed without any sign of her quarry. By
now her own shift supervisor would have marked her as absent and initiated a routine search to ascertain her location, health, and status. Her
unauthorized absence would go down on her permanent work record, she
knew, inhibiting opportunity for advancement and commendation. She
did not care. The second night shift arrived, and still the door to cubicle
eighty-two remained sealed.

What if he was inside, having suffered some serious harm? A dual
coronary arrhythmia, perhaps, with both hearts beating out of cadence.
Or a severe intestinal blockage. Curiosity turned to concern, which begat
fear. Rising from the resting position in which she had been settled for
more than a day, she struggled on stiffened legs to the nearest general
accessway and called for a domicile supervisor.

The female responsible for this section of living quarters responded
promptly, listened to Jhywinhuran's weary concerns, and agreed that the
situation she was describing demanded some sort of resolution. Accordingly, permission was obtained to make an unauthorized entry into private quarters. As she followed the supervisor down the corridor,
Jhywinhuran was beset with conflicting emotions. If something grave had

happened to Desvenbapur, she would be severely depressed. If, on the other truhand, there was nothing wrong, she would undoubtedly find herself on the receiving end of a well-deserved stream of imprecation.

She discovered that she could hardly breathe as the supervisor utilized an override to break the seal on the cubicle and slide back the door. They entered together. The interior of the compact living space was neat, clean, spotless; from the rest and relaxation chamber to the smaller area reserved for the carrying out of individual hygiene. In fact, it was more than spotless.

It had not been lived in for some time.

"There must be some mistake." Her gestures were clumsy, her words hesitant as she surveyed the immaculate, obviously untouched quarters. "His ident is on the door."

The supervisor checked her own scri!ber. Reflexively gesturing confusion, she checked it again. And a third time. When she looked up, the commingled movements of her limbs and antennae indicated more than simple puzzlement.

"You are right. There *is* a mistake. This living cubicle is unassigned."

Mandibles moving slowly against one another, Jhywinhuran stared at the senior female. "But his full ident is imprinted on the entrance."

"It certainly is. Be assured that I am no less curious than you to find out how and why it is there."

Jointly, they ran detailed searches. No assistant food preparator of any name had been placed in cubicle eighty-two by residential assignment. Yes, one named Desvenbapur had been transferred to the subsidiary kitchens. No, he could not be located. Perhaps his scri!ber was turned off or had run down without being noticed. Follow-up queries of every single worker assigned to food preparation in this sector revealed no knowledge of a Desvenbapur. Nor could anyone by that name be located *anywhere*, in any sector.

"Something is very wrong here," declared the supervisor as she concluded her searching.

Jhywinhuran was still working her scri!ber. "I agree, but what? He told me, told everyone he worked with, that he was being transferred to food preparation in this sector. His name is on the work roster."

"Just as his name is on the door to these quarters." The two females considered the situation. "Let me run one more search."

Jhywinhuran waited while the senior female waltzed the delicate fingers of her truhands over her unit. Moments later she looked up again, her antennae aimed directly at her visitor. "There is no record of a transfer to this sector being authorized for anyone in food preparation, or specifically, anyone named Desvenbapur."

"Then . . . he lied." Jhywinhuran could barely muster the appropriate clicks to underscore her reply.

"So it would seem. But why? Why would this friend of yours, or any thranx, lie about being shifted from one part of the hive to another?"

"I do not know." The sanitation worker stridulated softly. "But if he isn't here, and he isn't there, then where is he? And why is he wherever he is?"

"I do not know either, but unless something emerges to indicate otherwise, what we have here is unequivocal evidence of antisocial behavior. I am sure it will all become clear when he is located."

When he was not, something akin to alarm set in not only among those thranx charged with locating the errant assistant food preparator, but among their human associates as well.

Jhywinhuran found herself waiting in an empty interrogation chamber. It was of modest size and in no way remarkable except for the presence among the usual resting benches of a trio of very peculiar sculptures whose purpose she was unable to divine. They looked like tiny benches, much too small to provide surcease and comfort to even a juvenile thranx. Instead of being open and easily accessed, one side of each of the squarish objects was raised above the rest, so that even if you tried to settle your abdomen across it, the stiff raised portions would make it next to impossible.

The hive had been turned upside down in the search for the missing assistant food preparator. When it was determined to a specific degree of assurance that not only was he no longer present in the hive, but that his body could not be found, a startled Jhywinhuran had found herself called away from her labor and ordered to this room. There she sat, and waited, and wondered what in the name of the lowest level of the supreme hive was going on.

She did not have to wait long.

Four people filed into the chamber. Two of them between them had only as many limbs as she did. She had seen humans around the hive before, but not often. They did not frequent the section of the colony where she worked, and she had had no actual contact with them herself. From her predeparture studies she was able to discern that both genders were represented. As was common among humans, their skin and single-lensed eye color varied markedly. These and other superficial physical variations she expected. She also was not surprised when they sat down in two of the peculiar constructs whose function had so puzzled her. She winced inwardly, unable to see how any being, even one as flexible as a human, could call "relaxing" a posture that required the body to almost fold itself in half.

But she was startled when conversation commenced, and the humans participated—speaking not in their own language but in a crude, unsophisticated, yet impressively intelligible rendition of Low Thranx.

"How long have you known the assistant food preparator who calls himself Desvenbapur?" The human female blundered slightly over the correct pronunciation of the title.

Jhywinhuran hesitated, taken aback by both the nature of the question and its source. She looked to the two thranx present for advice, only to have the eldest gesture compliance. Not politely, either. Clearly, something serious was afoot.

"I met him on the *Zenruloim* on the journey out from Willow-Wane. He was pleasant company, and as there were only four of us bound for this world, we naturally struck up an acquaintance. I also met and became friends with the engineers Awlvirmubak and Durcenhofex."

"They do not concern us and are not involved in this matter," the eldest thranx explained, "because they are not only where they are, they are who they are."

She gestured bewilderment. "I don't understand."

"Neither do we," the elder responded. "That is one of the purposes of this meeting: to reach understanding." His antennae bobbed restlessly as he spoke, indicating no especial sentiment: only a continuing unease. "Your friend has gone missing."

"I know. I helped to file the report."

"No, you don't know," the elder corrected her. "I do not mean that he has gone missing in the accepted sense. I mean that he is nowhere to be found anywhere in the hive."

"Nor," added the male human somewhat melodramatically, "is his corpse."

"The inescapable conclusion," the younger of the two thranx told her, "is that he has gone outside."

"Outside?" Jhywinhuran's confusion gave way to disbelief. "You mean, he has left the colony? Voluntarily?"

The elder genuflected sadness mixed with concurrence. "So it must be assumed."

"But *why*?" Acknowledging her acceptance of the human's presence, she included them in her question as well as the pair of somber supervisors. "Why would he do such a thing? Why would any member of the colony?"

The female human crossed one leg completely over another, an intriguing gesture no thranx could emulate half so fluidly. Jhywinhuran wondered at its hidden meanings. "We were really hoping you could shed some light on that, Jhywinhuran."

Hearing her name emerge from an alien throat, complete to the appropriate whistle-and-click accentuation, was a novelty the sanitation worker did not have time to enjoy. "I assure you all I have no idea."

"Think," the elder prodded her. "This is important beyond anything you can imagine. We are already, with the aid of our human friends, searching the surface above and around the colony for this absent individual, but it would be of considerable use to know who and what we are searching for."

"You keep speaking of Desvenbapur as though he doesn't exist." Something deep inside her felt bound to rise, however feebly or ineffectively, to the defense of an acquaintance who had brazenly lied to her.

The two thranx exchanged gestures. It was left to the younger to explain. "He doesn't. *Crrik,* the individual you know as Desvenbapur certainly does, but that is not his identity. When your report was filed and it was determined that the individual was no longer residing within the colony, a thorough background check was run on him in the hopes of learning or at least obtaining some clue as to what might have prompted him to engage in such intemperate behavior. Given the seriousness of his apparent transgression, the check was correspondingly detailed.

"It included a search, via a surreptitious space-minus relay operated by our human friends, of records that extend all the way back to Willow-Wane—not only professional records but personal ones as well. A portion of the finished report was so extraordinary that despite the difficulty and expense a recheck was demanded. It only confirmed that which had preceded it."

"What did you find out?" The two humans were temporarily forgotten.

The younger supervisor continued the story. "Something this serious activates, as one of multiple automatic searches, a full family background check. The records of the Hive Ba show no mention of a Desvenbapur living or recently deceased."

None of the four thranx mandibles were capable of dropping, in the human sense, but Jhywinhuran succeeded in conveying her astonishment at this astounding announcement by means of a simple truhand gesture. "Then who is he?"

"We think we know," the elder told her. "He is very clever, this individual, far more resourceful than one would expect of an assistant food preparator."

"I always thought him so." Her horizontal mandibles clicked softly while the verticals remained motionless. She was more than a little dazed by this latest revelation.

"It all fits together." The younger supervisor was gesturing corroboration. "Tell me, Jhywinhuran: Did your absent friend at any time ever express a more-than-passing interest in the composition of poetry?"

This time she could only stare at her interrogators in stupefied silence. It did not matter. Her hush was sufficiently eloquent.

The senior supervisor continued, his mandibles moving methodically. "On Willow-Wane there was no Desvenbapur. Or Desvenhapur or Desvenkapur. Background investigation discovered a Desventapur, an elderly and well-known electronics mapper who lives in the Hive Wevk. Also a Desvenqapur, a harvester drone residing in Upper Hierxex." He shifted his abdomen on his resting bench.

"There is also a Desvengapur who is not only the right age, but also shows an interest in formal composition for purpose of performance."

"Is that the real person, the one we are talking about?" a shaky Jhywinhuran heard herself asking.

The supervisor gestured negativity. "Desvengapur is a mid-age female."

The younger of the pair took over, his speech becoming harsh and accusatory, the clicks sharper, his whistles shriller. "No living representative of the Hive Ba bears the name Desvenbapur. But on Willow-Wane there *was* an aspiring young poet sufficiently accomplished to be assigned the designation of soother. He managed to have himself appointed to the human outpost at Geswixt."

The human male chipped in. "Apparently this individual, for reasons we still do not know, desired contact with my kind."

"His name," the supervisor continued, "was Desvendapur. A real, existing person, according to all personnel background checks and official records."

A poet, she found herself thinking. A designated soother. No wonder her friend's "amateur" efforts had struck her as so wonderfully accomplished. There had been nothing amateurish about them, or about him, she reflected bleakly.

"He changed his name and his records." Her voice was dull, methodical, the words rising without difficulty to her mandibles. "He falsified his history and learned the trade of assistant food preparator. But why?"

"Apparently, in hopes of gaining assignment to the colony there," the female human responded. "Why he did this we still don't know. We'd certainly like to."

"Truly," declared the senior supervisor, "an explanation of his motivation would be most welcome. This Desvendapur is an individual who has been driven to take extreme measures."

Jhywinhuran indicated assent. "To make up a false identity, to equivocate repeatedly . . ." A sudden thought made her hesitate. "Wait. I can see how he could remake himself as an assistant food preparator named Desvenbapur, but what about his original self? Wouldn't it be missed, not only at Geswixt but elsewhere?"

"This Desvendapur's cleverness extends well beyond a talent for concocting agreeable phrases." The supervisor's tone was dark. "He participated in a short but unauthorized flight from Geswixt to the project outpost on Willow-Wane. On the return flight, the lifter that had conveyed him crashed in the mountains. It was presumed that everyone aboard perished in the fiery crash. Shortly thereafter, the name of one Desvenbapur appeared on the work rolls of the human outpost as an assistant food preparator."

She gestured astonishment. "How fortunate he was. That must have been a remarkable stroke of luck for him and for his plans, for I assume based on what you have told me that he must have been intending something like that for a long time."

"Certainly he was," the other supervisor readily agreed, "however there is now some question as to how 'lucky' he might have been."

"What are you implying, Venerable?" she stammered.

"The crash of his transportation on its return journey to Geswixt, leaving him an illegal and therefore unrecognized presence in the project outpost, is simply too convenient to be any longer considered a coincidence. Though much time has passed since this incident occurred, the appropriate authorities are even now reviewing the relevant records." He gestured with all four hands. "It is considered a distinct possibility that your friend contrived the crash of his transportation on its return flight to Geswixt in order to obliterate his old identity while providing an opportunity for him to create and adopt a new one."

While she was digesting this inconceivable volley of information, the female human commented, in that terse, tactless fashion for which humans were both famed and notorious, "What Eirmhenqibus is saying is that your absent friend, in addition to putting in jeopardy everything we have worked to achieve here, may also be a murderer." She had some difficulty with the appropriate accents for the thranx term for "one who kills its own kind," but Jhywinhuran had no trouble comprehending what had been said.

"I . . . I find that hard to believe."

"Then you are in good company in this room," the senior supervisor assured her. "Murder, falsification of identity, illegal assignation of profession, and now escapement. This Desvendapur has much to answer for."

"It is not something I would have expected of a soother." The other supervisor was quietly incredulous. "Your friend must be found, and quickly."

Both humans nodded assent. "This part of Earth was chosen for the colony not only because the climate is conducive to your kind," the female said, "but because it represents one of the last and largest regions on the planet in which the imprint of humankind has not been heavy. Very few people come here, and those that do travel about under strict supervision or professional guidance. But if anyone should see this Desvendapur, engaged in whatever purpose he is bent upon, he will immediately be recognized for what he is: an alien wandering about on a part of the Earth's surface where no alien is supposed to be."

"I do not think I need remind you," the male roughly told her, "about the delicate nature of the ongoing negotiations between your species and ours. Your . . . appearance . . . unfortunately, is off-putting to those of our kind who have not yet learned how to look beyond shape in the course of establishing relations. The great mass of humanity is still not entirely comfortable with the realization that there are other intelligent species, nor the possibility that some may be more intelligent than themselves. There exists a historical racial paranoia that is only slowly being eroded by contact with such as the thranx.

"The revelation that an illegal colony has been established here, in a part of the world where an alien presence is not officially authorized, could cast a serious pall on future as well as current relations between our respective species. In another ten or fifteen years, when the population of Earth has had a reasonable period of time in which to become used to your existence and appearance, the long-term existence of the colony will officially be made public. Realizing that your kind has lived among us in harmony and without friction for a studied length of time should, our psychologists tell us, greatly facilitate the formalizing of relations."

"But not yet," the female concluded. Jhywinhuran thought she looked tired, as if she had not slept in several days. "It is too soon—much too soon. The consequences that could result from premature disclosure are alarming."

The sanitation worker did not hesitate. In spite of any personal feelings she might retain for the engaging individual whose true name it appeared was Desvendapur, she was a dutiful and conscientious member of a hive. As such, she knew that the security and integrity of the community could not be compromised.

"I understand that he must be found and brought back before his existence is discovered by any passing humans. I will help in any way I can." She gestured sharply with a truhand. "Knowing him and being somewhat familiar with his nature, I can say that having gone to the trouble and extremes you have described, he may prove reluctant to comply."

It would have been better had one of the supervisors responded, but with the abruptness for which they were noted, it was the male human who replied first.

"If that proves to be the case, then of course we'll have to kill him."

19

An irritated Cheelo was about to respond to the alien's question, but before he could, a muted hum began to tickle his ears. Scanning the surrounding rain forest, he found his gaze being drawn to the tributary from which the striking anaconda had erupted. Ignoring the thranx's queries, he walked to the water's edge and squinted upstream. The hum grew no louder, but neither did it disappear.

"What are you doing?" Putting tentative pressure on his splinted middle leg, Desvendapur eyed the silent human curiously. "If you think after all this time that you're now going to persuade me that you are a naturalist by pretending to be engaged in some kind of profound observational behavior of the local fauna, you are—"

"Shut up!" Cheelo snapped. His tone more than the curt human words induced the poet to hold his peace. Or perhaps it was the hand gesture that accompanied the admonition; a sharp, downward chopping motion that Desvendapur had not encountered before.

The poet waited until he could stand the continuing silence no longer. Mindful of the human's warning, he kept his voice low as he moved forward to stand alongside the biped. The human's aspect and attitude were indicative of a sudden wariness.

"What's going on?"

"Don't you hear it? That vibrating sound?"

Desvendapur gestured affirmatively, then remembered to nod. "Certainly. While our sense of hearing is not as acute as yours, it is perfectly adequate." He tested the air with his antennae, seeking some radical new aroma, but caught nothing. "Some local animal, a forest dweller."

"Like hell it is." Putting out a hand, Cheelo urged the alien back into the undergrowth. Together they concealed themselves as best they could behind and beneath houseplants that here in their natural habitat grew to the size of small trees.

Wordlessly, he pointed at the eagle as it came gliding down the creek, its head panning slowly from side to side. Putting aside the queasiness that arose as a consequence of contact with soft, flexible mammalian flesh, Desvendapur indicated that he understood the situation. Only when he was certain that the eagle had passed well out of sight did Cheelo emerge from the brush and indicate that the thranx could do likewise.

"I do not understand." Antennae dipped and weaved balletically as Desvendapur gazed down the streambed, then turned back to the still-watchful human. "That was a particularly dangerous creature? Poisonous, perhaps, or stronger than it appeared?"

"That wasn't no damn bird at all. Eagles *scream*. They don't hum." Single-lensed brown eyes regarded the alien. "It was a machine. I've seen it before, or another one like it. I'm hoping it was nothing more than a routine, preprogrammed forest service overflight. I don't know what their inspection and censusing schedule is like. Didn't realize until I came here that the forest service used such sophisticated scanners. I guess they disguise them like the local critters so as not to alarm the fauna."

"This forest service you speak of may in fact not do that." Desvendapur eyed his human companion evenly.

Cheelo frowned. "Bug, is there something you're not telling me?"

Truhands crocheted the atmosphere. "There might be. Just as there is something you are not telling me. If I explain myself, will you reciprocate?"

"*Ay*. Yeah, sure." Still listening for any indication that the camouflaged scanner might be returning, Cheelo crossed his arms over his narrow chest and settled himself back against a tree.

"I suspect that cloaked device does not belong to any recognized human agency."

The perplexed human's expression contorted. "What do you mean, 'recognized'?"

"I think I know why it was so well disguised. It was not meant to be identified by your local authorities. It was designed to blend in with the local life-forms. And I think it was looking for *me*."

"For *you*?" Cheelo hesitated, then nodded knowingly. "Oh, right. Your fellow expedition members are looking for you. What is it? Past time for you to rejoin them?" Though still hopeful of finding some way of making money off the alien, Cheelo remained ambivalent about its presence and realized he wouldn't exactly be averse to its departure, either. It was slowing him down.

"Truly. But it has been time for me to rejoin them ever since I left."

The human shook his head impatiently. Explanations were not supposed to further confuse. "I don't get it."

"I am not supposed to be here."

"What? You snuck off on your own?" Cheelo chuckled softly. "How about that? A bug with balls."

"Since I have yet to master your extensive catalog of colloquialisms I will not comment on that observation. What I am saying is that I am not supposed to be here at all. In this place. On this planet."

This time Cheelo did not laugh. He stood away from the tree, his expression turning serious. "You mean your research expedition is an illegal one?"

Desvendapur hesitated only briefly. "How much can I trust you, Cheelo Montoya?"

"Completely." Expression blank, the human waited patiently.

"There is no research expedition." Turning his upper body slightly, the poet pointed eastward. "With the aid of certain select representatives of your own kind, a colony has been established in this part of your world."

"Colony? Of *bugs*?" Cheelo digested this, then shook his head sharply. "That's crazy! Even in a place as isolated as the Reserva Amazonia something like that would've been spotted before it got started."

Desvendapur begged to disagree. "Everything was done below the surface. Research, design, excavation, construction: everything. The colony's human sponsors provided and continue to provide the necessary cover to maintain our seclusion. Once the initial excavating was completed, expansion was not difficult. Or so the history that I studied of the colony declaims. I was assigned here. Unauthorized egress from the hive is strictly forbidden."

"This 'colony' of yours . . ." Cheelo hesitated uncertainly. This was bigger than he'd suspected. Much bigger. "It hasn't been authorized by the government, then? I mean, I don't exactly scan the media every day, but the big things, the major stories, you hear about them from other people. I've heard about your kind, but never anything about a bug colony."

"It is not authorized by your *visible* government," Desvendapur admitted readily. "Apparently only a few individuals from certain departments are involved. They have moved forward with this project on their own."

Like a child's building blocks, a crude but recognizable structure was assembling itself in Cheelo's brain. "So if this colony's been planted here on the sly, and nobody's supposed to know about it, and nobody from inside is supposed to go outside, then you're illegitimate twice over."

"That is correct."

Cheelo stood stunned, gaping at the calm, composed alien. Here he thought *he* was the one who had to be wary of discovery, and all along he had been traveling in the company of someone who had committed an offense beside which Cheelo Montoya's entire lifetime of minor misdeeds and infractions paled into insignificance. Every felony the part-time resident of Gatun and Golfito had committed had been provincial in nature, even the accidental killing in San José. Standing quietly before him was malfeasance on an interstellar scale.

He frowned. "Why're you telling *me* this?"

"To observe your reaction. I collect reactions." The thranx shifted on its trulegs, trying to spread his weight away from the injured, splinted limb. "I am not a researcher any more than you are a naturalist. I am a poet who seeks inspiration. I arranged to come here, to your world, in search of it. I illegally exited the colony in search of it." Like accusatory fingers, twin antennae were pointed directly at the biped. "It was in hopes of finding it that I went in search of humans who had not had prior contact with my kind."

Cheelo's thoughts swirled and collided. All the time the bug had been tagging along, it hadn't been studying the forest—it had been studying *him*. Not for scientific purposes, either. His bug was a goddamn artist, all right.

In his comparatively short lifetime Cheelo had thought of himself, envisioned himself, imagined himself as many things. A source of poetic inspiration was not one of them.

"What'll they do to you if they find you out here?" he asked pointedly.

"Take me back to the hive, to the colony. Debrief me. Ship me off-world as soon as proves feasible. Punishment will follow. Unless . . ."

"Unless what?"

"Unless my unauthorized sojourn here results in composition the likes of which has never been beheld before. I do not know how it is among humans, but among my kind great art excuses a multitude of transgressions. Additionally, all eminent artists are presumed to be at least partly mentally deranged."

Cheelo nodded. "Ay, I can see similarities." His expression darkened. "Just a minute. If nobody except these covert friends of your colony are supposed to know about its existence, and you've just told me all about it, then I'm compromised. You've compromised me." His eyes widened. "Shit, what'll they do to *me* if they find me in your company? I ain't going off to no bug world with you!"

"Obviously not. I imagine that either my people or yours will have to kill you to ensure your silence on the matter."

"My silence on the . . . ?" At that moment Cheelo wanted to reach out and choke the alien, except that constricting its neck would not result in a reduction in the supply of air to its lungs. It might be subject to suffocation in the coils of an anaconda, but not by any human. He could, however, by exerting diligence and all his strength, possibly break its neck. "Why'd you have to tell me all this? *Why?*" .

"You deserved to know. If that disguised scanner had discovered us and we had been picked up, you wouldn't have known the reason for it. Now you do. I did not have to tell you about the colony to compromise you. Simply being found in my company by searchers from the hive would be enough to doom you."

The biped stiffened. "Who's doomed? Not Cheelo Montoya! I've been hiding from searchers all my life! I've slipped safely in and out of places nobody else would go near. Unless I want them to, no bunch of goddamned illegal sweet-stinking bugs is going to find me, either!"

A thranx could only smile inwardly. "An intriguingly aggressive response for a self-proclaimed naturalist."

Cheelo started to shout something more, only to find himself strangling in mid-declaration. His lower jaw closed and his voice changed to a dangerous, angry mix of accusation and admiration. "Why you ugly, burrowing, big-eyed, toothless bug bastard. You think you're pretty clever, don't you?"

"That is a proven fact, not hypothesis," the thranx replied calmly. "Why not tell me what *you* are, man?"

"Sure. Ay, sure, why not? It doesn't matter. You can't exactly walk into the nearest police depot and turn me in, can you? Sure, I'll tell you." He gestured at the alien's thorax pouch. "Why don't you get out that scri!ber of yours and take it all down? You might get a goddamn poem or two out of it."

Oblivious to the human's sarcasm, an excited Desvendapur hurried to comply. Holding the compact instrument out toward the biped, the poet waited eagerly.

"I take things from people," Cheelo told him pugnaciously. "I was born without anything, I saw my mother die without anything, and I had a baby brother who died before he had a chance to know anything. I grew up learning that if you want anything in this world you've got to go out and get it, because nobody's going to give it to you. This is a pretty advanced planet. Lots of nice new technology, good medicine, easy to get around, a lot cleaner than it used to be. That much I learned from history. I do read, you know."

"I never doubted it." Desvendapur was absorbing not only the human's words, but his attitude, his posture, his wonderfully distorted facial expressions. Truly, the biped's ranting was a veritable fount of inspiration.

"Humankind's managed to get rid of a lot of things, a lot of the old troubles. But poverty isn't one of them. Not so far, not yet. I hear the sociologists argue about it a lot: whether there'll always be poor people no matter how rich the species becomes. Somebody always has to be on the bottom, no matter how high you raise the top." He shook his head sharply. "Me, I ain't going to stay on the bottom. When I found out I'd never be able to rise any other way, I started figuring out methods to take what I needed to lift me up. I'm not the only one, not by a flicker, but I'm better at it than some. That's why I'm standing here talking to you right now instead of licking my hospital dressings waiting to go in for a court-ordered selective mindwipe." There was something deeply gratifying about spilling his guts, even if only to an alien bug. Feeling more than a little reckless, he plunged on.

"I'm here right now because I killed somebody."

Desvendapur felt a thrill run through him. This was more than he could have hoped for: inspiration taken to and beyond a degree he could not have imagined in his wildest dreams. "You murdered another of your own kind?"

"It wasn't intentional," Cheelo protested. "I never meant to hurt nobody. Killing's bad for business. It just—happened. I needed the money. So I had to get away, to someplace where I could lose myself for a while." He gestured at the wild, all-enveloping rain forest. "This is a good place for that. Or it was, until I ran into you."

"You are still 'lost,' " Desvendapur assured him. "I will not give you away."

"You don't have to 'give me away.' " Cheelo's tone was accusing. "Like you said, all your brother bugs and their human friends have to do is find me with you and I'm history. Don't matter anyway. I was on my way out when you found me. I got an appointment. And you ain't helping me make it." Quietly, his hand strayed toward his gun.

"One more day." The thranx glanced skyward. "They haven't found me yet. I don't think they will, if I choose to continue hiding, but all I ask for is one more day in your company."

Cheelo's fingers hovered. Why wait? he told himself. Kill it now and move on. They'll find the body or they won't. Either way, he wouldn't be connected to it. As far as this unauthorized colony and its allies were concerned, he'd be just another solitary wanderer in the vast reaches of the rain forest.

But there was something in the alien's manner—an unrestrained eagerness, a desperation to learn, a need to achieve—that appealed strongly to something deep inside Cheelo Montoya. It wasn't that they were in any way alike: That was an absurd thought. Cheelo had never had a poetic or artistic impulse in his life, unless one counted the skill with which he relieved the unsuspecting and the unlucky of their valuables.

The camouflaged scanner had already passed this way. It was unlikely a second would be following it. Surely the resources of this secret colony were limited and any search it instituted, however frantic, must necessarily be circumspect. Otherwise it would attract the attention of the Reserva rangers or their own automatic monitoring devices. If he and the bug kept moving in the direction the eagle scanner had come from, they ought to be free of observation and safe from detection for quite a while.

Without really knowing why, he heard himself saying, "One day?"

The thranx nodded. Cheelo no longer thought the familiar gesture strange when executed by the alien. "One day. So that I may finish my note taking and observations and round them off smoothly and completely."

"I'm not sure I know what the hell you're talking about. I don't owe you nothing."

"No, you do not. Even though we are, in a way, spiritually of the same clan."

Cheelo frowned. "What are you babbling about?"

The thranx's tone did not change. "We are both outcasts, antisocials. And takers of life. I too am responsible for the death of another. All because I wish to compose something of importance."

There it was. This alien, this grossly oversized bug from another world, wanted to do something big, just like Cheelo Montoya.

No, he thought angrily, refusing to accept the analogy. We don't have anything in common! Not me and a goddamn bug! He said nothing aloud. What was there to say? He knew nothing of thranx society, of what it considered acceptable and what it did not, though he felt he could be certain of one thing: Surely among any intelligent species, the murder of one's fellows was considered inappropriate. He was wrong, but correct where the thranx were concerned.

"And if at the end of that time you remain tormented by uncertainties," Desvendapur was saying, "you can still kill me."

Cheelo started, his eyes widening slightly. "What makes you think I'd want to kill you?"

"It would be the logical thing to do." Two hands gestured in the direction of the human's holstered pistol. "I've seen your hands moving, up and down, back and forth in the direction of your concealed weapon, your gestures reflective of your changing mood. You have been thinking about it ever since we met. You could do it at any time."

"You're mighty confident I won't."

"No, I'm not." Antennae bobbed in a complex pattern. "I have been monitoring your pheromones. The levels rise and fall according to your state of mind. I know when you're thinking about killing me, and when you are not."

"You're reading my mind?" Cheelo gazed unblinkingly at the thranx.

"No. I'm reading your body odor. As I mentioned before, it is very strong. Even it is a source of suggestion to me." The heart-shaped head dipped slightly. "One more day."

"And then I can kill you? You just said yourself it would be the logical thing to do."

Again the alien nodded. "Very much so. But I don't think you will do it. If I did I would already have slipped away during the night."

Cheelo's tone was challenging. "What makes you so sure I won't do it?"

"Because you haven't already. And because doing the illogical thing, the unexpected, is what separates the exceptional individual from the great mass of the hive. Sometimes that individuality is not well regarded. In both our societies, iconoclasts and eccentrics are viewed with great suspicion."

"Well, I've sure as hell always been viewed with suspicion. One day." He considered. "All right. Tomorrow afternoon you go your way and I go mine."

"Agreed." The thranx gestured with both his scri!ber and with a foot-hand. "I already have enough material to nourish composition for several years. It wants only some framing, some greater context. If you would consent in the time we have remaining to us to answer a few questions, I will depart your company tomorrow very much content."

"Yeah, sure. But right now let's concentrate on getting away from *here*, okay?" Raising a hand, he pointed upstream. "Let's put some more distance between us and that airborne scanner."

Falling in alongside the human, Desvendapur held his scri!ber out, the better to pick up the biped's voice more clearly. "Please tell me: When you killed your fellow human, what did it feel like?"

Cheelo glanced over sharply, wishing he could read those compound eyes. But they only stared back, glittering in the light that filtered down through the canopy, siliceous gems set in blue-green chitin.

"What the hell kind of question is that?"

"A difficult one," the alien replied. "Easy answers make for weak poetry."

The interrogation, as Cheelo came to think of it, was relentless, continuing all through the remainder of the day and on into the night. What the thranx gained in response to queries that Cheelo felt waned from the irrelevant to the inane he could not imagine, but the alien seemed pleased by every reply, be it fleeting or lengthy. Cheelo endured it all, not really understanding the purpose, knowing that tomorrow he would be free of questions and questioner alike. Free to make the appointment in Golfito that would forever change his life.

He was awakened not by the sun or the chorusing of monkeys, not by demonstrative macaws or buzzing insects, but by a gentle prod to the shoulder.

"Later," he grumbled. "It's too early."

"I agree," came a familiar, soft, gently modulated voice, "but it is necessary. I do not think we are alone any longer."

Cheelo sat up fast, throwing off the blanket, instantly awake. "Your friends, come looking for you?"

"That is the peculiar thing. I see only evidence of passing, and it is not of the sort that traveling thranx would leave behind."

Cheelo frowned. "What sort of evidence?"

"Come and look."

Following the alien into the undergrowth, Cheelo was brought up short by a sight as expected as it was shocking. The pelts had been neatly stretched and hung to dry on racks fashioned of trimmed poles bound together with vine. There were signs of recent cooking as well as places where the soil had been compacted by repeated bootprints. No biologist, he still recognized the skin of the jaguar and the two margays. There was also a lightweight container that, on inspection, proved to be full of feathers plucked from dozens of macaws and other exotic rain forest birds.

Lowering the lid on the container, he found himself scanning the surrounding jungle anxiously.

"What strange human activity is this? Some peculiar ritual the local officials are required to perform?"

"It's a ritual, all right." Cheelo was already backing carefully out of the small, cramped clearing. "But it has nothing to do with local officials. Just the opposite." He nodded toward the forlorn skins drying in the heat of early morning. "This is a poacher camp."

"That is a term I am not familiar with." Scri!ber out, Desvendapur paralleled the human's retreat. He could not keep from turning to look back at the hollow-eyed skins hanging forlornly from their crudely rigged racks.

Cheelo's eyes darted from side to side, tree to bush, as he nervously scrutinized the surrounding forest. "Poachers slip into places like the

Reserva to steal whatever they can sell. Rare flowers for orchid collectors, rare bugs for insect collectors, exotic woods for furniture makers, mineral specimens, live birds and monkeys for the underground pet trade." He gestured at the covert encampment. "Bird feathers for decoration, skins for clothing."

"Clothing?" Desvendapur lowered his scri!ber as he looked back once more. "You mean, these people kill animals and strip off their skin so that humans can put them on?"

"That's about right." Alert for ants, snakes, and saw-jawed beetles, Cheelo pushed through a dense overlay of bright green leaves.

"But humans already have skin of their own. Beyond that, you manufacture what appears to be perfectly adequate artificial outerwear to protect your soft, sensitive exteriors from the elements. Why would anyone choose to wrap themselves in the skin of another living creature? Does the act involve some religious significance?"

"Some people might look at it that way." His mouth widened in a humorless grin. "I've seen rich folk who treat fashion like a religion."

"And they eat the flesh of the dead animal, too." Desvendapur struggled to convey his distaste but was not yet fluent enough to do so, having to resort to gestures to properly express his feelings on the matter.

"No. These people throw the rest of the animal away."

"So each creature is killed only for its epidermis?"

"Right. Unless they sell the teeth and claws, too. You getting enough inspiration out of this?"

"It all sounds vile and primitive. This mystifying mix of the sophisticated and the primal is all part of what marks you as a very peculiar species."

"You won't get no argument from me."

Though Desvendapur had no trouble keeping up, and in fact even with his broken middle leg moved more supply and easily through the forest than did the biped, he wondered aloud at the human's sudden desire for speed.

"The people running that camp would shoot you just as casually as they would a representative of an endangered species. Poaching in the Reserva is punishable by extensive mindwipe and a program of enforced social correctness. That's something I wouldn't ever submit to, and neither will whoever's smuggling out macaw feathers and cat pelts. We've already got your people looking for us. That's enough."

"Not quite enough."

Cheelo sucked in his breath. He could have kept going, could have tried to go around the muzzle of the weapon pointed in his direction, but that probably would have resulted in a journey of very brief duration.

There were two of them: very short men with very big guns. Their skin was the hue of burnished gold, their long black hair was tied unfashionably back, and they wore jungle mimic suits that allowed them to blend almost seamlessly into the landscape of bush and vine and tree. The tip of one rifle hovered uncomfortably close to Cheelo's nose.

He might have tried ducking, or slapping the barrel aside or grabbing it, or pulling his pistol if his antagonist had been operating alone. Unfortunately, he was not. His companion stood nearby but too far away to tackle, his own weapon held at the ready. Cheelo's fingers fell in the direction of his concealed holster. The poacher holding the rifle on him did not smile, did not speak. Only shook his head slowly, twice. Cheelo's hand drifted prominently away from his own weapon.

The other poacher stepped forward. After removing the pistol from its hiding place, he proceeded to pat the stranger down and remove his pack. Slinging Cheelo's belongings over one shoulder, he stepped aside to regard the thranx.

"What the hell is this, *cabrón?*"

Cheelo dropped his hands to his sides as the point of the rifle lowered from his nose to his chest. "That's an alien. A thranx. Don't you *ninlocos* watch the tridee?"

"Yeah, man." The other poacher laughed once, curtly. "And we have our own sensalude emporium here, too."

"It's a lonely life," the poacher shouldering Cheelo's backpack told him. "But it was good enough for my ancestors. Hapec and I do okay." The man's gaze darkened. "As long as nosybodies leave us alone to do our work." Dropping the backpack, he knelt and began going through its contents. After a while he looked up at his companion. "Not a ranger. Not a scientist, either." He eyed Cheelo speculatively as he rose. "He's a *pesadito*, a nobody."

"Good." His companion gestured with his rifle. "That means nobody'll miss him." The man's hard, unyielding gaze searched beyond the edgy Cheelo. "What do we do with the big bug?" Using the muzzle of the rifle he prodded Cheelo ungently in the stomach. "Where'd you get it, man, and what good is it?"

"Yeah," added his comrade. "What's an ugly alien thing like that doing in the Reserva, anyway? Does it speak Terranglo?"

Keeping a careful eye on the rifles, alert for any opportunity, Cheelo thought fast. "No, it doesn't. Something that looks like that? Are you kidding? It doesn't understand a word we're saying." Turning, he stared daggers at Desvendapur. "Its kind communicate by gestures. See, watch this." Raising both hands, he contorted his fingers strenuously at the thranx. The poet eyed the human's wiggling fingers askance. While he was not entirely sure of the newcomers' intentions, the fact that they were pointing weapons at Cheelo was something other than a testament to peaceful intentions. Their comments about his appearance did not trouble him, but their words, which despite Cheelo's ingenuous denial he understood with considerable faculty, caused him more than a little concern. The human's expressions he still could not read, but his companion's intent was clear enough: It might prove useful for one of them to feign ignorance of ongoing conversation. This he proceeded to do, replying to Cheelo's aimless manipulations with contrastingly eloquent gestures of his own. None of the humans had a clue what he was elucidating, but that was not the point. All that mattered was that they believed he and Cheelo were communicating.

"What did it say?" the nearer of the two poachers demanded to know.

Cheelo turned back to them. "It wants to know your intentions. I'd like to know myself."

"Sure," responded the other poacher agreeably. "First we're going to kill you, and then we're going to kill it, and then we're going to dump you both in the river." The muzzle of the second rifle shifted to point at the silent poet.

"You don't want to do that." Cheelo fought to keep his voice from shaking. He'd never begged anyone for anything before and he wasn't about to start now, but he wasn't ready to die, either.

The nearer poacher glanced over at his colleague and smiled unpleasantly. "Hear that, Hapec? Now he's telling us what we want." The rifle in his hands hummed softly with barely contained death. "We know what we want, man."

"I'm on my way up to Golfito, Costa Rica, to see Rudolf Ehrenhardt," Cheelo declared importantly. "He's expecting me on a matter of real importance."

"Too bad," responded the other poacher mirthlessly. "You're not going to make it."

He had wanted to lose himself, Cheelo reflected, and had done so. If these *ninlocos* didn't recognize the name of Rudolf Ehrenhardt, then he was in the middle of nowhere indeed. In a city, that name would have meant something, would have carried weight. Here, in the vast expanse of the Reserva, it was just a name. Of course, Ehrenhardt could not give a fig whether a hardscrabble lowlife like Cheelo Montoya lived or died. It was nothing to him. The cherished franchise promised to Cheelo would go to someone else. Since this pair did not know the name, it didn't matter anyway.

"Let us go," Cheelo pleaded. The second rifle was now pointed at the thranx, but he doubted he could wrestle the first away from its owner before his companion adjusted his aim and got off a shot. "We won't tell anyone you're around. What you're doing here is nothing to us." He spread his hands imploringly. "You don't understand. I *got* to make this appointment! It's my whole life, man."

"Sure." The poacher opposite laughed darkly. "We'll just trust you. That's how come Hapec and I have managed to bring this off for the past ten years: by trusting people. Now Hapec, he'd just off and shoot you right now. But me, I'm kind of a traditionalist. So I'll let you have any last words." He squinted past the thief, swatting away a hovering botfly. "You can ask the bug if it has any last gestures."

"You *can't* kill me!" Cheelo argued. "If you do, I won't be able to make my appointment!"

"Boy, that's tough. I'm all weepy inside." A finger nudged a trigger booster, and the hum from the rifle rose audibly.

Cheelo thought frantically. "Also, you'll have no way to communicate with the thranx."

The poacher shrugged. "Why would I worry about communicating with a dead alien body?"

"Because—because it's valuable. Probably valuable dead, but a lot more valuable alive."

The two wiry forest pillagers exchanged a glance. "Okay, *cabrón.* Talk. What's valuable about it?"

"You guys collect for the underground animal trade." He jerked a thumb in Desvendapur's direction. "Here's a specimen *nobody's* got, not even your richest, most private collector. If they'll buy a spotted tapir or a black jaguar, think what they'd pay for a live alien."

"Hey," declared the other poacher, "we know a couple of guys who got a number of aliens in their private zoos, but none of them are intelligent. That'd be pushing the limit."

"Who's going to know?"

On the verge of personal and financial triumph for the first time in his life, Cheelo was not to be denied now. He reasoned with all the skill at his command. Somehow, some way, he was going to make it back to Golfito in time to present the payment to Ehrenhardt. As for the thranx, he had ceased to think of it as a person, as a living, intelligent being like himself. It was a commodity, nothing more. He was bargaining with that commodity for his life.

"The bug doesn't talk, so it can't object. Nobody but your buyer and whoever he trusts will ever see it again. It can survive on terrestrial plants and stuff, so food's no problem. Come on, guys, you're not thinking *big* enough. Imagine what your top buyers would pay for something like this!"

It was evident from his expression that the nearest poacher was giving this heretofore unconsidered prospect careful consideration. Cheelo tried not to give him time to think it through.

"And if nobody bites on the offer, you can still kill us both later."

"We can kill you right now, man." Again the rifle bobbed. "We sell it, we don't need you."

"Sure you do. Because I'm the only one who can communicate with it. If you want it to come along peacefully, you need me to convince it to do so. You could try and catch it, roll it up in a net, fight with it, but it might get injured. Isn't an undamaged specimen always more valuable?"

"You stay right where you are," the poacher warned him. "You move, you try to run, you cross your eyes funny, you're dead. Understand?" Retreating slightly, he and his comrade entered into a conversation marked by intense whispering. Cheelo listened hard but could not make out what they were saying.

Eventually the discussion concluded, and the first poacher resumed his previous stance. "You still haven't told us what it's doing here."

"It's a naturalist," Cheelo informed them without hesitation. "Part of a small survey and study mission. But it's not authorized. So if this one turns up missing, the others can't go public for help. They're probably searching for him right now."

The other poacher reflexively glanced skyward. "If it's part of some alien science project, why would it come along quietly with us?"

Cheelo took a deep breath. "Because it wants to learn about humans. It trusts me. If I tell it we're going to go someplace where it can learn a lot about humankind, it'll take my word for it. Its cooperation will spare you a lot of trouble. By the time it catches on to what's going on, you'll already have it sold, crated, and shipped. Then it won't matter what it thinks."

Desvendapur listened to this exchange in silence. It was clear that his human companion was making up his story to forestall these two exceedingly antisocial types from shooting them. In this he so far appeared to be succeeding admirably. Meanwhile the poet kept silent and, as Cheelo had explained to the poachers, devoted himself to learning about humankind, a subject that was at present forcefully on display. He did not have to worry about either of the antisocials interpreting his hand movements because they were wholly unfamiliar with their meaning. As for them reading an expression, the inflexibly faced thranx had none to give away his true feelings.

"Why are you offering to be so helpful, *cabrón?*" The nearest poacher was studying him shrewdly. "What makes you think we won't kill you after we've sold the bug?"

Cheelo did his best to affect an air of disinterest. "I'd rather live for as long as possible. Besides, maybe whoever buys it will want to talk to it. That'd mean including me as part of the deal."

"You'd go along with that?" The other poacher was openly dubious.

"Sure, why not? The police are after me anyway."

"No shit? What'd you do, man?"

"Killed a tourist I was skragging. Bad luck, but that's not much of a defense in court. So you see, I'm probably on more wanted lists than you guys."

"And you think that maybe makes us some kind of brothers or something?" the nearer poacher asked.

Cheelo eyed him coldly. "No. If you thought that, I'd think you were pretty stupid."

For the first time, the poacher's expression softened. "You're okay, man. Twitch the wrong way and I'll still blow your stinking head off, but you're okay. All right. Explain to the bug that we're, um, collectors authorized to cull certain Reserva species that have bred to excess. We're carrying weapons to protect ourselves from dangerous forest predators. Tell the bug that we sympathize with its aims, that we've no love for the Reserva rangers who sometimes interfere with our work, and that we're going to take him to a museum." He glanced over at his colleague and chuckled. "A museum where he can learn a *lot* more about humans. Explain that it'll be well looked-after, and that you're coming along to translate. Tell it that after a couple of days we'll bring it back here so it can rejoin its colleagues. It'll have lots of swell stories to tell." He gestured with the rifle. "*Tell* it."

Turning, Cheelo stared into those expressionless compound eyes and began making snaky motions with his fingers. Would the bug understand? It had heard everything, but would it comprehend the need to keep silent and go along with the story? If not, at least one of them wasn't going to leave this patch of rain forest alive, and it would in all likelihood be the one with the fewest appendages.

He need not have worried. Desvendapur understood the situation quite well. He had no intention of speaking out. Clearly his human acquaintance had something in mind, a plan that would result in their salvation from these two virulently antisocial representatives of his own species. What that might be he did not know and could not imagine, unfamiliar as he was with the myriad mysterious workings of the human mind. Meanwhile he was delighted to observe and to listen. Already the experience had generated raw material enough for an entirely new suite, one that he would hopefully live long enough to render.

After several minutes of aimless, meaningless writhing, Cheelo turned around to confront their captors. "It has accepted my explanation and wants to know when we're going to leave."

"Tonight, man." The poacher gestured at his companion. Setting his rifle aside, Hapec moved off into the undergrowth. "I'm not going to tie you up because that might give your bug friend the wrong idea. Just don't do anything stupid."

Cheelo raised both hands, palms facing the poacher. "We've got an arrangement. Why should I risk it? If you can get me out of this hemisphere I'll be better off than I would if we'd never met." His gaze wandered to the patch of forest that had swallowed the other poacher. "We're going to walk at night? A GPS will show you the right way, but it won't light it for you."

The poacher hesitated uncertainly, then laughed anew. "You think we're going to walk? Man, if we had to rely on our feet the rangers would've caught us *years* ago. We've got an airtruck back in the trees. Mesyler two-ton carrying capacity, stealth construction, heat-signature-masked engine. Paid for, too. Not many people know this country like Hapec and me or how to get around the Reserva security net. We're *good*, man. We'll *fly* out. In an hour we'll be at a little place we keep just outside the Reserva boundary. You get to rest there while we put the word out to our regular people that we've got something special for sale." He grinned again. "You didn't think we were going to march you into Cuzco and stick you in a street stall with a price tag on your forehead, did you?"

Cheelo shrugged, trying to appear neither too smart nor unreasonably ignorant. "I don't know you *vatos*. I don't know how you operate. I wasn't assuming anything."

"Good, that's good." Extracting a smokeless stimstick from a shirt pocket, the poacher waited for it to ignite before slipping the aromatic mouthpiece between his lips. "Just don't assume that I won't fry your head the first time you piss me off."

20

While the poacher named Hapec busied himself breaking down the camp and carefully obliterating any memory of its existence, his colleague, whose name was Maruco, kept a watchful eye on their two prisoners. He concentrated his attention on the fidgety Cheelo, allowing Desvendapur to roam freely through the evaporating encampment. Whenever it looked as if the thranx might be wandering too far afield, Maruco directed his human prisoner to "call" the alien back. This Cheelo proceeded to do with much meaningless flailing of fingers. Desvendapur continued to fulfill his part in the masque by waiting for Cheelo to finish each charade before complying, not with the human's gestures, but with the directives the poet had already perfectly comprehended.

In this manner the two poachers remained ignorant of the alien's cognizance. Had Desvendapur possessed a weapon, he could simply have shot both of them. But all he had was the small cutting tool in his improvised survival kit. Granted complete surprise, he might have employed it successfully to incapacitate one of the two antisocials, but not both of them. They were too lively, too alert, too attuned to a life of imminent threat and danger. Additionally, while not directly suspicious of the alien in their midst, neither were they especially comfortable in the thranx's presence. Consequently, he was never able to get within a few meters of either of them before they began acting uneasy.

One such experimental advance caused Maruco to comment. "Tell the bug to keep its distance, man. God, but it's repulsive! Smells good, though. Myself, I think you're personally bent, but your suggestion is straight: Somebody *will* pay plenty for it." He shrugged, holding his rifle casually—though not casually enough. "Me, I wouldn't keep another intelligence in captivity, but I never understood the people who do keep animals. Hapec and I, we don't even keep monkeys."

"Why do you guys stick with this?" Cheelo was genuinely curious. His attention wandered without ever entirely ignoring the poacher's weapon. Given a reasonable chance of success, he'd make a grab for it. Such an opportunity had not yet presented itself. "Rangers and security scanners must be all over the Reserva. Is poaching a few skins and feathers that profitable?"

"Hapec and me, we do all right. But it's more than that. Our ancestors lived free here, hunting and fishing all over this country. They took what they wanted, when they needed it. When the Reserva was drawn up and its boundaries formalized, everybody who lived here was kicked out and resettled on the borders of their former homelands. All in the name of preserving a lousy bunch of plants and animals and a natural CO_2 exchanger for the atmosphere. Like the planet was going to run short on oxygen, anyway." His tone was bitter. "This is Hapec's and my way of getting a little back, of reasserting our ancestral claims to this land."

Cheelo nodded somberly. "I can understand that." Privately he thought the poacher's explanation was a facile rationalization heavily layered with pretentious bullshit. Their two captors kept slipping into the Reserva not to honor their ancestors but because they were making a nice, cushy, illicit living, and for no other reason. Taking revenge for some long-forgotten, sketchily remembered great-grandpa had nothing to do with it. He'd known small-time *ninlocos* like Hapec and Maruco all his life, had grown up with them. Maybe it made them feel a little better to conduct their miserable, self-serving offenses under the cover of an agreeable fiction. Cheelo Montoya didn't buy it for a minute. What the ingenuous insectile in his company thought of the situation he couldn't imagine. Nor could he find out if he wanted to, at least not for a while. To ensure that Cheelo's captors kept him alive it was necessary for the bug to continue to play mute.

Rustling noises rose from behind the encampment, back among the denser undergrowth. Cheelo strained to see. "So, this little place of yours: Where is it?"

"You'll see soon enough." As Maruco spoke, his partner began to remove from their stretchers and carefully fold the partially cured jaguar and margay pelts. When he had finished with that, he resumed breaking camp, reducing everything to a pile of poles, bindings, and disparate organic waste. This was then scattered among the concealing brush, to decay and disintegrate, along with any indication that people had ever spent any time at this particular spot.

"Must be rough." Cheelo was under no illusion that his attempts at casual conversation would ingratiate him with their captors, but in lieu of any alternative activity, it would have to suffice. "Having to tear down and make a new camp every time you come into the Reserva."

Maruco was dismissive. "Gets easier with practice. You learn what trees make the best hide stretchers, what vines are the most supple and easiest to work. Why do you give a damn?" He grinned nastily. "Thinking of going into competition?"

"Not me." Cheelo shook his head. "I'm a city boy."

"I figured. You skin different game."

As soon as the airtruck was loaded, the two captives were herded on board. Cheelo found nothing exceptional about the vehicle. He'd seen camouflaged stealth transport before. But Desvendapur was fascinated. It was the first complex piece of purely human technology he had encountered in person, and every facet of it, from the layout of the instrumentation to the design of the climate-controlled interior, was new to him. There was, of course, no place for him to sit down. For thranx purposes, the floor was more accommodating than the seats designed for humans. He chose to stand, balancing himself as the vehicle lifted in virtual silence from its hiding place to rise into the canopy.

Though it took four times as long as a straight flight would have, Maruco followed a course that kept them below spreading crests of the forest emergents, utilizing the canopy for cover whenever possible and only rising above it when the airtruck threatened to leave too expansive a path of destruction in the form of broken branches and snapped lianas in its wake. From time to time the closely entangled rain forest gave way to meandering streams and the occasional *cocha* that allowed him to fly low at higher speeds without leaving a trail behind.

Only when the first foothills hove into view among the mists and low-hanging clouds was Cheelo moved to comment. "I thought you said this place of yours was just outside the Reserva?"

"It is." Maruco spoke without turning while his partner kept a watchful eye and the muzzle of a rifle trained on their human captive. "If you're familiar with the area, then you know the western border of the Reserva runs right up this side of the Andes."

Cheelo watched the foothills give way rapidly to steep, green-shrouded slopes. "I know. I just assumed your place would be down low, where you could hide it in the trees."

Maruco smiled knowingly as the airtruck, following a gorge, commenced a steady climb. "That's what any rangers patrolling the fringes would think. So we set ourselves up right out in the open, up where it's barren and cold and uncomfortable. What stupid *chingóns* would stick themselves out on a treeless ridge for everybody to see? Not anybody running a poaching operation, right?"

"We've never had any trouble," Hapec chipped in. "Nobody checks on us or our little shack." He revealed a mouthful of gleaming, artificial, ceramic teeth. Light gold was currently a fashionable dental tint. "Anybody asks, we tell 'em we're running a private bird-watching operation."

"It's not a whole lie." Maruco was in a jovial mood. "We do watch birds. And if they're rare enough, we also snare and sell 'em."

As the airtruck entered the zone of cloud forest and the permanent mists that cloaked the mountainsides in lugubriously wandering blankets of gray and white, the poacher switched from manual to instrument driving. Earlier, the dehumidifier had shut down and the vehicle's internal climate control had switched over from cool to heat. Meanwhile Cheelo continued the meaningless banter that fooled no one. If provoked, either of the two poachers would as soon shoot him as spit on him. He knew it, and he knew they knew he knew it. But it was better than dead silence or trading insults. At least he might learn something.

Desvendapur certainly was. Not only the journey but the edgy conversation taking place between the three humans continued to provide him with an unbridled flow of suggestion, stimulation, and inspiration. Unable to freely utilize his scri!ber for fear that their captors might appropriate it, he concentrated on observing and remembering all that he could. Tenseness and barely concealed agitation were racial characteristics his kind had abandoned in favor of polite communion hundreds of years ago. In a highly organized society that chose to dwell underground in eternally close quarters, courtesy and politeness were not merely encouraged, they were an absolute necessity.

Humans, apparently, fought and argued at the slightest provocation. The energy they expended in such recurrent confrontations was breathtaking to behold: wasteful, but fascinating. It seemed they had stamina to spare. The most excitable thranx was more circumspect and conservative. The knowledge that they intended to sell him into some kind of captivity did not engage him half so much as their constant bickering. Captivity, if it occurred, would not be so bad. It would allow him to continue studying humankind at close quarters. He doubted, however, that his troubled human companion felt similarly.

It was him these antisocial humans wanted, not Cheelo Montoya. Neither did the poet have further need for the self-confessed thief. More than once Desvendapur thought about speaking up, revealing to the two poachers his fluency in their language. The only reason he did not was because he knew it would mean the death of his companion. While that would be, based on what he knew of Cheelo and what the man had told him, small loss to the species, it contravened any number of thranx rules of conduct. Recreant that he was, Desvendapur was not prepared to break with custom and culture to that extent. At least, not yet. For the moment it was more amusing to play the game, to listen to the new humans make comments about him convinced that he understood nothing of what they were saying.

After a substantial interval the airtruck rose out of the clouds and into sunshine so bright and unfiltered it was painful. In the pure, cerulean distance rose peaks that effortlessly crested five thousand meters. Just ahead, a stony, intermittently green plateau rolled off to the west: hills standing atop mountains. The only signs of habitation were a few detached farmhouses and long stretches of mountainside covered with phototropic sheeting to protect the potatoes and other crops thriving beneath.

On the eastern edge of a high ridge stood a modest, unspectacular domicile attached by a pedestrian corridor to a slightly larger structure. A roll-up door retracted as the airtruck approached. Guiding the vehicle in manually—use of its automatic docking system ran the risk of sending out faint but detectable signals curious rangers might pick up—Maruco brought it to a stop in the exact center of the garage when the appropriate telltale on the truck's console turned green. A flip of one switch and the vehicle settled gently to the smooth, impervious floor. The door rolled noisily shut behind them as the structure's internal heating panels roared to life.

Flanking their captives, the poachers led them through the access corridor to the main building, which was sparsely but comfortably furnished. Halfway there Hapec frowned at the alien.

"What's the matter with it?" He nodded pointedly.

Cheelo, who had been paying little attention to the thranx as he tried to memorize every detail of their prison, now turned to see that the bug was quivering. It took him only a moment to realize what was happening.

"He's cold."

"Cold?" Maruco let out a snort of disbelief as they passed a wall readout. "It's twenty-three in here."

"That's too cold for thranx. It told me it found the rain forest brisk. And it's much too dry in here. It needs at least ninety percent humidity and more like thirty-three, thirty-four degrees to be really comfortable."

"Shit!" Hapec muttered. "*I'll* die."

"No you won't. But it's liable to."

Grumbling under his breath, the other poacher addressed the house system, directing it to ratchet the interior climate up to something approaching the reported thranx minimum level of comfort.

"Maruco!" His companion protested as both the humidity and the temperature began to climb.

"Quit your bitching," the smaller of the two poachers snapped. "It's only for a little while. Couple of days, until we can finalize a deal. Shouldn't take any longer, not for something as special as this." He smiled fatuously at Desvendapur. "You're going to make us rich, you sickening pile of legs and feelers. So be comfortable for a while. We'll live with it." The poet regarded the antisocial human blankly and with perfect comprehension.

"And now you," the poacher informed his other captive coldly, "get tied up."

"You can't do that," Cheelo protested. "It'll . . . it will upset the alien. It's convinced you two are friendlies. Necklace me and you'll unsettle it."

"So let it be unsettled. If we have to, we'll tie it up as well." Hapec was already removing fasteners from a drawer.

"You could lose it. It could hurt itself struggling to get free, or even choke to death."

"We'll take the chance." Both poachers were moving toward the apprehensive Cheelo, Maruco with a rifle still aimed at him. "If it protests, we can always untie you. Don't make this hard for us, or for you."

"Yeah," Hapec warned him. "Consider yourself lucky. By rights, the ants ought to be scooping out the last of your eyeballs right now."

Having no choice in the matter, Cheelo submitted to having the plastic restraints secured around his wrists and ankles. When the poachers judged them tight enough, Maruco removed the safety strips and the plastic sealed itself, meltwelding shut at the joints. Glancing behind him, the poacher noted the alien's lack of reaction.

"Doesn't look like your bug buddy is too upset. Make it easy on yourself. Tell it this is all part of some weird human welcoming ritual."

"Tell it yourself," Cheelo spat, his anger making him thoughtless.

Hapec's hand started to come up, but he was restrained by his companion. "Don't give him any excuses. And we really don't want to upset our prize pretty if we can avoid it." Leaning close, Maruco stared hard into the snugly manacled thief's eyes. "You, on the other hand, I don't mind upsetting. Behave yourself, and you'll end up with a nice, free, private suborbital ride. Make trouble and we'll just have to sell the bug without an interpreter." Straightening, he turned to regard the thranx, which was presently engaged in a detailed examination of the kitchen facilities.

"What does it eat? Is it hungry?"

Subdued and unhappy, Cheelo replied in a reluctant mumble. "It's strictly vegetarian: hates the sight of meat. It can digest a lot of terrestrial plants. I don't know what kind are the most nourishing. I'll have to ask it." He held up his bound wrists. "Of course, I can't talk to it with my hands tied."

Maruco's expression twisted. It was clear neither poacher had thought of that when they'd secured him. With a knife, he slit the wrist bindings. "Okay, but as soon as you get the answers we need, you get tied up again. And no tricks."

Cheelo spread his palms wide. "What am I going to do? Tell it to call the rangers? Remember, it's here covertly, too." Turning his attention to Desvendapur, he began an elaborate wiggling and twisting of his fingers.

The poet paid dutiful attention to these meaningless gestures before replying with truhand and foothand gesticulations of his own. What he said with his hands was that Cheelo was a *pontik*, a particularly slow and stupid kind of grub. The two antisocials were *pepontiks*, or *pre-pontiks*, an even lower class of intelligence not bright enough to be classified as stupid. None of the three humans had the slightest idea what his complex gestures meant, of course, but it amused him to respond so.

Determining how best to reply not to Cheelo's meaningless inquiry but to the antisocial's actual query was a bigger problem. Since he could not speak, he would have to establish his dietary requirements in some other fashion. Turning away, he embarked on an up-close examination of the sink, leaving Cheelo to fend for explanations himself.

Deprived of support, Montoya improvised. "It's not hungry right now, and when it's not hungry it doesn't like to talk about food."

Maruco grunted. "We'll thaw out a selection of fruits and vegetables. It can pick out what it wants or needs. Meanwhile, I've got a sale to advertise. Hapec, you unload the truck." His partner nodded and headed for the access corridor that linked the two main buildings. The other poacher's gaze narrowed as he considered his one bound prisoner. "You bounce around enough to make me think you're trying to slip out of those seals, and I'll put a couple of 'em over your face." His smirk widened. "You can tell the bug it's part of the ritual." He glanced in Desvendapur's direction.

"I'm not going to check its pack, or container, or whatever that thing is riding on its back, because I don't want to upset it. I know it's not carrying any weapons because if it was it would have tried using them by now."

Cheelo nodded. "Like I told you: It was doing research. That's why it has cooperated so far. It's not armed." This, insofar as Cheelo knew, was the actual truth.

"Fine. We'll leave it at that—for now, anyway." Reaching down, the poacher slapped another self-sealing strap on the other man's wrists. In seconds they were tightly bound again. "That's so you can't 'talk' to it behind my back while I'm working."

Turning, he walked to a desk near the rear of the room and settled himself into a chair. Within minutes he was communicating with far-away places and the representatives of an orderly succession of individuals whose ethics were as impoverished as their bank accounts were expansive.

While a helpless Cheelo sat and fumed silently, the ever-inquisitive Desvendapur continued his exploration of the poachers' quarters. The temperature and humidity had risen to levels the poet found tolerable, if not entirely comfortable, and he was thoroughly enjoying a respite that he knew could not last. As he continued his examination of the room and its contents, Cheelo's expression underwent an extraordinary succession of contortions. None of them held any meaning for the poet, though it was clear by their frequency and urgency that the human was urging him to do something.

Desvendapur could not let himself be sold, of course. If no alternative presented itself, he was convinced that he could survive and even thrive in human captivity. But it was not the preferred option for the future. In human captivity, his performances would not be properly appreciated. He needed a thranx audience. Therefore, if possible, he had to find a way to return to the colony. Unable to see a way clear to doing that himself, he realized he would need Cheelo's assistance. That did not mean it was necessary to rush matters, and he had no intention of doing so. While the two antisocial humans desired to profit from his existence, Desvendapur suspected they would not hesitate to kill him if they felt sufficiently threatened. Surely Cheelo understood that.

Hapec soon returned from unloading and stabilizing the airtruck. Establishing himself in the kitchen area while his partner continued his steady stream of secured-transmission intercontinental conversation, the other poacher began meal preparations. For the moment, both captives found themselves largely, though never entirely, ignored.

Faced with a situation for which a lifetime of study and learning had not prepared him, Desvendapur was compelled to fall back on that one aspect of his personality that had never failed him: his imagination. As he pursued his examination of the domicile, he proceeded to lay out in his mind a sequence of actions in much the same way he would design an extended recitation, complete with appropriate revisions and adjustments.

None of this was apparent to the anxious Cheelo, who grew progressively more distraught in his bonds. Thanks to some fast thinking he had managed to buy some time, but, unlike a new communicator or tridee subscription, it was not guaranteed: There was no return policy in place in the event of dissatisfaction. The two poachers were not deep thinkers. Any little thing, any irritation of the moment or insignificant occurrence, might set them off. In that event he knew they might cast careful consideration and practicalities to the tepid wind that seeped upward from the cloud forest below, and blow his head off. He knew this because he and they were of a kind, representatives of that same subspecies of humanity that tends to *react* to awkward circumstance as opposed to thinking about it. Maruco and Hapec were too much like him for him to be comfortable around them. The devil he knew was himself.

Convinced he was at least not in imminent danger of being executed, he switched from watching them to tracking the movements of the thranx. It was impossible to know what the alien was thinking since he could not talk to it without giving away the fact that it understood Terranglo. He had to content himself with imagining. What did it make of all this? Did it care what happened to him? Cheelo knew he didn't care what happened to *it*, but right now his future prospects rested entirely with the many-legged insectoid. His life was in the bug's hands—all four of them.

If it forgot the scenario, if it deviated from the play and spoke aloud, then the poachers would quickly realize that they had no need of a translator. He would be rendered instantly extraneous. There were many steep precipices just east of the prefab abode into which a body could be thrown to be swallowed forever by rain forest, gully, and cloud. Silently he importuned the thranx to keep silent. Even if they found themselves sold, at least they would still be alive. Future prospects seemed considerably more promising when viewed from a perspective of abiding survival. Who could tell? With luck he might be able to persuade their buyers to make a brief stopover in Golfito.

He tried to cheer himself up. If the poachers and the bug just kept their heads this wouldn't turn out so bad. Didn't he need to hide out for a while? Wasn't that what he was doing down in the untrammeled rain forest in the first place? What better place to lie low—after he had finalized arrangements for his future with Ehrenhardt, of course—than the private zoo or collection of some incredibly rich patron who had just made a very expensive and very illegitimate purchase? As he had so many times in his desperate, frenetic life, he set about trying to mentally arrange events to his advantage. Even the bug was cooperating, maintaining silence while pretending to examine every object within the building.

He was giving Desvendapur too much credit. The thranx was not pretending. While the poachers ignored him, he took the time to study each individual example of human manufacture in great detail, paying particular attention to how the two humans operated their manifold devices. Once, the one called Hapec caught the thranx peering over his shoulder as he ran the cooker. The human gestured clumsily and ordered him to step farther back. Maintaining the fiction that he could not understand the man's speech, the poet obediently interpreted the gestures and moved away.

By mealtime Cheelo, though still nervous and worried about the poachers' state of mind, had resigned himself to his captivity. He cooperated while Hapec fed him listlessly, and he watched with as much interest as the poachers while Desvendapur picked through the assortment of rehydrated fruits and vegetables he was offered. When their prize captive seemed satisfied, the two men sat down to their own meal. Dinnertime conversation on their part consisted of coarse jokes, inconsequential natterings, and an impassioned discussion of how much money they were going to clear for selling the only representative of a recently contacted intelligent species into involuntary captivity. While salt, pepper, and hot sauce played a part in their dining, their conversation was seasoned by neither ethics nor morals.

When Desvendapur had eaten his fill, he stepped back from the exotic but nutritious banquet his captors had laid out before him, ambled over to a far corner, and casually picked up one of their rifles, cradling the lethal device in his right truhand and foothand. It took a moment before Hapec noticed the alien aiming the muzzle of the weapon at him.

"Hey. Uh, hey, Maruco!" The human's lower jaw descended, and his mouth remained open to no apparent purpose.

"Shit!" His eyes darting rapidly back and forth between his two prisoners, the other poacher pushed carefully away from the table. "Cheelo! Man, you tell the bug to put that *down*. It's holding a full charge, and the safety is off. Tell it it's liable to hurt itself. What's it doing, anyway? We're its friends, helping it to see and study more of our world. Go on, man: Remind it!"

"I can't tell him anything," Cheelo replied tersely. "My hands, remember?"

This time Maruco didn't hesitate. Rising slowly from his chair and keeping his eyes on the enigmatic thranx, he nervously edged his way over to where his other prisoner was secured. Using his knife, he once again released the captive's arms.

A relieved Cheelo promptly began rubbing circulation back into his wrists. "Hey, what about my legs?"

"What about your legs?" the poacher growled. "You don't talk to it with your feet."

"Free his legs." Desvendapur gestured with the rifle. Designed for thicker-digited, clumsier human hands, the weapon felt light in his arms. Manipulation and activation would be a simple matter.

"Sure, just be careful with that . . ." Maruco paused, the knife halting in midswipe, as he stared wide-eyed at the alien. *"Son-of-a-bitch-whore!"*

"You can talk!" Both poachers were gazing in open-mouthed disbelief at the suddenly voluble alien in their midst.

"Not very well, but my fluency is improving with practice. His legs?" Again the rifle moved.

Slowly, the poacher knelt and ran the blade across the restraining plastic. With a curt gasp of relief, Cheelo kicked his feet apart.

A thranx did not need to look out of the corner of its eyes to see action transpiring off to one side. Multiple lenses scanned a much wider field than human eyes could see, allowing for considerably greater peripheral vision. He shifted the tip of the weapon significantly in the direction of the larger human, who had risen and taken a step in the direction of the other gun.

"Although I am not familiar with the kind of result it produces, I believe I know how this weapon operates. I also believe that you should move the other way and stand alongside your friend."

"It's bluffing." Maruco began edging away from Cheelo, who had risen from the chair where he had been imprisoned and was now stomping about in an attempt to get circulation flowing to his feet again. "It doesn't know how to fire the gun."

"Yeah?" Keeping his hands in plain sight, Hapec slowly and carefully came around behind the table to join his colleague. "Then *you* go pick the other one up."

As he studied the weapon-wielding bug, Maruco spread his hands innocently wide, ignorant of the fact that the subject of his supplication did not know the meaning of the gesture.

"Okay, so you can talk. There's no need for this. We mean you no harm." Smiling ingratiatingly, he nodded at the now-standing Cheelo. "Our tying him up is just part of a special greeting and guest ritual."

"No it isn't," Desvendapur responded in his whispery but increasingly articulate Terranglo. "You forget that while I did not speak, I could listen. I have heard and understood everything that has been said since you first appeared before us in the forest. I know that you meant to kill us until Cheelo convinced you to sell us instead." He did not need to be familiar with the extraordinary diversity of human facial expression to interpret the one that now dominated the muscles of the poachers' countenances.

Still rubbing his wrists and flicking out his feet to stimulate the long-restrained muscles, Cheelo walked over to his alien companion. Having resigned himself to being sold as part of a package deal, he now found himself in a position he thought not to experience again for some time.

"You're full of surprises, bug."

The heart-shaped head and its great golden eyes turned toward him. "My name is Desvendapur."

"Ay, right." He reached out with both hands. "I'll take that now. Not that I don't think you can use it, but I'm probably a better shot than you." As the poet complaisantly handed over the weapon, Cheelo added by way of afterthought, "You *do* know how to use it, don't you? You weren't bluffing?"

"Oh, I'm sure I could have activated it. The firing mechanism is simple, and although the weapon is designed for human arms and hands, it fits well enough in mine. I would never have done so, of course."

"What's that?" Maruco strained to make certain he had heard properly.

"Although we have had to fight to defend ourselves in the past, and have evolved from primitive ancestors who battled constantly among themselves, we have become a peaceful species." Antennae bobbed elaborately. "I could never have shot you unless my life was directly threatened."

"It was threatened!" Cheelo reminded him.

The thranx shook its head, further surprising the poachers by its mastery and utilization of a common human gesture. "My freedom of movement was at risk, not my life. Although my preference is to return to the colony, I could have tolerated being transported to another part of your planet, could have lost myself in exposure to an entirely new environment and surroundings."

Maruco blinked. "Then why did you pick up the gun in the first place?"

"As I said, because for many reasons I would prefer to return to the hive. Also because my life and freedom of movement were not the only ones at stake." Both antennae dipped in Cheelo's direction.

A welter of conflicting emotion surged to the fore within the thief as the thranx's words sank in. It didn't object to being sold. It had picked up the rifle for his sake as much as for its own. Confronted by the rara avis of actual, genuine emotion, he had no idea how to respond, did not know what to say.

Screw it.

"Come on, Deswhel—Desvencrapur. We're outta here." With the rifle, he gestured at Maruco. "I want the airtruck. I told you, I've got an appointment to keep. If coaxed right, I think that truck'll make it all the way up to the isthmus."

Keeping his hands in plain sight, the angry poacher nodded in the direction of the accessway that connected the ridge-top living quarters to the shop and garage. "You'll leave us marooned here."

"Bullshit." Cheelo laughed, enjoying the turn of events fully. "Your buyers are going to come running, and they'll be bringing their own transportation." He grinned broadly. "Of course, they're not gonna be real happy with you when they find out that the prize you offered them decided not to hang around. Now, what about that truck?"

"It's an open design," Hapec told him. "Take it. I just have to unlock the navigation system."

"Like hell. All you have to do is activate the cencomp. You think I'm gonna give you a chance to program the engine for self-destruct? D'you think I was born dumb, like you two?" Maruco's expression tightened, but the poacher said nothing.

"Let's go." Cheelo gestured with the muzzle. "Despindo—Des, you follow me. We'll get as close to this colony of yours as you think we safely can, and I'll drop you there."

"Colony?" Maruco's small black eyes blinked. "What colony?"

Cheelo ignored him, waiting for the thranx's reply.

"Among my people I am guilty of the most egregious antisocial activity. They would confine me until I could be sent offworld for more formal punishment. So if you do not object, Cheelo Montoya, I would rather continue to travel in your company. For a little while longer, at least."

"No can do, big-eyes. This boy's jungle jaunt is over. I got to fly a long ways now, or I'm gonna be late for the dance. Besides, don't you have your poems, your compositions, to perform for your fellow bugs?"

The blue-green head swayed gently from side to side. "Insufficiently mitigating circumstances, I am afraid. I would far rather continue my ruminations, would much prefer to seek additional inspiration. Some day, of course, I will reveal them to all the hives. But not yet." Overhead lighting sparkled in his eyes, imparting to the multiple lenses a muted crystalline gleam. "There is still so much more I wish to do."

"Have it your way." An indifferent Cheelo gestured again with the rifle. Plenty of time to decide what to do with the bug once they were safely back down in the rain forest. As the two poachers stumbled off ahead of him, Maruco looked back over his shoulder.

"What were you saying about a colony? There's a whole colony of 'em here on Earth? Down in the Reserva? I never heard nothing about anything like that."

"Shut your face and keep moving. I know the truck's coded, so you're going to start it for me."

"Then it's true! There's an alien outpost in the Reserva that's being kept from the public." Rising excitement dominated the poacher's voice. "And you didn't say outpost; you said colony." He looked over at his partner. "This might be the biggest secret on the planet. Any one of the fifty big media groups would pay a lifetime annuity for that kind of information. It's worth a helluva lot more than one live bug." Once more he looked back at the stony-faced Cheelo.

"What do you say, *vato*? We've got the facilities here for communicating worldwide while hiding the source of the signal. We sell the information to the highest bidder and split it three ways. Nobody gets sold; nobody gets hurt. Plenty credit for everybody." When Cheelo failed to respond, Maruco's agitation increased. "Hell, we don't need *you* to sell it. But the Reserva's a big place, and this colony or base or whatever it is must be really well hid. Hapec and I are down there a lot, and we've sure never suspected anything like this was there. *You* know where it is. Whatever media group buys in ain't going to want to go hunting for the place. They'll want to set down right on top of it, before some competitor gets wind of what's going on." His voice fell slightly. "You *do* know where it is?"

"Pretty much," Cheelo lied. "Close enough so that anybody interested could find it within a week."

"Well come on then, man! Don't waft this off. We can be partners. All of us, we'll be rich."

"First you were going to kill me," Cheelo reminded him, his tone chilly. "Then you were going to sell me as a talking accessory to a bug."

"Heyyy," the poacher demurred, "it was nothing *personal*." They were approaching the garage. "That was just business. You're a businessman, *chingón*. That was business then; this is business now. You need our business contacts; we need what you know."

Cheelo found himself growing confused. The poacher's insinuating spiel was beguiling. "What about the bu—about Des. He may be an outcast among his own people, but he'd never agree to the premature exposure of the colony."

"*Chinga* the bug," Maruco snapped. "If it has a problem with this, blow its stinking guts out. We don't need it no more. What do you care? It's just a big, ugly, alien *bug*."

"It's intelligent. Probably more so than either of you two. Probably . . . probably more than me. It's . . . it's an artist."

Maruco laughed madly as they entered the garage. The airtruck rested where it had been parked, sleek and silent, its propulsion system fully recharged and awaiting only coded reactivation. With it at his disposal Cheelo knew he could reach Golfito. Or at least Gatun, where he had friends and could safely refuel.

His finger tightened imperceptibly on the rifle's trigger. "It's not funny. I used to think it was, but I've changed my mind. So now what the hell am I supposed to do? Trust you?"

"Yeah, you can trust us. Can't he, Hapec?"

"Sure. Why should we do anything? We need you to show the site to whoever buys the story," the other poacher observed. As he spoke, he was drifting to his left, toward a wall lined with tools.

"Don't even think about it." The muzzle of the rifle flicked sideways so that it was aimed straight at the bigger man's back. As soon as it shifted away from him, Maruco whirled. A compact, high-strung bundle of muscle and furious energy, he threw himself at Cheelo.

21

As he tried to bring the rifle around to bear on his attacker, Cheelo's finger contracted reflexively on the trigger. A tiny, very intense, and highly localized sonic boom echoed through the building. Hapec gazed down in disbelief at the small but lethal hole that the sonic burst had punched through him from stomach to spine. Even as he clasped both hands over the perforation, blood began to gush forth between his fingers. Mouth gaping in a silent "O" of surprise, he staggered toward the two combatants before sinking to his knees and then toppling languidly forward, like a brown iceberg calving from the face of a glacier, to the floor of the garage.

Maruco managed to grab the muzzle of the rifle before Cheelo could bring it around for a second shot. They struggled violently and in complete silence for possession of the weapon—until a second boom rattled the diminutive one-way windows that lined the walls of the enclosure.

Thorax pumping, Desvendapur pressed back against the airtruck and contemplated the bloody panorama spread out before him. Two humans lay dead on the floor, their body fluids leaking from their ruptured circulatory systems. Only one remained standing, the weapon dangling loosely from a hand. Heart pounding, chest heaving, Cheelo stood staring down at the body of Maruco lying at his feet like a broken doll.

Desvendapur had of course read of such violence, and he knew of it from the evidence of his own family history. Here was the sort of confrontation that harked back to the time when the AAnn had attacked Paszex and wiped out most of his ancestors. But despite holding the weapon earlier himself he had not really expected to have to use it. This was the first time he had ever witnessed such savagery in person. "This—

this is barbaric! A terrible thing!" Wonderful new phrases were already evolving unbidden in his brain, refusing to be ignored.

Cheelo took a deep breath. "It sure is. Now we'll never learn the activation code for the truck. We're stuck."

The poet's eyes rose to fix the surviving biped in their multilenticular stare. "I don't mean that. I mean that two sapient beings are dead."

Cheelo pushed out his lower lip. "Nothing terrible about that. Not as far as I'm concerned." His voice rose in protest. "Hey, you think I *wanted* to shoot them?" Desvendapur took a wary step in the direction of the accessway. "Take it easy. The conversation got kind of tense, I got a little confused, and they tried to jump me." When the alien did not respond, Cheelo became upset. "Look, I'm telling you the truth. They thought I was going to shoot them after they activated the truck. I wasn't going to. Sure, I *wanted* to, but I was going to leave them alive. All I wanted was out of here so I could get to my meeting. And before you go getting all bent out of joint, remember that they'd figured it out, about your being from a colony and all. If they'd been left here they still could've sold that information. Look at it like this: I had to shoot them to protect your people down in the Reserva."

"They might have tried to persuade others to go looking for the hive, but without specific coordinates they would never have found it. Never." Desvendapur continued to eye the biped accusingly, or at least in a manner that the defensive Cheelo continued to interpret as accusing.

"It doesn't matter," Cheelo finally declared curtly. "They're dead and we're not. Believe me, it's no loss to the species."

"The death of any sapient is a loss."

His human companion uttered several sharply intoned words whose meaning the thranx did not recognize. "I don't know about species wide, but there are sure some variations in our individual values." With the muzzle of the rifle he roughly nudged the corpse at his feet. Maruco the poacher did not move and would not poach again.

Walking over to the tool rack, Cheelo snapped the rifle into an empty charging cradle and turned to ponder the silent airtruck. "I can try to start this big bastard up, but unless these guys were completely confident in their isolation here, or were total idiots, there are probably about two million possible key codes." His gaze rose to the nearest of the one-way windows. "You saw the country around here on the way in. This place is really isolated. There's nothing nearby but some automated farming projects. We can try for one."

"I do not think so," Desvendapur argued.

"Why not?" His respiration slowly returning to normal, Cheelo stared at the thranx.

"While you were fighting with our captors I was hearing voices from their communicator. Someone with an especially authoritative voice was demanding to know where the one called Maruco had gone. When no response was forthcoming, the transmission was terminated with the words 'See you soon you little shit.' While I do not interpret that to mean that the speaker's appearance is imminent, it struck me as a promise to arrive in a finite period of time."

"You're right. Dammit!" Cheelo thought furiously. "I forgot about their bug buyers. We'd better not be around when they show up." A look of distaste on his face, he calmly contemplated the human debris staining the floor. "Help me with these two." Moving off, he searched for the manual door opener he knew had to exist.

"What are we going to do? Carry out some kind of formal burial ritual?" Despite his dismay at the carnage that had occurred, it would not prevent the poet from recording the details of what promised to be a particularly fascinating human rite.

"More like an informal one." Locating a control panel, Cheelo brushed touchplates, activating lights, servos, and an automatic washer before finding the one that operated the garage door. Cold, intensely dry air swept in from outside as the barrier rattled upward.

Working together, they hauled the bodies of the two poachers one at a time to the rim of the nearest obliging precipice and shoved them over the edge, watching as each limp lump of dead meat rolled and bumped its way into cloud-swathed oblivion. Desvendapur was disappointed by the lack of ceremony, having anticipated a certain amount of exotic alien chanting or dancing. But the biped who had become his companion mouthed only a few words, and none of them struck the poet as especially complimentary to or respectful of the deceased.

That onerous duty done, they returned to the deserted outpost where Desvendapur did his best to assist the human in cleansing the garage floor of blood. When he was satisfied, Cheelo stepped back to survey their work, wiping sweat from his forehead. Though the exudation of clear fluid by the biped's body as a means of maintaining its internal temperature was a process Desvendapur had already observed in the forest, he never ceased to be captivated by it.

"There!" Cheelo sighed tiredly. "When their buyers arrive, they won't know where their favorite *ninlocos* have hopped off to. They'll see that the airtruck is still here—we can't do anything about that—but that won't automatically lead them to assume that something's happened to them. They'll start a search, but one that's considered and unhurried. By the time they find the bodies, *if* they find the bodies, and figure out that maybe they ought to be looking for somebody like us—or like me, anyway—we'll both be safe and out of sight back down in the Reserva. I know if I follow the river it'll take me into Sintuya, where I can book a flight back to Lima. I still have enough time to make it to Golfito." Walking back to the wall, he yanked the sonic rifle free from the charging bracket.

"Expensive little toy, this." He rotated the sophisticated weapon in his hands. "So our trip up here wasn't a total loss. Let's help ourselves to the pantry and get out of here before nanny shows up."

"I cannot."

Cheelo blinked at the alien. "What d'you mean, 'you cannot'? You sure as hell can't stay here." He indicated a window that revealed the barren plateau outside. "Whoever comes looking for those two *ninlocos* won't hesitate about shoving you in a cage." Nobody'd make any money off it, either, he reflected.

"I will explain matters to them. That I wish to study them." Antennae bobbed. "Perhaps a mutual accommodation can be reached."

"You can take your goddamn studying for inspiration and . . . !" Cheelo calmed himself, remembering that the visibly flinching thranx was sensitive to the volume of the booming human voice. "You don't understand, Des. These people who are coming, they're gonna be nervous and on edge because they're unable to contact their two guys here. They'll come in fast and quiet, and if the first thing they see is a giant, big-eyed bug wandering around loose instead of properly caged up, they might not stop to smell the roses—or the alien that smells like one. They're liable to blast you into half a dozen pieces before you get the chance to 'explain matters' to them."

"They might not shoot first," Desvendapur argued.

"No, that's right. They might not." He pushed past the thranx, striding toward the corridor that led to the outpost's living quarters. "I'm going to start packing. You want to stay here and put your life in the hands of a bunch of senior *ninlocos* who aren't exactly experienced in the formalities of unanticipated interspecies contact, you go right ahead. Me, I'd rather put my trust in the monkeys. I'm heading down into the forest."

Left behind in the garage to meditate on his limited options, Desvendapur soon turned to follow the biped into the other part of the station.

"You don't understand, Cheelo Montoya. It is not that I *want* to remain here. The fact is that I have little choice in the matter."

Cheelo did not look up from where he was stuffing handfuls of concentrates from the outpost's food locker into his backpack. "Ay? Why's that?"

"Did you not notice that I was barely able to help you remove and dispose of the two cadavers? It was not because their weight was excessive. It was because the air here is far too dry for my kind. More importantly, the temperature is borderline freezing."

Pausing in his scavenging, Cheelo turned to regard the alien. "Okay, I can see where that could be a problem. But from here it's all downhill into the Reserva. The lower we go, the hotter and more humid it'll become and the better you'll feel."

The heart-shaped head slowly nodded acquiescence while truhands and antennae bobbed understandingly. "I know that is so. The difficult, and critical, question is: Will it become hot and humid enough soon enough?"

"I can't answer that," the human responded evenly. "I don't know what your tolerances are."

"I cannot answer it myself. But I fear to try it. By the wings that no longer fly, I do."

From hidden, long-unvisited depths Cheelo dragged up what little compassion remained in him. "Maybe we can rig you some kind of cold-weather gear. I'm no tailor, and I don't see an autogarb in this dump, but I suppose we could cut up some blankets or something. Your only alternatives are to wait here and hope you can talk faster than the people who are coming can shoot, or to strike out across this plateau and try and find another place far enough away that they won't search it."

The thranx indicated negativity. "If I am to walk, better to aim for a more accommodating climate than one I already know to be hostile." Turning, he gestured at the terrain beyond a window. "I would not make it across the first valley before my joints began to stiffen from the cold. And remember: I have one bad leg."

"And five good ones. Well, you think about it." Cheelo returned to his foraging. "Whatever you decide to do, I'll help you if I can—provided it doesn't cost me any more time."

In the end, Desvendapur decided that despite his increasing mastery of the human's language, he was neither confident nor fluent enough to risk an encounter with the dead poachers' customers. Already he had experience of the volatile nature of human response and its reaction to unforeseen events. Not knowing what to expect within the outpost that now failed to respond to their queries, whoever was coming in search of the absent poachers might well unload a rush of lethality in his direction before he could explain himself.

Whatever the chastisement meted out to him upon his return to the colony, it would not include summary execution. The question was, could he make it all the way down to the salubrious surroundings of the lowland rain forest? It seemed he had no choice but to try. Certainly the biped thought so. Having made the decision, the poet fell to scrounging sup-

plies of his own from the outpost's stores, relying on the human to elucidate the contents of the bewildering variety of multihued food packages
and containers.

When their respective packs were bulging with supplies, human and
thranx turned their attention to the question of how to insulate someone
whose anatomy did not remotely resemble that of an upright mammal.
Utilizing the clothing of the deceased proved impossible: None of it
would fit over Desvendapur's head or around his body. They settled for
wrapping his thorax and abdomen as best they could in several of the
high-altitude, lightweight blankets that covered two of the station's beds.
Unfortunately, these relied for their generous heating properties on picking up waved energy from a broadcast coil located in the floor of the single bedroom. Outside the buildings and beyond the coil's limited range,
the caloric elements woven into the blankets would go inert.

"That's the best I can do," an impatient Cheelo assured his chitinous
companion. "There's nothing else here that'd work any better. It's all tech
stuff. Stands to reason they'd bring in the most basic of everything they'd
need. In a town we could probably find some old-style, heavier wrappings." He nodded curtly toward the nearest window. "No telling how far
it is to the nearest village. I know I didn't see one on the way here."

"Nor did I," conceded Desvendapur. Wrapped in the blankets that the
human had clumsily cinched around him with cord, the thranx knew he
must present a highly incongruous sight. Contemplating himself in a
reflective surface, he removed his scri!ber from the thorax pouch that was
now hidden beneath the artificial covering and began to recite.

Cheelo looked on in disgust as he tightened a strap on his own pack.
"Don't you ever take a break from that composing?"

Winding up a stanza that oozed systemic emotion, the thranx paused
the instrument. "For someone like myself, to stop composing would be to
start to die."

The human grunted, one of its more primitive sounds, and activated
the doorplate. The composite barrier began to roll upward. Cold, sear-
ingly dry air rushed hungrily into the insulated structure, overwhelming
any warmth before it. Desvendapur's mandibles clacked shut to prevent
the deadly cold from entering his system via his mouth. At such times it
was useful not to have to open one's jaws to breathe. The biped had cut
two long, narrow slits in the blanket that covered the poet's thorax, allowing his spicules access to the air. Internally, his lungs constricted at the
intrusion of the frigid atmosphere. Trying not to shudder, he took a hesitant step forward.

"Let's go. The sooner we start downward, the sooner the air will start
to warm and to thicken with moisture."

Cheelo said nothing, nodding curtly as he followed him out of the garage.

There was a path, of sorts, made by what animal or animals Cheelo did not know. It was just wide enough for them to proceed along it in single file. Possibly the poachers themselves had enlarged it to allow access to the cloud forest and the rare creatures that dwelled in the little-visited ecosystem lying between plateau and jungle. Llamas would not have made such a track, but far-ranging carnivores like jaguars or the spectacled bear might have tramped back and forth along the same route for enough generations to have worn a path through the unrelenting greenery.

Far more comfortable in the cool mountain air than his companion, Cheelo would have quickly outdistanced him but for the fact that the thranx, utilizing all six legs, was much more sure-footed on the narrow path. Where the thief was forced to take extra care before negotiating an awkward dip or steep drop, Desvendapur simply ambled on, so that the distance between them never became too great.

At midday they paused to eat beside a miniature waterfall. Huge butterflies fluttered on wings of metallic hue, skating the edge of the spray, while mosquitoes danced among the lush ferns that framed the musical cataract. Cheelo was feeling fit and expansive, but it was plain that his many-legged companion was not doing nearly as well.

"C'mon, pick your antennae up," he urged the thranx. "We're doing good." Chewing a strip of reconstituted meat, he nodded at the clouds scudding along mournfully below them. "We'll be down to where it's revoltingly hot and sticky before you know it."

"That is what I am afraid of." Desvendapur huddled as best he could beneath the thin blankets that hung all too loosely around him. "That it will happen before I know of it."

"Is pessimism a common thranx characteristic?" Cheelo chided him playfully.

Without much success, the poet tried to tuck his exposed, unprotected limbs more tightly beneath him. "The human ability to adapt to extremes of climate is one we do not share. I find it difficult to believe that you are comfortable in these surroundings."

"Oh, it's on the brisk side; make no mistake about that. But now that we're off the high plateau and down in cloud forest there ought to be enough moisture in the air for you."

"Truly, the weight of the air is improving," Desvendapur admitted. "But it's still cold, so cold!"

"Eat your vegetables," he advised the thranx. How many times as a child had his mother admonished him to do just that? He smiled to himself at the remembrance. The smile did not last. She had told him things like that when she wasn't hitting him or bringing home a different visiting "uncle" every week or so. His expression darkened as he rose.

"C'mon, get up. We'll push it until you start feeling better." Gratefully, the poet struggled to his six feet, taking care not to shrug off any of the inadequate blankets or put too much pressure on the splinted middle limb.

But he did not start feeling better. Cheelo could not believe how rapidly the thranx's condition deteriorated. Within a short while after their meal the alien began to experience difficulty in walking.

"I . . . I am all right," Desvendapur replied in response to the human's query. "I just need to rest for a time-part."

"No." Cheelo was unbending. "No resting. Not here." Even as the thranx started to sink down onto its abdomen, Cheelo was reaching out to grab the bug and pull it back to its feet. The smooth, unyielding chitin of an upper arm was shockingly icy to the touch. "Shit, you're as cold as these rocks!"

Golden-hued compound eyes peered up at him. "My system is concentrating its body heat internally to protect vital organs. I can still walk. I just need to rest first, to gather my strength."

Cheelo's reply was grim. "You 'rest' for very long and you won't have to worry about gathering any strength." Why was he so concerned? What did it matter to him if the bug died? He could kick the body over the side of the narrow trail and into the gorge where the rich friends of the dead *ninlocos* would never find it. Continuing on alone, he would make better time. Soon he'd find himself down by the river, and then back in the outpost of civilization called Sintuya. Climate-controlled hotel rooms, real food, insect screens, and a quick flight to Lima or Iquitos, then on to Golfito and his appointment with Ehrenhardt. After a rapid electronic transfer of credit, his own franchise. Money, importance, fine clothes, sloe gin, and fast women. *Respect,* for Cheelo Montoya.

It had been promised to him and was all there for the taking. With all that in prospect, why should he exert himself on behalf of a bug, even an oversized, intelligent one? The thranx had brought him nothing but trouble. Oh sure, maybe it had saved his life up on the ridge, but if he'd never met it, he would never have found himself in that life-threatening situation. As if that wasn't reason enough, the insectoid was a criminal, an antisocial, among its own kind! It wasn't like he would be extending himself to help rescue some alien saint or important diplomat.

Des's limbs folded up against his abdomen and thorax as he sank down and huddled beneath the blankets. Even his upstanding antennae folded up, collapsing into tight curls to minimize heat loss. Cheelo stared. Ahead, the trail beckoned: a slender, rutted, dirt-and-mud track leading to one paved with gold. With luck—and if the trail held—he'd be down by nightfall and in Sintuya the following evening. He felt good, and as he went lower, the increasing amount of oxygen gave an additional boost to his spirits.

He took a couple of steps down the trail, turning to look back over a shoulder. "Come on. We can't stop here if we want to get out of the mountains by nightfall."

"A moment, just a moment," the thranx pleaded. Its voice was even wispier than usual.

Cheelo Montoya waited irritably as he gazed at the impenetrable, eternal clouds crawling up the green-clad slopes. "Ah, hell." Turning, he walked back to where the alien had slumped to the ground, all blue-green glaze and crumpled legs. Swinging his pack around so that it rested not against his spine and shoulders but across his chest, he turned his back to the poet, crouched, and bent forward.

"Come on. Get up and walk. It's downhill. Let one leg fall in front of the other."

"Fall?" The barely perceptible, protective transparent eye membrane trembled. "I do not follow your meaning."

"Hurry up!" Annoyed, impatient, and angry at himself, Cheelo had no time for stupid questions. "Put your upper limbs over my shoulders, here." He tapped himself. "Hang on tight. I'll carry you for a while. It'll warm up quick as we go down, and soon you'll be able to walk on your own again. You'll see."

"You—you would carry me?"

"Not if you squat there clicking and hissing! Stand up, dammit, before I have any more time to think about how dumb this is and change my mind."

It was an eerie, chilling sensation, the touch of hard, cold limbs against his shoulders, as if a gigantic crab were scrambling up his back. By utilizing all four front limbs the thranx was able to obtain a secure grip on the human's upper torso. Glancing down, Cheelo could see the gripping digits locked together across his chest beneath pack and straps. All sixteen of them. The embrace was secure without being constricting. The thranx was solidly built, but not unbearably heavy. He decided he could manage it for a while, especially since it was downhill all the way. The biggest danger would come from stumbling or tripping, not from collapsing beneath the moderate alien weight.

Twisting to look around and down, he saw the other four alien limbs hanging loose, two on either side of his legs and hips. Exquisite alien body scent filled his nostrils. Enveloped by perfume, he resumed the descent.

"Just hang on," he snapped irritably at his motionless burden. "You'll feel better as soon as it's warmer."

"Yes." Sensing the four alien mandibles moving against the flesh of his shoulder, Cheelo tried not to shudder. "As soon as it is warmer. I do not know how to thank you." The exotic alien syllables echoed eerily against his ear.

"Try shutting up for a while," his human bearer suggested. The poet obediently lapsed into silence.

The more relaxed beneath the extra weight he became, the faster Cheelo found he could move. By afternoon the pace of their descent had increased markedly. True to his word, the thranx maintained a merciful muteness, not even requesting that they stop for a meal. The alien's silent acquiescence suited Cheelo just fine.

By the time the shrouded sun had commenced its swift plunge behind the Andes in search of the distant Pacific, Cheelo estimated that they had descended almost halfway to the rain forest below. Tomorrow noontime would see them enter the outskirts of the lowlands, where the temperature and the humidity would reach levels uncomfortable to Cheelo but complaisant for the thranx.

"Time to get off," he told his passenger. Reacting slowly and with deliberation, the thranx released its hold on the human's torso and dropped to the ground.

"I could not have come this far without your aid." Clutching tightly at the blankets with both tru- and foothands, the poet singled out a log on which to spend the coming night, painfully straddling it with all four trulegs. The dead wood was damp and chilly against his exposed abdomen.

"Ay, you have to be feeling better." Without knowing why he bothered, Cheelo tried to cheer his companion. "It's warmer here, so you ought to be more comfortable."

"It is warmer," the thranx admitted. "But not so warm that I am comfortable."

"Tomorrow," Cheelo promised him. Kneeling beside his own pack, he searched for one of the smokeless fire sticks he had appropriated from the poacher outpost. The stick was intended to help start a blaze, but in the absence of any dry fuel he would just have to burn one stick after another until they made their own tiny campfire. They were as likely to find dry wood lying on the floor of a cloud forest as orchids sprouting on tundra.

As he prepared his simple meal Cheelo noticed that the thranx was not moving. "Aren't you going to eat?"

"Not hungry. Too cold." Antennae uncurled halfway but no further.

Shaking his head, Cheelo rose and walked over to examine the contents of the alien's pack. "For a space-traversing species you're not very adaptable."

"We evolved and still prefer to live underground." Even the thranx's usually elegant, graceful gestures were subdued. "It is difficult to adjust to extremes of climate when you do not experience them."

Cheelo shrugged as he rehydrated an assortment of dried fruit. At least water for food rehydration was not a problem in the cloud forest. With the onset of evening it was already beginning to precipitate out on his skin and clothing. Blankets or not, they would be compelled to endure at least one chill, moist night on the steep mountainside. Hot food and drink would help to minimize its effects.

Despite its obvious disinterest in the food, the thranx ate, albeit slowly and with care. Scarfing down his own meal, Cheelo watched the alien closely.

"Feel better?" he asked when both had finished. As always, it was fascinating to watch the bug clean its mandibles with its truhands. It put Cheelo in mind of a praying mantis gleaning the last bits of prey from its razor-sharp jaws.

"Yes, I do." A foothand traced a discreet pattern in the air while the two truhands continued their hygiene, causing Cheelo to reflect on the usefulness of possessing two sets of hands. "This gesture I am making is one of more than moderate thanks."

"Like this?" Cheelo's arm and hand contorted in an ungainly try at mimicry.

The alien did not laugh at or criticize the clumsy attempt. "You have the upper portion of the movement correct, but the lower should go this way." He demonstrated. Once again, Cheelo did his best to imitate the comparatively simple gesture.

"Better," declared Desvendapur. "Try it again."

"I'm doing the best I can." Muttering, Cheelo adjusted his arm. "Between shoulder and wrist I've only got three joints to your four."

"Near enough." The foothand extended and pulled back at a particular angle. "This is the gesture for agreement."

"So now I'm supposed to learn how to nod with my arm?" Cheelo smiled thinly.

The lesson was an improvement over charades. In this manner they passed the time until total darkness. They had to keep the lesson simple. Not because Cheelo was insufficiently flexible to approximate the thranx's gestures, but because there was no getting around the fact that the more elaborate ones required the use of two pairs of upper appendages. Despite his desire to learn, the thief could not see himself lying down and writhing all four limbs in the air like a beetle trapped on its back.

Morning arrived on the underside of a cloud, crisp and moist. Yawning, Cheelo turned over in his bedroll. The night had been clammy and cold, but not intolerably so. The temperature had stayed well above that common to the plateau high above.

He stretched as he sat up, letting his blanket tumble from his shoulders to bunch up around his waist. Glancing to his right, he saw that his alien companion was still asleep, huddled beneath its makeshift cold-weather gear, all eight limbs contracted tightly beneath its thorax and abdomen.

"Time to move," he announced unsympathetically. Rising, he scratched at himself. "Come on. If we get a good start we'll be all the way down by evening. I'll rehydrate some broccoli or some other green shit for you." Among the litany of terrestrial fruits and vegetables it had sampled, the thranx had proven particularly fond of broccoli. As far as Cheelo was concerned, this only reinforced the differences between their respective species.

When no response was forthcoming, either verbally or in the form of the by-now-familiar elegant gestures, Cheelo walked over and nudged the blue-green torso with a foot. "Rise and shine, Des. Not that you don't shine all the time."

To look at the thranx was to see nothing wrong. The same brushed, metallic blue-green sheen gleamed from wing cases and limbs, head and neck. The multiple lenses of the eyes, each as big as a human fist, threw back the early morning light in cascades of gold. But something was missing. It took Cheelo a long moment before it struck him.

It was an absence of fragrance.

There was no smell. The delicate, flowery miasma that was the thranx's signature perfume had vanished entirely. Bending over, he inhaled deeply of nothing but fresh mountain air. Then he saw that along with the enthralling alien scent something else had departed. Leaning forward, he gave an uncertain shove with both hands.

Stiff as if frozen, the thranx fell over onto its side, scavenged blankets fluttering briefly like dark wings. They had become a funereal shroud. Rigid legs and arms remained fixed in the positions in which they had last been held, folded tight and close to the body.

"Des? C'mon, I got no time to coddle bugs. Get up." Kneeling, he tentatively grasped one upper limb and tugged gently. It did not flex, and there was no reaction. Using both hands, he pulled harder.

A sharp, splintery crack split the air, and the uppermost joint, together with the truhand, came away in his startled fingers. Blood, dark red tinged with green, began to seep from the maimed limb. A shocked Cheelo straightened and threw the amputated length of alien appendage aside. The dismemberment had provoked neither reaction nor response. Stunned, Cheelo realized that Desvendapur was beyond both.

Sitting down hard, indifferent to the damp vegetation and the cold clamminess of the ground, a disbelieving Cheelo could only stare. The bug was dead. No, he corrected himself. No. The poet was dead. Desmelper . . . Dreshenwn . . .

Christ, he cursed silently. He still couldn't pronounce the alien's name. Now it was possible he never would, because the owner of that appellation could no longer lecture him on the fine points of thranx enunciation. He found himself wishing he'd paid more attention when the alien had talked about himself. He found himself wishing he'd paid more attention to a lot of things.

Well, it was too bad, but it wasn't his fault. Unpredictable destiny served as every sentient's copilot. Just because the thranx had met his here on a cold, wet mountainside in the central Andes didn't mean Cheelo Montoya had any obligation to follow its lead. *His* fate still lay somewhere in the future, first in Golfito and then in the remunerative flesh pits of Monterrey. His conscience was clear.

As for the bug, he owed it nothing. Hell, it didn't even belong on his *world*! The consequences it had suffered were the consummation of its own unforced, willful actions. No guilt concerning the final outcome attached to Cheelo or, for that matter, to anyone else. It was dead; things hadn't worked out; and Cheelo had seen it all before, albeit only among his own kind. No big deal. No big deal at all.

Then why did he feel so goddamn lousy?

This is ridiculous, he told himself. He'd done his best by the alien, just as it had by him. Neither of them had anything to be sorry for. If called before a court of judgment, both could have honestly proclaimed the verity of their conduct while traveling in each other's company. Besides, if the situation were reversed, if he, Cheelo Montoya, had been the one lying dead and motionless among the undergrowth, what would the thranx have done? Returned to its own people, for sure, and left him to rot forlorn and forgotten on the surface of the sodden earth.

Of course, Cheelo Montoya had nothing to leave behind.

He wavered. There was no one to coerce him, no accusatory visages staring at him from the depths of the cloud forest. Whatever urgency he felt came entirely from within, though from where within he could not have said. It made no sense, and he was nothing if not a sensible man. Everything he had ever learned, every ounce of self, all that there was that went to make him what was known as "him," shouted at him to pick up his gear and be on his way. Head down, get going, abandon the no-longer-needed campsite by the little waterfall. Seek out a comfortable room in beckoning Sintuya, arrange his flight, and claim the franchise that had been promised to him. His life had been one long litany of misery and failure. Until now.

Tightening his jaw, he rolled the body, blankets and all, into a dense mass of dark green brush. There it would lie hidden from above until the cloud forest claimed it. Not that the perpetual clouds needed any help in concealing objects on the ground from above.

Snatching up his backpack with a violent grab, he swung it onto his shoulders, checked the seals, and started resolutely down the trail. As he did so, he stumbled over something unyielding. Snapping off a muttered curse, he started to kick aside the piece of broken branch, only to see that the obstacle that had momentarily interrupted the resumption of his determined descent was not made of wood. It was the upper joint and hand he had unexpectedly wrenched from the thranx's body.

Divorced from the rest of the arm, it had assumed an air of artificiality. Surely those stiff, delicate digits were detached from some calcareous sculpture and not a living being. Sublime in its design, sleek and functional, it was of no use to its former owner anymore, and certainly not to him. Bending to pick it up, he examined it closely for a moment before tossing it indifferently over his shoulder and resuming his descent.

Down among the next line of vegetation he halted. Cloud forest trees bloomed intermittently year-round. Ahead rose one that was like a roaring blaze among green stone, an umbrella of brilliant crimson blossoms. Sunbirds sipped drunkenly at the bounteous nectar while giant electric blue morpho butterflies flitted among the branches like the scoured scales of some fantastic cerulean fish. Cheelo stood gazing at the breathtakingly beautiful sight for a long time. Then, without really knowing why, he turned around and began to retrace his steps.

22

Shannon didn't much care for her new posting, but it was a step up from covering tourism and reforestation projects. At least Iquitos had facilities, something to do at night, and climate-controlled shopping where city dwellers could escape from the oppressive heat and humidity. It could have been worse, she knew. The company might have assigned her to report on tropical research. That would have meant weeks at a time living out in the jungle with scientists who would condescend to her questions while resenting the imposition on their time, the access her presence provided to general media notwithstanding. Being assigned to the district office in Iquitos was better, much better.

It also offered the opportunity to do more than just report news. Hard to descry in the rain forest, traditional human-interest stories were plentiful in the city and its enjungled suburbs. Like the one that had presented itself this morning, for example. Plenty of reprobates and lowlifes tried to lose themselves in the vast reaches of the Reserva, but sooner or later their presence was detected by automatic monitoring devices and they found themselves a guest of the rangers.

The only thing different about this one was that instead of petty misappropriation of credit or common vandalism or illegal entry or poaching, the subject had been booked on a charge of murder. Iquitos could be a rough town, but homicide was uncommon. Advanced law-enforcement technology coupled with the threat of general instead of selective mind-wipe was usually enough to forestall most killings.

That was not what made this particular case intriguing, however. What made it interesting from a general media standpoint was that its progenitor had "a story." She was mildly curious to see if the teller was as crazy as his tale.

A guard was stationed outside the interview room; not surprising considering that the one incarcerated within stood accused of a capital crime. Having already been scanned for possession of weapons and other forbidden items, she identified herself to the sentry's satisfaction and was granted admittance. As the door slid into the wall he stood aside to let her enter.

The aspect of the solitary figure seated on the other side of the interview table was not promising, and she found herself worrying that she might well be wasting her time. Not that there was any especial demand on it at the moment. Pulling out and activating her recorder, she checked to make sure that the protective cover had retracted and that the lens was clean. Treated to repel dirt and grime, it flickered briefly in the subdued overhead light.

The brief flash caught the attention of the prisoner. When he lifted his head, she was able to get a better look at him. It did not improve her opinion. Neither did the way he looked at her, used to it as she was.

"I was expecting a reporter, not a treat." He leered unpleasantly. "How about we get the monkey cop to opaque the window?" He nodded toward the doorway.

"How about you keep your mouth and your eyes to yourself and you answer my questions?" she retorted flatly. "Otherwise, I'll waft and you can play with yourself until the official interrogators land on you again. They won't listen to your lunatic stories, either."

His macho bravado instantly deflated, the prisoner looked away. Fingers working uneasily against one another as if he didn't know what to do with them, he muttered a reply. "First you got to get me my personal belongings."

Her dyed and striped brows drew together. "What personal belongings? The report on you said you were picked up out in the forest with only the clothes on your back."

Leaning forward, he lowered his voice to a conspiratorial whisper. "When I saw that the rangers had me referenced, I buried my pack. Without what's in it you won't believe a word I say."

"I doubt I'll believe a word you say anyway, so what's the big deal? What's in your miserable pack that you had to hide from the rangers? Illegal narcotics? Gemstones?"

He grinned, this time knowingly. "Proof. Of my story."

Shaking her head sadly, she turned off the recorder. No point in wasting the cell. "There *is* no proof of your 'story.' Not in some mysterious buried backpack or anywhere else. Because your story's crazy. It makes no sense."

The smile tightened but did not disappear entirely. "Then why are *you* here?"

She shrugged diffidently. "Because it sounded different from the usual run-of-the mill rubbish we use for backscreen fillers. Because I thought you might be good for a new angle or two on how some miscreants try to mask themselves from the attentions of the legal process. So far I'm just annoyed, not enlightened."

"Go dig up my pack and I'll enlighten the hell out of you. The contents will enlighten you."

She sighed heavily. "I skimmed the report. There are *no* thranx in the Reserva. There are no thranx in this hemisphere. Their presence on Earth, like that of all representatives of newly contacted sentient species, is restricted to the one orbital station that's been equipped with proper diplomatic facilities. We have occasional closely supervised visits by especially important individuals holding the rank of eint or higher, but they are not allowed outside the official boundaries of Lombok or Geneva. Even if one somehow managed to end up here, it couldn't survive."

Inclining toward her again, he dropped his voice so low that she had to lean forward to make out the words. She did not relish the proximity. Despite the treatment accorded any incoming prisoner, he still stank strongly of his time spent in the Reserva and of his own disagreeable self.

"You're right. 'One' couldn't survive. But a properly prepared and equipped landing party could."

She rolled her eyes and looked away. She'd had just about enough of this homicidal *ninloco* and his pathetic fantasies. "Now you're trying to tell me that there's not one, but a whole landing party of thranx bashing around undetected inside the Reserva? What kind of moron do you take me for, Montoya? If the rangers can run down one human like yourself who's trying his damnedest to avoid them, don't you think they'd find something as alien as a thranx? Much less a whole landing party?"

"Not if it stayed underground and had human help," he shot back. "And I wasn't trying to avoid the rangers. Not anymore. I wanted to be picked up."

She frowned uncertainly, her irritation diminishing just enough for her to sustain a modicum of interest. "Underground? You're trying to tell me that there's an illegal thranx landing party operating inside the Reserva and underground?"

His countenance subsided into a complacent smirk. "Not a landing party. A hive. A colony." His tone had become insolent. "There aren't a dozen or so thranx in the Reserva—there are hundreds. And they're not peeking at plants or collecting butterflies—they're living there. And breeding."

She stared hard at him, at this slender, vainglorious *madrino* who sat with arms crossed and smile smug. He did not look away. She wanted to, but could not. Not quite yet.

"So what's in this pack of yours that would prove a claim as outrageous as that?"

"Then my 'crazy' story might be a little newsworthy?" He was taunting her now. She wouldn't let him get away with it.

"Give me the coordinates for this pack of yours and we'll see what's in it. If anything. If it exists."

"Oh, it exists all right." He glanced briefly toward the doorway. "But first we need to come to some kind of agreement. Officially recorded and witnessed."

"Agreement?" Shannon was not pleased. Her bureau's discretionary expense file was in proportion to her assignment. Iquitos wasn't Paris. "What kind of agreement?"

For the first time since she had entered the interview room he appeared to relax. "You don't think I'm going to give away the story of the century out of the goodness of my heart, do you?" For a moment, his eyes took on a faraway look and his voice fell to a whisper. "I *have* to get something back, because I've already missed my appointment. I forfeited the franchise. For this." He shook his head slowly, his tone disbelieving. "I *must* be crazy. One other thing: We tell it my way. I want editorial input."

She started to laugh, but then she saw that he was serious. "So now in addition to being a murderer you want to be a journalist?"

His eyes lowered. "That killing up in San José was unfortunate. An accident. It'll all come out at my hearing." The smile returned, sly and knowing. "It'll be a sealed hearing, you'll see. I know too much, and the government doesn't like people who know too much to run around loose babbling what they know. But it'll be worth it to you. I promise."

She sat up straight and turned her recorder back on. "Never mind all that other nonsense: What makes you think you know anything about telling a story?"

Pursing his lips, he blew her a kiss. She recoiled distastefully. "You just bought mine, didn't you?"

The pack was there, surprisingly far to the south, buried in a shallow pit between two gnarled strangler figs. Right where he'd said it would be. That in itself meant nothing. The presence of an identifiable, functioning thranx device inside was likewise conclusive of nothing except the owner's ability to obtain contraband through channels with which he was clearly familiar. The section of thranx arm, however, was another matter. It was sufficiently fresh and well-enough wrapped so that it had not yet begun to decompose, even under the relentless assault of the opportunistic rain forest. Taken together, they lent veracity if not proof to the prisoner's story.

The next time Shannon visited Montoya, she had company. Not rangers, but a pair of commentators from her company and one wizened, white-haired senior editor.

The prisoner eyed them with an amiable wariness. On the table between them lay the section of alien limb and the device that had been removed from the buried backpack. Neither appeared to have been touched, though in fact both had been carefully examined with a view toward verifying their authenticity. This had been done. Now it remained for the exceedingly curious media representatives to find out how these unlikely objects had come to be in the possession of a minor criminal whose erstwhile home lay far to the north on the American isthmus.

One of the reporters pushed the device across the table in Cheelo's direction. "We know that this is of alien manufacture, but we don't know what it does."

"I do. It's a scri!ber. I told you—Des was a poet. That means he did more than just put words together. Among the thranx, poetry is a performance art. I know: He performed a couple of times for me." A gaunt, regretful smile split his features. "I didn't get much out of it. Didn't understand the words or the gestures. There was a lot of clicking and whistling, too. But God, it was beautiful."

The reporter who had asked the question was about to laugh, but her companion put a restraining hand on her arm. Leaning forward, he spoke understandingly. "I'm Rodrigo Monteverde, from the parliament district. I haven't seen the kind of performance you're referring to myself, but I've talked to those who have. Your description fits."

"These thranx have performed for ranking officials. A couple have been on the tridee." The senior editor did not stir as he spoke. "He could have seen a recording."

Shannon gingerly pushed the length of amputated limb toward the prisoner. "What about this? What's this?"

Montoya lowered his gaze to the blue-green fingers. His insides knotted and a sharp pain shot through his gut, but to all outward appearances he was unaffected. "That? That was my friend." He looked up, smiling at Shannon before shifting his attention to the gray-hair who obviously called the shots.

"I'm offering you the biggest story of the last hundred years. You want it, or should I put out the word that I'm ready to talk to another media conglomerate?"

The senior editor retained his unshakable composure, but a hint of a smile toyed with one corner of his mouth. "We want it—if there's anything more to it. The question is, what do *you* want?" He nodded in the reporter's direction. "Ms. Shannon here has apprised me of your petition but did not supply any details."

All eyes were on him, components of expectant expressions. He reveled in the attention. It made him feel . . . big. "That's better! First, I want all charges pending or planning to be filed against me dropped."

"I understand you committed a murder." Shannon's tone was dry as dust. She didn't like him, Cheelo knew. That did not matter. What was vital was that she saw the opportunity to work on a big story. He was not the only one to whom the word was important. Much of the world still worked that way. "It was accidental, like I told you. The idiot had to go macho and grab the gun and there was a struggle. Nobody could prove premeditation. Scan the wife and you'll see that I'm telling the truth."

"Nevertheless," declared the senior editor inexorably, "you left an innocent man for dead."

"Fix it." Cheelo's tone was harsh and uncompromising. "I know what the media can do. After all charges are dropped, I want my permanent record expunged. I'd like to start over, clean."

"So you can fill it up again?" The editor sighed. "What you ask is doable. Expensive and awkward, but doable. Especially if what you say about scanning the wife holds up. What else?"

"Some credit in my account. I haven't settled on a sum yet. We can work that out together." His tone turned wistful. "You probably won't believe me, but by letting myself get picked up I sacrificed a lot more money than you can imagine. More than that, I gave up a career."

"How noble of you." As the editor spoke, all three reporters were taking notes. *Notes,* Cheelo thought silently. That's all any of us are: a bundle of somebody else's notes. When we die, we're all dependent on the notes made by others. Unless we take the time to make some ourselves.

"One more thing." He pushed the alien scri!ber toward Shannon. "I want everything that's on here published. I don't know what that means in this case, or how you'd go about doing it, because it's not like human poetry. But I want it *done.* I want it all published and disseminated. Among the thranx as well as here on Earth."

" 'Disseminated'?" Shannon eyed him archly.

"Hey, I'm poor, not stupid. I want Des's art—out there. For everybody to see."

"It won't mean anything to us, to humans," the second reporter pointed out.

"Maybe not, but the thranx are going to be exposed to it whether they like it or not. Once disclosed, they won't be able to ignore it. It's great stuff, important work. *Big* work." He squeezed his eyelids together. Hard. "Bigger than anything *I'll* ever do."

For the first time, the open hostility and contempt Shannon had been feeling began to give way to incertitude. "How do you know that, if you couldn't understand any of it?"

"I know because of the way Des believed in it, the way he talked about it, the way he showed it to me—even if I didn't understand much of it. I know because he gave up everything to try and achieve something important. I'm no artist—I can't sculpt, or paint, or weave light, or write real well. But I know passion when I see it." He brightened. "Yeah, that's what it was about Des. He was passionate." He tapped the scri!ber's protective casing. "This gadget is full of passion, and I want it splashed out there for everybody to see."

For the first time, the senior editor showed some animation. "Why? Why should you care what happens to the work of some obscure alien artist? The art means nothing to you. *He* meant nothing to you."

"I'm not sure. Maybe—maybe it's because I've always felt that everybody should stand for something, even if the rest of society doesn't agree on what that is, and that nobody should die for nothing. I've seen too many people die for nothing. I don't want it to happen to me, and I don't want it to happen to Des." With a shrug, he looked away, toward the single window that was too small for a prisoner to crawl through. Outside lay the city and beyond, the rain forest.

"It'll probably happen to me anyway. I'm not anything special. Never was and probably never will be. But I'm going to see to it that it doesn't happen to him."

While the reporters waited respectfully, the editor considered the prisoner's words. Eventually he looked back up at Cheelo. "All right. We agree to your terms. All of them. *Provided* there's something significant and real at the end of this alien rainbow of yours."

A mollified Cheelo leaned back in his chair. Despite the backpack, despite its unarguably alien contents, he was not sure until the very end that the media people would go for it. Unless he was very much mistaken, he would soon be walking the streets again. A dead thranx poet had cost him a career but bought him his freedom.

What the consequences of that freedom would be he could not have foreseen. He expected to be free. He did not expect to be famous.

Searching only within the section of rain forest specified by the thief allowed the reporters and their staff to locate the hive within a few weeks of Cheelo supplying them with coordinates. Worldwide revelation followed and outrage ensued. Exposed and confronted, the representatives of the colony and their covert human allies pleaded a case which for them could have only one outcome.

Their careful, cautious diplomacy undone, human and thranx emissaries scrambled to salvage what they could of a shattered process of prudent negotiation. Forced to advance all interspecies colloquy and bring forward proposals that were barely in the preliminary stages of synthesis, they hastened to compose and then sign the first formal treaties between humans and thranx some twenty to forty years before they were ready. Both species would simply have to deal with the unpredictable consequences. The alternative was a formal break in relations coupled with the possibility of open hostilities.

As for the Amazonian colony, it was allowed to remain only because humans were hastily granted reciprocal colonization privileges on the thranx homeworld of Hivehom in addition to the much smaller installation on Willow-Wane. A site was selected on what the bipeds soon came to call the Mediterranea Plateau, a dominion too bleak and cold and dry for the thranx to settle. Forced together by the circumstance of revelation, human and thranx rapidly discovered that they complemented one another in ways that could not have been predicted by formal diplomacy. The first tentative steps were taken to overcome each species' abhorrence of the hideous appearance of the other.

As for Cheelo Montoya, who only wanted to sink back into the backstreet society in which he had grown up, albeit with a bit more money, he found himself transformed from petty, remorseless street hustler into a paragon of interspecies first contact. It was a celebrity he did not seek and did not want, but once his part in the business was revealed he no longer had any choice in the matter. Eagerly sought out for interviews, thrust beneath world-spanning tridee pickups, he was repeatedly reminded of his personal inadequacies by questions he could not answer and requests for opinions that were beneath his ability to formulate. With his face thrust relentlessly before an inquisitive world, he lost any semblance of personal privacy. Poked, prodded, queried, challenged, the object of rumor and the subject of speculation, before long he found himself regretting that he had ever tried to make a single credit off his unsought relationship with the dead alien poet. Harried and harassed by a pitiless media and a bastard-loving populace, he died sooner than he should have, ennobled by a public whose historical appetite for falsely inculcated minor deities verged on the unbounded. His funeral was a sumptuous, splendid affair, trideed all over the planet as well as to all human and thranx-settled worlds. He would have decried the waste of money.

The monument they placed above his coffin, at least, was something big.

The thranx were less ingenuous. Forced by its exposure to accept on its merits the work of a monstrously antisocial artist who normally would have been resolutely ignored, the highly conservative thranx performance establishment proved unable to repudiate its worth. The power and passion with which the deceased Desvendapur had endowed his compositions would not be denied.

So it was that Cheelo Montoya, who did not want it, was forced to endure the fame that the renegade poet Desvendapur had sought. Offered a shocking amount for his memoirs, he had laboriously transcribed them for the media with the help of a small army of ghost writers. As he told it, the tale of his encounter and relationship with the renegade thranx artist took on a glamorous, heroic mien. Poetic, even, so that while later generations knew that a murderer and a poet were responsible for the forced, accelerated pace of human-thranx contact, the line became blurred as to who was which.

With tentative, cultivated, ceremonial contact shattered by the unscheduled revelations, relations between the species were advanced by perhaps half a century in spite of, and not because of, the exertions of well-meaning, hard-working, professional emissaries. There was precedent. History is often fashioned by insignificant individuals intent on matters of petty personal concern who have motives entirely irrelevant to carefully planned posterity. It was just as well.

Had humankind contacted the next intelligent race they encountered prior to formalizing relations with the thranx, the Commonwealth might very well never have come into existence. As for the duplicitous AAnn, their upset verged on outrage as they saw their traditional competitors for habitable worlds forge an ever-deepening relationship with the militarily strong but mentally unpredictable humans. Bereft of stratagems for countering the seemingly inevitable alliance, the government of the emperor sought the advice of any who might have an efficacious solution to propound.

As it happened, Lord Huudra Ap and Baron Keekil YN stood ready to supply one.

DIRGE

To John Haynes
Web-site designer *par excellence*

1

Kairuna was kneeling beside a flattened blue-brown bush that rose no higher than his knee, watching half a dozen dull yellow slugs with legs combine their efforts to spin a mutual home out of what appeared to be cerise silk. The nature of the instinct that impelled them to effortlessly meld their minuscule exertions would have to be identified by the xenologists. Absolved by his work classification of the need to analyze or classify, he was free to marvel and wonder at the intricate beauty of the delicate alien phenomenon. He felt sorry for the techs who were required to stop, stand, and interpret. Sometimes it was a lot better just to be able to look.

Straightening, he let his gaze rove over the endless forest. Well, not literally endless. The Earthlike pseudo evergreens only occupied the broad temperate belt that followed the planet's equator. A traveler journeying to north or south would eventually run out of forest and into one of the great ice caps that dominated the surface of Argus V. But since preliminary surveys from orbit had indicated that the forest belt varied between two and three thousand miles in width, there was plenty of room left between the brooding ice for trees.

And for ambulatory life, not all of which was as inconspicuous as silk-spinning slugs. In the two months they had been exploring the planet the surveyors had encountered a number of interesting and exotic larger life-forms. The local carnivores were efficient but not especially impressive—nothing the team couldn't deal with. Their presence added to the ambience of what was proving to be a chilly but otherwise hospitable world.

"Norway." Idar came up behind Kairuna, puffing hard and lugging her tripod-mounted census taker with her. "Western Canada. Tasmania."

Slapping her gloved hands together, she began to set up her instruments. Depending on how they were calibrated, they could take an image of a chosen section of ground together with an approximation of every kind and variety of life-form that dwelled therein.

"Kind of cold for me." Kairuna came from and preferred a warmer clime. The pristine atmosphere and the oxygen infused into it by the untouched forest helped to compensate for temperatures that, while remaining above freezing, precluded anyone but stoic fanatics from running around in short pants. He was glad of his insulated jacket and boots.

"Won't keep colonizers from coming." Idar squinted into an eyepiece, adjusted a readout, bent slightly to squint again. "Some folks would call this paradise."

"If so, it'll always be one with limited horizons." Kairuna gazed northward. They were working about a thousand miles south of the northern ice cap, but he still fancied he could see the glint from its leading edge sparkling on the sharp blue horizon.

"So it's not another New Riviera. What would be? But so far it looks as good or better than Proycon, and people are clamoring to settle there." Laboring behind her instrument, the census taker shrugged. "There's still plenty of room available for settlement. Oceans are small because so much of the planet's water is locked up in ice. People will like it here." Raising her head to look over the top of the eyepiece, she grinned. "Should be bonuses all around."

Kairuna contemplated the possibility and found it warming. The gruff voice that chose to dissent made him wince and smile at the same time.

"Bonuses! Ha! I wouldn't count on it!"

Both techs turned a rueful, knowing smile in the direction of the newcomer. Alwyn was a short, stocky, dyspeptic, highly experienced member of the survey mission's support team. Able to raise a shelter, arrange for purified water, or fix an enormous variety of instruments in the field with little more than a pocket repair kit, he was as valuable a member of the expedition as he was personally irritating. Nobody on board the *Chagos* liked him very much, not even his fellow corps members. In addition to recovery and repair, his other area of specialization seemed to be carping and bitching. He did not even have the good grace to shut up when he was working, forcing whichever tech or scientist whose gear he was rejuvenating to have to stand around and listen to his complaining.

He was, however, very good at what he did.

"Why shouldn't we?" The more argumentative Idar confronted the support specialist without hesitation. "It's been years since anybody found a world that was even remotely Earthlike." She gestured expansively at the forest. "Maybe it's only partly colonizable because of the ice caps, but the rest of it, the upper temperate forest lands like this, will draw settlers in droves. You know the rules: Everybody qualifies for a share in the primary finding and exploration benefits." She chuckled. "Even you, unless you want to sign over your presupposed nonexistent bonus to me."

"Thanks," the specialist muttered, "but I'll hang onto the designation, just in case I'm wrong and the government decides to play fair and honest with this one."

"With this one?" Kairuna's heavy black eyebrows arched. "How many primes for colonizable worlds have you been on?"

"Well, none, actually." The small, muscular form turned away. "This is my first."

"This is everybody's first." Kairuna mentioned the obvious while Idar adjusted her instrumentation slightly in order to take a new sighting. "There are a lot more ships out looking than there are habitable worlds being found."

"Right enough," Alwyn agreed. "And half of those seem to be full of giant bugs who've already laid claim to the place."

Idar looked up from the eyepiece of her taker. "The thranx are our friends."

"Yeah, sure," the tech groused. "The government keeps trying to convince us of that. Trying too hard, if you ask me. What about that covert colony they set up in the Reserva Amazonia? If it hadn't been for that wandering street thug stumbling into the place the rest of us still wouldn't know about that!"

"It was part of a secret government project." Kairuna watched something slim and elegant soar across the clear blue sky. At this distance he could not tell if its wings were fashioned of feather, membrane, or some as yet unidentified organic substance.

Alwyn was nodding vigorously. "Sure was. It was such a secret government project even the government didn't know about it. You ever seen a thranx? I mean, in person?" he challenged the bigger man.

"No," Kairuna confessed. "Only tridees."

"They're ugly little bastards. Like big crickets or mantids with an extra set of limbs." He shuddered. "I don't care what the lovey-dovey we're-all-sapients-together-in-this-galactic-arm propagandists mew. You won't catch me cuddling up next to no goddamn giant bug. And there are plenty of people who feel even stronger about it than I do. Me, if I ran into one, I'd step on it."

"The thranx are a little big to step on," Kairuna reminded him. "Especially for someone your size."

"And they might step back," Idar added without looking up from her work.

Alwyn thrust his chin forward belligerently. "Exactly my point. The galaxy's a vast, unfriendly, dangerous place."

"The more reason to make friends with those who inhabit it alongside us," Kairuna argued.

Lively blue eyes stared back up at him. "The more reason to be careful just who we nestle up to."

The discussion was interrupted—not by the weather or the indigenous wildlife, not by the need to continue working, but by a reverberant, insistent howl. Standing on the little knoll debating interstellar relationships while taking the measure of the alien forest, they turned as one in the direction of the wailing, sonorous bellow. It was unfamiliar to all of them.

"What the hell is that?" Alwyn had walked quickly to the edge of the knoll to gaze with even more than his usual wariness in the direction of the landing transport. Idar's recording was forgotten. Kairuna stood behind the two of them, staring over their heads in the direction of the mournful, insistent howl.

It came not from the vicinity of the landing transport but from the vehicle itself. It was Kairuna who finally recognized it.

"That's the general alert."

"General alert?" The census taker frowned back at him. "What the hell's a 'general alert'? I know all sorts of situation-specific alarms, but I've never heard of a general alert. Especially not on surface." Her expression was bemused as she stared down the hill in the direction of the camp that had sprung up around the landing field that had been cleared to allow shuttle craft a safe place to set down.

"I told you!" Alwyn was irritatingly triumphant. "You can't trust a new world, no matter how benign a face it presents."

In reference to faces, Kairuna wished the annoying service specialist would take his elsewhere. It did not matter that he might be right: The botanist was tired of listening to the other man's ranting.

"Come on," he urged them. "We'd better go and see what's happening."

"General alert." Nodding smugly, Alwyn joined them in descending from the densely forested knob and retracing their steps. "I knew it."

Surrounded by members of the *Chagos*'s staff, Burgess was staring intently at the tridee. Magnification was visual, not schematic, so he was able to observe the craft that had just joined them in orbit in all its alien glory. It was an impressive ship, at least twice the size of the *Chagos*. While the prevalent configuration was similar to that of the *Chagos* and all other vessels equipped with the universal variant of the KK drive, its design and execution differed in a multitude of significant respects.

"Not ours," one of the techs seated nearby murmured unnecessarily.

"Not thranx, either," the first officer added. "Unless they've been hiding something from us. Could it be one of those AAnn ships the thranx are always trying to warn us about?"

Burgess looked doubtful. "I've seen the AAnn schematics the thranx have provided. This design is much too sleek. Could it be Quillp?" Burgess longed for expertise in an area his crew, through no fault of their own, did not possess.

"I don't think so, Captain." Though far from positive, the first officer felt secure in hazarding a guess. If he was proved wrong, he would be delighted to admit the mistake. He hoped he was wrong. The inherent pacificity of the Quillp was well known.

Looking sharply to his left, Burgess snapped a question. "Any response to our queries, Tambri?"

The diminutive communications officer glanced over at him and shook her head. Her dark eyes were very wide. "Nothing, sir. I'm trying everything, from Terranglo through High and Low Thranx to straight mathematical theorems. They're chattering noisily among themselves—I can pick up the wash—but they're not talking to us."

"They will. Keep trying." Burgess turned back to the three-dimensional image floating in the air of the ship's bridge. "Who are they and what the blazes do they want here?"

"Maybe they've already claimed this world." The observation no one had wanted to voice came from the back of the command section. "Maybe they're here to inform us of a claim of prior rights."

"If that's the case," the first officer declared, "they've been mighty subtle about advertising any prior presence here. There isn't so much as an artifact on the planet, much less an orbital transmitter. There's nothing on either of the two small moons, or anywhere else in the system."

"That we've found yet, you mean." Having stated a contention, the dissenter felt bound to defend it. "We've only been here a couple of months."

"Okay, okay," Burgess muttered. "Let's everybody keep calm. Whatever the situation, we'll deal with it. We didn't expect to encounter sapience here, much less evidence of another space-traversing species. They're probably taking our measure as carefully as we are theirs." *But I wish they'd respond to our communications,* he thought tensely.

"Look there!" Someone in the growing crowd pointed.

A second, much smaller vessel was emerging from the side of the first. Winged and ported, obviously designed for atmospheric travel, it began to recede swiftly from the flank of its parent vessel. Its immediate purpose was self-evident. Anything else those aboard might intend could not be divined from tracking its progress.

"Get on to Pranchavit and the rest of the landing party," Burgess barked at the communications officer. "Tell them they're probably going to have company."

Once again the officer looked up from her instrumentation. "They'll want to know what kind of company, sir."

Burgess glanced over at the tridee holo. "Maybe they can tell us."

By the time Kairuna and his companions arrived at the camp, it was alive with questions and concerns, anxiety and confusion. No one seemed to know what was going on, including those who had recognized the audible signal for what it was. Now they troubled themselves with unsupported inferences and paranoid suppositions. In such company, Alwyn was in his element.

Pushing and shoving their way into an already crowded mess hall, the three late arrivals found themselves confined to the narrow remaining open space next to the rear wall. Up by the service door that led to the main stockroom, Jalen Maroto was waving his arms for quiet. When that didn't work, he put a compact amplifier to his lips and simply shouted everybody down.

"Shut up! If you'll just shut up, I'll tell you what's going on." As the crowd noise subsided he added apologetically, "Or at least, what we know."

"I know!" Alwyn was not afraid to proclaim theories where others were hesitant to venture facts. "Something local's finally showed up to cause trouble. What is it?" he demanded to know. "A herd of predators? A fast-mutating plague?"

"There's a plague, all right," the team leader declared through the amplifier, "but it's one we brought along with us." Delighted to take advantage of the emotional release, a number of the assembled turned their laughter in the specialist's direction. Unrepentant but temporarily subdued, he tried to meet the ridicule of each and every one of them with a defiant glare of his own.

"A ship has gone into orbit near the *Chagos*," Maroto informed scientists and support personnel alike. "We don't know where it's from, what species built it, or what their intentions are. So far nobody on the *Chagos*, including the people who are supposed to know about such things, has been able to pull a fact out of a big basket of ignorance."

"They're not thranx?" someone in the crowd wondered loudly, referring to the intelligent insectoid race with whom humankind had been cautiously developing relations over the past thirty years.

"We don't know who or what they are," Maroto replied, "because they're not responding to the *Chagos*'s repeated queries to identify themselves. If they're thranx, they're being mighty close-mouthed about it."

"The bugs may be ugly, but I've never heard of them going mute," Idar murmured softly.

"I know what they are." When no one reacted to his latest assertion of certitude, Alwyn assumed a plaintive tone. "Well? Doesn't anyone want to know what I know?"

"Nobody wants to know what you know, Alwyn, because you never know half of what you claim to know." Unlike his companions Kairuna had the advantage of being able to see over the heads of just about everyone in the crowd.

"Go ahead and mock." Alwyn was confident as ever. "These are the hostile, rampaging, bloodthirsty aliens we've always feared encountering as we extend our sphere of influence."

"I thought the AAnn were supposed to be the hostile aliens," Idar pointed out.

"That's what the thranx claim, but so far we've only the bugs' word for AAnn hostility. No, these are something new. New and hostile," he concluded with an assurance that regrettably was not born of proof.

"If they're hostile," a contrary Kairuna argued, "why are we still standing here talking? Why haven't they turned this site and all of us to dust?"

"Just you wait." Secure in his latent mistrust, the specialist glanced knowingly skyward.

Aside from the fact that scattering into the trees could be misinterpreted by those aboard the rapidly descending alien shuttle as a hostile gesture, there was—the feelings of a certain suspicious support specialist aside—no overwhelming reason to do so. The parent ship continued to swing in low orbit within viewing distance of the *Chagos*, moving neither toward nor away from the human vessel, its communicators silent, the identity of its occupants still a mystery. No one on board the *Chagos* was surprised when the alien shuttle braked atmosphere and began a swift, calculated curve that would put it on the surface directly in the midst of the survey team's encampment. Indeed, given the ongoing proximity of the two KK-drive craft, Burgess and his fellow staff officers would have been perplexed had the alien shuttle chosen to set down anywhere else.

"No component of the landing team is properly trained to handle a first contact," the *Chagos*'s second officer felt compelled to point out.

"Pranchavit has good people working for him," Burgess reminded the officer. "And Maroto's had offworld experience. Between our support personnel and the scientific complement I'm sure relations will develop in an orderly and prudent manner we can all be proud of."

"What if they can't communicate?" the first officer wondered. "Even the best intentions can go awry if misinterpreted."

"We don't have any choice." Burgess's expression was solemn. "I can't tell Pranchavit and Maroto to ignore the aliens. The rest of us will just have to maintain the alert and hope nothing untoward happens down below." Seeing the apprehension on the faces of his staff he added, "Look, there's nothing we can do from up here. Zdanko's contact team has been back on board for weeks because we didn't find any sentients on the surface in our first month here. Nobody could imagine that they'd show up later. It's never happened before."

"There must be something we can do," someone shouted wistfully from across the room.

"There is," the captain admitted. "Prayer would not be out of order. All of you please feel free to invoke whatever deities enjoin your affection." He turned back to the tridee. "Especially on behalf of those of us who are stuck down on the surface until this situation resolves itself."

Idar and Alwyn stood beside Kairuna as they had been instructed: assembled with the rest of the survey team between the cleared landing field and the trees ready to greet the arriving aliens. Argusian vertebrates soared high above the open grassland, scanning the surface for prey or seeds according to preference. A cool breeze kept the somber proceedings from becoming stiff, making it necessary for the anxious assembled to keep moving in order to stay warm.

"I don't get it." Both arms wrapped across her chest, Idar watched her breath congeal in the afternoon air. "What are we doing here? Not that I'm not as curious as the next person, but I don't see why our presence is necessary. We're not part of any formal first-contact squad."

"Neither is anyone else." Kairuna gestured skyward, once. "The official contact team is stuck up on the *Chagos*. So the job, and the burden, not to mention the responsibility, has been dumped on Pranchavit and Maroto." He gazed across the bobbing heads in the direction of the field, where the leaders of the survey team's scientific and support contingents stood side by side, watching the northern horizon and waiting for something to happen. "Better them than you or I."

"I could do a better job than any of 'em," Alwyn avowed. "At least I wouldn't be standing out there with my ass exposed to the four winds and no gun."

"You heard the appraisal from the experts on board the *Chagos*,"

Kairuna admonished him. "If these aliens intended hostilities they would already have attacked the ship."

"Not if they're still sizing us up and trying to gauge our strength," Alwyn shot back. "Or waiting to see if we're good to eat."

"What are you doing here, anyway?" Idar challenged him angrily. "If you're so worried about malicious aliens, what possessed you to apply for a position on a deep-space exploration run?"

"Let me guess." Kairuna responded before the other man could reply. "Money."

"Good guess." Alwyn tugged the brim of his warming cap down over his forehead, trying to shut out the wind. "But that's not the only reason. Earth was getting too dangerous. Too many people crammed into too many big cities. That's what the colonies are all about. Room to move around and keep clear of the crazies."

"So why didn't you apply to move to one of the Centaurus worlds, or New Riviera?" Idar wondered aloud. "With your technical qualifications you could have emigrated anywhere."

"It's the same there as on Earth," he responded without hesitation. "Too many lunatics. The only difference between Earth and the colonies is that the more adventurous nuts apply for emigration." He nodded skyward. "Deep space seemed the safer bet. At the time."

"It still is." Kairuna exuded quiet assurance. "I think you're going to be surprised. I think we're all going to be surprised."

"Yeah, we'll be surprised, all right," the specialist muttered. "That's why I'm standing back here, as far away from the designated greeting point as possible. Closer to the forest that way. At least in the woods we'll have a chance."

"You'll have a chance." Idar did not try to hide her distaste. "The rest of us aren't going anywhere. I've got work to do, and as soon as this formality is concluded, I'm going right back to it."

Not deigning to respond, Alwyn turned to his other companion. "What about you, Kai? You with me?"

"Only as far as dinner." The big man taunted him gently. "Why wait for disaster to strike, Alwyn? Why not make a break for the forest now, before the unspeakably horrid alien invaders arrive?"

"Because I'd have my pay docked for disobeying a general directive, and you know it. Go ahead and laugh. We'll see which one of us snickers last, and which of us is still able to do so."

"Hush!" Idar was staring to the north, where the first snow-covered mountains rose above miscolored alien trees. "I think it's coming."

At first nothing more than a distant point of light sifting down through an azure sky, the alien landing craft grew rapidly in size and dimension until its descending silhouette differentiated sharply from the framing clouds. Assembled between field and forest, fewer than a hundred human faces strained to make out the lines and design of the unknown vessel.

As it drew nearer still they saw that it boasted a peculiar arrangement of wheels instead of the familiar, all-purpose struts that extended from the underside of similar human and thranx craft. Half a dozen wings protruded from its flanks, running from the nose all the way back to the tail. This extravagance of lifting surfaces was counterbalanced by an absence of any visible antennae or weapons. Tinted bright yellow, the sides and undercarriage of the alien superstructure were flecked with unfamiliar and indecipherable mauve hieroglyphs.

The landing was smooth and almost silent, as if the pilots had been practicing on similar open fields for years. As the whine of multiple engines became tolerable, hands fell from ears to shade eyes as the craft turned to approach the crowd. There being no need for ceremony while engaged in survey, Pranchavit and Maroto were reduced to greeting the visitors in clean duty clothes. Kairuna smiled to himself. The prim head of the Argus scientific team, at least, was no doubt regretting the absence of his fancy dress uniform.

There was a stirring as the landing craft maintained speed during its turn, and a few of those gathered in front found themselves wondering if perhaps their desire for a good view of the proceedings might not be misplaced. But the many-winged alien lander pivoted neatly on its double set of nose wheels and lined up parallel to the crowd. Those in front relaxed. Nothing of an overtly offensive nature was in evidence. Kairuna knew of several researchers and techs who had armed themselves in defiance of directives. Pistols remained concealed by multiple layers of cold-weather clothing and bulky jackets.

Eagerness filled the air like a cool fog. What would the aliens look like? Would they be atavistically alarming like the thranx? Elegantly handsome and yet vaguely sinister like the AAnn? Or quaintly charming like the Quillp? Humankind had yet to voyage sufficiently far, had still to encounter enough intelligent species, to be blasé at the prospect of meeting still another.

Perhaps they would look like nothing the smooth-skinned simians in their glistening new KK-drive starships had yet met. They might be towering horrors or diminutive pacifists. Or diminutive horrors or towering pacifists. No one knew. The aliens had failed to respond to interrogatives from the *Chagos*, either verbally or visually. Kairuna and the rest of the survey team would be the first to gaze upon these new, previously unencountered alien countenances. He and his associates were acutely conscious of the singular privilege that was being accorded them.

Everyone had been thoroughly, if hastily, briefed. No matter what the aliens looked like, no matter how repulsive or absurd or disconcerting or surprising, all reaction was to be kept to a minimum. There was to be no cheering lest sudden loud noises upset the visitors. No wrinkling of faces, no distorted expressions that might be misinterpreted in the event the visitors communicated by similar means. No expansive gestures in case they asserted themselves in a manner akin to the highly gesticulatory thranx. Response to any overtures and all expressions of greeting would be made by Pranchavit and Maroto. Everyone else was welcome to watch, but in stillness and silence.

That did not prevent Idar from nudging Kairuna in the side as an opaque cylinder slowly and silently descended from the belly of the alien craft. It looked as if a particularly sleek bird was laying an oblong egg. Nearby, a grim-faced Alwyn patted his side.

"Not to worry. I'm carrying a regulation sideshot with a full clip."

"It won't be of much use to you in the brig," Idar hissed at him.

"Both of you, be quiet." Kairuna nodded. "They're coming out. Or something is." The possibility that the aliens might choose to make first contact through intermediaries such as mechanicals could not be discounted.

There were no mechanicals, however. The aliens had chosen to greet the tightly packed crowd of anxious bipeds in person. There were three of them. Nitrox breathers themselves, they were clad only in lightweight clothing of some unfamiliar fabric that shimmered in the bright, cold air, and no helmets or other headgear whatsoever.

The reaction to their appearance was a uniform gasp on the part of the assembled humans. Kairuna was unaware that his lower jaw dropped slightly, leaving him standing in full defiance of orders with a mock stupid expression on his face. Idar stood wide-eyed but with more presence of mind as well as person. Alwyn, whose left hand had been hovering in the vicinity of his concealed weapon, was moved to comment, but mindful of the general directive to keep quiet, he held his peace.

It was a good thing he had the forbearance to keep from drawing the gun. The aliens might not have reacted immediately to its emergence, but his fellow humans surely would have. It was not that his naturally suspicious nature was in any way mollified by the aliens' utterly unexpected and novel appearance, only that he was for once no less shocked than his companions.

2

The reaction on Earth to the announcement that yet another intelligent space-faring species had been discovered no longer dominated the news portion of the general media. People were more interested in the progress of the new settlements being opened in the Centaurus group, the results of the lottery to determine who would be granted emigration visas for New Riviera, the latest DNA-HGH gene splicing scandal involving the parents of would-be sports superstars, whether a new wholly artificial fat-free chocolate was safe for human consumption, and possible ballot fixing involving the two runoff candidates for world council representative from Oceania. As far as relations with nonhuman species were concerned, the vote on the possible expansion of the thranx colony in the Reserva Amazonia and a series of trade overtures from the AAnn Empire drew far more attention than anything that might have happened on far-distant Argus V.

Therefore officials were mildly surprised but hardly shocked when the *Chagos* materialized from the arcane torquing of space-plus into Mars orbit and commenced the far more gradual and easily monitored arc sunward toward Earth. On board was a contingent of officers from the survey and exploration party that had been exploring the Argus system. A sufficiently large, self-sustaining team had been left on the fifth planet of that benign, inviting sun, now named Treetrunk by its investigators, to continue the work of preparing it for an expanded series of studies and the possibility of eventual colonization.

The principal concern of Earth-based authority had been allayed when it was learned that the representatives of the Pitar, as their name for themselves was transcribed, were not native to Argus V but came from another nearby system entirely. Nor did they, according to admittedly preliminary discussions, have any claim on that particular world, nor any other in the Argus system. Out exploring on their own, they had picked up quantified radiation from the vicinity of Argus V only to discover that it emanated from another ship. Contact had been made, initiated by the Pitar themselves. In this instance of interspecies coming together it was humankind that had been discovered, and not humans who had done the discovering.

Shrouded in procedure and safe from the glare of sensation-seeking publicity, the appropriate personnel were designated and gathered to prepare for the arrival of the representatives of the latest in a series of recently encountered nonhuman species. By now a routine had been developed, rehearsed, and refined. Formal greetings and processing would take place on the island of Bali, a sufficiently isolated yet well-developed site that had been used for such purposes several times previously. In addition to its physical beauty, the island and its man-made shuttle landing strip were situated near the equator, thus allowing for the easiest and most economical lift-offs into orbit. Facilities for the elaboration of contact were already in place, and government operatives who knew how to best facilitate relations would be ready and waiting for the arrival of the incoming visitors.

Those on board the *Chagos* had yet to transmit pictures of the newly contacted creatures, but no one in the government contact offices on Bali or the reception facility that had been established on the nearby island of Lombok nor anyone else on Earth was in any particular hurry. The media could wait to image tridees in person—provided it was a slow newsday. The physical appearance of intelligent aliens had ceased to be an especially newsworthy event nearly a hundred years ago.

So while interested but far from agitated staff waited on Bali and Lombok for the arrival of the new aliens, the *Chagos* was directed into a parking orbit that would keep it isolated from other ships, shuttles, and orbiting stations until the appropriate authorities informed those on board that it was time for the representatives of the Pitar to be received. Quarantine and related biomedical canvassing had already been performed on the ship while it was traveling through space-plus and prior to orbit insertion. If such procedures had not been carried out in the safety of deep space, the *Chagos* would not have been permitted to take up orbit around Earth, much less disembark its esteemed passengers. As a craft equipped with the latest technology for carrying out survey and exploration, the facilities on board were the qualitative if not quantitative equal of anything available at any Earth-based medical agency. Had the tiniest indication of a possibly dangerous bacterium, virus, or other potentially infectious element been detected abiding on or within the Pitar, the *Cha-*

gos would have been stopped in lunar instead of terran orbit, where additional, more intensive tests could have been performed in perfect safety.

According to the exploration vessel's accomplished and experienced medical staff, the Pitar on board carried nothing harmful to humans individually or as a group. The aliens had been completely cooperative with their human hosts, readily acceding to any and all requests for blood, tissue samples, or scans by assorted instrumentation. In fact, they were as interested in the results of such procedures as the men and women who carried them out. To the irritation of their landed colleagues, the *Chagos*'s techs had chosen not to release any information via relay. Like their appearance, the biology of the Pitar remained confined to the storage facilities of the ship. Only enough information was transmitted to reassure the relevant departments in Zurich, Gauteng, and elsewhere that these dozen representatives of a new intelligence posed no medical threat to humankind.

Not only had they been cooperative where biological testing was concerned, the twelve Pitar who had been delegated to represent their civilization had shown no hesitation at leaving their friends and shipmates behind while entrusting their lives and futures to their new human acquaintances. Following a succession of polite, formal farewells, their own craft had departed for home to announce the mutual discovery. Though there had been plenty of volunteers from among the *Chagos*'s crew to travel with them, as the dozen chosen Pitar had elected to do in the company of their human counterparts, the Pitar preferred to proceed in a different fashion, according to their own traditions. Human travelers and ambassadors would be more than welcome in the very near future, Pranchavit and his superiors on the *Chagos* had been assured. The Pitar they were conveying to Earth would establish formal relations and commence arrangements for the exchange of diplomatic personnel.

Events were proceeding so smoothly and the declarations from the *Chagos* were so reassuring that after its first day in orbit no one thought it necessary to further monitor the newly arrived KK-drive craft. So it was that the release of a shuttlecraft from the starship's hold was not noticed until it was skimming the upper levels of the atmosphere, and was not remarked upon until an insecure watcher aboard one of the two nearby orbiting stations tentatively brought the matter of the unscheduled and unannounced trajectory to a superior. That individual regarded the confirming readout in puzzled and then stunned silence before demanding re-reconfirmation. When this was provided, a controlled state of all-hell-breaking-loose promptly went into effect on both stations.

When the situation was communicated to the surface, the relevant authorities had more than a little difficulty accepting the evidence.

Ground-based instrumentation confirmed not only the existence of the unauthorized shuttle descent but its path and velocity. No one panicked—no matter what was on board the vessel, it could not be terribly threatening. The shuttle was not large, was not disrupting normal atmospheric traffic patterns, and had promptly put itself in touch with and under the guidance of Denpasar authority. It had begun an unannounced descent but had subsequently taken time to carefully clear its final approach with ground control.

The contact personnel who were hastily summoned from downtime and off-duty to configure an appropriate reception team were bemused and in certain cases angry, but none of them were fearful. The shuttle was approaching openly, if irregularly. There was as yet no evidence of malice on the part of its crew: only a kind of ceremonious irreverence.

By the time the shuttle appeared beneath the low-hanging, moisture-heavy clouds, a proper if irritated greeting party had managed to assemble in the reception foyer that had been specifically designed to put first-time arrivals to Earth at ease. Several high-level executives were frantically checking each other's uniforms while lower-level functionaries busied themselves with more mundane preparations. Behind them, facilities for the unobtrusive scanning and recording of the visitors' shape, habits, and actions were being activated. Everyone wanted another hour, another half day, to ensure that everything was in order. As that was obviously not to be forthcoming, many of them substituted grumbling and muttering for the time they were not to be granted.

Guided in by both land-based and onboard instrumentation, the shuttle performed a near-perfect final approach and touchdown. As it did so, the morning cloud layer began to clear, dropping the humidity level somewhat and alleviating the discomfort the diplomatic staff felt in their hastily donned dress uniforms. After slowing, the shuttle turned at the far end of the artificial runway and taxied slowly over to the reception hall, bypassing the main terminal.

As soon as it stopped, several of the senior diplomats strode forward to await disembarkation. They were dressed neatly but not flashily, having no wish to overpower the traditionally disoriented visitors with an overabundance of personal color and light. They wore no arms, nor was any sort of formal military color guard in evidence. Everything about the ceremony had been designed to put cautious, hesitant visitors at ease while impressing upon them the friendliness as well as the determination of the united peoples of Earth.

The forward door opened, and a disembarkation ramp was lowered. The diplomats waited expectantly, naturally curious but far from anxious. After all, the explorers had already communicated the fact that the aliens were unaggressive nitrox breathers. Shape and size and the style of visible organs of perception were no longer a novelty to the team of experienced professionals.

No one was prepared for what they saw, and the shock that ran through the small cluster of official greeters was almost palpable enough to set the seismographs located at the base of Mount Agung to stuttering. Despite intensive training, despite the presence of men and women who were experienced as well as highly qualified, despite the cushion of written procedure and the absence of a need to improvise for virtually any conceivable situation, for a long, long moment no one in the clutch of official greeters and welcomers had anything to say. It was extraordinary. It was unprecedented.

Most remarkably of all, the temporary paralysis extended even to the perpetually jaded representatives of the media who were on hand for the occasion.

Siringh Pranchavit, the leader of the survey team that had been exploring Argus V, led the way, accompanied by several of his top aides. Not all were present, a number having been chosen to remain behind to continue the work on that promising new world. Accompanying the scientists and researchers were officers of the *Chagos* itself. Behind them and in advance of representative members of the ship's crew were the aliens. As attested, there were twelve of them. Half were male, the other half female. It could have been otherwise, of course, but among the diplomats and media reps present none would have bet half a credit on the separation of alien genders being anything other than what it appeared.

The Pitar were gorgeous. Drop-dead, overpoweringly, stunningly gorgeous. As beautiful as they were human. More properly, they were humanoid, but none present, least of all among the media reps who were now frantically scrambling to make certain their equipment was functioning properly, was prepared to bring up that distinction.

The males were magnificent. Without exception they were tall, though not intimidatingly so, with finely finessed lean musculature and faces that were devoid of blemish or whisker. Their countenances demanded revision of all previous descriptions of "chiseled" features. They were, as far as both the human men and women present were concerned, visually perfect.

As for the Pitarian females, the females were . . . The representatives of the media competed among themselves in a desperate search for superlatives that were neither jejune nor overworked.

Neither Pitarian gender manifested visible discomfort, though a certain understandable nervousness was reflected in their initial comments. After all, despite the reaction of the greeting team, they were participating in initial representations with a newly contacted space-traveling species, physical similarities notwithstanding. The warmth of the greeting that followed as soon as the dumfounded diplomats and their associates recovered their senses soon put the visitors at ease.

Their skin was a homogenous, unvarying bronze hue, made all the more striking by the extreme variance in hair and eye color that the *Chagos*'s scientists assured the members of the receiving team was natural. Blue hair and violet eyes were not uncommon. There were combinations of white and yellow, green and red, lavender and pink that would have seemed shocking on a human but which on the entirely perfect Pitar appeared utterly natural. Their voices, hastily trained in basic Terranglo during the space-plus journey from Argus, were uniformly resonant and mellifluous. They moved with the easy, pantherish grace of natural athletes and politely tolerated the wide-eyed stares of media and diplomatic personnel alike. Only occasional indications of nervousness betrayed what otherwise would have been a confrontation between two species completely at ease with one another.

As the shock wore off, the visitors were escorted into the receiving area. While stunned personnel took over and began processing the Pitarian representatives, Pranchavit and the senior members of his team were quickly drawn aside and hurried into a small conference room whose atmosphere was filled with disbelief mixed wildly with speculation. Kept outside, the desire of certain media reps to gain admittance bordered on the hysterical. Through it all the chief of the *Chagos*'s scientific complement maintained a calm, though clearly amused, composure.

"What kind of a joke is this?" As an assistant general secretary specializing in human-alien protocol, Dosei Anchpura carried more weight than her slight frame suggested. Presently she had parked her diplomatic skills just inside the door. Immediately behind her, on the other side of the soundproof barrier, media representatives fought to aim their pickup lenses over the shoulders of immovable security personnel.

"Joke?" Smiling absently, Pranchavit considered her question rhetorically. "What joke?" Next to him Werther Baumgartner, a sober xenologist pushing an active seventy, smirked and nudged his companion. "There is no joke."

"This is impossible!" Anchpura looked to her colleagues for support. "These Pitar—those people out there being guided through the processing lines—aren't aliens. They're human. Where'd you pick them up? From a live show on one of the orbiting stations before you came down? Without clearance, I might add, and here instead of across the strait at Lombok, where you belong. Although now that I see the joke, I understand your reasons, if not your motivation."

"Aye," Colin Brookstone put in. "What's come over you? It's a fine joke, I admit, but you'll soon have to call a halt to it."

"Siringh is telling you the truth." Smirk gone, Baumgartner was all serious now, and all scientist. "Believe me, the first time we set eyes on them our reaction was, if anything, more disbelieving than yours."

Ambassador-at-large al-Namqiz, who until now had been silent, sputtered a response. "But how can this be? They are as human as you or I, as anyone in this room." His attention shifted to the tightly packed horde of frantic media representatives who were still fighting to gain entrance to the meeting room. "More human."

Lionel Harris-Ferrolk, Baumgartner's companion in subdued mirth, was the possessor of a reputation that exceeded even that of his two nominal superiors. "Remarkable how after all these years of contact with sapient extraterrestrials we are still hostage to the superficiality of appearance." His reconstructed eyes, small but penetrating, swept over the diplomats assembled in the room. "You are all right, and you are all wrong. They are human to a remarkable degree—and yet not. Not quite."

Al-Namqiz sighed as he took a seat. What had promised to be a traditionally impressive yet routine meet-and-greet had turned into something extraordinary. Eventually he was going to have to face the media. He was not a man, after thirty-four years in the diplomatic service, who desired to do so without answers.

As his two slightly senior colleagues appeared willing to let him do the explaining, Harris-Ferrolk continued. "What we have in the Pitar is either the most remarkable instance of convergent evolution ever encountered, much less demonstrated, or else possible proof of the old theory that the dispersal of the origins of at least certain kinds of life throughout the galaxy, if not the universe, was by some form of seeds or spores, whether aboard meteorites, comets, or some as yet unidentified vector. The Pitar have been very cooperative. I ask you to keep in mind that despite the astonishing physical similarities, which I might add include internal as well as external features, preliminary studies reveal significant differences in DNA. As well, there are other factors at work that would never permit a Pitar to pass for human, or for that matter a human as Pitar."

From the back of the tense, crowded room, a terse question. "What about interbreeding?"

When Harris-Ferrolk looked nonplussed, the more relaxed Pranchavit spoke up. "That is a question I would have expected to come from a representative of the general media, not a member of the diplomatic corps. However, since it has been asked, based on our studies to date we do not believe that would be possible. The mere act of intercourse, which requires nothing more biologically complex than crude physical coupling, is another matter." For confirmation he glanced at his two colleagues, who both nodded.

"Physiological similarities extending beyond physical symmetry and external features suggest the latter should be possible. As we have explained, the Pitar have been most cooperative." He added drily, "You understand this is speculation only. There has been no experimental confirmation of any of this."

"They seem very subdued," someone else ventured.

"They are not demonstrative by nature. Certainly less so than a comparable group of humans would be," Pranchavit replied. "We do not know if this is a representative social trait or if they are simply being restrained in our presence. I can tell you that this is not a function of their isolation here on a strange world. Their manner was identical on Argus V, when they were in the company of their own people. Do not make the mistake of confusing their appearance with that of comparable human counterparts." The researcher shrugged. "Perhaps they are simply quiet by nature. Personally, I find it refreshing."

"Life spans?" someone else wondered aloud.

Pranchavit did not miss a beat. "From what we have been told and been able to glean, they are more long-lived than humans. Perhaps on the order of ten to fifteen percent."

"This may not be a properly framed scientific or diplomatic query," inquired one of the younger staff members restlessly, "but—do they *all* look like that?"

Baumgartner nodded somberly. "This group could be taken as typical, yes." In the back, someone whistled softly.

The others could indulge their curiosity. Al-Namqiz, charged with officially welcoming these unexpectedly attractive representatives of an alien species to Earth, was compelled to consider more practical concerns.

"What do they want? Have you talked with them about such things?"

Pranchavit nodded. "Good relations with us and everyone else they may meet. Beyond that we did not much go. Cultural exchanges, tourism, economic cooperation—my colleagues and I felt that these specific concerns did not fall within our purview to discuss."

Then he had not been cut out of the loop. Al-Namqiz felt much better. "I take it these are not formally accredited ambassadors, and therefore they cannot speak for their government on such matters."

"Only informally," Harris-Ferrolk admitted. "Remember that they were as surprised to encounter us at Argus as we were to see them. They no more had diplomats on board their vessel than we did on board the *Chagos*. Both our ship and theirs were on journeys of exploration. But it was felt by them that contact would be expedited if some of their people returned with us to present themselves to the rest of humankind."

"Expedited isn't the word." Al-Namqiz gestured in the direction of the door, against which the representatives of the media continued to throw themselves like seals heaving themselves up onto a beach. "As soon as they are presented on the tridee, there's going to be a frenzy of volunteers to go and 'visit' Pitar. Or accommodate their representatives here."

"We know." Pranchavit smiled thinly. "Most of our waking hours may be devoted to our research and the rest of our work, but my colleagues and I are not strangers to the human condition. We have been just as affected by their appearance as you all were when they stepped down from the shuttle. They are forthright and accommodating, but somewhat shy. They are willing to cooperate in mutual studies and learning, but only via formal, academic, accredited channels. They have no desire to stroll casually among us, or to allow us to do so among them. At least, that is the situation as it was explained to us. Whether it will change in the future or whether that is a firm and unalterable expression of the Pitarian social ethos it is much too early to say."

"When can you introduce us to them?" The face of the youngest member of the diplomatic team was alert and anxious.

In lieu of Pranchavit's sigh, Harris-Ferrolk responded. "We understand your eagerness. Following the usual final medical checks they must be officially welcomed and then queried. All this they have readily agreed to." He eyed the junior staff member sternly. "We must insist that they be treated no differently than the representatives of any other sapient species, such as the Quillp or the thranx."

"The thranx!" Someone in the back hooted in a reflexively derisive manner.

"Sure," another staff member murmured. "I'll treat them just like I would a thranx. Especially the one with the turquoise hair and the—"

"Quiet, all of you!" Turning in his seat, al-Namqiz glared at his clustered staff. "Difficult as it may be, we will do exactly as Mr. Harris-Ferrolk says. You are all of you professionals. Or at least, I have been given to believe that is the case. A position in a different service can readily be found for anyone who prefers to demonstrate otherwise." For the first time since the visiting scientist-explorers had arrived, there was complete silence in the conference room.

"That's better." The ambassador turned back to the grateful researchers. "If there is anything we need to know before commencing official interaction, however disagreeable or difficult it might be, I will rely on you to inform us and we will deal with it accordingly. Your work must be the foundation upon which we build our relations with these people. Thranx or Pitar, Quillp or anything else, the government of Earth and its colonies treats equally with all other intelligences." For the second time he glared at his staff. "Anyone here have a problem with that?" A single strained, uneasy cough was the only response. "Thank you."

Rising from his seat, he smiled at the three scientists and gestured toward the door. "Gentlemen and lady, if you will lead the way, we will make an attempt to deal with what I expect is by now a rapidly swelling and frenziedly impatient clutch of representatives of the world and off-world media. Meanwhile the immigration and medical people will have a chance to complete their work, and then you may introduce me to our newest interstellar friends. I would appreciate any additional information you can give me that might aid in my dealing with the media, not to mention the government, and that might facilitate the subsequent exchanges between myself, my staff, and our visitors."

It was not easy. While the ambassador took the podium and parceled out answers, the junior members of the diplomatic team and the crew of the *Chagos* were assailed by media reps promising ever-ballooning rewards for any information on the Pitar. Names, statistics, histories, preferences, dislikes, interviews, recorded images—small and then large fortunes were promised to those staff members who could provide them. On an exclusive basis, of course. Bidding reached a fever pitch when it was disclosed by one harried member of the starship's crew that at least a few of the Pitar had mastered a minimum of Terranglo on the journey out from Argus. The prospect of a first interview with one of the magnificent humanoids who could actually respond to questions sent the media reps into a veritable feeding frenzy.

Despite their best efforts and their most enticing blandishments, nothing came of their desperate entreaties. The aliens remained isolated and in media quarantine until such time as ambassador-at-large al-Namqiz and his staff felt they would be ready to meet the general public. Having been placed under the strictest of injunctions, none of the other members of the *Chagos*'s crew would talk, and the diplomatic staff had little hard information to dispense. As they learned more about their visitors, and with their permission, tiny dribbles of information were passed on to the salivating media.

Not everyone was instantly welcoming. There existed among the population of Earth a sizable minority whose opinion of intelligent aliens could best be described as cautiously paranoid and a smaller segment that was openly and vociferously xenophobic. The revelation years earlier of the secret thranx colony-base in the Reserva Amazonia had not hurt their cause, and they railed continuously and loudly in the media and in the hallways of government against forming anything like a close relationship with any alien species.

But even they were hard-pressed to find much mud to sling at the Pitar. Superficial it might be, but physical appearance went a long way toward swaying public opinion. In that respect humankind had changed little since the dawn of civilization.

Rightly or not, it was much easier for people sitting before their tridee to envision welcoming a Pitar into their home than a thranx whose appearance might well put them in mind of a cockroach or a giant ant. Still, there was commendable caution and a desire to proceed slowly and carefully among members of all pertinent scientific and governmental agencies.

Then the two Pitar who had become the most fluent of their brethren in Terranglo appeared on the global tridee. As soon as the first one smiled in response to a question, and before he could even answer, systematic caution and scientific restraint was overwhelmed by an outpouring of popular interest that would brook no further interference from any mere official source.

The government tried to keep matters under control but was overwhelmed. Against such a tsunamic outpouring of emotion from its constituents, confronted by an unprecedented outpouring of goodwill and even love, the inherent caution of elected representatives could not stand. The public wanted access to these beauteous, wondrous Pitar, and they wanted it *now*.

Some of the more critical who had contact with the Pitarian representatives thought them standoffish, but the majority put this down to an inherent shyness made all the more charming by their irresistible attractiveness. While not forthcoming, neither were they especially insular. Restricted despite the clamor for their presence to the official contact sites on Bali/Lombok and Zurich, they were quite willing to meet and speak with any humans who desired to pursue personal contact.

Permission to do so was highly sought after, and not only by researchers and professional xenologists. Members of the lay public proffered all sorts of blandishments to those in charge, who were hard put to turn down bribes for access that were often as inventive as they were compelling. But the authorities in charge of interspecies relations were admirably adamant. The Pitar could not be permitted to journey freely among humankind for at least a year, until formal relations had been cemented and all appropriate medical and scientific tests had been carried out. In this the Pitar themselves concurred, for if anything they were even more demanding and insistent that their own procedures be rigorously followed.

Through the world and off-world media humankind was treated to daily updates on the activities of the aliens. A craze for all things Pitarian swept the globe and spread rapidly to the colonies. Clothing, attitudes, gestures, words, phrases, hair colors—a host of Pitar imitations and imitators made their presence felt culturally. As for scientific advances the Pitar apparently had little to offer that was not already known to their hosts, though they were eager, in their formal and restrained fashion, to learn from humankind.

It would be fair to say that while humans became obsessed with their new acquaintances, the progress of interspecies relations with other intelligences suffered. The thranx in particular were neglected. Perhaps it was understandable that xenologists and specialists found it hard to find the time or enthusiasm to study chest-high bug-eyed antennae-waving insectoids when they could examine in detail physically perfect mammalian males and females instead. Similar sentiments were manifest among the general public.

While tens of thousands of requests for Pitarian attendance at innumerable social occasions poured into contact headquarters on Bali, not one asked for a date with a thranx—not even to talk. It was left to the professionals to maintain the minimum necessary contacts and to assuage hurt insectoid feelings.

Unfortunately, in order to know how to do that properly, considerable further human-thranx interaction was necessary. It was not immediately forthcoming.

3

Hathvupredek stood among the carefully tended jungle plants that thrived in the rich soil that overlay the subterranean, unseen colony and reflected on the alien world around her. She did not fear being seen. Ever since the premature but fortunately conciliatory revelation of the colony's existence some twenty human years previous, it had been possible for those dwelling in the hive below to walk freely on the surface of the world its dominant species egocentrically called Earth—within carefully prescribed parameters, of course. The councilor availed herself of the chance at every opportunity.

It was not Hivehom or Willow-Wane, but it was a beautiful world whose densest and least-disturbed tropical regions were reasonably close in general feel and appearance to that of home. Her ovipositors twitched as she settled herself down on a bench disguised to look like a fallen log, all six legs straddling the supportive cylinder.

In the undergrowth on her left a small, stealthy presence made itself known via a pungency that dominated everything in its vicinity. Her antennae dipped in its direction as she smelled the margay before she saw it. The secretive jungle cat dipped its head, eyes wide, as it took the measure of something too large and alien to eat. Like a puff of mottled yellow smoke, it evaporated into the surrounding verdure.

She did not turn as the organic crackle of crunching leaves and other forest detritus grew louder behind her. The voice was familiar, as was the gently brooding tone. A recent visitor to the colony, Adjami was a world representative from northern Africa. Fascinated by the thranx, he had chosen to linger beyond his designated time frame. In that time, he and the thranx senior councilor had struck up a more than professional acquaintance.

Eschewing ceremony, he sat down beside her, crossing his legs and heedless of the plant matter beneath that might stain his cool-suit. The heat did not trouble him, but he was thankful for the thermosensitive attire that relieved some of the onerous burden of the constant humidity.

They remained that way for some time: resting, soaking in the unspoken pleasure of one another's company, contemplating the surrounding undisturbed rain forest. Then Hathvupredek gestured and clicked a greeting with her mandibles and turned to look down at her companion of the moment. She did not have to hesitate or search for words or sounds, having reason to be proud of her fluency in Terranglo.

"What news for the hive from Bali?"

Reaching up, Adjami stroked his neatly trimmed black beard. His reply was peppered with clicks and whistles acquired from intense study of High Thranx. Many humans in the diplomatic service now utilized such thranx vocalizations, certain sounds providing efficacious shortcuts to specific phrases and intentions. Uncharted and largely unnoticed, a joint manner of speaking was evolving between the two species, or at least among those individuals whose work placed them in close contact with one another. A human diplomat whose hobby was linguistics had even proposed a name for it: Symbospeech. Begun as a game, a diversion, it was maturing into something much more significant. For the most part, the general population of both species remained unaware of its existence.

Especially since the advent of the Pitar.

"The proposed commerce treaty is still under discussion, with the usual adherents champing at the bit and the predictable opponents raining their suspicion on the slightest proposal." He flicked an inch-long ant off his left boot. Gnashing its jaws furiously, it landed in the leaves with an audible *plunk* before righting itself and scrambling away. "Two more cultural exchanges have been agreed upon, and there is finally some progress on the question of allowing the colony here to expand." That was the delicate matter that had brought him to the Reserva Amazonia in the first place.

"These individual humans who object to the details of the commerce treaty," she asked, "why are they so angry at us? Such exchanges can only benefit both our respective economies."

"As you know, the colonies are more enthusiastic." His sarcastic bent, never very far below the surface of his personality, singed the remembrance. "Swap all the painters and sculptors, poets and musicians you want and no one will say much against it. But when money is involved, tempers emerge and blood pressure rises."

"Our blood pressure does not fluctuate as wildly as yours," Hathvupredek murmured. "It can't, or we would blow up."

"Some of us do." Adjami sighed. "Politics can be such a disagreeable business. There are so many times when I wish I had followed my heart and studied archeology instead."

"I can sympathize. Myself, I wanted to be a *pin!!ster*."

He blinked uncertainly. "That is a term I am not familiar with."

"Someone who grows edible plants in an aesthetic manner. It combines your functions of farmer and sculptor. Easier to nurture a covenant with vegetables than with people. Plants do not argue."

Adjami grunted. "The ones in my homeland do. They grow reluctantly if at all. The ground there is obstinate." Reaching down, he dug through the leaf litter to raise up a fistful of dirt. "Not like here, where a little spit will bring forth all kinds of surprising growth."

"Perhaps we should expectorate more on behalf of mutual relations." Hathvupredek was not one to miss the opportunity to prod.

Adjami did not miss the gentle nudge. "I am impatient as well. Formalities should be moving along much faster. So they would be, if not for this recent distraction."

He did not need to elaborate. Ever since the discovery and subsequent arrival on Earth of the representatives of the species that called itself the Pitar, the expansion of human-thranx relations had been placed on a slow track. The government was devoting the majority of its attention in off-world matters to the new visitors, as its constituents demanded. Relations with the thranx were cast by the wayside, contact delegated to lower-ranking functionaries such as Adjami. Who wanted to meet with bugs when they could sit across the negotiating table from the shimmering, incredibly glamorous Slyl-Wett and her handsome corepresentative Coub-Baku?

Too polite to raise a ruckus, too stratified in their conduct to insist that the humans pay more attention to the development of relations, the thranx ground their mandibles in silence and tried to content themselves with what progress continued to be made. And there was progress, albeit at a glacial pace. Alliances and affiliations that the thranx felt should have been formalized in months now looked set to take years, perhaps decades. There was nothing they could do about it. They were trapped by the admiration humankind felt for the Pitar. Cause trouble, make noise, demand the attention and respect they deserved, and they would only be giving ammunition to their xenophobic enemies within the human community. Naturally patient, their limits were being tested.

They had no choice—not if they wanted relations to continue to progress and improve. Meanwhile, influential thranx who felt humankind wasn't worth the time and trouble were agitating the Grand Council on

Hivehom to break off all attempts at multiplying and enhancing relations in favor of maintaining only the loosest and most formal of associations. Who needed the humans, anyway? Yes, they were a numerous and powerful expanding species, but space was vast and there were others, like the Quillp, who were not so easily distracted.

Against this background of measured indifference from the human government and active opposition from the malcontents of both species, concerned individuals like Hathvupredek and Adjami struggled to sustain and strengthen the tenuous bonds between the two intelligences.

"Tell me." Adjami was rubbing a recently fallen leaf between his fingers, wondering what wondrous esoteric pharmaceuticals it might contain. "What do your people think about the Pitar? Officially they've been very reticent on the subject, but I've spent enough time in the company of your kind to recognize that more is being discussed in private than is being said openly." He smiled, showing a number of ceramic teeth. "Though short the requisite number of limbs, I have managed to acquire a small vocabulary of gestures."

She whistled softly, matching his amusement. "I have seen you watching. Many humans watch but do not see. Many see but do not learn. Many learn but easily forget." Truhands flashed. "There is no general consensus on the Pitar. The Grand Council continues to receive and absorb information. As you well know, this new intelligence is reluctant to disclose much about themselves. This invariably makes some of us suspicious."

Adjami looked away. Atop a dead tree, an oropendula was warbling. "It's said they are shy."

"Who says this?" Her tone was sharper than she intended; while more controlled than any human, neither were the thranx devoid of emotion. To calm herself, she recited one of the fifty-five mantras of Desvendapur. "Not the Pitar. To them their reticence to discuss and deal with many subjects is normal. It is the human media who have branded them bashful." Antennae coiled. "Humans evidently find such racial coyness becoming. My people are of a different mind."

"You said some of you find their ongoing restraint suspicious." Adjami gazed curiously into unfathomable, golden, compound eyes. "In what way?"

As would any thranx caught out by a direct question, Hathvupredek first considered what was known and then what was suspected before replying.

"We realize that despite appearances, the Pitar are not you. We are hardly experts in the analysis of mammalian behavior, much of which we regard as impulsive and indicative of an intelligence that occasionally veers into the retrograde. It is not even that we suspect the Pitar of hiding something."

"What could they hide?" Adjami added. "They immediately provided us with the coordinates for their twin homeworlds, which have subsequently been verified. I know of at least two KK-drive ships that have already made passing visits to both. They encountered nothing untoward at either stop, and were greeted in the same cordial, curious, restrained manner that the Pitar have demonstrated during their stay on Earth. There was no ambush, no indication of enormous fleets of armed vessels lying in wait or hiding to avoid discovery. It must be accepted that the Pitar are simply a reticent folk."

"So are the thranx." Despite the human's persuasive reasoning, the councilor knew that her superiors were far from ready to concede the Pitar's benevolence. "It is not that we are distrustful or even especially suspicious. We are simply more cautious in our dealings with other species." She shifted her position on the log bench. "This is not only a racial characteristic. Some of it certainly arises from our delicate dance of disharmony with the AAnn that has been ongoing now for more than three hundred and fifty of your years."

Adjami could not resist a dig. "We've been dealing with the AAnn for less than a hundred years and we've managed to get along. Sure, there have been occasional misunderstandings and minor confrontations, but we've always managed to smooth things over."

"The AAnn are spontaneous. In that they are far more like you than us. But when it suits their needs and aims they can also show patience. They are like a recurring virus that will not go away." All four hands gestured simultaneously. "We desire only to make certain that in the Pitar you have not encountered a species that is even more patient than the AAnn."

"A nicely diplomatic oblique damnation." Bending forward, Adjami picked up a long, thin leaf and chewed experimentally on the stem. It had a slight minty flavor characteristic of many of the alkaloid-laden plants that grew in the vicinity of the colony. "We're being careful."

"No you are not." Hathvupredek's atypical bluntness caught the visiting diplomat by surprise. "You are overcome by these Pitar, who so nearly resemble physically idealized visions of yourselves. You are dazzled. We are more analytical, more systematic in our appraisal of other intelligences."

Adjami spoke around the stem of the leaf that protruded from between his teeth. "So you're saying we're being naïve."

The councilor's ovipositors flattened slightly, the lowermost curl pressing against the back of her abdomen. "We think you are too welcoming. An engaging trait, but a dangerous one."

Adjami laughed gently. "We're not as ingenuous as you seem to believe. Sure, we've received the Pitar readily, even enthusiastically. But that doesn't mean they've been given the run of the planet or the colonies, or that the appropriate agencies aren't keeping an eye on them."

"We hope so." Hathvupredek's antennae abruptly snapped forward. "What is that?"

Adjami allowed his gaze to be led by the councilor's. "I don't see anything."

"Neither do I," his companion of the morning admitted, "but I smell it. Humans, coming this way. Many of them."

Scanning the trees, Adjami found himself unable to suppress a smile. "You're sure they're not Pitar?"

Hathvupredek missed the sarcasm. Or perhaps the councilor simply chose to overlook it. "Your bodily odors differ significantly. That of humans is much . . . stronger."

"Yes," Adjami confessed a bit reluctantly. "The variance has been noted." He continued to gaze into the forest. "I wonder what a large group is doing here? I'd think that researchers interested in the Reserva's wildlife would avoid the colony site, now that they know it's here."

"They do." Compound eyes and weaving antennae continued to take the measure of whatever was approaching. "As you are aware, visitation to the colony is strictly monitored and is restricted to accredited representatives of your governmental and scientific agencies. Random tourism is neither permitted nor encouraged."

Detecting a rising rustle of leaf litter being crushed underfoot, Adjami rose from his cross-legged seat. "Then I wonder who these could be?"

Man and thranx found out together when the band of perhaps thirty men and women emerged from the trees. The grim, focused expression on each camouflage-painted face was not encouraging, nor was the especially wild-eyed look worn by more than one. Their jungle clothing was in keeping with their obvious desire to blend into the rain forest background. While unsettling, none of this alarmed Adjami. The weapons they carried did.

"Praise be unto Him, what the hell is this?" His startled attention flicked swiftly between implacable, uncompromising countenances. "Who are you people, and how dare you infringe on a species sanctuary! Do you have any idea where you're trespassing?"

A middle-aged man wearing a loose, floppy camouflage hat turned and strode belligerently over to the diplomat. His tone was grindingly cold.

"We know exactly where we are, bug lover."

These people were well equipped, Adjami saw. Were they sufficiently well equipped to steal through the automatic sentries and security apparatus that protected the colony? Any unsanctioned intrusion might logically be expected to come from the air. How well was the colony prepared to protect itself from unauthorized encroachment on the ground?

"If you want to insult me you'll have to do better than that." Behind him, Adjami noted that Hathvupredek had quietly slipped off her bench and had begun to edge backward, toward the portal that led down into the hive.

Grunting an expletive, the armed intruder roughly shoved Adjami aside. The diplomat stumbled but managed to maintain his balance. Several of the trespassing humans had already hurried on ahead to cut off the councilor's retreat. Adjami's eyes grew wide as the full implications of what he was seeing sunk in.

"What do you think you're doing? This is a restricted, controlled area. I am Adjami L'Hafira, an elected representative to the world council! Leave at once before you force me to summon Reserva Security."

Looking him up and down, the man grinned unpleasantly. "With what? I don't see a communicator." With the muzzle of his rifle he gestured in Hathvupredek's direction. "You're just out for a morning stroll with your favorite roach, ain't you? Dirty bug lover. Traitor."

Fanatics, Adjami realized. These were the most extreme representatives of the sizable xenophobic contingent that was opposed to any human-thranx rapprochement. Every political group spawned its fringe element. Here before him were the most radical of that radical band.

"What are you going to do?" he heard himself stammering. He cursed himself for the fear that shook in his voice.

A calm reply can never overcome the wildness of a madman's expression. "Drive them out. Get them off our planet. Send them back to where they belong." The gun muzzle twitched. "We had too many bugs before they came here and we'll have too many after they've packed up and left, but at least we won't be expected to share our lives and homes and resources with them."

Adjami was not sure why he found himself backing up. It was not instinct. That would have dictated that he try to run, in which case they might ignore him. He was not their target, after all. As an experienced politician he could have tried arguing with them, if only to stall for time until local security became aware of the breach in its perimeter. Instead, he backed up, stumbled over and through the forest litter until he was standing in front of the thranx councilor. He could feel hard chitin bumping against his back, and his nostrils were filled with the sweet fragrance of blooming amaryllis.

"I . . . I won't permit this. If you people leave now, if you renew any complaints you may have through the proper channels, I will personally see to it that your views receive a hearing."

"We're done with hearings," snapped a short, frail woman who looked to be drowning in her bulky camouflage gear. To Adjami it appeared that the gun she was cradling was much too big for her. "Half the planetary government is composed of shortsighted idiots who don't see what these filthy creatures are up to, and the other half has sold out in return for commerce we don't need and promises of shared technology that haven't materialized. What's needed is for real humans to stand up and make a statement." With one hand she stroked the inside of her rifle, and in response several telltales sprang to life within the barrel. "A loud statement."

"Get out of the way," someone else said. Inside himself, Adjami shuddered. The voice that had spoken was neither hot nor cold, but something far worse. It was dead inside, the sound of a soul that had already committed ritual suicide and was prepared for death.

Nevertheless, the politician in him would not quit. He had dealt with difficult people all his life. Even when coping with fanatics there was often room to compromise.

"You've already made a strong statement simply by showing up here like this and successfully penetrating hive security." He gestured with a shake of his head. "Go on then; go further. Set off some noisy explosions and make a lot of smoke. The media will lap it up and be all over you for your opinions. There might be some fines assessed for trespassing, but you'll get your views splashed all over the tridee, and nobody will get hurt." Silence greeted his proposal. "What do you say?"

If the group had a leader, and such fringe organizations usually did, that personage chose not to manifest at that time. The middle-aged man who had spoken first provided a response.

"I say that we'll still have just as many bugs to deal with, and we won't tolerate being fined for 'trespassing' on our own soil." Using his rifle, he directed Adjami to move out of the line of fire. "You're a putrid, contaminated bug lover, but you're still human. Get out of the way."

One of the most overlooked components of true heroism is an abiding stubbornness in the face of danger. Lifting his arms out from his sides, Adjami held his ground. As with many accidental heroes, who are the most honest kind, if he had taken the time to consider what he was doing he probably would not have done it.

"No. I won't let you do this." The shakiness had vanished from his voice.

"You can't stop us," a voice in the armed crowd declared.

"And you cannot do this," he replied firmly.

"Sure we can." Raising her weapon, the frail woman with the too-large eyes fired.

Adjami looked down at himself in disbelief. The old-fashioned but still effective projectile weapon had produced a small hole in his shirt. The stain that was spreading from it resembled the rapidly expanding penumbra of a sunspot. It did not hurt in the way the representative believed it might. There was no stabbing pain, no overwhelming throb. Instead, the wound burned as if he had been jabbed with a hot fireplace poker.

Weakness overcame him, and he fell to his knees. Behind him a mellow, calm voice was murmuring in Terranglo. "Thank you for trying, my friend. Intelligence knows no shape. Neither does compassion. *Tchik ua! re!iq.*"

The rest of what Hathvupredek the councilor said was lost in the ensuing staccato of gunfire. When it was over the two bodies, one mammalian, the other insectoid, lay on the ground. The intruders resumed their advance, stepping over and ignoring them both.

There were no weapons in the hive. As guests of an indecisive planetary government representing a mistrustful species, it would have been impolite to stockpile anything that could have been construed as offensive. No one foresaw a need for guns or their presence on what was presumed to be hospitable ground.

Breaking in through one of the lightly barred surface entrances that had been constructed subsequent to official recognition of the colony's existence, the wrathful intruders met little resistance. Distributing grenades and bullets at every opportunity, they rampaged through the stunned hive firing indiscriminately at everyone and everything in their path, making no distinction between thranx "invaders" and human "traitors."

Peaceful though they were, thranx history was a litany of battle, of hive striving for supremacy over hive. More recently, they had been forced to deal with a frustrating, seemingly endless confrontation with the more militaristic AAnn. So the species was not unfamiliar with conflict, either on an individual or racial scale.

As soon as the scope and ferocity of the incursion became known, internal barriers were closed to restrict the range and movement of the aggressors. Arming themselves with tools and kitchen implements, lines of silent, determined thranx converged on the invaders. There was no question of waiting for help from the human authorities, who in response to the distress call from the colony were already on their way to the Reserva. The hive was in danger, and the hive had to be defended.

Many more thranx perished in repeated attempts to staunch the mindless slaughter. So too did several humans who were working or studying in the confines of the hive. The fanatics had come armed and ready to fight. But despite their determination and their murderous weaponry, they were not trained soldiers. The close confines of the hive, whose details were known to its inhabitants but foreign to the attackers, was likewise a detriment to their barbarous cause.

By the time the Reserva rangers arrived, many of the invaders were already deceased or dying, surrounded by small mountains of thranx dead. When the first soldiers disembarked from a transport hastily ordered inland from the nearest military base at Recife, it was nearly all over.

Acclaimed as martyrs by their fellow fanatics and accorded grudging admiration in less demonstrative quarters by their "civilized" xenophobic supporters, the ravagers of the Amazon hive achieved the media exposure the brave, luckless Adjami had foreseen for them. Fortunately, the response of the majority of the population was embarrassment and apology. Reparations proposed by a guilty government were refused with the explanation that the thranx did not believe in materialistic expressions of sorrow. On the other hand, the many letters and expressions of regret from ordinary citizens were received thankfully and with elaborate gestures of gratitude.

Not even such a catastrophe could obscure the effect the Pitar, who considerately offered condolences of their own to their fellow visitors to Earth, were having on human society. A pair (they never traveled alone) even visited the devastated hive to investigate the tragedy and offer commiseration on behalf of their government. Their compassionate presence was duly noted and monitored by the planetary media, who managed to give greater play to the mission of the Pitar than to the suffering of the hive's inhabitants, many of whom had lost friends, coworkers, and even relatives in the debacle.

While the media focused on the origins of the small but lethal fraternity of fanatics and strove to trace their sponsors, and the government representatives assigned to study the disaster tried to piece together evidence that might lead to proof of conspiracy and complicity beyond what was readily apparent, a meeting took place immediately after the confrontation that was to have much more far-reaching consequences for human-thranx relations than the aftermath of the savage raid itself. None present could have foreseen the results. Certainly none could have predicted the direction they would eventually take. In retrospect this was not surprising.

Who could have suspected that greater things would arise from dealing with the future of the dead than the future of the living?

4

Father Pyreau picked up the gun without thinking. Here, in the depths of the alien hive, he was having difficulty breathing. He was mildly claustrophobic, and wide-open spaces and lofty cathedrals were his preferred venue. Deep beneath the surface of the Amazonian earth, lost in a warren of high-tech thranx tunnels, he had long ago loosened his collar.

Lately there were many times, too many times, when he wanted to forget it altogether, to resign his position in the clergy and seek elsewhere the fulfillment that the church no longer gave him. He had been preparing for the regular Sunday service at the base when the emergency call had sounded. Swept up in the uncharacteristic alarm that followed, he had found himself on the transport rocketing inland before he knew what was going on. A superior officer had spotted him and, despite his initial protests, requisitioned his presence.

"I have a feeling your services are liable to be in demand, Padre." The major had not been very informative, but Pyreau could hardly disobey.

Before he knew what was happening they had descended rapidly into seemingly unbroken rain forest, only to find themselves welcomed into a subterranean flight hangar by a milling mass of whistling, clicking, frantically chattering insects. No, not insects, he'd reminded himself. The exotic, visiting thranx were insect*like*.

He had never received a full explanation of the proceedings, not even when he'd found himself thrust forward and carried along with the rest of the hastily organized strike team. The soldiers surrounding him had seemed to know little more than he, but gradually the word trickled back that a small but fanatical band of xenophobes had infiltrated the colony and were killing every thranx in sight as well as any visiting humans who tried to interfere with their bloodthirsty spree. A visiting diplomat and several esteemed researchers had been among the earliest casualties.

Swept into the depths, he had found himself caught in conditions that more closely resembled the traditional biblical hell than anything he had ever experienced before. A professional life that had previously been confined to conferring communion and counseling soldiers stationed at a peaceful tropical military base exploded in a succession of corridor-constricted concussions, flying body parts, the screams and shouts and whistles and clicks of the wounded and dying. Covered in blood both alien and human he had made his stunned, dazed way through the tunnels of death, bestowing what comfort he could on the injured and last rites on the deceased. This he had done in a spirit of faith and desperation regardless of the actual convictions of the departed. Atheists, agnostics, and true believers had received equal attention, there being no time to run dead soldiers' personal identity chits through his chaplain's scanner to ascertain the specifics of individual beliefs. Swirling, acrid smoke and the pungent stink of death had been his companions, and no angels had stepped out of the fiery gloom to assist his ministrations or ease his personal pain.

He had not run out of bodies when he suddenly realized that he had run out of companions. He was alone except for the righteous dead. Alone, and lost.

No, not quite lost. Another figure was stumbling down the fume-filled corridor toward him. It was human, male, its clothes torn and its exposed skin scarred. Dark blood smeared its face and arms, mixing with greasy camouflage paint. Against this grisly, dark smutch the whites of the man's eyes stood out like sculpted marbles. He carried a large, battered rifle and wore camouflage gear but no uniform.

He was not a soldier.

Espying the figure of the padre kneeling beside an inert thranx and a dead corporal, the half-mad, half-dead xenophobe drew his own conclusion. "Dirty bug lover! You're all gonna die! We're gonna kill every one of you egg mother suckers!" The muzzle of the rifle started to come up.

"I was only . . . !" Pyreau began. He did not finish the thought. It would do no good. Whatever reason the raving lunatic before him might once have possessed had been abandoned on the surface prior to his homicidal entry into the hive. It flared in his eyes and resounded in his voice.

All chaplains receive basic military training as a matter of course. At Pyreau's right hand lay a neuronic pistol. The green telltale pulsing in its handle showed that it still held a half charge. Whatever guided his fingers might have been divine intervention or simply the most basic, primitive need to survive. Picking up the pistol, he raised it as something loud and concussive echoed in his ears. A hot blade bit into the flesh of his left shoulder. Aiming more from reflex than training, he fired.

The figure of the xenophobe shuddered even as the madman got off a second shot. It missed Pyreau entirely, slamming into the corridor wall behind him and to his left. Nerves paralyzed, his assailant went down in a heap, the rifle tumbling from his fingers. Silence roared. Once again, Father Pyreau was the only one alive in the tunnel.

Mouth open in shock, he put the pistol down and thought to examine his shoulder. Blood leaked from what was no worse than a graze. Trying to rise, he found that his muscles had turned to rubber, his bones to putty. He could not stand.

Then hands were levering him to his feet, and they were not human. The voice that accompanied the helping digits was firm but soft, almost whispery, the consonants oddly musical, the vowels separately enunciated only with difficulty. What he remembered most of all later was a piquancy redolent of damp honeysuckle.

"Please try to use your legs. I cannot lift you by myself."

Admonished brain activated muscles, and Pyreau found himself erect amidst Armageddon. Stepping back, the thranx looked him up and down. "You wear the uniform of a soldier."

"I . . . I am a soldier, but a chaplain. Do you know what that is?"

Antennae searched in opposing directions to parse as much of the acrid atmosphere as possible. "I'm afraid not. You are with the rescue team that arrived promptly but too late."

"Yes." Pyreau nodded. "I'm sorry about that. We got here as fast as we could."

"I am certain that you did." A truhand gestured at the quiescent carnage surrounding them: waves of dead flesh frozen in midcollapse. "There will be trouble over this. Loud whistling and clicking and abundant recriminations to go around." Golden compound eyes rose to meet the padre's. "Enough for both species. What does a chaplain do?"

Pyreau gestured helplessly at the massed bodies, the majority of which were thranx. "I represent one of humankind's principal religions and, when necessary, all of them. I provide spiritual counsel to the men and women of the unit I happen to be assigned to, lead them in prayer on certain traditional days and also in private, minister to the sick at heart, and perform specific ceremonies that have religious overtones, such as the burying of the dead."

A truhand and foothand rose to gesture in the direction of the fanatic Pyreau had just shot. "You certainly ministered to him."

Pyreau did not look back—not because he was incapable of it, but because he did not want to. "I had no choice. It was him or me. Although

I believe in a life after death, I'm in no hurry to trade this one for the other. It will come in its proper sequence, as it does to all of us."

"An interesting assertion of belief." Reaching up and across with a foothand, the thranx tapped his own right shoulder with all four fingers. In the manner of thranx body decoration, a small, glistening black circle was inlaid in the hard blue-green chitin. Even in the dim light of the damaged corridor it shimmered with iridescence. "Do you know what this insignia signifies?"

"I'm afraid I don't." The young priest badly wanted a drink of water. "I haven't paid much attention to the details of contact between your kind and mine. There hasn't been much new information available."

"I know." The thranx made a gesture that the good father did not recognize for the expression of resignation that it was. "Your people are preoccupied with the Pitar. About them you want to know everything." This observation was quietly stated and in no way accusing, but Pyreau felt oddly embarrassed just the same.

"It's not my job to decide what appears on the tridee. I have nothing to do with the media. If it means anything, I'd like to know more about both species." To prove that he'd been listening, he nodded slightly in the direction of the black inlay. "What does it signify?"

This time all four hands wove a quick but complex pattern in the air. "It means that we are colleagues."

"Excuse me?"

"I am . . . I do not have an exact translation that would fit a Terranglo term with which I am familiar. You might call me a consulting physicist of the soul. I am also a counselor. It is a traditional calling that was in place even in pretechnological times. When a member of the hive has a question that cannot be answered by anyone else, by a specialist or teacher or artist, they come to such as myself. We attempt to comprehend the incomprehensible, to understand that which has no explanation, and to provide some solace in the absence of cognition. We are the last resort when reason and logic fail, a repository of compassion in the face of a cold and indifferent universe." He ambled forward on four legs to examine the body of the xenophobe Pyreau had just killed. "Of course, we make a lot of it up as we go along, but in searching there is truth, and sometimes, even to our own astonishment, we manage to get something right."

"You—you're a priest?" Pyreau struggled to recall what was known about the thranx, or at least what he himself had studied. "I didn't think . . . didn't know you people had priests. I didn't even know you had religion."

"That by any other name, as one of your famous writers once

avowed." With its largely fixed, inflexible countenance the thranx could not smile, but Pyreau had the impression of gentle amusement nonetheless. "Semantics are irrelevant in the face of the spirit."

"Do you believe in God?" Pyreau asked without thinking.

"In your sense, no. In ours . . . This is not a question easily or casually answered. Do you find it so?" The valentine-shaped head cocked sideways.

"Some of my superiors do. I don't. I was taught to believe, but I was also taught to question."

"Ah, *crri!kk,* those eternal antagonists. Always making existence more difficult and complicated than we would like it to be. But no one asked us, did they? My name is Shanvordesep." The soft alien voice grew suddenly alarmed. "Are you going to lose consciousness? You do not look so good."

"Just . . . thirsty. I am Cirey Pyreau." Pyreau muttered the response as he looked past the thranx and down the corridor, wondering when someone would find him. He had completely lost contact with the rest of his unit.

"As opposed to ultimate questions of divinity and existence, that much is easily remedied." Reaching back with a truhand, the thranx drew a cylinder of some shiny spun material from the pouch slung across his thorax and held it out to Pyreau, who eyed it uncertainly. The coiled drinking spout was unfamiliar to him.

"Like this." The thranx demonstrated briefly before passing the cylinder back to the padre.

Pyreau took it shakily. Probably he ought to have first smelled of the contents, but he was too tired and thirsty to care. Besides, there were times when a man had to take the word and judgment of another on faith, even if the individual in question came equipped with one too many pair of limbs.

The water was cold, fresh, and tasted better than the finest Chardonnay. Despite his desperate thirst he was mindful not to drink all of it, making sure to hand it back to its owner at least half full. With his right forearm he wiped the back of his mouth. The blood on the sleeve had already dried.

"What do we do now?" he wondered aloud.

Although the blue-green body remained facing him, the head swiveled an astonishing amount, enabling the thranx to look almost directly back over its shoulder. "I suppose we wait. I could go for help, but in the confusion I'm not sure your comrades would respond readily to my entreaties. If they are proper soldiers they will be following the orders of their superiors. In such a situation they are unlikely to listen to someone such as myself." Antennae twitched and mandibles clicked. "I am sure someone will find us before long."

Without pause or obvious attempt to change the subject, Shanvordesep crouched to examine the body of the nearest thranx. Curled tightly, all eight limbs had been drawn up against the body. Its head was missing, blown to bits by an explosive shell, nerves and longitudinal supportive muscle protruding from the open neck.

"I am given to understand that you recycle your dead differently from us."

Pyreau was appalled, though he was careful to control his expression in the event the thranx might comprehend it. "We don't recycle our dead. We give them, in most cases, a proper and dignified burial."

Still investigating the corpse, Shanvordesep looked back and up at the human. "You bury them in the ground. Then what happens to them?"

"They rest there." Pyreau wondered why he was being asked to explain the obvious.

"And then what happens to them? Later?"

Pyreau shrugged. "Unless special preservative techniques or coffins have been employed, they remain so until their containers break down. After that, their bodies are—"

"Recycled," the thranx finished for him. "There are only small differences in our approach, primarily in the matter of enclosure. We choose to recycle immediately, your kind over time. It has always been thus in the hive. Admittedly, there are details that do demarcate certain specific differences, but taken as a whole our traditions are not so very different." He straightened, his head coming just up to the priest's chest.

"I believe there are other similarities that might usefully be explored." A truhand gestured toward a section of corridor comparatively free of corpses. "Would you like to discuss them? It seems that for the foreseeable future we have nothing if not time."

Debate religion with an alien? One that reminded him more of the large mantids he had seen delicately poised beneath the eaves of the buildings back at the base than a fellow seminarian? Why not? As Shanvordesep sensibly pointed out, the only thing they had to kill now was time.

The last thing he expected was for a bug-eyed, eight-limbed alien insectoid to reinforce his faltering faith, but that was exactly what happened. For his part, he was able to enlighten the intensely curious thranx on matters of human spirituality. It developed in the course of their conversation that Shanvordesep was less than satisfied with the present organization of the ancient order to which he belonged and from which he drew his calling. It had not kept pace with the culture, he felt, or with such unanticipated revelations as the existence of other intelligent species elsewhere in the cosmos.

The longer they talked, the more Father Pyreau felt that here, beneath his gleaming exoskeleton, was a fellow spirit. Initial half-serious thoughts of trying to convert the thranx, if such a thing were even acceptable or possible, gave way to an open mutual exchange of beliefs and disbeliefs, of certitudes and unanswered queries, of a desire to understand the great mysteries while carrying out useful and practical work in the only reality they knew.

They were alone together in the corridor for a long time. When the first patrolling triad of hive gleaners found them, man and thranx were locked in animated conversation. Returned to troops who had thought him lost, Pyreau was accorded a hero's welcome. He did his best to demur in the face of all the accolades, pointing out that he had done little more than survive and wait for rescue. But his comrades would have none of it. He was recommended for several citations. As a matter of course and though chaplains rarely wore such decorations, he was awarded the same battle ribbon as was the hastily engaged infantry who had fought to save the hive: crossed antennae on a field of blue-green. He found the ornate medal altogether too embarrassing and kept it hidden away in its sealed presentation box.

When he requested a leave of absence from duty it was readily granted. Given what he had been through, it was understandable to his superiors that he might require some rest and relaxation. Subjected to combat conditions, even a chaplain could suffer the contemporary high-tech equivalent of shell shock.

It was an assessment Father Pyreau made no effort to confirm or deny. All that mattered was that he be set free to resume his dialogue with the thranx advisor Shanvordesep. For his part, the thranx readily welcomed his new friend into the hive. Together they plunged into weeks of intense discussion of matters spiritual, studying one another's beliefs, learning their histories, discovering how representatives of both species perceived the same eternal conundrums.

Months later, they had done much more than exchange views and acquire wisdom. They had ascertained possibilities and identified solutions. They had determined how best to apply insubstantialties to reality and resolve contradictions. They were ready to act.

All they needed now was a sponsor.

"Found a new church? Are you both crazy?" Martine Herzalt Lorengau sat upright and stiff in a chair as she regarded the pair of unlikely visitors.

"I'm assuming that blatant insanity manifests itself similarly among the thranx, of course."

"I can assure you that we are not mad." The insectoid gestured casually, in a manner the gangly, pinch-faced human might recognize. "Only hopeful."

Beside him, Father Pyreau hastened to support and reaffirm his friend. "We came to you because we have been turned down everywhere else."

A hint of a smile struggled with the corners of Lorengau's mouth but could not break through. The barriers were too great. "As a businesswoman of some repute, let me tell you that is about as piss-poor an opening for a request for investment as I have ever heard. Nothing like starting out by telling me that everyone else you've talked to thinks that you're fools."

"This is to be an investment in people, and the future." Pyreau met the woman's unnervingly deep-set, large eyes without flinching and tried not to squirm in his chair. He ought to be used to this by now, he told himself. The milieu as well as the rejection. Nevertheless, he persevered. What else could he do?

"Even if I wanted to waste money on such a ludicrous enterprise, why would I choose to support one that purports, according to your proposal, to spiritually link humans with thranx? Why not humans with Pitar? In that, at least, I could see some possible return."

"The return from such an investment would not be monetary," Pyreau replied earnestly.

"With the Pitar involved, it might be." Her voice falling, she grumbled under her breath. "Missed the boat on that one. But we're catching up." Leaning forward slightly, the high, black leather back of the expensive chair rising behind her like a throne, she regarded each of them in turn. "I'm still not sure how you managed to secure an appointment with me. My time is valuable." Her tone darkened. "If nothing comes of this meeting, and I fail to see how it can, someone else is going to end up paying for it."

"There are those who do sympathize with our aspirations." Shanvordesep concluded his reply with a soft, descending whistle.

The industrialist's demeanor remained unencouraging. "If you did any research at all before coming here you should know that I am an atheist."

Pyreau nodded. "We know. Our proposed religious venue would be open to all."

This time the smile emerged. It was a smile that had on more than one occasion struck terror into the heart of a competitor. "Now you are simply being asinine and worse, wasting my time." A hand moved toward a row of tactile perceivers.

"We mean to do this thing. If we can establish a congregation capable of accommodating the beliefs and feelings of two entirely different species, making room for the different beliefs inherent in one species will be simple by comparison."

The dismissive fingers that terminated in perfect nails hesitated. "It won't include me. I don't believe in anything."

"But you do," Pyreau argued energetically. "Everyone believes in something. If you don't believe in a supreme deity, then you are convinced of its nonexistence. Conviction is founded on dogma, which is supported by belief."

Martine Lorengau blinked. "I am a businesswoman, not a philosopher. I have neither the time nor the inclination to waste on theology or metaphysics."

"You have a soul," Pyreau assured her softly.

This time she laughed, a sound that contrasted startlingly with her speaking voice. "I could cite you hundreds of people who would disagree."

"That which lies within every sapient being and cannot be quantified needs feeding." Truhands reflexively wove a complex pattern in the air before the intimidating desk. Knowing that the female human comprehended not a single wave of fingers or hands complicated Shanvordesep's response. Trying to communicate without gestures was akin to speaking with only half the words at one's command. Nevertheless, he tried.

"I assure you," she replied, smiling, "that I am fully fed. All of my psychological needs are well taken care of."

"Then you have completely recovered from and are entirely over the unfortunate deaths of your husband and daughter," Pyreau said.

Jaws slightly parted, Lorengau turned to stare sharply and unblinkingly at the unrepentant priest. When next she spoke, her tone was icy and dangerous.

"How dare you. How *dare* you mention that in my presence."

This time Pyreau was not intimidated. "One who stands every day naked before God can dare anything." Simultaneously relentless and compassionate, he continued. "The accident was eleven years ago. One of your company planes was returning to Gauteng from Harare. To this day no one is sure why it went down into the Zambezi. Everyone on board was killed."

"I know what happened." Slumping slowly back in the great leather chair, Lorengau suddenly seemed in danger of being swallowed by it, of becoming even thinner, until she disappeared into one of the supple ebony tucks. "I wasn't much of a believer before that. Afterward . . ." Her gaze rose. "I'm curious. What sort of colossal personal arrogance makes you think your proposed denomination has anything to offer someone like me?"

"We can't say for certain that it would," Pyreau replied without hesitation. "We can be certain that nothing else does. Who knows what revelations may manifest themselves in the commingling of the beliefs of two entirely different species? Different ways of thinking, of looking at the universe, of both approaching and answering abstruse questions."

"There will be no restrictions, no constricting internal laws requiring adherence to unprovable dogmas," Shanvordesep added. "It will be open to all. Not only humans and thranx, but members of any other species who wish to join. It will remain resolutely apolitical, a noted concern of your kind, and as equally accommodating of traditional thranx hierarchical concerns, an interest of my people."

There was silence in the room. "What do you hope to achieve with this?" Lorengau finally asked. "Power, wealth? Inner peace? Acclamation within your own vocations?"

Pyreau looked over at his companion and saw Shanvordesep gesture encouragingly. "We don't know. That is, we're not sure. A place where individuals who are in need but who feel unsatisfied by other ideologies can come for succor and assistance. A refuge capable of offering more than words. We know that regardless of the beliefs it propounds, every church is ultimately accountable to a secular bottom line." He indicated his companion. "Shanvordesep has experience in such matters, far more so than I."

Lorengau pursed her lips. "So not only am I being asked to support this dubious, unfocused enterprise, I am also supposed to turn over control of a large sum of credit to an alien. Not even a Pitar, at that."

"It is a wonderful thing about mathematics that it responds with equanimity to skilled manipulation regardless of shape." The thranx calmly ignored the slight.

If the industrialist was testing him, he evidently passed. "This is a waste of time and money. In that my opinion obviously does not differ from that of everyone else you have contacted in search of support. However . . ."

If a divine blessing could be accounted in one word, Father Pyreau thought, the woman seated grandly before them had just intoned it.

"I have no time to waste—but I do have a lot of money. As you are aware, after the accident I never remarried. Mwithi was the finest man I ever met, and the only one who never expressed the slightest interest in my money. I've been looking for someone like him ever since. So far I have been grievously disappointed. As for my daughter . . ." She did not choke, Pyreau noted, but she did pause ever so briefly to gather herself. "You have your angels; I have mine. So, you want my money? To under-write this numinous folly of yours?"

"We do, *crri!kk,*" Shanvordesep acknowledged.

"I suppose you'll want to lease or build a headquarters, or temple, or whatever kind of specialized structure you end up conceptualizing."

"We intend to keep our facilities as modest as our goals," Pyreau assured her. "I have always been doubtful of vast cathedrals and temples and mosques and the like. If God, or some great spirit, or whatever it is that we cannot yet give a name to is truly within us, then I don't see why it matters that what lies without be constructed on such a grand scale. All my life I have wondered about preachers who shout, as if God were deaf."

"All I know is that when that plane went down he didn't listen to me," she snapped. "But that's in the past."

"Then you will support us?" Unable to sit in a human chair, Shan-vordesep had been forced to stand the entire time on all six legs. Now he rose, sitting back on four, the better to see eye to eye with the industrialist.

"I will underwrite your foolishness, yes. For as long as it continues to amuse me." Adopting a mocking tone, one slim hand fluttered diffidently in the air. "Who knows? I might even pay you a visit now and again, just to see how you are wasting my money."

Shanvordesep fumbled with his thorax pouch. "We intend to become self-supporting within the first year."

"Indeed?" She waved off his efforts to find whatever it was that he was searching for. "No, no. Don't show me any projections, any figures. I'll just spot the holes in them and discourage you. Madness needs to remain insular or it becomes hostage to reality and loses its charm. I'm not doing this because I think you're going to make money, or even repay me. I'm doing it for a diversion. As an amusement."

Having accomplished what they had come for, Pyreau knew they ought to depart. Shanvordesep was gesturing precisely that. But the good father had never been one to leave well enough alone. If that had been the case he would not have found himself in his present circumstances, shar-ing a hypothesized future with an alien bug while begging money from the contemptuous and cynical affluent.

"We don't consider the undertaking amusing. Despite what you may think, this is not farce. We see a need that is not being fulfilled."

For a horrible moment he feared he had gone too far, that he had abused this powerful woman's hospitality to the point where she would withdraw her offer. Then she laughed for a second time, and he relaxed.

"If you're not in the business of amusing, then why am I enjoying this so much? Why do I find the whole endeavor so comical?"

"Perhaps," ventured Shanvordesep quietly, "because it has satisfied a need."

She turned on him. "A need? I don't have any 'need.' What need?"

"One that you have yet to identify, obviously." The thranx bowed slightly and began to back away from the desk. "You are a fascinating species. I never cease to be amazed at your ability to pretend things that exist do not, and to ignore logic and reason in favor of what you would like to believe."

Lorengau shrugged slightly. "So our nature is more whimsical than that of the thranx. Whose wouldn't be?" Activating a screen set into her desk that was shielded from their view, she manipulated controls with the fingers of one hand. "I'll want my husband and daughter's names prominently displayed on the list of contributors, of course, as well as on the front of your first tabernacle, or whatever you end up calling your places of gathering."

Pyreau glanced at his eight-limbed colleague. "We don't plan to do that sort of thing. This is to be a refuge from the realities of the world, not a reminder of them. I have always found that the prominent placement of contributors' names on the outside of structures intended for religious purposes only reminds those who are unable to do likewise of their comparative insignificance, if only in a temporal, nonspiritual way. We are trying to get away from such things."

"But we will find a way to acknowledge your gift," Shanvordesep put in quickly. "One that I believe will more than satisfy your wishes."

Shaking her head slowly, Lorengau's speculative gaze passed from human to thranx. "I can't make up my mind if you two are truly dedicated or just arrogant." She sighed softly. "People are going to find out about this, you know."

"We intend that they should," Shanvordesep declared.

"There's going to be a lot more amusement, much of it directed my way. Not to my face, of course. But people will laugh at me."

"Someday they will bless you." Pyreau made the assurance with as much feeling as he could muster.

"Oh, I'm sure," she muttered sardonically. "What name have you picked for this creed of yours, anyway?"

That much, at least, he and Shanvordesep had worked out beforehand, Pyreau thought with relief. "Nothing complex. Nothing overbearing or intimidating. We were thinking of calling it the United Church."

"How original. And yourselves?" She eyed him with some interest. "Will you still be a priest, Father Pyreau?"

"I think so, though that is still to be worked out."

"And your many-legged, golden-eyed friend?"

Pyreau turned to the thranx, and this time it was the solemn-visaged pastor who smiled. "In a difficult moment early in our encounter Shanvordesep once referred to himself as the 'last resort' of his . . . flock is not quite the right word, but it will do. And that is what he will be once we begin: the last resort."

5

As it had for thousands of years, Mount Agung was steaming softly. The thranx who were strolling along the beach hardly glanced in its direction. They had never questioned why humankind had chosen to situate one of the two original sites for greeting and processing visitors to their world in the midst of a necklace of islands noted for their exceptional volcanic activity. Perhaps this question had occurred to their hosts, who had on more than one occasion alluded to the possibility of moving the facility to the large land mass that lay to the south.

There were three thranx: Nilwengerex, a specialist in human culture; Joshumabad, recently arrived from Hivehom; and Yeicurpilal, the second-highest-ranking representative of her species on Earth. In the company of the two younger males she made her way along the shore, careful to keep well away from the water. The protection from large, potentially deadly waves afforded by the offshore reef was not adequate to completely reassure any thranx.

Joshumabad would not, and perhaps could not, let go of the theme that prevented him as well as his companions from enjoying their morning stroll beneath the warm equatorial sun. It was understandable. The concern he continued to express was the reason for his being there.

"Those on the Grand Council feel like they are caught at the terminus of a dead-end tunnel with a starving *memn!!toct* at the open end. They do not know whether to run, estivate, or start digging."

Yeicurpilal's six unshod feet left multiple impressions in the slightly damp sand. A warm tropical breeze whispered through her ovipositors. Though past the age suitable for procreation and unable to vent any more eggs, she was still straight and sturdy of limb. The delicate lavender tint maturity had imparted to her exoskeleton was highlighted by the angle taken by the rays of the still rising sun, and her compound eyes glistened with intelligence.

"Why are they so upset?" Yeicurpilal gestured with a truhand in the direction of the island of Bali that lay just across the deep, swift body of water known as the Selat Lombok. "Our relations with the humans are good. Negotiations are proceeding on a host of mutually important matters, from trade and commerce to exchanges in the arts. I realize that agreements are not being finalized as rapidly as some might like, but neither are they at a standstill."

Less comfortable in the alien surroundings than his companions, the recently arrived Joshumabad kept much of his attention focused on the ground beneath his feet. He was careful to avoid anything that hinted of the organic. While he had confidence in the greater experience of his associates, neither of them were experts on local life-forms. Though the likelihood of them encountering anything that could prove toxic to their offworld biologies was small, he was not the type to take chances.

"Everyone is nervous. Not only those on the council, but those who are assigned to many of the advisory committees. These mammals are aggressive, intelligent, and technologically advanced. The council very much wants them as a counterweight, if not as formal allies, in this part of the Arm to restrain the adventurism of the AAnn."

"We are on course to achieve that." Yeicurpilal bent to pick up a piece of driftwood. It had a lovely grain. Swinging it back and forth in the manner of strolling humans she had observed, she caused the nervous Joshumabad to put more distance between them. Disturbed at the pleasure she felt as a consequence of the result she had produced, she flung the stick aside. It landed in the water and began to drift away on the slight current. Was the same likely to happen to thranx hopes for this world and its peculiar, frustrating, sometimes maddening inhabitants?

"What is the council afraid of?" she asked when she had disposed of the stick.

"Being preempted by these Pitar. We have perused all the reports. It has been noted how the humans are far more comfortable in the presence of the Pitar than they are with us."

"They are not more comfortable," Nilwengerex declared firmly, speaking for the first time. "They are infatuated. I have some limited experience in intraspecies contact, with the Quillp as well as the AAnn, and I have never seen anything like this. It is not so much that they believe everything the Pitar say, or take all of it at face value, as the fact that they want so desperately to believe their own perceptions. These are, as you know, colored by the external appearance of the Pitar, who according to what my human colleagues have told me in response to my inquiries represent everything that is physically perfect in the human imagination."

Joshumabad considered. A bird, one of this fecund world's many acrobatic aerial life-forms, momentarily distracted him as it flew by overhead. He would have had even a harder time concentrating had he known that the sea eagle was evaluating him as a potential meal.

"How can they be so accepting? Physical appearance has nothing to do with the trustworthiness and dependability of another. It does not matter if one is speaking of an individual or, as in this instance, an entire species. Even a *hou!p* knows to look deeper."

"They are mesmerized by the superficiality of external beauty as embodied in these visitors." Nilwengerex was a staid, humorless male, Yeicurpilal mused, but ruthlessly good at his work. She ranked him near the bottom of potential companions and at the very top as an advisor. Whether he was aware of her opinion she did not know. Males did not challenge senior females in matters of personality. He knew his position within the hive and was content with it.

"I do not understand." Joshumabad executed a complex gesture indicative of internal confusion. "They are manifestly intelligent, fast learners, enthusiastic explorers. Yet in the presence of these Pitar they slough off several hundred years of social maturity. If we were to encounter a sapient species that resembled the thranx ideal we would be welcoming, but not . . ."

"Sappy." Nilwengerex picked up a shell and began to examine the intricate, brightly tinted calcareous whorls. "As usual, the humans have a word for it, even if that is one they themselves would not apply to their present condition. However, nothing prevents me from using it." He handed the shell to Joshumabad, who extended a truhand to accept it reluctantly. To have refused would have constituted a small but inescapable insult.

"Interestingly," the culture specialist continued, "they are very much aware of their own insupportable reaction. At least, the more intelligent among them are. The great fevered mass of humankind seems largely oblivious. They wish only to expand and enhance contact with their new friends. Deeper consequences do not concern them."

"What about the reception accorded our delegation by these Pitar?" The representative of the Grand Council was not at all comfortable with the information he was receiving.

"Formal and polite," Yeicurpilal told him. "Insofar as we have been able to determine by cross-referencing with our human friends, these new aliens are treating us no differently than they are their human hosts. In that respect they are displaying more diplomatic maturity than the humans themselves."

"What is the opinion of our perceivers?" Joshumabad matched her stride for stride while Nilwengerex wandered off to inspect the gelatinous mass of some tentacled creature that the sea had regurgitated onto the shore.

"Inconclusive. Contact is too recent and infrequent to reach any formal conclusions." She glanced sideways at him. "The council has been kept fully informed by space-minus communications. They know all this. Why are you asking questions to which answers have already been given?"

Feeling a chill, Joshumabad found himself longing for the low-lying clouds of Hivehom. "I wanted to hear it directly from you. Oftentimes official reports inadvertently leave out the most significant particulars. Even visual transcripts can neglect information that is inherent in person-to-person gestures and glances." He turned his attention back to the cultural specialist, who had concluded his examination of the dying jellyfish and hurried to rejoin them.

"I am interested in your informal opinion, Nilwengerex. What do you, personally, think of these Pitar? Beyond what you have contributed to the official reports."

Nilwengerex pondered a reply. The sky was very blue, and beyond it, Hivehom very far away. Yet he did not feel as estranged on this world as he had on Trix, for example, or even at his first posting, on the benign globe known as Willow-Wane.

"I haven't made up my mind. Nor have any of my colleagues. We felt that we were just beginning to comprehend these humans, to come to some understanding of how their very different minds work, when one of their deep-space exploration teams returned with these Pitar in tow. Their unannounced appearance was as much of a shock to us as it was to the rest of humankind. So we have been forced to adjust our work and reallocate our resources to study not one but two new alien, mammalian species. It has been something of a strain. Under such circumstances, you and the council will have to learn to be patient. We are learning as much as we can as fast as we can.

"Unfortunately, access to the Pitar is restricted. More than restricted: It is virtually unattainable. Constantly attended and surrounded as they are by ardent humans, it is almost impossible to procure unescorted contact with them."

"They are willing enough to talk to us," Yeicurpilal put in, "but reluctant to insist lest they irritate the humans. After all, it is their world on which we all are visitors. A polite guest does not make demands that might displease their hosts."

"I know that the Pitar claim to occupy only two worlds, in conjoining orbits in the same system. Though they possess vessels capable of journeying in space-plus they are not eager colonizers. By way of contrast, we have to date settled five worlds and the humans seven. Population disparities aside, do you think they are dangerous, these Pitar?" It was a question Joshumabad had put off asking until he felt more comfortable in the cultural specialist's presence.

A sharp, high whistle sounded from Nilwengerex. Startled by the unnatural alien sound, several small, rainbow-colored lorikeets burst from the cover of nearby brush and took wing. When the whistling laughter finally died down, the smallest of the three strolling thranx readily replied.

"We do not know enough about them to say, but one thing I do know: They can't be any more dangerous than these humans."

It was not the kind of response Joshumabad had expected, and his responsive gestures showed clearly that he was taken aback. "How can you avow such a thing? We have not only many representatives on this world, but an expanding, functioning colony. If what you say now is true, then there are lives at risk."

"I do not deny it." The dour attaché appeared engrossed in the pale blue sea, as though he had a death wish of his own. Joshumabad did not like him very much, but he respected the other male's knowledge. "Yet each day I spend on this world I find myself liking these humans more and more."

Joshumabad halted abruptly, the sand warm beneath his feet. "Now I am thoroughly confused. Which is it? Which observation do I convey to my superiors when I return to Hivehom to make my report in person? Are these bipeds dangerous or not?"

He might have expected clarification from the senior diplomat among them. Instead, Yeicurpilal only succeeded in muddying the waters further. "That's it exactly."

Joshumabad held firm. "That cannot be it exactly. Either these humans are a threat to us or they are not."

Yeicurpilal was not swayed by the visiting representative's determination to secure a straight answer. "They are warlike and peaceful, brutal and sensitive, ignorant and understanding. This planet is a big ball of raging contradictions. And the worst of it is, while they recognize these inconsistencies within themselves, they seem powerless to do anything about them."

"You have to give me something more," Joshumabad pleaded. "I can't present myself to the Grand Council with conclusions like that!"

"First of all," Nilwengerex assured him, "they are only observations, not conclusions. I can *tell* you that my colleagues and I who have been studying these people do not believe they pose any direct threat to the thranx."

"*Crri!kk,* that's something, anyway." Joshumabad was visibly relieved.

"I said no 'direct' threat," the attaché reminded him. "Their racial volatility makes their future actions unpredictable. We have been making progress in many areas of cooperation, most notably in the matter of commercial and scientific exchanges. The greatest difficulty we are being forced to try to overcome is the fact that in shape we so nearly resemble the small arthropods that are, numerically at least, the dominant life-form on this world, and with whom humans have been engaged in a battle for survival since the dawn of their own evolution. As you must know by now, they attach an enormous and irrational importance to physical appearance." His tone had turned even drier than usual. "Witness their immediate and unwarranted attraction to these Pitar. Through no fault of their own, these newly contacted bipeds are inadvertently responsible for the marked setback in our developing relations with the humans."

The council representative was silent for a while as the three resumed their stroll. Much more at home on the alien beach, Yeicurpilal and Nilwengerex reviewed every plant and animal they encountered, striving to identify them according to the taxonomy that had been supplied by human scientists.

"Then I am to inform the council that relations continue to advance successfully, but at a slower pace than previously?"

Yeicurpilal gestured concurrence. "That is what I would report."

"And when might they be expected to accelerate again?"

Yeicurpilal looked to Nilwengerex for a considered response. The attaché was reluctant to commit himself. "It is difficult to say. My own personal opinion, based on observation and the small knowledge I have gained of these people, is that it will not happen until the novelty of the Pitars' appearance has run its course. Unfortunately, it shows no signs of relenting. The humans are as entranced by their newfound near-duplicates today as they were when first they were brought here."

"Is there nothing we can do to regain appropriate attention?" The unexpected situation was new and confusing, as unprecedented in Joshumabad's experience as it was in everyone else's. They had not had such trouble relating to the Quillp, or even to the AAnn.

"If we are too forceful in our demands," Yeicurpilal informed him, "I fear that the humans will take umbrage at our attempts, thus rendering the situation even more awkward than it is now. It is my recommendation— and Eint Gowendormet, who is chief of our mission here, concurs—that we proceed according to our standard plan of contact while waiting for the ferment surrounding the discovery of the Pitar to run its course."

Joshumabad brooded on this. "The council will not be pleased. The desire to fully engage a strong species such as this as a counterweight to the endless adventurism of the AAnn is resolute."

Yeicurpilal gestured powerlessness. "It cannot be helped. During my sojourn on this world I have learned a number of things about our hosts. One is that they cannot be pushed, shoved, forced, or cajoled into doing something that does not originate with them, even if it is manifestly to their benefit. It is better to hint and suggest and let them believe that the idea originates with them. When dealing with humans, patience is not merely to be advocated, it is imperative. There is no other way to work with them."

"I am sorry," Nilwengerex added, "but that is the way of things here. If these Pitar had not revealed themselves to a human exploration team, maturation of our mutual relations would be on schedule. You cannot imagine the exceptional forbearance we are required to show in our daily dealings with them. Whatever its wishes and needs, the Grand Council must learn to do the same."

A visibly unhappy Joshumabad indicated understanding. "And our tentative connection with the Pitar? We of course must seek to establish formal relations with them as well. Though it does not fall within your purview, I presume your staff has taken the necessary preliminary steps forced upon them by circumstance?"

Yeicurpilal replied thoughtfully. "We have made the appropriate overtures. It is not so much that they have been rebuffed as that the Pitar have no time for us. They seem to be as ensnared by the humans as the humans are by them, though for the Pitar this fascination is reflected in a more intense and subdued attitude. Unable to study them firsthand, our specialists are reduced to speculating on their motivations. It cannot be determined if they are reclusive, wary, secretive, guarded, paranoid, fearful, all of the aforementioned, or simply shy. Without more intimate contact their racial psychology cannot be resolved. It is hoped time will provide us with access."

Joshumabad considered. "What is your personal opinion of them? Aside from the knowledge that has been compiled by such as this one." He indicated Nilwengerex, who took no offense at being referred to obliquely.

Antennae twitched meaningfully. "I don't like them."

The representative of the council gestured tersely. "*Crri!!kk,* that is concise, anyway. Why not?"

Yeicurpilal looked away. "You asked for an opinion not based on known fact. That is my opinion."

"Foolish," Nilwengerex proclaimed. "Xenologically impertinent. Even an opinion must be founded on a base of knowledge." He inclined both antennae in Joshumabad's direction. "I have no fear of these Pitar, nor love of them. I feel the same about the humans. My reactions and published convictions are based on factual material."

"There is room here for maneuver." In his mind Joshumabad was already compiling the report he would make to the Grand Council. "We will continue on course with the humans without forcing the issue of closer relations. These must develop as a consequence of natural processes. As for the Pitar, you will maintain contact with their representatives here on Earth until we can make arrangements to have a separate delegation received on Hivehom. Separated from humans, relations between us will advance at an acceptable pace." A seagull defecated nearby, and he observed the process with interest.

"Meanwhile, the current pace of diplomacy is not acceptable."

Yeicurpilal looked at him sharply. "But we have just told you that—"

"It does not matter." Joshumabad's interruption conveyed the importance of what he was saying far more than mere words and gestures could have. "The council is not satisfied." He used all four hands for emphasis. "If you cannot accelerate the signing of agreements with humankind, the council is perfectly willing to appoint others to your present positions in the hopes they may do better. This is not a threat, but merely a communication to be taken under advisement."

"I'm so glad it's not a threat." Even when he appeared to be ignoring his companions, Nilwengerex heard everything. "It does not matter. According to what you have been telling us, the council wants us to stay the course, not force matters but speed things up. I am sorry that does not strike you as a contradiction."

"It does not matter what I think." Being possessed of a highly amenable and easygoing personality, Joshumabad was noticeably unhappy at the direction the conversation had taken. Not that he had any choice. His mandate called for him to visit, learn, report, and deliver instructions. This he had done and would continue to do, no matter how unpleasantly he was received.

Yeicurpilal hastened to intervene between the two, conversationally as well as physically. "Nilwengerex is right. We are doing our best here. All the wishes of the council will not make the humans move any faster."

"Not even as fast as that larva." With a foothand, Nilwengerex pointed off to his left.

The girl who was running out of the palm trees and down onto the beach could not have been more than eight or nine. Even when inclined fully forward to make use of all six legs, the three thranx were taller. Leaning back on trulegs only, they would tower over her. She was as brown as the scattered pieces of shattered driftwood that studded the shore like so many gypsy hieroglyphs, with straight dark hair and dancing eyes the color of small black shells. Laughing and giggling, she bent to pick up a stick and throw it toward Sulawesi. It did not quite reach the water.

Turning slightly and bending in quest of another missile, she caught sight of the thranx. Having halted at her unscheduled intrusion, the aliens stood watching quietly. Joshumabad in particular was at once captivated and repelled. From his preflight studies he knew what very young humans looked like, but this was the first time he had seen one in the flesh. The unexpected encounter left him only momentarily speechless.

"Is . . . is it dangerous?"

"Not usually." Nilwengerex responded in his usual dry, clipped tones. "Not one this small. The adolescents are potentially lethal. Unlike us, their bodies assume adult form and bulk preposterously in advance of their minds. But one such as this should be quite harmless, though even infants are capable of surprising violence."

Straightening, the little girl came toward them. She was wide-eyed and unafraid.

"What should we do?" Joshumabad fought hard to suppress the panic that was rising within him.

"Nothing," Yeicurpilal informed him. "Remain as you are. Let the larva come to us."

Not without some concern, Joshumabad did as he was told. The girl halted a couple of arm's lengths away, one finger pressing against her lower lip. "Hello, bugs. What are you doing here?"

"What are *you* doing here?" Nilwengerex asked her in Terranglo so fluent that Joshumabad was startled. He knew the specialist was competent in the local language, but he'd had no idea he was so skilled. "This is a restricted area. Only authorized adult humans are supposed to have access." He looked beyond her. "How did you get in?"

"Hole in the fence," she replied without hesitation. "Maman says the big storm last week made it." She glanced back over a shoulder, though not to the degree a thranx could manage, and gestured importantly with one finger. "We're having a picnic."

Nilwengerex looked to his superior. "We must report this violation."

Yeicurpilal indicated resignation. "Of course. The humans will be most upset."

"At this point any kind of reaction we can get from them would be welcome. The council's official impatience notwithstanding—" He arched his antennae significantly in Joshumabad's direction. "—I look forward to the resumption of proper negotiations and exchanges." So saying, he stepped toward the child.

Joshumabad's instinctive reaction was to restrain the other male. Aware that Nilwengerex was the specialist in thranx-human interaction and he only a recently arrived newcomer, he held back. Lowering his head, Nilwengerex extended a truhand in an odd fashion.

"I am Nilwengerex. These are my friends, Yeicurpilal and Joshumabad. We are pleased to meet you."

"Hi. I'm Tomea." Reaching out, she took the extended truhand and shook it up and down. Joshumabad was impressed at how readily and easily Nilwengerex flowed with the gesture, which the representative quickly recognized as the most common human method of greeting. "It's nice to meet you. I've heard Maman and her friends talking about you." The doubly perforated organ located in the center of her face expanded and contracted several times. Following this, the corners of the flexible mouth curved upward and the jaws parted, exposing white teeth.

"You smell nice."

"Tomea!" The voice was deeper than the girl's, the tone agitated. "Tomea, where are y—?"

A subjective peroration split the air, startling Joshumabad who instinctively retreated several body lengths. Yeicurpilal did likewise, but Nilwengerex released the girl's fingers and stepped back only reluctantly. Chances to study human larvae were rare. He had yet to encounter one that readily accepted contact.

The female who came running down the beach was not very large. The thin, loose folds of her single garment fluttered like bird wings around her slim body. Reaching the girl, she clutched her by the shoulder with a severity that stunned Joshumabad. Turning her away, the mature female lectured her offspring as they walked back the way they had come. Occasionally the adult human glanced back at the three motionless thranx as if fearing pursuit. Joshumabad could not be sure, but it appeared to him that the larva was protesting the intervention.

"Do they always treat their progeny so roughly?" The visiting representative watched the adult human march her young off the sand and back into the trees.

"Frequently." Nilwengerex did not turn away until the two humans had been swallowed up by the palm grove. "It is a component of the naturally aggressive nature of the adults that is passed down to their brood. From my studies, it is clear to me that the humans themselves have little idea why they act in such a fashion, except that they always have."

"It may be a reflection of the fact that among mammals the young do not go through a pupal stage where all they can do is passively listen and learn." Yeicurpilal had evidently done ample reading and research on her own into the habits of these peculiar creatures.

"The break in the fence must be reported so it can be repaired." Nilwengerex glanced again at the representative of the Grand Council. "Not to keep us from wandering beyond the restricted area, but to keep curious and potentially dangerous humans out. No one wants a repetition of the Amazon hive incident."

"Certainly not I," Joshumabad agreed with feeling. He turned back. "It is growing late, and I would rather not be caught outside the compound after dark. You two may be comfortable in the night of this world, but I am not." Reflecting his agitation, his antennae bobbed and weaved aimlessly. "Yet despite such revelations, all reports indicate that those of you stationed here enjoy your contact with these humans."

"They are all right," Nilwengerex conceded. "They simply have a surplus of energy that they have never been able to channel properly. When our relations have become sufficiently close, it is hypothesized by those specialists concerned with such matters that we may be able to offer them some assistance in such matters."

"*If* our relations become sufficiently close," a brooding Joshumabad reminded him. "Too much energy, you say?"

"Not I," Nilwengerex corrected him. "Our students of alien psychology. Though I would not dispute their assessment."

"*Chrri!k,* at least it has done them well. They have advanced rapidly."

Yeicurpilal had been silent for a while. Now she spoke anew. "Only technologically."

Joshumabad eyed her curiously. "Your words are straightforward, but your gestures are circumspect. What else do you mean to say?"

The Grand Council's second-in-command on Earth regarded the visitor evenly. "You saw the reaction of the adult to our interaction with the larva. It does not matter if juveniles are involved or not, or only adults, or specialists, or even those who seek to help us bond with their kind. Beneath every interaction, whether successful or a failure, hopeful or uncertain, enthusiastic or rote, the undertones are the same. Sometimes they are subtle, sometimes blatant, but they are almost never absent."

Indicating confusion, Joshumabad turned to Nilwengerex for clarification. "What is she talking about?"

"These humans," the specialist informed him. "They are indeed technologically advanced. Even a cursory study of their history shows that they have overcome extraordinary odds and exceptional difficulties to reach the place where they are today, having successfully preserved their own world while settling many others. In spite of this, what the senior female says is indisputable. One does not have to be a qualified xenologist to see it."

"See what?" Joshumabad demanded impatiently.

Nilwengerex regarded the visitor quietly. "That they are not happy."

6

Minister Saluafata was not nervous about meeting his Pitarian counter-part. Having on occasion dealt with the eminently reasonable yet harrow-ingly grotesque-looking thranx, he anticipated no difficulty in sitting down at the table with one or more nonhumans who resembled tridee luminaries more than visiting aliens. He looked forward to the forthcom-ing interaction. Only the outcome concerned him.

This was to be no ordinary meeting. Much more was at stake today than superficial agreements on cultural exchange or travel rights. Such matters could be, and were being, handled by assistant ministers and second-echelon diplomats. Only for something as important as this was someone of Saluafata's stature personally involved.

That stature extended to his physical as well as mental proportions. Though not particularly rangy, the minister was huge. A legacy of his chiefly forefathers, he was almost as wide as he was tall, and very little of it was fat. A walking door plug, some of his colleagues and underlings had called him. More adept at plugging crises than doorways, Saluafata was used to disarming initially intimidated adversaries with a smile as wide as the lagoon that framed his island home. When that failed to soothe nervous opposites, a song or two sung in his startlingly accom-plished falsetto inevitably produced grins and delighted laughter.

Like a whale that had been subjected to reverse evolution and had reclaimed its hind legs, he settled himself into the chair at one end of the table. His personal secretary Ymir sat down on his left while the prim and always correct second undersecretary for Extraterrestrial Affairs, Mandan HoOdam, assumed the empty seat on his right. Carafes of chilled water were positioned in front of the delegates, along with small cobalt crystal bowls of assorted nuts. The Pitarians, it had been learned, had developed a liking for such terrestrial food.

A guard stood at either end of the room. Neither of them carried visible weapons—the operative word, Saluafata knew, being *visible*. The meeting place was a cheerful hemisphere with a single wide window that overlooked the placid tropical sea beyond. Set high on a Balinese hillside, the carefree beaches of Sanur were visible in the distance. They were filled with visitors cavorting in the warm waters, none of whom were aware of the somber significance of the meeting that was about to take place. All but a few were employed by the planetary government in the service of extraterrestrial relations. Overdeveloped Bali had long since ceased to be a stopping point for gallivanting tourists.

The entire facility needed to be moved, Saluafata mused. With the increase in deep space exploration and expansion, it had outgrown the available site. Nor did he suspect that he was the only diplomat or worker who felt uneasy laboring in the shadow of the periodically active volcanoes that dominated the island and this part of the world. Already, bureaus and agencies in need of additional room were being shifted southward, to the east coast of the southern continent. There was a surplus of flat, empty land there, and an enormous shuttleport was being built to service the increasing volume of offworld travel.

HoOdam murmured while scanning the privatized contents of her reader. An invisible beam from the reader periodically bounced off her retinas and back to the device, indicating that the individual gazing down at it was lawfully entitled to do so. If that proved not to be the case, the print on the screen would have remained as invisible as the security beam.

"What do you think, Api? Will they be difficult?"

He shrugged, and the movement took measurable time to travel from his columnar neck all the way down his enormous shoulders to his upper arms. "There's no way to tell in advance, Mandy. So far it's our government that has been doing most of the giving. The Pitar have been more than friendly; they've proven themselves amenable. But this is the first time we've proposed anything on this scale." Reaching forward, he poured himself a glass of water. Since there was no established protocol for dealing with the Pitar, he had no basis to fear that his simple gesture might be breaking it.

"What if they refuse?" Recorder at the ready, Ymir was running a hand repeatedly through his short, blonde hair. Saluafata recognized the nervous habit but did not point it out. Everyone was edgy, and it was a harmless enough release. The Pitar were not like the thranx, who saw every gesture, no matter how inconsequential, as the equivalent of a ver-

bal comment. When dealing with the insectoids, a person had to be conscious of his every movement lest unexpected confusion or, worse, unintended offense be given. The Pitar did use their hands occasionally, but
not as a component of interpersonal communication. That a hardworking
handful of them had already become fluent in Terranglo only added to the
ease of interchange. They were much better at it than the thranx.

Of course, he reminded himself, their speaking apparatus was far better suited to the task. Technically, the higher compliments were due the
thranx who had mastered human speech. As always, when compared to
the Pitar, the insectoids came off looking bad. But who wouldn't, the
minister mused? Alongside the Pitar, everyone tended to appear ungainly
and graceless.

He had resolved that the conference would not be affected by such
superficialities of aspect. Personalities would not become involved. The
forthcoming talks were too important, the matter at hand too consequential, to founder in a sea of perfunctory perception. He would not allow
himself to be distracted. Besides, if not as attractive as the Pitar, he could
be much more charming.

A soft musical tone chimed twice. Pushing back the specially ordered
oversized chair, he and his colleagues rose as the Pitarian delegation
entered. He recognized Urin-Delm and Jpar-Vhet from previous encounters. Both males were tall, muscular, perfectly formed, and wore the
familiar blank Pitarian expression of noncommittal. They were clad in
simple gray jumpsuits unadorned except for embroidered insignia that
identified them as to both name and function. They flanked a mature
female who . . . They flanked . . .

The minister swallowed hard as humans and Pitar alike took their
seats more or less simultaneously. To his secretary he whispered, "Close
your mouth."

Even by Pitarian standards of beauty the female was extraordinary.
Hair the hue of turquoise framed her face like the ultimate expression of
the Zuni silversmith's art. Her eyes were a deep royal purple. Lips that
did not belong in any species' diplomatic service were lightly parted, and
the molecules of air that rode in and out of that exquisite mouth were
repeatedly blessed. As for the rest of her, perfection was too mild a word
to serve as an adequate description. In a space of less than a minute,
Apileaa Saluafata, minister for Extraterrestrial Affairs, virtually forgot
who he was.

A nudge in his capacious side rudely induced his fall from heaven.
Though much taken by the appearance of all three Pitar, Undersecretary
HoOdam had retained a semblance of self-control.

"You're staring, Api. And we have business to do."

Indeed, having taken their seats, the three Pitar were observing their human counterparts in expectant silence. One had already begun sorting through the salted nuts on the table in front of him.

Unable to meet the ameythstine eyes of the alien seated across from him, a disconcerted Saluafata removed his own reader from its case and scrolled down the list of items that had been placed on the agenda. The cool, detached print helped him to regain his personal and professional equilibrium. But it was not easy. Every time he looked up, the purple eyes of his counterpart were there, gazing across the conference table in his direction. They made him want to think of anything except business. It did not help when she spoke first.

"The Dominion of the Twin Worlds extends its greetings to the people of Earth on this congenial day. We look forward to listening to whatever you have to say."

Diplomats should not have voices like that, the minister felt. It conferred an unfair advantage on the speaker that had nothing whatsoever to do with the issues under discussion. It made him think of somnolent days on deserted beaches, of hammocks caressed by emollient breezes, and cold, tangy fruit drinks placed close at hand. It made him think of . . .

"We receive the representatives of the Dominion," he heard himself responding, "in friendship and with high hopes for a mutually agreeable and successful culmination of our discussions. I presume that you have all had an opportunity to examine the formal proposal that was conveyed to your equivalent agency or department?"

To Saluafata's disappointment, it was the male seated across from Ymir who next spoke. As for himself, he wanted only to sit and listen to the female speak, to have her words nuzzle his ears like the lingering warmth of a perfect sunset on the eyes. Not that there was anything wrong with the male's voice, as the first cracks in HoOdam's armor of diplomatic distance showed.

"The matter has been studied," the irresponsibly handsome male responded. "You wish our permission to begin settling your people on the world you have chosen to call Argus Five, also Treetrunk."

Saluafata nodded. Flanking him, Ymir and HoOdam struggled to present a businesslike demeanor. That did not keep them from stealing surreptitious glances at the radiant comeliness of the three Pitar. If the visitors noticed this unprofessional attention or took exception to it they gave no sign. Presumably, the minister thought, they were used to it by now.

"That is correct." The special chair provided enough room for him to shift importantly on the reinforced seat. "Naturally, we understand that you may have hesitations. Let me assure you that my government is prepared to compensate or negotiate further on any particular objectionable aspects of this proposal, no matter how numerous. We are willing to work with you on this for as long as may be necessary to ensure that both sides are completely comfortable with the ultimate resolution of the matter. We can offer you . . ."

"There are no hesitations." The female cut him off softly. "There are no objections. The Dominion of the Twin Worlds does not object to the settlement of the world known as Treetrunk by the people of Earth."

Having prepared himself and his staff for lengthy, difficult negotiations, for an extended period of give-and-take, for argument and dissention, the minister was more than a little taken aback by the unexpected and to all intents and purposes unqualified grant of rights. He stalled for a few moments to gather his swirling thoughts.

"I need to make certain we understand one another." He addressed the female. For him her companions had ceased to exist, though not for Ymir or HoOdam. "You are saying that you grant us permission to settle as many colonists as we wish on the one habitable world of the system in question, without restriction or covenant?"

The male on the left of the woman with the look of a shallow sea replied. "Without restriction or covenant, yes. You may begin whenever you wish. We will not interfere."

"I don't understand." HoOdam felt compelled to speak up. "The extremes for favorable existence of your species fall within the same tolerances as ours. You could settle Argus Five as readily as we. Furthermore, it lies much nearer your homeworlds than does Earth or any of its developed colonies. Why are you leaving it to us?"

As they so often did, the three Pitar put their heads close together and conferred in whispers that were even softer than their usual speech. When they moved apart again, the woman in the middle explained.

"We explore, as your first ship to visit Treetrunk discovered. But we do not settle. We do not colonize." She smiled, and her countenance far outshone the light from the overhead glowstrips. "Our population is stable and has been so for some time. Believing as we do that the Twin Worlds are the most perfect of all habitable places in this galaxy, or at least in this part of this arm, we see no reason to stray from them. None of our people would willingly do so, even if our government was to offer incentives. They are quite happy where they are, and know that their offspring will be as content there as are they. We do not seek to spread ourselves more widely throughout the firmament."

The other male spoke up. "The stars are home to dangerous, uncouth, uncivilized creatures. We wish to know they are there so we can defend against any that might prove hostile. Among those we have met only yours suits our limited desire for offworld contact. We want as little as possible to do with the others." He shivered visibly. "Such as these over-bearing AAnn and hideous thranx."

Frowning, Ymir piped up. "The thranx aren't so hid—*umph!*" Turning a hurt face to Saluafata, the secretary used the bottom of one foot to rub the other where the minister's heavy shoe had descended. Discarding laborious diplomatic niceties in favor of alacrity, Saluafata had cut the secretary off in mid objection.

Let them find every space-going sapient species except homo sapiens abhorrent, the minister mused. Unreasonable and xenophobic such an attitude might be, but it only increased humankind's leverage in relations and negotiations. Still, he could hardly believe his good fortune. Not only would the council be delighted, such an astoundingly successful arrangement could only enhance his personal prospects for advancement.

Still, he could not escape the feeling that he was overlooking something significant. He sought certitude.

"Though colonizable space on Treetrunk is limited due to the conditions that prevail over much of the northern and southern portions of the planet, there is room for settlement by more than one species. You are certain your people do not want to share? We already have such an arrangement with the thranx, both here on Earth and elsewhere."

"No thank you," replied the female evenly. "In addition to the reasons I have already given, we find Treetrunk both too cold and too barren to be enticing. Also, our present thrust of exploration lies in the direction of the galactic center, away from your Earth as well as the Argus system. Even if we sought it, there is no reason for potential conflict."

"Better for you to concern yourselves with the expansionist AAnn, thranx, and other aggressive colonizing species than with us," the male on the right proclaimed. "Bearing such considerations in mind, you would do well to begin your settlement of Treetrunk as quickly as possible."

"I'm sure that when I convey the results of this conference to my government it will want to do just that," the minister assured the Pitar. "Local climatic considerations on Treetrunk will keep the pace of development below that of such worlds as Amropolous and New Riviera, but I know that as a first step the scientific outpost that is there now will be expanded as rapidly as possible." Putting both massive hands together, he leaned forward and rested them on the table.

"Now that I have your most gracious concession on the principal matter at hand, we can proceed to a discussion of congruous minutiae. Specifically, how much and what sort of compensation does your government want in return for allowing us unrestricted settlement privileges on Treetrunk? I would imagine that trade credits would prove the most amenable, provided we have anything you want. If there is something else you wish that is within my government's power to grant, I have the authority to recommend that it be given to you."

For a second time the three Pitar conferred, giving Saluafata and his cohorts the opportunity to gaze long and lingeringly at their fetching alien counterparts.

"I am not sure we understand," the female finally declared. "We want nothing from you."

"Nothing?" HoOdam blurted. "No compensation at all?" So stupefied was she by the response that bordered on the ingenuous that she did not even notice Saluafata's disapproving glower.

"How can we claim compensation?" The female concluded with one of the few, restrained Pitarian body gestures. Saluafata recognized it and enjoyed it. "Treetrunk is not ours to give. It is an empty world. We wish only to see you, our friends and close relations, settle and enjoy and populate it. The coincidence of stellar proximity grants us no special claim to it."

Saluafata took the risk of pointing out something now in the hopes of avoiding disagreement or confusion later. Everything said at the conference was being recorded. Neither he nor the council wanted the Pitar or anyone else coming back years later insisting that a certain right had not been granted, that specific permissions had not been obtained.

"By galactic standards the Argus system lies much nearer the Twin Worlds than it does to Earth or any of its colonies. Members of the scientific team that you encountered there were told that your people had visited Treetrunk previously. To our way of thinking, that does give you the right of prior claim. Yet you wish to waive this privilege without recompense?"

"Quite," the male on the right stated. "We have no use for the place. We are certain your people will find much success there, will multiply and fill the narrow ecological niche that is suited to mammals. We encourage you in this."

"After all," the other male added with an inviting smile, "why waste it? You want the place; we do not. Take it and welcome, and in friendship."

"We will of course make periodic visits to monitor your progress." The female's smile, aimed exclusively at Saluafata, melted any lingering concerns. "It should be interesting to observe how your people spread themselves across a new world, since it is something we do not do and have never done ourselves."

The minister found himself beaming back. "Naturally your people will always be welcome on the world you have so generously yielded to us, as well as here on Earth."

"Then if there is nothing more to discuss . . ." The Pitarian representative left the implication dangling.

"Your people are fond of markings on documents," one of the two males pointed out.

Saluafata would rather have spent the next hour staring into the amethyst windows that were the female's eyes, but while he might be feeling like a love-struck schoolboy, he was not one. With regret, he broke the hypnotic connection and sat back in his seat. The buttressed chair groaned as he shifted his weight.

"Yes, I'm afraid it's a tradition even a contemporary government adheres to. If you do not object, that is," he added hastily, wondering what he would do if they did.

"We do not," the female replied, to the minister's relief. "We only find it a curious but harmless anachronism." Again the supple smile that could melt lead. "We will be happy to put the written equivalent of our names to any material of your choosing."

The official signing of the settlement agreement took place in the rooftop assembly chamber, a dome of iridescent, polarized glass that provided a much more dramatic backdrop to the ceremonies than the tiny conference room in which the unexpectedly meteoric negotiations had taken place two weeks previously. Given the presence of not one but several of the glamorous Pitar there was no shortage of media coverage and attention.

Though outranked by several more prominent signees, a restrained Saluafata dominated the proceedings with his sheer presence, his royal dimensions invariably singled out for comment by the tridee commentators. And when senior representatives of the world government returned to their homes and offices in distant Zurich, Washington, Beijing, and Delhi, it was the minister who remained behind to conclude the ceremonies and to see to the ultimate satisfaction of the visiting aliens. This appeared to be as much to their liking as to his.

Much as he luxuriated in the presence of the seductive Pitar, it was not all pleasure. There was business to be conducted. There had to be, or the aliens would have ignored him. Frivolity and fun did not seem to be part of their interspecies lexicon. Polite, pleasant, ingratiating even, they drew the line at convivial intimacy. It was a wall that the immensely gregarious minister was determined to break down. Within the government, subordinates and superiors alike were fond of remarking that Saluafata's girth was exceeded only by his charm. The contrast between sharp mind and boyish charisma struck everyone who came in contact with him, if one could call a man who weighed nearly two hundred kilos "boyish."

Yet his most sincere efforts to break down their inherent reserve resulted in nothing more than courteous smiles from the Pitar. Masking his disappointment, he persisted in his attempts, all the while conducting the people's business.

This was difficult to do on a beach, where accompanied by Ymir he met four of the Pitar for an informal discussion on issues of mutual interest. It was difficult because one of them was the female who had presided over the negotiations that gave rights of colonization of Argus V to the people of Earth.

Slightly more hot natured than the average human, the Pitar enjoyed relaxing if not stiffly basking in the tropical sun. This they normally did in the absence of clothes. Even though the beach lay within the diplomatic compound and was screened and guarded, they had reluctantly agreed to make concessions to the inexplicable vagaries of contemporary human culture. Swimsuits had been provided for all four. The most they would tolerate were small swimsuits. Very small. Guards and privacy screens notwithstanding, the utter absence of these strategic strips of fabric might well have provoked a riot among the ever-hungry media.

Focusing on the business of diplomacy, or anything else for that matter, in the presence of the gem-eyed, statuesque female was not easy. Despite the envy others might feel at his perceived good fortune, Saluafata actually worked harder at such times to earn his stipend than he did in more formal surroundings.

As they sat in folding beach chairs that were the property of the government and gazed at the unruffled silken surface of the lagoon, the minister confined his comments to matters of mutual interest. He did not try to make small talk. The Pitar did not engage in small talk, a characteristic that had been noted and remarked upon as early as their initial contact with the crew of the *Chagos*. But that did not mean that a speaker as voluble as Saluafata could not insinuate casual queries into an otherwise formal diplomatic conversation.

Noting that Ymir was cavorting in the water with a pair of support personnel from Administration, the minister leaned into the sun shadow of the female Pitar's shape. "The water here is safe and warm, but I don't see any of your people enjoying it."

Piercing eyes turned to meet his, and she smiled at him: the standard polite, noncommittal Pitarian smile. "We see oceans as a resource. There is no other reason to enter them except for harvesting and development."

To someone like Saluafata, raised on an island in the middle of the Pacific, such an opinion constituted a kind of heresy. Or would have, had it come from a human. Still, he found it hard to believe that the oh-so-similar Pitar did not even indulge in recreational bathing. It was an observation, however, that allowed him to segue to a minor but curious point of diplomatic contention.

"You know that my government has now made more than several appeals to allow some of our representatives to visit the Twin Worlds." Though his smile was far more open and genuine than hers, it won him no response. "Reciprocal cultural exchanges are a useful way of building and cementing long-term friendships."

"We have no objection to such exchanges," she reminded him. As she shifted in the seat, her barely covered golden alien backside only centimeters above the hot sand, he struggled to keep his thoughts focused on the current business. "We have already concluded numerous agreements permitting such contact."

"Yes, but all of them call for Pitarian cultural groups to visit Earth, or one of the colonies. No permission has yet been granted allowing the equivalent human organizations access to either of the Twin Worlds."

"It is just a matter of time." This time when she smiled, it struck him as just a smidgen more genuine and less academic. Or was he reading into her expression that which he wanted to be there? "Your people have to understand, Minister Saluafata, that the natural reticence and shyness of my kind far exceeds their own. Confined as we are to the two homeworlds of our origin, we are intimidated by races that have spread themselves to other worlds, other star systems. This feeling is not restricted to humankind. We have yet to allow the thranx or any other newly contacted species access to the Twin Worlds." Still speaking, she turned away from him to face the lagoon.

"I am sure it will come with time. But your government has to understand that access to the ancestral home of the Dominion is for us a most sensitive matter. Your people must be patient and not try to force the issue, especially when relations between us are maturing at such a satisfactory pace." Reaching over, she touched the side of his forearm with long, lissome fingers. Though manifestly casual and anything but overtly erotic, the contact sent a shock through his entire expansive frame.

"It's just that we don't see any reason for your hesitation." Despite his pleasurable unease, he refused to be distracted. "If true friendship is to be extended across the parsecs . . ."

She touched him again, and this time her fingers ran down his exposed skin from elbow to wrist. "Please, Minister Saluafata. It is very much such a pleasant day, and so good to—how is it said?—take a break from the relentlessness of duty. Do not spoil it by pressing me or my colleagues for a response we are not authorized to give. I can only reiterate that your people must have some patience with us." This time he chose to believe that the scintillating smile came from the heart. "After all, we have not even been aware of one another's existence for but a short time. Allow us our privacy."

He grinned back. "It's not for me to take away. I'm just doing my job by conveying the petitions of my superiors. Myself, I don't care if your people choose to keep your homeworlds cloistered forever, so long as you come and visit us once in a while and we maintain amicable relations."

"You are a gracious and understanding representative of your kind, Minister Saluafata. I can see why your people appointed you to such a significant position."

"I've seen how your kind favor formality in interspecies relations." He gestured amiably in the direction of the sand, the sea, and the tropical sky. "But just here, just now, couldn't you break with your tradition for a few hours? Long enough to call me 'Api'? It would please me." His grin widened irresistibly. "Think of it as a diplomatic concession to improved relations."

" 'Api.' " She considered him thoughtfully. "A small name for so large an individual."

"It's a common trait among my particular, very small tribe."

"You are a tribe all by yourself, Api."

It was the first time he, or perhaps anyone else, had heard a representative of the Pitar make a joke. He was encouraged beyond reason.

"I'm not involved with the extensive studies that have been undertaken and are still ongoing in attempts to resolve our respective biologies, but I have read the reports—at least, the informal ones. I have neither the time nor the training to delve into the scientific literature. One thing I believe we've had some trouble resolving is the matter of aging. You seem to do it so much better than us."

She executed a Pitarian gesture of understanding. "It is not something we work at. Biology is what it is. It does not play favorites. Believe me, there are aspects to it where your abilities far exceed ours."

"There are millions of humans who, after seeing you, would disagree. Take yourself, for example. Unlike with most human females, it's impossible to tell if you've had or have not had children."

The look she turned on him was so sharp and sudden it shocked him. "What makes you ask that?"

He hastened to recover. "Nothing particular. I was just making conversation." His smile seemed to settle her. "I did not mean to intrude, or to violate any social taboos. Remember, we are still learning about each other."

"That is true. You should excuse me. I should not have reacted the way that I did."

But she had, Saluafata reflected, and he could not help wondering why. He proceeded gently. "Then if I'm not probing an area that's restricted or off-limits, may I ask if you have had children?"

"No, I have not given birth to any offspring." She smiled as she said it, but to the perceptive Saluafata she still seemed sensitive about the matter.

He was about to investigate further when she suddenly turned to him and once more placed a hand on his arm. The difference was that this time, she did not remove it.

"As long as you have brought forth the subject of mutually investigative biology," she murmured in a voice that was as unchanged as it was inherently seductive, "you must know that it has been theorized that sexual relations between Pitar and human are regarded as physically possible. All preliminary studies of the relevant architecture would seem to favor it. There can of course be no issue as a consequence of such contact. All that is wanting for confirmed results to be promulgated is a sufficiency of experimental data."

"I actually wasn't aware that much of anything had been done to resolve the conjectures." He swallowed with some difficulty. "Such matters are reserved for study by the scientific community and do not fall within the ken of the diplomatic ministry." Glancing up the beach, he saw that the other three Pitar had wandered off by themselves. Frolicking in the shallow water, Ymir and the two administrative assistants had moved far away.

The alien was very close to him now, and the sun and sand were very warm. "We have more latitude in such matters." As she whispered to him, her hand moved from his arm. "As a dedicated servant of the Dominion, I am always ready to add to the growing body of scientific and cultural knowledge my people are accumulating about your kind. Experiments in the field need not always be officially authorized."

There were questions he wanted to ask her, elucidations he sought, but as her hand moved he forgot all about them.

7

Heather Wixom struggled triumphantly to the top of the ridge. She could have taken a lifter there and had herself dropped off, but that would have denied her the sense of accomplishment she felt from having made the time-consuming ascent on her own. Technically, it had been easy: dense but navigable native forest; pauses to examine the indigenous wildlife while it hesitated long enough to stare at the slim, alien, human intrusion; and at the top, tolerant slopes that were kind to her booted feet.

From one of the larger boles directly below her rose the dirge of a gnarter. The tree itself put her in mind of a spruce with a skin problem, many of the evergreens that gave Treetrunk its popular name tending to shed copious amounts of bark at the slightest shift in the weather. As for the gnarter, it was a lumpy, eight-legged mass of slow-moving brown and dark blue fur that lived in selected tree hollows while regarding the world out of large, mournful eyes dominated by hourglass-shaped blue pupils. It had been suggested that it looked like the product of a union between a cuttlefish, a koala, and a caterpillar. A prolific inhabitant of the boreal forests, it did not often stray this far south.

It was luxuriating in the "warm" weather, Wixom decided as she tugged the sealfast of her insulating coat tighter around her neck. Treetrunk had rapidly revealed to its new inhabitants how fecund the frigid northern and far southern climes were. The temperate zone that tracked the equator was home to a correspondingly greater variety of life, of which the gnarter was by no means the most outlandish example.

Another was the hoat, a puma-sized predator that impaled its prey on spikelike teeth that grew horizontally from its expansive mouth and flattened jaws. Alone on the hilltop, she kept a careful eye out for it and its less imposing relations. Treetrunk was far from being tamed, its indigenous life-forms anything but domesticated. That was one of the great joys of settling a new world, she knew. It was one of the reasons that, restless and unmarried, she had traded a comfortable and predictable life as an up-and-coming urban planner on New Riviera for the incertitude of laying out new communities from scratch on Argus V.

The weight of the shocker in her left pocket made her grin to herself. No need for quite so potent a weapon of self-defense on placid, easygoing, semitropical New Riviera. There, unwelcome advances could usually be discouraged by the judicious application of a few sharp words.

Unlimbering her backpack, she unfolded the extensible stabilizing pod and attached the siter to the clip on top. Activated, the unit provided a heads-up display that allowed her to place buildings and infrastructure wherever she wished, creating a virtual community anywhere the unit's viewfinder was aimed. Warehouses, shuttleport, access roads, communications, water and sewerage, power transmission pylons—everything could be constructed with the touch of a few controls, could be sized to fit and arranged as she preferred without a single spadeful of dirt having to be overturned.

As she began to lay out the access routes from the growing town of Rajput to the proposed suburban extension, she made adjustments for the terrain, utilizing the unit to banish rock and earth that was in the wrong place and move it to where it was needed. As many trees as possible would be spared, but it was not really a major concern. Between the tundra lines, Treetrunk was a solid belt of native forest, and provisions had already been made to preserve the bulk of it in reserves. A renewable resource if properly looked after, its woods would provide income to the colonists in the form of everything from exotic furniture to tourism.

As she contrived the new town the unit recorded those decisions that she wished to convey to the planning board. In so doing she allowed herself room to maneuver, occasionally indulging in personal fancies that she knew the board would disavow. It was a game: She did as she pleased, the board remonstrated with her, and they compromised. In the end she got what she wanted while permitting the board members to believe that they had prevailed in every matter. The ego involved in the repetitive confrontations meant nothing to her: It was the results that mattered. Her psychological skills had contributed as much to her success on New Riviera as had her talent for organizing and planning.

The board would want the power distribution center to go there, she suspected. She moved it six blocks east. After due debate, she would concede the point, thereby allowing herself room to place the observation and restaurant complex exactly where she wanted it. That mattered. She didn't give two gnarter moans about the location of the power center.

"You are very intense."

The comment did not cause her to jump out of her skin, but her heart certainly thumped momentarily harder. Whirling, she prepared to unload a choice selection of suitably modified expletives on the head of whoever had snuck up behind her. Thinking she was alone and concentrating on the work at hand, she had been doubly oblivious to her immediate surroundings. The surprise had been total, and someone was going to pay.

The instant she caught sight of her soft-footed visitor, the flood of insults she was ready to deliver caught in her throat. From past experience ruefully familiar with their propensity for elaborate gags, she was expecting one or more of her colleagues from Rajput. What she got instead was an alien.

To be precise, a Pitar.

She was better prepared to deal with a marauding hoat.

He gazed down at her with interest, his expression noncommittal, his mouth set in a thin, inscrutable line. The heavy cold-weather attire he wore obscured most of the famed Olympian alien torso, but she could see enough to tell that from the neck downward his build did not differ significantly from the bronzed Greek-god proportions that were the Pitarian norm. She knew they often visited Treetrunk to offer their quiet assistance and to monitor, out of curiosity, the progress of the colony's development. Since they laid claim to nothing, and in fact were effusive in offering their help to the small but steady stream of arriving settlers, the government saw no reason why they should not be granted unrestricted access to the burgeoning, energetic new communities.

Wixom knew of several occasions where the aliens' assistance had been vital in helping small new municipalities overcome difficult local conditions. How the Pitar knew when an outlying hamlet was in trouble no one knew, but when it was they invariably appeared in their sleek shuttles, providing aid and support without having to be asked. No thranx vessel ever did anything like that, she reflected, shuddering a little at the thought of the giant, grotesque bugs running freely through the colony. Admittedly, the nearest thranx system lay a respectable distance from Treetrunk while the Twin Worlds of the Dominion were near neighbors in terms of space-plus travel. Nor was it that the thranx were indifferent or standoffish. They simply preferred to follow procedure in all things, including matters of aid and assistance. In this as in everything else they were methodical where humans were impulsive. Pitarian methodology appeared to fall somewhere in-between.

In any event, she relaxed as soon as she identified her visitor. He had steel-gray eyes and pale orange hair that put her in mind of ripening tangerines. Framed by a soft, protective hood, his features were predictably perfect. As he stood there on the windswept rock slope she grew aware that he was waiting for her to say something. The fact that she had never met a Pitar and knew nothing of their language was a poor excuse for her continued nonresponsiveness, but it was all that she had. Quick-witted, sharp-tongued, and completely at ease as she was among members of the opposite gender of her own kind, in the presence of this minor male mammalian divinity, she stood as if struck dumb, completely at a loss for movement as well as for words.

Apparently detecting that something was amiss, the visitor spoke again. "I seem to have startled you. Such was not my intent. Do you require medical attention?"

I am not going to swoon, she told herself firmly. Women of my experience and education do not swoon. Besides which, swooning is an atavistic reaction more properly applicable to the proper ladies of the nineteenth century. This facile forensic explication, however, did nothing to reconcile the physical and emotional insurrection that was raging within her.

The Pitarian male helped. He helped by moving: by bending and picking up a rock. He examined it before tossing it casually aside. It clattered against the scree, and the sound and motion served to jolt her out of her trance. Forging an effort of will, she turned away from him and back to her work. Her mind, however, was not intent on laying out accessways, waterlines, or communication lines-of-sight.

The alien was very close to her. She wanted to tell him—no, to order him—to move away, but for some reason her brain seemed to have lost contact with her vocal apparatus. All she could say was "Yes, I'm an intense person, both in my work and in the rest of my life."

"Intensity is good." Leaning close, the Pitar tried to resolve her heads-up display. This put his head very near to her own. She could smell the flat but not unpleasant alien scent, could feel the gossamer caress of inhuman breath. Her fingers on the controls of the siter started to tremble, and she angrily thrust them down at her side.

"What are you doing here?" I sound inane, she thought angrily. An inane twelve-year-old; that's what I've become. Conscious of the fact that she was bringing no credit either to herself or to her species, she fought to reestablish the kind of control that the alien's unexpected appearance had shattered.

"Only having a quiet look around, as you humans say."

Just as she was starting to recover some equilibrium, he smiled at her, and she found that she had to begin all over again.

"As you know, we are fascinated by the entire concept of leaving the comforting confines of a homeworld to settle upon another. It is a concept entirely foreign to us. But we want to see you succeed here, on Treetrunk. So in order to learn how to be of better assistance, we travel and we observe." His expression flattened once again. "You do not mind if I observe you?"

"Suit yourself," she replied indifferently. Within, she was yearning for him to observe her for a good, long time. Oh, how she wanted him to observe her! She had heard stories, they had all heard stories, about the . . . relationships that under just the right circumstances could develop between individual humans and Pitar. There were those who insisted these were nothing more than that—just stories. Rumors fed and fueled by the perversely imaginative. Though looking at this Pitar, tall and straight and so obviously muscular beneath his cold-weather gear, she could well believe that . . .

Stop it, she told herself! Male he may be, but he's also an alien. Don't ignore him, but don't trade your dignity and self-respect for some unsupportable foolish flight of fancy. Respond to his questions, and to nothing else.

"You are doing what?" he inquired politely, and the slight grammatical deviation helped to remind her of who and what he was. She returned her attention to her instrumentation.

"I work for the planetary planning agency. It's my job to search out and recommend the best locations for the individual components of a new development, as well as to design and suggest overall schematics. It's a task that does require some intensity of purpose, as you observed."

"I am very impressed," the Pitar told her, and for utterly inexplicable reasons this perfunctory comment caused her breathing to accelerate. "I am only a simple observer and could never manage the complex interdisciplinary tools necessary to perform such a task."

"It's not that difficult," she responded. "Having a new, state-of-the-art siter helps a lot. Here, I'll show you." Stepping aside, she allowed him to peer directly into the eyepiece that queued the heads-up display.

The Pitar asked several questions, struggling with his command of Terranglo, before stepping back. "It appears to be a very efficient device. Your technology is good."

She could not decide if she was blushing or if her cheeks were simply reddened from having been exposed to the cold air during the climb. "I don't make it; I'm just trained to use it. From what I read and see on the tridee, your technology's good, too."

"We have done well enough. Concentrating solely on developing the Twin Worlds has both helped and forced us to concentrate our energies. Our two local asteroid belts supply ample resources, and we are careful not to overexploit those that are not renewable. Of late our society has grown somewhat stagnant, but contact with your people has suggested ways and means of revitalizing our development, as well as solving problems that previously seemed insurmountable. For that we thank you, and are most grateful for the contact between our two species. We are especially glad to see you doing so well here on Treetrunk."

"Your people have been so helpful ever since the first settlement went in." She hesitated briefly, fearful of committing some unseen faux pas. She was a planner, not a diplomat. "Some of us have become . . . fond of you."

"Your demonstrations of affection have been remarked upon." His tone was dry and formal, and she wasn't sure whether she was grateful for that or not. "We find it peculiar that a great deal of it has to do with our appearance, which we ourselves find in no way remarkable and over which we have no control. Nevertheless, anything that facilitates better relations between us is to be welcomed." From within his protective hood a smile emerged that warmed her to the tips of her boots. "Your mate must be proud to be conjoined to so competent a worker."

"Thanks for the compliment, but I'm not marri . . . mated."

"No children, then?" His tone was unchanged, academic.

"Not yet, but I'm hoping to have a couple someday." She fiddled absently with the controls of the siter.

He looked past her, into the shallow valley that would soon be home to another two or three thousand humans. "As am I. Our reproductive and birth systems are extraordinarily similar."

"So I've heard." She looked away from the siter and back up at him. "Why haven't you had any children?"

His smile faded, and he made a gesture she did not recognize. "For one thing, the time is not right for me. That is one area where our physiologies differ. Not only are our females fertile only for a limited time each year, but the same is true for the males. We do not enjoy the flexibility of year-round breeding that you do."

"Oh, I don't know." She responded with a mixture of consideration and playfulness. "I know plenty of people who would prefer that kind of biological arrangement. It would make a lot of things easier." Reaching out, she tentatively placed a hand on his arm. She could feel the power even through layers of winter clothing that exceeded her own. "So that means you can't get anyone pregnant right now?"

He made the Pitarian gesture for agreement, a smooth dipping of the right shoulder. "That is correct."

"Not that you could anyhow," she murmured as she embarked on a fairly explicit explanation of the intricacies of how certain specific on-site structures ought to be erected.

* * *

From the preliminary settlement of Chagos Downs to the carefully laid-out capital city of Weald, the colony grew rapidly. The pure, unpolluted air energized new colonists the instant they stepped off their transport shuttles. Sometimes bitterly cold winters, when it seemed as if the entire planet were about to succumb to the glaciers that were advancing slowly from both north and south to squeeze the habitable belt around the planet's midsection in an icy vise, gave way to an explosively vibrant spring and therapeutic summer. As predicted by its discoverers, Treetrunk was no New Riviera, but it was a highly amenable place to live. Those who arrived from other worlds to make their homes there generally had few regrets.

There were always malcontents who would never be happy anywhere, who really believed they *could* get all their squirrels up one tree. Grumbling and complaining, they packed up and left, always in search of the paradise world that existed only in their imaginations. Their number was a trickle compared to the steady stream of satisfied newcomers. Families began to put down roots, new enterprises were begun, education centers expanded rapidly.

Operating out of her own tiny prefabricated habitation, a crazy lady preached the gospel of a church that as yet had no recognized name but which aimed to include and encompass all forms of intelligent life. Bound by tradition and unable as yet to envision themselves praying alongside, for example, a brace of thranx, colonists new and old laughed at and teased the earnest evangelist. A few, a very few, occasionally stopped to listen, finding the ravings of what appeared to be a rational fanatic entertaining if not convincing.

Following in the gridded footsteps of the planners, the colony expanded. Outposts became waypoints; waypoints became stations; stations became the cores of small communities. Imports gave way to locally produced goods and services. New industries congealed, from small crafts and manufacturing that made use of the planet's extensive hardwood forests to a pair of mines that extracted useful metals from beneath the surface.

The colony was well on its way to advancing from dependent to transitional autonomous status, with its own independent world government, when the *Glistener* entered into orbit above Weald. A small, compact deep-space vessel engaged in scientific exploration, it stopped to pay its respects to the inhabitants of the new human colony world before continuing on its planned course through the upper Orion Arm in the general direction of the galactic center.

Visitors from the ship were greeted with full courtesy and formalities, if not warmly. Though naturally suspicious of outsiders, the settlers could not very well refuse to welcome representatives of a race with which humankind enjoyed officially cordial relations. The thranx were granted permission to visit several communities. Each group was accompanied by experienced members of the planetary government who saw to it that the visitors' plans and itineraries were well publicized in advance. The majority of colonists had never seen a thranx, and it would not do to have children or susceptible individuals panic at the sight of them. That would have been discourteous.

There was little need to worry. The thranx intended a short visit at best. A species that favored 100 percent humidity and air temperature to match, they were not at all comfortable in the brisk, wintry atmosphere of Treetrunk. Despite their personal discomfort, their inborn concern and curiosity caused them to persevere, if only for the brief duration of their stay.

Dutifully, they admired the energy exhibited by the human settlers and gestured approvingly at the skill with which the colony had been laid out and was being developed. Their hosts thanked them when appropriate while privately wishing to be rid of the inquisitive, talkative, pleasantly odiferous bugs so they could get back to the business of building the colony.

Unlike her fellows, there was one senior thranx who seemed, in spite of the unkind climate, reluctant to leave. Every question her hosts answered sparked another two or three. Interested in everything, she was satisfied by nothing. While her hosts despaired of satisfying her, she continued blithely on her way, inquiring endlessly about the most inconsequential matters.

"The local population is approaching six hundred thousand," her weary guide informed her. "Of these, some two hundred thousand plus are concentrated in and around Weald, with another ninety-five thousand at Chagos Downs. Allowing for geological constraints, the rest are scattered in small communities and outlying camps that follow the equator."

"You are not expanding to north and south as well?" Cocooned within cold-weather gear that exceeded in insulating properties anything a human would wear except at the poles, the thranx's face was barely visible. Twin antennae peeped hesitantly from beneath the brim of the headgear.

The guide sighed tiredly. "Of course we will, but for right now there's no reason to do so. The most amenable zone is being promoted first. When our settlements meet on the other side of the planet, that will be the time to expand into the colder forests."

The senior thranx nodded, a gesture they had developed the habit of using among themselves as well as in the presence of humans. "Then you are doing well here?"

"Extremely well." The guide could not help but add, "In addition to the regular runs from Earth and the occasional visit from New Riviera or Proycon, the Pitar have been really supportive. Not just with verbal encouragement, but with material assistance as well. Especially during the first two years of settlement, the help they provided was invaluable."

If the thranx understood this observation to be a dig at her kind for not offering more, she did not acknowledge its tone. "We are glad that you received the aid that you needed. You are fortunate. The expanding colonization efforts in our own sphere of exploration require our full attention, as no species has offered to assist *our* efforts. In addition, we have a long-running, ongoing disputation with the race you know as the AAnn, which complicates and inhibits our efforts."

"The AAnn don't bother us here." Unwittingly, the guide had assumed a marginally superior air.

"*Chur!kk,* the AAnn are very shrewd." A truhand encased in insulating fabric waved at the much taller guide, who comprehended nothing of the meaning behind the gesture. "Thinking oneself safe from them, bound by alliances and agreements, secure behind a thin barrier of treaties and covenants, is the most dangerous attitude a people can have."

"Well, I'm not a diplomat, but all I can say is that they haven't given us any trouble."

"Have they paid you a visit?"

The guide blinked. "Several times, I believe. I only settled here last year myself. But yes, ships of the Empire have called at Treetrunk. If I remember correctly they had a look around, extended their hopes for a successful enterprise on the part of the colonial government, took some straightforward and innocuous scientific readings, and left. I understand that their visits were very brief." He couldn't keep from smiling. "No doubt they found it a bit nippy for their liking."

Once more the thranx gestured. "The AAnn require an ambient temperature similar to ours, but infinitely drier than even your kind prefers." A pair of hands wagged in his direction. "Ensure that those who monitor your scanning instrumentation are well trained and remain alert. Nothing is more dangerous than a well-wishing AAnn."

"We'll have a care," the guide replied with polite nonchalance.

Whether the thranx detected something in her host's voice or if she simply decided to have a further say in the matter the man never knew, but the heavily bundled insectoid turned to him with an effort and met his eyes with hers. Leastwise, he thought she did. When gazing at compound eyes, it is difficult to tell for certain exactly where they are focused.

"We are always astonished at the confidence you humans display in the face of a lethal and indifferent universe. Have a care that your confidence does not exceed your ability to sustain it."

"Thank you for that solicitous homily," he replied tartly. "We know what we're doing here."

"Does anyone know what they're doing anywhere? Individual or species, it does not seem to matter. We are all of us sapients adrift together in a cosmos in which the largest single constituent of matter seems to be composed of unanswered questions." Turning away, she started up along the path that would lead them back to the terminus where the ground skimmer would pick them up. "I have seen enough. I'm cold, and ready to return to my cubicle on board the *Glistener*."

I'm ready for you to do so too, he murmured silently. Most of us here on Treetrunk have better things to do than escort garrulous bugs around, answering their inane questions while trying to ponder their cryptic aphorisms. Even if, he reflected, one or two did smell like attar of frangipani.

8

Trohanov was relaxing in his cabin with one of the few tridee recordings he hadn't already watched on the run out from Earth. It was some trifle about a genetically engineered lone avenger on an endless voyage of self-discovery whose ultimate denouement the creators of the entertainment had left purposely obscure. The protagonist struck him as shallow and his paramour devoid of depth, but they were both pleasant to look upon.

Presently, their beguiling three-dimensional forms were occupied in an activity that, while not in any wise significant to the advancement of the plot, was nonetheless engaging. So it was with some ire that he acknowledged the insistent hail from the bridge.

"Hollis, I'm off duty!" he barked, knowing that the omnidirectional pickup would convey his tone as well as his words to the ship's second-in-command. "Maybe that doesn't mean much to you, but when you reach my age you learn to treasure every little—"

The second officer interrupted him, which while not unprecedented, was unusual. She also sounded worried, but that was normal for Hollis. "Captain, you'd better come up here."

"Why?" Even as he objected, he was swinging his legs out of the bed. "We made the transition from space-plus without incident, and this system holds no surprises. What's wrong with the ship?"

"It's not the ship, sir. At least, Kharall says it's not."

"All right, all right!" Grumbling to himself as he slipped into his one-piece duty suit, he damned the regulations that required a vessel's captain and senior officers to always be available for consultation.

No one confronted him as he made his way via lift and corridor to the bridge. Whatever had upset Hollis, it had not caused any panic on the ship. He encountered no frightened faces, no individuals racing to and fro in panic. This had better be a real problem, he thought irritably, or he was going to have serious words with his second.

Nor did there appear to be any reason for distress on the bridge itself. There was Kharall, bent toward his console as if by bringing his face a few millimeters closer to the readouts he could discern details that would not otherwise be evident. Everyone else assigned to the second shift was in position and to all intents and purposes engrossed in their work. A few chatted softly, their attitudes anything but indicative of imminent disaster. No voices were raised, though the expressions on several faces as he entered were expectant.

Expectant of what? He had no idea yet what was going on, or why Hollis had thought it necessary to summon him from the middle of his rest period. Only one thing was he certain of: He would have some answers very quickly.

Turning slightly to his right, he strode purposefully over to where Hollis was conferring with Meeker, the ship's communications specialist. Both looked up at his approach. Hollis didn't wait for the captain to speak.

"We're a fraction of an au out from Treetrunk, just cutting the orbit of Argus Six, and there's still no response."

He replied instantly. "So their beacon's down."

"All of them?" She met his gaze unflinchingly. "All three?"

"It's possible," he shot back, though internally he was already beginning to argue with himself.

Meeker joined in. She was a small woman with big ears, ragged black hair cropped short in what Trohanov had always thought a very unflattering cut, and she had a surprisingly large voice that was the aural equivalent of her occasional opinions.

"One okay. Two maybe. Three never."

"Never say never." Trohanov was not ready to concede, though if professionally challenged he would have been compelled to agree with his communications officer. "Treetrunk's still a new world, only been settled for a few years."

"Four," Meeker corrected him.

"Okay, four, dammit." Ahead, through the narrow, curved port, could be seen only stars and the still distant dot of Argus V, their destination. "A multiple beacon failure is still possible, especially on a world as recently colonized as this one."

"There's no response from the shuttleport at Weald, either." Meeker was conciliatory but insistent.

"So their communications are down also. It means they're having some problems, that's all." As he spoke he leaned closer to the communications console, studying the readouts closely.

Meeker turned her child-troll's face up to his. "There's no background noise. No tridee, no chat, nothing. Not even a hiss. From a communications standpoint, the planet's dead."

Her choice of words upset Trohanov, but he didn't let it show. "Okay, that's bad. Maybe real bad. Let's not anybody jump to any conclusions. I've known several people who jumped to conclusions and they invariably came to a bad end."

"What happened to them?" Hollis asked softly.

He flicked deep-set cinnamon eyes at her. "They landed in holes. Maintain preset course for orbital insertion. There's nothing to suggest we should do otherwise. Keep everyone on alert."

"What about the rest of the crew?"

"Leave 'em alone. There's no reason to tell them anything until we have something definite to tell. Those who are sleeping might need all they can get." Reaching down, he put a strong hand on Meeker's shoulder. "Keep monitoring everything that sputters and let me know the instant you hear anything, even if it's just bad language." She nodded once. In charge of words, Meeker was not one to waste them.

Hollis regarded the captain speculatively. "I suppose there's no reason for you to stay here, sir. You might as well go back to bed. We'll call you when we know something."

He glanced sideways at the starship's silent, flickering instrumentation, his expression set. "Like hell," he growled softly.

They settled into orbit without incident. As expected, they were the only vessel present. Treetrunk was an outpost, a comparatively new settlement far from Earth and the other colonies. KK-drive ships called infrequently, and only on official business. In the ellipsoidal cargo compartment that comprised the bulk of the vessel's superstructure was a consignment of goods from New Riviera. Subsequent to delivery, the space-plus transport would move on to Proycon. Everything about the run, from its payload to its course, was conventional.

On the chill world below, however, something was not.

Meeker had been at it for another six hours straight when Trohanov finally lost patience. By now all three shifts were awake, with rumor and controversy rampant among the crew. It was time to resolve ignorance.

"Run the check on shuttle number two. I'm going down. Hollis, as per procedure you're in charge until I get back." He turned to leave.

"What about the cargo, sir? We have three full loads. The company will scream if we have to make an extra drop."

"Let 'em howl. There's some kind of trouble down below, and until we know the nature, extent, and degree of the local emergency it's more prudent to hold onto the shipment than to start delivering it. As soon as we know what's going on we'll start shifting containers. Until then, ship is to remain on alert and everyone is to stand by. I'll field complaints from those who are supposed to be on downtime later. Right now the first thing we need to do is find out why this place is electronically comatose."

Nothing untoward materialized to interfere with the shuttle's descent. The view out the small, thick ports was uneventful, the surface a water-color wash of white, brown, and green. Trohanov and the half dozen crew he'd chosen to accompany him spoke little as the shuttle struck atmo-sphere and began to vibrate. At such times each man and woman had thoughts enough to occupy their minds. At the captain's direction, all wore sidearms. Procedure, he thought. In the absence of knowledge it was always reassuring to be able to fall back on procedure.

Nothing in the literature, or the regulations, or his experience pre-pared him for what they found, however.

As the shuttle dropped beneath the thick clouds and into calm air the pilot reported the absence of any signal from the capital's port. There was heavy overcast but no rain or snow, the atmosphere being as eerily silent as the surface. In the absence of the usual datastream to take control of the shuttle's instruments and guide it in, the pilots were forced to locate the landing strip themselves. "On final approach," one of the pilots said, and Trohanov and his people scrunched a little deeper back into their seats. Down, down . . .

The shuttle accelerated violently and without warning. He found himself wrenched sideways, then pressed back into the seat. Several of the crew gasped, but no one screamed and there was no panic. They were still airborne, and the shuttle's engines throbbed with restored power. Moments later the voice of the pilot echoed through the passen-ger compartment.

"Sorry about that, everyone. Obviously, we made a last-second pull-up. We're going to have to try and find a field or something to set down in. We can't use either of the two landing strips at Weald shuttleport." There was a short pause while the atmospheric craft began to bend around in a tight curve, though the arc it executed was no more constricted than the pilot's voice. "They've been destroyed."

It took some time for the pilots to locate a suitable site. Relying on the shuttle's landing skids, they made a bumpy, jolting, but successful touchdown. Before the craft had slid to a stop Trohanov was out of his seat and harness and racing forward.

The view out the cockpit's wide double port was maddeningly unin-formative: tall evergreens, distant tree-swathed hills, a nearby pond whose inhabitants were only now starting to return following the shuttle's noisy landing. Everything appeared peaceful and serene.

"Where are we?"

Solnhofen, the copilot, pointed to a readout. "About two kilometers southwest of the southern runway. This appears to be a natural meadow."

Bending over to peer out the port, Trohanov nodded once. "I don't see any signs of catastrophe. You said the landing strips were destroyed?"

"Yes, sir." The pilot's face was ashen. "We didn't get a good look at the city itself—too busy with the descent. Neither Lillie nor I have had to do a manual landing since flight school."

"Forget it. You both did great. Could you tell what caused the damage?"

The two pilots exchanged a glance. "No, Captain," a regretful Solnhofen told him. "It was as Dik said. We were too busy just trying to get down in one piece."

"Right." Turning, a couple of steps brought Trohanov back into the passenger compartment. Everyone was out of harness, fidgety and anticipative. "We're going for a walk. Check your sidearms and make sure they're not just decorative. I want everyone's weapon and communications gear fully powered up." They stared at him expectantly, and he realized they were waiting for an explanation. In the absence of one, he improvised as best he could.

"Something bad has happened here. We don't know what yet, but we're going to find out."

"That's not our job, Captain," someone pointed out. "We're a class three KK-drive deep-space cargo carrier, and that's all we are."

"You can file a formal complaint about being forced to function outside your job classification with the company later. Right now everybody here comes with me. I've been in Weald twice before, once as recently as last year, so I'm at least sort of familiar with the municipal layout. Stick close and don't wander off. No matter what we find, we'll be back here before dark." He looked over his shoulder, toward the cockpit.

"You two stay on board. I don't want you going outside, not even to smell the tree sap. If anything real disturbing should start to show itself, you lift off and return to ship."

"Disturbing?" The pilot looked uncertain. "Like what, Captain?"

"Like I don't know—yet. Use your own judgment." He tapped the communicator on his duty belt. "We'll keep in touch."

Stepping out of the shuttle, it was difficult to believe that anything was amiss. Indigenous wildlife filled the nearby forest and the open meadow with intermittent alien song. Arboreal life-forms flitted among the trees and skittered through the waist-high blue-bladed ground cover. Plotting a simple straight line, Trohanov led his people away from the shuttle and into the woods.

The gently rolling ground did not slow them, and the absence of dense underbrush except in isolated copses allowed rapid progress. With the shuttleport lying to their northeast, Trohanov calculated, if they maintained their current pace they ought to reach the southernmost outskirts of the city by midafternoon. That would not allow much time for exploring, but they ought to be able to secure transport into the city center. Someone at Administration would be able to clear things up and to explain the nature of whatever emergency had befallen the colony.

But there was no transport readily available in the southern suburbs of Weald. There was very little left of the suburb they entered, or for that matter of the rest of the city.

Its inhabitants, it was revealed, were as dead as their communications.

Whatever smoke and flame had risen from the ruins had long since burned itself out. Except for the occasional darting shape of a native scavenger working the dead, the city was devoid of movement. Finding and righting a small skimmer that still retained half its power charge, they succeeded in covering considerably more ground than they would have been able to do on foot.

The destruction was selective as opposed to total. Many of the city's buildings were still intact, from individual or group habitations to municipal facilities such as the central water-treatment plant. But the center of the city, where Administration had been located, was a spacious, silent crater. Ramparts of fused glass sloped down to a pile of vitreous slag in the center. On the northern outskirts of the city, a similar pit marked the spot where the colony's intersystem space-minus communications shaft and facility had been located.

All that afternoon they scoured the capital in search of survivors, and found none. Those bodies that had not been incinerated by shot or subsequent fire displayed indisputable evidence of having been shattered by violence. Come early evening Trohanov found himself kneeling alongside an entire family. Trapped inside a small shop, they had evidently attempted to make a stand against whatever had ravaged their community. Signs that a blockaded doorway had been smashed inward lay scattered everywhere.

Whatever weapon had been used to kill them was thorough and messy. Though no forensic pathologist, Trohanov could see as clearly as anyone that something had struck each of the bodies and blown them apart. The remains of the father lay in the middle of the floor, where he had apparently attempted to intercept the intruders. Back in a corner they found the corpse of the mother splattered over those of two preadolescent boys. In a warmer climate the stench in the room, as elsewhere in the city, would have been overpowering. The cold, clear air of Treetrunk had helped to slow decomposition and decay. Otherwise, it would have been impossible for the crew to have continued their investigation.

As it was, several of the small group became sick at different times that afternoon. The slaughter gave every indication of having been carried out in a relentless and methodical fashion. Returning to the shuttle, Trohanov informed Hollis and the rest of his crew of what he and the others had found and took care to relay the visual information they had managed to collect. Returning to the ship, they compressed and sent it on its way to Earth, entangling it with the first quantum receiver that acknowledged their transmission.

In the silence of the bulbous ship no one slept. As soon as Trohanov felt able, he took a larger team back down to the surface. This time they set down near the colony's first community and second city, the municipality that had been named Chagos Downs after the ship that had originally explored the Argus system. There was no shuttleport at the Downs, but there were landing facilities for suborbital aircraft. Unfortunately, those facilities had suffered the same fate as their much larger counterpart at Weald, and the crew once again had to set down in the nearest available field.

Chagos Downs was a mirror image of disaster, albeit on a smaller scale. The same conditions applied as they had encountered in the capital: Many structures had been left standing and intact, some with no sign of damage at all, while others had been completely reduced. As before, there were no survivors. Like the inhabitants of Weald, the citizens of the Downs had been slaughtered where they had been found; attempting to surrender to unknown assailants, lying in bed, slumped over instruments and other devices while busy at work, caught preparing meals, on the streets, and in hallways. From the eldest patient in the hospital to the youngest infant, no one had been spared.

Whoever, whatever had committed the atrocity had been relentlessly thorough in seeing to it that not one survivor was left breathing to comment on the cataclysm. Trohanov knew it was not his responsibility to try and find out who was responsible. The crew member who had spoken out earlier doubtless had being doing no more than voicing the concerns and opinion of many of his colleagues. They were crew on a deep-space transport: not soldiers, not mass-homicide investigators, not government operatives. Whatever had happened on Treetrunk was terrible, but it was not their business to try and fix responsibility. Nor could Trohanov leave his ship under Hollis's command to resume its voyage while he remained behind to await the first official response from Earth. Pragmatically, he and his companions could do nothing with the anger and helpless fury that boiled within them except bottle it.

Reluctantly, they returned to the ship and resumed their itinerary. Until the day and hour of their deaths, the memory of what they had seen never left them, remaining as clear and sharp as the air of the devastated world itself.

Little had changed when the three warships emerged from space-plus dangerously close to the planetary mass. Settling into equidistant orbit, their instrumentation between them covering and monitoring every meter of the cloud-swathed globe beneath, they dropped nine shuttle craft into the clouds and clear air below. Each was far larger than that of the cargo ship that had preceded them. On board were soldiers as coldly efficient and highly trained as Earth and its colonies could produce, armed with the most advanced weaponry their military research institutes could manufacture.

Setting down simultaneously at predetermined locations in the planet's habitable equatorial zone, the independently functional squads immediately established defensible perimeters around their respective shuttles. Once these landing sites were secured, ground transports were unloaded from the craft and boarded by half of each squadron's personnel. Leaving the entrenched perimeters that now surrounded the heavily defended shuttle craft, these armed skimmers and their smaller escorts moved out in carefully designated search-and-rescue patterns.

They found little changed and nothing significantly different from the halting, barely adequate pair of reports that had been filed by the crew of the cargo transport that had first made the grisly discovery. Fanning out from their landing sites, they checked the towns first, then moved on to isolated hamlets, individual farms, mines, and tiny frontier outposts. The degree of physical destruction varied, but nowhere did they find anyone alive, nor any record in any of the surviving instrumentalities of what had happened.

As soon as the military commander of the expedition was satisfied that no threat remained on the surface, at least insofar as his troops could determine, the members of the scientific team were allowed to descend. Forced to remain on their assigned ship while the soldiers secured the ground, they were in a quiet frenzy of fervor to begin their work. Over their protests each was assigned an armed guard. Until some answers were forthcoming the military was taking no chances. Pathologists and recorders, biologists and scanners were forced to operate under the watchful eyes of edgy soldiers.

The scientists' escorts were not uneasy because they feared attack. Indeed, they would have welcomed it. To the last man and woman they had seen too much death on what had previously been considered a mellow, pastoral, even boring world. Women clutching infants, old men slain in the doorways of their homes, children shot down in the street: It was too much for some of them. Those who gutted their way through the last of the patrols wanted something to shoot at, something to kill. No plague had wiped out the inhabitants of Argus V, no secretive native uprising had surprised the colonists in their beds. The evidence was indisputable that advanced killing technology had been at work in the peaceful forests and meadows.

The question that was on everyone's mind—soldier, scientist, and starship crew alike—was, Whose?

Derwent was tired of trideeing bodies. After the first sickening couple of days his stomach settled down and he was able to go about his job more or less normally and at a faster pace. The labor was necessary, he knew. Not only so that relatives on other worlds could identify slain relations but so that the research team being put together back on Earth would have as much information to work with as possible. Hudson, his partner, was reciting into her recorder in her familiar monotone. It was her job to render a preliminary judgment on cause of death.

Dozens of additional personnel were active in other districts. Since landing, no one had enjoyed a day off. Given the condition of many of the bodies there was no time to spare. Not with hundreds of thousands of corpses to evaluate. For teams such as Derwent and Hudson, long hours in unpleasant conditions had become the norm. Every body, or remnant thereof, had to be dutifully recorded and evaluated.

Outside the ruins of the small country inn a corporal and two privates stood guard, *stood* being perhaps too strong a word. Derwent didn't mind when the three sat down and set their weapons aside, conversing quietly among themselves. The small skimmer that had transported the team and its supplies rested nearby, powered down and open to intrusion. The recording specialist was not worried. From the time the first squad of marines had touched down they had encountered no opposition. Nor had any trouble manifested itself since. Nothing interfered with the work of the pathologists or coroners.

Whatever had exterminated the population of Argus V was nowhere in evidence. If the relentless and thorough attackers had suffered casualties they had been careful to take their dead and wounded away with them, as well as erase any evidence of their existence. Only human bloodstains and fragments of human bodies were found. The use of generic and not especially sophisticated weapons of destruction precluded the rapid identification of the killers. Nothing remained of their handiwork except the corpses of their victims.

To the psychologists, that suggested that the assailants feared retribution. As well they should. There wasn't a soldier among the relieving force who did not go to bed night after night dreaming of imaginary alien necks to wring.

Derwent was more of a realist. Knowing nothing of those who had destroyed the colony, it was premature to assign blame even to imaginary enemies. For all they knew the invading force might have been renegade humans from one of the other colony worlds.

"What motivation could another colony possibly have for carrying out a massacre like this?" Hudson had challenged him. Light glinted off her implanted lenses. She was a pert, spirited lady whom the adjective *vivacious* fit in more ways than one, and she was not slow to defend an opinion.

Phlegmatic and blunt, Derwent argued for the sake of dissention. They were not a particularly well-matched team, but their personal disagreements did not hamper their work.

"How should I know? Not having the mind-set of a mass murderer myself, I can't begin to imagine a reason." He stepped over the body of an eight-year-old boy whose head and legs had gone missing.

"Then shut up," she told him curtly. "If you can't give reasons, you don't have a hypothesis."

"Oh so?" Swinging his recorder around the front room of the inn, he made sure to keep the extensive damage to the back wall in frame. "All right, I'll guess. Maybe somebody was jealous about the amount of aid these people were receiving. Maybe they thought they could steal whatever was really valuable and save themselves some hard work. Maybe a grudge developed between this colony and another."

"None of those makes any sense." She was bent over the remains of a middle-aged couple who had died in each other's arms. "Even if one of them did, or if several of them did, all of them taken together with another half dozen added don't serve to rationalize the annihilation of six hundred thousand people. Humans don't do this sort of thing."

Derwent laughed curtly. "Read your prehistory."

"All right," she conceded, "they don't do it *anymore*. We haven't turned on ourselves to this extent since the conclusion of the Second Dark Ages."

"Then aliens are responsible."

"Nothing is certain yet," she reminded him. "No conclusions have been drawn. It's too soon, and the evidence is still being assembled. We won't be the ones to render the final judgment anyway. You know that. It will be decided back on Earth." She fell to murmuring into her recorder.

Derwent had already finished upstairs. Four guests had been staying at the inn at the time of the attack. Besides the proprietor's family there was also a second couple who had worked for the owners. The number of deceased jibed with the records a search team had accessed in the nearest town, except for a Sithwa Pirivi, age twenty, whose body had not yet been located. That meant nothing, he knew. The young woman might have been elsewhere at the time of the attack, visiting friends, shopping in town, or simply out hiking, and would have been killed there instead of in the vicinity of the inn where she worked. It was going to take time to fill in the blanks in the record of Treetrunk's exterminated population. People traveled, both for reasons of work and recreation, and did not always perish where they lived.

The chore of recording and evaluating the tens of thousands of decomposing dead was a distressing and difficult task. Not everyone adjusted as efficiently or pragmatically as the team of Derwent and Hudson. As time wore on many had to be relieved, some only long enough to recover their equilibrium, others permanently. Throughout the appalling work the teams and their support groups persevered. The number of identified dead rose from the tens of thousands into the hundreds of thousands.

And still there were no answers. Working alongside their conscripted civilian counterparts, practitioners of military forensics struggled with the available evidence in an increasingly frustrating and futile attempt to try and identify the perpetrators of the atrocity. The executioners had left nothing behind, not even footprints. If they had utilized weapons firing explosive projectiles they had gathered up every shell casing, intact or fragmentary, so its origin could not be identified.

One aspect of the attack the researchers felt confident in propounding: It had taken the colonists completely by surprise. How else to explain the utter absence in surviving records of any reference to the invasion? If someone had jotted a report or warning down on a piece of paper, or whispered frantically into a personal recorder, there was no record of it. It was as if the population had stood blithely by while whoever was responsible for their brutal demise had proceeded methodically with their gruesome work. The pathology teams were specifically instructed to look for any such surviving testimony.

"You'd think there'd be a note somewhere." Having finished his work at the inn, Derwent was wandering through the reception area while Hudson tidied up the last of her responsibilities. "A sketch drawn by some poor terrified kid, or a description buried in a coded file."

"There isn't an intact file left on the planet subsequent to the day of the final encounter." Hudson rose from where she had been crouching. "Not only were these people surprised by their attackers, they were surprised repeatedly. It's crazy. But I agree with you. No matter how much of a shock this attack was to the populace, someone ought to have left a recoverable message somewhere." She looked up at him out of her colorless implants. "It wouldn't take much. A couple of words. 'Humans did this' would be enough to get started on. Or 'Thranx here, killing everybody.' Or 'Unknown aliens have landed.' Anything, anything at all."

Derwent nodded as he lowered his instrument and started outside. "Anything's better than nothing. And right now, nothing is what we got. I don't suppose you've heard any different from any of the other teams?" As he strode toward the skimmer, their military escort reluctantly bestirred themselves.

She shook her head. "It doesn't seem to matter if you're working out in the country, like us, or downtown in one of the bigger communities. It's the same everywhere. All dead, and nothing to implicate the possible killers." She hazarded a thin smile. "Somebody'll find something somewhere. You don't slaughter six hundred thousand people without leaving a few clues behind. It's only a matter of time."

"Better be soon." Climbing into the skimmer, Derwent settled himself into his seat. Their next stop was a small vegetable farm located six kilometers northwest of the inn. He had no doubt what they would find there. "I hear that back on Earth and the colonies people are raging at their local government ministers. That's not surprising. They want a face to attach to this enemy."

"Revenge may be a primitive emotion, but it's one that's likely to always be with us." Given her smaller frame, it required more of an effort on Hudson's part to board the vehicle. As the soldiers began to pile in and take up their positions she strapped herself in next to Derwent, making sure first that her precious recorder was secured. "I'd like to personally eviscerate a few of whoever's responsible for this myself."

As the skimmer whined to life and began to lift he looked at her in surprise. "Seriously? You never struck me as the violent type."

She glanced over at him, her petite features not far from his own. The optiplants glittered like herkimer diamonds. "I never saw two hundred dead children all huddled together in one place before, either."

Derwent remembered the school, and his teeth clenched. Everyone had their limits. Despite his outwardly stoic demeanor he wanted to find something to hold responsible as badly as did everyone else. He wanted something to kill. Sure, he was first and foremost a professional, and he prided himself on his professional detachment.

But when it came down to it, no matter how hard he tried to affect an air of indifference and aloofness, he was only human.

9

The outrage and anger felt by the rest of humankind at the awful butchery that had taken place on Treetrunk were shared by every known sentient species. Ships of the thranx, the Pitar, the Quillp, and others were instructed as well as warned to be on the lookout for any unfamiliar or infrequently encountered species that might have the technological capability to perpetrate planetary genocide on the scale it had been committed on Argus V. This request from Earth was readily, even eagerly, complied with. In addition, the thranx and the Pitar of their own accord sent out ships whose mission was specifically to search for the home of an as yet unidentified and unknown race of maniacal aliens.

Nor did humans neglect to investigate possible motivations that might have arisen from within their own tortured racial history. Like any colony, Treetrunk had been settled by a heterogeneous broth of folk of every ethnic, religious, and social background. Nevertheless, the possibility that some powerful group, either from Earth itself or one of its distant colonies, held a grudge against a significant component of Treetrunk's population could not be and was not ex officio ruled out. In the absence of explanation, no prospect, no matter how outrageous, was automatically discounted. Every theory was investigated, every suggestion taken, every lead acted upon.

But despite the remorseless and dedicated perseverance of both humans and their alien allies alike, nearly a year passed without so much as a single hint or clue emerging as to the identity of the perpetrators of the carnage. Human exploration and development of Earth's recognized sphere of influence were slowed as xenophobia and fear on Earth and its existing colonies gained sway over those who favored continued expansion. Few people were anxious to settle on new worlds knowing that the butchers of Treetrunk's six hundred thousand were still out there—unpunished, unidentified, and unknown—ready to annihilate the next rush of humans rash enough to try and settle themselves on yet another empty, inviting world.

On Earth and elsewhere recriminations raged among a distraught and frustrated populace. How could such a catastrophe have been allowed to happen? Who had been negligent? In the absence of answers blame was readily placed elsewhere. Many who were innocent of oversight or neglect became inevitable scapegoats. There was finger-pointing in the media and in private, there were riots and accusations, while lawsuits and calumny raged aplenty. The only thing there was a dearth of was answers.

Inevitably, gradually, the rotating military and forensic teams that were assigned to investigate Treetrunk completed their work. As one contingent after another was withdrawn, that hospitable world with its ringing waterfalls, racing streams, and globe-girdling forests was abandoned to its indigenous life-forms. No possibility had been overlooked, not even the remote chance that some advanced native civilization had managed to keep in hiding while their planet was settled, only to emerge one day to murder every unwary, unprepared settler. The highest form of life on Argus V was an arboreal saurian with sloe eyes and an accusative yip. Although it displayed some rudimentary tool-using behavior, it could not cope with the larger, dull-witted carnivores that preyed upon it, much less wipe out so much as a handful of well-armed humans.

Reldmuurtinjak was a member of one of several thranx teams that had offered their services to help try to resolve the appalling riddle. Together with specialists from the Pitar and Quillp worlds, they, along with their human counterparts, poured over and through the scant available evidence, finding very little light in the unwholesome darkness that now shrouded the planet.

If anything, the exceedingly organized thranx were more frustrated than their human colleagues. Such things simply did not happen in a part of the galaxy where sentience and civilization held sway. Yes, death and dissention and violent disagreement were still present, but they could always be explained if not justified. In the absence of reason, there were still reasons.

Reldmuurtinjak was working in the ruins of one of Weald's few surviving administrative buildings when he looked up long enough to observe the tall human advancing toward him. He had never met a human being prior to being assigned to this grim duty. Scrutinizing the barren devastation for clues was difficult enough for him: He could only imagine what it must have been like for the first human crews forced to deal with thousands of corpses lying amidst the destruction.

Like the rest of his kind he had heard a lot about the humans. Visuals had helped to put to rest some of the more outrageous tales that had been told about them. They did not tower over thranx; they were simply tall. Most could not bend their bodies into rubbery knots; they were merely flexible. And despite their ridiculous tailless longitudinal axis, they did not fall over. At least, not very often. While excitable and edgy, they could also relax and be pleasant. Personally, he found this last open to dispute. During his sojourn on Treetrunk, the researcher had not seen very many of them relax.

The one who now approached looked uneasy but not nervous. His name was Lee, and Reldmuurtinjak had struck up a causal, casual relationship with him as their respective groups labored side by side in search of answers in the ruins of Argus V's capital city. Unusually intense even for a human, he spent more time in the company of the thranx than did any other of his colleagues. Reldmuurtinjak wondered at this. He was soon to find out the reason why.

Lee peered down at where the thranx was working in a slight depression in the floor. The space had somehow survived the collapse of the upper two floors. Lying within the shallow bowl was an intact desk together with contents. Typically, none of the desk's linking electronics had survived the devastation, but there were always hopes of finding notes, scribblings, jottings that might shed some light on what had happened. Using a translating scanner, Reldmuurtinjak was examining these now, neatly filing each sheet of treated synthesized cellulose into one of three piles.

"Any luck?" the pale-haired human inquired rhetorically.

Reldmuurtinjak replied as expected. "There is much surviving information. Unfortunately, none of it is relevant to our inquiry."

Nodding to indicate that he understood, the human turned sideways and slip-slid cautiously down into the dimple in the stelacrete floor. "Your people are very good at this kind of work. You never seem to get tired, or bored."

Reldmuurtinjak struggled to reply in his recently acquired Terranglo, even as the lanky human sought to address him in Low Thranx. Their conversation was a melange of both, an uncertain brew of slippery human vowels and fricative thranx clicks and whistles. The ungainly but evolving interspecies patois had unofficially been dubbed Symbospeech, and the name had stuck. As yet, the results were far from justifying even so semigrandiose an appellation. But with each encounter between the species, the shared vernacular grew.

"We are accustomed to slow, methodical work." Reldmuurtinjak did not look up from his labor. It was not necessary, since there were few human gestures critical to interpret. Aural conversation conveyed the majority of their communication. "We are glad to help."

"You know, some of my coworkers—not myself, understand—have wondered about that. Of all the other intelligent species, you and the Pitar were the first to volunteer your assistance." He looked distinctly uncomfortable, but Reldmuurtinjak had not dealt with enough humans for long enough to be able to interpret the extravagant range of human facial expressions. "There's been talk—I haven't participated in it myself—that maybe, and I hope you won't be offended by this, that maybe a rogue element of your people might have had something to do with this."

It took a moment for the import of the human's words to sink in and for the thranx to review it in his mind to make certain that he had not heard incorrectly.

" 'With this'?" Putting down the four tools he was handling simultaneously, he now turned face and antennae up to the human. "I believe I understand the implications of what you are saying. I just do not want to."

Lee raised both hands in a gesture unfamiliar to Reldmuurtinjak. "Hey, it's not me! I don't give any credence to it for a moment." To emphasize his stance on the matter he concluded with a fairly fluent double click from the back of his throat. "I just think you ought to know what's being said about you. Not about you personally, understand. About some hypothetical thranx who might have had a hypothetical part in the real tragedy."

Utilizing the by-now common human gesture, the researcher nodded deliberately. "There is tragedy in what you say, but it has nothing to do with what happened to this world." He turned slowly back to his work.

The human started to edge a little closer and then, uncertain, held his ground. "I don't believe a word of it, of course. I mean, it doesn't make any sense. What would the thranx, any thranx, have to gain by participating in such a bloodbath? Not new lands to settle. Your kind get chilled in Earth's tropical regions. You'd be uncomfortable here on a midsummer's afternoon, like today. Most of the year you'd just freeze."

"Quite true," Reldmuurtinjak agreed, trying to bundle his own cold-climate attire more tightly around his thorax. "We have no use for this world."

"And we've had contact with each other for more than half a century now, with no major conflicts or disputes. Just the usual ranting and raving from xenophobes on both sides." He went silent.

As the human appeared to be awaiting a response, Reldmuurtinjak supplied the one he thought the biped might be waiting to hear. "Those thranx who are suspicious of and wish no contact with your kind inveigh against it because they are frightened of your unpredictability."

Lee frowned uncertainly. "Not our proclivity to violence?"

"No. Recognizing that aggressiveness is not an uncommon characteristic among sentient species, we are not unsettled to find it among your
kind. Our ancestors fought one another as ruthlessly as did yours. And we
have been dealing with the feints and depredations of the far more belligerent AAnn for more than two hundred and fifty of your years. But the
actions of the AAnn are more or less predictable. Those of your kind are
not." Now he looked up from his work. "At least, the formula for mutual
understanding is still in the developmental stage."

Kneeling down alongside the insectoid, Lee was caught up in a per-
vasive scent of gardenia. "Look, I want to apologize for my friends. You
have to understand that every human, here and on all our worlds, is
intensely frustrated at our inability to identify the people or peoples who
were responsible for the horror that happened here."

Glistening compound eyes considered the flexible, enigmatic alien
face. Reldmuurtinjak could not decipher what might be hidden there, but
he did detect the concern in the mammal's voice. "We are frustrated too,
but it does not lead us to make groundless accusations."

An embarrassed Lee looked away. "It's a human thing. In the absence
of someone to blame, blame anyone. I'm afraid that's not going to change
until we find out what happened here."

"Then relations between us are likely to be poisoned for some time."
The thranx's voice was soft as always, the tone cool and uninflected.
"Because my people have found nothing any more conclusive here than
have yours."

This time they were silent in tandem for a while before Lee spoke
again. "It does strike some of us as peculiar that among the known sentient species capable of rendering assistance only the AAnn have declined
to send research teams here to help with the search for leads."

"*Kil!!ck,* that does not surprise us. The AAnn are a treacherous and
dangerous people. They will kill when it is to their advantage and retreat
in a confusion of apologies when strongly confronted. That is what
makes dealing with them so infuriating. One moment they will be happy
to trade keenly but fairly, the next they will ambush and destroy. If caught
out, they are masters of repentance. In the absence of surety one must
always be on guard against them."

Lee considered thoughtfully. "You're not the first to hint that the
AAnn might be responsible for this. Until the puzzle is solved, everyone
is suspect. Even apostate humans."

That startled the thranx researcher. "You would suspect your own
kind of such an atrocity?"

"Such things have happened in the past. In the First and Second Dark Ages."

"But why? What possible motivation could there be?"

As his legs began to cramp, Lee settled himself into a more comfortable seated position. "You spoke of the xenophobes among your own kind who don't want to have more than the most minimal contact with us. Ours are more zealous than yours. There are fanatics who'll do anything to keep our respective species from growing closer together." With a sweep of one arm he gestured at the devastation that surrounded them. "It's not out of the realm of possibility that they might resort to measures as extreme as this so they could blame the result on the thranx, or on non-humans in general."

"Then you have motivation." Although he spoke the words, the possibility that the scenario the human had just described might actually have taken place remained barely conceivable to Reldmuurtinjak.

"Motivation, yes, but seemingly insupportable means of acting on it." Lee shifted his backside against the hard floor. "Though powerful, with many undeclared supporters, it's hard to envision how the xenophobes could have mustered sufficient military-style strength to carry out such a devastating assault on another world—much less erase any and all evidence of their participation. What happened to the Amazon hive was one thing. Obliterating the population of an entire colony is something else again. If such was actually the case it would answer one question, though."

"Which one?" Reldmuurtinjak executed a gesture of ongoing confusion. "There are so many."

Lee was not sophisticated enough to catch the delicate hint of humor. "How the invaders were able to achieve such complete surprise. Battalions of arriving fellow humans, even heavily armed fellow humans, would not be questioned. Not until it was too late. They could have spread themselves throughout the colony before attacking simultaneously at multiple points in response to some prearranged signal. Evidence of their perfidy could have been gathered up and destroyed after the fact." His tone was flat. "As I said, in the absence of the guilty, everyone is suspect. Even ourselves."

"I am glad to know that we are not alone." The thranx had a well-developed sense of sarcasm. "Better your people should look to the AAnn, press them on their absence from the collective effort to unearth explanations, and watch the skies of your other colonies."

"Everyone from New Riviera to Cachalot is on alert," Lee assured the bug. "Every arriving ship has to undergo checks and quarantine that would have been unthinkable just a couple of years ago. It's a monumental inconvenience, but most people understand the need."

"Inconvenience is better than genocide." Examining a torn length of the familiar white human writing material, Reldmuurtinjak patiently set it in one of the three piles that were rising slowly beside him. "What have you heard from the central coordinating authority? Is there any news?"

Leaning back against a melted mass of plastic that had once been a storage locker, Lee sighed resignedly. They were all tired from their fruitless researches. Arriving in orbit around Treetrunk, everyone had been flush with energy and enthusiasm, each man and woman in his complement certain they would be the one to find the key that would unlock the mystery of the colony's destruction. As the days wore on and became weeks, then months, nascent eagerness gave way to uncertainty, then to resignation, and lastly to a kind of professional ennui. No one expected the next building, the next box, the next electronic file, to provide anything more informative than the routine details of everyday life leading up to the disaster. He wondered if the thranx ran a similar gauntlet of discouraging emotion. If so, they did not show it—at least, not in any fashion a watching, wondering human could decipher.

"No," he replied. "Not a thing. I heard that a Quillp team working east of Chagos Downs thought they'd stumbled onto the wreckage of a downed nonhuman shuttle, but it turned out to be a privately registered aircraft. Strictly suborbital. Hundred percent human design and manufacture." In response to the unasked corollary he added, "No evidence of arms or armament was found in its vicinity, so it must have been local."

Reldmuurtinjak was intrigued. "Among my kind individuals do not have access to their own shuttlecraft. There are private suborbital vehicles capable of very high-speed flight, but nothing that is competent for extraatmospheric travel. No individual entity smaller than a hive operates its own flights into orbit."

"In that we are different," Lee explained. "Among my kind large nongovernmental organizations engaged in trade and commerce often operate their own vessels, which are naturally equipped with proprietary shuttles. There are also certain very wealthy individuals who have access to privately owned and operated ships, even starships, together with their associated shuttlecraft. It's not common, but it's not unheard of, either. That's the most likely explanation for what the Quillp found. Remember what I told you earlier about the possibility of fanatic human xenophobes mounting their own attack on the settlements. The first step in plotting something like that would be to obtain adequate untraceable interstellar transportation. That means acquiring not only starships, but also unused or unregistered landing capability."

Reldmuurtinjak indicated that he understood. "Nothing else, then?"

Lee shook his head regretfully. "Only rumors that the money and resolve to keep our work here going is drying up. There are people on Earth and the colonies who want to concentrate the relevant research resources elsewhere."

"As in finding a species to blame for what took place."

Lee did not dispute the thranx's observation. How could he, when he had alluded to as much himself? "I'm afraid so."

"Would that not play into the hands of renegade humans, if it is indeed such who are responsible?" Truhands and foothands worked through the mass of debris in a digital ballet.

"Possibly. I hope those in charge keep that in mind when they make their final decision." Raising up, he looked around the ravaged interior of the building. "Personally, I'd hate to see the last humans abandon this beautiful world without taking some answers away with them."

"You said 'abandon.' If I grasp the meaning correctly, your authorities are not planning a recolonization?"

Lee eyed the insectoid in dismay before realizing that the thranx doubtless felt different about such matters, as they did about so many things. "It wouldn't matter if they were or not. No human would settle here now, no matter how potentially profitable or life affirming. Despite its physical beauty, Treetrunk is seen as a world of death. Humans are . . . not always scientific in their response to such occurrences. For any of my kind to even think of resettling the Argus system, an incontrovertible explanation of what happened here must first be presented. Even then, I'm not sure very many people would want to live in the psychic vicinity of six hundred thousand dead."

" 'Psychic vicinity'? What is that? Is it near Weald?"

Despite the serious turn of conversation, Lee had to smile. "It's a state of mind, not an administrative boundary. Just take my word for it. No one will move here until they know for certain what annihilated their predecessors, and maybe not even then."

"Six hundred thousand dead." Reldmuurtinjak repeated the figure in Low Thranx. To Lee the melancholy mantra was a succession of ephemeral whisperings framed by an eloquence of musical whistles and clicks. It sounded even more foreboding in Low Thranx than it did in Terranglo. "All the dead have been accounted for, then?"

"Less some twenty-two thousand presumed incinerated or otherwise utterly obliterated." Along with the rest of his associates the young researcher had been compelled to deal with such deranged statistics daily, but that did not make them any easier to take, or the images they conjured up unbidden any simpler to banish. Six . . . hundred . . . thousand. An inconceivable number, an unreal chronicle of annihilation.

As for the identities of the missing twenty-two thousand, they had been culled from the litany of the known deceased. There would be no burial for them, and their memorials would be anonymous. Lee had seen pictures, tridee recordings, drawings from life that had survived in schools and residences. The faces of the exterminated swam before him: wide-eyed, innocent, oblivious to the fate that was soon to befall them. The weight of the dead was crushing.

All of a sudden he wanted out. He'd had enough. Let someone else be the hero. To an unknown more perspicacious than himself he bequeathed the honor of unraveling the great enigma. Climbing to his feet, he regarded the industrious, methodical thranx without envy.

"That's it. I've done my share here. I'm going to put in for transfer. I can't take this anymore." Focusing on the alien helped him to avoid looking at the surrounding desolation, kept him from hearing the screams of the dying or envisioning their helpless, terrified faces.

Reldmuurtinjak looked up from his work, his valentine-shaped head facing that of the taller human squarely. In the subdued light that filtered into the depression between floors, his blue-green exoskeleton shone dully. "Psychic vicinity beginning to affect you?"

"Something like that." Glancing around to see if any of his colleagues were watching, he lowered his voice. "I hope it's one of your kind that finds the answer. I hope it's a thranx."

Reldmuurtinjak gestured to express curiosity, even though he knew the human would in all probability not be familiar enough with thranx body language to appreciate the sensitivity of the response.

"Why? What difference does it make to the ultimate resolution?"

"Because I don't want to think that your people are responsible. Not even a group of fanatics. Because I enjoy talking with you and others of your kind. Because unlike some of my uncertain, suspicious colleagues and friends and relatives back home I want to see that relationship deepen." Reaching out, he extended a hand, palm downward and fingers slightly apart, toward the insectoid's smooth, shiny skull. "Because I like you."

Twisting his inflexible upper body around as much as he was able, Reldmuurtinjak dipped his head forward until both antennae made contact with the human's hand. It was a gesture of greeting and farewell that was becoming more common among mammalian and insectoid acquaintances, one that took into account humankind's regrettable lack of a flexible cerebral sensing mechanism. Smiling, Lee turned and moved to rejoin his friends.

Reldmuurtinjak regarded him for a moment longer, then returned to his work. It was as monotonous, boring, and unrewarding as ever—but without pausing to consider the reasons, he found that he was feeling a little better about it.

10

As starships went, the battered, downsized craft that stumbled inelegantly out of space-plus in the vicinity of Argus VII was singularly unimpressive. The parabolic fan that promulgated its KK-type drive field was inefficiently aligned and indicative of low-grade manufacture. Further proof that the vessel was the product of a struggling as opposed to a surging technology could be found in the design and execution of the main body. Any ship of human, thranx, or AAnn fabrication was superior.

But it was no derelict. It moved, and it was guided by its builders, who took what pride they could in a vessel that represented the pinnacle of their own meager science. All ships might not be equal, nor their engineering, but the crew of the odd little craft took pride in their species and its limited yet very real accomplishments.

The Unop-Patha were not well known. They occupied a single system whose sun they called Unatha, after the Great Being they traditionally believed had given birth to the first of their kind. Ill equipped for long-range exploring, they kept close to home and sent out no more than a couple of ships at a time to maintain contact and relations with the far more vigorous sentients who occupied the same general area of the Arm. Humankind knew of them largely through the thranx, who had enjoyed contact with the species for well over a hundred years.

The Unop-Patha were neither bold nor threatening, finding the maintenance of even formal relations with other intelligent races a strain on their limited resources. An easy conquest for an aggressive, expansionist people like the AAnn, their world and its scanty assets were not even worthy of the force required to take it over. Their very worthlessness assured their continued independence.

Occasionally they sent one of their few space-plus-capable ships voyaging. Not in search of resources they were unable to exploit, or worlds they were incapable of settling, but because they were as curious as any developed people, albeit with a timorous curiosity. Treetrunk drew their attention not so much because of the tragedy that had befallen that human colony but because it lay within the limited range of the best of their vessels. They were aware of the catastrophe, of course. Every intelligence within that part of the Arm that had access to travel in space-plus or that had space-minus communications capabilities knew.

Their arrival was immediately noted and their presence challenged by one of the two warships from Earth that remained in orbit around the planet. It took a few moments for the analysts on board the cruiser *Shaka* to convince themselves of the identity of the visitors. Setting aside initial impressions, they did not take the abused, apparently innocuous appearance of the much smaller vessel at face value. Everything and anything in Treetrunk's vicinity had to be thoroughly checked out.

As soon as ship-to-ship communications were established and the taxonomy of the Unop-Patha crew confirmed, the visitors were allowed to proceed as they wished. Travel to or visitation of the surface of Treetrunk was circumscribed but not forbidden, provided that any landing parties first obtained appropriate clearance from the military authorities on board the *Shaka*.

The Unop-Patha accepted these restrictions obeisantly, having neither the desire nor the inclination to challenge the far more powerful human craft. Their own carried virtually no armament, its crew instead relying for defense on their transparent helplessness. Nevertheless, their presence and actions were closely monitored by sensitive instruments on both warships. Though nearly a year had passed since the destruction of Argus V, no one had forgotten that whatever had extirpated its population had accomplished the evil with the aid of complete surprise. Certainly the Unop-Patha and their pitiable vessel looked harmless, but they would nevertheless be watched carefully and scanned periodically until they left the system or reentered space-plus.

The Unop-Patha did not avail themselves of the opportunity to descend to the surface of Treetrunk. They could not afford nor could their single shuttle craft tolerate more than a few such trips, and they chose not to expend one visiting a world whose horrors were well known. Instead, they contented themselves with dropping into as low an orbit as they could manage and making observations from altitude, even though they would have found the climate congenial and the gravity light.

A week of such scrutiny proved sufficient to satisfy their modest scientific needs. Signaling their intention to move on, their polite appreciation was acknowledged by the officer on board the *Shaka* who had been given charge of such matters. A request to take measurements and read-ings throughout the remainder of the Argus system was promptly granted. The unassuming scientists on board the Unop-Patha craft were particu-larly interested in Argus VI, a gas giant of unusual composition. Though located in an orbit comparatively close to Treetrunk, its banded bulk did not appear to exert any gravitational effect on that far more salubrious world, hinting at the absence of a solid core. While much material on the gaseous sphere and the rest of the Argus system was obtainable from human sources, the Unop-Patha humbly preferred to carry out their own investigations.

Accelerating slowly away from Treetrunk, the Unop-Patha naviga-tors plotted a course that would insert them into orbit around the sixth planet of Argus within a couple of days. As they moved off, tugged along by the greatly subdued glow of their minimally powered drive, they were traveling slowly enough to take readings on the two moons of Treetrunk. Rocky, airless, small, and astronomically undistinguished, these had been of no especial interest to the colonizing humans. Their dimensions, com-position, and other relevant information had been automatically recorded, filed, and forgotten in the rush to settle the glamorous, accommodating world nearby.

The Unop-Patha were not sophisticated, but they were thorough. Patience was a virtue of science that did not demand advanced technol-ogy to practice. So they slowed still further, to ensure that their specialists would be able to complete their readings.

It was while passing the inner and smaller of the two chunks of rock that one of the three communications technicians, engaged in monitoring background noise, thought she might have detected an anomaly. Accorded only minimal attention by her colleagues at first, she persisted, finding the duration and bandwidth of the noise perplexing. Her perseverance finally engaged the interest of a superior, who while initially skeptical, soon found himself studying the relevant readouts through the twin lenses of puzzlement and surprise.

The electromagnetic nonconformity was brought to the attention of the family group that was in command. After due debate and discussion it was decided to pause in the vicinity of the moon just long enough to investigate the abnormality before moving on to the sixth planet as planned. A cursory inquiry would cost little and would not involve the use of much time or equipment. The very low gravity of the moon meant that the coddled and sometimes troublesome shuttle craft would not have to be used. A pair of much smaller repair vehicles could be employed to explore the cratered surface.

Each utilitarian vessel could accommodate a maximum of four, but two were adequate to fly and operate the compact craft. Taking silent leave of their respective air locks, they fired programmed bursts from their tiny engines as they descended toward the scabrous surface of the noticeably ellipsoidal moon. The feeble electronic anomaly that had sparked the unplanned visit grew no stronger as they tracked it, suggesting emission from a natural source.

The reality turned out to be anything but.

The pilot of the first ship altered his trajectory as soon as visual contact was made, directing his backup to do the same. Anxious communications flew back and forth between the two repair craft and the starship.

"A vessel of some kind it is, MotherTwo." The pilot and his companion did not have to use instruments to reach their conclusion. The silhouette that was floating above the crater was unmistakably synthetic.

"Can you it identify, TwelveSon?" came the apprehensive response.

Both Unop-Patha stared at the quiescent, shadowed object that lay in front of and below them. "Ours it is not, but that without saying goes." Alongside the pilot, his companion hazarded a guess.

"FortyDaughter here being. Human maybe it is, because it on a moon sits that a human world orbits it does."

"Real you speak, FortyDaughter," came the reply. "However any space-going species belonging to it could. Including maybe sentience unknown that the population of this world made dead."

However reasonable and indeed, unavoidable, the verbalization of such a possibility was, it was seriously disconcerting to the crew of both observing repair craft. Yet there was no sign of movement or life from the unidentifiable ship, nor any indication that anything aboard, organic or artificial, was aware of their presence.

"Very small it is," the pilot of the second repair vessel reported. "No larger than our own. Not capable of space-plus travel it is, would I estimate."

His colleague in the other ship continued the reportage. "No generating projector visible is, nor anything that an analogous structure might be called. Old it looks. If elsewhere encountered, not capable of flight of any kind would I think it. Almost at the end of a decelerating synchronous orbit it appears to be. If not for the slightness of this moon's weak gravity I imagine it long ago into the surface would have crashed." When no response was forthcoming, he inquired hesitantly, "Closer looking should we take?"

This time the ensuing silence from the starship was understandable: The commanding family was taking the request under advisement and discussing it with the heads of the other dominant families. The pilot was not sure whether to be happy or despondent when the response that was finally forthcoming was affirmative.

"Distance where and when possible keep," the pilots of the two investigating craft were admonished. "Remove yourselves if any hint of trouble or hostility there is. Scrutiny we perform will, recordings you take will, and when done all a report to the human authorities we make will."

TwelveSon waited for FortyDaughter to bring her little ship up alongside his. Together they advanced on the silent, inactive alien craft. No, silent not, he reminded himself. It continued to emit its feeble, intermittent electronic sputter.

What if a scout ship of the unknown ravening species that had annihilated Argus V it was? He could feel his copilot shivering and shuddering alongside him. Together they sloughed off an inordinate amount of nervous energy. He knew that FortyDaughter and her companion must be experiencing similar terrors. He wanted to turn around, to flee this dark, dead place and return to the familiar family warmth and comfort of the starship. Wanted to, but did not. The Unop-Patha were not particularly courageous, but they were persistent. Oftentimes all that kept them stumbling down the road of progress was the fear of being laughed at.

The two investigating repair craft were soon close enough to the alien vessel for their integral manipulative armature to reach out and touch it, should the pilots wish to do so.

"How the emission is?" FortyDaughter inquired.

"Unchanged still," came the reply from the starship. "No reaction from the subject craft?"

"Nothing," TwelveSon reported. "No movement, no lights internal or external visible are." Carefully he edged his ship along the length of the silent vessel. Within the repair craft all was hushed. "A lock I have maybe found. Sealed it is." Plaintively he inquired, "Can return to ship now maybe?"

"No. Families further information wish. Conclusiveness is sought."

"Conclusiveness points to nothing living here," TwelveSon's copilot murmured. "Automatic emission only there is. Not even signal we are sure it is. Energy release from broken equipment or failed instrumentation could well be. Let the humans further probe." Tilting his round, heavily furred head back, he surveyed their grim surroundings. "Unpleasant this place is. Dead ship in a dying orbit above a dead moon."

"Conclusiveness sought is." The directive from the starship was tranquil but unrelenting. "Search lock external release for. Try."

"Not even certain builder-owners of ship oxygen breathe." Grumbling, FortyDaughter maneuvered the manipulative arms of her craft into position above the possible lock door that TwelveSon had located. Unfortunately, there were indications of exactly the sort of controls they were looking for. Unfortunately, these responded to the pilot's gentle, precise handling. The lock or seal slid into its retaining wall, revealing a small alcove beyond. Both pilots maneuvered their ships close enough to shine lights within. They were unable to ascertain the identity of the instrumentation and internal engineering. Both dreaded the directives that reached them subsequently.

"Enter and explore. The source of the emission try to establish."

"I here will remain to keep watch," TwelveSon immediately offered.

"No," argued FortyDaughter. "You better at such exploration than we are. You enter, watch we will keep."

The dispute was settled from the ship. "TwelveSon and ThirtyOne-Son enter will. FortyDaughter watch will keep. Care to be taken."

"Care to be taken." Muttering, TwelveSon released himself from his restraints, disconnected himself from the repair craft, and prepared to follow his copilot into the repair craft's tiny lock.

It was a cramped space whose confines made donning a suit for outside work more difficult than it ought to have been. Normally, such suits would be put on in one of the much larger main locks on board the starship. When they had dropped away, no one had anticipated any reason why they might have to make use of pressure suits. It took some scrambling, but after dancing awkwardly around each other for a while, both pilots were suitably outfitted.

They exchanged a brief but intense clinch before turning and opening the door to the outside. Gravity barely strong enough to keep the alien vessel from drifting off into space allowed them to float gently down to its curved metal skin. Ahead, the open alien lock loomed. Above and behind them, they could see the concerned faces of FortyDaughter and her companion anxiously following their progress through the viewport of their hovering repair craft.

The sooner they completed their examination, the faster they could return to the warm embrace of the starship. TwelveSon led the way forward. Memories of the empty, shattered world below rose unbidden into his consciousness. Something had utterly annihilated the population of a seemingly benign world. Admittedly, the six hundred thousand who had perished had been aliens, but they had been intelligent and warm-blooded like the Unop-Patha. Whatever had ruthlessly slaughtered them might not be discriminatory in its taste for extermination. True, the ship they were about to board was unpretentious, far too small to harbor weapons of mass destruction or very many warlike individuals even if they were smaller in stature than the Unop-Patha. But it was more than a matter of numbers. TwelveSon did not want to encounter even one rampaging, murderous alien.

As they entered the lock both he and ThirtyOneSon agreed that the placement of controls and instruments suggested that the lock, and by inference the rest of the derelict vessel, had been designed with beings bigger than the Unop-Patha in mind. TwelveSon was not sure whether to be relieved or further intimidated by this conclusion. Trying to determine its composition, he studied a blank screen of alien manufacture while his companion scanned the inner door and its seals. The screen and its design were far more sophisticated than anything comparable aboard the starship.

ThirtyOneSon turned to him, staring out of his suit's head bubble. "There's no atmosphere on this craft. If there ever was one it has all away leaked."

"It could be there was aboard never anyone." Moving to the inner door, TwelveSon began running his four stubby fingers around the edge. It was darker here, away from the outer portal. "It might have been accidentally from the surface of the fifth planet launched, or from a human starship, or from a vessel of the attacking species. Or it might a true derelict be that has here for generations lain."

"Not many generations," ThirtyOneSon reminded him. "The colonizing humans had not this world for very long occupied before they wiped out were."

"I realize that, but there is still—"

He let out an involuntary yelp and leaped backward as the inner door began to open. The paltry gravity would have sent him crashing headfirst into the ceiling had not an alert ThirtyOneSon reacted in time to grab his companion's lower leg as he began to soar past. Even as ThirtyOneSon pulled his friend back down toward the floor, he was already stumbling toward the outer portal.

"What is it, what happening is?" FortyDaughter's alarmed voice crackled over their simple bubbleset speakers.

"The inner lock door cycling is," TwelveSon reported as he regained both his emotional and physical equilibrium. Together, he and ThirtyOneSon halted themselves in the frame of the outer doorway, watching and waiting.

The inner barrier continued to withdraw until the way was clear. Beyond, they could make out a corridor and more alien instrumentation. A few lights shone dimly. In the stillness of the airless moon, nothing moved.

"In the course of your inspection one of your hands must a still active control have brushed," ThirtyOneSon remarked to his companion. When the pilot, still breathing hard, did not reply, the slightly larger of the pair added, "We should a survey of the interior make."

TwelveSon looked over at him. "I would rather not."

ThirtyOneSon did not possess an especially imaginative personality, a quality that was a definite asset in their present circumstance. His tone was maternal-stern. "We should a survey make," he insisted firmly. "Having been the opportunity granted, we will chastised be if we without doing so return."

"No one will know if . . . oh, wait," an unhappy TwelveSon muttered. They had already reported to the other repair ship that the inner lock was open. Even if ThirtyOneSon had concurred, it was too late to back out now. With great reluctance, the pilot started back into the lock and toward the ominously gaping inner gateway.

The absence of breathable atmosphere was encouraging. Surely there was nothing left alive aboard the solitary little vessel. As they penetrated deeper within, keeping close to one another, growing confidence began to override his unease. As an exemplar of alien engineering the ship struck him as more primitive than what he had seen of the best of contemporary human and thranx and AAnn technology, but it was still more advanced than anything aboard his own vessel. A sudden thought struck him: If by chance the humans did not know this was here, perhaps he and his people could claim right of salvage. There might be much to learn from the empty, abandoned craft. It depended how advanced it actually was. Arrogated technology was of little use to those who appropriated it if its design and details were beyond comprehension.

ThirtyOneSon bumped into him, knocking him slightly forward and in the light gravity, nearly off his feet. TwelveSon whirled irritably on his companion. "Watch where you stepping are! And don't so close follow. There plenty of room in here for the two of üs is."

That was when he noticed that the hair on his friend's head, face, and neck was standing straight out. ThirtyOneSon was looking to their left, and pointing. "You mean, there plenty of room for the three of us is."

A shape was rising from the shadows. It continued to rise until it towered over the two terrified Unop-Patha. TwelveSon was too frightened to move forward, back, or scramble for a hiding place. More than four times their mass, the ghostly apparition had a similar bipolar body but with much longer limbs. What they could see of its face and head inside a helmet were almost as shaggy as those of an Unop-Patha, but the eyes were far too small and the mouth too large. As details continued to resolve themselves in the feeble light, he and his companion began to relax.

It was a human. Then this was a human vessel, or so they now supposed. But where had the human come from, and why was there only one of them? If this was a scientific vessel engaged in an exploratory jaunt from one of the two huge warships orbiting the planet, TwelveSon would have expected it to house several scientists. And if that was the case, why was this individual wearing an environment suit and not working in a pressurized compartment?

An accident! They had stumbled across a human survey or scientific craft engaged in exploration of this moon. It had run into difficulty and become stranded here. It might be from one of the warships or—he hardly dared countenance the possibility—it might have been caught and trapped here when Treetrunk had been set upon by its unknown homicidal invaders. Overlooked by the otherwise maniacally thorough attackers, its crew had survived.

Except there did not seem to be any crew. Looking past the single tottering figure TwelveSon was unable to discern any others, either erect or lying down. The little vessel was large enough to accommodate a number of individuals the size of the average human. Possibly they were active in another compartment. If this craft was not a component of the present orbiting human detachment and if it had been here since the attack on the fifth planet, then supplies of every kind would be running very low. Retiring to the confines of sealed suits would have allowed the marooned crew to conserve their remaining air by in effect pressurizing only their bodies in lieu of their surroundings. He marveled at the environmental technology that would let so small a craft keep its occupants alive for such an extended period.

Of course, how far and how long any onboard supplies lasted was in direct proportion to the number of crew. The fewer the occupants, the longer the reserves would last. Once again he peered past the awkward bulk of the human. There was still no sign of the rest of the crew.

"Why is it not to communicate trying?" ThirtyOneSon was eying the human intently. This was the first one either of them had ever encountered in person instead of via a communications transmission or study manual.

"Perhaps it see us does not." TwelveSon weighed how best to proceed. "Or perhaps it is not to open communications authorized and is for one of its superiors waiting."

"That may be," ThirtyOneSon conceded, "but I sure it sees us am. How could it not? We right here in front of it are."

"Protocol it from acknowledging us may prevent. The AAnn like that are, and the thranx somewhat less so. We far less about this species know than we do many others."

"So what do we do? Just here for the rest of them to show up wait?"

ThirtyOneSon looked around uneasily. "I this place do not like. I want to back on the ship be."

"No less than I." Protocol be damned, TwelveSon decided. He was not going to stand here waiting on the aliens forever. If his actions resulted in a reprimand, he would accept it with good grace. Anything to accelerate matters so he and his friend could return to their vessel. Thirty-OneSon would support his actions.

Moving forward, he reached out and touched the leg of the human. When it failed to react, he grabbed the flexible material of its suit and tugged on it. This finally produced a response. Turning toward the two Unop-Patha the human glanced down. His eyes widened, the framing flesh pulling back to expose more of the whitish orb, and his mouth opened and began to move.

Wrenching himself away from the Unop-Patha's grasp, the human stumbled backward until it was pressed up against the wall. It stood there staring at them, its mouth still working, arms splayed wide and flattened tightly against the composite material of the bulwark.

TwelveSon took a step forward, then hesitated. Hardly a specialist in interspecies contact, he was once again unsure how to proceed. "Is it to communicate trying or not? It looking right at us is."

"No." In his stolid, unimaginative way ThirtyOneSon was firm. "It not looking at us is. It looking behind us is." Turning as one, the two Unop-Patha examined the space behind them. They saw nothing exceptional, nothing to differentiate it from the rest of the vessel's interior.

"Whatever it is seeing not here is, but in its mind is." ThirtyOneSon's tone was somber. "I don't think I to see it want."

"But at it look! Surely it trying to communicate is." Baffled by the human's reactions, TwelveSon was at a loss as to what to do next. "See how open and active its mouth is? Humans communicate that way, as we do know; by means of modulated sound waves."

"Different frequencies," ThirtyOneSon commented thoughtfully. "We would not its words anyway understand, but specialists on the ship have to the principal human tongue access. Our people may not fluent be, but the necessary data in the library should be." He contemplated the task at hand. "We must back to the ship get this one."

TwelveSon reluctantly agreed. Since he and his companion could not talk to the human, they would have to somehow induce it to follow them into the presence of those who could. Stepping forward, he executed several simple gestures, hoping the human would get the idea. Then he and ThirtyOneSon turned to start back the way they had come.

"It not following is," ThirtyOneSon observed. "It still just standing there staring at the opposite wall is." He peered past the human and down the empty corridor. "Maybe for the rest of the crew it waiting is."

"I'm beginning to think there no rest of the crew is." TwelveSon's thoughts were tumbling. "If there were they ought to have by now arrived. This a very small ship is."

A contemplative ThirtyOneSon was quiet for a moment. "Then this being a sole survivor of the accident that trapped this vessel here is."

"I beginning to think so am." TwelveSon hesitated. "Unless the others, if there are others, are all dead, or otherwise immobilized."

"I don't know about you, but I not looking am." The larger Unop-Patha was adamant. "We our family mandate here and more have fulfilled, by this craft entering and one human finding. Let FortyDaughter or others from the ship explore further. We leavetaking are owed."

"I agree. But one last time let us try." He turned back toward the human, who had not shifted from its splayed stance against the wall. "If it will with us come and our communications people can with it make contact, others may not hunt for answers to difficult questions have to."

"Yes," his companion readily agreed, "and if it a lost craft from one of the orbiting warships is, we valuable merit for performing a rescue should acquire."

"Wonder make one it does, though." TwelveSon had approached to within arm's reach of the much more massive human. "If that the case is you would expect the humans both of these moons to be scouring, as well as the planetary surface in search of their lost comrade. And to have informed our ship upon arriving here that one of theirs had missing gone."

"Communication the key is," ThirtyOneSon observed. "Once that established is, then the human all such questions for us can answer."

Reaching out for the second time TwelveSon grabbed the human, this time reaching up over his head to tug on the creature's arm. Its helmeted head jerked around sharply, and the Unop-Patha could see the large facial orifice gaping and moving once again. But the human would not leave its place flattened against the wall.

Bemused, TwelveSon stepped back—only to see that his companion had retreated several steps and was staring mutely up at the alien. "Now what is it?"

It took ThirtyOneSon a moment to respond. "Your suit's transmission pickup. Off internal communication switch and change to—" He glanced down at the wrist console he had been fingering. "—eighty-six point three dash eleven."

"Why, what the point is?" TwelveSon looked from his friend back up at the immovable alien. "Don't tell me you understand it can?"

"Yes." ThirtyOneSon's words were barely audible. "Yes, I can understand it. Just listen, and you will, too."

Bewildered and a bit angry, TwelveSon proceeded to do as his companion suggested. As soon as he entered the recommended frequency into his suit instrumentation his ears were assailed by the voice of the alien, and he understood the truth of what ThirtyOneSon had told him. He found that he could indeed understand the human.

It screaming was.

11

"They're saying *what*?"

Having not been told to stand at ease, the orderly remained at attention in the anteroom, surrounded by the Victorian-era bric-a-brac that was the commander's favored décor. "They claim to have rescued a human from the inner moon, sir. They say—" The orderly glanced down at his reader to the printout of the report to make certain he was recounting everything accurately. "—that they found one live human in a single small vessel on the far side of the moon. Beyond being alive, they cannot testify as to his condition, though they believe it to be marginal."

"This is preposterous." As she spoke, Commander Lahtehoja was sealing up the sides of her lightweight duty boots. "Neither we nor the *Shaka* are missing any personnel, and I would be more than a little upset to learn that all shuttle craft and lifeboats were not accounted for. I know that the level of boredom is high among the crews, but if some people have gone for an unauthorized joyride I am not going to be pleased."

With each sentence the commander's voice had diminished. Eyes set front, body stiff and ramrod straight, the orderly knew what that meant. In contrast to others, when Lahtehoja grew quiet it meant she was really angry. When a soldier had to strain to hear the commander's words, it was time to look for a hole to hide in.

He pivoted sharply to follow her as she exited the commander's quarters and headed for the bridge, moving with the same long, purposeful, relentless strides that had made her a champion quintathlete in her days at the Academy. Crew they encountered stopped whatever they were doing to snap to attention and salute, gestures that she acknowledged perfunctorily. Anyone who had thought that inspection and survey duty at ill-fated

Treetrunk would be a walk through an aerogel had neglected to note the name of the commander currently in charge.

A lift carried them to the auxiliary bridge blister situated on the upper-middle portion of the big ship. Far forward, the immense projection fan of the KK drive dominated the field of vision. With the warship rotated to face the planet, the white-girdled globe of Treetrunk loomed in the view dome.

More salutes and salutations greeted her arrival. Lahtehoja did not move to take her seat but instead strode directly over to confront the officer on duty. Captain Miles vaan Leuderwolk was a paunchy, easygoing career officer who favored a shaved head and imposing beard. For all his rough appearance he was known to laugh frequently and easily. He looked like he should have been spending his days serving lager in a beer garden instead of directing a warship. Those who served under him were inordinately fond of their easygoing master. No such rumor had ever been attached to Lahtehoja.

"What do we have, Miles?" The commander's eyes were black, small, and intense as a laser. You had to look for them, but nobody wanted to find them.

The captain of the *Ronin* wore his bemusement as artlessly as his beard. "You read the report from central communications?"

"I've heard it." A flick of the head in the orderly's direction was sufficient to explain. "Who are these Unop-Patha? I'm not familiar with their kind."

"I'll tell you on the way to B hold." Vaan Leuderwolk smiled through his beard. "I don't know much about them, either. Just the basics. They have very little contact with us, and we with them. When they popped out of space-plus here a few weeks ago they requested and were subsequently granted permission to do some cultural and scientific survey work."

Lahtehoja led the way, forcing the captain and the orderly to have to hurry to keep up. "I don't remember being notified of this arrival."

Leuderwolk shrugged. "It happened when you were on sleep shift. "Buthefasi over on the *Alexander Nevsky* didn't deem it important enough to bother you."

Lahtehoja muttered something under her breath but did not comment further. She knew it was a failing of hers that she felt the need to know everything about everything that was going on under her command. A good commander had to know how to delegate, a skill that was not among her strengths. Nevertheless, although Buthefasi had acted properly, this was one particular she was sorry she had missed.

Her ignorance was soon to be rectified, however.

Having just listened to as concise a briefing as the relevant department had been able to prepare with virtually no notice at all, vaan Leuderwolk filled her in on what was known about the Unop-Patha as it had been related to him. Occasionally she would nod her understanding or interrupt to ask a precise, terse question. By the time they reached B hold she felt she knew as much about these Unop-Patha as did the captain of the *Ronin*.

They were waiting for her: half a dozen child-sized aliens with round, almost tubby bodies, big eyes, and no visible ears. What she could see of their bodies was covered with a thick, coarse, green-brown hair. They wore miniature space suits and had removed their headgear. Small black noses with four openings peeped out from near the top of the skull, just barely visible within the dense fur.

Lahtehoja and her small entourage halted before them. A specialist eighth-class wearing the insignia of communications walked over, saluted, and accepted the commander's admonition to stand easy with obvious relief.

Lahtehoja glanced automatically at the man's ident. "What do we have here, Mr. Waitangi?"

The specialist was prepared. "Their vessel hailed ours, Commander, and requested permission to come alongside. They claimed to have found and picked up a lone human from a marooned ship drifting in low synchronous orbit on the far side of the nearer moon." As he spoke the specialist frequently glanced down at the oversized reader he held, the rapid but controlled movement of his eyes automatically scrolling the information it displayed. "We had to run the transmission three times to make sure we had it straight." He smiled tolerantly at the waiting, curious aliens. "Their communications technology is pretty primitive."

"Apparently it was good enough to find this person when neither we nor any of our predecessors in this system could."

The specialist's smile vanished instantly. "Naturally, they want to transfer him, but they say that they can't."

Lahtehoja's neatly highlighted brows drew together, and her voice fell slightly. "Why not?"

The young man hurried his response. "They say that when they try, he—we've determined from their description that the individual in question is male—he resists. Sometimes violently."

The commander nodded knowingly. "And they're afraid he'll hurt one of them or do some damage to their ship. I can understand that, noting the disparity in our respective sizes."

"Excuse me, Commander, but that's not the reason." The specialist assumed an apologetic air. "They say that they have him safely isolated on their ship, but they're afraid he'll hurt himself."

"Hmm." Lahtehoja eyed the inquisitive, clearly awed visitors with new respect. "So we don't know much about these Unop-Patha, but we see that they understand compassion. I'll accept that as a basis for working with any alien species. Ask them if they will permit some of our medical personnel to go aboard their ship and remove this person they have so obligingly rescued."

With a nod, the specialist turned to face the visitors. As he spoke through the translator that hung from around his neck he crouched to bring his face more in line with those of the aliens he was addressing—and also to assume a less intimidating aspect.

It took a few moments, what with the specialist's need to adjust the translator each time human or alien spoke. Unlike High Thranx, for example, or Pitar, no one on board the warship spoke Unathian. There was no need for it.

Eventually the specialist rose. The look of satisfaction on his face preceded his announcement. "They say that they have no objection, but suggest that anyone we wish to send to visit their vessel be chosen as much for physical dimensions as for pertinent skills."

"Thoughtful of them." The commander turned her head in vaan Leuderwolk's direction. "Find me some short doctors and nurses and have them assembled here. Let's see what these people have found." In a less authoritative tone she added, "What the devil is one lone individual doing stuck out here, of all places, and where the hell did he come from?"

"I'm as curious to know as you are, Ludmilla." The captain watched as the petite aliens began redonning their rudimentary suit helmets. "Who wouldn't be?"

It took several hours for the hastily assembled medical team to be transported to the Unathian vessel and to return. They made the transfer in a couple of the *Ronin*'s accessory craft—not because Lahtehoja and vaan Leuderwolk did not trust the patently inoffensive Unop-Patha, but because the transportation the aliens courteously offered to provide would have been too cramped even for the purposely diminutive group of physicians and assistants.

Lahtehoja was back on the bridge attending to the normal workday duties of a task-group commander when she was notified that the medical team had returned. Leaving the *Ronin* under designated cluster command, she and vaan Leuderwolk took an express lift to the infirmary. Lieutenant Colonel Holomusa, chief of medical staff, was waiting for them in the reception area. Cursed with the face and frame of a caricatured undertaker, he resorted to scanning makeup to enliven his otherwise doleful appearance. For all that, he was an upbeat and merry fellow, exactly the sort a patient confined in an infirmary would want to see coming toward them.

He was not smiling now, however. Lahtehoja did not like to see confusion and uncertainty spread like a mask across the faces of those under her command. She especially did not like to see it dominating the usually cheerful countenance of a ranking physician.

"I can see the prognosis in your face." She sighed. "Educate me."

Holomusa glanced down at his reader. "Anglo-Oceanic male, height one hundred and seventy-two centimeters, weight fifty-one kilos." Noting her questioning look he added, "The reduced body weight doesn't appear to fit naturally on his frame. He has the underlying musculature of a much stockier man. One doesn't have to be a physician to be able to tell just by looking at him that his health has suffered—psychologically as well as physiologically. In other words, he's had to deal with shock to his nervous system as well as an insufficiency of food. Naturally, each magnifies the deleterious effects of the other." The chief medical officer swallowed. "After examining him, I'd say it's a wonder he's not in worse shape. Given his condition, it's something of a surprise that he's even alive."

Vaan Leuderwolk spoke up. "To what do you attribute his survival, Ben?"

The physician made a noncommittal gesture with his reader. "Better to ask him that. It certainly wasn't a sound and satisfying diet. He's suffering from an impressive catalogue of nutritional deficiencies." He nodded in the direction of the recovery chamber. "Not vitamins, though. Pills can help, but they're no substitute for solid food."

Lahtehoja turned toward the silent, shuttered chamber where their mysterious visitant lay. "You're feeding him now?"

"In a manner of speaking." Holomusa chuckled softly. "He's receiving a steady flow of osmotic fluids."

Vaan Leuderwolk nodded knowingly. "When will he be able to sit up and take solid food?"

"Yes, and how soon can we talk to him?" Lahtehoja had to restrain herself from carrying the conversation into the recovery room. Commander of the visiting force she might be, but within the confines of the infirmary it was Holomusa who was in charge.

"I don't know," the chief medical officer replied candidly.

The commander ground her teeth—a bad habit she had never quite been able to break. "That's not the kind of answer I expect from my staff. I don't deal in incertitude."

"You think I like to?" Among the complement of the *Ronin*, the chief physician was one of the few the commander could not intimidate. "Non-specific as it is, that's my prognosis. The man's comatose. I'm not going to try and force him out of it. Push his condition and we could lose him permanently."

As always, Lahtehoja was ready with a sharp retort. Instead of delivering it to the unblinking physician, she sighed again and raised her gaze ceilingward. "All right, Ben. It's your call. What happened when you went aboard the Unathian ship?"

"They took us to the room where they were holding him." Holomusa's tone was even, professional, but vaan Leuderwolk could tell that the physician had been shaken by the incident. "He was curled up in a corner, not quite fully fetal, but on the way. As soon as I saw the state he was in I ordered everyone else to remain in the corridor and out of his line of sight. I'm not a big man, but the Unop-Patha are a lot smaller, and I had to bend low to fit through the doorway."

"What did he do when you entered his 'space'?" Lahtehoja's voice was flat, unemotional, analyzing.

"Started whimpering," the physician told her without missing a beat. "I've seen disturbed men and women, people who have suffered a severe mental shock, try to dig their way into the floor or climb through the walls. This is the first time I've seen one try to crawl into himself." Behind the three officers, the commander's orderly stood mesmerized by the doctor's tale.

"As soon as I saw that there was a very real chance of him hurting himself, I stopped where I was. Trying to make eye contact, I just started talking to him. Anything I could think of, whatever came to mind, so he would hear a familiar, nonthreatening, hopefully soothing human voice. My object was to get him to relax, to slow his heart rate, which I supposed might be dangerously high, and to get him to trust me."

"And did you?" With one ear Lahtehoja was straining to hear sounds from the recovery chamber, but the only audible noise besides that of their own voices were the soft beeps and hums of efficient, indifferent instruments.

"Long enough to stick him with an osmotic hypo that pumped him full of tranquilizer. I was ready to jump him, to call for help, or to flee back out the doorway depending on his reaction. Funny—all he did was slip quietly into unconsciousness. Never uttered a sound. We squeezed him back through the door, off that claustrophobic Unathian ship and onto one of ours. He's been sleeping soundly until about an hour ago, when he woke up."

"Woke up?" Vaan Leuderwolk blinked. "I thought you said he was comatose."

"All right, maybe 'woke up' is an overstatement. He opened his eyes and he's breathing on his own. Other than that, there's nothing there. Severe trauma." He spread his hands helplessly. "Not much I can do here. Sure, we're trained and equipped to deal with a whole range of combat psychoses, but wherever this guy has retreated to, he's gone deep. I could try to pull him out—"

"Why don't you?" Lahtehoja prompted him.

"Like I said. Because if I make a mistake, I could drive him down deeper into the pit. Deep enough so that he might never come out. I'm not prepared to take that responsibility."

"Suppose I change my mind and order you to try?"

The chief medical officer stiffened slightly. "Then I would respectfully relinquish my post and report to the brig. I assure you that in that event every one of my subordinates will follow me, one by one."

"Take it easy, Ben," she soothed him. "I had to ask. I have no intention of trying to countermand or supersede a medical decision. Damn! That means we'll have to take him back to Earth for treatment without knowing his history. We'll end up seeing his story on the tridee like everyone else."

"If he ever recovers enough to tell his story," the cautious physician reminded her.

"What about physical details?" vaan Leuderwolk prompted the other man. "Identification, clothing, indication of possible origin?"

"His garments were filthy." Fastidious physician that he was, Holomusa's expression wrinkled at the distasteful memory. "My inclination was to have them burned." At the look of alarm that spread over the faces of the commander and the captain the physician hastened to reassure them. "Ai, don't have a stroke in my presence! Rest assured that everything has been properly preserved for future examination. I can tell you that his garments disclosed nothing spectacular or specific, which was in itself telling. They were clothes such as anyone might wear around the house—or on a ship. Casual and domestic. No uniform. Nothing in his pockets or sealed secretively in the fabric of his clothing.

"He carried no identification. Nothing. I have been informed that the suit he was wearing when the Unop-Patha found him is a very old model. It was in bad shape, barely pressure-safe. Certainly would never have passed inspection on this ship, or on any private vessel that valued its certificate. It showed evidence of having been repaired, restored, and refitted more times than is legal. I spoke of burning our mystery man's clothing. His space suit should have been burned before he stepped into it."

"Yet it kept him alive," vaan Leuderwolk pointed out. "On the inner moon."

"In what circumstances?" Lahtehoja's brain was running hot. "Did the colony have a scientific station there? Some kind of observation post, perhaps for weather watchers?"

"Sorry to disappoint you, Commander." Vaan Leuderwolk knew what his superior was thinking. His thoughts had rushed down the same path of possibilities—until some basic research had shot them down. "According to every available record on Treetrunk there was not recently and never was any kind of colonial outpost or base of any kind on either of the planet's two moons. They're too small and their orbits are too irregular to make them of much use in that regard, and like most relatively new, rapidly expanding colonies, this one had no resources to spare on scientific frivolities. Their standard-issue communications satellites did the same kind of work more easily and cheaper." He paused briefly.

"Of course, whatever annihilated the population took the time and care to destroy anything that might have been capable of recording what was taking place at the time. Including all communications and monitoring satellites."

Lahtehoja grunted. "So we don't even know where this poor bastard is from."

Holomusa shook his head sadly. "Not based on his appearance, his suit, or his clothes, no. We can't even say if he's from Treetrunk or some passing ship that subsequently vanished. And that's all we have to go on."

"Not quite," the always calculating commander countered. "There's the vessel the Unop-Patha found him in." Badly as she wanted to speak to the survivor, it could wait. Turning to the *Ronin*'s captain, she issued the order for a change of orbit.

Starting at opposite ends, two teams of investigators would examine the exterior of the unknown survivor's ship while a third plumbed its interior. Should they encounter anything of significance, it would be removed to the cruiser's labs for more detailed analysis. Following this preliminary survey and investigation the tiny ship itself would be brought aboard the warship, where further studies could continue in a controlled environment during the flight back to Earth.

Even if the Unop-Patha had not provided details of the vessel's location, it would have been easy to find. The inner moon was not large. But anyone not making a deliberate search of its far side, she reflected, would never have picked up the incredibly feeble remnant of a signal that the diminutive craft was emitting. Identifying it proved surprisingly easy.

It was a lifeboat. A lifeboat from a KK-drive ship. What it was doing crewed by a single psychotic on the inner moon of Argus V no one could say. It was only when the *Ronin* was several days out from Treetrunk and deep in space-plus that a team of inspecting engineers brought the news.

Certain details had led them to one unlikely but inescapable conclusion. The lifeboat had not been launched from a ship. Leastwise, not in recent memory. Instead, it had been used to travel from a planetary surface to the satellite where it had been found. A one-way trip with no possibility of return or of traveling anywhere else. A suicide run—or one of ultimate desperation. Tests of microscopic particles clinging to its interior confirmed the obvious: that Treetrunk had been the origin of the battered vessel's most recent and final flight.

What was an ancient, oft-repaired, and amateurishly refitted lifeboat doing on a colony world like Treetrunk in the first place? That was a question for which the most detailed examination of the boat failed to supply an answer. The craft's on-board instruments had recorded only flight data, and there was no magic bottle full of answers hidden away in a cabinet or storage locker waiting to be opened. Only its presumed pilot, navigator, crew, and sole survivor could provide an explanation.

And he wasn't talking.

The government intended to keep the matter as quiet as possible for as long as possible. Revelation that someone might have survived the Treetrunk massacre, much less have been a living witness to its destruction, would have sparked an outcry and concurrent media frenzy unprecedented in the history of interstellar colonization. Under the resultant pressure for information it might have proven well-nigh impossible for the physicians assigned to the case to perform their work properly. It was decided at the highest levels that the comatose survivor's privacy would be protected at all costs, along with that of the specialists who were charged with doing their utmost to try to revive him.

The hospital was located in a quiet suburb of Kavieng, on the Pacific island of New Ireland. It was as isolated from the mainstream of world culture and tridee attention as it was possible for such a facility to be while remaining close to relevant government centers of operation on Bali and in Brisbane. Originally a center for research into and treatment of tropical diseases, over the years it had been expanded and modified to serve the needs of a wide area, including and beyond the Bismarck Sea. Workers on the regional tuna and lobster farms were among its regular clients.

Not everyone knew what the unconscious man in room fifty-four had been admitted for, nor the cause of his condition. An unusually large number of visiting doctors came and went from his bedside, prescribing, consulting, and conversing among themselves. Some were rumored to be specialists from as far away as Europe and North America, and several members of the staff recognized one especially famous neurosurgeon who was noted for never leaving his distinguished practice in Gangzhou.

It did not matter how many physicians visited room fifty-four, however. The condition and status of the patient it housed did not change.

The hospital's regular staff attended to his conventional, daily needs. He was fed and hydrated intravenously. Fifth-floor nurses bathed and changed him, making sure the monopole braces that suspended him in a clinical magnetic field above his resting place did not fail and drop him to the bed or surge and fling him against the ceiling. Such lifters, which held a patient aloft in a strong magnetic field, were usually reserved for seriously injured patients such as critical burn victims, and its employment simply to ensure the comfort of one who could not express feelings of pain puzzled some of the staff. But orders were orders, and since the facility was notably free of critical cases at that time it did not become anything more serious than a topic of conversation.

That the patient was someone special was evident not only from the parade of specialists who visited his room but from the presence of the two plainclothes guards who were always present outside his door. These men and women were polite but uninformative, insisting to inquisitive staff that they had no more idea who the man in room fifty-four's bed was than they did. They had been assigned to watch and protect. There was no need for them to know anything more, and frankly, they preferred it that way.

So the equatorial days slid into equatorial nights, with the tropical sun dropping systematically behind the distant high island of New Hanover, without more than a few people at the very top level of hospital administration knowing that the silent, unimpressive figure who lay motionless in corner room fifty-four was the most important patient on the entire planet.

Certainly Irene Tse was unaware of his prominence. Unlike some of her colleagues, she worked the graveyard shift because it allowed her to spend many of her daylight hours diving. Wearing their compact rebreathers, she and her friends would spend endless hours in the waters framing the dozens of small islands that speckled the ocean surrounding New Ireland and New Hanover, observing what was still the world's most diverse and impressive aggregation of underwater life. Widowed at twenty-three when her husband had been crushed in a stampede of panicked three hundred kilo bluefin tuna, at thirty she had yet to remarry. A lively and spirited personality, she had been attracted to a number of men and several women, but attraction was not love, affection not passion.

As far as the motionless man in fifty-four was concerned, identified on his charts as a Mr. Jones, to her he was just another patient who needed to be cared for, an insensible lump of humanity who might or might not one day emerge to a greater or lesser degree from his present state of catalepsy. At two o'clock in the morning she greeted the guards, both of whom were engrossed in watching a live windsand race from central Asia. Even though they all knew each other by sight now, she was required to produce her ident as well as being physically recognized by both retinal and heartwave scanners.

Once passed into the room, she began by checking the monitors. It was not necessary for her to record their readings, as these were transmitted directly to the hospital's central monitoring facility. Activating the levitator, she changed the bed and sponge-bathed the patient while he hung suspended in the field, the atoms of his body temporarily magnetized. When she shut down the field he was lowered gently in fresh hospital gown onto the newly changed bed.

She was preparing to move the osmotic fluid injector to a new area of his torso when she felt something touch her arm.

She might have stopped breathing for a second or two. She wasn't sure. What she was certain of was that fingers had moved against her skin. Looking down, she saw that the patient's left hand had brushed her wrist. Fallen against it, no doubt. As she was preparing to make a note of the phenomenon, two of the fingers, the middle and the index, rose. Trembling, they lightly grazed her for a second time before falling back, as if exhausted by their own nominal weight.

Looking up, she saw that the two fingers were not all that had moved. The patient's head was inclined toward her—though that may simply have been where it fell, she reminded herself. The open eyes did not startle her—they opened every morning, to stare at nothing, and closed every night. It was the moisture at one corner that was unexpected. It could easily have been the result of a miss with the soft towel following the evening bath. There was a quick and easy way to tell.

Leaning forward and reaching over, she wiped at the bare trickle with a finger and brought it to her lips. Her tongue communicated the unmistakable taste of salt. The moisture was a tear.

Why she voiced her thoughts she never knew. It was not a conscious decision, simply part of an automatic response. "I'll call the duty doctor," she whispered tightly. As she started to turn to do so, all five of the fingers on the patient's left hand suddenly uncurled and reached up to grab her wrist in a grip of iron.

Lips fluttered, lips that had been kept moist through the judicious application of treated cloths and expensive salve. For the first time in the month and a day since the patient had been brought into the hospital and placed in his bed, a sound emerged from the hitherto unused throat. She had to lean close to sculpt a word from the whisper.

"Don't . . ."

Transfixed by the single word, by the man's blank stare, and by the utterly unexpected firmness of his grasp on her wrist, Tse stood there, not moving, waiting to see what would happen next. She could break the hold if she tried, she felt, but what effect might that have on the patient, who obviously wanted her to remain? He had spoken—she was certain of that. Could he also now hear?

"I'll stay," she told him, "but let go of my arm. You're hurting me."

The fingers relaxed, released her, slumped away from her wrist. In minutes, she knew, someone at Hospital Central would have noted the surge in physiological activity within the room. The duty doctor and staff might already be on their way.

Sure enough, they piled into the room a couple of minutes later, crowding around the bed as close as they dared without impeding the patient's access to air. Among the panting arrivals was an imposing woman in expensive designer garb and a tall, lanky older man wearing the uniform of a high-ranking military officer. They competed for space and attention with Dr. Chimbu, who bent low over the patient.

"Mr. Jones, can you hear me?" When no response was forthcoming from the motionless figure in the bed, the doctor looked expectantly up at the woman in the expensive suit. After exchanging a glance with the officer, he nodded solemnly and tried again—but differently.

"Mr. Mallory. Alwyn Mallory, can you hear me?" The doctor licked his lips. "If you can hear me, can you give us a sign of some kind?"

The single, barely perceptible nod the patient managed by way of response generated more activity in the room than a speech from the president of the world federation. Bodies flew through the outer door, startling the guards. More decorously dressed but heavily armed individuals appeared moments later. In the interim, a steadfast Dr. Chimbu tried to keep at a proper distance those who sought to crowd the bed. Only the woman in the suit would not be denied.

"Mr. Mallory," she whispered in a compassionate and gracious tone, "you are on Earth. You are safe. You were brought here from the inner moon of Argus Five. Treetrunk. You were found there on a badly jury-rigged lifeboat of outmoded design, in a spacesuit that was supplying you with a seriously reduced flow of air, presumably to conserve dwindling supplies." She swallowed delicately. "It is presumed by some that you came from Treetrunk itself. Others feel you reached the moon from a passing ship. We—everyone—would like very much to know which is the truth of the matter." When no response was forthcoming she glanced back at the stone-faced officer and tried again.

"Please, Mr. Mallory. If you can say anything, anything at all, do try to do so."

The prone shape on the bed lay still and silent. Its lips did not move; its arms remained listless at its sides. Then very suddenly, without any warning whatsoever, it began screaming.

"Out, everyone out!" Chimbu was already working on the patient, giving orders, directing nurses. The startled woman and her entourage were ejected from the room, despite the halfhearted protests of the man in uniform. Only Chimbu, two assistants who had arrived with him, and Tse, standing by the door, stayed.

When the patient had been sedated and was once more resting quietly, eyes closed, heart rate and other vitals stabilized, Chimbu drew the nurse aside.

"I saw what happened on the monitor replay. He grabbed your wrist. Is that correct?"

She nodded slowly. "First I felt something—him—touch me. Then he grabbed me."

"You touched his face in the vicinity of his left eye and then put your finger to your mouth." Chimbu's words were composed, professional. "What was that about?"

"I saw moisture there. I thought it might be left from the bath I had just administered. It was salty. He was tearing."

The doctor nodded. "He also moved his lips. The pickups that are in place are sensitive, but they're not perfect. *Did he say anything to you?*" The quiet intensity in the physician's voice unsettled her. Chimbu was no automaton, but around the hospital he was not noted for exhibiting a wide range of emotion.

She licked her lips before replying. "Yes. He said, 'Don't.' "

"That's all?" The doctor's expression wrinkled. " 'Don't'?"

She nodded, and he seemed disappointed. "Don't 'what'?"

"I had the impression he didn't want me to leave."

"Ah." Chimbu looked back at the stabilized, immobile patient for a long moment. "Then stay. If he even hinted that he might want you to stay, you should stay."

"Doctor? I have to complete my rounds." What was happening here? she found herself wondering.

"Not anymore," he informed her firmly. "As of right now you are relieved of all other duties. Replacements are already being scheduled. From this moment you are assigned to this patient exclusively. Furthermore, you are being placed on extended half-day shifts." Raising a hand, he forestalled her imminent objections. "You're also on double pay. No, triple." Murmuring more to himself than to her, he added, "Administration will approve it on my recommendation. They don't have any choice in the matter anyway." Raising his eyes back to hers, he remembered that he was speaking to another human being and not to a mechanical or a recorder.

"I would like to make arrangements to move another bed in here, so you can sleep in the room when you're not officially on duty."

She gaped at him. "Doctor? I take pride in my work, but I have a life outside it, you know."

"I know; I know." He made mollifying gestures. "You'll be fully compensated for your sacrifice. And if the patient begins speaking rationally to others, you will be permitted to leave. On extended vacation, at hospital expense."

Her eyes widened. " 'Permitted' to leave? What is this?" Looking past him, she focused on the man in the bed. The ordinary, now officially semi-comatose man whose brief stirring had aroused an unexpected tidal wave of activity. "Who is this 'Mr. Jones' that you called Alwyn Mallory?"

"You're a good nurse, Tse. You don't miss much." Chimbu pushed his physician's probe back from his forehead to the crest of his skull so that it pressed tightly against the receding hairline. "You know about Treetrunk?"

She searched his face. He looked suddenly tired, weighed down by unexpected and unsought responsibility. "I'm not dead, so of course I know. What's that to do with this Mallory person?"

"If you're going to attend him you have to know, so you might as well know now." The hospital's chief of staff was as serious as Tse had ever seen him. "He *may* be a survivor of the massacre."

Overwhelmed by the implication, for a long moment she had nothing to say. Finally she stammered, "There are no survivors of what happened on Treetrunk."

"You heard what the woman from the bureau said. He was found in a lifeboat on the planet's inner moon, traumatized and speechless. He might be a refugee from a passing ship, or someone a disgruntled crew kicked out. Or . . . he might be a survivor of the catastrophe. The only survivor." He peered deep into her startled eyes. "You understand now? *Do you?*"

"Yes, Doctor." As much as anyone could understand the impossible, she thought.

"He wants you to stay. Or he might have meant something else when he whispered 'Don't' to you. We don't know yet. We don't know anything. No one knows except him." Turning, he gazed speculatively at the figure in the bed. "His reactiveness tonight might have been a one-time fluke. Or it might be the harbinger of future stirrings. We can't take any chances with this man. He might be nothing important. Or he might be able to manage only another sentence or two. They might be sentences twenty billion humans are waiting to hear." He took a step back from her.

"Until we know what he meant when he said 'Don't' to you, you are to stay with him. Continue with your usual duties. Bathe him, check his hydration and nutrients and medicine drip. Stay close." His tone softened. "I know you're not a statue, not a machine. You can use the room's tridee. Whatever you want to make you as personally comfortable as possible will be sent in. The room monitors will remain on, recording twenty-four hours a day just as they have been for more than a month, so you don't have to worry about missing something of significance. If one of his eyelids twitches, it will be noted and recorded."

"What—" She tried to gather herself, to make sense of everything that had happened in the past few frenetic minutes. "—what else should I do?"

Reaching out to her, Chimbu gently squeezed her shoulder. "Be here. For him. If he wants to whisper, you listen. If he wants to converse, you talk."

She nodded. "Do you want me . . . Do you want me to ask him about Treetrunk?"

The doctor considered. "No. The important thing right now is to encourage any progress in his condition. I'm still the Chief of Staff here, and I'll shield you. From the government, from the military. So will my colleagues. If he speaks, let him talk about whatever he wants. If he improves enough, we'll consider putting questions to him later. In the meantime his health is the most important thing. Don't worry—if he lets something important or relevant slip, it will be recorded." He released her shoulder.

Around them, curative instrumentation and devices hummed and clicked softly. On the bed, a single figure lay unmoving. Tse and Chimbu contemplated it together.

"Is there anything else, Doctor?"

"Yes," Chimbu murmured. "If the opportunity arises, be kind to him. He needs it."

12

Having heard only one word in the course of one month, Tse did not expect tirades to spill from the mouth of the afflicted. But she was surprised when, upon awakening on the morning of the fourth day after being moved into the room, she sat up rubbing sleep from her eyes to find Alwyn Mallory staring at her.

Nothing else had changed; nothing in the room had been disturbed, though she knew that down in Central doctors and other important people must by now be glued to viewscreens in response to the patient's action. It must be demanding a tremendous effort on their part, she reflected as she turned and slid her legs off the inflatable bed, for them to stay out of the room.

Not only was he staring at her, he had raised his head slightly to get a better look. Now it fell back, the inches it had inclined forward proving too much for the man's weakened muscles to sustain.

"Don't stress yourself," she heard herself saying to him. "I'll come over there." Aware that monitors were everywhere, including the bathroom, she simply slipped out of the sleeping gauze and into her uniform.

By the time she sat down in the chair that had been placed by the right side of the bed, he had ignored her advice to remain still and had turned his head to face her. Then he smiled. So brightly unexpected was it, so warm and full of thanks, of the simple joy of being alive, that this time it was her own eye she found herself daubing at.

"Well, that's better." It was all she could think of to say.

"Who are you? Where am I?" His lips moved slowly, with careful deliberation, as if each syllable had to be constructed and approved by a separate portion of his brain before he attempted its actual verbalization.

"You're in Golman Memorial Hospital, South Pacific Region. I am your duty nurse, Irene Tse."

"I'd shake your hand, Irene, but you told me not to stress myself." A different sort of smile this time, more calculating, reflective of looming uncertainties. "I don't like taking orders, but you I think I'll listen to. Not because I have to, but because it pleases me." Defying her admonition, he raised his head again, holding it up longer this time. With each movement, each word, he seemed to grow stronger, not weaker. "You said 'South Pacific Region.' I'm on Earth?"

As she glanced over at his readouts in what she hoped was an inconspicuous manner, she did not comment on the obvious. He looked around, inspecting the room.

"How long have I been asleep?" His eyebrows tried to knot. "They must have knocked me out for the jump here."

"No one knocked you out. You traveled to Earth and arrived here in a cataleptic state." Reflexively, she put a hand on his lower arm. "As of this morning, you've been here in hospital thirty-four days."

"Thirty-four . . . ?" Leaning back against the pillow, he gazed pensively at the ceiling. "Not asleep. In coma." She nodded gravely. "I didn't wake up at all? I mean, if I did I don't remember it, but it's hard to think of being unconscious all that time. I don't feel like I've been out for more than a day or two."

"The mind plays wonderful tricks on the body." She smiled reassuringly. "Sometimes the body plays back."

She was acutely aware of the omnidirectional pickups that were judiciously placed around the room, of the fact that everything that was being said or done was being observed and recorded by a multitude of devices. It shamed her. Whatever he had gone through, this man deserved his privacy. It might never be given back to him, she knew. Issues of an order of magnitude greater than the personal desires of one man were at stake.

"Who found me?" Though he had asked a question, it seemed to her that his thoughts were concentrated elsewhere. He had posed it almost absently.

"I don't know." Before she could finish, her recorder vibrated gently against her. Removing it, she found information on the remotely activated page. "Some people called the Unop-Patha. A minor race about which not much is known except that they're shy and inoffensive. They just happened to be in the right place to pick up the signal from your ship." A line of questions appeared on the screen immediately after this information. Consenting only to the first, she firmly tucked the recorder back in its holder. "I understand that the vessel they found you in was of an old, discontinued type and wasn't in very good condition."

He laughed then, a good sign. It was followed by a spate of coughing that was not. Unable to raise his hand all the way to manage it, he let her slip the drinking tube between his lips. When she felt he'd had enough, she gently withdrew it from his mouth.

"That's enough for now. You've been on osmotics for a long time, and you don't want to shock your system with too much real drink and food too soon."

"Yes I do," he shot back. "I want to shock the hell out of it. I want tea, and coffee, and twenty-year-old bourbon. I want fish, and canned goods, and crispy vegetables, and cremated dead cow."

Her mouth was firm. "How about some applesauce?"

"How about you—?" He broke off his rejoinder and inhaled deeply, slowly. "I can't argue with you. I can't argue with anybody right now. 'Applesauce'!" Astonishingly, his expression grew mischievous. It was about the last thing she would have expected. "Will you feed it to me?"

Mindful of their significant unseen audience, she kept her response coolly professional. "That is part of my job."

"Good! Then I will have some applesauce."

When he said nothing more, she hazarded a cautious prompt. "Don't you want to talk some more?"

Now he was grinning broadly. "Applesauce. Your idea."

Afterward he slept, ignorant of the frenzy of activity his awakening had galvanized within government and military circles. Indifferent to a flood of entreaties, she refused to wake him early or otherwise intrude on the peacefulness that seemed to have come over the rechristened Alwyn Mallory. True to his word, Dr. Chimbu and the rest of the medical team supervising the precious patient's care backed her decision.

Two more days passed in recovery for Mallory. Two days during which the inner workings of government lurched forward in a state of semiparalysis. Two days in which extraordinary efforts somehow succeeded in keeping an always ravenous media ignorant of the lone man in room fifty-four of the Golman Memorial Hospital on the island of New Ireland. The intentional isolation helped. Even in the latter half of the twenty-fourth century, New Ireland was not an easy place to visit.

In those forty-eight hours Mallory went from barely being able to raise his head to being able to feed himself, from hesitating in the clouded search for words to talking voluminously. His apparent progress was underlain by the very real medical fear that he could lapse back into coma at any moment. Chimbu and others put their careers on the line by supporting nurse Tse's determination not to pressure the man in their care for details or ask if he knew anything about what had happened on Treetrunk.

Following lunch on the third day, her forbearance and the medical staff's conviction were rewarded.

"A couple of days ago, when I mentioned the kind of ship you'd been found in, you laughed at me." She came toward the bed, having just dumped his lunch dishes and utensils in the room's recycler.

This time he only chuckled. "I remember. You said that it was old and not in very good condition. That's hardly surprising." When he was alert, like now, she found that his eyes had a wonderful twinkle. "It was an old lifeboat, freighter class. I got it cheap, since the masters of the cargo ship that left it behind on Treetrunk knew it would cost too much to renovate it to the point where it could pass a safety-board inspection again. Fixing it up, puttering around with its innards, was my hobby. Kept me busy whenever I started to think too much. I never expected it to actually fly anywhere again, much less offworld." His gaze met hers. "Did you know that I was a member of the original survey team of the *Chagos?*"

The name meant nothing to her, and she told him so. Down in Central, where hospital communications had been linked in half a dozen ways with centers of power all across the planet, technicians scrambled while several of their superiors digested the patient's disclosure in stunned silence.

To Mallory, however, the innocently ignorant Tse clearly required elaboration. "The *Chagos* was the starship that discovered and carried out the first surveys of Treetrunk. Since there was no reason for the people who brought me from there to here to presume that kind of personal connection, I guess no one made it. Also, I used to space under the name Alwyn Lleywynth." He grinned. "Finally got tired of people not being able to spell or say it, and had it changed officially when I settled on Treetrunk."

"That's interesting," she told him, nodding. "I have a feeling that you're right and that no one made the connection." They would be making it now, she knew without a glance at any of the pickups. Making connections and trying to draw conclusions.

"I was good at what I did. I'm also an accomplished bitcher, which didn't endear me to many of my colleagues, I'm afraid. But in spite of my customary complaining, I liked Treetrunk. Liked it a lot. Enough to ask for my release and stay behind when the *Chagos* finally left. I helped build the place, worked on some of the first infrastructure for Weald and a lot of smaller towns. Always kept to myself as much as I could, though. I didn't much care to be around people. It was one of the reasons I originally went into deep space. It was one of the reasons I chose a new world to be my home and final resting place." His voice fell slightly. "That's all changed now. When I get out of here I think I might like to settle down in New York, or Lala, or Joburg. I want people around me now. Lots of people. Swarms of 'em."

Without warning, he began to tremble, the covering sheet shivering above his torso like rapidly advancing bleached fog. The contrast between his strengthening voice and frail body could not have been more dramatic. When she started to rise, he lifted an arm to detain her.

"I'm all right," he whispered shakily. "I'm all right." His expression pleaded. "Would you—I swear I'm not trying anything here—would you just, hold me? For a moment. Just . . . hold me."

Rising from her chair, she tentatively took a seat on the bed alongside him. Bending low, she put her arms around his shoulders. Immediately his head slid into the crook of her arm, like a bird finding its nest. Hesitant at first, she brought her legs up onto the bed and slid them carefully next to his. Then she lay down beside him.

More than an hour had passed when she awoke, quietly surprised to discover that she had fallen asleep next to him. Around her the machines ticked and whispered. The room was unchanged. No one had disturbed them.

Moving her head, she found that he was awake, staring at her, his eyes swallowing every inch of her as if she were a cool, invigorating potion, a silent libation for the soul. Uncertain and a little confused at what she was feeling, she sat up quickly on the side of the bed.

"Relax. Take it easy," he told her. Then he smiled afresh. "Hey, did you hear what I just said? Me, telling you to relax and take it easy. Want me to check your vitals?"

She had to smile back. This man, who had obviously been through an experience too horrible to imagine, was irrepressible. She found herself liking him instead of pitying him. He sensed the shift in her attitude and was pleased.

"So you became a citizen of Treetrunk." She rested a hand on his upper arm, not entirely for therapeutic purposes this time.

"Yes," he told her. The smile faded away, and he began to shake again. In response to her look of alarm he willed his body to relax, forced the muscles to still. "It's okay. I'm not going to scream again."

She blinked. "You remember screaming?"

"I remember." He nodded. "I just couldn't stop it. I didn't want to stop it. It was so easy, to scream. It blotted everything out. A little." He began to fidget beneath the sheet. "I'm sick of lying down. Help me sit up."

Immediately she reached for the bed's remote. "I can raise you to any angle you—"

"No, goddammit!" He was emphatic. "I want to sit up! Me, not the damn bed."

She assisted him, wondering as she did so what Dr. Chimbu would have to say about stressing the patient. But no one interrupted them, either in person or via communicator, and with her aid in a couple of minutes he was sitting up straight, his back propped against the pillows.

"How do you feel?" Her concern was a mixture of professionalism and—something else. "Any nausea? That would be normal."

"Not for me it wouldn't. A little dizzy, maybe. That's all." Looking past her, his gaze focused for the first time on the view through the room's large window. From his location in a top-floor corner of the hospital he could see palm trees and ships in the harbor and the blue, blue water of a tropical sea. A flock of flying foxes was flapping from east to west over the harbor, a dark motile cloud scattered among towering white cumulus.

Turning to her, he asked in a calm, quiet voice and without warning, "Would you like to know what happened to my adopted home? To Argus Five, also known as Treetrunk?"

Down in Central, and in linked monitoring stations all across the globe, instant pandemonium ensued.

13

It was a good life. Mallory was happy with his decision to resign his position on the *Chagos* in order to become one of the first settlers of the new world. That choice would not make him rich, but perhaps his progeny, if he ever had any, would one day find it useful to be able to boast that their great-grandfather, or whatever, had been among the original surveyors and colonizers of Argus V.

Despite his irascible, often contentious personality, he had no difficulty finding work. As a jack-of-all-trades on KK-drive craft like the *Chagos* and a retired ship's engineer—and at a precocious age, at that—he was a master of many skills that were highly valued in the new colony. Disdaining seductive offers from the rapidly burgeoning municipality of Weald and the innumerable companies and concerns that specialized in abetting the development of new colonies, he set himself up as an independent consultant. Wealth did not flow in his direction, but he made a more than adequate living. In his ample free time he visited many of the beautiful and as yet unexplored regions of the temperate equatorial belt or enjoyed the home and shop whose construction he had supervised. Its isolation on an uninhabited mountainside deep within a choice patch of virgin alien woods gave him the freedom to tinker with the surplus freighter-class lifeboat he had purchased on a whim for an astonishingly modest sum.

When he needed credit he would choose from among the many standing assignments on offer. Given the headlong forward expansion of the colony, these were always in plentiful supply. There were few newly arriving settlers with his knowledge and experience. His expertise was eagerly sought.

In this manner five years passed during which Mallory, while not entirely happy—such a state of existence not being in his nature—was forced to concede that he was less discontented than usual. When compelled to visit the city for those necessary items he could not manufacture or grow himself, he tolerated the occasional company of others. As a known recluse who was irritable by nature, he was not sought out except when his professional abilities were in demand. This suited both him and everyone else on the planet just fine.

He did not hear the general announcement that interrupted all tridee programming. That particular morning was unusually bright and clear, even for pristine, unpolluted Treetrunk. As the sun rose and warmed his mountainside he ate a leisurely breakfast on the hand-hewn porch and then prepared to spend a stimulating and enjoyable day working in the simple shed that housed his shop and hobbies.

The walk from his home to the outbuilding was a short one. Though he had built a covered walkway to shield him from the rain and snow of Argus V's wet season, he had no need of it that day. The sun was out, and there was hardly a cloud in the sky. The shed itself was a single large enclosed structure stained brown and green to match the surrounding trees. Such a large, unmasked building would have attracted the attention of the passing curious. Having no wish to be disturbed and being fanatical in his desire for privacy, Mallory had caused both his home and workplace to be camouflaged from the rapidly expanding population. Newcomers in particular he sought to avoid. They were invariably effusive and friendly, two qualities he did not seek in neighbors.

Four months before, he had taken the old lifeboat out for a short flight from the capital district over to Demure and back. While successful and as smooth as could be expected, the journey had predictably loosened some internal components. Entering the open boat, he found his tools where he had last left them and settled down happily to effect the necessary repairs.

Several times during the morning he thought he heard the echo of distant, dull booming. Despite the absence of clouds when he had made the walk from home to shop, he put the noise down to an approaching thunderstorm. Rough weather could blow up on Treetrunk at any time, and with summer approaching abrupt atmospheric disturbances could be expected. Or it might have been a construction team excavating new foundations for large buildings on the outskirts of Weald itself. Or perhaps it was simply boisterous adolescents working mischief closer to his home. He gave the random, sporadic echoes barely a second thought.

It was nearly two when, sweaty but satisfied, he set the industrial-strength tools aside and resolved to get something to eat. As he often did, he'd labored through the lunch hour. One of the pleasures of working for oneself, he reflected as he wiped at his face and rose to leave the lifeboat, was the freedom to eat when one was hungry instead of when it was expected.

Exiting the shed, he started back toward the house—and stopped. Shading his eyes with one hand, he stared in the direction of the capital. Rising into the crystalline air, smoke from numerous sources drifted together to form an enormous dirty brown cloud that had begun to block out the sun. *What the hell . . . ?* he thought.

Moving a little faster, he hurried back to the house. Some kind of widespread industrial disaster had struck Weald. At the moment he could not imagine its nature. Modern fire prevention techniques prevented destructive blazes from spreading freely from house to house, building to building. Yet the distant glow of flames and widely separated pillars of smoke suggested not only spreading, but that the conflagration had broken out simultaneously in different parts of the city.

Hurrying straight to his den, he activated the tridee and waited for the first three-dimensional image to congeal above the floor. Colors and shapes appeared, but did not coalesce. No matter how much he fiddled with the controls he could not induce the flickering polygons and sparking clouds to come together into anything recognizable. Similar static dominated every infochute. Then he lost the static, too. The air in the room was silent.

Something was very wrong.

Not panicked yet, but anxious and concerned, he rushed back outside. If anything, the smoke cloud had grown larger in his absence. He couldn't be certain, but it seemed as if new smoke pillars were appearing even as he watched. The recurrent booms he had heard before were sounding more frequently now.

He had never seen a city under attack, but he had seen tridee recordings, both fictional and historical. Who would assault a defenseless colony and why, he struggled to imagine. His first thought was of the AAnn. The thranx insisted the aggressive reptilian species would jump on any advantage it could find. But Treetrunk was much too cold to suit them, far from the nearest of their own worlds, and did not even lie along a potentially Empire-threatening vector. Nor was it a storehouse of valuable resources that could not be found elsewhere.

The same reasons only more so applied to the thranx. Like the great majority of humankind his feelings toward the insectoids was ambivalent. They wanted to be friends, but most people were not anxious to jump at the opportunity. Distance remained largely because of the species' appearance. Having spent thousands of years battling the thranx's much smaller very distant terrestrial relatives, it would take time before people were ready to invite them into their homes.

Who else, then? he wondered as he stood stunned and watching the distant destruction blossom. Surely not the Quillp, as inoffensive a species as humans had yet encountered. Still, the Quillp were colonizers and settlers, too, and their sphere of influence lay much closer to that of the rapidly expanding humans than did the empire of the AAnn, though not the thranx.

Might it be a new, previously unencountered race? Standing there on the mountainside watching the city he had helped to found burn, that seemed to him at that moment the most likely explanation. Whoever it was, they were technologically sophisticated.

Retreating back into the house, he returned to the porch carrying a handheld scoper. Methodically, he played it over the perimeter of the great cloud, then scanned the interior. There was no sign of aircraft. The descending explosives were extra-atmospheric. They were being launched from orbit and then guided to their targets with precision. A more distant pillar of rising smoke marked the location of the city's shuttleport. Two others indicated the sites of outlying towns.

While thorough, the intent of the attack was apparently not to annihilate completely. Had that been the case, he would not have heard multiple booms while he had been working on his salvaged lifeboat: only one overwhelming one as a single nuke obliterated the entire city. Instead, it was still there, albeit burning furiously. He did not doubt that the attackers, whoever they were, possessed such weapons of mass destruction or the ability to manufacture them. Any sentience sufficiently advanced to negotiate space-plus had to first achieve nuclear technology. You couldn't learn to manipulate the components of other space until you had mastered the minutiae of this one.

What were they after? What did they want? If total obliteration was not their aim, it suggested they wanted something intact. He couldn't imagine anything that an invading force could not have acquired simply through threat. The only explanation, he decided, was that the attackers wanted to protect their identity. Based on the collapse of planetary communications and on what he could see from the front of his home, it was a hypothesis that gained credence with every passing moment. He had no doubt that the space-minus communications facility near the shuttleport was one of the first sites to be targeted. Almost certainly the other one at Chagos Downs had suffered a similar fate.

If so, it suggested that the aliens knew what targets to hit first and where to find them. That put the lie to the notion that the attackers were a new, previously unknown and unencountered species. There were always KK-drive ships in orbit around Treetrunk, and they would have noted and communicated the presence of any alien vessels embarked on a survey of strategically important locations. Therefore the attackers must have arrived with a carefully laid-out, premeditated plan of assault based on prior research already in hand.

Even so, the unannounced arrival of one or more large alien craft would have been noted by the government and as a matter of course passed along to the citizenry through the usual media channels. He had seen no such bulletin on the tridee, not the previous night or this morning during breakfast, when everything had been operating fine.

He was missing something, he realized. Something important. Whatever it was, the authorities had missed it as well. Not that there was much they could do to stave off a determined attack by a properly equipped military force. As a new, developing colony Treetrunk had only domestic policing weaponry of its own. Humankind was not at war with any of the known intelligent species. Disagreements that revolved around matters of commerce and settlement were settled by discussion, sometimes loud but never physical. Interstellar war on a large scale was too complex and expensive a proposition to be viable. Even the AAnn realized that and limited their occasional depredations, usually in thranx territory, to isolated, confinable piratical acts. No one thought of assaulting an entire world.

Until now, he told himself grimly.

Having returned to the notably aggressive AAnn, his thoughts once again considered what reason the bipedal reptilians might have for launching so violent an assault on an innocuous colony world. Try as he might, he could not conceive of one. Of course, he was speculating from the standpoint of human motivation. The AAnn might have reasons for attacking Treetrunk that were quite incomprehensible to him or to any other human.

He needed information. In the absence of the usual tridee chutes, he would have to try something else.

Rushing back into the shop, he activated the antique communications console on board the lifeboat. Designed to scan and decipher every possible corner of the spectrum that might contain downloadable information, under his direction it began by checking the bands that carried information from ship to ship and ship to ground. There was plenty of chatter, but it was all in colors and hisses unknown to the unit. It was the attackers, he decided. Talking among themselves. It was maddening to know that he was seeing and hearing the answers to his most pressing questions but could not decrypt them.

Changing focus, he sampled more familiar bandwidth. As expected, all the usual tridee chutes were either dead or suffocating in visual static. Weald was silent. So were Chagos Downs and Waldburg and every other town that boasted its own chute or uplink. Nothing came from above, the dozen or so communications satellites proving as quiet as their land-based transmitters and translators. Destroyed during the initial attack, most probably. It was what he would have done. Blind and isolate your prey first, then butcher at leisure.

He had almost given up hope and had decided to fly his truck as close to the city's outskirts as he dared in hopes of learning what was happening when something flickered in the lifeboat's viewing alcove. It was smaller than similar images would have been in his house because the display space was smaller.

What he was picking up, distorted and intermittent, came from a mobile remote, an automated unit that was the property of one of Treetrunk's two independent media concerns. He identified it by the small rotating logo that hovered above the floor of the lifeboat. There was sound but no commentary. Whoever had been traveling with the unit was quite likely dead, murdered by the invaders. Since communications both local and extraplanetary had been among the invaders' first targets it was not unreasonable to assume that everyone back at the media concern's main offices were dead by now as well.

Unconcerned and oblivious to the fate of its human operators, the independently powered robot soldiered on, obediently transmitting tridee images to a base unit that probably no longer existed. No home or commercial receiver could pick up its pictures. For one thing, such interception of a commercial signal would have been illegal. It would take a skilled technician working with specialized equipment to make the grab. Someone like Mallory, for example, working with something like a lifeboat's all-encompassing emergency instrumentation.

Sitting alone in the boat's cockpit, he watched in stunned silence as the mobile unit's pickup roved the city. There was fire everywhere, and smoke that obscured many of the images. Trained to seek out the visible, the unit kept moving. In the absence of directives from an accompanying commentator or its home base, it relied on the fallback instructions programmed into its memory.

Not every building was on fire. Some had been spared or missed. Others had been melted, and gaping, smoking craters marked the prior location of those that had been completely obliterated. A man appeared from off-image left, running at an angle across the pickup's field of view. Dirty and bleeding, his clothes torn, he carried a baby in his arms while a teenage boy ran along parallel to him. The man kept looking around as if in search of help or a refuge. He might have been an office worker or a technician or a civil servant.

The boy looked back, and as he did so, his head vanished in a rainbow puff of blood, brains, bone, and flame. Ducking to his left, the man tried to bend as low as possible while shielding the child in his arms. One of his legs exploded, and he went down. Unlike the teen, who had perished in silence, a horrified Mallory heard him scream. The mobile remote picked up the shrill sound with detached efficiency.

Dumped from cradling arms, the infant went rolling across the street. It too was screaming. One leg gone, the man began to pull himself across the street toward the child. As Mallory bit down on the back of one index finger hard enough to draw blood, shapes appeared out of the smoke, advancing from the left. There were two of them, tall and straight, clad in protective helmets and bulky body armor. One of them walked up to the crawling man, put the tip of a long, unrecognizable instrument against the side of his head, and activated the device. The man's head blew apart, blood and fragments of bone splattering against the armored legs. The killer's companion walked over to the squalling infant and without hesitation repeated the action. Mallory ordered his body to breathe.

The mobile unit moved sideways, traveling along the street, emotionlessly following its programming. When it found a scene that would trip something within its set of internal commands, it would stop and focus, then move on again. Twice Mallory lost the image; both times frantic manipulation of the lifeboat's outdated but still functional instrumentation brought it back. As he worked at the controls something large and powerful screamed past overhead, loud enough to be heard within the lifeboat that was inside the shed. Transfixed by the images he was seeing on the tridee, he ignored the sonorous echo of the object's passing.

Drifting aimlessly in a fallback news search pattern, the mobile reached Weald's central plaza. Carefully and lovingly laid out to resemble a series of concentric gardens, the square had been planted with blossoming plants and exotic growths gathered from all over Treetrunk. Many of these careful transplants were dead or dying now, incinerated or blasted from their planters. The square's central fountain, a gift from the populace of the enormously successful colony of New Riviera, was a shapeless lump of ceramic and composite slag. Water from broken source pipes ran in a steady, aimless stream into surrounding drains.

Several air repulsion-type vehicles were clustered together near the center of the square, hard by the demolished fountain. All boasted protrusions that, while not immediately identifiable, were easily recognized as weapons. More of the armored body shapes were moving about nearby. In addition, there were a large number of figures engaged in other activities.

The mobile moved in closer. For some reason it was not immediately noticed by the invaders. Or perhaps, having already destroyed all known communications facilities, they felt no urgency to eliminate a single mobile device of obviously mechanical origins. The tridee image in the lifeboat flickered and danced. Cursing, hammering on the console, Mallory fought to stabilize it.

A small vehicle arrived and halted. Several of the more lightly clad figures moved to its side and helped those aboard to unload. Mallory leaned forward slightly, expecting to see valuable electronic components or containers full of informational recordings. The objects the aliens disbursed were somewhat larger, though equally recognizable.

Bodies.

Whether they were dead or simply paralyzed Mallory could not tell. In any event, none of the dozen or so exhibited any visible signs of damage. They were all, insofar as he could tell from the unsteady, intermittent image, female. Ranging in approximate age from fourteen to forty, they were carefully laid out on a prepared portable platform.

Other figures came forward. They carried small devices that Mallory at first thought were sidearms. They were not. Three of the figures immediately set to work on the nearest of the neatly laid out torsos. Silently, stolidly, having no one to lament with, Mallory watched as the aliens carefully and efficiently sliced into the abdomen and removed, insofar as he was able to tell, the complete set of female reproductive organs: uterus, fallopian tubes, ovaries, everything. Wet and glistening, these were smoothly transferred to a waiting container from which smoke/mist drifted, indicating that its interior was either very hot or very cold.

Their excision completed, they moved on to the next body in line, that of a girl who looked to be close to but not quite twenty. Whether the woman they left behind was still alive or not Mallory could not tell. It did not matter to the aliens, who made no attempt to close the gaping wound they left behind, and he found that he did not want to know.

He wanted to look away, to stare at something else, to put what he was seeing out of his mind, but he could not. The mobile unit, following its programming, continued to focus on the grisly biopsies, following the horribly inevitable course of one after another. So stunned was Mallory's system by what he was witnessing that the shock was sufficient to suppress even his nausea reflex. At least, it was until he saw one of the eviscerated women twitch and try to sit up. Not through any dint of empathy but operating strictly from efficiency, one of the patrolling armored figures noticed the movement and shot her before she could rise far enough to comprehend the gaping crater in her belly. She had been granted the mercy of indifference.

Devoid of involvement beyond its unemotional programming, the mobile was relentless. It watched, it transmitted, it commented not. Pausing before the seventh helpless, prone figure, one of the alien exenteraters paused to adjust his protective gear. In the course of so doing it momentarily removed its helmet. Reacting to this action, a companion did likewise. Mallory stared. Humans. Other humans. Then he took note of the subtle differences, of the prismatically colored hair, the too-perfect posture, the sculpted countenances. Not human.

Pitar.

Why? he felt himself screaming silently. Why, why, why? What reason could there be for the Pitar to attack an inoffensive and harmless colony like Treetrunk without warning, without reason? It made no sense. Exultant madness ruled the day, and dementia had taken control of the plenum. And what were the invaders doing, what could they possibly want, with the preserved reproductive organs of human females?

To these hopeless questions he could configure no rational answers. It made no sense, none whatsoever. Surely the Pitar knew the consequences of their actions! Not only humankind but sentience throughout the Arm would react with outrage, with anger, and then with retribution. Whatever they hoped to gain through the successful fulfillment of this atrocity would be infinitely transcended by the devastation a united and fully mobilized humankind would wreak on the perpetrators of the outrage.

Which would only happen, he realized with abrupt, exquisite clarity, if the identity of the perpetrators became known.

He was already moving when one of the body-armored Pitar finally took notice of the hovering mobile, turned directly toward it, raised a weapon, and fired. By the time the tridee image vanished, Mallory was out of the shed and racing back toward the house.

There was no need for structures and facilities on Treetrunk to be camouflaged. Who would want to attack a colony with a restricted habitation zone, limited industry, and still underexploited resources? Only someone who wished to be avoided by his fellow settlers would seek to distance himself from them and to make an effort to conceal his abode. There were no true hermits on Argus V, but there were a number who cherished their privacy. Among these, only one had the skill and the wherewithal to render himself and his habitation semivisible.

That wouldn't save him, Mallory knew. It might keep him from discovery by the invading forces for a while, but eventually they would seek him out. They had to. The horrors they were committing demanded no one be left alive to speak of what had been done. The Pitar would scour the habitation zone for colonists and the cold wastes of the north and south for exploration parties. If they carried life detectors they would be able to track down and analyze even minor ambulatory patterns. On such instruments a human being left a signature as clear and sharp as a tridee paragon. Only a deep cave or oceanic environment could mask the individual autograph, and he didn't doubt that the Pitar would search beneath the ground and sea as well.

He couldn't remember from the last time he had viewed the news if any KK-drive ships were currently in orbit. If they were, none were likely to be warships. Undoubtedly their unlucky crews had been among the first to fall victim to the Pitarian treachery. Vessels stopping at Argus could not continue to disappear without notice, but given recent shipping patterns he estimated it might be several months before another called at Treetrunk. Several months would give the Pitar more than enough time to search the length and breadth of the planet for possible survivors and then depart without notice.

They would know where to look: what zones were being surveyed for minerals or development; what areas were under consideration for future expansion; where important communications, power-generating, and transportation facilities were situated. And why not? After the first several calls, their regular visits to Treetrunk had ceased to be restricted. Why circumscribe the movements of amiable, considerate, congenial friends? All the time they had been helping the colony to expand, they had been recording and consolidating data for the day of the attack.

They might not immediately notice his home and shop, isolated and concealed as they were on the side of the mountain. But after securing the few cities they would methodically move on to the larger towns, then the smaller villages, and finally to outlying farms, infrastructure postings, and individual structures. Even the forest would be no refuge. It would be expected that some people would flee into the Argusian wilderness in search of safety. Ruthless and relentless, the well-prepared Pitar would have anticipated that and would have come prepared for it. Mallory's expression tightened. After the cities and towns, there would be hunts. Human hunts.

Any ships, satellites, or free-orbiting maintenance craft would already have been captured or destroyed. A competent attacking force would first secure the space around a world before turning its attention to the helpless surface. Shuttleports and airfields would be next in line for destruction or occupation, together with any craft capable of flight that happened to be on the ground. Once confident of having eliminated a target's ability to fight or flee in atmosphere or free space, invaders could settle down to methodically exterminating the local population.

A few companies and citizens operated aircraft of their own, he knew. But such craft, while they might preserve their owners for a while longer, could not escape the attentions of much faster, higher-flying, orbit-capable shuttle craft. Anything with the ability to reach orbit required the long runways and support facilities of a port, or in an emergency a spacious open field or dry lake. Nothing robust enough to escape the pull of the planet's gravity could take off straight up. That would require a craft with a short, explosive propulsion system: one designed to generate a single sustained but brief burst of speed before its motive source gave out.

In short, a lifeboat. Alwyn Mallory had a lifeboat. It was intact, more or less. It was internally equipped and provisioned, more or less.

The question was, could it exceed orbital velocity, more or less?

Having no options, he did not hesitate. If he remained where he was he would undoubtedly survive longer than the great majority of his unfortunate fellow colonists. It might be a matter of days, it might be a matter of weeks, but eventually the Pitar would come for him, as they would for everyone else. He did not intend to wait helplessly for that moment, like a rat chittering impotently at the back of its burrow.

Without hesitation, he tore through his once orderly home, ripping into cabinets and storage lockers. Anything that might prove remotely useful he threw into the transport cart from his shop. Food, medical supplies, reading material, raw electronic components, clothing, small tools—all found their way into the bowels of the old lifeboat. There was plenty of room. Designed to carry and care for a dozen people, it would soon be serving as refuge for only one. He would be short of everything but space.

It took him less than a day to scavenge his home of several years, the home where he had expected to live out a long and reasonably contented life. With luck he might see it again someday, but he did not stand around dwelling on distant possibilities. The lifeboat would be his home now. Or it would if he could escape the attention of the Pitar. When the last bar of sustenance had been thrown aboard, the last potentially useful tool stowed away, he rigged a line to fill the boat's tanks with water. There was none aboard, just as the craft was devoid of food. It had been so when he had purchased it, everything useful and portable having long since been salvaged by the previous owners.

One tank leaked copiously before he noticed it. Despite the urgency and desperation of the moment he had to laugh at the idea of fleeing into the cold, heartless vacuum of space with water sloshing around his feet. It was a short, terse laugh. He had neither the time nor the inclination to indulge in any extended bouts of hilarity. Outside, down the mountain and beyond the woods, the beautiful, the glamorous, the estimable Pitar were slaughtering and eviscerating. The noble Pitar. The neighborly Pitar.

He had to get away. Somehow he had to avoid the blanket of detection they must even now be expanding across the planet. It was possible that the spider's web was not yet complete. All that was necessary was for one fly to get through. Throughout the night he slaved intently on readying his wings.

Two hours before sunrise he was ready. As to whether the lifeboat was, the answer would come from the trying. The proof would be in the doing. If his preparations proved inadequate, if trouble arose that was beyond his power to amend, well then, he would die no slower than if he fell into the hands of the invaders.

Settling himself into the cockpit he ran a final check. Those instruments that still functioned, many of which he had personally repaired or replaced, insisted that their respective components were functional. He found himself wishing he had spent more time with each and every one, that he had taken a little extra effort with each installation and connection. But it had all been a lark, a time killer, something to amuse himself with in his idle hours. Now his life would depend on the skill with which he had indulged in a hobby.

Was there anything he had forgotten, anything that had been omitted? Once committed to the launch sequence he would not be able to change his mind, to remember something overlooked. He did not trust the old lifeboat, or for that matter his own skill at restoration, to recover from an abort sequence. Deciding to go, he would go, and devil take the consequences.

Then he did remember something. Spending as much time as he did in the shop, and away from home attending to various work assignments, he tended to miss a good deal of live entertainment and news. When not watching the tridee, it was set to record. It would have recorded informational bulletins. It would have recorded presentations and sports from the capital and elsewhere throughout the colony. Unfortunately, the last transmissions it would have recorded were unwatchable garbage.

But the images he had recently viewed on the lifeboat, the singular movements and images that had been transmitted by the orphaned media mobile, would have been recorded by its own built-in unit, and should be available for playback.

He did not have time to check. Opening the console, he dug inside until he found what he was looking for. Removing the tiny mollysphere, he slipped incontrovertible proof of Pitarian perfidy into a pocket, shut himself into the lifeboat, force-sealed the reluctant lock, and settled into the pilot's seat and harness. He was no qualified pilot, not of a craft the size of the lifeboat or of anything else. But the whole concept behind such a vessel, the notion that underlay its very design, was that it had to be able to be operated in a moment of emergency by utterly unqualified passengers. As an ex–ship's engineer he was far better prepared than the average citizen to operate a lifeboat's instrumentation, even a design as antiquated as the one that now enfolded him.

The star Argus would soon be making its presence known above the eastern horizon. While the Pitar were certainly equipped with all manner of sophisticated tracking devices, he saw no reason to make their search any easier by providing the additional possibility of visual identification. He could do nothing about the lifeboat's initial liftoff signature. It would be noisy and bright, but only until he reached escape velocity. At that point he would have to risk shutting it down.

A preflight check of the weather indicated the presence of a small storm to the northwest. What he wanted was a hurricane, or some severe thunderstorms. Anything to help mask evidence of his liftoff. The modest rain event would have to do. Programming the shed's roof and the boat's navigation to the best of his ability, he tightened the harness as much as his body would tolerate, then waited.

Even if he was detected lifting off, nothing but a shuttle that happened to be in the immediate vicinity stood a chance of intercepting the vertically ascending lifeboat. Not that it mattered. Once out in space, drifting free, he could be tracked down and eliminated by an orbiting shuttle. Or, if he was extremely lucky, a warship might actually have to bestir itself for a moment or two to chase him down. If nothing else, he might at least inconvenience a few of the invaders.

Or having analyzed his craft and realizing it had no space-plus capability, they might simply decide to ignore him, letting him float aimlessly in the vastness of space until his supplies and atmosphere ran out. He suspected that was a forlorn hope. Having already witnessed evidence of their thoroughness, he did not expect that the Pitar would leave anyone alive, not even a lone soul adrift between worlds without any hope of returning to one. He might be found, and that they could not permit.

He had to try, though. Anything was better than sitting and waiting for death to come knocking. Better to kick back and keep on kicking for as long as was possible.

A pleasant feminine voice announced that departure was imminent. He had taken special care with reprogramming the boat's methodical, businesslike tone. Now he was glad that he had. It might be the last voice besides his own he ever heard. A loud whine permeated the air, and the cockpit began to vibrate around him. There was no port, but the forward viewscreen showed the roof of the shed parting like a pair of flat, featureless hands. Beyond, black sky and scattered stars became visible in the lucent night of Treetrunk. The whine became an irritation, the vibration in his seat and harness almost soothing. A final massage, he mused. The solicitous attentions of a mechanical undertaker.

Something shoved him hard in the chest, and he gasped sharply. The receded roof panels disappeared, and the stars rotated wildly. In minutes he had punctured roiling cloud—the storm that was drenching the forest to the northwest. Minutes later he burst free, like a fist punching through stuffing, to find that the stars had multiplied beyond counting. The pressure on his chest lessened; the hand that had shoved him gradually withdrew. Small unstowed objects began floating about the cockpit. His stomach churned, and his inner ear insisted he was falling. And so he was—falling up.

Free of Treetrunk's gravity, he was still alive, the embracing lifeboat still intact around him. Loosening his restraints, he hastened to check the readouts. Designed to locate and skew a vector for any nearby ship, the lifeboat was already searching for presumptive help. Prior to liftoff he had thoroughly disabled the automatic beacon designed to signal the lifeboat's presence to other vessels. There was no help to be found here, and he did not want any nearby craft to pick him up. He would blow the lock first and die cleanly in the emptiness of the void.

The relevant readouts made no sense. Testing for malfunctions, he found none. There were no ships within detection range, which meant that it was possible there was nothing to detect him as he raced, silent and small, away from the surface of Argus V. That was impossible. Where were the Pitarian starships, their transports and shuttles? They could only be one place, he realized.

On the other side of the planet. For the moment, Treetrunk was screening him from detection.

It was not how he would have conducted an invasion. But the more he thought about it, and he had time for nothing else, the more he realized that his extraordinary luck was the product not of alien stupidity but of a quite understandable succession of factors. Having destroyed or captured everything in orbit around Treetrunk before commencing the actual physical invasion, the Pitar had no doubt already secured or rendered useless all three of the colony's shuttleports and any orbit-capable craft located on the ground. That and the two space-minus interstellar communications facilities would have been their first ground-based targets.

With the ports and their complement of vessels accounted for in the first stages of the attack, there was no reason to suppose anything like a rogue lifeboat might be present elsewhere on the planet, much less anything in operable condition. In the first flush of what surely must look to be a complete and unqualified triumph, they might relax their surveillance just a little—just enough for a single minuscule, almost undetectable craft to make its escape ridiculously perpendicular from the planet's surface on the opposite side of the world from the attacking armada. No shuttle craft would lift off at the angle he had taken.

He wanted badly to record the size and strength of that invading force, but even if he had possessed the maneuvering capability necessary to sufficiently alter the lifeboat's course he would not have done it. If he tried to move into a position to observe them, then surely the far more sophisticated instrumentation on board a modern warship would detect his presence first.

So he continued to speed outward from the devastated surface, leaving warmth and atmosphere and ongoing horror behind, heading for the only destination the lifeboat had a chance of reaching before its limited supplies began to run out. He had programmed the boat to aim for the inner moon. Not because it was closer, but because it was far smaller than its more distant relative. It was a less likely place to hide, a much more modest potential refuge. As such, if the Pitar thought to consider such possibilities, there was the chance they might conduct a cursory survey of the more accommodating satellite while passing over its relatively insignificant cousin.

The inner moon of Argus V generated barely enough gravity to hold itself together, let alone affix anything to its surface. Maneuvering the lifeboat as delicately as his limited skills and the remaining propulsive capability allowed, he dropped the craft into lower and lower orbit until eventually it was hovering only a short distance above the floor of a suitable impact crater. With the boat's motive power all but exhausted, he ran multiple checks of the restored vessel's status.

He had power. He had air. There were no detectable leaks. Hull integrity was intact. Having positioned himself to the best of his ability, he settled down to wait and to deal with dangers as serious as those posed by the Pitar: loneliness and silence.

The first days and weeks were a cycle of rising, eating, and watching the readouts for signs of passing or patrolling ships. With each succeeding day that the instruments remained quiet and the screens blank his confidence grew. By the end of the first month he felt certain he had escaped the notice of the invading Pitar entirely. As the end of the second month approached he began to fear that he had.

It was terrible in the lifeboat. The psychic weight of airless void on one side and lifeless rock on the other began to press inexorably on his spirit. He felt his very self squeezed between resignation and isolation. Yes, he had foiled the Pitar. Yes, he was still alive when every other human being on Treetrunk was probably dead. But to what end? To thumb his nose at invaders who were not now and never had been aware of his existence? So he could die out here, alone, not even surrounded by the corpses of his fellow settlers? As the days continued to pass, the minutes slowing to a visible crawl, he began to wonder if he had made the right decision. Resistance, survival at any cost—what was it worth? Did it have meaning, or had it been nothing more than the instinctive reflex of a clever ape?

Growing desperate, he even risked some of his precious air by going outside in a suit. The barren, lifeless surface of the dwarf moon drove him back inside where at least there was warmth and recorded sound and visuals. After a while he stopped watching them, too, unable to bear the sight of happy, living humans. The boat was stable in its absurdly low orbit, but his mind began to drift. Gravity is only a local constant and does not hold thoughts.

By the third month his hastily assembled supplies began to run out. He found that he did not care. To conserve air he began to live in a suit, choosing to shrink the available atmosphere around him. He did it because it was expected of him, to preserve life, and not because he had any especial desire any longer to do so. A sufficiency of water to sustain existence for a little while longer remained, but he was out of food. That was a good thing, he decided. He would weaken and eventually pass out and not know when the last air available to his suit was exhausted. His body would remain untouched by Pitar or decomposition, preserved in the perfect coldness of space that had already established its imperturbable grasp on the rest of the ship.

He had been drifting, drifting, for a long time, sucking less and less often at the plastic teat of the water tube in his helmet, when something hazarded to ruffle his sleep. Irritated at the interruption, he rose from his seat and moved to locate the source of the disturbance. Before he could find it, it found him, and he started to scream. After that, he remembered little except the screaming.

As it turned out, except for a few inexplicable outbursts, no one could hear the screaming but him. It went on and on, forever . . .

14

" . . . Forever."

Tse said nothing. Sliding her hand down his arm, she took his right hand in both of hers. Lifting it, she brought it up to her lips and kissed it gently, then pressed it against her cheek, not giving a damn what any vexed bureaucrats or disapproving hospital personnel watching on distant monitors might think. As he continued to stare out the window at the blue water and gently swaying palms, tears were running down Mallory's cheeks, copious and unstoppable. His respiration was normal, his heart rate steady, but he could not stop crying. Eventually, he simply ran out of water.

"A part of me is here, alive. Another part is back on Treetrunk, with my friends and associates, dead. A third and last part is floating, floating on an inner moon, raving mad."

"I'm here," she told him softly. "I'm alive."

"Yes." Smiling again, he wiped at his eyes with the sleeve of his hospital gown. "Thank God for small favors. Not you, Irene. There's nothing 'small' about you. May I call you Irene?"

"Mr. Mallory, you may call me anything you want." Lowering his hand, she squeezed it very tightly before lowering it back to the bed. "You've earned that right."

"I don't want it as a 'right.' I want it from a friend."

"However you wish," she told him softly.

The moment was broken, though not shattered, as Dr. Chimbu, several military and civilian personnel Tse did not recognize, and two medical technicians entered the room. Though they filled it, there was no frenzy, no pushing or shoving. Everyone, including the solemn-visaged officers, was quiet and respectful.

"Mr. Mallory," Chimbu began gently, "we don't want to crowd you. If there are too many people in here now, just say so and we'll have some leave."

The man in the bed grinned. He had not let go of the nurse's hand, and she did not draw it away. "Too many people? There aren't enough. There can never be enough for me, not ever again."

Standing behind the chief medical officer, a handsome woman in a colonel's uniform was no longer able to restrain herself. It was an attitude plainly shared by everyone around her.

"Mr. Mallory, as I'm sure you can understand there are some of us who very badly would like to ask you some questions. If you don't feel up to it . . ."

"Ask away." He smiled up at Tse. "And how about some real food? Applesauce is fine—preferably on a large eland sirloin, with fried potatoes. And gravy. And shellfish—any kind of shellfish."

Tse glanced expectantly at Chimbu, who looked reluctant but eventually nodded. "A *small* sirloin," he could not forbear from adding.

The elegant soldier was hesitating, spurring Mallory to prompt her. "Go ahead and ask what you will. You won't upset me. I've done my time in upset land."

"Very well. Mr. Mallory, I'm sure you know that everything that has happened in your vicinity since you were brought here has been carefully monitored. I'm sure you must understand that given the reception the Pitar have been accorded here on Earth and elsewhere, coupled with the fact that over a period of some five years they have displayed nothing even remotely like the behavior you have described—the story you just told is difficult for the rest of us to accept." The hospital room was dead silent as everyone waited to see how the patient would react.

Mallory's reply was low, but perfectly intelligible. "So you think I'm a liar?"

"Nobody said that," another officer hastened to add. "Nobody's calling you a liar." He looked to the woman, then back down at the ravaged figure in the bed. "You've been through a terrible ordeal, sir. It's a miracle that you survived, much less with your body and your . . ." Aware he had stumbled into awkward territory, he broke off.

Mallory finished the thought for him. "My mind intact?" His eyes searched the attentive gathering. "You think I may have hallucinated what happened on Treetrunk? How about the six hundred thousand dead or missing?" His voice rose perceptibly. "That's one hell of a hallucination."

"No one disputes the destruction of Treetrunk." The female officer's tone was tender, but hardly condescending. "That is something no human being would dare try to deny. What Major Rothenburg and the rest of us are wondering is if you actually saw what you say you saw, or if your mind, overwhelmed by the horror, invented something, however implausible, to mask or blot out an even worse reality."

"Worse reality? Worse than genocide? Worse than female reproductive organ evisceration and theft?" He shook his head slowly. "Ma'am, all I can say is, you must have a greater capacity for inventing horror than I do."

From his position near the end of the bed, Chimbu spoke up. "Mr. Mallory, Colonel Nadurovina is an eminent military psychiatrist specializing in combat and combat-related disorders. She doesn't mean to impugn your veracity. Like the rest of us, she only wants what's best for you—and to get at the truth."

"The truth!?!" His voice bordering on hysteria, the patient leaned sharply forward in the bed. Nearby, a medtech activated the osmotic hypo he held behind his back and started forward. Startled by the unexpected violence of his response, Tse let go of Mallory's hand. But she did not stand up or retreat from her position alongside him. Seeing the sudden fear in her face, he made an effort to regain his composure.

"I've told you the truth. Whether you believe it or not is up to you." Staring hard at the circle of the curious, he added warningly, "You'd better, because there's no guarantee the Pitar won't try something like it again. Unless, of course, they got everything they needed from Treetrunk."

"Human female reproductive organs?" Rothenburg's tone laid bare his skepticism. "You'll excuse me, Mr. Mallory, if that doesn't strike some of us as unsound grounds for rationalizing an assault on a colony. To gain a strategic advantage or base, yes; to acquire a world rich in rare metals and minerals, perhaps; or even to try and intimidate the occupying species into conceding possession, possibly. But what you say makes no sense."

"Deliver us from the blindered workings of the military mind," he muttered. "What's the military doing here anyway?"

"When six hundred thousand people are slaughtered without mercy or warning, it becomes a military matter," a man behind Rothenburg replied stiffly.

Mallory grunted and leaned back against his pillows. "For what it's worth, it doesn't make any sense to me, either. Pitar and human can't generate offspring, but at the same time I can't put the kind of organized organ-gathering I witnessed down to morbid scientific curiosity or aimless disemboweling. The Pitar I saw looked like they knew exactly what they wanted and how to go about getting it. They had storage containers ready to store their . . . handiwork. What they did was for a reason. If they had other motives for annihilating Treetrunk, then they're the only ones who can tell you about them." He made an obscene gesture, heedless of who might be watching via relay on distant monitors.

"Me, I think we should put every weapon we can find on every ship that can be mustered and blow them out of existence all the way back to their beloved bastard Dominion, and then seed both their precious Twin Worlds with radioactive dust that has a nice, long half-life. How about it? Why don't you put the question to a couple of their local representatives? Gauge their reaction. They'll lie, of course. Fluently. They're doubtless convinced they obliterated any evidence of their treachery. Which they did—except for me." The bluster and bravado abruptly leaked out of him like the air from a balloon subject to deep-sea pressures. His voice became small and frightened, as if two distinct personalities were fighting for space in the same body.

"They don't know about me, do they? They don't know I'm here . . . ?"

"Easy," Tse told him, leaning closer and stroking his arm with her fingers. "Be calm, Alwyn. Nobody knows you're here." She looked anxiously over at Chimbu. "Do they?"

The chief physician shook his head. His words spelled confidence. "Only the upper echelon of the hospital staff knows about Mr. Mallory's origins. Beyond the people presently assembled in this room, there are a handful of government officials who had to be informed."

Colonel Nadurovina added soothingly, "You would be surprised who knows and who does not, who was deliberately informed and who was kept in the dark. You are safe here, Mr. Mallory. If you look in the hallway you will not see much, if you look out your window you will see less, but it would take vaster weaponry than we believe the Pitar or any other species possesses to reach you." She smiled, and it did not seem forced or artificial. "At this moment you may very well be, Mr. Mallory, the best-protected individual in this portion of the Orion Arm. The members of the world council are not as well looked after."

"Then you do believe me." She might not be in charge, but Nadurovina acted as if she was, so he directed half his attention to her. Whether she was aware of it or not, the rest had been settled on Irene Tse.

"We believe you saw something. We believe that a powerful and inimical sentience is responsible for the eradication of human life on Treetrunk. Whether those two things are one and the same we cannot accept on the word of one man found drifting in space starving, near death, and out of his mind." This time her smile was wry. "Surely you can appreciate the sensitivity of my position and that of my colleagues who are charged with rendering a decision in this matter."

"Question the Pitar," Mallory shot back. "Corner them and press them. Ask them what they might want with human organs and judge their reaction."

A plump man in civilian clothes who had hitherto been silent now pushed his way forward. "I am Jenju Burriyip. I represent the world council." His lips curved upward. "Those members who have been informed, anyway. Please tell me, Mr. Mallory, how I am supposed to confront the representatives of what to this point has been a likeable, good-natured species and inquire politely if they might perchance have in an off moment slaughtered six hundred thousand of my fellow beings?"

"How should I know?" the patient snapped curtly. "I'm no diplomat."

Burriyip nodded solemnly. "That is exactly my point, Mr. Mallory. If, and please bear with me when I say 'if,' what you have told us has somehow become confused by your condition, or distorted because you have suffered physically, or has otherwise been altered in your mind, and we wrongly accuse the Pitar, however obliquely, then we stand to forfeit some nice, useful, popular new friends. If word got out, the government could fall."

"Listen to me." Mallory chose his words slowly and carefully. "The Pitar are not nice. They are not ever going to be 'useful.' They murdered six hundred thousand men, women, and children, for what depraved reasons of their own I can't say. And if they only had to do it once to get what they wanted or needed, and never do anything like it again, then they will have done worse than what they did. They will have gotten away with it."

Burriyip was immovable. "I said 'if,' Mr. Mallory. No one is ready to discount your theory out of hand."

"Goddammit, it's not a theory!" He looked as if he was going to start crying again but pulled himself together with an effort. The hypo wielder held his ground. "Then you won't confront the Pitar?"

The representative sighed heavily. "I am sorry, Mr. Mallory, but to accuse an entire race of interspecies genocide on the word of one man . . . We cannot. You have to understand that. You do not have to like it, but you do have to understand."

"I understand that if you don't do something you're going to have humankind dancing and laughing down through the years hand in hand with the worst enemies in its history, and that they're the ones who are going to be laughing the hardest. If they do laugh, that is."

"We will do something, Mr. Mallory." Nadurovina tried her best to mollify him. "We will find out who is lying and who is telling the truth."

"And most of all," Rothenburg added, "we're going to find out who or what was responsible for what happened on Argus V."

"Not if you don't ask the right people the right questions." Closing his eyes, Mallory slumped deeper into the pillows.

Tse held his wrist, not trusting the machines. "That's enough. He's only recently emerged from his coma, and this is more activity than he should have to endure."

Chimbu rose. "Nurse Tse is right. We should leave so he can get some rest."

"When can we talk to him again?" Despite his professional skepticism, Rothenburg felt concern for the man in the bed.

"Not before tomorrow." Chimbu began to urge everyone out of the room, an insistent father herding his flock. "If you don't want to communicate with a mind that might be playing tricks on itself, allow it to rest. If his vitals continue to strengthen and he is willing, we'll try this again tomorrow."

"Maybe once he's rested some more he'll remember something else," Rothenburg murmured as he stepped out into the corridor.

"Like who actually committed the atrocity?" Nadurovina followed her colleague down the hall.

"Then you don't believe his story?" Absently, Rothenburg saluted the two guards who were posted at the far end of the walkway.

"I don't know. The Pitar as exterminators? And for such an obscure reason? One that might well devolve from some unhappy or repressed childhood sexual experience of the patient's? I could not find anything in his records, but that does not mean there is nothing of the kind buried deep within his memories." They entered the hospital lift and stood back from the closing doors. "That does not mean he is not telling the truth. The question remains, is it the truth as it actually is or merely the truth as his traumatized self sees it?"

Rothenburg considered. "Burriyip meant it when he said the government couldn't confront the Pitar."

"I know. We cannot, either. Not without a specific directive from above, one that I do not think will be forthcoming. Ever since the first encounter, people have been mesmerized by the Pitar."

Rothenburg nodded knowingly. "My wife has two outfits inspired by Pitarian design. She'd find the very idea of them killing one human grotesquely laughable, let alone hundreds of thousands. If we challenge or accuse them in any way, there'll be diplomatic bedlam. Careers will be ruined, or at the very least any hopes for advancement aborted. In that respect Burriyip wasn't understating the gravity of the situation. Such a confrontation really could bring down the government."

"I agree. Neither the government nor the military can directly confront the Pitar. But someone else can."

"Someone else?" Rothenburg's uncertainty showed in his expression. "Who else could possibly . . . ?" He halted in midquery. "You can't be thinking what I think you're thinking."

Nadurovina did not smile. Her posture was as regimented as her thinking. "Tell me true, Erhard: Haven't you ever, watching such happenings on the tridee, had the desire one time in your life to gamble a million credits or so on a single throw of the dice, or spin of the futures' globe?"

They stepped out of the lift and into a main hallway, busy with nurses and medtechs, doctors and support personnel. The two by now familiar uniformed officers hardly rated a glance.

"We could lose him," Rothenburg warned her. "The shock might be too much, even if the Pitar are involved only in his imagination. Fantasy can kill as readily as reality."

"I'll speak to Chimbu about it. Medication and specialists will be standing by at all times in the next room, ready to intervene."

"What about the Pitar? What makes you think one of them will agree to see him?"

The colonel's mouth twitched. "How could they refuse? Compassionate and neighborly as they are, it would look funny if they declined to offer their deepest sympathies to the sole survivor of the Treetrunk holocaust. Anyone who agrees to pay their respects will be intimately screened for the carrying of anything even potentially inimical, of course, before being allowed to come within a hundred kilometers of this island, much less this hospital. Much less Mr. Alwyn Mallory's presence."

"Even so," Rothenburg felt compelled to point out as they turned a corner, "determined assassins invariably find a way."

Nadurovina nodded thoughtfully. "In that event we would have something of an answer by roundabout means, wouldn't we?" Rothenburg did not know what to say in response to this cool, detached calculation. "But I do not think that will be a problem. The Pitar may very well believe that we are testing them with words. If they are the responsible party, as Mallory continues to insist, then they will gladly go along with any test they believe will help to remove them from the list of suspected peoples. If they are not responsible and their participation in the atrocity is nothing more than a figment of Mr. Mallory's addled imagination, no harm will have been done."

"Not to human-Pitar relations, maybe," Rothenburg objected, "but what about to the patient?"

"Time to roll the dice, Erhard."

He smiled thinly at his colleague. "Easy to say when it's not your sanity that's at stake."

His retort clearly troubled her. "In spite of what you may think, I don't recommend this course of action easily or without qualms, Major. However inchoate, I am quite aware that Mr. Mallory is our only connection with whatever happened on Treetrunk. I have no more desire to see him lose his strengthening grasp on reality than you or anyone else. But I am the senior officer here, and I am the one being pressured for answers. Not informed speculation, not reasoned hypotheses, but answers. Whatever happens if we confront Mr. Mallory with his terrors, whatever the consequences, I am the one who will have to answer for them. I am prepared to take that risk."

"Again, with somebody else's dice." Rothenburg refused to let his colleague and superior off the hook. "In spite of initial impressions I find myself liking this Mallory."

"It is not his likability that is at stake here. For what it is worth, I like him, too. But in the resolution of this frightful mystery, neither his life, nor mine, nor yours, means anything."

"All right. I'll cosign on the requisite directives so long as you accept ultimate responsibility."

She found herself walking toward the exit. Outside were languid breezes and the scent of orchids, the warm, moist aroma of mother Earth. Upstairs lay a lonely, frightened man who might hold the key to cataclysm, if only they could drag the proof or denial of it out of him.

"As senior officer on site, I have no choice. So I might as well do it willingly. You will commence the necessary arrangements?"

He nodded. "I'll handle my end of things. How long before you think you can have one or more of them here?"

"One should do, I think. If we make too much of a show of it they may become suspicious. We want them to react, not anticipate. I will discuss with Dr. Chimbu a means of monitoring Mr. Mallory's reactions even more effectively than we do now. We will need to record everything that happens in the finest detail for study later."

"In case he locks up, or blanks out again, or dies?" Resigned to the turn of events Rothenburg might be, but he was not happy about them.

Nadurovina ignored the sarcasm. "Yes. In case any of those eventualities unfortunately come to pass. I hope they will not."

"What about having the nurse present—Tsue or Tsoy or whatever her name is?"

"Irene Tse. She should be there. She is good for him. She does a lot of little things."

Rothenburg was moved to reluctant admiration. "You don't miss much, do you, Colonel?"

"No, Major. It is my job not to."

15

He was tall and bronzed, regal of posture and sleek of muscle, faultless of demeanor and enchanting of smile. Wherever they went, heads turned; men out of admiration, women from a plethora of confused but animated emotion. In other words, he was a typical Pitarian male, no more or less spectacular than any other of his kind. Walking alongside him Nadurovina felt slighted, but not overawed.

His name was Dmis-Atel. A tertiary assistant from the southwest branch of his embassy, he had flown to New Ireland at the request of the authorities there to pay his respects, it was said, to a survivor of the Treetrunk bloodbath. Protesting that no such survivors were known to exist, the Pitar had been informed through the most secret channels that this was most probably the case, but in the event it was not, it would be gracious of them to bestow their guileless commiserations in person. And in the far more likely event that it was a clever falsehood being perpetrated by certain unscrupulous individuals for amoral reasons of their own, perhaps a perceptive Pitar could shed some light on the matter by examining it from a nonhuman perspective.

Once the situation had been explained to them thus, the Pitar did not hesitate. Representative Dmis was placed by his embassy on the first available aerial transport and charged with rendering whatever sympathy or service he could in the matter, as the occasion might demand. Rothenburg had met him at the airport and escorted him to the hospital, where he had been taken in hand by a calm, unruffled Nadurovina.

"I am anxious to see this person."

The Pitar moved with effortless, graceful strides that gave him the appearance of flowing over the floor. One was tempted to bend low for a look at the bottoms of his feet to see if they were actually touching the ground. The Pitar did everything effortlessly and well. Nadurovina was no more immune than her friends to the spell they cast. Only her innate professionalism allowed her to maintain a greater degree of detachment. Did they also slaughter the innocent effortlessly and without strain?

"He does not know that you are coming." They turned into a corridor through double doors that shouted *Restricted Entry—Authorized Personnel Only* and headed for the lift. Every step of the way, hidden scanners were examining every aspect of their bodies, from the material of their clothing to the contents of their digestive systems. Specific instruments searched for explosive components in their bloodstreams and toxins in their saliva. By the time they reached the corner room on the northwest end of the fifth floor they had been subjected to as thorough a noninvasive analysis as contemporary technology could contrive. This despite the fact that Nadurovina and her associates were fairly certain that the Pitar would not make an attempt on the patient's person. To do so would amount to an admission of guilt or, at the very least, a stain on their saintly mien that would be difficult to wash away. Armed and highly trained personnel would be close at hand in any case, ready to intervene at the slightest provocation.

The Pitar did not give indication of being under any unusual stress, but then, the Pitar never did. It was difficult for the most perceptive at the best of times to tell what they were thinking. They never lost their temper or burst out in uncontrolled laughter. Like their physical appearance, their demeanor was always perfect.

They were alone in the lift. Nadurovina knew that a battery of observers was waiting in the room next to the patient's, with dozens more cemented to remote monitors and pickups. Every movement of the visiting Pitar would be scrutinized, every word deconstructed, every shift in expression analyzed.

The door loomed ahead. The Pitar looked over and down to smile gently at her. "Are the guards for us or for this individual?"

"For him. As you can imagine we've been very interested in what he's had to say about the destruction of his adopted homeworld."

"And what has he said?" The Hellenically perfect countenance betrayed no concern, the body movements no agitation.

The military psychiatrist smiled back. "You can ask him yourself." After identifying herself and her guest to the guards, they were allowed to pass. "I think you'll find him an interesting subject."

Still no visible reaction. Why should she have expected anything different? Opening the door, she entered first.

Mallory was sitting up in the bed with Tse in a chair at his side. It was a tableau that had become intimately familiar to Nadurovina over the past week. In that time the patient had put on weight and regained lost muscle tone. Much could be attributed to the attention he had received from the nurse, whose devotion to the single patient whose care she had been charged with looking after exceeded anything that could reasonably have been expected.

Here it was. The moment of confrontation. She could feel the eyes behind the multiple pickups glued to their screens, watching, waiting.

"Good morning, Mr. Mallory, Ms. Tse. I hope you do not mind, but I have brought a guest." Stepping aside, she bequeathed to the man in the bed an unobstructed view of the visitor.

Mallory's eyes shifted. He saw the Pitar. As importantly, the Pitar saw him. Nadurovina was not above holding her breath, ready to intervene, spring aside, or call for help as the occasion should demand. She did not know exactly what to expect. No one did. In their intense discussions prior to this moment she believed that she and her colleagues had imagined and discussed every possible scenario.

They were wrong.

"A Pitar." Mallory's voice was calm, controlled, absolutely devoid of fear or panic. "Here." His gaze shifted to the psychiatrist, and he did something even more remarkable. He smiled. "Another of your tests? A little experiment, maybe?"

"Dmis is a member of the delegation that is headquartered on Lombok," she explained. "He is a real Pitar, not an actor made up to look like one."

"I can see that." Did his tone darken ever so slightly, or was Nadurovina reading into it one of the things for which she and her associates were searching? "I know what a Pitar looks like."

She tensed but made no move to interfere when the alien moved toward the bed. Outside, beyond the wall, she knew that the strike team of armed commandos would have reacted to the alien's approach by automatically advancing to another level of readiness. To her relief he halted at the foot of the bed.

"So. You survived the disturbing incident that overwhelmed Argus Five."

"That's right. I did." Mallory met the alien's inscrutable gaze without flinching. "I saw what happened there."

The Pitar made a small, almost imperceptible gesture whose meaning no one in the room comprehended. "My people are very concerned about what took place."

Mallory's mouth set in a tight line. There was no trembling, no quivering that Nadurovina could see. A glance at the readouts of the instruments that monitored the patient's vitals showed little change, certainly not enough to be considered significant.

"I'll bet they are."

"What did you see happen there, man?"

Seated next to Mallory, Tse listened quietly to the conversation, one hand resting on the patient's forearm. Reaching up, Mallory affected an air of mock forgetfulness.

"I'm not sure . . . Oh yeah, it's coming back to me now. Let's see. Your people were there." Once more the mocking smile. Did the Pitar stiffen? Again, the psychiatrist couldn't be certain. Being in the room, standing to one side and observing, was like watching a chess match with living pieces.

"Yes, that's right. Your people. I recall it quite clearly. They were killing everybody. Destroying anything and everything that might record or otherwise indicate what they were doing. Your people are real thorough. Real thorough motherfuckers."

Nadurovina felt compelled to play the role she had assigned herself. "Please, Mr. Mallory. Dmis is a diplomatic representative."

"That's kind of a contradiction, Doc. There's nothing diplomatic about the Pitar."

The alien's expression did not change. He seemed more fascinated than upset by the patient. "You are a very imaginative person, Mr. Mallory. Very inventive. The Pitar do not kill except in self-defense. I am no physician, but I think the dreadful experience you have obviously suffered must have at least temporarily unhinged your mind. Why my people should figure prominently in your delusions I cannot think, but it is not very flattering."

"I'm not delusional. It wasn't delusion. I know what I saw. Your people attacked without warning, trading on friendship acquired through five years of joyful, kindly contact to achieve complete surprise. You slaughtered anything on two legs. It didn't make any sense to me then, and it doesn't make any sense to me now."

"Ah," Dmis murmured, "an admission that confirms the diagnosis."

"No, you don't understand. What doesn't make any sense to me is what you needed with the reproductive organs of human females. I saw them being removed with surgical precision from one woman after another and carefully packed away in what I believe now to be cryogenic containers. What do you do with them? Eat 'em? Venerate them? Use them in some kind of unimaginably barbaric conceptual art? Tell me, diplomat Dmis. I'm really curious to know."

"As am I," the Pitar replied. "Curious to know what sort of human mind can invent such absurdities."

Nadurovina interrupted. "If this is upsetting you too much, Dmis, we can leave."

"No, no." The alien did not appear in the least perturbed by the accusations that were coming from the bed. "It is interesting. As do all of my kind, I want to know as much as possible about humans. Even their mental aberrations. This is a useful occasion."

Mallory nodded agreeably. "Useful for me, too. See, I want to know all about the Pitar, because it will help me to understand how better to kill you."

"I have to tell you, Mr. Mallory, that I understand what is happening here and that I truly sympathize. With ongoing care of the quality you are obviously receiving I am certain that your condition will improve. Meanwhile, I am intrigued by your misconceptions." He smiled over at Nadurovina. "Is there anything I can do to help?"

"Yeah," Mallory declared without hesitation. He proceeded to describe an act that was an anatomical impossibility, even for the limber Pitar. Nadurovina choked slightly, but the alien took no apparent offense.

"Another elaborate fantasy. Naturally, Mr. Mallory, you have proof to underline and support your fantasies. Images of this imaginary assault, perhaps, or voice records, or a corroborating witness."

"No," the man in the bed muttered. "You know damn well that I don't. If I did, you wouldn't be standing there grinning like an underfed Buddha. You wouldn't even have been brought here. Somebody would've shot you on sight." His smile widened. "I'd gladly do that myself except that where my mental state is concerned plenty of these 'specialists' happen to agree with you, or at least are willing to consider the possibility. I could get up from this bed, right now, and put my hands around your blemish-free throat and squeeze until all the life leaked out of you." For the second time, Nadurovina tensed.

"I do not think even if you were healthy you would be physically capable of such a feat," the much taller Dmis replied calmly. "As it is, you are weakened from your misfortune, and I am considerably larger and stronger than you."

"I can see that, but you've never experienced the kind of strength that uncontrolled fury can give a human being." He glanced at the anxious psychiatrist. "Don't worry, Doc. Much as I'd like to I'm not planning on leaving this bed for a while. Not even for the sheer pleasure of feeling a Pitarian neck under my fingers." He turned his attention back to the alien. "I'm saving myself, you see. I want to kill many more than just one of you."

Dmis looked to his escort. "I hope Mr. Mallory is receiving appropriate medication for his condition. It would distress me to think that he might one day attack someone else, perhaps believing that they were Pitar."

"I can assure you that his treatment regimen takes all possibilities into account," Nadurovina told the alien, succeeding in answering him truthfully without committing herself to any specifics.

"This has been most interesting." The Pitar leaned slightly over the foot of the bed in Mallory's direction and beamed benignly. "When you have invented some proof to give support to your expressive delusions, you must see to it that I am notified. It would be educational to continue this discussion. In the absence of anything additional, however, I must return to my mission and make a report." Stepping back, he turned his full attention to the psychiatrist.

"I would like to be kept informed of Mr. Mallory's progress, as a matter of personal interest. It is distressing to see any sentient being slide so far into fantasy. But it is quite understandable. Among my kind it is also common to build a mental wall around a terrible experience as a way of dealing with the consequences. In the absence of truth, the patient has invented elaborate imaginings to avoid having to deal with a large, threatening blank spot in his memory. I am sure that with time and your good offices these delusions will gradually begin to fade away."

"I'm sure he will continue to improve," she replied noncommittally as she gestured toward the doorway. The Pitar preceded her into the hall.

Nine and a half hours later Irene Tse burst from room fifty-four in panic. From behind her and within the room came a cacophony of instruments shattering and furniture breaking. Above it all rose an inhuman howling, the piteous shrieks of an unhinged mind teetering on the razor edge of sanity.

Nadurovina was interrupted in quarters where she had just sat down to dine with her husband. Tearing back to the hospital at velocities that threatened to send her vehicle spinning out of control, she blew through the entrance and past startled hospital personnel in her race to reach the building's top story.

Shoving her way through the crowd that had gathered at one end of the floor, she espied Tse and ungently forced a path to where the nurse was sitting. Though the psychiatrist was not in uniform, the medtech who was attending to the nurse recognized the officer and gave way.

Trembling, Tse was holding her face in her hands. Blood from a deep scratch had welled up to stain the upper right sleeve of her duty blouse. Settling in behind her, the medtech began to treat the wound.

Nadurovina had no time for niceties. "What happened?" Reaching forward, she grabbed the younger woman's wrists and roughly pulled them away from her face. "Look at me, nurse!" Tse's tear-stained face lifted to meet the psychiatrist's.

"I . . . I don't know. It just happened. One minute everything was fine. I was just clearing away the dinner tray when it happened."

Nadurovina glanced in the direction of the room but was unable to see anything but surging, swirling bodies. If it was this confused and chaotic now, she reflected, what must it have been like ten minutes ago?

"When what happened? Talk to me, nurse. Was it . . . Did the Pitar . . . ?"

"Pitar?" Blinking, Tse reached up and rubbed at her eyes with the unstained sleeve of her uniform. "What Pitar? There are no Pitar here." Realization penetrated the younger woman's understanding as Nadurovina heaved a vast sigh of relief. Despite every precaution, despite all the round-the-clock, state-of-the-art security, there was always the possibility, the fear, that if the aliens were guilty of Mallory's charges or if they had simply taken a severe disliking to him they might somehow manage to get to him. Evidently they had not.

On the other hand, their apparent absence and lack of involvement in whatever had taken place in the hospital room meant they were still, in the eyes of uncommitted justice, as innocent as Dmis had claimed.

Tse was babbling quietly. "He just went crazy. One minute he was finishing the last of his ice cream and passing me the tray, smiling and happy, and then . . ." The slow shaking of her head was visible evidence of her disbelief. "It was like a bomb went off inside him."

"Is he . . . all right?" With her initial concerns allayed, Nadurovina could afford to be more compassionate.

"I guess so. I don't know." The younger woman's expression pleaded for understanding. "I tried to help, tried to calm him down, but it was like he couldn't hear me. He started throwing things, breaking things." As if still not believing it was there, she reached up to feel the cut the medtech had just finished bandaging. "I ran, both to protect myself and to get help." She looked toward the room. "It's been quiet for a little while, so I guess they got him calmed down. I hope . . . I hope they didn't have to hurt him."

"He's had the best people the staff of this hospital can boast attending to him on permanent rotating duty." The psychiatrist tried to sound reassuring. "I am certain he will be all right."

"What do you think happened, Doctor?"

"I don't know, either, Irene. But I can hazard a guess. He has experienced a delayed psychological reaction to the Pitar's visit. You saw how calm he was in the alien's presence. It was the last thing I would have expected, whether his story is true or not. Somehow he held it all in, kept perfect control of his reactions and emotions. Then I expect he tried to forget all about it. And he managed to do it—until his system could not take any more. When you told me it was like a bomb went off inside him you were probably closer to the truth than you realize." She shook her head.

"People have this belief that fusionable material contains the most explosive type of energy." Reaching up, she tapped her forehead. "Myself, I have always believed it was trapped in here." Her expression somber, she knelt to face the shaken woman and put a comforting hand on the other's knee. "If you would like to be relieved of this assignment, I will see to it that the order is cut."

Tse swallowed and wiped at her eyes again. "No. I'll stay on."

Silently pleased, an admiring Nadurovina straightened. "Your devotion to your job is commendable. I will make sure that you are properly compensated for your dedication."

Tse looked up at her. "I'm not staying on because I'm devoted to my job."

Nadurovina hesitated only briefly. "Oh. So that is how it is."

The younger woman nodded. "That's how it is."

The psychiatrist's mouth tightened. "I don't approve. It is not professional."

Tse responded with an awkward, choking laugh. "You're telling me. I didn't plan it, you know. I had no idea anything like this would happen."

"I am not sure that any of us ever do, dear." The older woman sighed. "I won't say anything. As long as it does not appear to be interfering with your professional duties, I will not raise any objections to your staying on."

Reaching up, Tse took the other woman's hand in hers and mustered the best smile she could. "Thank you."

With a last nod, Nadurovina turned and pushed back into the crowd. This time she was held up by a guard, but from within the room Chimbu must have seen her because she heard his voice call out for her to be admitted.

The hospital room did indeed look as if a bomb had gone off within. Of the patient there was no sign.

"We moved him across the hall into fifty-two." A weary Chimbu looked harried and strained. "Along with anything else that was worth moving. He's sleeping now, under sedation." Without further comment he indicated their surroundings.

The destruction was impressive, Nadurovina saw. Hard to believe one short, malnourished, sick patient still in the middle stages of recovery had been able to wreak so much havoc in so brief a span. Chimbu saw the question in her face.

"Nurse Tse called the medtech staff on duty immediately, but they hesitated to interfere out of concern he might seriously injure himself. It took the duty physician a few minutes to get here and issue orders. At that time the patient was still going strong. Five orderlies needed to coordinate their efforts to get him down long enough for one of them to administer a sedative. They finally made the decision to jump him when it looked like he was going to make a run for the window."

Nadurovina glanced in the direction of the specially retrofitted safety glass. It was strong enough to stop an explosive shell. She found herself wondering if it would have been enough to thwart the crazed Mallory. The window was still closed. "What about self-inflicted damage?"

"Nothing too serious. Minor cuts and bruises. I've talked to Tse, and I think it's pretty clear what set him off."

The psychiatrist nodded. "I have also spoken with her." As she conversed with the chief medical officer she scanned the room. Expensive instrumentation had been smashed, cables ripped from the walls and monitors, furniture crushed. Bent and twisted, a chair lay in one corner like a beached anemone. Even the bed coverings had been shredded. Bending to pick up a plastic cup, she saw that pieces had been chewed out of the rim. The tornado that had gone back to sleep in Alwyn Mallory's brain had reawakened. Remembering the shaken, frightened nurse, Nadurovina was thankful no one had been hurt.

What would Mallory do when he began to come out of his sedative-induced sleep? By that time if the hospital staff had done its job properly a new set of monitoring equipment should be in place and operational. There was no guarantee the patient would not resume where he had left off, raging and destructive, endangering all those around him as well as himself. Tse's intervention could be crucial, she knew. Steeling herself, she headed for the hallway to talk to the nurse.

Her considerable powers of persuasion were not required. Tse was anxious to return to Mallory's side. She listened quietly to the older woman's instructions, taking on that advice she thought useful and wordlessly ignoring the rest. By this time she felt she knew Alwyn Mallory better than anyone else. Ultimately, when he next awoke she was the one who would have to make the first, critical decisions.

In furniture, facilities, and layout room fifty-two was a mirror image of the one a berserking Mallory had wrecked. Under the influence of the powerful sedative he slept all through the rest of the day and on into the night. Tse dozed off beside him, unwilling to make use of the inflatable bed that had been provided for her. When she awoke, it was to find the first tendrils of daylight creeping through the window and the patient lying with eyes open, staring silently at her.

Surprised, she started slightly, relaxing only when he smiled.

"I was a bad boy, wasn't I, nurse?"

"How are you feeling?"

Even before he could answer she was automatically checking the monitors alongside his bed. She knew they would read more or less normal. If anything serious had manifested itself during the night, doctors and other nurses would have attended to the problem, invariably waking her in the process. But she had to ask.

"Tired. A little sore." Reaching up, he felt of the pellucid epidermal seal that had closed a cut on his forehead. "I don't remember many details. Just a lot of noise."

Her tone was quietly reproving. "That would have been you smashing up everything within reach in the other room."

"Other room?" Raising up slightly, he scrutinized his new surroundings, noting the reversed layout and the altered view through the large window. "I don't remember being moved."

"They had to knock you out. It took five orderlies."

"Five, eh?" He seemed perversely pleased. "I imagine this is going to go on my bill."

Putting a hand over her mouth she covered the laugh she was unable to suppress. This was supposed to be a serious moment, one in which she admonished the invalid for his unacceptable actions and discussed with him how to prevent a recurrence. Instead, she found herself giggling and grinning at the irrepressible patient's every other comment. Furthermore, she discovered that she didn't give a damn about the reactions of those individuals whose attention might be fixed to distant peeping monitors.

"I have a feeling the government is picking up the cost of your stay."

"Really?" Pushing down against the mattress, he sat up. "Maybe I'll trash this one later. Yeah, one room a week. That would fit the way I'm feeling."

Making an effort to be serious, she wagged a warning finger at him. "I'd think twice about that. Keep it up and you'll be spending most of your time under sedation. You won't be any good to anyone in that condition."

His smile evaporated and he looked away from her. "Who gives a good goddamn?"

"I do," she replied simply.

That brought his head back around. Outside, the equatorial sun was climbing rapidly, flooding the room with diffused but still sharply defining light. The window glass darkened slightly in response, moderating the illumination and temperature level in the room.

His tone was subdued, thankful. "I'd like to be able to say it was worth everything I went through just to hear those two words."

She put a hand on his. "I don't expect that kind of oblique praise, Alwyn. I don't need it."

"Then you believe me?" Despite his outward bravado, she could sense that veiled desperation underlined his words.

"I believe you," she replied sympathetically, "but to convince others will require more than your word. Surely you can see their side. You can't accuse an entire species of genocide and inconceivable acts without something more to back it up than the word of one man. Or even the words of a shipful. You mustn't feel singled out."

"But I do feel singled out," he told her. "I *was* singled out. I survived. I'm the only one who survived. Why me? Why not someone with a better nature, or great artistic talent? Why not a composer or a writer, or a mother with three kids? I'm a cynical, misanthropic, short-tempered, semiretired son of a bitch. If there was any justice in this universe I'd have been one of the first to die."

"That would have been a pity."

His gaze narrowed slightly. "Yeah? Why?"

Her fingers tightened around his. "Because then we couldn't be having this conversation."

He stared at her for a moment longer. Then he began to cry. Not silently this time, nor in great racking sobs, but normally, the way any man would cry when overwhelmed by irresistible emotion. The very ordinariness of it was a profound relief to her.

He stopped so suddenly that she was alarmed.

"Alwyn, what is it, what's wrong?"

"Nothing's wrong." He wiped at his eyes almost angrily, as if trying to punish them for their betrayal of his fancied indifference. "I just remembered something."

"Is it important?"

"I think so." He was nodding slowly. "It's proof."

Nadurovina was not the first into the room. Rothenburg was faster. Chimbu followed behind, accompanied by an orderly. There were others who wanted to join them, but the chief medical officer had ruled against any more being present at any one time. Given the patient's recent deranged outburst, the doctor did not want to do anything to make him feel pressured. That included crowding his space.

On the bed, Mallory was nodding wisely to himself. "This is about as much privacy as I thought I had."

Rothenburg would not be denied. "You said you remembered proof. I heard you. I heard you distinctly. What kind of proof?"

Mallory eyed the intelligence officer unflinchingly. "You think I invented that story about the Pitar. You all think I'm nuts, that my mind is conjuring illusions to cover what I actually saw. That's what that smiling Pitarian bastard you flew in to confront me with would like you to think, too."

"Change our minds." Ignoring the cautioning looks he was receiving from Nadurovina, Rothenburg challenged the other man openly. "Make us look stupid. Go on, do it! Shove the truth right in my face."

Mallory held the Major's eyes for a moment longer, then dropped his gaze and looked down at the bed. "I can't. Not yet."

An exasperated Nadurovina kept her voice level. "Why not? You said you had proof."

"That's the right tense, Colonel. *Had* is the operative word here."

Rothenburg wanted to lurch forward, to shove the seated nurse away from the bed, reach down, and violently shake the infuriating man hiding beneath the covers until he made sense. "All right. You 'had' proof. What kind? It would have to be convincing beyond doubt."

Mallory coolly met the officer's angry glare. "How about a few hours of verifiable media-grade recording of the Pitar ravaging Treetrunk? Shooting down adults and children, razing buildings, stalking through the streets in body armor? Surgical teams carefully eviscerating women and preserving their internal organs?" His body had begun to tremble again, but his voice held steady. "How about it, Major? Would that constitute sufficient 'proof'?"

"Yes." Rothenburg straightened. "Yes, once cleared beyond doubt of possible falsification and professionally verified, that would probably suffice. Where is it?"

The man in the bed was shaking his head slowly. "I don't know."

"You don't . . . ?" Rothenburg began, but held himself back when Nadurovina grabbed his shoulder.

"I mean," Mallory muttered as he struggled with himself, "I know, but I don't know. I *think* I can find it." He wore a look of honest helplessness. "I hid it."

Glancing up at a small dot in the ceiling, Rothenburg barked directives. "Security recheck! I want to know that this entire building is scan-shielded, not just this room. Do it now." When a reply in the affirmative sounded from a concealed speaker, he nodded sharply and turned back to Mallory. "Very well. You have a recording, but you hid it somewhere. You think you can find it. Where do we look?"

"You'd never locate it. I'll have to do it. Retrace my steps." He smiled wanly and gripped Tse's hand tightly. "It's the only way."

"Why?" Rothenburg prompted him. "Just tell us where on Treetrunk you concealed this recording and there'll be a recovery team on site within days."

"It's not on Treetrunk," he told the officer. "It's on the inner moon." His expression turned apologetic. "Under a rock. I didn't want to leave it on the lifeboat in case the Pitar detected my emissions and picked me up."

Rothenburg looked like a fighter who had just taken a combination to the head and body. "After the Unop-Patha delivered you to the *Ronin*, your lifeboat was brought aboard and thoroughly checked over. Nothing was found, of course. But if that was your reference point for what you buried, how are you going to find it now? As moons go, I understand that Treetrunk One is pretty small. But it's still a moon."

"All I can do is try."

"You'll have help." Rothenburg's mind was racing ahead—planning, directing, plotting logistics. "What kind of container did you bury the recording in? Metal?" he concluded hopefully.

"Sorry. I used a small composite sealtight. Impervious to extremes of heat and cold, maintains a good vacuum."

"What was the recording medium?" Nadurovina asked.

"Standard home-recording mollysphere. A big one, centimeter in diameter. High grade—I could afford quality stuff. Also composite material, of course."

"Which means we'll have a hard time running a materials scan through rock." The major took a step back from the bed. "It doesn't matter. We'll find it if we have to take the whole planetoid apart grain by grain."

"I think I can save you a lot of time." Mallory leaned back against the pillows. "At least, I hope so."

"Just a minute." Chimbu broke his silence. "I'm not sure that's such a good idea. If you go back to where you were found, there's no telling how you'll react. The experience could cause you to flash back and relive the trauma you originally suffered. You could lapse back into coma."

"I'm sorry, Doctor," Rothenburg began, "but the overriding importance of this dictates that your authority is . . ."

Mallory cut him off. "Take it easy, Major. I'm coming." He shifted his attention to the troubled Chimbu. "I don't have any choice. I owe it to six hundred thousand dead neighbors."

"If you experience a serious relapse," the chief medical officer warned him stiffly, "this time you might not come out of it in as little as a month's time. You might not come out of it at all." He looked sharply at Rothenburg. "Then you'll have neither proof nor witness."

"A witness without proof is worthless," the officer shot back. Remembering the man in the bed, he added less stridently, "Nothing personal, Mallory."

"Up yours," the patient responded without hesitation. "I'm going."

"Good. I'll initiate the necessary arrangements." Rothenburg eyed the doctor. "You'll certify that he's well enough to travel."

"Since that wasn't phrased as a question," a diffident Chimbu replied, "I don't suppose it matters what I say."

"You'll come along," the officer continued inexorably, "to supervise his medical care." His gaze shifted to the side of the bed. "As will you, Nurse Tse."

"I have no problem with that." She continued to hold Mallory's hand in hers.

"A one-centimeter diameter composite mollysphere." Exhaling slowly, Nadurovina rubbed tiredly at her forehead. "I hope his mind will be clear enough to remember its location."

"Screw his mind," Rothenburg snapped. "His sense of direction is all I'm concerned about." Remembering the figure in the bed he added, "No offense."

"For a repeatedly offensive person, at least you're appropriately apologetic," a serene Mallory informed him.

16

The long journey to the Argus system was accomplished via military transport. Mallory was given a commanding officer's suite with two adjoining orderly's quarters. Tse was ensconced in one and Chimbu in the other. Though he objected strenuously to the profusion of monitoring instrumentation that had been placed in the suite, his protests were courteously ignored. Until the greater matter at hand was resolved, Alwyn Mallory would not be allowed to go to the bathroom unsupervised. He was too important—so important that the KK-drive dreadnought conveying him back to Treetrunk traveled englobed in a cruiser-and-destroyer convoy.

It was an incredibly costly escort for one man. But Rothenburg could have asked for half a fleet and had the request granted. Out of concern for secrecy, he did not. The movement of a small task force would not be overly remarked upon. Military vessels made the run to Argus periodically. Mallory's escort was certainly of unusual size, but not aberrantly so.

As one by one the ships executed the drop from space-plus back into space-normal, there was outwardly nothing wrong with the convoy's first passenger. How much he was holding inside only he knew. Nadurovina worried herself sick about him. To a lesser extent so did Chimbu and Rothenburg and the few others who knew what a full-strength task force was doing visiting the devastated Argus system. Of those close to medical science's most important patient, only Tse was relaxed and confident.

"He's stronger than you think," she told Nadurovina one morning over real coffee and calorie-free beignets.

"Taxonomically speaking, I realize that Alwyn Mallory is one tough son of a bitch." The psychiatrist sponged coffee with a beignet. "I also know that he puts up a strong defensive front that conceals what he is really feeling. He would not be human if it were otherwise. We are both aware that despite his jaunty demeanor and tough exterior he is never very far from the edge. He proved that when he became violent and wrecked his original hospital room." Her voice fell slightly. "What happened before can happen again. As the physician nominally in charge of overseeing his state of mind, I am far from prepared to piss off that possibility."

"I didn't mean to make light of it." Tse had lost weight during the past weeks, Nadurovina noticed, while Mallory had put it back on. Diet, concern, or fear? "I know Alwyn's sanity has survived a terrible shock." She smiled hesitantly over the rim of her cup. "He likes to say that the hinges of his mind are intact, but rusty."

"Has he said anything more about the location of this recording he claims to have made?"

Around them, crew shuffled back and forth from the food wall to tables, chattering in small groups or eating in solitude. The crew of the dreadnought knew only that they were making a visit to Treetrunk. Rumor had it that the stop was intended as a grisly object lesson, to emphasize that those who staffed the giant military KK-drive starships must never stray from alertness. This erroneous scuttlebutt was encouraged.

Not 'claims to,' " Tse countered primly. "Made. It's real. All we have to do is find it."

Nadurovina sipped at her coffee. She had taken quite a liking to the younger woman, motherly concern she kept well hidden. Nothing could be allowed to affect their professional relationship.

"I wish I had your confidence. This is a very expensive little excursion. We have no choice, of course, but to follow up on the only clue that has bequeathed itself to us. The world council realizes that. Even so, they were reluctant to authorize the escort force that Rothenburg insisted on. For his part, he refused to take your Mr. Mallory off-world without it."

"Major Rothenburg is afraid that the Pitar might try something, isn't he?"

"He just wants to be prepared. That's his nature. A consummate alpha personality."

"I want Alwyn to find the mollysphere, of course," Tse murmured, "but more to prove that he's been telling the truth all along than for any other reason."

Nadurovina was slightly taken aback. "What about bringing the butchers of the six hundred thousand to justice?"

Tse hesitated momentarily. "If Alwyn's right and the Pitar were responsible, if they did all the terrible things he says they did and he can bring forth proof of it, it will mean war, won't it?"

The psychiatrist nodded slowly. "One does not need an advanced degree in human psychology to envision the explosion of rage that would result. Personally, I cannot see anything less than all-out hostilities satisfying the atavistic revenge response that would ensue. The limits of such a conflict would remain to be defined, of course."

Tse looked unhappy. "There are interstellar wars with limits?"

"We have no experience in such matters, but if the thranx are to be believed, they have been engaged in just such a contest with the AAnn for more than two hundred and fifty years. I do not see anything that time-consuming happening in this case." She looked thoughtful. "We do not have the patience or the forbearance of the thranx. Or so the relevant literature insists. Myself, I have never met one of the bugs. Someday I think I would like to do so."

"Not me." Tse spoke with conviction. "I don't care how intelligent they are. Every time I see one I'm reminded of the time I snuck into my mother's pantry looking for candy and a bunch of cockroaches fell out on me. I was washing my hair for days afterwards."

"They do not look like cockroaches. Haven't you seen the tridees? More like mantids."

"I don't like them either." Tse pushed back from the table. "I don't like anything that eats with multiple mouthparts, or has honeycombed eyes, or walks on more than four legs."

"You are phobic. I am surprised. A woman with scientific training like yourself."

"I'm not perfect," Tse contended. "Everybody's afraid of something. Major Rothenburg is afraid of not having everything sufficiently organized. Dr. Chimbu is afraid of losing a patient. You are afraid of Alwyn losing his mind again."

"And Alwyn Mallory is afraid of the Pitar," the psychiatrist concluded.

"No. You're wrong there." There wasn't a hint of doubt in the nurse's voice. "Alwyn isn't afraid of the Pitar. He hates them. What he's afraid of is himself."

Consistent, disciplined activity was the norm on the bridge behind him as Rothenburg gazed out the port. Mallory was right, he reflected. Treetrunk One was not much of a moon. Easily overlooked, it was hardly worthy of the astronomical designation. Looking at it put him more in mind of a captured asteroid than a moon. But it was more than large enough to hide a small ship behind. Something as small as a lifeboat would be swallowed entirely.

He had seen the tridees of the tiny vessel Mallory had used to escape the holocaust that had swept over Treetrunk. The interior had immediately struck him as uninhabitable. The outside was worse. Somehow the irascible engineer had not only coerced it into lifting off without exploding on ignition, but had managed to coax it to the point of achieving escape velocity. Without its outmoded navigation equipment to automatically hone in on a destination, Rothenburg knew it would have gone sailing silently off into the starfield, never to be seen or heard from again.

Instead a quirk of luck had led to its being found by ingenuous aliens and its pilot being returned to his people. Subsequent events had precipitated a sequence of scarcely credible concurrences culminating in the arrival proximate to the minor satellite of Treetrunk of the most powerful expeditionary force this sector of starfield had ever seen. It was hardly to be believed.

Rothenburg believed it, just as he believed that in a very short while that same pilot was going to embark on a return visit to the scene of his recent madness. All the medical technology human science and experience could muster was going to be brought to bear on that singular individual to ensure that a recurrence of his dementia did not take place. Even so, Rothenburg knew that nothing was certain. The best minds and the most skilled techniques could not warrant that upon setting foot on Treetrunk One Alwyn Mallory would not go stark raving mad or lapse into coma or otherwise react in a fashion guaranteed to drive Rothenburg, Nadurovina, and everyone else connected with the current enterprise a little crazed themselves.

They could only hope and do their best and put more trust than they wanted to in the ministrations of an ordinary duty nurse with a less-than-extensive professional history.

As so often happens at such times, events progressed in ways unforeseen by even the most adept prognosticators. Mallory allowed himself to be suited up without complaint or hesitation, joking at the ongoing process and lending a hand when and where he was able. Meantime, while everyone was focusing on the indispensable patient, they neglected to consider the condition of his personal attendant. Having never worn an environment suit before, much less been outside a ship in space, Irene Tse was rapidly working herself into a state of near hysteria.

The consequences of this were as salutary as they were unforeseen. Instead of being left to worry about himself, Mallory spent the last moments before disembarking working to soothe and reassure the nurse. Only when he was convinced of her well-being did he condescend to board the military repair vehicle that would carry them from the vast cocoon of the dreadnought to the surface of the tiny moon below. This time it was he who gripped her hand reassuringly.

They were not alone. A small flotilla of armed lifeboats, repair craft, and other vessels awaited, hovering like so many incandescent bees around a darkened, mottled hive. Their operators had been primed to respond instantly to any requests from Mallory—once these had been quietly cleared by Major Rothenburg or one of the two extensively briefed lieutenants who were assisting him.

The major's declaration that if circumstances demanded it they would tear the moon apart to find the mollysphere was held in abeyance. Stir up the satellite's surface and they might bury the inestimably precious recording permanently. Or worse, the abysmally low gravity might allow it to drift off into space. In respect of everything that could go wrong, each ship kept its preassigned distance. Only one descended, with infinite deliberation and care, to the surface of the moon itself.

It did not quite achieve touchdown. Hovering just above the battered, eroded surface, it adjusted its position until the best records available insisted it was occupying the exact same coordinates as the patient's lifeboat had previously. Even the north-south axis of the repair craft was oriented identically. Stepping outside, Mallory theoretically should be able to recognize his surroundings, theoretically ought to be capable of retracing his steps to the spot where he had buried the recording.

Theoretically.

He entered the lock effortlessly and without apparent trepidation. Two techs preceded him while a third accompanied a visibly agitated Tse. She was controlling herself with an effort, insistent upon being included in the excursion, knowing that if Mallory suffered a relapse she wanted to be with him. She needed to be with him, and not just for his sake. Their relationship had progressed beyond that. Nadurovina followed her into the lock while a fourth tech signaled to those on the other side of the barrier that all was well and the landing party was ready to proceed.

All was not well, but Tse knew how to utilize various mind- and breath-control techniques to stabilize her system. Such skills were part of her training. It was the first time she had used them on herself, however, and not on a patient. Controlling her emotions was another matter entirely. Somehow she managed that as well.

The outer door opened, and the dusky light of Treetrunk's star poured in. The first pair of techs exited efficiently, one after the other floating gently down to the rocky surface. In defiance of proper procedure, Mallory insisted on taking Tse's hand and egressing with her. To everyone's unspoken relief, the tandem descent was accomplished without incident.

Once the entire landing party had left the repair craft, Mallory moved clear of the group and sought to establish his bearings. If the larger vessel was positioned exactly the same as his lifeboat had been when he had been marooned here, then there ought to be a hill resembling a broken tooth approximately forty degrees to his right. Turning in that direction, he was gratified to see that the landmark was exactly where and how he remembered it. Approximately fifty meters from where he was standing there would be a small, shallow crater. As he paced off the span, the others followed at a respectful distance. No one watched his movements with more intensity than Irene Tse.

The crater was a little farther than he remembered it, but it was unarguably the same depression. To make certain, he walked off the diameter. Seven meters, more or less. Remembrances were lining up like winning numbers on a gambling machine, with a jackpot payoff at the end no bigger than a fingernail. Looking back at the hovering repair craft to properly orient himself, he drew a mental line in the rock between the ship and the snaggle-topped hill. Walking to the half-meter-high rim of the crater, he looked down at its edge, searching for the large, flat rock he had placed there. It had a distinctive triangular shape, which was why he had chosen it.

The rock was not there.

Frowning behind the faceplate of his suit, he followed the crater's rim to the right. Still no sign of the marker he had carefully left behind. When he had walked perhaps a fifth of the way around the crater he retraced his steps and began searching in the other direction. Tse advanced to join him. The consequent intimacy was only physical. Anything they said to one another could be overheard clearly by everyone else in the group, as well as by the crew of the repair craft and, via relay, everyone listening back on board the dreadnought.

"It's here." Mallory paused long enough to look over at Tse, their faceplates nearly touching. "I know it's here."

"Of course it is," she told him reassuringly. "It's only natural for you to be a little disoriented. It's been a long time, and you had other things on your mind when you hid it."

"I'm not disoriented!" Seeing her flinch behind the faceplate he hastened to apologize. "Really, I know exactly where I am. Sometimes my words still get all mixed up, but not my actions. Everything is just as I remembered it." Turning, he indicated the location and position of the repair craft, the jagged hilltop looming in the distance, the shallow circular crater. "This is all correct. Everything is where it should be. Except for that damn rock."

"Which damn rock?" she inquired quietly. "I'll help you look for it." Turning her head, she glanced back in the direction of the assembled group. "We'll all help."

Mallory hesitated. It was his rock, his potential vindication, and he wanted to find the damn thing. But it wasn't where it was supposed to be.

Maybe he was forgetting something. Or maybe he was imagining it after the fact. Maybe . . . maybe the Pitar who had visited him in the hospital room had been right all along and his brain was inventing elaborate cover-ups for his debased memory. Panic threatened to rise in his throat like vomit.

"Okay, sure. Why not? Everyone can have a look. The important thing is not who finds the rock but finding it, right?" Smiling tenderly behind her faceplate, Tse nodded encouragement. The others gathered around.

"We're looking for a flat stone about this big." Mallory used his hands to trace size and shape in the vacuum. "About eight centimeters thick. No other distinguishing features."

"What color is it?" asked one of the techs from the ship.

Mallory had to laugh. "Look around. You've got a choice of two: dark gray and darker gray. It's the shape that's significant."

The party split, half searching to the left, the other half marching methodically in the opposite direction. When they met unsuccessfully on the other side of the crater they passed each other and kept going. By the time they met again, back at the original starting point, discouragement and the first flickerings of serious mistrust were beginning to make their psychological presence felt among several of the searchers.

"Are there any other identifying landmarks?" Nadurovina probed as gently as she could. It would not do to challenge the patient too forcefully or say anything accusatory. Upsetting him could only have deleterious mental consequences.

She need not have worried. Mallory was already actively upsetting himself. The strain showed clearly on his face.

If he had imagined burying the mollysphere, then maybe he had imagined having it. If he had imagined having it, who knows what else his mind had invented? The presence of the Pitar? Not the devastation of Treetrunk—that was real enough. All too much proof of the atrocity was hanging in the sky on the other side of the small moon. Under incredible psychological pressure and mental stress, had he written on the blank sheet of his memory an elaborate scenario that had never taken place, that was the product of an overheated imagination instead of cold, composed reportage?

He could see the faces of his companions through the transparencies of their faceplates, could see the skepticism stirring in their expressions. Outwardly they remained committed and supportive, but within themselves they were beginning to question, to wonder, and he lay square at the nexus of their mounting uncertainties.

Where was that damn rock? A man could contrive any number of chimeras, but a rock was a real thing: solid and unforgiving, a piece of stellar matter made hard and cold. Ignoring the accusing stares, he focused on the surface on both sides of the crater: scanning, searching, scrutinizing. There were plenty of rocks, hundreds of rocks. Some were the right size, but none were quite the proper shape, and not one was where it had been when he'd first decided on the hiding spot.

"We have to go back." The voice of the tech reverberated like a bell in Mallory's helmet: tolling failure, ringing fiasco. He was studying a gauge. "Overall, group air is down to fifteen percent. Return to ship is standard security procedure."

Tse remained at Mallory's side. "It's okay, Alwyn. While the suits are recharged we'll have something to eat and drink. We'll talk about it, and you can collect your thoughts. Then we'll try again." She smiled hopefully. "Maybe all you need is a fresh start."

"That's right." Though it was not required of her, Nadurovina did her best to encourage him. "If you stepped out of the ship facing the wrong way, you could have started off on the wrong tangent right at the beginning."

"We'll recheck the location and orientation of the repair boat, too." Rothenburg's tone belied the helpfulness of his words. "If it's off even a few degrees it would mess everything up."

Everything was already messed up, Mallory thought apprehensively. The repair craft was properly positioned. He knew that was the case because the cracked hill stood exactly where it ought to be. So did the crater. He knew it was the right crater not only because it was situated precisely where it belonged, but because it was the proper size, shape, and depth. He *remembered*. There was nothing wrong with his memory—unless he was so seriously impaired that his imaginings had become that real to him. If that was the case, then maybe what he thought was reality was in fact the foundation of his madness. Maybe he wasn't even here, on this runt rock of a satellite. Maybe he was lying in a hospital somewhere back on Earth, with a solicitous but otherwise disinterested Tse bending over him. He'd been given a lot of medication, he knew. Maybe his return to Treetrunk was drug-induced instead of Kurita-Kinoshita powered.

"Alwyn, don't look like that!" Tse was at his side, gripping his suit and shaking him. "You're scaring me."

Blinking, he nodded slowly as he met her gaze. "It's nice to have company. I'm scaring me, too." Gently disengaging his arm, he turned to look at and past the crater rim. "This is *right*. Everything is right. It's just as I remember it. The rock should be here. The recording should be under it."

He became aware that the two techs were now flanking him. "Mr.

Mallory, sir," one of them was saying inside his helmet, "we're running low on air. Regulations require that we return to the ship for recharging."

Angry and confused, he allowed himself to be led back toward the waiting repair boat. Aware that their words were common currency via the suit channel, none of his companions voiced their thoughts or feelings. Vacuum helped to dissipate the growing tension, but could not banish it entirely.

Halfway back to the ship, Mallory halted as if shot. When he whirled to confront Rothenburg, the officer recoiled slightly but held his ground. He did not care for the look on the patient's face.

"When the technicians from the *Ronin* retrieved my lifeboat, what method did they use?"

"Excuse me?" Taken aback by the abruptness of the question as well as the confrontation, Rothenburg stalled for time.

"How did they reclaim it?" Mallory was in a fit of impatience, not madness. "Did they use a tractor beam from the big ship, did service personnel adjust its position before signaling for it to be taken aboard, did they try to fire the boat's engine? What recovery techniques were employed?"

"I don't know," the major admitted. "But I can find out." Switching to suit to boat to mothership relay, Rothenburg conveyed the query while Mallory and the rest of the party waited. Not in silence, though, or in contentment.

"Really, Mr. Mallory," the tech standing on his right declared. "Suit air is approaching ten percent. We absolutely must return to the boat."

"You go on if you want to." All of Mallory's attention was focused on Rothenburg, waiting for a reply, waiting for an explanation. "I'm not finished here yet. Ten percent is more than I need." At his side, a hesitant but supportive Tse stood with him. With an effort of will, she avoided looking down at her own suit gauge.

Rothenburg finally switched back to suit-to-suit. "Two manned repair craft were used to move your old boat from here to the *Ronin*. They were smaller than the one we came down on, but larger than your lifeboat."

"Propulsion systems." With that Mallory turned and began to retrace their original line from the repair ship, not walking deliberately this time but moving in long, bounding strides through the low gravity. Each time he touched down his feet kicked up a cloud of slow-settling dust—dust and small rocks.

Nadurovina was visibly concerned, and Tse's expression bordered on the frantic; but Rothenburg saw and understood. By running Mallory was not just returning as rapidly as possible to the crater: He was delivering a lesson in physics. Ignoring the rising plaints of the technicians, the major raced after the retreating patient.

Arriving at the crater's edge he found Mallory once more searching the terrain. Not along the crater's rim this time, but beyond. Well beyond. Without a word he moved off to one side and commenced hunting on his own. He heard Nadurovina long before she reached him.

"What's going on? You heard the tech. We have to return to the ship!"

"Five minutes," the excited officer told her. "Another five minutes. Then we'll all go back together. Right, Mallory?"

"Right," the spirited reply came. Some private epiphany had restored the patient's spirits even as they had revived Rothenburg's enthusiasm for the mission. "Five minutes. And if we don't find it then, we'll come back and spend some real time looking for it. Everybody, five minutes! Look for the rock."

Tse fell to searching alongside him. "I thought you told us that you placed it on the rim of the little crater, Alwyn. In a line between your lifeboat and the broken hill."

"I did." Not looking up, he continued moving methodically over the airless landscape, head down, searching, searching. "But when repair craft came from the *Ronin* to recover my lifeboat, one of them might have positioned itself with its grapplers facing that way." He rose just long enough to point directly behind them, back toward the waiting boat. "When it fired its thrusters to commence the return to the cruiser, the exhaust blast would have come *this* way." One arm swept around in a wide, swooping arc that terminated with his hand pointed toward the ragged promontory. "It would have blown dust and debris in the direction of the hill."

Her eyes widened slightly. "And rocks."

He nodded vigorously. "Maybe even a few big rocks. Maybe even one shaped like a triangle."

They found it with six percent air remaining in their suits. There was nothing under it. Another man might have been crushed by the sphere's absence, but not Mallory. He recognized every rill in the stone, every pore, every crack. It was his rock, the one he had positioned as a marker over the container holding the recording. Half mad at the time he might have been, but the sane half had known what it was doing. Of that infinitely priceless little sealtight there was no sign.

"It's here." Carefully he put the rock down. "For God's sake, everyone watch where you step." His head was in constant motion, minutely scrutinizing the surface around the feet of his companions as well as his own.

Nadurovina studied the gently rolling, dust- and grit-covered terrain.

"We'll need dozens of searchers. Even with numbers it could take months to find anything in this."

"If the exhaust blast from the repair vehicle blew a rock this size so far from the crater's rim, the container holding the recording would have been blown ten times as far." Rothenburg was looking not at his feet, but off in the distance.

"Not necessarily," Mallory argued. "It could have been blasted down into the dust, or become caught up against another rock, or the rim of one of these smaller craters. It could be an arm's length from here, or a hundred."

The major was nodding. He was doing what he did best, what he most enjoyed: organizing. "Everyone will be properly instructed. We'll bring shape sensors in, and have some simple mesh boxes made up for sifting dust. We'll find it." His tone was decisive.

"Unless it was blown off into space," one of the techs contended. "The gravity here is so weak."

"That is a possibility." The ever-rational Rothenburg was compelled to entertain the unthinkable. "But to push away from the surface the thrusters on the repair craft that retrieved his lifeboat would have been directed downward. I would lay odds that the container is still here somewhere, buried in the dust or jammed up against a redeeming rock." The muscles of his face were tight. "We have to believe that."

Had the Unop-Patha chanced to return to the inner moon of Argus V they would have been astonished to find more than a hundred space-suited humans busying themselves like ants on a portion of the insignificant satellite's surface. Finding humans more than a little baffling anyway, the frenetic activity being carried out in the complete silence of the void would only have added to their bewilderment.

Responding to Rothenburg's directive, the task force was prepared to remain on station for a month. Settling in for a long, monotonous stay proved unnecessary.

The young ensign who entered the cafeteria two days later had not even taken the time to remove her sweat-stained undersuit. Accompanied by two companions and a senior officer she made her way to the table in the far corner and presented herself to a questioning Nadurovina with a crisp salute. Without further ado she swung a small metallic bag from her side to her front, unsealed it, reached inside, and removed an object that she placed gently on the table.

"Is this it?" she asked without preamble.

Resting on the table, between a chicken sandwich on cracked wheat and a rangeweed salad, was the most important single object in the Arm. It did not look like much. The tumble it had taken from the back blast of the rescuing repair craft's thrusters had left its surface pitted and one corner crumpled. The seal, however, was intact.

Mallory was surprised at how steady his fingers were as he reached across table and food to pick it up. Almost casually, he disregarded the seal. The lid flipped open. Inside lay a small, gleaming, one-centimeter-in-diameter silvery sphere that glistened metallically beneath the overhead lights of the cafeteria, even though there was no metal in it.

Unable to contain herself, Irene Tse threw her arms around Mallory's neck and shoulders and hugged him so hard that the psychiatrist feared he would drop the container. There was little chance of that. For the foreseeable future it was wedded to the patient's hand: a small, square, silvered sixth digit. The former patient, she corrected herself. Standing by the side of the table, the ensign who had found the box beamed proudly. No one had acknowledged her question. No one had to.

A somber Tse stared at the unprepossessing contents of the box. "So much tragedy in such a tiny space."

Mallory nodded. "It's full of death. Death, and justification. I wish the two weren't joined." Putting it back in the sealtight, he closed the lid but did not try to reactivate the container. Frankly, he was unsure if the battered seal could be repowered. "Intelligent beings are going to die because of what's on that mollysphere. A lot of intelligent beings."

"I hope so, sir," one of the other soldiers who had accompanied the ensign declared. Standing at attention, he was not smiling. "One of my cousins and his family were colonists on Treetrunk."

"Better no one jumps to any conclusions." Pushing back from the table, Nadurovina rose. "We must go inform Rothenburg and the rest of the staff. Meanwhile, let's pray that the sphere is still functional and that it contains more than tridee of Argusian fauna and scenes of settlement life." She started for the doorway.

Mallory and Tse followed. She was leaning against him. "I don't care what happens now, or if the sphere operates, or what's on it. Finding it vindicates you, Alwyn."

"I know. But I don't care if I'm absolved. I want what I saw and experienced to be vindicated. Not me." In what should have been a moment of triumph, his expression was forlorn, his tone bleak. "The psyche is exonerated. Let's hope the same holds true for the technology."

17

Herringale had been chosen by lot from the pool of qualified candidates. Inoffensive, gentle voiced, with a physical profile from which all the rough edges had long since been buffed by time, he was one of those faceless but professional bureaucrats who do most of the work for little of the recognition. An engraved plaque now and again or an extra day's paid vacation were all the extra reward someone of his position and demeanor could reasonably expect.

Now he was waiting to receive Suin-Bimt, the ranking Pitar on Earth. He was not nervous, and in fact was looking forward to it. He would control himself, he knew. His life had been spent in controlling himself. It was one of the reasons he had been chosen to conduct the interview.

The conference chamber was very large for two. An enormous curved window, seemingly poured in one piece and unsupported by braces throughout its length, overlooked the Bodensee. Ancient castles were visible along the lakeshore, and snow crowned the majestic rampart of the northern Alps. Gleaming golden, a meeting table capable of seating thirty in comfort shone behind him. He and Suin would not need it. They would use two comfortable chairs and a small round table instead.

The Pitar entered from the far corridor, the doors sliding silently apart to admit him. Locating Herringale as his host rose, Suin altered course toward him. When he extended a hand in the customary human fashion, the much smaller human took it politely, then gestured that they both should sit.

Outside, pleasure boats cruised the calm waters of the immense alpine lake. The sun shone brightly, filtered by the glass. On the small table between them stood two tall glasses and a citrine pitcher filled with ice water. Suin took in the view and smiled.

"This is very pleasant. I was told my presence was required here, so I came. Not for long, I hope. I have a full schedule today."

"It shouldn't take much of your time." Fingering the arm of his chair, Herringale activated the player. A large rectangular heads-up display darkened in the center of the window, blocking out a portion of the villatic view of the lake and mountains. "I've been asked to watch a recording with you and seek your comments. It's been cleaned up a little, but I'm told it's more or less identical to the original. There's water, and glasses. If you need anything else, ask me."

"What kind of recording?" The Dominion's ambassador settled back in the easy chair. "One of your frenetic entertainment features? Or is it music? I quite like your music."

"There's no music," Herringale told him quietly, "and it's not entertainment."

The display flickered briefly. An added title appeared, giving time, date, and length as well as other relevant vitals. Herringale was watching the Pitar, not the display. He had already seen the recording. More than once.

Everything that appeared was from the point of view of a moving recorder. The images drifted dreamily in the air in front of the window, rendered in soft tridee or what the ancients would have called bas-relief. Adjusting the display controls would have brought them forward in full three dimensions, but Herringale and his superiors saw no need for that. There was enough to comprehend in the reduced format.

Suin watched for a while without commenting. Insofar as Herringale could tell, the Pitar's expression did not change. Twice, he turned slightly to pour himself a glass of water. Only when the recording reached its end did the alien turn to regard his host. During the replay the ambassador had shown no emotion, had offered no comment.

"Very imaginative. And very insulting. I am forced to inquire as to the rationale behind such an expensive travesty. Your entertainment people are very clever, but this is not in any wise amusing."

"We are in agreement on that," Herringale informed him stiffly. "It is not amusing. Nor was what you have just seen the product of our 'entertainment' people. It is a tridee media recording, broadcast on Treetrunk at the time of its invasion and recorded by an alert citizen who had access to more professional equipment than the average resident."

"Absurd." The Pitar's voice was unchanged. "No record of the devastation of that unfortunate world exists. If it did, it would have come to light long before now."

"It was hidden," Herringale explained. "And only recently recovered."

The Pitar shifted his position in the cradling chair. "I had been given to understand that your people had scoured the surface of Argus Five and continue to do so without finding anything remotely like what you have just forced me to watch."

"That is so. However, this recording was not found on Treetrunk. It lay buried and unnoticed on Treetrunk One, the smaller of that martyred world's two moons. A refugee who fled during the invasion concealed it there. He is the same person who made the recording."

Ambassador Suin was repeatedly making the Pitarian gesture that signified negativity. "No one escaped the destruction. Your own people say so." He shifted his legs preparatory to rising. "I do not like this game, and I have important work to supervise."

"Oh, please." Herringale leaned forward sharply. "Humor me a moment longer. This really is very important."

Impatient and reluctant, the ambassador retained his seat. "I disagree, but very well. A few moments more, and then I really must go."

"Yes. Just a few moments. Does the name Alwyn Mallory mean anything to you?"

The Pitar's expression rippled. "No. Is this person attached to the diplomatic mission here?"

"Hardly. He's not even attached to the government. One of your people on the other side of the planet, a diplomatic attaché named Dmis, has met him."

"I do not know that name, either. I am not expected to know the names of everyone assigned to duty on your world, any more than you would be required to identify everyone working in the diplomatic arm of your government."

Herringale nodded. "Maybe you should contact and converse with Dmis. He met Mr. Mallory, so he knows that he is a real person. We also know that Mr. Mallory is a real person—an unusually independent and resourceful one. Among other things, Alwyn Mallory is an ex–starship engineer. As a hobby, he obtained and restored a ship's lifeboat of antiquated design. It was adequate to convey him to the far side of the moon in question, together with a copy he had made of this remote media broadcast. To ensure its safety, he buried the recording on the moon. It has only recently been recovered."

"A very disturbing story." Suin pressed outer edges of his hands together in the formal Pitarian manner. Like all his kind he was an extraordinarily handsome individual, tall and regal. Granted unlimited access to the skills of Earth's finest cosmetic surgeons, Herringale knew he could never look half so imposing.

"The recording has been authenticated. Among the methods employed to do this was the extensive excavation of the specific locales imaged in the tridee. Everything matches up, from the ruined buildings to the traces of blood found in the city of Weald's central square." He found that he was compelled to take a swallow of cold water. "I am told that such traces are extensive. Having viewed the recording several times previously, even as a nonexpert I can understand this."

"I am leaving now." The ambassador moved to rise. Herringale rose with him. The Pitar towered over the soft-bodied, middle-aged diplomat.

"We have many questions." Herringale's voice was as calm as when he had first greeted the alien. "Foremost among these is the desire to know the reason behind the careful evisceration of so many females and the concurrent careful preservation of their reproductive organs. I admit that I am personally interested. I have two daughters of approximately the same age as the young women who are shown in the recording being disemboweled while still alive." Without realizing what he was doing, he reached out to pluck at the ambassador's sleeve. "Please, won't you explain? I'm really, really curious."

Suin stared down at him. "I intend to register a formal protest with my government. To waste my time with such nonsense is bad enough, but to subject me to additional slander borders on wanton malice."

"Go ahead and register," Herringale told him. Something was rising within the career diplomat, and he fought hard to suppress it. Professional self-control was a major reason, after all, why he had been chosen for this morning's work. "It is possible your complaint will arrive before my government's formal declaration of war."

The ambassador finally showed some emotion, though it was as subdued as all such Pitarian reactions. "What kind of joke are you making? You can't mean that your people would begin a war based on a single recording purportedly made by a lone human?"

"The recording has been validated. Mr. Mallory's reminiscences have been validated. The decision of the world council was unanimous. The colonies have been informed, and their respective individual councils wholeheartedly concur. In effect, the war has already begun. It will be interesting to observe the consequences. There are those pundits who insist that interstellar war is an oxymoron. We are about to find out." Despite efforts to control himself, his tone darkened somewhat. "Your people are about to find out."

"Is there no stopping this travesty?"

Herringale gazed up at the much taller alien. He found that he was not intimidated. "Beginning at six o'clock tonight, Greenwich mean time, the recording made by Mr. Mallory will be broadcast across the planet and on all the colonies. It will be flanked by detailed information explaining the nature of the recording and how it came to be. The program will be followed by the official announcement of mobilization. Reservists are already reporting to their positions and their ships. I have been asked to conclude this meeting, Ambassador Suin, by informing you that you and your entire staff are under arrest, and heretofore should regard yourselves as prisoners of war." This time it was the sallow-faced human who smiled.

"You cannot reciprocate, of course, since you have never allowed us to establish a formal mission on either of the Twin Worlds. In the light of what we now know, such puzzling decisions on your part strike us as ever more suspicious."

"Are there to be no ends to these insults?" Suin drew himself up to his full, impressive height. "By your own laws, my staff and I have diplomatic immunity."

"I'm sorry, but after viewing that recording there is little inclination among any of my people, be they members of the diplomatic corps or the local janitorial staff or the general populace, to grant any kind of immunity to any Pitar. In fact, I can honestly say that if the privilege were bestowed upon me, I would take great pleasure in cutting you into smaller and smaller pieces of raw meat right here in this room, even at the risk of permanently staining a very expensive and historically important floor covering."

Suin was striding toward the doorway. "I refuse to stand here and be subjected to continued insult and innuendo."

"You don't have to," Herringale called after him. "You can keep going and be subject to continued insult and innuendo later."

Herringale was not quite finished with the ambassador. Confronted beyond the doorway by a quartet of heavily armed and armored security personnel, the Pitar surprised them by drawing a weapon of unknown type from a hidden compartment within his left pants leg. It must have been a well-shielded compartment in order for the diplomat to have successfully blinded the security scanners that monitored all comings and goings to the inner chancellery. There was no need for a diplomat to carry a weapon, Herringale mused as he ducked down behind one of the chairs, unless the possessor had something to fear—or was particularly paranoid.

They never found out in Suin's case because, after wounding two of the guards, the Pitarian ambassador died in a blaze of gunfire as he attempted to flee the building. An offer to remand the remainder of his colleagues into protective custody was declined with disdain. Following the general broadcast of the Mallory record, as it came to be known, a mob stormed the building housing the Pitarian embassy in Zurich. Defending themselves, the Pitar killed several dozen people before the military could intervene. The aliens perished to the last.

Similar confrontations took place wherever Pitar could be found, from the supposedly inviolate compound on Bali to more isolated urban facilities in Brisbane, Delhi, and Lala. Within twenty-four hours of the worldwide broadcast of the unexpurgated recording, not a Pitar was left alive on Earth.

At the time, there were two Pitarian vessels in orbit. In attempting to flee, one was blown apart while the other managed to escape. It being impossible to track a ship in space-plus, the pursuing humans terminated the chase halfway between the moon and distant Mars.

All the while, warships and supply vessels were in the process of assembling—not only in the vicinity of Earth, but around its far-flung colonies as well. From Proycon to Centaurus, from New Riviera to Mantis, ships and personnel gathered. There was no singing of patriotic songs, no mass rallies of fervid supporters. It was all business, serious business, and was organized and conducted accordingly.

Some hoped that the Pitar would admit their crime and capitulate, following which suitable punishment and penalization could be decided upon. Others prayed that the aliens would resist. As the Twin Worlds of the Dominion did not lie that far from either the galactic plane or the expanding human sphere of influence, an answer to these questions was expected soon.

Once they had been informed of Pitarian responsibility for the Treetrunk atrocity, outrage was general among every other civilized species. It did not translate into action, however. The quarrel was between humankind and Pitar, and it would be left to those two civilizations to settle the matter. The Quillp, the Unop-Patha, and everyone else expressed their regret and sorrow and then stood back to see which species would prevail. In this regard the AAnn proffered their condolences as fervently as anyone else, while quietly hoping that both powerful space-going races would permanently and severely incapacitate one another in the coming conflict.

Among the thranx the reaction was one of subdued fury. Arising as they did from an ancient line that had succeeded partly by venerating a single egg-laying queen, they were especially sensitive to any violation of the reproductive system. What the Pitar had done to and with human females sent a ripple of rage through every hive. Even as the humans methodically assembled a vast force to attack the Twin Worlds, vexatious debate seethed among the thranx on how best to respond to the unimaginable barbarity.

"It does not involve us."

Sprawled atop a convenient log, Wirmbatusek regarded the lake. It was a small body of water surrounded by dense tropical forest, a refuge high in the mountains of Lombok. Nearby, Asperveden was waltzing with a birdwing butterfly, letting it flutter from one truhand to another. Perhaps the huge, iridescent green ornithop recognized a distant alien cousin. More likely it just found the thranx's chitinous digits a convenient place to rest.

"Of course it involves us."

Raising a truhand, Asperveden examined the exquisite creature. Compound eye met compound eye. Beautiful, the attaché mused. What the butterfly felt was not recorded. Eventually it tired of the game and flew off, soaring up into the tall vine-draped hardwoods, a pair of thin emerald slabs throwing back the sun.

Wirmbatusek turned his head and antennae in the direction of his friend and coworker. "Keeping a constant watch on the AAnn is enough to worry about. Why would the Grand Council choose to weaken our own defenses to support a massive effort to punish a race that has done nothing to us?"

Exhibiting uncharacteristic daring, Asperveden walked forward until all four trulegs were in the water. Astonished at his own boldness, he stood and watched as the tepid, algae-stained green liquid swirled gently around his limbs. Where he was standing the lake was perhaps ten centimeters deep.

Wirmbatusek's antennae twitched nervously. "Are you insane? Get out of there! Suppose the soil is soft and you begin to sink? Don't expect me to pull you out."

The slightly smaller thranx gestured for his companion to be calm. "Have no fear. The surface underfoot is firm and unyielding. These Pitar have violated every accepted norm of civilized behavior."

"No one disputes that." Wirmbatusek watched a line of ants marching along the base of the log. To a single ant, the insectoid thranx might well have been a vision of God. "No one disagrees with the humans' urge to seek revenge. We would doubtless react similarly, albeit less noisily, if the barbarity had been visited upon us. But it was not. What happened on Argus Five does not concern us."

"Why not? Because only mammals died? Because only human females were dishonored?"

"It is too facile to say that we should help the humans." Sliding off the log, Wirmbatusek settled himself on his trulegs. Using all four hands he daintily picked bits of bark and other debris from his gleaming blue-green exoskeleton and the thorax pouch that hung from his second major body segment. "First, they have not asked us, or any other species, for assistance. Next, it is not incumbent on the thranx to aid them because there is no treaty or agreement between our two races particularizing any such action. There are no reasons for us to become involved and many why we should keep our distance. For one thing, like so much else about them the martial capability of these Pitar is unknown. We could end up having allied ourselves with the losing side." He flicked a fallen leaf from his abdomen.

"I would not bet against the humans in a war." Finally starting to grow uneasy at the feel of water lapping around his legs, Asperveden carefully backed out of the shallows.

"Nor would I, but neither would I choose to gamble with the neutrality that preserves our civilization unscathed. War is not a lark, and gambling on it not entertainment."

One foot at a time, Asperveden shook water from his impermeable chitin. "The estimable Desvendapur would have much to say about this situation."

"No doubt, if he was living. I wish I could have seen him perform. To my knowledge none of his poetry dealt with war, despite the gravity of his clan and family history." The larger thranx followed a pair of hornbills as they glided across the lake. "What makes you think the humans would accept our help even if it were to be offered? A great many of them despise us and cannot even stand to be in our presence. Those of us here and at the Amazon hive are isolated from such individual conflicts."

"I realize that our relations are still developing." Feeling the first pangs of morning hunger, Asperveden began to remove food from his own pouch. "I am not naïve. Much work remains to be done to bring our two peoples together to the point where trust is accepted instead of debated, and genuine friendship is not an isolated occurrence." Biting into a starch loaf with all four opposing jaws, he chewed reflectively. "This conflict would be a perfect opportunity to do just that."

Approaching his friend, Wirmbatusek waited to be offered food, withholding his own offering until the smaller thranx made the appropriate gesture. "More than strategic concerns are involved in this. As many thranx are suspicious of the humans as they are of us. It is hard enough to arrange for meetings, for cultural exchanges, for agreements on minor matters. An alliance that includes provisions for mutual defense lies far in the future."

"It need not require a formal association." Asperveden executed the appropriate hand gestures, following which his friend responded in kind. They exchanged food. "The arrangement could be temporary, and understood as such by both sides. Assistance in time of and solely for the duration of conflict, superseding all current agreements, after which the previous status is resumed."

Wirmbatusek considered. "I am envisioning several fully armed hive warships emerging from space-plus at safe distance beyond the orbit of this world's moon. I am envisioning the human reaction. I am not sanguine about what I am seeing."

"Hive ships need not enter this system. A mutual rendezvous point elsewhere could be agreed upon." Asperveden refused to acknowledge the impossibility of his hypothetical proposal. "The humans would be grateful. It would advance our relationship and improve our mutual prospects immeasurably."

Swallowing, Wirmbatusek began to hunt in his pouch for the spiral-spouted drink bottle. "If we are victorious. If the Pitar should win, we would have acquired their enmity for nothing."

"Not true," Asperveden argued. "We would still have gained the gratitude of the humans."

"Would we?" Slipping the decorated drinking tube between his jaws, the larger worker began to sip sugary, nutritious liquid. "You ascribe to humans a quality of gratefulness I have yet to see demonstrated." He passed the bottle over. "First I would like to see one invite me into its home without an expression of disgust on its face. Then I might consider rendering it some assistance. If we remain neutral we are detached in the eyes of Pitar and human alike. We risk nothing. That is what the Quillp, and the Unop-Patha, and even the AAnn are doing. Why should we do any differently?"

Asperveden contemplated the tranquil lake, the intriguingly different indigenous wildlife, the warm, clear, morning air, and felt himself troubled. "I do not know. Perhaps because we are better than they?"

Wirmbatusek chose to comment via a sequence of circumspect clicks. "Anything else?"

"Nothing that could be construed as conclusive. Only that, unlike many who count themselves true progeny of the First Queen, I happen to *like* humans."

"So do I," Wirmbatusek confessed freely. "But that does not mean I am ready to march out of the hive to sacrifice limb and life alongside them."

18

The armada was unlike anything that humankind, or for that matter any of the other species that happened to dwell in that same portion of the Arm, had seen before. Less what was necessary to protect and defend Earth and its other colonies, every armed vessel propelled by a KK-drive was assigned a position and time to rendezvous on the outskirts of the Dominion. It was believed that the Pitar would meet them there, somewhere in the vicinity of their system's twelfth and outermost world. It was also conceded that Pitarian vessels ranging far and wide would at least make an attempt to assault one or more of the human populated worlds, if only to divert attention from their own.

Neither threat materialized. Human strategists were perplexed. The xenologists who had studied the Pitar were not.

Levi was one of those who was not. Others like him had been assigned to the armada, one to a ship so that in the event of catastrophe all the members of his group and the valuable knowledge they represented could not be lost in a single blow. If not the fleetest of mind or the most experienced member of the team that had studied the Pitar since first contact, he was acknowledged the senior member of the group. His opinion was solicited and respected. He found himself on the *Wellington*, seconded to the general staff.

It was subsequent to a meeting where the plan of first attack was being finalized that he found himself, thoroughly preoccupied with the critical matters at hand, strolling aimlessly through the great ship. As big as anything mobile that mankind had yet put in space, the *Wellington* was an impressive achievement. Four rings of armaments located in evenly spaced weapons blisters girdled the main body of the dreadnought. The KK-drive generating fan that spread out before it and pulled it through space-plus was the size of a small town. Between fan, hydrogen spark plug, and the main body of the ship were five defensive-screen generators. No more powerful or fearsome ship cruised the cosmos. It was a supreme example of contemporary human technology, an other-than-light vessel representing a confluence of all that human civilization had thus far accomplished.

That it was designed expressly to blow things up placed it squarely in the mainstream of human technological achievement.

Meyer Levi was a civilian attached to a military expedition. He was an old man who ought to have been reclining in a soft chair in a library, fronted by a tridee screen and surrounded by real books, a hot drink steaming on a nearby table, and a rumpled dog lying at his feet. Instead he found himself inconceivably far from home and anything akin to such imaginary comforts.

Despite the absence on the system's outer fringes of any armed confrontation, no one believed that the Pitar were simply going to allow the invading humans to put punishing landing parties down on the surface of the Twin Worlds unopposed. The timing and manner of their resistance was yet to be determined. But one by one, the warships of Earth and its colonies had emerged from space-plus into Pitarian space, uncontested and unchallenged. Now fully assembled in normal space, the armada was ready to take the next step of moving toward the system's sun and positioning itself around the Twin Worlds.

Nor had the Pitar sent ships to attack Earth itself or any of its more lightly defended colonies. There had been no reaction at all from the tall, elegant humanoids. Their representatives on Earth and elsewhere had died fighting, refusing to suffer imprisonment. All remaining Pitar, the entire population, was on their two homeworlds, presumably cognizant of and awaiting the arrival of a vast assemblage of ships crewed by tens of thousands of angry, revenge-minded humans.

What were they overlooking? Levi found himself wondering. Surely the Pitar were going to resist, were not going to commit racial suicide. But that was essentially what their isolated representatives on Earth had done. Did the entire species have a death wish that humankind had been put in the position of inadvertently satisfying?

The armada was in motion, a great swath of ships and science, when the answer came to him. Rushing as fast as his aged legs would carry him, he hurried toward the bridge. In the vastness of the great ship he lost his way several times, despite the instructions available to him in each lift.

When he finally succeeded in finding his way to the central, shielded core of the *Wellington*, he had to identify himself several times before he could gain access to Fouad. She was seated in the captain's command chair, in charge of the ship but not the strategy it would execute. That was the province of the group of general officers seated off to one side, facing one another across a wide, oval table from which projected upward a perfect three-dimensional portrait of the Pitarian system. A cloud of glowing pinpoints was moving toward the sun at its center, each pinpoint a ship. Levi was put in mind of midges attacking a dog.

"Hello, Mr. Levi." Her musician's hands rested on controls; her trained soprano voice commanded more destructive power than humankind had ignorantly unleashed upon itself since the beginning of its struggling civilization. "Feeling well?"

"Tired," he told her. "Tired, and worried."

"We're all worried," she replied. Before her hovered a tridimensional image similar to the one being closely scrutinized by the general staff, only somewhat reduced in scale. "Everyone is waiting for something to happen."

"What will you do if the Pitar do not respond?" Fascinated as always by technology he did not understand, Levi stared at the perfect, hovering representation of the space in which the ship was moving.

"Place ourselves in orbit around the first of the Twin Worlds. Deliver the ultimatum drawn up by the world council." She shrugged without smiling. "React to their reaction. If they continue to do nothing, the first landing parties will go down. These will be backed by heavy armor and orbital firepower. Once our forces have acquired a beachhead on the surface the choices remaining to the Pitar will be considerably reduced. Basically, they'll have to decide whether to opt for capitulation or seppuku. After securing the outer of the Twin Worlds, the armada will move on to the second and hopefully repeat the process."

Levi nodded. "What happens if they do submit without a fight?"

Fouad looked at him closely. "Is that what you think is going to happen?"

"No, but at this point the possibility cannot be entirely discounted."

She turned away from him, back to the glowing, in-depth representation. "That's not my department. I'll do what the general staff tells me to do. They in turn have their orders from the world council. All I know is that there's a predetermined sequence of actions whose degree of reaction is calibrated according to how the Pitar respond." Her jawline firmed. "To one extent or another, they are to be punished for what they did on Treetrunk."

"You asked me what I thought was going to happen." Levi watched her expectantly.

The captain's interest was piqued. "You have an idea?"

"I think so. You know, among the original Twelve Tribes the Levites were the scholars. I do not feel like I belong here, on a warship, preparing to engage in mass destruction."

"Your unhappiness is noted," she replied curtly. "Tell me what you think."

"I've studied the Pitar ever since they first arrived on Earth aboard the *Chagos*."

"I know that." Her tone was impatient. "Get to the point, old man. In case you haven't noticed, there's an invasion in progress."

"Sorry. There are a number of ways I could put it scientifically, but I see no need to couch an opinion in complex systematic jargon. Suffice to say that the Pitar are homebodies."

"They don't colonize. They told us that from the first." Fouad tried to divide her attention between the clustered general staff, the view tridee before her and its accompanying heads-up displays, and the lugubrious sage standing next to her seat. "It was one of the reasons their complicity in the massacre was so hard for so many to accept."

"They're not just homebodies. They're fanatical about the Twin Worlds. Except for occasional excursions to places like Earth and Hive-hom, and deviate adventures such as Treetrunk, they do not leave their home system. Not only are they not colonizers, they are not big on straightforward exploration. They simply do not like to leave home."

"Which means what? You do have a point, don't you?"

"I think so. What I am trying to say is that all the energy, and effort, and advanced technological development we have put into spreading ourselves outward, they have focused inward."

She frowned and idly adjusted the neural jack above her left ear that allowed her direct communication with the rest of the armada, her own staff, and the *Wellington*'s intelligence center. "So you're saying that . . . ?"

A little anxious himself now, Levi interrupted her in order to state the thought. "Everything we have put into offense, they may have concentrated on defense."

It was not long thereafter that the *Wellington* was rocked by explosion and near catastrophe, and the armada found itself fully and desperately engaged.

Extending in their respective orbits outward from Pitar's star were three worlds of various mien, none suitable for permanent habitation. Then the closely aligned planets numbered four and five, the Twin Worlds of the Pitarian Dominion. Between the fifth planet and the sixth, which happened also to be the first of four gas giants, was not one but two asteroid belts. While one lay in the normal plane of the ecliptic, the second occupied an orbit almost perpendicular to the first. Among this mass of planetary debris were a good many planetoidal objects of considerable size.

Every one of which had been transformed by the Pitar into an armed and shielded attack-and-support station.

In those first lunatic moments frantic commands ricocheted between ships at the speed of light. Humans and their machines slipped instantly into battle mode, each functioning efficiently and effectively. In this it was difficult to say who had the greater advantage. Machines offered speed and reliability, humans the ability to improvise in response to the unexpected. Organic and inorganic had spent several hundred years evolving in tandem to perfect the art of combat.

On the other hand, in spite of the unprecedented ferocity of the human assault and despite all their racial introspection and paranoia, the Pitar did not fold up and slink quietly back to their homeworlds.

Interstellar space is unimaginably vast. Even between planets there is room enough to lose a thousand ships. But the physics that can follow the tracks of tiny comets and minuscule asteroids are also adept at locating the operational drives designed to push vessels through space-plus. And a vessel that is propelled by anything less takes months to journey from one planetary body to another.

So while humans and Pitar swam in inky nothingness, their respective machines utilized far more sensitive instruments than eyes and ears to plot each other's courses. Every time a ship of the armada attempted to pass within the orbits of the intersecting asteroid belts it found itself confronted by two or more Pitarian warcraft. Each human vessel was parsecs from home while support for the defending ships was, astronomically speaking, an eye blink away.

And the Pitar were capable. Avoiding confrontation wherever possible, they concentrated exclusively on countering any approach to the Twin Worlds. Initially, fear of active counterattack dominated much of the general staff's strategic thinking. As the days became weeks and the weeks months it became clear that Pitarian tactics included such thrusts only insofar as they related to their defense. No attempt was made, even by a single suicidal ship, to threaten Earth or any of the colony worlds. Everything the Pitar had, every armed vessel they could throw into the conflict, remained close to home. Not one ventured beyond the Pitarian heliosphere.

The attacking humans tried everything. When a deliberate concentration of forces in one place was met by an energetic and equivalent Pitarian response, the battle planners went to the opposite extreme by suggesting an attempted englobement of one of the Twin Worlds. Reacting aggressively and quickly, the Pitar promptly dispersed their forces in precisely the most opportune fashion to counter the widespread assault. Probes of sectors presumed weak were beaten back by Pitarian forces of unexpected strength.

Missiles launched at the fifth world were detected, tracked, intercepted and destroyed. The residents of the Dominion suffered no casualties as a result of the invasion of their system. Requests to parley were met with strident animosity. It became clear that while humans had originally taken an immediate liking to the Pitar, the humanoid aliens felt very differently about their smaller mammalian counterparts. This did not take the form of outright loathing: The Pitar were too courtly for that. It was more on the order of a general contempt for the human species as a whole. The Pitar would not talk, would not discuss any sort of armistice with the lowly humans, until every last ship of the armada had left the sacred system of the Twin Worlds.

It didn't matter, since they refused to apologize for what they had done on Treetrunk or discuss handing over those responsible. One Pitar spoke for all, and all Pitar spoke for one. Admitting no guilt, they therefore dispersed it among themselves and repeatedly commanded the disgusting, detestable invading beings to depart, as their very presence constituted a corruption in the sight of the hallowed Dominion.

Their attitude helped Levi and his colleagues to unravel the rationale behind many prior enigmas: why no embassy had been allowed to open on either of the Twin Worlds, for example, and why visits to the Dominion had been prohibited. It had nothing to do with racial shyness or reticence. The Pitar were not coy—they were overbearing. Nasty, uncouth humans could not be allowed to defile the purity of the homeworlds.

To what end their plundering force had removed the reproductive organs of thousands of human females from Treetrunk continued to remain a mystery. Here it was left to an admixture of Levi's people and researching biologists to speculate on possible reasons. Many were put forth, some fantastic, not a few revolting. Among the facts that were assembled in the ongoing attempt to build an explanation was the realization that from the moment the Pitar had been contacted until the day when the armada had emerged from space-plus on the outskirts of the Dominion, no one had ever seen a Pitarian child.

Had some factor still unknown, psychological or biological, caused them to stop reproducing? In carrying out the atrocity on Treetrunk, were they seeking a means for ensuring the continuation of their species? Had that means been found and implemented, and if so, did humankind really want to be informed of the methodology? Many people on Earth and elsewhere had relatives who had perished in the extermination of intelligent life on Argus V. Levi and his colleagues were not so sure that they would be happier or otherwise better off to learn precisely what had happened to some of their deceased relations.

Certainly the Pitar did nothing to enlighten their attackers. Even tentative requests for explanations were dismissed out of hand. They would not talk, coldly refusing all attempts at communication with what they could now openly admit to regarding as an inferior life-form. Levi and the rest of the scientists and researchers who accompanied the armada grew increasingly frustrated. The uniformed masses who crewed the ships labored under no such mental strain. Some of them, too, had lost friends or kin on Treetrunk. Their interests were much more focused: They did not need to understand; all they wanted to do was kill Pitar.

Five months into the attack the ships of the armada and their frustrated personnel began to be rotated. New ships arrived from Earth and the colonies crewed by eager, fresh enlistees. They opposed an enemy whose soldiers faced no long journeys through space-plus, who could find ease and relaxation within a day's flight of their duty station. In battle they found themselves confronting concentrations of ships that could be quickly and easily repaired and restocked. It was the classic battlefield situation of an overextended attacker trying to break down the defenses of a determined and well-entrenched enemy, translocated to an interstellar environment.

Eight months passed without any change in the line of battle. The Pitar would not permit a single human vessel of any size to cross beyond the orbits of the intersecting asteroid belts. The attacking humans would not give up. Determination and not skill or strategy became the defining factor on both sides.

While ships might stand still, weapons research did not. For every new means of attack the humans refined and threw into combat, the Pitar developed a counter. High-energy beams were met with high-energy deflectors. Subatomic particle guns designed to disrupt communications on board opposing vessels were intercepted and shunted harmlessly into space-plus by low-power versions of deep-space drives. Larger, faster missiles were met with small interceptors that were faster and more agile still. Space was filled with the scattering of shattered matter from fusion weapons that never reached their intended targets.

Now and then a ship engaged in skirmishing would take a hit, suffering damage or on rare occasions, implosion. At such moments hundreds, even thousands of lives would be snuffed out of existence, vanishing into the icy limbo of the void. Each such loss made the Pitar more intractable and the humans more unforgiving.

Finally admitting after ten months of failed attack that they were unable to break through the defenses of the Dominion, the general staff debated how best to proceed. Breaking off the offensive was unthinkable: Now spread across a number of worlds, humankind would not hear of it. Ending the confrontation would imply that the Pitar had won, that they had consummated their barbarism without suffering any penalty. Such an abomination could not be tolerated.

It was remarked that while no human warship had been able to reach either of the Pitar homeworlds, neither had any of the aliens' craft been able to travel a sufficiently safe distance from those twin planets to safely engage its full drive and make the jump to space-plus. Trapped in the glare of human vigilance, the Pitar were effectively confined to their homeworlds. Other species, however, were not.

On the face of it, the notion of a blockade in space seemed unworkable. Even the comparatively tiny distances between planets allowed ample room for a ship to enter into or emerge from space-plus. Once back in normal space, however, any and every such vessel was vulnerable.

The word was passed, though not without trepidation. How would neutral intelligences such as the Quillp react to being banned from an entire system with which they had no quarrel? More importantly, how would the combative and powerful AAnn react to a unilateral attempt to restrict their access to a people with whom they enjoyed amicable if not affectionate relations?

Before such a tactic could be tried, it was the turn of the diplomats to go on the offensive. The Quillp were puzzled. But while the ornithorps were expansionists, colonizing empty worlds in the manner of humankind, they were by nature inherently unaggressive. As might have been expected, the Unop-Patha wanted nothing whatsoever to do with the ongoing conflict, preferring to stay as far away from both the arrogant Pitar and the demonstrably demented humans as possible. Several minor species, each confined to a single inhabitable world, were not important enough to enter into the equation.

Among known intelligences with enough strength to affect the balance, that left the AAnn and the thranx. The insectoids were not only amenable to the pronouncement, but had from the start been quietly supportive of the human attack on the Dominion.

The AAnn were more difficult to factor. Following intense lobbying by human diplomats, they agreed not to send any of their vessels into the Pitarian system until the military impasse there had been resolved in favor of one side or the other. Their understanding was marked by repeated thranx warnings to the effect that if the Pitar should succeed in seriously degrading humankind's military capability, it would not be past the AAnn to take advantage of the situation. In such an event, probing AAnn attacks on one or more human colonies could reasonably be anticipated.

The world council and the general staff separately advised the distressed thranx that even in the event of an unanticipated catastrophic human defeat in battle, sufficient forces had been held in reserve to ensure the safety of Earth and every one of its colonies. The thranx accepted this reassurance with a certain aplomb, but remained privately watchful and troubled. It was wonderful to observe the passionate confidence displayed by the humans, but confidence had never been of much use against the AAnn.

With every species that could possibly be impacted having been contacted and dealt with, the general staff formally announced the imposition of the blockade. Safe and assured on their twin homeworlds, the Pitar were neither impressed nor intimidated. Tens of thousands of individuals on hundreds of ships actively supported by the populations of multiple worlds maintained and strengthened the stalemate.

It was not a static standoff. From time to time specially designated components of the blockading human fleet would attempt to penetrate the seemingly immutable Pitarian defenses. Each time, utilizing newly conceived tactics and weaponry, their crews would set off full of faith and in high spirits. Each time they would return, thwarted and dispirited. And there were those terrible times when some did not return at all.

Wars of attrition are not always won by the besiegers, no matter how resourceful and resolved. Having nowhere to go, no hidden retreat, no refuge held in reserve, the Pitar fought with incredible tenacity and determination. Though their ships would hurl themselves entire, crew and all, into an enemy attacking pattern in order to disrupt it and preserve possession of a seemingly minor, insignificant asteroid, they would not commit a single vessel to an attack. Their philosophy of war was wholly defensive, to protect the twin homeworlds at all cost but not to otherwise directly challenge an invader.

The members of the armada's commanding general staff were rotated along with enlisted personnel and low-ranking civilian affiliates, but they were united in their frustration. As one admiral put it, the blockade was war conducted entirely under cover of night, where night covered nothing. There could be no surprise attacks launched on an alerted, technologically sophisticated species. Instrumentation that never slept saw to that. Mind could only do so much before it was necessary for machine to take over. For a soldier it was hard to sustain the energy and alertness demanded of a fight with an enemy one could not see. Even the enemy's worlds were no more than another bright couple of points of light in the galactic sky.

Yet no one thought of giving up. Treetrunk could not be forgotten. Even so, despite the comparative recentness of the outrage, it was already starting to fade a little in the minds of a small but growing segment of the population. The media strove to maintain interest, but a blockade is not like a series of dramatic encounters in space. The battle for control of stasis did not play as well on the evening tridee as an invasion.

Something had to be done. Something had to happen to change the unacceptable status quo, and both military and civilian strategists realized that in that regard sooner would be better than later. By now more than a year had passed since the *Wellington* and the rest of the armada had entered the system of the Pitarian Dominion to the cheers and vengeful shouts of the majority of humankind. Almost that much time had passed since there had been any perceptible change in that status. In the interim, the cheers had given way to grudging acceptance of the blockade, and the vengeful shouts to orchestrated growlings of support. The military was aware of the threat of germinating discontent, but there was nothing more they could do than what they were already doing.

Others, however, had different ideas.

19

"Why should we help them any more than we already have? Why should the hives, *cruk!ck*, get involved?"

"Yes," another member of the circle agreed. "There is no compelling reason for putting thranx lives at risk." Leaning back, the speaker raised all four hands in order to gesture simultaneously. "These humans do not even like us!"

"I can just see," still a third sarcastically declared, "these humans risking their own lives to aid us if the situation were reversed. Put them in a tunnel with only us facing danger, and they will turn and run the other way."

When the dissenters had had their say, the Tri-Eint Debreljinav activated the pickup before her and was respectfully conceded queen's dominance. Since the advent of hormonal extracts that had enabled any thranx female to lay fertile eggs, the lineage of hereditary queendom had vanished from thranx civilization. Subsequent to the enforced abdication of procreative royalty, many heraldic vestiges of those primitive times had assumed highly formalized places in thranx culture. One such was the rotating speaking position of queen's dominance.

No member of the Grand Council was more respected than Debreljinav. Not many were older; few were as perceptive. Chosen leader of both the hive Jin and the clan Av, she had advanced to the exalted position of eint at an unusually early age, retaining the post while acquiring honor and prestige over the years. Now she could rise no higher, being one of those the great mass hive of thranx had chosen to govern not only Hivehom but the colony worlds as well.

"It is clear what benefits accrue to us if we remain neutral, like the

Quillp. But what might we lose by doing so, and what more might we gain by becoming actively involved?"

An eint seated among the opposition responded without hesitation. "We lose nothing because we have nothing to gain." Sympathetic stridulation by those of like mind momentarily filled the room with the din of a hundred improperly tuned violas.

"Nothing?" a supporter of intervention argued. "We have cordial relations with the humans. Aiding them in their war would, if not make formal allies of them, leave them in our debt. When the next serious confrontation with the AAnn arises—and make no mistake, it will arise—we will be able to call upon these tumultuous mammals for assistance. Just the ability to do that will give even the most belligerent among the emperor's court pause."

"Who says the AAnn fear the humans?" a voice shouted from the other side. "What makes you think the scaled people factor the mammals into their equations?"

"Because while the AAnn may be malicious and rapacious, they are not stupid." This time it was supportive stridulations that rose in volume from the other side of the table.

The racing noise receded as Debreljinav prefigured her speech with an appropriate gesture. "Do the humans truly hate us so much that they would even refuse our help?"

A representative of one of the technical classifications rose. He was not an eint and was present, along with a number of others, because he possessed the ability to contribute special insight into specific aspects of the debate.

"Only a small number of xenophobes and fanatics among the bipeds actually hate us. Among the rest there are many who openly enjoy our company and are not afraid to say so." Compound eyes swept the attentive chamber. "The vast majority of humans belong to neither grouping. This mass remains unsure of us and our motives."

"Ingrates!" a leader of the opposition bellowed. There was discord until the Tri-Eint Sevrepesut could restore order and return dominance to the patient female standing off to his left.

Intimidated, the specialist waited for Debreljinav's gesture of encouragement to respond to the interruptive expletive. "Humans have short memories but—"

"Fine candidates for allies in time of trouble!" another representative of the skeptical shouted.

"But they are capable of grand kindnesses and gratitude. I believe that those who advocate intercession are correct. In so doing we would gain valuable allies against the AAnn, and against any others who might one day threaten the great hive." Whistles of derision and rising stridulation threatened to drown him out, but this time the specialist would not be denied.

"The AAnn Empire is strong and growing more powerful by the day! If we will not aid the humans in their just fight against the Pitar to make them our allies, then we must aid them so that the AAnn cannot. Or is that a possibility that the distinguished eints prefer not to ponder?"

The reaction from supporters of intervention as well as those of the opposition showed that it was a notion that had not been much discussed. Everyone hoped that in an ideal cosmos the humans would ally themselves with the thranx against the AAnn. Few cared to contemplate the consequences should the aggressive, militaristically accomplished mammals choose to take the side of the predacious reptilians instead.

"The humans would never support the AAnn in a disagreement with us." The eint who ventured this observation did not sound very convincing even to herself.

"Why not?" a supporter of intervention countered. "One of your own has just pointed out how much they dislike us."

"We must make them like us." Debreljinav's declaration carried the full force and weight of her considerable personality. "We cannot afford it to be otherwise."

"It will not be any easy task." The Eint Jouteszimfeq was anything but encouraging as he looked around the circle. "I have tried to study everything there is to be known about the humans. Individually they are sound, but their mass psychology is unstable. Small, insignificant things can induce vast swings in their collective consciousness. Worse, these critical effectives can in themselves be meaningless and unsupported. But by the time realization sets in, the damage has already been done." His antennae parted to sense the greatest possible number of his fellow debaters.

"We must move actively to prevent this from happening. Although it does not sound in and of itself especially scientific, making the humans 'like' us should be among our very first priorities. Simultaneously, we must endeavor to deal with those thranx who have difficulty tolerating the sight, sound, and presence of humans."

"Don't you mean the smell?" someone who wished not to be identified interjected. General whistling followed, eventually to be suppressed by Debreljinav's four-armed gesturing.

"I myself am rather more concerned with the eventual disposition of human muscle than their scent." Respectful quiet again filled the chamber. "If we cannot induce the humans to become our allies, then we must strive to make them our friends. Since we can do nothing about our shape and ancestry, which is what appears to constitute the principal basis of human dislike for us, we must find other ways of convincing them that we are worthy of their trust." Antennae spread and at the ready, she gazed around the chamber. "As a tri-eint among you, I am open to suggestions."

There were almost as many positive suggestions as there were opposing views. Unlike in ancient times, those in the minority did not suffer to have assorted limbs amputated as a consequence of losing an argument. In place of jaws and teeth and primitive weapons, only sharp words were employed. In many instances, these cut deeply enough.

Field Marshal MacCunn was conversing with Admiral Yirghiz when a comtech interrupted them. Yirghiz accepted the missive, perused it briefly, and then passed it on to MacCunn. The field marshal's face featured the protuberant, bony brows of a very early Cro-Magnon. It saddled him with an unfortunate countenance that was the source of many jokes among those within his command. Having risen from the ranks himself, he was delighted to so painlessly be of service to his troops.

"What's this about an alien task force entering Pitarian space?"

Yirghiz rose as general quarters sounded. "I haven't a clue, Hamish—but I have a feeling we're about to find out. I only hope that it's neutral, or if not, that it isn't materializing in response to a coordinated effort with the Pitar."

The bandy-legged MacCunn had to employ a longer stride to keep pace with the lanky admiral. "That would imply some sort of offensive gesture on the part of the Pitar, something totally out of character for them."

"I concur." Yirghiz nodded sharply. "Which doesn't mean we can afford to take the possibility lightly. Hence the automatic call to general quarters."

Long before the two senior officers reached the bridge at the center of the *Tamerlane*, the great warship and the rest of the blockading fleet on this side of the Dominion's sun were on full battle alert, ready to extend a polite, formal welcome to the as yet unrecognized newcomers, or to blow them out of the firmament, as the occasion demanded.

MacCunn took up his position alongside the admiral. Yirghiz was barking orders before his backside contacted the contoured command chair. "Incoming—identification!"

Captain Coulis was ready with a response. "Not ours. Not Pitar." A generally subdued murmur of relief sighed its way around the bridge at this announcement. "Thranx."

Both senior officers frowned. Their confusion had plenty of company among the rest of the bridge complement. "What are the bugs doing here?" MacCunn wondered aloud. "And with a task force, albeit a small one." He glanced in the captain's direction. "It is a small one?"

Coulis was studying a fully dimensional tridee replete with brightly hued embedded analyses. "One dreadnought. Not *Wellington*-class, taking into account that thranx design differs from ours. Nothing else appears to be bigger than destroyer-class. No cruisers, no smaller escorting craft."

"Odd configuration." Yirghiz frowned. "Too weak to participate in a serious fight, much more impressive than is required for a social call." He raised his voice as he again addressed Coulis. "Hail them, Captain, and find out what they're doing here. They're aware of the quarantine. See if you can find out what they want."

"Initial intership communications protocol is already being delimited, sir," the captain replied. At the moment her eyes were as busy as her fingers.

Answer and explanation arrived simultaneously mere moments later. Coulis swiveled around in her seat to address the two senior officers. Her expression effectively communicated her confusion.

"The vessels are indeed thranx, gentlemen. They are carrying a representative of the Grand Council of the Great Hive." Her gaze traveled from one senior officer to the other. "It wants to come aboard."

This was not the sort of decision either of the two men had expected to have to make when they had arisen at the start of the current shift. Yirghiz responded while MacCunn eloquently said nothing.

"This is your ship, Captain. Not being a strategic judgment, the decision whether or not to receive visitors is entirely yours."

"I'm a starship captain," Coulis replied. "This is a matter for diplomats."

Now MacCunn spoke up. "Not when a vessel is on combat station. No, it's your call, Captain."

Coulis rubbed at an uncooperative eyebrow. "No ship of the armada has seen any action for several weeks now. The next tactics are still in the process of being schematized. I see no reason to refuse such a request from a neutral power." She smiled laconically. "If it's secrets of military technology the thranx are after there are far easier ways to steal them."

"I've never met a thranx. Walked around tridee holos, but never encountered one in the flesh." Yirghiz was curious. "Let's see what they want here."

MacCunn grunted softly. "To try and ascertain who's winning, I would imagine. If that's the case, they'll need to use their imaginations."

Both men and everyone else on the *Tamerlane* and within the armada who obtained a good look at the thranx craft were suitably impressed. The KK-drive type vessels were sleek and well fitted out, their design and construction bespeaking a technology as advanced as anything human-kind could devise. Nor just because the alien dreadnought massed almost as much as the *Wellington* or the *Tamerlane* could it be assumed that it was the most powerful ship in the thranx arsenal.

Insisting that any formalities be kept to a minimum, the insectoid emissary transferred to one of the flagship's locks via a small shuttle. There was some confusion resulting in a delay in the visitor being wel-comed when it was discovered that he had a personal escort, but the mat-ter was quickly resolved without rancor. As Coulis pointed out, it was natural to expect so high ranking an individual of any species to be accompanied by attendants. It was explained by the thranx that the emis-sary's two escorts were necessary to look after her health and not her security, and those on board the flagship could well believe it as soon as that worthy was helped from the shuttle's lock.

The thranx was very old. One of her ovipositors had been surgically removed, the consequence of a disease that was not mentioned. The other double-curled egg-laying appendage had lost so much of its natural spring that it lay nearly flat against her back. Instead of the familiar smooth blue-green, her exoskeleton was a rich, deep purple, the chitin worn rough and pebbly in places. The golden compound eyes did not shine as brightly as did those of her solicitous escorts, but the antennae were ever-moving and alert. The characteristically soft thranx voice was strong, spilling words and clicks and whistles without vacillation.

MacCunn and Yirghiz met her with translator in tow. That individ-ual's presence was not required. The emissary spoke very good Terranglo. For his part, Yirghiz looked forward to trying out his stock of memorized Thranx phrases. He was terrible at grammar and could not figure out how to properly integrate the requisite gestures into the conversation, but he was a good whistler and an excellent mimic. Becoming truly fluent in the combination of Terranglo words and Thranx expressions that was evolv-ing into a kind of mutual patois among the young of both species was beyond an old soldier like himself, but he had felt bound to try. He had also memorized a cache of stock AAnn phrases and could manage brief declarations in the single Pitar dialect. By contrast, the field marshal was a linguistic mute. But then, Yirghiz reminded himself with a hidden smile, MacCunn wasn't much of a conversationalist in his own tongue.

"Welcome aboard." Stepping forward, the admiral introduced him-self and the field marshal before extending a hand palm down, fingers slightly spread and inclined upward. The elderly alien's antennae dipped forward to brush his fingertips.

"I am the Di-Eint Haajujurprox. From the Great Hive I bring you greetings and the taste of friendship."

"We are pleased to receive you." A delighted Yirghiz waved off the translator who was standing by, a young woman who was plainly relieved that her skills apparently would not be necessary. The bug's Terranglo was mellifluous and only slightly inflected. The insectoids had a much easier time with the simpler human tongue than humans did with the complex combination of words, clicks, whistles, and gestures that constituted High Thranx.

Alongside him, he observed MacCunn striving to appear inconspicuous as he inhaled repeatedly of the air in the lock. In the vicinity of the three thranx it had become suffused with the aromatic essence of a complex perfume. In respect of scent, age had not dimmed the emissary's personal bouquet.

"Won't you please walk with us?" Turning, Yirghiz led the way.

As they strolled toward the lift that would take them to a comfortable and private room he noted that unlike the images of thranx he had seen, the emissary never rose up on her four trulegs. She required the use of all six to ambulate adequately. Though wondering how old, in human terms, the visitor might be, he was too polite to ask. Among the thranx such a question might be regarded as normal and natural, or it might be considered intrusive. He did not know. Regardless, it had nothing to do with conventional diplomacy. But he was still curious.

They made small talk until they arrived at the senior officer's lounge. This was cleared, and the diplomatic party made itself comfortable. While the di-eint settled herself onto a makeshift couch of cushions placed end to end on the floor, her escorts remained standing. So did the four armed soldiers who had escorted MacCunn and Yirghiz. While their superiors conversed, the common soldiers eyed one another with unfettered interest.

"This is no place for a casual call," MacCunn began without further preamble. "Your government is aware of the quarantine that we have placed around the inhabited worlds of this system, and the conflict that is ongoing here." He started to cough and reached for a glass of water. When he had recovered sufficiently, he continued.

"We know that your ships are not simply 'passing through.' No one travels through space-plus without a definite destination in mind. So I think—we think—that it's safe to assume you came here to speak with us." He gestured absently, wishing he had Yirghiz's command of alien gesticulation. "We have to ask, Why here, when all previous diplomatic contact has taken place between your representatives and ours on Earth or Hivehom?"

"It was decided," the elderly di-eint replied evenly, "that since the matter to be discussed most directly involved the unfortunate situation here, it would be best to communicate directly with those of your kind who are most intimately involved." Her antennae dipped sharply forward. Somewhat startled, MacCunn drew back slightly. Yirghiz did not move.

"You know that we are outraged at what the Pitar did to your colony of Treetrunk. As sentient beings, their actions there horrified every hive. Ever since, there has been much discussion among my kind as to whether it would be appropriate for us to make our displeasure known in a more proactive fashion." Her finely shaped head continually shifted from one human to the other, even though the exceptional peripheral vision provided by her compound eyes meant that she could survey nearly the entire room without moving it at all. The cranial posturing was to assure the two senior humans that she was indeed focusing her attention on them.

Glancing in MacCunn's direction, Yirghiz saw no enlightenment there. Perhaps the field marshal was preoccupied with his persistent bowel problems, the admiral mused. That was not the case. MacCunn simply had nothing to say and was content to let his colleague take the lead in composing their response. It did not mean he was not paying attention.

"Could you be more specific as to what you mean when you say 'more proactive'?"

"I have come here on behalf of the Great Hive authorized to propose a formal military alliance between our peoples. We want to help you in your fight against these Pitar," the di-eint stated.

This time MacCunn was quick to respond. "Why?" he asked curtly. "So you were outraged by what they did on Treetrunk. All intelligent species were outraged. Only you are offering to help. Outrage is by itself an insufficient reason for actively engaging in interstellar warfare."

"Is it?" Many-lensed eyes shifted to face the field marshal. When he did not respond, the di-eint gestured acknowledgment. "Very well. It is as you say. There are other reasons. While a large faction finds the outrage sufficient for us to respond, they are not a majority. It was necessary to build an adequate consensus, corollary by corollary." She shifted her awkward position on the queue of cushions.

"As you know, we have been locked in an ongoing battle with the Empire of the AAnn since before your kind encountered ours. The AAnn are a devious, ruthless, expansionist race."

"We've had no trouble with the AAnn," Yirghiz felt compelled to point out.

"The AAnn are also very patient. They are evaluating your

resources." The elderly alien leaned toward them. "They are especially interested in the present conflict. While they are too clever to aid the Pitar directly, they are delighted to watch them deplete your resources."

MacCunn frowned. "Why should they care who wins? As you say, they are completely neutral."

"On the face of it, they are. But the Pitar have nothing the AAnn want and pose no threat to their strategies. The Pitar are not colonizers. Humans are, very much so. As are the AAnn. As both spheres of influence continue to expand, they will inevitably begin to overlap. There will come a time when tenancy of a new world falls into dispute. If the Pitar succeed in severely weakening you, or are still tying down a large portion of your military strength, the AAnn will not hesitate to take advantage of the situation that results."

The field marshal was nodding slowly. This was an explanation he had heard before and could understand. "So by helping us against the Pitar you hope to ensure that our strength is not diminished, and that it will be available as a counterweight to future AAnn expansion."

She did not nod. Adoption of human gestures was a habitude for the young. But she did indicate her acknowledgment. "We also expect this alliance to operate in the opposite direction."

"Of course you do." As much was obvious to Yirghiz. "If your government is going to send its citizens to risk their lives on our behalf, it would be unreasonable not to expect the same from us. If the AAnn attack you, you'd want to be able to ask for our help."

"It'll never happen." MacCunn was darkly assured. "The world council will never vote to send ships and personnel to help defend—" He started to say what was in his mind, and hastily substituted something else. "—your kind."

With their fixed exoskeleton the thranx were incapable of smiling. Nor were the relevant inflections detectable even to the more linguistically adept Yirghiz. It did not matter. The di-eint's response contained sufficient inherent sarcasm.

"Bugs, you mean."

MacCunn replied calmly. "I didn't say that."

"You do not have to. It doesn't matter." The di-eint's antennae dipped and bobbed. "My government is prepared to leave the question of what degree of response your kind would provide should such a confrontation arise for future discussion. Our overriding concern is to assist you now."

"Before the Pitar can weaken us to the point where we might be unable to effectively resist the incursions of the AAnn."

"You may draw your own conclusions. The important thing is that you accept. And there is another reason."

Yirghiz was growing impatient to return to the bridge. "What else?"

"We happen to like you. Not all of my kind feel thusly, but a great many do. We do not like the Pitar. Not after what they have done, showing neither remorse nor repentance. But for an accident of biology it might have been a thranx world they despoiled. On a more informal level, I am compelled to say that *I* like you."

Yirghiz's instinct was to reply in kind, but he found he could not. However convivial it might be, the creature seated opposite him was still simply too . . . buggy. That was not a rational, scientific response, he knew, but he could not help it. Like so many he knew, he remained a prisoner of his racial history, of memories of thousands of years of competing with far smaller distant cousins of the thranx for food, for space, for very existence.

That would not prevent him, however, from accepting their help.

"It's not within my purview to agree to so momentous a proposition." He gestured in the field marshal's direction. "No one on this ship or in the armada has that power. Believe me, I personally would be glad to accept all and any additional assistance, regardless of its origin."

"Because you are going nowhere here," Haajujurprox told him.

MacCunn bridled. "We are making progress. With each engagement the Pitar lose ships and fighters. We're wearing them down."

"And they are wearing you down. We are quite capable of monitoring human opinion. In a war of attrition conducted in the vastness of interstellar space, it is the well-emplaced defenders who usually win. With the forces at your command you cannot break through their defenses."

"Our land-based production plants and orbital assembly facilities are turning out newer and better ships and weapons." The field marshal's voice was tight.

"As are the Pitar, who have the advantage of bringing them to bear sooner and more easily than you can. It is not unreasonable to imagine that they might succeed in out-producing you. They have the resources of two planets as highly developed as Earth operating in close proximity to one another, whereas your subsidiary colony worlds are widely scattered. The raw resources of not one but two extensive asteroid belts are theirs to draw upon. Your position here becomes less, not more, tenable over time."

MacCunn swallowed hard. "Denigrating the efforts of the people you propose to help strikes me as a peculiar way to initiate an alliance."

"Truth is not denigration," the elderly thranx countered. "Mathematics is not prejudiced and does not take sides." Glancing down, she consulted a delicate device strapped to the forepart of one truhand. "By this time your world council should have reached a decision on our offer.

Our arrival here, you see, was timed to coincide with the very secret debate that has been taking place within your government for several of your weeks."

MacCunn and Yirghiz exchanged a startled glance. The look was sufficient between friends to convey the awareness that neither man knew something relevant that he had neglected to tell the other.

As if choreographed, both senior officers' private readers vibrated for attention. Removing the instruments, the two men read in silence. Despite herself, Haajujurprox was impatient to receive more than visual reactions from the humans.

Sighing heavily, Yirghiz slipped his recorder back into its holster. "The actual communication was received before you set foot on this ship. It took the time we have spent talking to decode, recheck, and decode the recheck. If your skills in battle are as precise as the timing of your diplomacy, your help will be most welcome indeed."

The di-eint interpreted this promptly. "Then your government is agreed?"

MacCunn nodded briskly. "Any help you want to give us is hereby accepted. Details of a full alliance will continue to be discussed and debated. But in the interim, if you should happen to extirpate a Pitarian warship or two, the people of Earth and its colonies will be pleased not to look too deeply into questions of your motivation."

"Excellent." Haajujurprox started to rise, began to tremble, and slumped back toward the cushions. Her twin escorts rushed to assist the elderly di-eint.

Without realizing it, Yirghiz had started to do the same. It had been an instinctive gesture. Now he stood more slowly, watching as the two younger thranx assisted their elder in rising. One helped to support her while the other carefully removed the line of cushions from beneath the aged abdomen so that she would not have to step awkwardly over them.

Why had he started to go to her aid? The admiral found himself caught in a welter of unexpected emotions. Intelligent beyond doubt she was, but the emissary was still virtually a giant bug. He didn't like bugs. But he found that he was very much starting to like this one.

Not a bug, he told himself firmly. It's only the shape. Ignore the shape—or learn to see it differently.

MacCunn was speaking softly in his usual, clipped, formal tones. "We will work with the commanders of your vessels to include them in our general battle schematics. We certainly don't expect them to lead any thrusts, but their status as active reserves will be most welcome."

The di-eint rotated her head to a greater extreme than any human could manage in order to look back at the senior officer. "Don't you trust us, Field Marshal MacCunn? Or do you need to first see dead thranx bodies floating in space to be convinced of our earnestness in this matter?" When he started to reply, she raised a hand to forestall him. Yirghiz was quietly amazed to see him comply.

"No, do not try to explain yourself. Though I have not experienced them personally, I am well aware of human feelings toward my kind. You cannot help it. In this and many other ways you are still prisoners of your primitive past. Given time and effort, we hope to be able to effect changes in that."

Yirghiz stepped into the uncomfortable breach. "Blowing a few Pitarian warships out of existence would be an excellent way to begin."

Haajujurprox gesticulated acknowledgment, not pausing to wonder if any of the humans in the room understood the meaning of the gesture.

Flanking their superiors, the two thranx and four human soldiers formed up an escort. The meeting concluded, they found themselves eying each other very differently than they had been when it had first commenced. The thranx studied the flexible, flowing movements of their bipedal counterparts with bemused curiosity, while the human soldiers could not keep themselves from inhaling deeply and repeatedly. Of such small exchanges are great events fashioned.

MacCunn was constitutionally unable to keep himself from discussing strategy, even during what should have been a walk marked by casual conversation.

"Your task force will complement our ships nicely in sector twelve. We've been weaker there than I would like for nearly two months now."

"Task force?" Haajujurprox adjusted her valentine-shaped head to peer up at him.

"The one dreadnought you brought and the escorts that are accompanying it." MacCunn smiled, wondering if the venerable thranx knew the meaning and intent of the expression.

"My dear Field Marshal MacCunn, *cl!rrik,* that is no task force. That is our scouting force. Subsequent to the final approval by your full government of the terms of our mutual arrangement, a substantial portion of the Hive fleet will arrive here within days. Less what is required to maintain the adequate defense of Hivehom, Trix, Willow-Wane, and Calm Nursery, of course. While the AAnn wait in hopes of seeing you weakened, they would be more eager still to take advantage of any perceived frailty on our part."

MacCunn looked at Yirghiz, who was silent but visibly elated. "Then we can expect the assistance of a few more of your warships?"

"It is recognized that if the defense of Pitar is to be broken, any adjustment in the balance of forces must be significant. Otherwise the effort would be wasted."

The two senior officers indicated their agreement, reiterating that the blockading force would be grateful for any help, no matter how limited or unobtrusive.

Six days later two hundred and sixty-five thranx warships dropped out of space-plus around Pitar's sun.

20

The arrival of the unexpectedly impressive thranx forces was met with a unanimity of cheers and a spontaneous outpouring of warmth among the humans who crewed the ships charged with enforcing the quarantine around the defiant and venomous Dominion. The reaction on Earth and throughout the colonies was less homogenous. While delighted at the offer of assistance, a good deal of suspicion was voiced over the terms of the proposal.

The opposition to any formal agreement was led by the highly visible and equally vocal xenophobe faction. Dubious at having to deal on equal terms with giant bugs, the prospect of fighting alongside them and possibly at some point in the future for them drove the most extreme groups into paroxysms of fury. Consequent outbreaks of violence protesting the agreement, while distressing, were effectively contained by the world government. Despite vigorous attempts to do so, these could unfortunately not be concealed from an active and perceptive media. Agitated debate over the virtues and drawbacks of the understanding continued even as thranx warships prepared to go into battle alongside their human counterparts.

The reaction among the thranx was equally divisive, but deliberated with considerably more restraint. In the end the desires and self-serving rationales of both governments prevailed: Thranx warships would fight alongside those of the armada.

It was a moment in time fraught with significance when the order for the first combined attack was transmitted. Several dozen ships began to probe forward on a wide astronomical front, their movement and positioning coordinated by hastily forged closed communications. Throughout the armada tension ran higher than usual. No one knew how well human forces would operate alongside those of the insectoids.

Activity in normal space exposed ships and personnel to counterattack by Pitarian forces. It was impossible to conduct any kind of fight in space-plus, a realm of nonconforming physics where the customary definitions of matter and energy no longer held sway. But on low drive power, conventional weapons could wreak havoc in minutes. Ships could be damaged or destroyed, and thousands could lose their lives. Advancing to within accurate bombardment range of a target world in space-plus was of course impossible. The stress of emerging into a planet's gravitational field, even at a distance where its effects would be greatly reduced, would impact on the sensitive alignment of a ship's KK-drive field and tear it apart as soon as it emerged back into normal space.

So the commingled fleets advanced as rapidly as was feasible, knowing that the Pitar could not shift ships to meet them any faster than they were already traveling. Computation systems stood ready to orchestrate flights of explosives and high-energy weapons. All personnel were at battle stations and on full alert. Over the previous year many such confrontations had riven space in the vicinity of the twin asteroid belts and the innermost gas giant. Everyone hoped this battle would be different than those.

Detecting the incoming ships, the Pitar promptly allocated a force large enough to counter the incursion. As soon as far-ranging instrumentation descried this enemy activity, another human-thranx battle group began to move inward from its position on the far side of the Dominion's sun. As before, their location and movement was noted by the Pitar, and as previously, a sufficiency of warships was reassigned to intercept them.

Within an hour the entire armada, augmented by the substantial thranx force, was in motion, as were all available Pitarian craft. It was very much like a gigantic chess game, one that involved hundreds of pieces of varying strength engaged in simultaneous motion on an interplanetary scale. Aboard the *Tamerlane* as aboard every ship in the armada, there was hope that the final and deciding battle might at last be at hand: that with the addition of the thranx force the blockaders might at last have enough strength to overwhelm and beat their way past the Pitarian defenders.

It was not to be.

Watching the constantly shifting readout within the flagship's main battle tridee, the lowliest ensign saw what was happening at the same time as general officers like Yirghiz and MacCunn. At first no one could believe it. The ship's battle instrumentation, which automatically compensated for far punier human senses, was quickly checked for error.

Nothing was malfunctioning, and subsidiary instruments confirmed the accuracy of all primary modalities.

Pinpoints of light were rising from the vicinity of both the Twin Worlds. Ascending and racing outward along the appropriate vectors to support existing Pitarian defenders. They were prodigal in number, not staggeringly so but still disappointingly abundant. The Pitar had been holding a substantial number of perfectly good ships in reserve, not employing them even for routine patrol or to help rotate ships and crews. Designed to furnish an entirely unsuspected line of defense for the Twin Worlds, their masters were now forced to use them in order to counter the unexpectedly augmented human attack.

MacCunn, for one, did not have to wait for the official report from remote sensors. The moving pinpoints were difficult to count, but he could estimate.

The offensive was called off before any ships could engage. There was no point in risking personnel and material to fight to yet another draw. The efficacy of Pitarian ships, weapons, and tactics had already been amply demonstrated. No one wished to risk thousands of lives to secure a reiteration of what was already well known.

No one died in the aborted sortie, but the sense of disappointment that spread throughout the armada was crushing. Expecting a decisive battle, the ships had instead withdrawn without either side having loosed a single missile or fired so much as a ranging shot. The thranx had broken the status quo, and the Pitar had promptly reestablished it. The thranx commander, a di-eint himself, was apologetic. They would try harder next time. But no more thranx vessels could be expected to participate than those that had already arrived. The rest of the thranx fleet was obliged to remain on home station to defend their respective worlds.

The government of Earth and its colonies tried to minimize the aftermath. No ships had been lost in the most recent engagement, and not a single soldier had died. Furthermore, the clandestine strength of the Pitar had been exposed. They had been forced to reveal the extent of their reserves. As a military argument it was a good one, but it carried little weight with the discontented people of Earth and associated worlds.

Besides, what proof was there that the Pitar were not concealing still additional martial capacity? That the next assault, however greatly enhanced, would not be met by a similar counteraction? What if the Pitar had yet to divulge their full strength? These were questions a cautious military could not answer. The reaction on Earth and elsewhere, once more led by the xenophobes, was not salutary.

To break the deadlock around the Twin Worlds of the Pitarian

Dominion a radical improvement in weaponry or change in tactics was obviously required. But what?

The one development no one expected was that both would occur simultaneously and as a consequence of the same research, or that it would be the thranx who first hit upon the singular idea.

In addition to the cultural and diplomatic exchanges that had permeated relations between human and thranx since the time of first contact, there was a quiet but continuous exchange of scientific information. Discovering that the human interstellar KK-drive was more efficient than their own, the thranx promptly adopted and incorporated into their own vessels specific aspects of its design. Human engineers and researchers also benefited from the results of thousands of years of thranx research. Largely ignored and overlooked by their respective governments, as well as by the fanatics on both sides, the scientists went about their work in stolid, systematic fashion. Which is to say they mutually engaged in the monotonous, boring, dull, everyday work that constitutes the vast bulk of what ordinary people think of as science.

Space-minus communications delivered information and accepted cautious propositions. Arcane theories were debated and hypotheses scrutinized. Good things arose from these communications, though nothing very dramatic.

Until a small group of thranx physicists decided to broach an idea to a visiting party of human colleagues.

The engineers were on Hivehom to explain certain aspects of KK-drive manufacture to their thranx counterparts. They were practical men and women who were far more interested in application than theory. As such, they were bemused by the physicists' insistence; for that matter, so were their thranx counterparts.

It was left to a senior member of the local research group to make the presentation. Humans and thranx alike had gathered to hear him in the casual surroundings of an underground esplanade. Organized water spilled in a systematic, tranquil manner from the ceiling, suffusing the air with the music of its falling while saturating the circumscribed atmosphere of the sizable chamber with additional moisture. The thranx delighted in its feel. Wearing as little as mutual modesty would allow, their human visitors tolerated the incredible humidity as best they were able, having long since learned that working with the thranx on one of their worlds meant sweating not just while at work, but every minute of every day.

Couvinpasdar was aware of all the eyes on him, compound and single-lensed alike. He could not interpret many of the multitudinous human facial expressions but would not have been wrong in supposing that they were the fleshy equivalent of the progressive gestures of skepticism being propounded by his fellow thranx. While humans and hive members chatted in the increasingly convenient and maturing language of Symbospeech, the young physicist set up the small image generator he had brought with him. When he was ready, he was forced to gesture and call for attention, so indifferent to his proposed presentation were the members of his audience.

"I extend gratefulness to all who have taken time from their busy schedules to grant me a few moments worthy of their contemplation, especially our visiting human friends, whom I know find the controlled climate here in the inner levels of the hive less than homelike." Perspiration pouring down their bodies, the watching, slightly impatient bipeds could only agree.

Activating the projector that was attuned to his voice patterns, Couvinpasdar walked around and occasionally through the images it generated as he spoke, pointing out specific details and occasionally using a truhand to manipulate them. Some of his audience granted him their full attention, while that of others wandered. Around them, unaware that an important demonstration of combat physics was being presented in their midst, thranx strolled and clicked and whistled in pairs or small groups. To one of the humans who also happened to be something of a historian, reflecting later on the demonstration, it was as if Robert Oppenheimer had exposed the design and schematics of the first atomic bomb on a busy day in New York's Central Park. Few of the busy, preoccupied thranx gave the unusual gathering more than a passing glance. Those who did look ignored the shifting, shimmering projection in favor of scrutinizing the loose-limbed, gangly bipeds.

"We have found that your kind are very good at conceptualizing basic scientific breakthroughs," Couvinpasdar was saying. One of the attendant humans murmured something, and a couple of her companions responded with soft coughing noises—human laughter, the young physicist knew. He did not let it distract him. "Thranx are very good at finding improvements in existing engineering and other practical applications that humans often overlook." No laughter this time.

"My research group has been studying the problem of how it might be possible to break the defenses that surround the Pitar. Very early in our discussions we came to the conclusion that this could not be done with existing weapons, not as long as the Pitar match ship for ship. Furthermore, any vessel mounting a radical and potentially advantageous new weapon would immediately be set upon by the Pitar in all their strength. Therefore it was decided that any new weapon must also incorporate into its scheme and make use of a corresponding shift in strategy." The projection mutated.

Floating before the assembled audience was one of the smallest ships any of them had ever seen. It was, in fact, smaller than the lifeboats that were carried about most ships. But it was neither lifeboat nor repair vessel nor intership shuttle. There was the KK-drive field projection fan, severely shrunken and modified, and behind it—absurdly close behind it—the main body of the vessel. A single tiny weapons blister on a standard body-girdling belt ran around the median of the ship. Its diminutive size rendered it virtually inoffensive. Atop the craft was a structure that at first glance resembled a lifeboat launcher. In the context of the ship's ridiculously small size it struck several of the onlookers as a structural extravagance.

Speaking in a mixture of Low Thranx, Terranglo, and Symbospeech, Couvinpasdar elaborated on the design. "We call this a stingship. As you can see, it is quite an unpretentious design. It is designed to carry a crew of two: one human and one thranx." He indicated the locations on the schematic. "One here, and the other here, on opposite sides of the vessel. They are intended to complement, not back up, one another. To carry out its intended mission with maximum efficiency, the stingship is designed to be flown by two pilots operating in tandem."

"Doing what, *currukk?*" a thranx member of the audience inquired. "The vessel is too small to do any real damage. Even a small Pitarian or AAnn warship would easily blast it out of the sky." The questioner gestured at the center of the model. "It is not even large enough to generate its own defensive screen."

"The stingship relies on agility for its defense," Couvinpasdar replied.

"With a drive attenuated to that size," one of the humans pointed out, "the vessel is not capable of interstellar travel."

"It is not intended to be," the physicist explained. "Stingships are meant to be carried, in sizable numbers, in the holds of larger craft. Dreadnought-class ships, or preferably, a new class of vessels specially built for the purpose."

"How did you work out the physics of a KK-drive that size?" another of the humans wanted to know.

"Engineering on the subatomic level is an art among my colleagues," Couvinpasdar informed her. "However, the proposed stingship propulsion system is still not the smallest drive we have contemplated. This is."

So saying he ran his fingers through the projection. The stingship model gave way to something appreciably smaller. If it was another diminutive ship, several members of the audience felt, it would function well only as a joke.

"By the Final Tunnel," the senior thranx scientist in the gathering clicked, "what is *that* supposed to be?"

"Maybe it's a KK-drive powered coffin," one of the humans commented drily, "for commending bodies to space who want to say their final farewells to their surviving comrades in a great big hurry." This time the laughter, both human and thranx, was more general.

Couvinpasdar gestured polite acknowledgment of the amusement, but his tone did not change. "The KK-drive unit you see here is only theoretically possible. Something of this reduced size has never been brooded before, much less built." His blue-green, hard-shelled fingers shuffled within the projection. "This is not a ship. Fitted behind the miniature drive is a sizable thermonuclear device. As you can see, the drive-driven explosive fits into the launcher on top of the stingship. Because of size considerations, and to preserve the exceptional maneuverability of the two-person vessel, only one such device is carried by each craft."

Laughter had given way to contemplative quiet. "So the stingship, hypothetically avoiding the attention of an enemy's weapons systems, penetrates its defenses as far as possible before releasing or firing this drive-driven missile. What's to prevent the enemy from simply blowing it out of the void?"

"This is not a normal missile," the young thranx physicist reminded his questioner. "It is powered not by conventional propulsion systems, but by a KK drive. Furthermore, it is being launched from a craft that is itself KK-drive driven. Some shells may indeed be intercepted and destroyed." Subdued light glinted off enthusiastic compound eyes. "But imagine the effect of several thousand such weapons deployed simultaneously across a wide sphere of conflict. It would be impossible for an enemy to detect, far less predict and intercept, the course of every single incoming munition.

One of the thranx who had not yet spoken now ventured a question. "The defense screens generated by Pitarian ships are very good. At distance, they can disperse even the energy released by a fusion explosion."

Couvinpasdar efficiently adjusted the projection. Ship models vanished, to be replaced by more intimate schematics decorated with fancies of mathematics. "That is so, but the thermonuclear device that rides behind the drive is only part of the effectiveness of the system. Once the SCCAM shell detects a target, at a safe distance from its launching stingship so as not to compromise that vessel's drive field, its own field warps into deliberate and irrevocable overdrive. This means it will be attracted to the nearest gravity well of size. In this instance, that would be the corresponding drive field of the target vessel." His eyes roved his now very solemn and attentive audience from which all suggestion of humor had fled.

"The computations have been crunched many times, and the consequences are inescapable. No defensive screen known can resist the effect of a KK drive on overload. Impacting on the active field of an enemy vessel, the resultant sudden and excessive gravitational distortion would rend both asunder. At the very least its drive would be permanently disabled, rendering the ship unable to move and effectively helpless."

One of the humans had an objection. "Then all an enemy vessel has to do to avoid such a hazardous interaction is shut down its drive whenever closing stingships or these SCCAM shells are detected. Without a substantial gravity well to attract it, at combat distances the shells are likely to speed right on past."

Couvinpasdar gestured to indicate that this objection too had been anticipated. "Except that the shell's sensors have already locked in on the coordinates and course of the target. A ship's defensive screens are powered by its KK drive. Turn off the drive to eliminate the attracting gravity well, and you also lose your screens. With screens down, a ship is then open and vulnerable to the effects of the thermonuclear device carried by the SCCAM shell." He watched his audience for reaction. "By either means or both, the enemy is completely destroyed or is rendered incapable of further maneuvering."

A long, thoughtful pause followed before another of the thranx spoke up. "The system is not perfect. Their proposed exceptional maneuverability notwithstanding, some of these unscreened stingships will still encounter enemy fire that they cannot evade. Ships and pilots will be hit."

"Two crew per ship. A far more acceptable ratio than if even a single cruiser is lost."

The human woman who had first spoken had set aside her sarcasm. "Why one human and one thranx pilot? Why not two humans or two thranx?"

"Because research has shown that our minds and bodies work in different ways. Because under the duress of combat, studies prove that humans do certain things well and thranx other things better. Because we complement one another."

The assembled scientists fell to arguing. Some debated with quiet intensity while others clustered around Couvinpasdar, bombarding him with questions that arrived as fast as if they were propelled by downsized

KK drives of their own. The discussion consumed the remainder of the day and ran on into and through the night, the majority of the group forgetting or disdaining to eat. By morning everyone was exhausted. But out of acrimony and skepticism and doubt had come hope.

Following the designs and delimitations of Couvinpasdar's research group, a single stingship was fabricated. Out at the testing station beyond a moon of Hivehom's largest gas giant, it was activated. It did not succumb to the peculiar distortions of space-plus, nor did it tear itself to pieces and kill its two pilots. Others were built, the inaugural design tightened and refined in the process.

The first symbiotically cached concussive armed missile was built. True to the predictions of Couvinpasdar and his associates, when its absurdly tiny drive system was sent into deliberate overload, the shell promptly threw itself at a drone target vessel programmed to avoid and escape. The drone did not. When their drive fields intersected, both ship and shell vanished in an entirely satisfactory and supernally bright dissolution of energy-encumbered particles. It was a very gratifying demonstration.

Couvinpasdar and his colleagues accepted the honors and commendations bestowed upon them by both thranx and human authorities with quiet grace—and in traditional thranx fashion, promptly returned to their work. Though they had earned and were entitled to a rest, they replied with an old thranx metaphor to the effect that "no burrow was ever finished."

Eight years after humankind had taken pleasure in its first contact with the imposing Pitar and three years following the destruction of the colony of Treetrunk, the commingled human-thranx armada once more threw its combined strength against the defenses surrounding the Twin Worlds of the Pitarian Dominion. But this time the probe by hundreds of capital warships was augmented by a prodigious swarm of tiny stingships each armed with a single self-propelled SCCAM shell.

Caught in the annihilation sphere of hundreds of explosive devices, or swept by devastating beams of coherent energy, dozens of stingships and their pilots evanesced out of existence, many before they even had a chance to launch their weapons. Dozens more accomplished their runs and were destroyed before they could escape.

But Pitarian warships found themselves riven and ruptured from the aftereffects of their own overloaded drives, while others switched off their fields and screens only to be annihilated by precision-targeted thermonuclear devices. On the opposite side of the sun from the Twin Worlds, the hitherto impenetrable defensive sphere protecting the Dominion began to implode under the unexpected new kind of assault. In the end it collapsed like a balloon. Once a single hole had been punctured in the curvature, the rest of the orb simply caved in.

MacCunn was not there to exhort his troops. The field marshal had died six months before, a victim of his failed digestive system, when the outcome of the conflict was as much in doubt as it had been when the first assault had been launched against the Twin Worlds. His friend and colleague Admiral Hyargas Yirghiz was present at the final Pitarian collapse, however. Standing before the main battle tridee on the bridge of the damaged but still very battle-worthy *Tamerlane*, he watched in silent satisfaction as the surviving stingships returned to their mothercraft and the main body of the armada advanced to within orbital bombardment range of both worlds.

After three years of struggle there was no wish among the attackers to annihilate the population. Different degrees of punishment to be applied as circumstances dictated had been worked out by the world council of humankind and the Grand Council of the thranx. All depended on how the Pitar reacted to their defeat.

They reacted as if they had not been defeated. From the surfaces of both planets, ground-based missiles fired from hardened launchers streaked upward toward the assembled invaders. A few did damage, but most were easily knocked down or brushed aside. One by one, their flight paths were tracked, traced, and the launching facilities destroyed. Small red flowers erupted on the surface of both the Twin Worlds, blossoms of nuclear death.

And still the Pitar fought on.

It was finally deemed necessary to land troops, an eventuality the senior officers had hoped to avoid. Unrelenting Pitarian hostility left them with no choice. The thranx participated in this exercise only as observers. Their alliance with humankind did not extend to providing support for ground action. Thranx enough had died crewing ships of the armada, as well as aboard the tiny, seemingly insignificant but ultimately lethal stingships that had at last altered the course of battle.

To dispassionate observers the concluding consequences were inconceivable. The Pitar would not surrender. Every community was armed. Those who capitulated did so only as a convenience of deception, turning on and slaughtering their captors the instant the humans' guard was down. Even Pitarian progeny knew how to pick up and fire a small weapon or rush a pod of human soldiers with explosives strapped to their bodies.

Scientists wished to preserve at least a remnant of Pitarian civilization in hopes of being able to study and perhaps understand their rabid xenophobia. It proved impossible. Whenever cornered and weaponless, the Pitar always managed to find a way to kill themselves, if not their enemies. Remembering the atrocity of Treetrunk, individual human soldiers were not inclined to go out of their way to ensure the survival of any Pitar.

Still, through the use of stun guns, soporific gas, and other nonlethal weapons, a small number were captured alive. They refused to be studied. Noncooperative and virulent to the last, they turned on their captors when possible, committed suicide when they could not, or retreated into a kind of voluntary madness until their minds and bodies finally expired of natural causes.

In the end, three habitable but unpopulated worlds remained as a consequence of the conflict—one human, two Pitarian. They are not often visited.

The research teams that followed the departure of the armada gleaned what clues they could from the ruins of Pitarian civilization. What they found was not so much that the Pitar had been incontrovertible xenophobes as they had been irredeemable narcissists. Unable to countenance the ongoing existence of any intelligent life-form but their own, they had deliberately set out to steal as much knowledge as they could from humankind before turning on Earth and its colonies. Hivehom and the thranx would have been next, or possibly the inoffensive and blandly expansionist Quillp. But the Pitar had a problem.

Every other sentient species was capable of outbreeding them. Unlike humans or thranx, Pitarian females ovulated only once a year. It helped to explain why no children were present on any of the ships that visited Earth or its colony worlds, why none participated in any of the infrequent cultural exchange programs. The occasional Pitarian progeny was precious.

The stolen reproductive organs of the several thousand human females on Treetrunk who had been surgically eviscerated were found—floating in carefully maintained tank batteries, rank upon rank of disembodied uteruses, ovaries, and fallopian tubes. The eggs of human females were removed, their DNA modified; they were then inseminated with Pitarian sperm and were replaced—returned to their natural cavities to follow the "normal" progression of plenteous human pregnancy. Once sufficiently matured, each embryo was then removed and implanted in a suitable Pitarian female for the sole purpose of giving birth.

Surrogate mothership of Pitarian offspring by living human females, even if it had been proposed to and accepted by qualified women, was a thought no Pitar could countenance. So they attempted to thieve the organs and eggs they needed in hopes of enlarging the population of the Twin Worlds to the point where they could successfully challenge the more prolific species that infested an otherwise unpolluted galaxy. The complete destruction of Treetrunk had been carried out to mask their real intentions.

How awful for a noble Pitar to have to live in a cosmos swarming with lesser humans and thranx, Quillp and AAnn, Unop-Patha and other debased species. But having confined themselves to their two perfect worlds, they could not begin to cleanse their portion of the galaxy until they had significantly increased their numerical strength. It was decided that a naïve, biologically similar humankind would unknowingly provide the means. And might have, had not a single sullen and solitary human succeeded in escaping the holocaust with proof of what had taken place.

The armada was disbanded, its constituent vessels returning to Earth or to their respective colony worlds. The vast majority of surviving stingships were decommissioned—but not all. Mindful of the expanding empire of the AAnn, who had watched the conflict with the Pitar with pitiless, impenitent interest, an active fleet and its buttressing reserve was maintained. The thranx returned to their own interests.

Following an initial outpouring of human gratitude for the insectoids' assistance in defeating the Pitar, there came a gradual return to normalcy, to the business of living lives and devoting time to more insular concerns. Colonies continued to expand, and potential colonies continued to develop. Worlds such as Wolophon III and Amropolus that technically fell within the human sphere of exploration but were too redolent of greenhouse effect for human comfort were conceded to the busy thranx, while humankind's chitinous friends willingly turned over to the more cold-tolerant bipeds information on planets they found too frigid to conveniently accommodate their kind. Given an extensive technological effort, each species *could* colonize the other's preferred worlds, of course, but the mutual trade-off in climatological comfort zones made infinitely more sense. Interstellar distances being what they were, there was no real perception of one species intruding on the space of another.

The AAnn watched these developments unhappily. Unable to challenge the maturing human-thranx axis directly, they pondered less confrontational means of impeding the resolution of a deeper, stronger alliance. There were many ways of doing this, at which the insidiously artful AAnn were masters. Their advantage lay in the fact that a great many humans and thranx remained ultimately suspicious of one another, and of any expansion of intimate contact.

With a little luck, and much shrewd manipulation of opportune circumstances, sagacious AAnn nobles and their skillful xenologists felt it might even be possible to bring both transient allies into open conflict with one another.

The AAnn set to work.

DIUTURNITY'S
DAWN

We shall not cease from exploration, and the end of all
our exploring will be to arrive where we started,
and know the place for the first time.
—T. S. Eliot, 1942

1

Bugs.

Hundreds of bugs. Thousands of them, many nearly as tall as she. All chittering and clicking and waving their feathery antennae at one another as they went about their daily business. Magnified by the heat and the more than 90 percent humidity they favored, the atmosphere in the teeming underground avenue was saturated with the natural perfume emitted by their massed bodies. Understandably, they stared at her, their gloriously red-and-gold compound eyes tracking her progress. When she felt it necessary, she would respond to their inquiring gazes with a *crr!lk* of acknowledgment. Astonished to hear a human speaking High Thranx, their multiple mouthparts would invariably twitch in startled response. Such moments made her smile—though she was careful not to expose her teeth. Through such small diplomacies were relations between species improved for the better.

They were not bugs, of course. Though commonly used to describe the highly intelligent insectoids, that word was typically insensitive human shorthand. The thranx were arthropods, insect*like* but internally very different from their primitive Terran look-alikes. Four-armed and four-legged, or two-armed and six-legged—depending on the needs of the moment—they had helped humankind finally defeat the invidious Pitar. That notable achievement was now more than thirty years in the past. Since then, relations between the two victorious species had improved considerably over the suspicions and uncertainty attendant upon First Contact.

Stagnated would be a more accurate description, she mused. In certain specific instances, it could even be argued that they had decayed. As a second-level consul attached to the human embassy on Hivehom, it was the job of Fanielle Anjou and her colleagues to see that they did not worsen any further. Those who entertained higher hopes found themselves frustrated by the sluggish pace of diplomacy on both sides.

The electrostatic wicking of the shorts and shirt she wore reduced the effect of the oppressive humidity by more than half, and the electronic cooler integrated into her neatly cocked cap did much to mitigate the heat, but there was no way to pretend she was comfortable. It had been worse on the transport capsule that had brought her into the inner city, even though the commuting thranx had politely allotted her more space than they would have one of their own. As she wiped at her face, she reflected on the eternal low-tech usefulness of an absorbent handkerchief.

Diplomatic offices were on this level, but another half quadrant forward. She passed a nursery, where larval thranx were cared for and educated while awaiting metamorphosis; an eating establishment, with its rows of padded benches on which a tired thranx could stretch out on its abdomen, legs dangling comfortably on either side; and a large public information screen. The activities it proffered were utterly alien to her. Despite nearly ninety years of casual contact, and much closer interaction during the Humanx-Pitar War, humans still knew all too little about the enigmatic eight-limbed acquaintances with whom they shared the Orion Arm of the galaxy.

The public announcements that periodically echoed above the constant clacking of busy mandibles were all in Low Thranx. She had not mastered either language, but for a human, she was considered fluent—at least by her colleagues. What the thranx thought of her attempts to speak their complex language she did not know. No doubt they considered soft lips and a flexible tongue poor substitutes for hard mandibles.

At least, she thought, I can make myself understood. That was more than many of her click-challenged coworkers could claim.

An adult female with two adolescents in tow passed close by. Unlike human postpubescents, the pair of youngsters were perfect downsized versions of the adult. They were in the premolt stage, preparing to shed their hard exoskeletons preparatory to growing into another size. Both had their antennae pointed rigidly and impolitely in the direction of the bizarre biped coming in toward them. As she strode past, Anjou overheard one chitter excitedly.

"But Birth Mother, it's so soft and pulpy! How can it stand upright like that? And on only *two* legs!"

Anjou did not hear the birth mother's answer. From what the diplomat knew of thranx culture, the reply was most likely in the form of some mild chastisement coupled with an attempt at explanation. What the latter would consist of would probably be highly imaginative. The average hive dweller knew as much about human physiology as a hydroengineer whose business it was to work on the venerable water system of London knew about a thranx's internal plumbing.

The particular burrow complex she was traversing was home to, among other segments, the Diplomatic Contact section. Its sub-burrow loomed just ahead. The main entrance, with its impressive portico of anodized metal and floating holoed worlds, presented no problem. Entering the lift and hallway that lay beyond, however, forced her to watch out for low-hanging appliances. Here her short stature was a positive advantage. Her male colleagues dreaded having to visit anything smaller than a main burrow corridor. If Jexter Henry, who stood a shade under two meters tall, wanted to spend some time in a city like Daret, his travels would be restricted to the main corridors. As a consequence, he was essentially confined to the human outpost at Azerick.

Thoughts of that establishment, of its comfortable surroundings on the temperate Mediterranea Plateau on the largest of Hivehom's four continents, did not improve her mood. At least, she reflected as she turned into a tertiary access tunnel, the Contact facilities were located in a brand-new section of the city. Being the capital not only of Hivehom but of the entire thranx expansion, Daret had been among the first burrows to transform itself from a traditional hive into a real city. As a diplomatic representative, she had been allowed to visit the older, archeologically important sections of the metropolis, with their early nurseries, food storehouses, and primitive arsenals. She had maintained a smile—tight lipped, of course, so as not to expose her teeth—throughout, but had no desire to repeat the tour. Even to a nonclaustrophobe, the ancient quarter of the city was oppressive.

As she passed through the unobtrusive security scan, the male thranx of midage who had been following her ever since her arrival in Daret was at last compelled to abandon his pursuit and continue on past the entrance. He was not disappointed. Though he possessed within his backpack the means for evading the security system, now was not the time to employ it. That would come later, when the fractionated time-part was deemed right by himself and his compeers.

Even fanatics have a sense of timing.

Unaware that she had been followed, Anjou presented her thranx security chit to a series of scanners. It took her longer to gain entrance to the facility than thranx who ambled up from behind and passed her, since the automated security system had to not only verify that the pass she carried was indeed a match to her particular cerebral emissions, but that she was of the species claimed by the embedded photons. The eye scan that served to pass most thranx was of no use in identifying humans, with their oversized, single-lensed oculars.

Eventually she reached the corridor that led to Haflunormet's office. He greeted her with a cheerful click and whistle, to which she replied to the best of her increasing fluency in Low Thranx. He also inclined his head slightly forward, presenting his feathery antennae. Bowing in turn, she reached up and flicked them gently with the tips of her index fingers before allowing them to make contact with her forehead. Formalities concluded, he employed both a truhand and foothand to direct her to one of the three benches that fronted the freeform arc of his workstation. Composed of a wondrously light yet strong beryllium-titanium alloy, it was anodized with a flux that gave it the look of a dark, fine-grained wood.

There were no windows in the chamber because there was nothing to look out upon. Dwellers within the ground throughout most of their history, the thranx were equally comfortable on the surface, but a complex assortment of reasons kept their communities underground. A human forced to work every day in such confinement would have found it suffocating, despite the excellent simscene of luxuriant jungle that filled one wall with color, depth, and a farrago of fragrance.

"I bid you good digging, Fanielle." The Terran diplomat and her thranx counterpart had been on a first-name basis for several months now. As he settled himself back on his elongated seat, she retired to one of the low visitors' benches. Instead of lying prone on her chest and stomach while straddling it head-forward in the thranx manner, she simply sat down on the soft artificial padding. It made for a perfectly comfortable perch, if one discounted the absence of any back support. It was certainly preferable to sitting on the floor.

She did not need to see Haflunormet to recognize him. Every individual thranx emitted a distinctive personal perfume, each more aromatic and sweet-scented than the next. A visit to a city the size of Daret could easily overpower the olfactory sensitive. To her, entering a thranx hive was like plunging into a sea of freshly plucked tropical flowers. Even those humans who disliked the appearance of the thranx were hard put to remain hostile in their astonishingly fragrant presence.

Unfortunately, she reflected, a way had yet to be found that could effectively transmit true smell via tridee. It was too bad. If every human could meet a thranx face-to-face, the continuing uncertain and unsettled state of relations between the two species might be at least partially alleviated.

The improvement in Haflunormet's Terranglo had kept pace with her growing fluency in both Low and the more difficult High Thranx. "I trust you had a pleasant journey from Azerick?"

"The flight was smooth enough, if that's what you mean." She shifted her rear on the near end of the long, narrow cushion, wishing for something to rest her spine against. "The tube transport from the port into Daret was a little slow."

"It's a busy time of year. Fourth cycle of the Dry Season here."

She chuckled softly. "You have a dry season?" It had rained hard and steady ever since the atmospheric shuttle had begun its descent into Daret Port East.

"Taste in atmospheric conditions is relative." Haflunormet gestured expressively with both truhands. "I don't see how you humans stand that high, cold desert you call the Med'ranna Plat'u."

Anjou tried not to think of the pleasant, temperate hillsides where the human outpost was situated. Despite the best efforts of her specialized attire, she was sweating profusely. Though she had grown personally fond of Haflunormet, she couldn't wait to get out of the chamber, with its low ceiling and windowless environment, and back onto the surface.

"I see that you are uncomfortable."

His observation startled her. "I didn't know you had become so adept at interpreting human expressions."

"It is difficult." He gestured casually. "It takes continuous effort for us to realize that those species equipped with flexible epidermi utilize them to convey the same kinds of meanings that we do with our hands. And your skin is more elastic than that of the AAnn, the sentient race you most closely resemble physically. I have had to work hard with my study visuals."

"You watch my face; I observe your limb movements." She gestured decorously. "By such studies do we learn from each other."

He rose from behind the workstation. "Enough to know that you would be more at ease outside the city." Approaching until he was standing next to her on all four trulegs, he reached up with a foothand and gently urged her in the direction of the portal.

"Let's take a riser to the surface, *keerkt*. It will be just as hot and humid, but I know that your kind respond with favor to the unrestricted flow of open air." He made a short gesture of curious indifference. "A peculiar affectation, but a harmless one."

She was more than tempted. "What about security?"

Compound eyes flashing golden beneath the overhead illumination, he indicated reassurance. "We can talk freely in the Park. There are many secure places."

She did not need further convincing. Together, they exited his work chamber and retraced her steps as far as the main corridor. Instead of continuing on past Security, they turned down another narrow passageway that terminated at a bank of oval gateways. Her head just did clear the entrance to the one he selected, but she had to bend slightly at the waist to avoid bumping it on the ceiling of the internal transport motile. Nearly all her male and most of her female colleagues would have been forced to sit on the floor.

Haflunormet coded in a destination, and in seconds they were ascending at a rapid rate of speed. When the riser halted and the portal reopened, she was greeted by a vista of tangled alien rain forest, wondrous aromas, and ferine screeching. The ostensible wildness was illusory. The bulk of the terrain that lay directly above the subterranean capital consisted of carefully tended parkland. The filtered water sources, holoed directions that appeared at the wave of a truhand, concealed emergency communications devices, artfully disguised food-procuring facilities, and other technologically inconspicuous paraphernalia scattered strategically along the path Haflunormet chose pointed to the highly domesticated nature of the "jungle track" down which they began strolling. In appearance, the forest they were entering was little different from those undomesticated tracts that survived elsewhere on Hivehom. But this one had been tamed.

Not only did the heat and humidity not assault her as they exited the riser, it was actually cooler and drier on the surface than in the vast hive conurbation below. Repressing a smile, she hoped it was not too chilly out for Haflunormet. Their divergent preferences in climatic conditions provided numerous opportunities for amusement. In contrast to their weather, the thranx sense of humor was noticeably drier than that of humans. The intent of traditional human slapstick, for example, escaped them completely. To a thranx, a pie in the face was food wasted; nothing more. In contrast, whistling thranx were often clearly amused by conflations that humans found nothing more than common coincidence.

We still, she reflected as she strolled down the path alongside the thranx diplomat, have so very much to learn about one another.

A quartet of *qinks* bobbled past over their heads, gyrating from one tree to another. Both mating pairs capered around each other, performing an intricate mating dance in the air. As she understood it from the Biology Department, qinks only mated in fours, the twofold coupling bolstering the chances of producing viable offspring instead of unsettling it. Like little helicopters, the multiwinged qinks whirled overhead in tiny, tight circles. This meant that at any one time, one or two of the participants was actually flying backward. Ordinarily, it would put that individual at risk from lurking predators. But since qinks only flew the mating dance in tetrads, two of them were always keeping an eye on the sky ahead at all times.

She lengthened her stride, not wishing to be standing directly beneath the whirling aerialists when the time came for them to consummate their performance. Though his legs were markedly shorter than hers, Haflunormet had six of them at his disposal and had no trouble matching the pace. In a sprint, she knew, she could easily outrun him and most other thranx. With his three sets of legs and greater endurance, over a distance he would catch up to and surpass her.

Qinks and sprints, witticisms and woes, she reflected. All grist for the mill of diplomacy. Haflunormet felt similarly, though he was inherently more pessimistic than his human counterpart. Or maybe it was patience, she decided. Humans frequently mistook the immoderate patience of the intelligent arthropods for pessimism.

"How are you coming with arranging that meeting we spoke about?" she asked him. In presenting the question, she employed a combination of human words and thranx words, clicks, and whistles. This useful and informal shorthand manner of speaking was gaining increasing favor among not only the diplomatic but the scientific staff at Azerick. Combined with thranx gestures and the resident humans' best attempts to imitate these utilizing only two hands instead of four, it formed a kind of casual symbolic speech. This allowed thranx to practice their Terranglo and humans the opportunity to train their throats in the elaborate vocalizations of the thranx.

"*Krrik*, it is proceeding slowly. Discouragingly so. I think the physicists are not the only ones who are absorbed in the study of inertia." He glanced over and up at her to make sure she understood the last term correctly. As she did not immediately laugh in the human manner, he could not be certain she had understood his attempt at humor. Of all the humans he had met—admittedly this was not a large number—Anjou was the most consistently serious. Perhaps, he ruminated, this was why she got along so well with the thranx. To Haflunormet it appeared she sometimes acted in this manner to the detriment of her relationship with her fellow mammals.

Watching her step easily alongside him, he tried to admire the play of her muscles, obscenely visible beneath the semitransparent epidermis. Diplomat or no, he found he could not do it. There was simply too much movement, too much visible play within the anatomical structure. In this it resembled that of the AAnn, but the reptiloids' internal composition was concealed by tough, reflective, leathery scales. If a person peered closely at a human, individual blood vessels could be seen not only beneath the skin but forming rills and ridges above it. Their entire corporeal structure was, inarguably, turned inside out.

He forced himself not to look away. It would be impolite. This female was his hive counterpart. Much as the sight unsettled his stomachs, he was determined to maintain visual contact. As to the sharp, distinctive, and wholly unpleasant smell that emanated from the biped, he steadfastly refused to dwell on it. No matter how their future relations evolved, he realized that there were some things that could not be changed through negotiation.

He worked to pay attention, realizing that the tottering upright stinking blob was speaking. No, he corrected himself resolutely: It was a graceful, fluid biped who was addressing him. Formal diplomacy aside, the thranx were exceedingly polite: a consequence of having evolved in surroundings so confined that humans could not even conceive of the social forces that had been at work. To the thranx, of course, they did not seem confined at all, but perfectly normal and natural. It was wide-open aboveground spaces that tended to occasionally make them nervous. Consequently, their conquest of space had been a more impressive feat than that of humans. Psychology was harder to engineer than spacecraft.

Anjou was deep in thought as they turned a bend in the trail. Eint Carwenduved was Haflunormet's superior. Because of the rigid thranx chain of diplomatic command, only she could properly accept a formal proposal from the Terran government and pass it on to the Grand Council for discussion and consideration. It had taken a select group of forward-thinking statespeople from half a dozen human settled worlds almost two years to finally hammer out a preliminary proposal for establishing closer ties between their respective species. This had not even been voted on by the Congress on Terra, yet the signatories felt that opening negotiations with their thranx counterparts at the same time as the details were being debated on the human homeworld would, if nothing else, serve to accelerate mutual consideration of the delicate issues involved.

It was an acknowledged diplomatic ploy, a means of forcing reluctant individuals on both sides to consider politically highly sensitive issues they might otherwise prefer to ignore. Easy enough for the executive director of the colony world of Kansastan to ignore the question of closer human-thranx relations—but not if he felt that his thranx counterpart on Humus was ready to vote on the matter. Merely having the proposals presented for contemplation forced those to whom they were delivered to deliberate their possible ramifications. A good deal of the work of real diplomacy consisted of engaging such individual uncertainties.

Just agreeing on what was technically a compilation of informal suggestions was a triumph for those thranx and humans involved. Others, they knew, were actively working to discourage the implementation of even one of the proposals. One way to do this was to persuade those in positions to actually make decisions to simply ignore anything relevant that crossed their desks. Hence Anjou's intense desire to have a face-to-face meeting with Eint Carwenduved. Haflunormet's superincumbent could not only present proposals to the Grand Council; she could go so far as to make recommendations.

Through Haflunormet, Anjou had been trying to arrange such a meeting for more than six months. Patience or pessimism, whatever one chose to call it, the seemingly endless procrastination was driving her crazy. She could not give vent to her true feelings, however—not in front of Haflunormet. The xenologists had been firm on that from the beginning. She had yet to meet a thranx who would not recoil in distaste at what was to them an often explosive human outburst of emotion.

Anyway, she told herself, diplomats do not do that sort of thing. So the fact that she wanted to stop right there and then in the middle of the domesticated alien jungle and scream out her frustration to curious qinks and any other exotics within range of her voice had to remain nothing more than a passing fancy. But the desire did not wane quickly, she realized.

The delay was not Haflunormet's fault. She knew that. Thranx diplomacy made the human equivalent appear to progress at lightning speed. There was nothing to be done about it but persist, stay polite, and keep her hopes up.

"Why the continuing reluctance?" She gazed over at glittering compound eyes that were more advanced than that of any terrestrial insect. "It's just a meeting. It needn't even last very long."

Haflunormet stepped, one set of legs at a time, over an artfully positioned *zell* root. "Eint Carwenduved continues to study the proposals."

"I know that—she's been 'studying' them for the better part of a year." At once, Anjou regretted her tone, even though it was unlikely that Haflunormet was aware of its significance. His knowledge of human gestures, facial expressions, and linguistic peculiarities was improving rapidly, however, so she was more concerned than she would have been a few months ago.

He did not react as if he detected any bitterness, however. "You must understand, Fanielle, that such things take more time to be resolved among my kind than they seem to among yours. Carwenduved must be certain of herself before she commits to any course of action because she will inevitably be held responsible for relevant consequences."

Which was a fancy and not altogether alien way of saying that the eint was stalling, Anjou knew.

"The eint marvels at your earnestness," Haflunormet continued. "She sees no need for a 'face-to-face,' as you call it." As the thranx diplomat spoke, he absently employed a truhand to preen his left antenna.

"My people believe strongly that personal contact is an important component of diplomacy."

Haflunormet indicated understanding. "You do realize that not all my kind take pleasure from being in your physical presence." He hastened to qualify his comment. "I did not mean you personally, of course! I meant humans in general."

"I know what you meant." Anjou was not naïve. She was fully aware that most thranx, especially those who had experienced little or no contact with humans, found the presence of her kind physically unappealing. It was something she had worked hard to overcome, in everything from her attire to her manner of speaking. "But as a diplomat, I am entitled to certain accommodations." This time her tone was firm. "Eint Carwenduved realizes this as well."

"I know that she does." Haflunormet sighed, the air wheezing gently from the breathing spicules that lined his b-thorax. "Your patience gains you merit in her eyes as well as in mine, Fanielle."

What patience? she thought. I'm going crazy here, hanging around up at Azerick waiting for your mommy bug to deign to see me. She promptly shunted the undiplomatic and very unthranxlike thought aside.

Instead of thinking antithranx thoughts, what might she make use of that the thranx themselves would react to? Perhaps she had been stalking the impasse from the wrong direction. Perhaps she had been thinking too many human thoughts.

How would a thranx diplomat gain speedier access to a counterpart? It would have to be something informal, she knew. The delicate intricacies and involved traditions of thranx hive government were still largely a mystery to the human researchers charged with interpreting them. More was known about thranx culture and society in general. Mightn't there be something there she could apply?

She halted so suddenly that Haflunormet was momentarily alarmed. Both antennae fluttered in her direction. "Is something the matter, Fanielle? If you are feeling stressed by the local conditions, we can find you a climate-controlled chamber in which to revitalize—though I personally find the weather outside today a bit on the cool side."

"Yes," she told him. "Yes, I am feeling a little—a little faint." She put the back of one hand to her forehead in a melodramatic gesture any human would have found amusing, but which the anxious thranx could only view as potentially alarming. "It happens to us—at such times."

He indicated confusion. "Of what 'times' are you speaking?"

"Oh, that's right. You don't know. I haven't told you before now, have I? An oversight on my part. You see—I'm pregnant, Haflunormet. With, um—" She thought of the dancing qinks. "—quadruplets." Unfamiliar with the nature or frequency of human birthing, the anxious diplomat ought to accept her admission at face value. He did.

"*Srr!lk!* You should have told me!" Setting aside his instinctive distaste for such contact, he took her free hand in both his foothands. "Do you want to lie down? Can I get you fluid? Do you wish an internal lubrication?"

"Uh, no thanks," she replied hastily, dropping the hand from her forehead even as she wondered what an on-the-spot internal lubrication meant to a thranx female.

In a determined gesture of interspecies concern, Haflunormet continued to hold her hand, doing his best to ignore the unnatural warmth that radiated from the pulpy flesh. He realized how much he had come to like this particular human. If something were to happen to her while she was in his company, not only would it reflect on his individual and family history, he would regret it personally.

"How are your eggs? Excuse me," he corrected himself, "your live feti. Fetuses?" Despite his disquiet, he could not bring himself to contemplate the wriggling, unshelled larvae that must even now be jostling for room within her womb. He tried to lighten the moment. "As you possess no ovipositors that I could observe going into pre-laying spasm, I had no visual clue to your condition."

"It's all right. I'll be fine." Meeting his gaze, which she assumed reflected his concern even though his compound eyes could not convey anything like such a complex emotion, she announced firmly, "Tell Eint Carwenduved that the pregnant human Fanielle Anjou is making a formal *Bryn'ja* request."

Haflunormet started, his antennae twitching. Then he simultaneously whistled his amusement and understanding. "The news will place the eint in a difficult position."

That's the idea, she thought, wincing perceptibly for effect. If she understood the pertinent aspect of thranx culture correctly, no adult could refuse a first Bryn'ja request from a female who was about to lay. Such a compunction applied equally to ordinary citizens, respected poets, noted teachers, and everyone within the hive irrespective of function. It even applied to diplomats.

Of course, it was a blatant lie. Surely, she told herself, the first time in history one had been employed in the service of diplomacy. She would have to make sure her colleagues at Azerick were informed of her "condition" lest the always thorough thranx decided to check on it with a second source. Once her rather abrupt pregnancy was verified, it would be interesting to see how the thranx would react. Time would at last become a factor. To refuse a first Bryn'ja request from a gravid female until after she laid her eggs would earn the refuser significant opprobrium. Her only real concern was whether or not the custom would apply across species lines. And if it did, would it be subject to the same onerous, lingering deliberation as every other communication she had asked Haflunormet to pass along to the chamber of the eint? Could any thranx authority move at more than a sluggard's pace, no matter the incidental circumstances?

The official response was as revealing as it was gratifying. So much of successful diplomacy was not about knowing how to do something, or when, but how to step just ever so slightly outside the boundaries of traditional, formal negotiation without falling into the pit of cultural transgression.

Within thirty-two hours, she received acknowledgment of her long-sought-after appointment.

2

The Bwyl were furious. They had been ever since the revelation of the presence on Willow-Wane of the covert human outpost there, with its clandestine attempts to bring humans and thranx closer together, had been divulged to an unknowing hive public more than eighty years earlier. It was bad enough, from the standpoint of the Bwyl, that humans and the thranx had cooperated in a war against the Pitar that was no hive's business. The disclosure that the soft-bodied, bipedal mammals had been allowed to establish what amounted to a de facto colony on a developed thranx world amounted to cultural sacrilege. The purity of the Great Hive had been defiled.

Worse still, the vast majority of thranx had reacted indecisively at best, indifferently at worst, to the announcement. Now that the war against the Pitar lay nearly in the receding past, where humans were concerned the average burrower seemed to hold little in the way of strong opinion. So long as the humans posed no overt threat to the Great Hive and did not ally themselves with the bellicose AAnn, the typical worker was content to ignore them. And if the respective life tunnels of the two species happened to intersect now and then, why, it would only be polite to pause and allow those traveling crosswise to pass without confrontation.

It was all very bewildering to the Bwyl. What about the sanctity of the hive? Where was traditional deference to poetic purity? Bad enough to allow these red-blood-pumping creatures access outside the usual restricted diplomatic missions. To allow ordinary citizens to mix with them at will, without proper safeguards or preliminary acculturation, was to invite cultural degradation and worse. What was a newly metamorphosed adolescent to think when confronted with sophisticated sentients who wore their skeletons on the *inside* and peered at the universe out of single-lensed eyes?

It was not to be tolerated. But the Bwyl, though a multihive fellowship, were few in number. They could not influence the councils proportionately. They did have many who were sympathetic to their aims, but who were afraid to express their beliefs openly. The Bwyl base of support was large, but diffuse.

It did not matter. They could wait no longer. Already, there was talk at significant hive levels of formalizing a much closer alliance with the humans. True, such talk had been rampant since the end of the Humanx-Pitar War. Lately, though, it had taken on a certain urgency. Important eints who believed they could make use of the humans as a bulwark against the adventurism of the AAnn had been pressing for more than talk. Regrettably, they found sympathetic hearing organs among traitorous members of the lower councils. Now dialogue threatened to become action, and action, decision. For the sake of the Great Hive, this had to be prevented.

Which was why the Bwyl had called the meeting on Willow-Wane. Its members were not alone in their stand. There were two other interhival societies that had on more than one occasion expressed similar sentiments. Representatives of the S!k and the Arba had arrived on Willow-Wane only days before to participate in the critical discussion.

Now the twineight gathered on the shore of the River Niivuodd, chattering amiably among themselves. To passersby they looked for all the world like a group of taskmates out for a day's relaxation. They carried food and drink and humming amusements, and talked of inconsequentialities. But their intentions were far more serious than an afternoon's casual distraction. They had not joined together beneath Willow-Wane's searing sun for purposes of frolic.

When all had assembled by the river's shore and settled themselves in a half circle facing the water and one another, and when assurance came from posted sentries that no patrollers, first class or otherwise, were lingering in the vicinity, Tunborelarba of the Arba waved all four hands for quiet and proceeded to open the solemn convocation with a pugnacious, if not downright martial, paean to the virtues of the Great Hive. His fine words and whistles encompassed them all, from outworld visitors to their resolute Willow-Wane hosts.

Then Beskodnebwyl of the Bwyl rose on his four trulegs and declaimed what all of them were thinking. Overhead, a flock of silver *taiax* flew past, dipping and looping to snap in unison at the smaller arthropods that filled the steamy afternoon air. Their sedate *ke-uk, chitt-*

chitt, ke-uk-uk did not interrupt the flow of the charismatic speaker's words.

"We are gathered here because we agree that anything deeper than the traditional, polite, formal relations that exist between sentients of different species is an abomination that is not to be tolerated." Attentive antennae and glittering compound eyes were focused in his direction. Near the back, the ovipositors of a young female S!k as fanatical as she was attractive contracted in response to the forcefulness of the Bwyl's words.

"There are those among the hives of several of the burrowed worlds who believe that a stronger relationship can be forged with these humans. These fools dwell in the nursery of delusion. The bipeds are too different—not only in appearance, but in culture, actions, psychohistory, and every other standard that is used to take the measure of another species. Our alliance with them for the duration of the latter part of the Pitarian War was superficial and designed to achieve maximum diplomatic benefit in a limited period of time."

"Principally to forestall the designs of the AAnn," an Abra could not refrain from pointing out.

Beskodnebwyl did not upbraid his impassioned listener for the discourteous interruption. All were allies in this place: supporters of a similar philosophy. He had no intention of alienating a collaborator over a point of etiquette.

"That is so. Yet despite what appears to us to be the obvious, there are among our own kind those who are sufficiently deluded to desire to place the security and sanctity of the Great Hive itself at risk. They intend to do this by forging ties with these humans of a nature so intimate I can scarcely bring myself to contemplate it. You will understand my feelings when you receive the detailed reports that will be provided to all of you at the close of this gathering. All I can say without going into further particulars is that there are varieties and types of corruption not even new larvae can dream of."

"They must be blind!" someone chirruped above a chorus of lesser clicking.

For a second time, Beskodnebwyl deferred his right to criticize an outburst. "There are all kinds of blindness, many of which have nothing to do with the sense of sight. It is these we must correct, even at the risk of carrying out bitter antisocial behavior. The very ancestral integrity of the Great Hive is at stake." Reaching back into a thorax pouch, he withdrew a compact projector and spurred it to life. Immediately, a semitransparent globe appeared before the body of thranx assembled by the river. It was a representation of an attractive world even the most galographically sophisticated among them did not recognize.

"The planet Dawn, as the humans have named it. A fetching place, by all description. Newly settled and growing rapidly. There is also, in this subversive spirit of specious cooperation that presently exists between our respective species, a sizable burrow located beneath the swamps and savannas of the minor southern continent."

"What has this to do with us and our avowed purpose?" a female S!k inquired reasonably.

Manipulating the projector, Beskodnebwyl increased the magnification substantially, until they found themselves eying one of the distorted, sprawling aboveground conurbations that had become more and more familiar recently in the information media. Frivolously tall, slim edifices, not only unaesthetic but impractical, thrust absurdly all the way up into the weather. Extensive agricultural facilities bumped up against a surprising amount of undeveloped green space. Free-standing bodies of water were spotted with fishing craft. Clearly visible were all the mysterious accouterments of a characteristic aboveground human hive.

"There is to be a fair held on Dawn, to be situated not far outside the capital city of Aurora." Beskodnebwyl continued to manipulate the details of the holo as he explained. "A cultural fair, exhibiting the best and newest of human music and arts."

"Is that not a contradiction in terms?" someone ventured. Amused whistling spilled from the assembled to drift across the river.

"Obviously, not to humans, it isn't," Beskodnebwyl observed when the laughter had died down. "This gathering will also present contributions from the local thranx of the southern continent." He leaned forward, stretching his b-thorax, his antennae quivering with barely concealed passion. "It is to be a wholly cross-cultural, cross-species event—the first of its kind on Dawn. In addition to presentations by the locals, a number of important artists from nearby settled worlds, both human and thranx, are also to participate. For so young a colony, it promises to be a most prestigious and important convocation, a watershed in the settlement's evolution." He drew himself back, pausing and gesturing for emphasis.

"We of the Bwyl also intend that it shall be so, and in a manner that will leave a deep and lasting impression on perceptive sentients everywhere. We hope that you of the S!k and the Abra will join us in making our own presentation at this fair."

"Which will consist of?" The senior Abra present waved an antenna inquiringly.

Beskodnebwyl did not hesitate, nor did his tone change. "We hope to disrupt the fair, and in doing so push the course of human-thranx relations back onto a proper level, by killing as many of the participants as possible. Operating under the guise of the ancient Protectors, we hope to make our case so irresistibly to all citizens of the Greater Hive that they will have no choice but to see the correctness of our doctrine." He indicated first-degree confidence.

"The humans will respond immediately to our actions, of course. Once word of our involvement and efforts is disseminated, they will enter the fair and kill us as quickly as they can. With luck, some of us will escape to carry on the necessary work. Those of us who do not will be recycled knowing that they gave their essence to preserve the Great Hive, much as our ancestors did in the course of thousands of ancient battles. This cause is nobler than any of those, because it is carried out on behalf of the entire Great Hive itself." He switched deliberately to the rougher but more straightforward Low Thranx.

"Males and females of the S!k and the Abra: Will you join with your hive mates the Bwyl in this great and noble undertaking?"

Animated discussion followed, lively but by no means uniform. Clearly, there remained among the disputants considerable difference of opinion. Having chosen directness over diplomacy, Beskodnebwyl had no leeway for hesitation. Nor had he intended to leave any.

"How would you intend to do this thing?" Velhurmeabra of the Abra was clearly taken aback by the proposal and not afraid to say so. "Will the humans have in place no precautions against such an eventuality, no guards?"

"Why should they?" Beskodnebwyl replied expansively. "It is a cultural fair, not a military caucus. As to the actual methods to be employed in the carrying out of our intentions, we have already spent much time refining our options."

"What about introducing into the atmosphere of the gathering a powerful cyanotoxin?" one of the more enthusiastic S!k proposed.

"For the same reason that we cannot spread a lethal hemolument." This time the images generated by Beskodnebwyl's handheld projector were more detailed, full of charts and sketches that floated in midair before the assemblage. "Human blood binds oxygen through the use of iron, not the usual copper. I am assured that given enough time and resources, suitable poisons could be engineered for use against them. We have neither. By the same token, biological agents that would devastate us are just as likely to pass harmlessly through their systems. For example, the *gin!gas* wasting disease for which no cure has yet been discovered degrades chitin. I am told that malignant as it is, it might at most cause the hair and fingernails of some humans to fall out. That is hardly the bold statement we wish to make."

"Then what do you propose to do?" Uhlenfirs!k of the S!k asked, then waited quietly.

Beskodnebwyl underlined his response with deliberate movements of antennae and truhands. Behind him, an aquatic *hermot* splashed in the river, pursuing a school of hard-shelled *couvine*, predator and prey alike oblivious to the convocation on the nearby bank vigorously contemplating mass murder.

"Explosives have the advantage of not discriminating between species. Volunteers have already been chosen. They will infiltrate this detestable fair and wreak such havoc as cannot be imagined. The fact that individuals will be free to do their work independent of any central control ensures that even if one or more are detected and forced to abort their mission, the others will be able to proceed unimpaired. Additionally, every operative will enter adequately armed for their personal defense."

The nominal leaders of the S!k and the Abra conferred, supported by their most able aides. When they were through, Velhurmeabra of the Abra faced his expectant counterparts across the semicircle.

"While we of the Abra and the S!k feel much as you do with regard to this too rapid and too intimate mixing of species, we have decided not to participate in your plans to disrupt the cultural fair on the world of Dawn. While we are not entirely opposed to the use of violent means of dissuasion, indiscriminate bombing of so large a gathering will inevitably slay or injure numerous artists as well as ordinary visitors."

One of the S!k spoke up. "The killing of an artist is an abomination unto itself. The stifling of any fount of creativity, however modest, diminishes us all."

Beskodnebwyl gestured understanding. He had expected this line of objection. "Humans feel otherwise. They make no such sharp distinctions between, say, composers of music and purifiers of water. It is further proof of their degraded culture."

"But you cannot guarantee," Velhurmeabra continued inexorably, "that only human artists will die."

"Unfortunately," Beskodnebwyl responded, "explosives are notoriously undiscriminating. It is conceded that thranx will also perish in the making of our statement. It is unavoidable."

"Then we cannot participate actively," the Abra concluded.

Beskodnebwyl pounced on an inflection. " 'Actively'?"

The leader of the S!k spoke up. "We have no legs to provide you, no antennae to aid you, no eyes to share. But—" He hesitated only for emphasis. "—we wish you well in the enterprise, which seems almost certain to accomplish the goals you have set out for it. While not participating directly, we can perhaps provide some small encouragement."

"In any event, we will do nothing to discourage you from burrowing in this chosen direction," the Abra concluded.

It was not all that Beskodnebwyl had hoped for. But logistical support would be useful and would free up the dedicated members of the Bwyl to carry out the more active components of the scheme. The Abra and the S!k could not overcome the deep-seated cultural prejudice against the killing of artists. Only the Bwyl had progressed far enough to do that. But the support of the others would be welcomed. They wished to share in the credit for the ultimate disruption of human-thranx integration, but not in the ultimate risk.

It was better than outright dissension, Beskodnebwyl knew. The Abra and the S!k had access to materials and contacts and useful facilities that were denied the Bwyl. When the deed was done, the truth would come out. Credit would be apportioned where due. Beskodnebwyl was not concerned with the refining of such matters. He carried nothing for credit. He wanted only to put a halt to this abhorrent, noisome mixing of species.

If the Burrow Master was with them, they would do precisely that— once and for all time.

Elkannah Skettle stepped off the shuttle and examined the world spread out before him with great interest. Ahead, he saw Lawlor and Martine passing rapidly through Customs. Pierrot, Botha, Nevisrighne, and the others were somewhere in the crowd behind him that was still filing off the transport vehicle. They had grown used to traveling together yet keeping their distance from one another.

The port facilities were efficient, the port's equipment spotless, the smiles on the faces of the local officials almost painfully welcoming. And why shouldn't they be? he mused. Dawn was a new world, bursting with opportunity, unclaimed lands, fortunes yet to be made. The climate was salubrious, the terrain inviting, the local flora and fauna reasonably pacific. A fine place to live and an enchanting place to visit.

Provided, he knew as he smiled pleasantly at the young woman who passed him through the body scanner, it could be kept free of bugs.

Not that there was anything inherently wrong with the bugs, he reflected as he presented himself to Customs. Or with the Quillp, or the AAnn, or any of the diverse other intelligent races with whom humankind shared this corner of the Orion Arm. He had reason of his own to be grateful to the bugs. Without the aid they had rendered to humankind in the Pitarian War, a favorite grandniece of his might not have survived the fighting. Military assistance in the midst of conflict was always welcome.

But the idea that relations should proceed beyond *that* was simply intolerable to one who loved his kind. The thranx might be all twirling antennae and sweet smells on the surface, but they were as alien as any sentient species humanity had yet encountered. The revelation that they had an actual colony in the Amazon Basin had been enough to trigger simmering outrage not only in men like himself, but in many who previously had given little thought to the problem.

And it *was* a problem. How could humankind ever be certain of its safety, of its very future, if empty-headed authorities allowed aliens to expand beyond the customary, restricted diplomatic and commercial sites where they were allowed? The notion that such growth should not only be permitted but encouraged and codified was sufficient to prod Skettle and those of like mind to move beyond protest to action. Negotiations, he knew, were presently at a delicate stage and could go either forward or back. A well-timed statement might be enough to put a stop to foolishness that bordered on the seditious.

Unlike others who felt similarly, Skettle did not think those humans who blindly advocated intimate ties with the thranx were traitors. They were simply ignorant. The bugs had deceived them. They were very clever, the thranx. Polite to a fault, ever conscious of the feelings of others, they had lulled supposedly astute people into a false sense of security the likes of which humankind had never before experienced.

But not all of us, he thought resolutely as he presented his travel case for inspection.

He waited while it passed beneath the Customs scanner. His corpus had already been cleared. Now it remained only for his luggage to do the same. Lawlor was the only potential weak link in the group, he knew. The man tended to exhibit unease even when no threat was apparent. That was why Skettle had chosen to carry this particular case. Old men were not usually the first to be suspected of smuggling.

With a tip of his cap and a practiced smile, the earnest young inspector passed him through. Picking up his case on the other side of the scanner, Skettle resumed his trek through the terminal, staying in the middle of the stream of disembarking passengers. Compared to those on major worlds like Terra or Amropolus, the terminal was not large. The scanner had detected nothing inside his case beyond the expected: clothing, vacation gear, personal communicator—the usual unremarkable assortment of travel goods.

It had not, however, performed a detailed analysis of the luggage itself. Even had it undergone that thorough an examination, the local authorities would still have been hard pressed to prove anything. Had they noted the composition of Lawlor's case, and Martine's, and subjected them to observation by a trained physical chemist, however, they would no doubt have been persuaded to investigate further.

Each of the three cases was composed of a different set of materials. When certain specific sections of the trio were cut up and then layered together in the appropriate proportions, then treated with a commonly available binding fluid, the result was neat little squares of an extraordinarily dynamic explosive. Utilizing this product, Elkannah Skettle and his colleagues intended for the widely advertised Dawn Intercultural Fair to give off even more heat than its organizers intended.

Everything had been carefully prepared in advance. It was meant for the deadly consequences to be blamed on unknown provocateurs working together with renegade thranx elements, but the apportionment of blame was not really crucial. What mattered was the disruption, and preferably the destruction, of the fair itself. If nothing else, it would put an end to what was supposed to be an exchange of "culture" among the races. What nonsense! Skettle chuckled to himself. The idea that humans and bugs should create art in common, that thranx culture should be allowed to contaminate human painting, music, song, or sculpture, would have been laughable if it was not so dangerous. Such aesthetic degradation could not be allowed. Were no one but Skettle and his associates thinking of the children as yet unborn? He thought, as he had so very many times, of the brave forebears of his own organization who had given their lives in the attempt years before to wipe out the foul thranx colony located in the Reserva Amazonia. Their sacrifice would not go unavenged.

The Preservers took separate transport to the small hotel they had booked. Located on the outskirts of Aurora, capital of the semitropical colony, the establishment overlooked a small natural lake and was within easy commuting distance of the fair. Following a suitable pause after checking in, they assembled by ones and twos in a prereserved commons room. There they bantered trivialities while Botha checked for hidden sensors and erected an industrial-strength sound envelope. There was no reason to suspect the presence of the former and no demonstrated need for the latter, but they were taking no chances—especially when the hand weapons they had contracted for were due to arrive with their local contact later in the day.

Feeling secure, they activated the tridee and waited the necessary few seconds for the room unit to warm up. As soon as the menu appeared in the air on the far side of the room, Pierrot directed it to provide them with as much local background on the fair as was available for viewing, commencing with material recorded as recently as ten days prior to their arrival.

The site was expanding impressively. Portable structures had been raised on the far side of the main lake, facilities for transport vehicles had been prepared underground, a high-speed transport link with the city continuing on to the shuttleport had been constructed and tested, and the usual virtually invisible molegel had been suspended in place above the entire site to shield it from any adverse weather, since Dawn did not yet possess the advanced climate-moderating facilities of more technologically mature worlds. Most of the larger exhibits were already in place and undergoing final checkout.

"Show us the thranx pavilions," Skettle ordered the tridee. Obediently, it supplied perfectly formed floating images on one side with a running printed commentary, in addition to the accompanying audio, on the other. Cerebral plug-ins were available, as was to be expected in any decent hostelry. Skettle disdained their use in favor of group observation.

"Look at that grotesquerie." Pierrot called for magnification, and the tridee unit complied. "What can that abomination possibly be?" She was shaking her head disdainfully.

"Some kind of organic sculpture, I would guess." Botha possessed more imagination than most of them, Skettle included. "It's not so bad, if you ignore the color scheme."

"Remember," Skettle announced, "it's not the content of the fair that we're here to terminate. We're not art critics." A few laughs rose above the ongoing commentary from the tridee. "It's the possibility that such content may lead to a freedom for thranx on human worlds that will let them infiltrate and eventually dominate our very lives, from the way we create to the way we live." This time his words were greeted not with laughter, but with grim muttering.

They watched for more than an hour, until Nevisrighne could take it no more. Rising, he walked over to the room's food service bay and ordered a chilled alcoholic fruit drink. "I'm sorry, but I can't watch anymore. Too many bugs for one morning."

"Time we finalized more than observations, anyway." Botha looked expectantly to Skettle.

The old man nodded, his fine gray beard bobbing prominently. "All right. I know you're all anxious to begin the actual work, but we must be careful not to rush matters. Now that the time for action is so near, it is all the more imperative that we exercise restraint and caution. The last thing we need is to attract the attention of local authorities."

Pierrot made a rude noise. "Security here is primitive compared to even New Riviera."

"General security, most likely," Skettle agreed. "But because of the sensitive nature of the fair, more than local government is involved. As a consequence, there will be extra precautions in place. Not only those of Earth, but from Hivehom as well."

No one followed Skettle's observation with any abrupt, disparaging comments. They had a healthy respect for thranx technology. But technology only added to the challenge. As to the eventual success of their mission, none among them had the slightest doubt. They were each of them well and truly dedicated to their avowed cause.

From his luggage Botha produced a purpose-built three-dimensional diagram of the fair site. It was exceptionally thorough. As well it ought to be, Skettle reflected, since he and half a dozen sympathetic associates of the Preservers had worked at refining and improving it almost constantly ever since the idea of the fair had been proposed and acted upon. It was safe to say that even the fair organizations themselves did not possess a schematic any more detailed than the one that presently floated before the oddly hushed crowd in the commons room.

Everything from food service to sewerage to controlling electronics to items as simple and straightforward as disposal bins were reflected in the diagram. There was nothing that could not be expanded and rotated so that the finest detail of construction and integration could be analyzed. Though not of a technical mien himself, Skettle could admire the artistry that had gone into the compilation of the schematic. It was a most beautiful diagram of destruction.

Fanning out to preselected locations throughout the fair, at the height of general festivities, he and his companions would install and try to simultaneously detonate the blended explosives. An impartial, emotionless beholder might have observed that among the myriad devices intended to be planted throughout the fair, not one was designed to impact upon the integrated fire-control facilities. With a cutting-edge emergency plant designed to cope instantly with even a minor blaze, the destruction of such facilities would seem to an outside observer to be a priority for a group of terrorists planning wholesale destruction. That such a contingency was nowhere in evidence was a tribute not to oversight or ignorance, but to the skill of Botha and the team he had worked with back on Earth.

It was astonishing, Skettle mused as he admired the schematic, how few people ever gave a thought to the fact that the time-proven, complex, fire-fighting chemicals used to put out unwanted blazes were composed of a precise chemical mixture that could also, in combination with certain laboriously engineered additional elements, stimulate instead of suffocate the very flames they were designed to extinguish. The anticipated, indeed hoped-for, attempt of the local emergency command to fight the blazes to be fomented by the Preservers would result not in a smothering of those conflagrations, but in their enhancement. Skettle smiled inwardly. The resulting chaos and confusion should contribute nicely to the blossoming cataclysm.

Botha assured him that upon contact with the materials to be spread by the multiple explosions, foams and liquids intended for combating out-of-control blazes would themselves be turned into a substance suitable for supplementing the very conflagrations they were designed to quench. By the time a sufficiency of nonreactive chemical retardants and suppressants could be brought from Aurora City, much of the glorious but debauched fair should be reduced to wind-blown cinders among which would drift the carbonized components of as many baked bugs as possible.

The consequent reaction among the human populace of this portion of the galaxy upon learning that the destruction had been cosponsored by thranx opposed to any deeper alliance among their respective species ought to put a clamp on any enthusiastic treaty making for some time to come, Skettle knew. Which thranx? Skettle's associates back on Earth had spent much time devising a complete bug terrorist hierarchy, the veracity of which *might* eventually be disproved. But by that time, the delay in negotiations that would result would give him and the rest of the Preservers ample time to spread their message to a more alerted population. Relations between human and thranx would progress no farther than humankind's relations with any other intelligent species.

That was as things should be, he mused. But education required time. This they would gain from the chaos that would be bought by the destruction of the fair. It would have the added beneficial effect of destroying the viability of any further such profane convocations. The Humanx Intercultural Fair on Dawn would be the first and last of its kind.

The fire in his eyes and those of his companions was a precursor to the greater conflagration that within a few days would engulf thousands of unsuspecting visitors.

It was not a blaze that was amenable to reason.

3

Cullen Karasi stood on the edge of the spectacular escarpment that overlooked the Mountain of the Mourners and reflected that he was a very
long way from home. Comagrave lay on the rim of the bubble of human
exploration, more parsecs from Earth than was comfortable to think
about. If not for the well-established colony in the nearby system of
Repler and the discovery of valuable mineral deposits on Burley, it was
doubtful humankind would have pushed so far so quickly into this section
of the Arm. By KK drive, the capital of the AAnn Empire, Blassussar,
was closer than Terra.

This latter fact was not lost upon the AAnn, who freely coveted
Comagrave. A semidesert planet whose ecological parameters all fell
near the center of their habitable paradigms, it was ideally suited to their
kind. To survive on its surface, humans had to exercise caution. In this
regard, however, it was no worse than many desertified parts of Earth
itself and was more accommodating than others. Survey after survey
revealed a wealth of mineral and biological potentiality—not to mention
additional archeological treasures yet to be unearthed. With proper preparation and development, humans would do well enough here.

Humankind's claim was clear, indisputable, and grudgingly recognized by the AAnn. In return for permission to establish a limited number
of observational outposts, strictly for purposes of study and education,
the reluctant reptiloids had offered to put their knowledge and expertise at
the service of the colonists. Despite certain reservations within the Terran
government, it was an offer that could not be denied. The AAnn had forgotten more about surviving on desert-type worlds than humans had ever
known, and the government on Earth was far, far away.

Certainly, Cullen reflected, the assistance his team had so far received from the AAnn had been a great help. It was they who had provided material aid when funds from his supporting foundation had been temporarily reduced. It was they who had saved thousands of credits by knowing the best places to establish safe camps. AAnn geologists invariably knew where to locate the deep wells that were necessary to tap Comagrave's elusive aquifers, which made settlement expansion as well as long-term scientific work in the field possible. And it was his AAnn peer, the scientist Riimadu CRRYNN, who had been the first to descry the secret of the Mourners.

That was why a base camp had been set up near the edge of the great escarpment. Below him, the sheer sandstone wall fell away more than a thousand meters to the flat valley floor below. Only the narrow and intermittent River Failings meandered through this desiccated vale, an echo of the immense watercourse that had once dominated this part of the continent. Already, field teams had gathered ample evidence that Comagrave had once enjoyed a much wetter and greener past. Whether this was the reason, or one of the reasons, for the demise of the Comagravian civilization and the highly advanced people who had called themselves the Sauun had yet to be determined.

Already, human exoarcheologists had accomplished much. Ruins of sizable cities were to be found on every continent. There was evidence of extensive agriculture, mining, and manufacturing—all the detritus of an advanced culture. And yet, tens of thousands of years ago, it had all perished. Nor was there any proof that the Sauun had achieved more than rudimentary space travel. Preliminary surveys of the planet's three moons revealed the ruins of only automatic stations, with no provision for habitation or development.

This did not jibe with the level of scientific achievement visible in their abandoned cities. There were gaps in technological evolvement where none ought to exist. It was the presence of such gaps in the Comagravian historical record and the desire to fill them in that drew researchers like Cullen to a world so distant.

Behind him, portative digging equipment hummed softly as fellow team members and advanced students strove to bring to the light the answers that hopefully lay buried beneath the hard, rocky surface of the escarpment. A vanager cried as it dipped and soared above the valley floor. With a leathery wingspan equal to that of a small aircraft, the indigenous scavenger could stay aloft indefinitely, carrying its two offspring in a pouch beneath its neck. Vanagers lived in the clouds, mated while aloft, and raised their progeny without ever touching the ground. To feed, they dove and plucked what they could from the surface or snatched it out of the air. Long ago they had lost all but rudimentary evidence of legs and feet. A vanager caught on the ground could only flop about clumsily, its great wings useless until a gust of wind sent it aloft once more. Or so the biologists insisted.

Far across the valley, the Mountain of the Mourners stared back at him. Literally. Hewn from the solid green-black diorite of the mountain from which they seemed to be emerging, the Twelve Mourners were at eye level with the top of the escarpment. Counting elaborate headdresses whose significance had yet to be interpreted, they averaged some fifteen hundred meters in height. How they had been carved, when and with what tools, was another of the many mysteries that Comagrave proffered in abundance.

With such gigantic representations of their kind available for study, there was no wondering what the Sauun had looked like. Tall and slim, with long, humanoid faces and horizontally slitted eyes, the colossal carvings were clad in flowing robes embellished with elaborate decorations and intricate designs. Despite their immense size, the Twelve had been depicted with extraordinary care and detail. Who they had been, no one yet knew. Knowing that the Sauun had progressed beyond kingdoms to a modern, planetwide government, all manner of possibilities had been proposed. The Twelve could be famous artists, or scientists, or the carvers themselves. Or politicians, or criminals, or individuals chosen at random, or composites of a theoretical species ideal. Cullen and his colleagues did not know, and they burned to find out. On one verity they were pretty much agreed: It seemed unlikely any civilization would go to the trouble of chiseling fifteen-hundred-meter-high images out of solid rock, finishing and polishing them with extraordinary care, to perpetuate the memory of a dozen nonentities. Whoever the Twelve were, they represented personages of some importance in the history of Comagrave.

It was the AAnn Riimadu who had first noticed that the enormous, solemn eyes of the graven icons were aligned on a level with the top of the escarpment. It was he who had theorized that the pupilless orbs were each and every pair subtly positioned so that they all focused on approximately the same spot—the one where Cullen's crew was presently engaged in exploration. Cullen owed the AAnn a debt that would be hard to repay. At the very least, they would share in the subsequent fame and profit of any discovery.

Riimadu was the only AAnn attached to the project. When he was not on site, Cullen missed the alien's expertise. Like all his kind, the AAnn exoarcheologist displayed an instinctive feel for the makeup of the ground. Adopting his suggestions had already saved the team days of hard work. With most of the busy crew untroubled by the AAnn scientist's presence from the start, one concern of Cullen's had been removed early in the process of excavation.

He did have to be careful to keep Riimadu and Pilwondepat apart. Though diplomacy was not a province of his expertise, Cullen knew enough of the traditional enmity that existed between AAnn and thranx to see to it that the two resident alien researchers encountered one another as infrequently as possible. Unlike the AAnn, who took an active part in the excavation, Pilwondepat was present as an observer only, on behalf of several thranx institutes. They had as much interest in ancient races as did humankind, but Comagrave was not to their liking. Though humans could survive and even prosper on a desert world, to the thranx it was an exceedingly uncomfortable place to be.

While humans had to worry only about sunburn because of Comagrave's comparatively thin atmosphere and take an occasional slug from a bottle of supplemental oxygen, and while Riimadu strolled around in perfect comfort, poor Pilwondepat lumbered about burdened by all manner of gear designed to supply him with the extra oxygen thranx required, as well as special equipment to keep his body properly moist. To a creature who thrived in high heat and even higher humidity, the climate of Comagrave was withering. Unprotected and unequipped, a thranx like Pilwondepat would perish within a few days, shriveled like an old apple. That was assuming it could keep warm at night, when surface temperatures dropped to a level tolerable to both humans and AAnn but positively deadly to a thranx.

So Pilwondepat was not comfortable with his assignment. He kept to his specially equipped portable dome as much as possible and only emerged to take recordings and make notes. When he spoke, it was with difficulty, through a special unit that covered his mandibles and moistened the air that flowed down his throat. Cullen felt sorry for him. The eight-limbed exoarcheologist must have done something unpopular to have come to a world so disagreeable to his kind.

As he turned to head back to camp, Cullen could feel the immense green-black bulges of the eyes of the Twelve drilling into the back of his neck. If only they could speak, he thought. If only they were not made of stone. And if only the Sauun had left some surviving record of what had happened to their civilization. It was such riddles that drove curious men and women to willingly endure harsh conditions on isolated outpost worlds. It was what had driven Cullen Karasi from a successful family business to the study of ancient alien civilizations.

The resolution to all the great unanswered questions lay somewhere on Comagrave, he was certain: buried in an abandoned city, secreted within a protected metal vesicle, locked in the overlying lines of incredibly complex Sauun code that Cullen's colleagues working elsewhere on the planet had not been able to fully decipher. The first requirement of a good archeologist was curiosity, but the second was patience. Just as one could not hurry history, so too could the unveiling of its mysteries not be rushed.

But waiting for the key was hell.

Meanwhile, each individual science team hoped theirs would be the one to bring to light the Rosetta that would unlock the enigma of the Sauun. While Cullen's hopes were as high as those of any of his colleagues, realistically he knew he was not likely to be the one to make the meaningful breakthrough. As others labored to interpret the riddles of the abandoned Sauun cities, he was stuck on a distant plateau whose isolation was notable even for an empty world like Comagrave. More than he cared to admit, he was relying for direction on the unofficial counsel and expertise of a visiting alien.

"I would not sstep there." As he spoke, Riimadu underscored his words with a second-degree gesture of admonition.

The AAnn's Terranglo was remarkably proficient. Seeing nothing but a few bumps in the ground ahead of him, Cullen nonetheless eased to his left before resuming his advance. He had come to trust the alien's instincts.

"I don't see anything," he commented as soon as he had drawn alongside the other biped. Unlike the insectoid thranx, the anatomy of the scaled, sharp-eyed AAnn was fairly similar to that of humans. The AAnn had evolved from a reptilelike ancestor, and they shared with humans the same upright bisymmetrical build and the same large single-lensed eyes, though their hands and feet each boasted one less digit than their human equivalents. They had no external ears, vertical pupils like cats, and highly flexible, prominent tails that they used to supplement their serpentine, courtly language of gestures. But for these details of design, and the bright, iridescent scales that covered their bodies, they might pass at a distance for wandering bald primates. In build they were slim, slightly shorter on average than humans, and muscular. Sexual dimorphism was more subtle than in primates, so that Cullen had to be certain who he was talking to before addressing individuals of the species as male or female.

Riimadu had established himself as male from the day he had first been allowed to visit and conduct observations of the human archeological team. Now he unslung a small, painstakingly embossed leather pouch from around his neck and right shoulder. Despite the dry heat that radiated from the rocks atop the plateau, he was not panting, and AAnn did not sweat. While Cullen and his coworkers perspired profusely, Riimadu was very much at home in the hot, arid climate.

"Look and learn," the alien hissed softly as he tossed the pouch. It landed atop one of the slight bumps in the ground. Soundlessly, it was jolted half a dozen centimeters into the air, fell to the ground nearby, and lay motionless. Striding forward, his limber tail flicking from side to side, Riimadu recovered the pouch. Cullen noted that this time the AAnn handled it with extra care.

Bringing it back, he held it out for the human to inspect. Three small brown spines had pierced the bottom of the pouch. One went all the way through the fine leather to emerge from the other side.

"Defenssive mechanissm for an endemic ssoil-browsser. Not a predator." Using his clawed fingers, Riimadu slowly extracted one of the spines from the pouch. Its tip was so sharp it seemed to narrow down to nothingness.

"Poisonous?" Cullen examined the needlelike implement respectfully.

"Analyssiss will be required. With your permission." Removing the other pair of spines one by one, the AAnn carefully placed them within the pouch's padded interior.

"I wonder if they would have gone through the sole of my boot." Turning away from the no-longer-innocuous, quiescent mounds, Cullen continued back toward the site.

"While I am a firm believer in dynamic experimentation in the field," Riimadu responded, "I did not feel it would be entirely ethical to utilize you for ssuch a purposse without firsst sseeking your conssent." He hissed softly, an exhalation that Cullen had come to recognize as AAnn laughter. While the reptiloids were by nature more solemn than the thranx, and positively wooden alongside the Quillp, that they possessed and displayed a sense of humor could not be denied. It was the subject matter that was occasionally off-putting.

"I appreciate the consideration," he told the alien dryly. "My feet hurt plenty as it is." The AAnn did not react, taking the comment at face value. Well, Cullen mused, one couldn't expect every witticism to make the whimsical jump between species.

The ability to espy hazardous camouflaged fauna was something he had come to expect from Riimadu. He told the AAnn so as he thanked him more directly.

"You humanss are alwayss looking up, or ahead," the exoarcheologist commented. "Anywhere but where you sshould. On a world like Vussus-sica you need to keep your attention focussed much more often on the ground in front of you."

Vussussica was the name the AAnn had given to Comagrave. It was rumored that certain elements among the Imperial survey services had never fully relinquished their claim to the distant world humans had begun to explore long before the first AAnn ships had arrived in orbit around its sun. Subsequent to the conclusive imprinting by both sides of the formal agreements regarding Comagrave's future status, it was presumed that these dissident elements had been suppressed. Certainly no one had mentioned them to Cullen or to any of his staff. To Riimadu they were of no consequence. "A hisstorical footnote," he had called them when asked to expound his own feelings on the matter.

On an entirely practical level, Cullen did not know what he would have done without the AAnn's help. It was Riimadu who had suspected that the eyes of the Mourners held a secret, and it was he who had triangulated the gazes of the twelve monoliths and chosen this site for excavation. That they had so far failed to find evidence of anything more significant than local subsurface life-forms like the spine shooter did not mean the site was barren of potential discovery, only that they had more work to do and deeper to dig. Certainly the preliminary subterranean scan had generated some interesting anomalies highly suggestive of the presence of unnatural stratification. Digging proceeded by hand only to protect the topmost layer of whatever they might uncover. Thereafter, once they knew what they were dealing with, more advanced excavation tools could be brought into play according to the fragility of the site. They knew they were onto *something*. They just did not, as yet, know what.

Patience, he reminded himself.

A thickly bundled figure was lurching clumsily along the western edge of the main excavation. Setting his hopes of discovery aside, Cullen spared a brief rush of sympathy for the awkwardly garbed Pilwondepat.

Despite making use of all six legs for locomotion, the thranx scientist was still tottering. The humidifier that was wrapped around his b-thorax covered his breathing spicules completely. It was not quite silent and made him sound like he was wheezing even though the source of the sound was entirely mechanical. Though the device drew moisture from the air, there was not enough in the atmosphere of Comagrave to satisfy even the hardiest thranx. The humidifier's draw had to be supplemented by the contents of a lightweight bottle that rode on the scientist's back. Coupled with leg and body wraps that helped to retain body moisture, Pilwondepat resembled a child's toy engaged in a clumsy and ineffectual attempt to break free of its packaging.

Only the scientist's head was completely unprotected, allowing him to observe without obstruction. The chafing of his chitin from the dryness of the air was plain to see, even though Cullen knew the exoarcheologist employed several specially formulated creams to maintain his exoskeleton's shine and character. The site administrator had often wondered what awful blunder the thranx had committed to get himself assigned to Comagrave. He had been shocked to eventually learn that Pilwondepat had actually requested the assignment.

"What are you?" he had asked in an unguarded moment. "Some kind of masochist?"

Pilwondepat had clicked to the contrary. "The love of self-suffering is a human trait. I simply felt the opportunities here too intriguing to eschew. Like you, I want to know what happened to these people—to their cities, and to their dream of space travel that was never fulfilled despite their having apparently achieved an equivalent level of technology in all other aspects of science."

"But to volunteer for duty on a world so blatantly inhospitable to your kind . . . ," Cullen had continued.

The visiting scientist had responded with a cryptic gesture the human had been unable to access in his pictionary of thranx gestures. "This is the world where the Sauun lived. As a field researcher, you must know yourself that recordings and records are no substitute for working on site."

Cullen recalled the brief but instructive conversation as he watched the thranx totter to the edge of the excavation. If the eight-limbed academic's dedication did not exceed his own, it certainly matched it. Despite the appalling conditions, his hard-shelled counterpart rarely complained. As he put it, the fascination of the Sauun enigma helped to moisten more than his curiosity.

Advancing in front of Cullen, Riimadu approached the thranx from behind and addressed the scientist in his own language. "*Srr!iik,* you musst be careful here, or you will fall in."

Pilwondepat looked back and up at the AAnn, who loomed over him, though not by as much as would the average human. "I have six legs. Have a care for your own footing, and don't worry about mine."

"I worry about everyone'ss footing on thiss world." Leaning forward, Riimadu peered into the excavation. Neatly partitioned with cubing beams of light, the hole was now some thirty meters in diameter and seven deep. At the bottom, humans labored in thin, lightweight clothing, exuding salt-laden body water as they worked. Their skins, in a variety of colors, rippled unsettlingly in the light of Vussussica's midday sun. Unlike AAnn or thranx, their epidermal layers were incredibly fragile. Why, even a feeble thranx could split them from neck to ankle with a single sharpened claw!

They were very quick, though. Agility was their compensation for lack of external toughness. To an AAnn or thranx, the human body

seemed composed of lumps of malleable material, stretching and squash-
ing unpleasantly in response to the slightest muscular twitch. Their
anatomy had no gravity, no deliberation. The AAnn would have found
them amusing, had they not been both gifted and prolific. And dangerous.
The Pitarian War had revealed their true capabilities. To the AAnn, who
had remained neutral throughout the conflict, the war had been exceedingly instructive.

Lurching forward, he leaned his body weight against the thranx's
right side. Pilwondepat's foothands slid over the edge of the excavation,
dirt and gravel sliding away beneath them as he scrambled to retain a
foothold. Under such pressure, a biped would have taken a serious tumble
into the open excavation. The thranx's four trulegs kept him from falling.

Turning his head sharply, the thranx's compound eyes glared up at
the AAnn. "That was deliberate!"

"I kiss the ssand beneath your feet if it wass sso." Gesturing apologetically, the AAnn exoarcheologist stepped back. Sharp teeth flashed
between powerful, scaly jaws. "Why would I do ssuch a thing? Esspecially to a fellow sstudent of the unknown."

"Why do the AAnn strike and retreat, hit and retire?" As he regained
his composure, Pilwondepat held his ground, determined not to give the
AAnn the satisfaction of seeing him flee. "Always testing, your kind.
Always probing for weaknesses—not only of individuals, but of worlds
and alliances." The thranx gestured with a truhand. "I don't even blame
you, Riimadu. You can't help yourself—it's your nature. But don't push
me again. I may not be as strong, but I have better leverage than you."

The AAnn was visibly amused. "Colleague, are you challenging me
to a fight?"

"Don't be absurd. We are both here as guests and on sufferance of the
human establishment, *crrllk*. They are not fond of either of us, and must
regard our presence here as an imposition and distraction from their
work."

"Not the human Cullen." With the tip of his highly flexible tail, the
AAnn gestured to where the human in charge was descending the earthen
steps that had been cut into the side of the excavation. "He knowss that it
wass I who found thiss ssite, and I can assure you that he iss properly
grateful."

Pilwondepat turned away. He knew the AAnn was right. The human
Cullen Karasi owed the AAnn his gratitude. Pilwondepat possessed no
such leverage with the human, or with any of his coworkers. Stumbling to
and fro among them, weighed down by the humidifying equipment that
kept him alive if not entirely comfortable, he noted their sideways stares
and heard their murmurings of disapproval. The archeological team rep-

resented a cross section of humanity, though a well-educated one. There were among them some who actively espoused closer ties with the thranx. They were opposed by those who fervently desired that the two dissimilar species keep their distance from one another. The majority listened to the diverse arguments of their fellows and tried to make up their as-yet-undecided minds. Pilwondepat feared that his personal comportment under trying circumstances was insufficient to elevate the status of his people in the humans' eyes. At every opportunity, he did his best to counteract the sorry image he was certain he was presenting.

If only he could get rid of the awkward, encumbering survival gear! Within his private dome he could do so, and actually relax. But those few humans curious enough to pay him a visit did not linger. Coupled with the temperature on the plateau, the 96 percent humidity Pilwondepat favored within his living quarters soon drove them out. There was nothing he could do about it. If he lowered the humidity in the dome to a level humans would find comfortable, that would leave him miserable all of the time, instead of just when he was working outside.

So he tried to learn their language, a form of communication as slippery and fluid as their bodies, and make friends where he could. Meanwhile he was forced to watch as Riimadu strolled freely about the site, interacting effortlessly with the humans, sharing the same basic body structure and single-lensed eyes, and positively luxuriating in what for the AAnn was an ideal climate.

Had the reptiloid deliberately nudged him in an attempt to send him tumbling over the edge into the excavation, or had it been an accident? One could never be sure of anything except their innate cunning where the AAnn were concerned. They would gesture first-degree humor while cutting the ground out from beneath you. Yet he could not complain. The humans, who had far less experience of the AAnn than did the thranx, continued to remain ambivalent in their attitude toward them. Humans, Pilwondepat had noted in the course of his studies, had a tendency to react against assertions they themselves had not proven. Accuse the AAnn, insult them, insist on their intrinsic perfidy, and well-meaning humans were likely to leap to their defense.

It was infuriating. The thranx knew the AAnn, knew what they were capable of. Humans did not want to hear it. So the insectoids had to proceed discreetly in all matters involving the scaled ones, whether in personal relationships or at the diplomatic level. Humans would have to learn the truth about the AAnn by themselves. Like others of his kind, Pilwondepat only hoped this education would not prove too painful.

For their part, the AAnn were being more patient and proceeding more slowly in their developing relations with humankind than the thranx had ever known them to do with any newly contacted species. This knowledge allowed Pilwondepat to smile internally. Having to proceed with such unaccustomed caution must be causing the AAnn Imperial hierarchy a great deal of discomfort. He certainly hoped so.

Meanwhile, he was but one representative of his family, clan, and hive, isolated on a world of great mysteries, dependent on the unpredictable humans for continued permission to work among them and, indeed, for his very survival. That many of them viewed his presence among them with suspicion and xenophobia he could not help. He could only do his work and try, when the opportunity presented itself, to make friends. For some reason he enjoyed greater sympathy from human females than from the males. This, he had been told before embarking on his assignment, was a likely possibility, and he should be prepared to take advantage of it.

It had to do, he had been informed, with the thranx body odor, which nearly all primates found exceedingly pleasant. More than once, human workers had commented upon it, and he had been forced to resort to his translator to ascertain the meaning of strangely emollient words like *jasmine* and *frangipani*.

With a sigh, he started around the edge of the excavation. It was time to do some work among the human field staff. That meant making his way to the bottom of the excavation. In the absence of a familiar ramp, he would have to cope with human-fashioned "steps." It was uncivilized and awkward, but he dared not ask for help. Special treatment was the one thing he was determined not to request. Many humans did not realize that thranx, built low to the ground, were terrible climbers despite boasting the use of eight limbs.

A young worker named Kwase saw the scientist struggling at the top of the first step. Putting down his soil evaporator, the young man turned and vaulted up the earthen staircase to confront the alien. Smiling encouragingly, he made a cup of both hands in front of his own legs. Quickly discerning the sturdy biped's intent, Pilwondepat gratefully dipped both antennae in the mammal's direction before carefully placing one foothand in the proffered fleshy stirrup and resuming his descent.

Brr!!asc—we make progress! he told himself with satisfaction. The annoyed look on Riimadu's glistening face as he observed the human voluntarily assisting the thranx was even worth a few deep breaths of inadequate, desiccated air.

The bottom of the excavation was no familiar homeworld burrow, he mused when he finally hopped down off the last step, but it was far more calming than the wind-blown, lonely surface.

4

Fanielle watched the Hysingrausen Wall slide past beneath the aircar's wings. Running east to west across this portion of the central continent, the immense, forest-fringed limestone rampart was interrupted only by a succession of enormous waterfalls that spilled over the three-thousand-meter rim. Despite the heavy flow, most evaporated before they reached the ground. Only a very few, the offspring of mighty rivers that arose in the northern mountains beyond the Mediterranea Plateau, thundered against rocks at the base of the wall.

The majestic geologic feature had kept the thranx from making anything more than cursory explorations of the high tableland. Humans were delighted to be allowed to establish themselves in a sizable region the thranx had ignored, and many thranx were pleased to see humans making use of an uplifted portion of their planet that was to them the perfect picture of a half-frozen hell.

She sealed her field jacket as the aircar, once clear of the strong downdrafts that raked the wall, commenced a gradual descent. The afternoon temperature at Azerick Station was sixteen degrees C. Bracing to a human, unbearably frigid and dry to a thranx. Azerick did not receive many visitors from the heavily populated lowlands. Most of the thranx who were assigned to help facilitate the station's development stayed down in Chitteranx, in the rain forest, where the humidity and heat were pleasantly overpowering. A few unlucky souls were assigned permanently to the human outpost. Being thranx, they rarely gave voice to their displeasure. Only someone like Anjou, who had learned to interpret many of their gestures, could tell how unhappy they were.

In less than two weeks she would have her meeting with the eint. She intended to be forceful but congenial. There were years worth of particulars that needed to be discussed, lists of individual items that needed to be addressed in detail. She would have to pick and choose carefully so as not to offend, or bore, or isolate her estimable audience. Haflunormet was a good soul, but during the time they had worked with each other he had been able to offer little more than sympathetic encouragement on issues of real import. Working at last with someone who could actually make decisions promised to be enlightening as well as effective.

There was so much to prepare. She worried about overwhelming the eint with minutiae before paradigms could be agreed upon.

The aircar set down gently amid the quasi-coniferous forest that covered the plateau. While the trees resembled nothing arboreal on Earth, at least they were green. Jeremy was waiting for her. They embraced decorously. Other moves would have to wait for greater privacy.

He took her bag as they walked through the terminal. "I hear you finally got your meeting with a higher-up. Some of us were beginning to wonder if any of the diplomatic staff here ever would."

"You know the thranx." They turned a corner, squeezing past chattering travelers outbound on the aircar that had just arrived. "Caution in everything."

He made a rude noise. "It's more than that. It's deliberate. They're trying to stay friends, close friends, without committing themselves to anything definite. The Pitarian War was an exception, brought on by exceptional circumstances. Now they've reverted to the hive norm." Outside, he placed her bag in the transport capsule. In seconds, they were racing along a grassy trail split by the glistening metallic strip of a powerguide.

"I don't think that's the case at all, Jeremy." Leaning back in the seat, she watched the forest whiz past. At this speed, details vanished in a green blur, and travelers could almost imagine they were speeding through the far more familiar woods of Canada or Siberia.

He shrugged diffidently. "Well, if anybody should know, it's you, Fannie. You've spent more time among them than anyone else on staff. Personally, I don't see how you stand the climate and the crowding inside their hives." Reaching out, he took one of her hands in his and with a fingertip began to trace abstract designs on the back. "I'd rather have you spend more time here, you know. It's not real great for my ego to think that you prefer a bug's company to mine."

She smiled and let him toy with her hand and fingers. Little sparks seemed to materialize with each contact. "Unfortunately, while humankind has conquered deep space, cured the most serious primitive diseases, and spread itself across a small portion of one galactic arm, we have yet to solve the unfathomable complexities of the male ego."

His fingers jetéed up her arm. "Chaos theory. That's the ticket."

The darkened capsule arrived at Azerick with both passengers considerably relaxed in mind and body. Jeremy bid her a reluctant farewell, leaving her to compose the report she would present in person to the ambassador. Upgrading the embassy here to full settlement status was one item on the crowded agenda. The humans wanted it—for one thing, it would mean promotions all around—but the thranx were reluctant. Granting such status implied recognition of a condition existing between the two species that they were not sure they were prepared to acknowledge.

She showered and redressed, leaving off the field jacket since the station was heated to an Earth-ideal standard of twenty-two degrees, with humidity to match. Ambassador Toroni was anxious to hear her preliminary report. Details could come later.

Smiles and congratulations awaited her in the main conference room. Outside, the forest of the Mediterranea Plateau, as the resident humans had come to call it, marched away toward distant high mountains. A smattering of applause greeted her rising. She did not blush, was not uncomfortable. The acclaim had been earned.

Spreading a brace of viewers out before her, she folded her hands and waited as the ambassador rose. There were eight other people in the room, most of whom she knew well. Living in an outpost on an alien world left little room for people to be strangers.

"First," he said, "I want to extend my personal congratulations to Fanielle Anjou for securing what we had come to believe might never come to pass: an appointment to discuss, and to present, multiple items of diplomatic importance on which we have all been working for years. While the method of finally obtaining this long-sought-after meeting may have been unorthodox, I think I can say safely that no strenuous objections will be raised at higher levels."

"Especially since 'higher levels' have no idea what a Bryn'ja request is," Gail Hwang observed tartly.

"Funny, you don't look pregnant." From his seat next to the ambassador, Jorge Sertoa grinned down at her. "Who's the father?"

"Probably that thranx she's been seeing so much of," someone else put in quickly. Laughter rolled the length of the table.

"I don't think so." Aram Mieleski pursed his lips as he rested his chin thoughtfully on the tips of his fingers. "The delivery mechanism involved is so different that . . ."

"Oh, shut up, Aram," Gail chided him. "I swear, if ever anybody needed a humor transplant . . ."

"Emotional conditions cannot be transferred between individuals," an unruffled Mieleski calmly observed, by his words confirming the necessity of her observation.

"What will you do," Enrique Thorvald asked seriously, "if the thranx continue to inquire as to your condition?"

"They'll be informed that I lost the multiple larvae prior to giving birth." Anjou held one of her readers before her. "I've worked it all out. If anything, that should gain me even more sympathy. And it doesn't hurt that Eint Carwenduved, with whom I am to meet, is female."

"Yeah," Sertoa muttered. "You can compare the glaze on your ovipositors." While basically a good guy, Jorge Sertoa was among several outspoken members of the outpost staff who were less than enthusiastic about cementing deeper relations with their hosts.

"And I bet you'd like to be there to see that." Her rejoinder prompted more laughter and defused what could have been an awkward moment. Putting the jovial banter to rest, she hefted the reader and commenced delivering her formal report. They would all receive copies in due course, but this way questions could be asked as soon as they were formulated. Ambassador Toroni was a firm believer in encouraging staff interaction.

When she concluded, less than an hour later, there were fewer queries than she had anticipated. Her accomplishment in securing the official meeting was duly applauded once again, but most of the questions thrown her way concerned maintaining the security of the ruse she had invented to gain the appointment rather than what she was actually going to discuss when it finally came to fruition.

"It all depends," she commented by way of summation, "on how much authority I'm given going into the meeting."

All eyes shifted to Toroni. Running a hand through his shock of white hair, he leaned back in his chair and considered. For an ambassador appointed to what was arguably the most important nonhuman populated world known, he was casual in manner and laid-back in his work habits. It was an attitude much appreciated by those who labored under him. Azerick was a lonely enough place to be stationed without being forced to toil for some inflexible martinet.

"If it were up to me, Fanielle, I'd give you permission to vet and sign treaties. But you know I can't do that. I don't have that capability myself. As soon as we adjourn here, I'll get on the deep-space communicator and find out just how far the authorities on Earth are prepared to let you go. One thing you can be sure of: You won't be allowed to negotiate anything controversial."

"I already know that," she responded.

"But we might be able to procure more authority for you than you think, by trumpeting the importance of this meeting, how it's likely not to be repeated for some time, the sensitive nature of relations between you and this Eint Carwenduved—I intend to call in every favor and promise I've been stockpiling." He leaned forward. "I want you to have as much autonomy going in as we can manage. This is the first real breakthrough we've had in months, and I don't want to squander it."

"Even so, sir," Sertoa began, "we don't want Fanielle to agree to anything hasty." He smiled deferentially at her. "Careful perusal and dissection of any potential covenant is demanded before the authority to sign can be conferred."

"Loosen up, Jorge," she told him. "No matter what I manage to get the eint to agree to, I don't think you have to worry about some thranx sharing your bathroom anytime soon."

It was an exceedingly mild put-down, but whether for that reason or one unknown, Sertoa said nothing more for the duration of the meeting.

"I've been working on proceeding to the next step in securing a stronger alliance among our respective species." Holding up her reader, she touched a contact and waited the couple of seconds necessary to transfer the relevant documentation to everyone else's handheld. "If the eint doesn't dismiss it out of hand, I intend to at least broach a number of possibilities for future discussion."

"Such as what?" Hwang asked with obvious interest.

"A lasting, permanent alliance. Nothing held back. Military presence on one another's worlds, mutual command of tactics and weaponry, joint colonization of which this plateau and the Amazon Basin are only the most preliminary sorties." Someone whistled.

"You don't want much, do you, Fanielle?" Genna Erlich observed.

"You're talking about the kind of treaty that would require not only a vote of the full Terran Congress, but approval by majorities on all the settled worlds." Mieleski's tone was somber. "It's a very adventurous program."

"What are we here for, if not to press for closer relations?" Toroni smiled paternally. "Though you've certainly chosen an ambitious agenda for yourself, Fanielle."

"Everything depends on the eint's reaction to my prefatory suggestions," she replied a bit defensively. "Depending on how things go, I might not even have the chance to make known my more elaborate proposals."

"Quite right." Rising, Toroni indicated that the conference was at an end. "I look forward to reading all the details of your report, Fanielle. With luck, we should within a couple of days have some guidelines from Earth detailing how you will be allowed to proceed. I myself am optimistic, and intend to frame the request for those guidelines in the most anxious manner possible.

"In the meantime, we all of us have much to study, and to digest. I take it you are amenable to criticisms and suggestions, Ms. Anjou?"

"Always," she replied, at the same time hoping there would not be too many. Putting what had previously been an informal succession of guidelines into presentation format was going to take most of the time she had remaining until her meeting with the eint. The last thing she needed was a flood of well meaning but essentially superfluous advice.

Only when word came back from Earth that she was to have essentially a free hand in making proposals—though she could not commit to anything more significant than, for example, the Intercultural Fair about to get under way on the colony world of Dawn—did she realize how truly important the encounter would be. Though usually an island of calm amid her often frazzled colleagues, she finally had to take some minor medication to still her nerves.

I am going to go in there, she told herself, as the chosen representative of my entire species, knowing that I have gained that access on the back of a lie. But while the burden was making her increasingly uneasy, she would not have turned the meeting over to one of her colleagues for all the suor melt on Barabbas.

As the time for her to return to Daret drew near, she found herself relying more than ever on Jeremy's strong, self-assured presence. A microbiologist, he had no diplomatic ax to grind, nothing of a professional nature to gain from her success or failure. He was interested only in her and their future together; not in her mission. It was a gratifying change from the characteristic infighting and arguing that took place within the highly competitive diplomatic hierarchy.

When the day scheduled for departure finally did arrive and she had little to take with her but her hopes and anxieties, he took time off from his lab work to join her for the brief journey in the transport capsule that would convey her to the settlement airport.

Once more, the great green forest of the Mediterranea Plateau was rushing past outside the transport's port. To the thranx, it was their deepest jungle, the most biologically mysterious region left on their homeworld. Visiting human researchers, strolling about comfortably in pants and shirts, were making valuable reports and passing on the results of their research to their thranx counterparts, who would have required special gear and attire simply to survive in the temperate-cool lower oxygen environment humans found perfectly amenable. Similar revelations were being made by thranx researchers stationed in the deep Amazon and

Congo Basins on Earth. Of such serendipitous exchanges of data and knowledge were scientific alliances, if not diplomatic ones, strengthened. During the high-speed commute they held hands and talked. Jeremy's research was going exceptionally well, and everyone at the outpost was talking about Fanielle's breakthrough in securing a meeting with a thranx who ranked high enough to actually make decisions as well as recommendations.

"I'm not going to be able to get near you when you get back," he told her teasingly. "You'll be blanketed by representatives of the media."

"If this visit is a success," she reminded him.

"There are no *ifs* where you're concerned, lady-mine."

"Maybe not where I'm concerned, but diplomacy is something else again." Why, she wondered, did someone who was perfectly comfortable trolling the corridors of interstellar power suddenly and so frequently in this man's presence devolve to the maturity level of a sixteen-year-old? She had long ago become convinced it was due to a recessive gene on the Y chromosome.

"Just like you're something else again." Leaning forward, he kissed her as passionately as the time remaining to the airport conveniently allowed, then rose. "I could use something to drink. Do you want anything before—?"

She became aware of the pain as vision returned. It seemed to increase in proportion to the intensity of the light that splashed across her retinas. Memory loaded in increasingly large chunks: who she was, where she ought to be, what she was supposed to be doing. Too much of it failed to jibe with what she was feeling and seeing. Though the first words she heard were in themselves entirely innocent, their import was uncompromisingly ominous.

"She's awake."

She recognized the voice. Ambassador Toroni had a distinctive, measured way of speaking, slightly nasal but memorable. It matched his face, which moments later was smiling down into her own. There was relief in his countenance, but no humor.

A voice she did not recognize said, "I'll leave you alone with her for a while. Her vitals are fine, but she's liable to be less than completely coherent until the comprehensive neural block has fully worn off. The aerogels will keep her comfortable. If anything untoward occurs, or something doesn't look right, just hit the alert."

"Thank you, nurse."

Nurse. Anjou liked the sound of that even less than the absence of humor in her superior's expression. She struggled to sit up. Reading the

relevant cerebral commands from the patch fastened to the back of her
skull and ascertaining that rising did not contradict her medical profile,
the bed complied.

Sitting up, she found that the light did not hurt as much. In addition to
Toroni, Sertoa was also present. He did not even try to fake a smile.
"Hello, Fanielle. How—how are you feeling?"

"Sleepy. Confused. Something hurts. No," she corrected herself,
"everything hurts, but something is muting it." Looking past them,
searching the hospital room, she did not see a third face. Especially not
the one she sought. "I've been in an accident."

Toroni nodded, very slowly. "What's the last thing you remember,
my dear?"

"Packing to go to Daret. No," she corrected herself quickly, inspired
perhaps by their stricken looks. "I was already on my way there. On the
transport to the airport. With—" She looked past them again. "—Jeremy
Hyguens."

"He was a good friend of yours," Sertoa commented softly.

"Yes. We are—" She broke off as Toroni threw the other man a look
of quiet exasperation.

He was. That was what Sertoa had said. *He was.* She sank back into the
cushioning aerogel, wishing it was solid enough to smother her. When she
had finished crying, when the tears had subsided enough for her to form
words again, she believed that she heard herself whispering, "What . . .
happened?"

Bernard Toroni sat down on the edge of the bed, the transparent aerogel dimpling under his extra weight. He wanted to take this exceptional
young woman's hand, to hold it tightly, to make things better. But that
was not a procedure allowed for in the diplomatic syllabus, and circumstances dictated that he keep a certain distance. He did not want to keep
his distance, though. He wanted to hold her the way he had once held his
own children back on Earth, before he had begun to receive assignments
to other worlds.

"You were on a transport capsule in line for the airport. There was an
empty cargo carrier on the strip ahead of you. No one knows exactly how
it happened, but there was a program failure. The cargo unit's drive field
reversed. The two capsules hit very hard."

"The kinetic energy released—" Sertoa started to say before a look
from Toroni silenced him.

"Once engaged, transport capsule fields don't 'reverse.' The programs are designed to be fail-safe. At worst, onboard in-line safeties
should have cut its drive. Had that happened, your capsule's onboard sensors would have had time to detect the failure ahead and bring it to a stop

prior to impact." He paused for reflection. "There were a total of twelve people on board the capsule you were traveling in. You and a fellow named Muu Nulofa from Engineering were the only survivors."

"Jeremy—" She did not swallow particularly hard, but her throat was on fire.

Toroni shifted his position on the edge of the bed. No one else had been willing to pay this first visit. "The lifesavers who extricated you from what was left of the capsule found his body sprawled across yours. They theorize that the extra . . . padding . . . is what saved your chest from being crushed when the front wall of your cubicle caved in. There was nothing they could do for him. Cerebral and internal hemorrhaging." He hesitated. "I did not know the man, but I have since spoken to some of his colleagues. They all describe him as a fine human being who was dedicated to his work. And to . . . other things."

Her eyes rose to meet his. He did not enjoy the experience, but he respected the woman in the bed far too much to look away. "Did they also tell you we had been discussing marriage?"

"No." The ambassador's lips tightened. "No, nobody mentioned that to me."

She relieved him by turning her head to one side, letting the warm aerogel supply the support her muscles no longer cared to provide. "We didn't talk about it much except among ourselves. There were too many other distractions. Professional—" She choked softly on the word.

It was quiet in the room. No one spoke for many minutes: the two men remaining silent out of respect, the woman because she no longer had anything to say. Behind her eyes, something had gone away.

"It's very interesting," Toroni finally murmured. When she failed to react, he added, "Unprecedented, certainly."

Moving with a slowness that had as its source something deeper and more profound than medication, she rolled her head back in his direction. "What is?"

"The expression of concern. On a personal level. From our hosts."

She frowned ever so slightly. "I don't understand."

"Some of the recently communicated terminology is unique to our translator's experience. I am told there are nuances involved they have never before seen expressed." He mustered a fatherly smile. "There are several from your contact Haflunormet, as well as from other contacts you have made among the locals. Of particular note is the one from Eint Carwenduved. Not only are deepest regrets expressed, but she wishes to assure us that as soon as you are able to resume work, she looks forward now more than ever to making your acquaintance."

"Your meeting is still on." Sertoa looked pleased. "You'll carry into it with you the extra benefit of added sympathy."

Her mind stirred, roiled, thoughts and emotions crashing into one another before slipping away in opposing directions. "No I won't," she responded tersely.

Toroni blinked. "I'm sorry, my dear?"

The look in her eyes was very different from the one that had commanded her countenance only moments earlier. "I won't be carrying sympathy or anything else into that meeting because I'm not going to be in attendance. I'm not going, Bernard. I'm finished here. Finished with Hivehom, finished with the bu—with the thranx, finished with everything." She turned away, until all she could see was the aerogel support. The portion in front of her face opaqued when she closed her eyes. "I want—I need to go home."

The ambassador considered. In the course of his distinguished career he had been faced with similar situations before. Some had even been inflected with highly emotional overtones. But never before anything like this. Never. That did not keep him from pressing forward as he knew he must.

"Fanielle," he told her as tenderly as he could, "you *have* to do this. No one else here at the mission has managed to achieve as intimate a rapport with our hosts. No one else is as facilely comfortable with their ways, with their habits or mannerisms. *You are the best qualified to take this meeting.* That's why you were given the assignment of trying to secure it in the first place. It's your moment of triumph. You have to take it."

From the vicinity of the aerogel came the agonizingly stillborn response. "I don't want it anymore."

Hating himself, Toroni refused to let it, or her, go. Both were too important. "It's not a question of you wanting or not wanting it. You have to do it because no one else can do it as well. This is a highly sensitive moment in the development of relations between our species and the thranx. Perhaps even a milestone. We won't know until we see the fruits of our labors begin to blossom. The fruits of your labors, Fanielle. Do you really want to cast aside everything you've worked for here?"

"I've already cast it, Bernard. Find somebody else to go. Find somebody else to take my place."

Swallowing determinedly, he leaned toward her, careful not to initiate a significant disturbance within the highly responsive aerogel. "Don't you think, Fanielle, that if I felt someone, anyone else, was sufficiently qualified I would have assigned them to the task already? Before coming here to see you?"

Deep within, a certain component of her shattered self was pleased by the sincere words of a man she greatly respected. But like so much else that was Fanielle Anjou, that part of her was hiding now, isolated and shunted aside by the nightmare that had overwhelmed her life.

"I told you, Bernard. I don't care. It's not important anymore."

He nodded slowly, even though she was not looking at him. Or at anything else. The ensuing silence lasted longer than its predecessor. Once again, it was the ambassador who broke it.

"Program failure. Transport capsule drive fields just don't go into reverse. The system is replete with fail-safes—every one of which failed. The engineers are working on it, working hard. They're good people, but they're baffled. They cannot afford to be, because we must know what caused the accident. If we don't know, then we cannot with any certainty prevent a repetition. Of the accident. If," he concluded concisely, "it was an accident."

It was enough to turn her head. "Bernard?"

Sertoa took his turn. "Fanielle, you know as well as any of us that there are elements, some of them with substantial backing, both among the thranx and our own kind who will do anything to prevent the kind of union between our species that the enlightened among us seek. I'm not talking about the great mass of undecideds on both sides. I'm talking about the kind of blatant, old-fashioned fanaticism we thought we had evolved beyond."

Slowly, she digested what her colleague was saying. Contemplated it from an assortment of viewpoints. In the end, every one of them was equally ugly.

"You think someone deliberately reprogrammed that cargo capsule to reverse and smash into the one that was taking me to the airport?"

"We don't know that." Toroni was relieved to see some small flicker of alertness return to his junior colleague's expression, even if it was thus far focused entirely on concern for something unconnected to professional interests. "At this point it is only speculation. But I am not the only one to have considered it. Azerick Authority is pondering the possibility with utmost seriousness. If, and I caution if, the hypothesis should turn out to have any basis in fact, it would mean that our entire modus here will have to undergo the most strict review. We will continue to press forward with our work, of course. More fiercely than ever. But we will have to do many things differently."

She heard everything he said, but in manner muted. Her own thoughts were churning. "Somebody would kill a dozen innocent people just to get to me, to keep me from a stupid meeting?"

"Not stupid." The strength of her response allowed the ambassador to employ a stronger tone of his own. "Highly important. Possible milestone."

"And maybe it wasn't someone," Sertoa added. "Maybe it was some thing." He eyed her sternly. "The thranx have their own fanatics, remember."

"But to resort to killing a diplomat . . ." Her voice trailed away into disbelief.

"Why not?" Turning, Sertoa began pacing slowly, waving his hands to emphasize his words. "If successful, they set back our efforts until we can find someone else capable of achieving your kind of personal rapport with their kind. If discovered, word reaches Earth that thranx have carried out a mass killing of humans here on Hivehom. Either way, they achieve at least one of their ends."

"Which is why," Toroni went on, "no word of our suspicions is being allowed to go beyond Azerick. Officially, there was a programming failure. A transport accident. Nothing more. Unofficially, desperate unease is being bounced between worlds at high speed and without regard to the cost."

She was silent for a moment, wrapped in a cocoon of conflicting concerns. "What will you do if the investigating authorities determine that the crash was no accident, and that thranx were responsible?"

Bernard Toroni had been in the service all his professional life, had ridden the currents of diplomatic ebb and flow until all the rough edges had been knocked off him long ago, leaving him polished and smooth. Nothing surprised him; nothing could crack his learned demeanor; nothing could get a grip on his emotions. For the first time since he could remember, maybe for the first time ever, he was shaken.

"I don't know, Fanielle. I don't think anybody does. The reaction on Earth, among the colonies . . ." He swallowed hard. "It would result in . . . a setback."

She nodded, the movement a barely perceptible stirring against the aerogel. "If it's true, then someone—" She glared disapprovingly at Sertoa. "—some*one*, will go to any length to keep me from meeting with Eint Carwenduved."

Toroni's face betrayed nothing. "To keep you from doing so, yes. You specifically, Fanielle."

She gazed back at him evenly, more awake now than at any time since the two men had first entered the room. "You're a very cunning man, Bernard Toroni."

He shrugged, his face a perfect blank. "I'm a professional in the diplomatic service, Fanielle. Nothing more."

She turned her gaze to the ceiling. It displayed a soundless, peaceful holo of drifting clouds. In the distance was a small rainbow. She did not see it, just as she no longer saw peace. That had been taken from her. Forever? She chose not to think about it. Forever was a very long time.

"How soon will they let me out of here?"

The ambassador's tone was glib, controlled. "In a day or two, if you like. Then there will need to be a period of rest. You are one bipedal contusion from head to toe. But nothing significant was damaged. Nothing was broken."

"I wouldn't say that," she whispered wearily. "So . . . I will follow through with the lie, and make the meeting. You must be pleased, Bernard." Seeing the look on his face finally gave her the means to again consider the feelings of others. "I'm sorry. That wasn't fair."

"It doesn't matter." He rose from the side of the bed. "I'm used to it. It's part of my job." He hesitated briefly before continuing. Noting his superior's expression, Sertoa nodded solemnly and left the room. "There is one other thing. At least you will no longer have to worry about lying when you refer to the Bryn'ja request."

She did not reply: just stared up at him.

"The staff here knows nothing is broken or damaged because when you were brought in from the wreck you underwent the most thorough medical scan the facilities here are capable of rendering. I am more sorry than I can ever say, Fanielle, but there is no point in keeping it from you. Truth always seems to emerge before it is convenient for us to have it do so. When you meet with Eint Carwenduved you will be able to do so as someone who has not obtained an encounter on the basis of a prevarication."

She examined the implications of his words from a distance. It only made her that much more determined to confound those who might have done this to her. To her, and to one other, and to a future that now would never have the chance to be.

Her voice as taut as duralloy stressed to the point of destruction, she gazed up from the bed out of damp eyes and asked him softly, "Do they know how long I've been pregnant?"

5

It certainly was a lovely world, Elkannah Skettle reflected as he and Botha took their ease along the shore of City Lake. New pathways had been laid to accommodate the anticipated tide of guests. Transparent lobes thrust out over the lake's surface so that visiting children could experience the illusion of walking on water while delighting in the play of native and introduced aquatics swimming just beneath their feet. A multitude of chromatic-winged flyers swooped and darted above the shimmering splay of water, making fearless dives to pluck small, wriggling creatures from the depths. They filled the air with an unexpectedly sonorous honking, surprisingly tolerant of the increasing numbers of visitors who had begun to throng the lakeshore prior to the official opening of the fair.

Too bad it all had to be marred by the presence of thranx.

For all that he had devoted much of the previous decades to decrying humankind's intensifying relationship with the insectoids and then taking his philosophy and intentions underground, Skettle had seen very few thranx in person. Observing them on the tridee was no longer a problem. The disgusting creatures were all over the media. You could hardly find one delivery source out of the thousands available where they were not eventually to be encountered; all bulging compound eyes, wriggly antennae, and obscene multiple mouthparts. If anything, meeting them in person was even worse.

He could sense the same robust revulsion in the shorter, darker man who matched him stride for stride. Botha was not especially talkative, ill at ease in get-togethers even of his own kind. But there was nothing subdued about his dislike of the bugs. Equipped with poor social skills, he had to be watched over constantly lest his deeply felt feelings manifest themselves in ways that could be dangerous to his friends as well as to himself. Skettle had taken it upon himself to do this, which was why he had insisted that the engineer be paired off with him today. Hatred is healthy, he had assured Botha on more than one occasion. But it must be moderated by wisdom. To be effective, ruthlessness must be appropriately timed.

So when they passed a mated pair of the creatures, all suffocating scents and pearly aquamarine exoskeletons, he shifted his weight just enough to nudge Botha off stride. Wearing a hurt look, the stumpy engineer blinked up at him in confusion.

"What was that about, Elkannah?"

"Keep walking. Keep looking at the wildlife on the lake. That's better." When he was certain they were well out of earshot of any other visitor, and after checking to make sure that his individual privacy field was at full strength, Skettle absently placed an open palm in front of his face to confound any possible distant lip-readers and proceeded to explain.

"How often must I remind you, friend Botha, to conceal your true feelings toward the bugs?"

The smaller man's expression changed to one of honest surprise. "I wasn't! . . . Was I?"

"Your face is pure plastic, Piet." The older man stroked his beard. "I at least can rely on these long gray whiskers to hide emotions that might otherwise escape. If you will persist in using a biannual depilatory, you must be prepared to monitor every wrinkle of your lips, every arch of your brow, every twitch of your cheek muscles."

Botha replied while considering something on the ground—which also allowed him to conceal his lip movements from potential far-seeing viewers. "I'm sorry. You're right—I need to be more aware. Especially now, when we are so close to accomplishing something really important. But is it really necessary to be so careful, every minute? We've both seen non-Preservers who obviously feel as we do yet aren't afraid to express themselves visually."

"That's because it doesn't matter if somebody confronts them, or questions them." Raising a hand, Skettle waved at a passing couple. Charming little girls they had with them, too. "Without appearing effusive, we must seem to be among those in favor of closer, not more distant, ties to these bug beings. We must not merely deflect suspicion; we must embrace it, engulf it. Then it can be safely disposed of, the way targeted eukocytes kill cancer cells."

Botha nodded understandingly. Except for the thranx presence, which would not begin to become truly onerous for another day or two until the full panoply of the fair was thrown open to the public, he was quite pleased with how things had been going. The weather, the freshness of the unspoiled atmosphere, the subtle tingling tastes and aromas of a new world: all were meant to be enjoyed.

Several times that day they tarried to eat something, or sit and have a drink. These many pauses allowed time for reflection. They also allowed Botha, through the sophisticated instrumentation woven into his attire, to coordinate the actual final layout of the fairgrounds with the multiple schematics he had spent nearly a year preparing. The inconspicuous display that occasionally flashed onto the organic readout that floated atop his left pupil would have gone utterly unnoticed by anyone but a very attentive lover.

By late afternoon they had covered a good deal of ground. Having studied stolen diagrams of the grounds for months prior to actually arriving on Dawn, they were able to avoid dead ends and cover only those areas it was absolutely necessary for them to visit and confirm in person.

"We could do another quadrant." Botha had perfected the art of reading the optical display without squinting. "They won't close for another hour yet." When the fair opened officially, they both knew, the grounds would remain accessible to visitors around the clock. This was very convenient for their own purposes, which did not include nocturnal sight-seeing.

"No need to rush things." Skettle was sitting in a chair floating above a small pond. Trained leeshkats, local amphibians, popped up in cleverly choreographed rhyme-time to spit sparkling fountains into the air. Despite the seeming randomness of their alien exertions, not a drop of water fell on giggling, appreciative patrons of the small snack bar. Flowers flush with streaks of pink and vermilion swayed atop flexible aqueous roots. "We'll come back and finish up tomorrow."

"Fine with me. Everything matches up with the charts we've been using. I haven't seen anything yet that will complicate our planting of charges." Frowning abruptly, Botha spun in his seat. His chair rocked playfully with the sharp movement. "What is that awful screeching?"

"Poetry reading." As he pointed with one hand, Skettle took a sip from the self-chilling glass of his tall, teal fruit drink. "Watch your expression, Piet."

From atop a rotating mobile platform drawn by picture-perfect simulacra of eight-legged *covuk!k* from Willow-Wane, an ornately attired thranx was declaiming melodiously. Enchanted by his exotic appearance, quaint mode of transportation, silvery clicks and whistles, and a wafting fragrance redolent of crushed orchids, a sizable crowd trailed behind. They hung on the poet's every gesture and sound. Though the majority of the entranced entourage was human and could understand little of the actual meaning of what was being said, they were fascinated nonetheless. The few thranx tourists in the procession endeavored to translate as best they could, and to convey some sense of the trenchant artistry that underlay the courtly performance.

"Look at those people, slavishly hanging on that filthy bug's wretched croakings!" Botha had to turn away from the noisome spectacle, so repellent did he find it. "What's wrong with them?"

"They have not been educated." Far more in control of himself than his companion was, Skettle took a longer swallow of his drink, then eyed the nearly empty glass appreciatively. "This is very good. We will have to try and take some concentrate back with us. It is the task of such as ourselves, Piet, to educate them. That is why we are here." He listened for another moment as the procession wandered out of earshot. "Desvendapur."

"What?" Botha blinked at him.

"That was the thranx poet who escaped from their treacherous outpost in the western Amazon. Before your time, really—but I remember it quite well. I spent more time than it was worth trying to see what even a few disoriented, misguided humans found in his so-called poetic random barks and gargles. None of it ever made the least sense to me. Absolutely worthless drivel."

"Apparently not to a bug," Botha commented.

Skettle emancipated his empty glass, watched as it carefully negotiated a path between diners and drinkers on its way back to the kitchen. "Who knows what a bug thinks? Who cares? Let's get back to the hotel and find out how the others did."

Botha slipped out of his chair. It rocked briefly in his absence, then steadied to await the next set of perambulating buttocks. "Hopefully, Pierrot hasn't blown up anything prematurely."

"If she has, she better have included herself." Skettle did not look in Botha's direction, for which the smaller man was grateful. He admired, even revered, Elkannah Skettle as much as any member of the cause. But the old man could scare you sometimes, without even intending to. Something in his manner, in his mental makeup, was skewed: a powerful ego skimming swiftly across the ice of the mind on skates fashioned of parallel psychoses.

That did not make him any less of a leader in Botha's eyes. You just had to be wary of his occasional . . . moods.

Like his companions, Beskodnebwyl found Dawn unappealing. Had the authorities in charge not decided to hold this misconceived melange of a fair in the middle of the hottest month on the northern continent of the colony, he did not think he could have stood being outside for very long without proper survival gear. The idea of spending a winter on such a world . . .

As it was, it was near noon and he was still chilly. Afternoon would be better. The local temperature tended to reach its most intense just before sunset. Nothing could be done about the dryness of the atmosphere, however. Like the temperature, the local humidity fell just within the limits of what was tolerable. He felt some sympathy for the thranx who were actually participating in the fair. They did not have his flexibility, could not always come and go when the weather suited them best.

It was not enough sympathy to keep him from watching them die, however.

Flanked by Sijnilarget, Meuvonpehif, and Tioparquevekk, he wandered in apparently incessant spirals that in fact were designed to carry him and his square of four to a specific destination. Not one of the many clever amusements that had been constructed by the resident humans, nor any of the engagingly familiar displays that had been erected by the invited thranx, distracted the Bwyl from their chosen course. The four resisted all such blandishments, ignoring lights and music, recitations and performances, disdaining to sample even the finest examples of thranx foodstuffs imported by invitees from Hivehom, Willow-Wane, Eurmet, and elsewhere. They had no time to partake of such diversions. The truly dedicated are not easily swayed from their intendment.

The closer they got to their destination, the more edgy they became. It was not necessary to conceal the emotions running through them, however, because certain movements of limbs and antennae that would have been highly suggestive to another thranx meant nothing to the humans among whom they passed, and all other thranx were busy operating exhibits. The fair infrastructure had been designed, laid out, and was being run solely by the hosting humans of Dawn.

Even if they were confronted at the wrong time or in the wrong place, Beskodnebwyl knew, they could easily plead ignorance.

No one challenged them as they reached the building that had been constructed on the shore. A large portion of it extended out over the lake. This bulky apparatus was to be expected, since the building's task was to integrate communications within the fairgrounds, both private and public. Concessions, restaurants, exhibits, and most of all, Security—all depended on the gleaming new transmission and relay system to supply their needs. This it did admirably, in manner mostly automated.

Working with data extracted from restricted reports, a mated pair of renegade scientists sympathetic to the Bwyl cause had developed a wonderful set of miniaturized explosives easily deliverable by hand. At their chamber in the temporary hivelike structure the humans and their thranx advisors had built to provide comfortable climate-controlled lodgings for thranx visitors to and workers at the fair, the Bwyl had left a small packing case containing an assortment of favorite drinks. One drink container held enough of the explosives to kill a significant number of people.

Utilized throughout the fair, they would quickly cause widespread havoc. When the source of the havoc was identified as thranx, it should not be enough to start a war, but should prove more than sufficient to place a freeze on the upgrading of diplomatic relations that would last for years at a minimum.

They located and memorized several entrances to the structure, which was to be one of their principal targets. All were secured, as Beskodnebwyl and his companions knew they would be. Beskodnebwyl and Tioparquevekk kept watch while Sijnilarget and Meuvonpehif inspected the security arrangements.

"Difficulties?" Beskodnebwyl asked as soon as they returned. Few humans had passed their way. Those that glanced in the direction of the four thranx had assumed they were part of the fair maintenance staff. A reasonable, if totally incorrect, assumption.

"Not many." Sijnilarget was peering through a device that no human would have recognized. "Though important to the smooth functioning of the fair, this is not a military installation. I would estimate less than ten time-parts to gain entry without setting off any alarms. Admittedly, I have not had as much time as I would like to study human designs of this nature, but I see nothing insurmountable. Regardless of the sentient species that designs them, security systems for oxygen breathers adhere to certain fundamental patterns."

Beskodnebwyl gestured his understanding. "Gaining entrance is the difficult part. Once inside, it becomes a simple matter of setting and timing a couple of containers. In the absence of communications, the chaos we will create will only be magnified."

"There may be human guards inside," Tioparquevekk cautioned. "Or at least maintenance workers we may have to deal with."

Meuvonpehif flicked her truhands sharply forward, producing a small cracking sound as chitin snapped against chitin. "You concern yourself with getting us in. The rest of us will handle matters should any unfortunate humans decide to try and intercede."

"Anyone observing our activities must be silenced." Sijnilarget deliberately spoke in Low Thranx to emphasize the crudity of his response. "They must not be allowed to raise the alarm."

"We don't even know if there will be any humans to be encountered in what must surely be a largely automatic operation." Beskodnebwyl continued to shield Tioparquevekk's instrumentation with his body. "No one enters a strange burrow looking for trouble. How are you coming?"

"Almost finished." Tioparquevekk hovered over his equipment. "I have analyzed and ascertained the requisite patterns. All that remains is to record them and then run a phantom, to ensure that everything will work on the day we choose to act." He went silent, busy with all four hands and sixteen digits.

"Hey!"

Beskodnebwyl, whose knowledge of human speech forms verged on fluency, recognized the word as an exclamation of accusation. What mattered, he knew from his painstaking studies, was the intensity with which it was delivered, and whether querulousness was implied. It struck him that in this instance all the relevant ingredients were involved.

"What are you doing there?" The human who had spoken now adopted a tone more belligerent than curious. Beskodnebwyl did not panic. There were only two of the bipeds, and they were not clad in the attire of the several maintenance teams that serviced the fair. That meant they were only casual fair-goers, not unlike himself and his three companions. Behind him, he could sense Tioparquevekk concluding his work and hastily downpacking his equipment. Despite a rising sense of anxiety, the other three thranx worked smoothly and efficiently. With four hands, they were not prone to fumbling.

If this human did not occupy an official position, what right did it have to bark accusingly at Beskodnebwyl and his companions? Assuming a defensive stance, he moved forward to confront the human. It was rangy, even for its kind. Standing tall on his four trulegs, Beskodnebwyl could not have raised his head to the level of the biped's chest. Nonetheless, he was not intimidated. Proximity to the lumbering, lurching mammal brought on feelings of disgust and mild nausea, not fear.

"I will tell you as soon as you have shown me your license."

Looking bemused, the two men halted. The taller one continued to do all the talking. "What license?"

"The one that gives you the authority to challenge peaceful visitors to this fair." Behind him, Beskodnebwyl sensed his companions shifting their stances to form the rest of a traditional defensive four-headed square. Whatever happened now must be resolved quietly, he knew, lest the confrontation draw unwanted attention.

The smaller of the pair spoke up, speaking to his friend. "Not only talkative bugs, but sarcastic ones." His hand, Beskodnebwyl noted, was hovering over a slight bulge in the garment that covered his lower body. The Bwyl was not worried. If the human flourished a weapon, Sijnilarget, Meuvonpehif, and Tioparquevekk would be ready to respond with firepower of their own. Though differing greatly from thranx in their physical makeup, human bodies reacted similarly to an encounter with high-velocity explosive pellets.

The taller one's tone became slightly less combative. "I asked you what you were doing here." His head bobbed in a gesture Beskodnebwyl knew was meant to indicate the building behind them. "This isn't part of the fair exhibit. There's nothing here for the public to see."

"We know," Meuvonpehif commented readily in her heavily accented Terranglo. "It's the central communications facility."

Beskodnebwyl was furious enough to reach back and snap one of the female's antennae. By her physical reaction, he could see that she recognized her error almost as soon as she made it. Perhaps, he hoped agitatedly, the humans would find the comment innocuous.

They did not.

The tall man chose to continue to direct his words to Beskodnebwyl. "Is it really? That's interesting. How do you know that? It isn't marked as such on the outside."

"Its function is quite obvious," Beskodnebwyl replied a bit too quickly. "The necessary apparatus for the transmission of information dominates the roofline."

The human nodded again. Beskodnebwyl thought his expression now indicated thoughtfulness, but it was difficult to tell. Mastering the range of human facial expressions took time and patience. "So you've been studying the communications center from other vantage points besides this one. That's even more interesting. I wonder what the Dawn police would make of your interest?"

The biped was preternaturally perceptive, Beskodnebwyl thought tightly. This was threatening to get out of hand. He could feel his companions shifting their stances behind him, preparatory to . . .

He was contemplating how best to dispose of the humans' bodies when the short human appeared to lose control of himself. Drawing the bulge from his shirt, he aimed a device that was as lethal-looking as it was compact directly at Beskodnebwyl's head.

"Goddamn dirty bugs want to get their filthy claws on everything!"

Reacting almost instantaneously, the trio of thranx behind Beskodnebwyl extracted from their thorax pouches weapons of their own. Confronted unexpectedly by thrice his number, the stocky biped hesitated, unsure now how to proceed, his initial bravado much reduced by the revelation that his intended victims were armed. He stared at them, glanced up at his companion, then back at the thranx. Like the rest of him, the muzzle of his weapon wavered.

Admirably calm, the tall human stepped between his friend and the armed defensive square. "Now, this I would not have expected. Piet is quite right: It is unthinkable to have disgusting, germ-ridden quasi-insects such as yourselves stumbling about this close to a vital human installation. It inevitably raises the question of why you would want to do so. The presence of concealed weapons at a peaceable venue like this fair greatly enhances those questions. As does the undeniable skill and readiness with which they have just now been deployed. Yet you are not members of an officially recognized organization."

"I dispute nothing you say, but what does it prove save that thranx are always ready to defend themselves from reasonless attack?" Beskodnebwyl was watching the tall human carefully. The man's stocky companion he had already dismissed as unimportant, despite the fact that he was the one holding the weapon.

"It may prove a very odd thing indeed." The human smiled, fully exposing his teeth. Beskodnebwyl had to force himself not to turn away from the distasteful sight. "It suggests that you and I may be here for the same purpose."

Beskodnebwyl had nothing to frown with, and the human could not understand the thranx's gestures. It was left to inadequate words to convey subtleties of meaning. "And what purpose could that possibly be?"

"Elkannah?" the shorter man murmured uneasily. "Are you sure about this?"

"I always trust my instincts, Piet. If there's another explanation, we'll divine it in short order." Turning his attention back to Beskodnebwyl, he continued as calmly as if requesting a change of shuttle seat assignment. "You and your dirt-dwelling friends are here to disrupt this fair, aren't you? You're planning to do something to, or with, local communications. You are here to cause trouble."

This was it, Beskodnebwyl reflected. They would have to kill both bipeds, and kill them quickly. All it would take would be a gesture from him. The humans would not recognize it, and so the one holding the gun would not have time to react. But . . . he was curious.

"That's the kind of observation that could get an individual killed. Why shouldn't it?"

"Because my friends and I are here for the same reason. From civility, we plan to bring forth chaos. We don't like your kind, you see. Among us are many, too many I fear, misguided people who think we should cuddle up to you bugs, make you part of our cultural and political lives, let you set up your teeming, odious colonies on our own worlds. That sort of thing is reprehensible, unnatural, and must be prevented at all costs." He stopped, waiting while the bugs digested his words.

"How very astonishing." At a gesture, the trio behind him lowered, but did not put up, their weapons. Somewhat reluctantly, the shorter human did likewise. "Your speech is admirable, except that for sake of veracity the word phrase for *stinking soft flesh* should be substituted for the derogatory term *bugs.*"

The biped smiled again. Beskodnebwyl found he was better able to tolerate it this time. "I think we may be able to come to an understanding. If we do not cooperate, our natural antipathies will surely undo our respective plans. Ours do not especially involve the communications facility. Your plan is just to destroy it?"

"Yes," Meuvonpehif replied before Beskodnebwyl could silence her.

The biped looked in her direction. "You are lying. Such as you would not come all this way, smuggling in weapons as well as intentions, just to render the visitors to and promoters of this abomination of a fair unable to communicate with one another. You must have something more extensive planned." He returned his gaze to Beskodnebwyl. "I will reiterate: If we do not cooperate, we will end up at cross-purposes, when what we both want is the same result."

Beskodnebwyl nodded, an absurdly easy human gesture to imitate. "We intend to set off explosives not only here but throughout the length and breadth of the depravity." Behind him, he heard Tioparquevekk and Sijnilarget inhale sharply in disbelief. "The more fair-goers—human and thranx alike—that we can kill or incapacitate, the stronger will be the reaction among your kind."

Again the human nodded—approvingly, Beskodnebwyl thought. "We plan to make use of some custom-built explosive devices. As I understand it, the more creative types we execute, the angrier will be the response from your infernal hives."

"Quite correct." Beskodnebwyl found himself staring up at the human. Used to dwelling underground, the human's greater physical stature did not intimidate him. That sort of psychological positioning was for open-air dwellers only. "You confirm what we already believe: that your kind are inherently violent and murderous, and must be kept as far away as possible from a truly civilized society such as our own."

"We want nothing less. Back on Earth, you know, we step on bugs all the time. Have been doing so since the beginning of our recorded history."

"What more can be expected," Beskodnebwyl responded, "from a species that flops about like ambulatory sacks of iron-based blood and loose meat?"

Skettle's smile faded slightly. "We understand each other, then. We will not interfere with whatever it is you intend to do, and you will not interfere with us. Working separately but with the same goal in mind, we will with our endeavors here succeed in putting relations between our species where they belong: at a distance sufficient to ensure that we have to do no more than tolerate your presence in the same galactic arm as ourselves."

"I could have put it better," Beskodnebwyl replied, "but your words will do. It may even be that we will, over the next several days, find reason to cooperate more closely in carrying out our respective efforts, and might even try to synchronize our operations in hopes of achieving maximum outcome."

"That's a fine idea." Skettle started to retrace his steps. At no time did he turn his back on the bugs. "We should arrange for some of us to meet daily to continue this exchange of information. How about at the Syxbex Restaurant, on the lakeshore?"

"That location will be eminently satisfactory." Beskodnebwyl maintained the defensive square, watching as the pair of bipeds retreated. "We want to be sure to avoid any misunderstandings."

When we have done what we came for, he mused, we will also find a way to kill you. Loose antennae could not be allowed to flutter about. Besides, it would give him pleasure to preside over the demise of so forthrightly antagonistic a human. He raised a foothand in the human gesture of farewell.

Skettle waved back, thinking as he and Botha turned the first available sheltering corner that he was going to delight in seeing this particular bug's skull cracked and its brains oozing out over the colorful pavement that had been laid down for the fair.

There is nothing in art, in philosophy, or in politics to match the fervor of mutual cooperation among discordant bands of fanatics.

6

The supply station had a spectacular setting. Located on a low rise over-looking a vast salt pan smoking with geysers, mud pools, and hot lakes, it doubled as a geothermal research station for the score of scientists and their support teams studying the wonderfully bewildering variety of silicate and sulfuric minerals that gushed forth from the bowels of the planet. These often differed markedly from their terrestrial analogs. Every week of exploration, sometimes every day, elicited new cries of discovery from delighted geologists.

In addition to being crammed full of mineralogical revelations, the thermal wilderness was awash in beauty. While yellow and its variations were the predominant colors, there were also rich varieties of blue, green, and red thanks to the presence of the tough, active, endemic bacteria that thrived in the thermal pools. Occasionally, a brisk south wind would sweep through the valley, brushing away the clouds of steam to expose kilometer after kilometer of roaring geysers, gurgling hot springs, plopping mud holes, and steaming rivers. A certain species of thermotropic eel-like creature nearly two meters long had biologists almost coming to blows over its taxonomy. Was it a highly advanced worm or an exceedingly primitive fish? Or something entirely new to science?

On the rare occasions when it rained, the combination of steam, fog, and drizzle made it impossible to see more than a meter in front of one's face even at high noon. At such times fieldwork was restricted. Unseen, the tentative network of hastily laid prefab pathways could not be negotiated in safety, and even aircar work was halted. The resident scientists would cluster in frustrated, argumentative knots inside the air-conditioned labs and living quarters, anxious to be released from regulations even though they knew these had been drawn up with their own safety in mind. But when was there ever a scientist who paid proper attention to personal safety when a host of new discoveries lay close at hand?

Brockton was working on a robot probe designed to take samples from the hottest vents when he felt the first vibration. It was accompanied by a muted rumble, as if one of the back doors had been opened. A glance showed that both of the big service bay barriers were still shut. With a shrug, he returned to his work. He was alone in the shop except for the automatics, Norquist and Oppervann having decided to take a long lunch. They did not have many opportunities to interact with the scientific staff and took every chance to do so. To improve their education, both men insisted. To try to put the make on one of several attractive unattached ladies among the staff, Brockton knew.

Nothing more than casual flirting for him. He had a wife and two kids on Tharce IV. He was here because he didn't mind the desert, and because in a year on Comagrave he could make the equivalent of three years' salary back home. His family understood. When his contract was up, he would be able to take a whole year off doing nothing but watching his kids grow.

Though considered a party-killer, he got along well with his workmates. His skills, honed through fifteen years of experience, were greatly appreciated by both his colleagues and his employers, and he did not try to play the disapproving father figure to his predominantly younger coworkers. Removing his hands from the interior of the probe, he shut the access panel, picked up the nearby magnetic welder, and began to reverse the polarity on the interior latches. Once flopped, they would hold the panel shut as securely as if it had been melted into place.

There it was again. A second tremor, stronger than the first. He had picked up enough geology from hanging around the station's scientists to know that where geysers and thermal pools are present, stronger seismic activity was to be expected. But this didn't feel like one of the numerous minor temblors he had experienced many times during the preceding months. It had a different feel to it—more of a bump than a rumble.

The station was constructed on a flexor foundation that was designed to distribute any shock evenly across its base. Anything short of a tectonic convulsion would be dissipated by the integrated flexors before it could cause any damage. The contractors had known what they were doing. Though he had not worked in construction, Brockton had seen enough to know good work from bad. Upon arriving, he had taken an off day to make his own inspection of the station and its outlying structures. Everything had looked reassuringly solid.

That was when the ground fell away and the roof started to come down on top of him.

The roar that accompanied the collapse was frightful, a caustic clamor in the ears that masked the screams of those crowded into the central dining area for lunch. Feeling the floor fall away beneath him, he grabbed wildly for the probe. It was plunging downward as well, until he managed to hit the open programming panel. Bluish light emerging from its flat underside, the probe rose and steadied on its tiny repulsion field. Brockton's terrifyingly rapid descent slowed. Kicking the field up to full power, he found that the probe could muster just enough lift to keep them both aloft. For how long he did not know.

Then the rest of the roof came down.

Guiding the probe, he made a mad dash for the nearest crumpled doorway. He just did manage to slip through a rip in the crumpling, warping fabric. Outside in the glare and steam of the day, he turned his head to look back in the direction of the station. Keeping both arms and legs wrapped tightly around the laboring device, he tried to make some sense of what he was seeing.

The entire station—central hub, communications tower, living quarters, lab modules, service departments, hygienics plant—was collapsing in upon itself. No, not upon itself, he saw through the rising, swirling mists. Into a gaping cauldron. A roaring river of boiling water had suddenly manifested itself directly beneath the station. With nothing to support it, the advanced flexor foundation was no more useful than a row of wooden pilings.

Despite the damp heat, he was having chills. Rising above the groans and grindings of imploding buildings were the screams of those trapped inside. A few who had been near the front exits had tried to escape that way, only to find there was no place to escape to. Like those they had left behind, they died before they could reach solid ground, crushed beneath the subsiding structures or boiled alive in the torrent that had burst forth beneath their feet.

In less than an hour there was nothing left of the supply station. It had been swept away, down the steaming cataract that now gushed from the side of the rise and into the nearest expanse of hot lake. A couple who had been out all morning studying cyanotic bacteria returned in their aircar and pried his cramped arms and legs off the probe that had saved his life. Another researcher returned later that evening. He was accompanied by the resident AAnn advisor. Decamping on a mound of solid, well-vegetated ground half a kilometer away, the numbed survivors tried to make sense of what had happened.

Brockton knew what had happened. He had survived to feel his wife next to him once more, and to hold his children. As soon as rescue teams arrived, he was putting in for a pysch dismissal. He doubted he would have any trouble getting one. Not after what he had seen.

Norquist, Oppervann, all those other fine men and women—all gone. If the rescue teams were really lucky, they might be able to recover some bones. Sitting on the ground beneath an orgthic bush, he hardly heard what the others were saying. It was starting to get dark, and he was cold. Surrounded by hell, he was cold. Of everything his fellow survivors said prior to the angelic arrival of the first rescue craft, only a few words of the AAnn, speaking in clumsy Terranglo, remained forever stuck in his memory.

"*Ssstt*, we told your engineerss not to build on that ssite!"

The stitcher's harpoon struck the underside of the aircar with a familiar shrill *thwack*. Leaning cautiously over the side, Elrosa saw it wriggle out from under the sand, all three of its protruding, bulbous eyes triangulating on him, their intended prey. He wondered what, if anything, the voracious alien mind behind them was thinking. As he thrust his scanner over the side of the vehicle, he watched as the meter-long harpoon was slowly retracted. The stitchers learned quickly: It would not expend its killing mechanism on the armored underbelly of the aircar again.

So powerful was the expelled harpoon of a stitcher that it could penetrate the underside of a normal vehicle. Elrosa and Lu's aircar was not normal. It had been given a ventral sheathing of glistening golden percote that would have been more appropriate to a military transport. Nothing merely organic could penetrate that layer of sprayed-on armor. It reduced the aircar's speed and range, but not significantly. And it allowed the two biologists to proceed in comparative safety with their study of several varieties of desert-dwelling predator.

Another hopeful *thwack*. Another subsurface hunter disappointed. This was turning out to be an excellent study area.

The stitchers were one of several unique carnivores that lived and hunted beneath Dawn's scattered sand seas. They impaled their prey on long, sharp harpoons built up of concentric layers of hardened calcium carbonate. It was as if a human had learned how to sharpen a femur, spear it into prey, and reel the resultant kill back in by means of the ligaments still attached to the bone. Since no one had yet dissected a stitcher, the means by which their harpoons were propelled at such remarkable velocity remained open to explication. Elrosa favored compressed air as a nontoxic and readily renewable means of propulsion. Lu came down on behalf of those who postulated the existence of multiple knots of rapid-twitch muscle fibers.

They were not out today to catch and dismember—only to take measurements. Elrosa was duly excited by the work they had accomplished over the past several days. There were more stitchers per cubic kilometer of sand sea in this area than anyone had previously encountered anywhere else. Lu thought it might be a mating territory. Stitchers mating—now that would be a ripe subject for a monograph!

Another lackluster *thunk* sounded as a harpoon struck the impenetrable underside of the aircar. He smiled to himself. It would be useful to know if the stitchers considered the low-flying intruder a threat or a possible meal. Perhaps both, he mused. Previous fieldwork indicated that the predators sometimes appeared to hunt in tandem, or even in small groups. He and Lu had seen no evidence of pack hunting thus far, but like everything else on Comagrave, organic or otherwise, very little was known with assurance.

Behind him, his partner shouted a verbal command to the aircar console. It complied, and they found themselves jetting silently forward, leaving frustrated stitchers goggling in their wake. Only the predators' eyes and expended harpoons were visible above the surface of the dune.

Another sand-filled depression beckoned. With luck, they might find a line or two of migrating geulons, or a new species. So recently arrived were humans on Comagrave's surface that it was the unfortunate biologist indeed who did not return from a field trip without at least several new species to record. Taxonomy was almost as exciting as actually encountering the creatures in question.

Leaning over the open side of the car, careful to keep himself as small a target as possible for anything inimical that might be lying camouflaged under the sand, he directed Lu to shift them another ten meters northward.

"That's good!" He gestured with his upraised right hand. "This looks like a promising spot."

His assumption was correct. Every day, they grew more skilled at predicting the movements of the planet's endemic wildlife. No sooner had the aircar hummed to a halt than not one but three loud *thwack*s, one after another like shots from a gun, rapped on the underside of the vehicle.

Lu joined his friend at the edge. The air suspension craft hovered effortlessly some three meters above the sand. "There!" Lu pointed to where a brace of eyeballs, like pale white melons, protruded from the sand. Recorders were brought into play.

As they clicked away, Elrosa heard a decidedly different kind of *thunk*. It was higher in pitch, more immediate, and sharper of sonic detail. Turning, his eyes widened slightly as he saw the meter-long calcareous lance quivering upright in the deck. It had penetrated the plastic sheeting to a depth of a fifth of a meter. As he stared, a soft whistling sound drew his gaze upward.

"Look out!" Throwing himself to the side, he just did avoid the descending tip of the stitcher harpoon. It slammed into the deck centimeters from his scrambling right foot.

Rolling over, Lu stared in astonishment at the impressive weapon. "They know that there's food up here—us—that they can't get at from below. So they've started firing into the air, hoping to impale us on the way down. Amazing!"

The aircar was equipped with a retractable cover, but one designed to offer protection only from the weather. A harpoon would go through it like a vibrablade through gelatin. As Elrosa climbed to his feet and took a step toward the control console, a vast whistling suddenly filled the air, as of an approaching dustdevil. Lu let out an inarticulate cry and dove for the open hatch that led to the tiny, enclosed head.

He didn't make it.

Assembling silently beneath the sand, the pack of stitchers must have fired at least fifty harpoons.

Though its power pack was approaching empty, the aircar was still hovering in place when one of the several search teams sent out to look for the two biologists finally found it. Of the two biologists who had been aboard, there remained only bloodstains on the deck, and on the side where their harpoon-impaled bodies had been dragged from within by the hungry stitchers. Studying the scene of quiet butchery, the newcomers conversed in subdued whispers interrupted only by the occasional *thwack*s of harpoons striking their craft's underside and armored roof.

When the sole AAnn aboard suggested that perhaps she and her kind should take over field study of the stitchers, or at least supervise the work, the human in charge readily agreed. If the AAnn wanted to deal with such cunning carnivores until such time as enough was known about them to work their territories in comparative safety, he saw no reason to argue. Let the reptiloids be the ones to put their lives at risk.

"There will be less rissk for uss," the AAnn assured him sympathetically. "We are ussed to living in the ssandss, among thosse kindss of creaturess that make their homes thussly. You will, of coursse, receive copiess of all reportss as they are prepared, and will be kept fully up to date on all our progress."

"Fieldwork is usually better carried out by the many than by the few," the dejected human supervisor concluded. Another time, under different circumstances, he might have felt otherwise, but he was distraught over the unexpected loss of two of his colleagues. Besides, where was the harm in sharing field assignments with the willing AAnn? They were more at home in this kind of country than any human, and their willing-ness to share data had already been demonstrated. Let them do some of the hard work. With an entire new world to study, catalog, analyze, and report on, his staff was already stretched thin. They could find plenty to occupy themselves besides stitchers.

"I don't understand." Hibbing stood by the side of the glassine tower and stared dubiously at the readouts embedded in its smooth, curving side. "Everything was fine as of this time yesterday." Nearby, Tyree and Sou-vingnon were examining the contents of the relay box that hugged the side of the tower close to the ground.

Tyree glanced up. "Everything's working, sir. The extractors just aren't pulling any water."

Turning, Hibbing saw his eyewrap darken as he gazed eastward. The site that had been chosen for the main settlement on Comagrave com-manded a sweeping view of the spectacular Carmine Cliffs, a geologic upthrust averaging a thousand meters in height that ran for hundreds of kilometers from north to south. Below and to the west were the Bergemon Salt Flats, a perfectly flat pan devoid of vegetation, subsurface liquids, or tectonic instabilities. To the north lay the maze of narrow canyons known as the Fingerlings. One of the most biologically rich areas on the planet, it was but a short journey from the outskirts of Comabraeth community.

Beneath the settlement site, hydrologists had located a sizable prehis-toric aquifer big enough to provide a six-hundred-year supply for a city of half a million. A better place to establish the colonial capital of Coma-grave could not be found on the planet. There was water in abundance, more than ample landing space for shuttles and aircraft out on the pan, biological and geological riches practically within walking distance. Months had passed without a hint of trouble, during which time the vil-lage had grown into a thriving small town of more than ten thousand. There was talk of formalizing it as the capital of the incipient colony.

And now the water, every million acre-feet of it, was gone. Or so his hydrotechs were telling him.

Reluctantly, he lowered his gaze from the glorious, multihued vista spread out before him. Comagrave was not yet developed enough to be able to accommodate tourists, and his position never allowed him longer than a minute or two to be one himself. "How could this happen?"

Souvingnon rose to confront the administrator. At his feet, Tyree con-tinued to fiddle with instrumentation, as if by so doing he could somehow will the water to return. "There are possibilities. Since the original dis-covery dated the top layer of water to several hundreds of thousands of T-standard years ago, it seems pretty clear to me that the only way it would suddenly vanish is if some radical new regional development did something to affect the underground geology."

Hibbing nodded slowly. "And the only new regional development is us."

Souvingnon gestured in the direction of the extraction tower and the attached processing and filtration plant. "Everything above ground is working perfectly. So we have to assume that the problem is subterranean in nature. Personally, I've never heard of an aquifer that big disappearing this fast. But this is a new world. Geology isn't even a perfect science on Earth." He turned thoughtful. "This region might not be as seismically stable as the original surveyors first assumed. There might have been a catastrophic collapse in the shale strata underlying the aquiferic sands. It could have been set off by the continual vibrations of shuttlecraft landing and, especially, taking off."

"That doesn't sound very reasonable."

Souvingnon sighed. "Since we don't have a reasonable explanation for what's happening, I'm starting a search for unreasonable ones. The aquifer is broad, but not deep. Realistically, a subterranean collapse on such a scale is unlikely. Theoretically, it's possible."

"What can we do?" Hibbing turned back in the direction of the town. "I've already activated emergency rationing procedures. I'm responsible for the health and well-being of nearly fifteen thousand people, Souvingnon, every one of whom needs to drink and occasionally to wash. We don't have a waste problem—the solid-waste decomposing system needs no water—but I'm going to have to start having supplies tanked in from the Broughlach River. That's three hundred k's from here. A couple of months of that will bankrupt our municipal operating budget. As you know, initial planetary R and D stopped supplementing that over a year ago."

And I'll be replaced, he thought to himself. They'll send me somewhere quiet and out of the way to decompose, just like the town's solid waste. Hibbing did not want to be replaced. He liked his job, liked the beauty and solitude that Comagrave could boast in plenty. It was why he had applied for the position of colonial administrator in the first place.

"We can drill elsewhere." Souvingnon pointed across the valley, to the colorful crimson rampart. "Maybe at the base of the cliffs."

"Maybe." Hibbing was dubious. "But the initial hydro surveys chose this spot because there was water in plenty here. And if the shuttle landings are responsible for what has happened, who's to say the underground water table hasn't been collapsed everywhere in the vicinity?"

Tyree finally rose from his inspection, brushing dust from his hands. "We could ask the AAnn."

The AAnn had a very small deeded scientific outpost to the west of the town, near the edge of the salt pan. They had no view of multihued cliffs, no easy access to the valleys of the Fingerlings. As Hibbing understood it, there were no more than forty individuals working at the reptiloids' outpost at any one time. Insofar as he knew, they had their own water supply. An emergency line could be laid across the pancake-flat edge of the pan from the alien outpost to the town in a fraction of the time and cost it would take to build one to the Broughlach River.

If the AAnn had water to spare, and if they were so inclined.

Hibbing considered. Town storage was at 80 percent of capacity. Within a few days, like it or not, they would be tanking in water from the distant Broughlach.

"Let's pay our scaly neighbors a visit," he told his engineers softly.

Coblaath SSCDDG met them outside. Standing at the entrance to the AAnn outpost, it was difficult to tell that there was any kind of installation at the edge of the pan at all. That was because, in keeping with AAnn preference and design, the great majority of it was located underground.

"Very hot insside for humanss," the outpost commander informed them. "You like it warm. We like it hot."

That was an understatement, Hibbing knew. Vacationing AAnn would have no compunctions at setting up sand baths and scale scratchers inside a working oven. And they liked even less moisture in the air than did humans.

"I appreciate your concern for our welfare." Hibbing was new to this. He was an administrator, not a diplomat. But having explained the dire situation to his superiors via deep-space beam, he had been given emergency leave to do whatever he thought necessary and best to alleviate the situation.

"You heard what has happened to our water supply?"

The AAnn executed a gesture of third-degree commiseration coupled with fourth-degree understanding, all of which looked like nothing more than gratuitous hand waving to Hibbing. "A terrible missfortune. Who can explain ssuch a thing? We have never encountered ssuch a phenomenon oursselves, and we have ssettled many worldss very ssimilar to Vussussica."

Hibbing ignored the use of the AAnn cognomen. He was not here to argue the fine points of diplomatic terminology. He had come for help.

"You heard what my engineers have theorized."

Coblaath gestured, then nodded. "Thiss head movement iss the correct one, yess?"

Hibbing smiled broadly. "That's correct, yes."

The AAnn commander drew himself up proudly. "I have been prac-
tissing. My people perussed your hydrology report. Your engineerss
appear to have analyzed the ssituation mosst thoroughly. We ssurmise
that there iss at leasst one, perhapss sseveral vertical upthrusstss of impermeable rock between here and your sstation. Thiss accident of geology
keepss our aquifer sseparate from yourss."

"And you still have plenty of water?" Hibbing tried not to show too
much interest, wondering in the midst of his caution if the vertical-
pupiled, lizardlike alien would recognize such concern even if it was
manifested.

"Truly ample. The equal of what ussed to lie beneath your own
esstablishment, I am told." As the pointed tongue flicked in Hibbing's
direction, the administrator tried not to flinch. "Enough to sspare whatever you need, perhapss even on a permanent bassiss." He gestured reassurance. "After all, we have only a tiny outposst here, and require very
little water for our own needss. Why sshould you, our friendss, not make
good usse of it?"

Hibbing was taken aback. The period of difficult, extended negotiations he had been prepared to embark upon in order to secure the minimal
amount necessary to keep the station going had not only not materialized,
but here was the AAnn commander offering him all the water he
needed—and for an unlimited, or at least unspecified, time into the
future. The money alone that would be saved . . .

"I hardly know what to say, Commander Coblaath. I had not
expected such a generous offer."

The AAnn's tail switched sideways in yet another gesture of
significance Hibbing was unable to interpret. "While it ssleepss underground, the water doess no one any good. We can help you with the engineering. If we begin a pumping sstation here while your people lay pipe
from your end, it will sshorten the time until you can receive our water."

"Yes, of course it would." Hibbing had gone from being apprehensive
to feeling positively buoyant. But while he had seemingly achieved all he
had come for, and much more, the negotiations were not yet completed.
"What would you require in the way of payment? My staff and I don't
expect you to give us access to this water out of the goodness of your
hearts."

"But that iss why we are doing thiss." Coblaath managed to sound, if
not look, surprised. "We would not let our good friendss want for water.
We assk only one thing."

Hibbing waited, trying to hide his unease. "What might that be,
Commander?"

"We wissh only to be accorded equal sstatuss in thiss region. To be free to go where we wissh, to do our own sscientific work without having firsst to ssubmit it for approval to your ressearch authority, to move about as we require. A little freedom of action, that iss all. Iss not too much to assk in return for ssaving your largesst community on Vussussica—your pardon, on Comagrave. Iss it?"

Hibbing hesitated. Did he have that kind of authority? The AAnn wasn't asking for equal colony status, or control over anything. Simply the ability to cut out the red tape that hampered the free movement of his own staff. What harm could there be in acceding? It wasn't as if Comagrave was home to military secrets that needed to be protected. The money this would save . . .

And he had been given the authority to deal with the emergency as best he saw fit, hadn't he? If the authorities back on Earth didn't like it, they could deal with the agreement after the fact. Meanwhile, the station would have all the water it needed, and the AAnn would have a reason to continue to maintain cordial relations with the staff and inhabitants. If anything, Hibbing felt, in agreeing he was doing something to promote better interspecies relations.

"I think I can safely say there will be no problem in getting my people to agree to such a simple and straightforward request. That's really all you want in return?"

"That iss all." The commander extended a hand in imitation of the human gesture. "Thiss is the proper indication, iss it not?"

Hibbing took the proffered hand. The three fingers and opposable thumb were tipped with sharp claws that had been painted with colorful whorls. He felt hard scales slide against his own soft flesh. The sensation was not unpleasant. He was charmed by the AAnn's effort to mimic human ways.

"Indeed it is. I extend my thanks and that of my entire staff, not to mention those of everyone resident in the town."

"Tell them on behalf of mysself and the Imperial Board of Intersspeciess Relationss that I am mosst delighted we were able to help. Truly."

Like everyone else on Comagrave, Pilwondepat kept abreast—or more properly, athorax—of weekly happenings through reports that were freely available via the planetary net. Not only did it help him to stay well informed and aid him in his own research, but it was an excellent way to practice his Terranglo. The only information available in Low or High Thranx came via sealed communiqués or direct orders from the tiny thranx complement living on sufferance at Comabraeth community. During the past months he had become used not only to speaking in Terranglo, but to thinking in it. It made him less thranx, but not necessarily more human.

Presently, he was perusing a seemingly minor account about a poisoning that had occurred in the Talathropic Pond ecosystem. The Talathropics lay nearly a thousand miles from Comabraeth. A human resources-analysis team had been following up a stock satellite report, prospecting on the ground for possible ore bodies of certain metals, when one of their number had been bitten by a local arthropod. The man's circulatory system had reacted severely—so much so that he had not been expected to live. The site was too far from Comabraeth for help to reach the afflicted in time.

Only the presence in the same area of an AAnn troika that was taking mineral samples made the difference, as the AAnn possessed on their craft a small lab for synthesizing regenerative proteins. Ratiocination of the toxin's molecular structure allowed them to concoct a crude antidote that saved the man's life. As the report detailed, his friends were effusively grateful for the reptiloids' swift and efficacious intervention.

By itself, the article was a mere annoyance. While happy that the human who had been bitten had survived, Pilwondepat was irritated that it was the AAnn who had received gratitude for the deed. Then he began to think. Probably, he decided, the only problem was that, isolated in his self-contained chamber on the edge of the escarpment, he had too much time to think. But . . .

Wasn't it odd that a human should be bitten by a viperous indigene far from any human assistance, only to encounter AAnn working the same vicinity who just happened to have among their mineralogical gear a fully equipped portable lab for doing organic chemical synthesis that included among its research files sufficient data and material for calibrating human as well as AAnn biologenes? Was it more than odd, or did he need to turn the chamber's humidifier up yet another notch?

Something else pricked at his mind. Resetting the viewer, he began searching for similar articles, or even dissimilar ones that might involve human-AAnn interactions. Anything so long as it smacked of oddness.

Gradually, as the night wore on and everyone else in the camp slowly slipped into deep, relaxing sleep, what he began to find were examples of something more than apparently unrelated oddities, the least of which smelled even stronger than the most odoriferous of his human associates.

And much more ominous.

7

It was a part of Daret she had never seen before, that no human had seen before, and it was spectacular. Accustomed to the crowded warrens of the capital hive, the last thing Anjou had expected to find was open space underground.

She felt as if she were walking in a park lifted from some elegant imperial past on Earth. To be sure, the scattered furnishings and artwork were utterly alien, and the botanical decor was unfamiliar; but the sense of luxury and good taste was apparent everywhere, even to a visiting human. Small waterfalls cascaded down slopes that had been sculpted from the raw rock out of which the high-domed chamber had been hollowed, their flow vanishing into the myriad conduits that were the lifeblood of the hive. The arching ceiling glowed with yellow-and-blue light supplied not by artificial lights but by hundreds of transplanted fungi. Mist swirled gracefully, only to be caught and borne away by concealed fans to be recycled through hidden ducts.

A small *myrk* peeped out from beneath spatulate, blue-veined leaves. Crouching, Fanielle extended a hand, and the palm-sized creature crept hesitantly over to her, ambulating on four legs nearly hidden by its dense coat of black-and-blue fur. It had the huge eyes and sensitive nostrils of an animal accustomed to living underground. As it sniffed cautiously of her open hand and then moved close so she could scratch it, she reflected that these were the kinds of furred creatures the thranx were used to dealing with: tiny, harmless, mewling things that had shared their hives and tunnels for millennia. It cooed delightedly and pressed up against her caressing fingertips.

In another part of the Arm, the tiny balls of fluff had stood up, shed most of their fur, and achieved a level of technology equal to that of any other space-traversing species. This was difficult for many thranx to accept. One shooed furry creatures out of the way, or paused to observe their strange behavior. One did not converse with or enter into treaties with them. One especially did not sign agreements that could be construed as even a partial surrendering of sovereignty.

Yet that was the ultimate end to which Anjou and those of like mind within the diplomatic corps strove. It was proving an uphill battle on both sides, against superstition, fear, prejudice, uncertainty, and inertia. She thought of Jeremy and imagined him waiting for her back in Azerick. Jeremy, with his quiet, confident smile and the way his face would light up at the news that another new kind of spore had been discovered. Jeremy, with his enveloping, comforting arms, and soft lips. Jeremy, with . . .

Jeremy was no more, and there was to be no more of him. She shuddered violently, uncontrollably, and angrily shoved the back of a hand against her moistening right eye.

"Are you feeling unwell, *crr!!kk*?"

Whirling, she found herself gazing into the face of the oldest thranx she had ever seen. Even the venerable female's ovipositors had turned a dark purple. Her chitin was the color of raw amethyst, the glow of her great golden compound eyes was significantly dimmed, and her antennae hung forward in limp arcs. At least two trulegs gleamed more brightly than their counterparts, showing that they had undergone forced regeneration, and one truhand was purple composite, suggestive of injury so severe it could not be regrown and had been replaced with a prosthesis. But the voice, though muted, was strong, and the concern it reflected genuine.

"I'm all right, thanks." Though she stood straighter, she still found herself at eye level with the sage. Most humans towered over the arthropods: not Fanielle. Whether they appreciated having a diplomat to deal with who came down to their level physically she did not know. Haflunormet had never commented on her height.

"You are the attaché who sought this appointment, are you not?" The valentine-shaped head cocked slightly to one side.

"I am Fanielle Anjou, yes. You are Eint Carwenduved?" A simple gesture on the part of the elderly thranx was confirmation enough. "I very badly want to talk to you about—"

The venerable eint interrupted, pointing with the artificial truhand. "Let us go and sit by the *prolerea*, and listen to the music of the waters singing. We can talk there."

The thranx moved slowly and with deliberation, picking her steps as if each one might be her last. She did not appear to be that feeble, Anjou reflected. Ancient, to be sure, but still capable of flexibility and movement. The human hoped her host's mind had the same capacity.

They paused at a little alcove close by one of the many small waterfalls. This one tumbled and tinkled over a succession of metal leaves, each droplet generating a musical tone. Looming above was a bush with a thick trunk that threw out great splays of bright pink-and-black flowers. The fragrance from so many blossoms reeking of cinnamon and honey was almost overpowering.

Reaching up, the eint plucked one and pressed it to her face. Anjou could see the multiple mouthparts working as the thranx devoured the center of the bloom. When it was half consumed, she extended the remainder to Anjou.

"I am told that your people can safely ingest this. Would you care to try it?"

Anjou did not, but diplomats are often called upon to extend themselves in peculiar ways on behalf of their profession. Accepting the remnant, she saw several centimeter-long structures protruding from its underside. Plucking one, she showed it to the thranx, who gestured encouragingly. Popping the alien pistil into her mouth, she bit down tentatively.

Flavor and a sugary sensation exploded across her suspicious taste buds. The pulp was so sweet it almost hurt her teeth. As she passed the blossom back, she needed no encouragement to finish what she had been given. It was superb.

"Very nutritious." Finishing off the remaining pistils, the eint set the bloom casually aside. In a subterranean garden as immaculate and ornate as this, Anjou doubted the debris would remain unattended to for very long.

"About the proposed treaty details," she began, the lingering sweetness still effervescing throughout the inside of her mouth, "have you had time to scrutinize the details?"

"*Ssslcci,* I have done little else these past major time-parts." Reaching out with a longer foothand, the eint put four hard-shelled fingers against the human's belly. "I cannot imagine what it must feel like to give live birth. I am told it is painful, and can well imagine it."

"It's not comfortable." Anjou was not pleased by the rapid change of subject, but did not try to force the conversation. "In ancient times, I'm told it was often fatal."

The eint gestured restrained disbelief. "Eggs are better. They do not kick. Now then, about this treaty of yours. It's very substantial. Mere translation took a goodly amount of time."

"A treaty is not a poem," Anjou admitted. "Nothing must be left open to misinterpretation."

"I assure you it was not. The entire series of documents was vetted most thoroughly."

"I know that you are in a position to make real decisions." Anjou leaned forward, trying to suppress her excitement. "That you can recommend directly to the Grand Council. What do you think of the proposals?"

The distinguished female caressed a blossom bud with tru- and foothand, bending the petals back ever so gently. "I love these flowers. I love the look of them, and the smell, and especially the taste." Dimmed but far from dead eyes regarded the watching human. "If you bring the plant into your sleeping chamber, it fills it with perfume—but only for a few days. Then it withers and dies. I would hate to see the very good relationship that presently exists between our species perish from too much contiguity."

Anjou was not put off. "That won't happen."

"Is that so?" The distinguished female set the barren bloom aside. "So in addition to giving birth to this document, you can also predict the future?"

"No, no, of course not. I'm just saying that safeguards will be put in place to ensure that we don't intrude on each other. Close friends don't have to live together under the same roof."

Antennae bobbed and dipped. "That is what the council will say. I can tell you right now what the response will be if I propose your treaties for ratification. I don't have to tell you, of course, but I rather like you, Fanielle Anjou. And not simply because you are eggfull." A truhand reached out to stroke the woman's forearm. The superannuated chitin was still smooth and cool to the touch.

"You obviously believe deeply in these proposals on a personal as well as a professional level."

"I am not alone," she responded. "There are many who believe as strongly in the interdependent future of our two species as do I."

"And it is not to be denied that there are those in the hives who feel similarly, and who are not hesitant to express themselves in the strongest terms." The matriarch's essence filled the air, stronger even than the surrounding, lovingly tended flowers. "But they are not a majority. Nor are those who angrily oppose any contact with your kind beyond that which is absolutely necessary. The bulk of the Greater Hive remains undecided. The words in your proposal are reassuring, and well thought out, but they are not wholly convincing. Furthermore, they are only words." Reaching back, she removed a small tube from the embroidered pack on her thorax and sniffed deeply of one end by holding it flush against first one set of breathing spicules, then the other.

"We have to start with words." Anjou shifted her seat. "When we have agreed on certain words, then relevant deeds can be implemented. But treaties must come before action." Am I getting through to this ancient? she wondered. What was the eint thinking? Unlike face-to-face negotiations with another human, there was no way to tell from simply looking at the eint what was going through her mind. The chitinous countenance was inflexible.

"You speak well for your proposals, you and those who side with you. As for myself, I belong to that great, surging, heaving mass of egg-layers and tenders that has not yet made up its mind." A truhand wagged in Anjou's direction, and she did not need a visual guide to interpret its significance. "Push us too hard, young female, and we will wall up our tunnels away from you. You will not be able to reach us."

Anjou struggled to remain confident. It wasn't easy; the eint was offering little in the way of encouragement. "Then as they are written, you disagree with the basic tenets of the covenants?"

"I did not say that." Plucking a smaller, darker branch from the nearby foliage, the eint munched contentedly on azure petals. Her mouth-parts made fastidious grinding noises as they masticated the succulent herbage. "What I think, what the majority of those I represent and those I deal with daily in council think, is that your kind and mine have a perfectly good relationship right now. There is no need to extend it further, except insofar as concerns the AAnn."

Anjou watched something small and metallic flit through the surrounding undergrowth. "We have no quarrel with the AAnn. Therefore we can't promise you any more assistance as regards them than what already exists. If they were to make some kind of serious frontal attack on a thranx world, that would be different. We would be bound, even in the absence of a formal military treaty, to render aid because of the help you gave us during the Pitarian War."

"Would you, my dear?" Carwenduved studied the human closely, wishing she understood the meaning of those remarkable twists and contortions that flowed through the biped's flexible epidermis. "There is no formal reciprocation. You are not obligated to assist us, just as we were not obligated to help you against the Pitar. There is no treaty, no pact that requires you to provide such military assistance. We helped you against the Pitar because we thought it was the right thing to do. In the event we are assaulted by the AAnn, will your people believe similarly?"

Diplomat though she was, it was too big a lie for Anjou to countenance. Besides, the eint probably knew in detail whereof she spoke. "I can't answer that, Carwenduved. It would depend on the circumstances. I can tell you that humans have always stood up against injustice, no matter where it has occurred."

"That is good to know. Is it so even among those of you who refer to us as 'bugs,' and would like to squash us underfoot like our tiny namesakes that occupy your worlds?"

"Shapeism is conspicuous among the thranx as well as among my people. It is a primitive animosity that will eventually die out."

"As it must also among my kind." The eint sighed, her b-thorax expanding and contracting sharply. "But for now, it exists, and must be dealt with." She stirred on her bench. "Although I admit there are those on the council who would like to forge a tighter relationship with your kind, they are outnumbered by the many who believe that the present situation is perfectly satisfactory. They see no need to dig the two burrows closer together. You have your worlds; we have ours. While we can share the same environments, we have different preferences. We like hot, humid worlds with a higher oxygen content than yourselves. From our point of view, you like to live in dry, cold places where no thranx would be comfortable for very long, and where depending on the relevant extremes we need special equipment to survive. There is no direct competition. Therefore, there is no need to modify the formalities that presently exist between us. The galaxy is a big place, and our explorations and exploitations need never overlap."

Anjou could not hide her disappointment. She had worked so hard to secure this meeting, and except for some casual, albeit friendly, chitchat, it was going nowhere. The eint was polite, but firm. "It could be so much more. The way our species worked together during the Pitarian War showed that."

"More than what, *yrriik*? What more could we wish for than what we already have? Trade proceeds as trade always does, according to the benefits that accrue to those participating. There is mutual respect, and even a certain degree of sometimes grudging mutual admiration for each other's unique qualities. There is even beginning to be appreciation on a deeper level, as witness occasional events like this intercultural fair on your new colony world of Pawn."

" 'Dawn,' " Anjou politely corrected her. "But it's not the same. It's not what it could be." Held in check since she had arrived, excitement finally overcame her professional equivocation. "We've never encountered anyone like the thranx. Physically, socially, you're completely different from us. Yet we enjoy so many of the same things. Not only art, but even humor. I don't know anyone who has spent time among you who has not made a permanent friendship or two."

She was waving her arms about now. Instead of alarming the elderly eint, it relaxed the alien. Speaking frequently as they did with their four arms, it was a pleasure for a thranx to see a human similarly utilizing her limbs. Carwenduved studied the movements with interest, wondering at the meaning of each individual gesture. She would have been disappointed to learn that nearly all served only to emphasize and did not carry specific meanings of their own.

"Friendship is a fine thing," the eint declared when Anjou finally ran down. "But you speak as one who has spent more time among us than most of your kind. Others are not so sanguine. What is to say that a closer, tighter association might not harm rather than help relations between our kinds? In the absence of proof, continued caution would seem to be the best course."

Here, at least, was a line of objection Anjou had anticipated and prepared for. "There are the outposts here, at Azerick, and in the Amazon Basin on Earth. In both places, humans and thranx have developed a working relationship that goes beyond the formal. Everyone gets along. There have been just one or two reported incidents of violent conflict between settlers, scientists, and locals. The more time our people spend in one another's company, the closer grows the bond between them. We have seen this happen over and over again. There is occasionally some mutual distaste involving appearance, but this soon passes as everyone gets to know everyone else." She nodded at the eint. "Your own reports, I am sure, show similar maturation."

"No one disputes that our species can get along, or that individuals can become fond of one another." Reaching out with a foothand, she ran the two center fingers down Anjou's arm. "*I* am growing fond of *you*. Your persistence gains you merit. And I must confess that I myself . . ." She looked away—or at least, Anjou thought that she did. With those compound eyes, it was hard to tell. "I am inclined to think that the proposals you set forth in these documents should be given serious consideration."

Anjou contained herself. Out of the cool, calm resistance of the conversation had come the first glimmer of hope. "It would be," she replied with as much gravity as her small voice could muster, "the greatest thing to happen to our two species since each of us independently detected the presence of intelligent life beyond our respective homeworlds. Think of it! An alliance between two different intelligences that for the first time in this part of the galaxy advanced beyond the usual agreements on trade and culture. Thranx would be able to visit any human world they wished, at any time. Humans would gain reciprocity of movement with the Greater Hive. We would share government, thus reducing many large expenses. And no potentially antagonistic species would dare to threaten so powerful a regional alliance. You would be safe forever from possible depredations on the part of the AAnn."

"Don't underestimate the determination and capability of the AAnn." The eint gestured first-degree vigilance. "They are afraid of nothing. Cautious, yes. Deliberate and calculating, yes. But afraid, no. You are right, of course. Such an all-encompassing alliance would give them considerable pause, and would therefore be to our great advantage. But it goes beyond the military commitment the Great Hive seeks."

Anjou sat back. "I don't see you ever acquiring the one without the other." It was time for bluntness, no matter how unpleasant. "Despite what I said earlier, I personally don't see the great mass of humankind going to war to save the thranx. To save a human-thranx society, or humanx as some of us have taken to calling it, that would happen without debate."

"And I don't see the council moving in the direction of sharing government and dissolving at one dig all the usual barriers that stand between us."

Anjou wished there was another representative she could caucus with, someone else she could turn to for advice on how to proceed. But there was not. She was alone. The eint had agreed to see her, and only her, because of the Bryn'ja. There were at present no other diplomats serving at Azerick who happened to be pregnant.

"Will you at least present the formal proposal to the other members of the council?"

"They have much to occupy their time, and are very busy. Not only are they responsible for the stable operation of government here on Hivehom; they must consider progress and development on our own colony worlds."

"And wouldn't those functions be easier if they could be shared?"

The eint whistled quiet amusement. "You are righteously dedicated in this matter, I see."

"I, and those who think like me, dearly desire what we believe to be best for both our peoples."

"Well, the Pitarian War certainly gave a boost to your aspirations. There are those among the thranx who would sign such a treaty tomorrow. Unfortunately, they do not lie in council. But yes, I will present the relevant documents for consideration."

Anjou's heart leaped. It was not everything she had hoped for, but it was realistically as much as she could have expected from the visit.

"And now, enough of interstellar diplomacy, of debating the fate of worlds." Rising from her supportive bench, the rickety eint clasped Anjou's right hand in a foothand. "Such softness! One cannot only feel the warmth, but see blood vessels beneath the skin. I marvel that it does not tear as easily as a leaf."

Anjou let her hand lie freely in the hard chitinous grasp. It was like holding hands with a crab. "Amazing stuff, human skin. I'm afraid we don't take care of it the way we should."

"Yet if torn, it bleeds more slowly than do we." Antennae dipped forward, stroking the human's exposed arm. "And this business of exuding salt water through your epidermal layer. Most bizarre."

"No less strange than breathing through one's neck," Anjou responded. "Or employing a set of limbs alternately as hands or feet. Or smelling through feathers that stick out of one's head."

"You speak querulously of normal things." Tugging gently, the eint drew Anjou away from the bower where they had been talking to lead her down another garden path. "Not being a biologist, I take it you have never seen a nursery, or visited a pupation station."

"No," Anjou admitted. At the eint's words, images swam in her mind of glistening larvae and newly matured adult thranx bursting forth from swollen body cases.

"*Srr!!lpp,* if you're going to speak of merging our civilizations, our cultures, you need to know more than what they show you at formal briefings." The two fingers and two thumbs that had been holding Anjou's hand moved around to her lower back and pressed, urging her forward.

"You will come with me now, Fanielle Anjou. It's time you met the kids."

8

"Maman, look at the funny-looking man walking the big bug!"

The well-dressed woman leaned over and whispered urgently to the little girl, who looked to be about seven. "Hush now, Iolette. It's not polite to call someone funny-looking. It's only his clothes that are different. And he's not walking the big bug; they're walking together. That's a thranx, sweetheart. They're not really bugs. They just look a lot like bugs."

From the other side of the seven-year-old, her father bent over to speak. "A bug is an insect, sweetheart. The thranx are not insects. They're people, just like you and me, and they're supposed to be very smart."

The little girl's black ringlets hovered about her forehead as she looked sharply up at her father. "Can we go meet them, Dadan? Can we say hello?"

Mother and father exchanged a glance. "I don't know, sweetheart," the mother murmured. "Are you sure you really want to? I thought you told me that bugs were yucky."

The girl was insistent. Perhaps it was the play of color of the thranx's iridescent blue-green exoskeleton, or the flash of light from the red-banded golden compound eyes. Something drew her in its direction. "But Dadan says thranx are not bugs. Please, Maman, please!"

The woman hesitated, but her husband was encouraging. "This is supposed to be an intercultural fair, Peal. It would give her something to talk about in her next age-group mixer back home. I'll bet none of her friends have ever met a thranx in person."

"They haven't, Dadan." Ringlets and wide blue eyes swung around on the reluctant mother. "Please, Maman!"

"What can it hurt, Peal?" the husband wondered aloud. "Actually, I wouldn't mind face-to-facing one of the things myself. And if that guy at its side isn't walking it, maybe he's some kind of handler or something. See, they're wearing similar symbols. I'm sure it's safe." A sudden thought made him smile. "I know! It's some kind of wandering exhibit, as opposed to all the static displays we've been seeing on stages and in tubes."

Under assault from two sources, the woman finally relented. "Well, if you're certain it's safe . . ." Making sure her daughter's fingers were grasped firmly within her own, she glanced down one last time. "You stay close to Maman, Iolette."

"That larva has been staring at me for some time." Twikanrozex gestured with antennae and truhand in the direction of the dark-haired little girl who was eagerly leading her parents toward him and his companion.

"Girl," Briann corrected his friend. "It's a little girl, not a larva. I know that for you they amount to the same thing, but I promise you no human parent wants its offspring, however cute, referred to as a larva. The word brings up unpleasant atavistic racial memories."

"*Little girl.* I will remember. But I think *larva* is a better description. Compact."

"I won't argue with you." Glancing down at himself, Briann made sure his robe was straight. As always, he wanted to make a good impression. Good impressions first, they had been told. Conversions later.

The approaching adults looked uncomfortable. The woman, Briann noted, studiously avoided looking directly at Twikanrozex. "Hello," the man began, "I hope you don't mind, but my daughter expressed a desire to . . ."

"Can I touch it, Dadan. Can I touch it?" Wide-eyed, the little girl was bouncing up and down with barely repressed energy and excitement.

"You have to excuse our daughter," the woman began apologetically. "She's never seen a thranx before. We come from New Riviera, and we've only seen thranx there on the tridee. So you can understand that—" She broke off abruptly, clearly distracted by something unexpected. "What is that *exquisite* fragrance?"

Briann repressed a smile. It was always the women who noticed it first. "I think you're probably referring to the body odor of my companion." He indicated Twikanrozex, who stood patiently. The sensitivity of humans to thranx body scent was no mystery to him. One had only to breathe in that of humans to understand the attraction.

"Really?" The woman had come unglued. Her eyelids were fluttering as she inhaled deeply. "I've heard about it, read about it, but it's not the same. Words just don't—they don't . . ."

"Peal, control yourself." The man breathed in and did smile. "I can't quite place it myself. Attar of plumeria? Essence of protea?"

"Everyone responds a little differently because of subtle variations in the neural connection between their olfactory nerve endings and the brain. And no two thranx seem to smell exactly alike." Briann was always gratified when the hesitant and sometimes openly hostile drew near enough to get a whiff of his friend. Twikanrozex's personal perfume was a better introduction to his species than any carefully scripted salutation.

As her mother stood swaying slightly, her eyes half closed in a private ecstasy of olfaction, the little girl broke free of the woman's diminished grip and rushed forward. Twikanrozex recoiled ever so slightly. Remembering the eighty-fourth maxim propounded by the founders Shanvordesep and Cirey Pyreau allowed him to relax and accept the assault. Human offspring, he had been told, were by nature far more physically forward and demonstrative than their thranx counterparts, not least because they already had arms and legs since they did not experience pupation. So when the girl reached out to lightly touch his thorax, he did not flinch.

"Iolette." The woman was coming out of her fragrance-suffused haze. "Maybe you shouldn't—"

"It's all right," Briann was quick to reassure her. "This is what the fair is about, really. Not rides and exhibits and food." He nodded to where the wide-eyed girl was enthusiastically exploring his companion. "This." When the woman looked uncertain, her husband put a reassuring arm around her.

Dropping to all sixes to bring himself closer to the young biped's level, Twikanrozex dipped his head in her direction. "Would you like to feel my antennae? That's what we smell with."

Reaching out and up, the girl gently let the feathery projections slide through her small fingers. "They're soft! Like feathers." She looked the alien directly in the eyes, utterly unafraid of its proximity. "You people smell really nice, but you sure are funny-looking!"

"And you are funny-looking to us, child," Twikanrozex replied without hesitation. The young one had said "people" instead of "bugs." Of such tiny steps were enduring relationships forged. "We can't imagine smelling the world through holes in the middle of our faces."

Giggling, the girl put a finger to the tip of her nose and pushed it first to one side, then the other. In response, Twikanrozex wriggled his antennae. This led to further giggling and brought forth a smile on the woman's face that was wondrous to behold. For the first time since her daughter had insisted on the confrontation, the mother looked relaxed.

"How about," Twikanrozex suggested, "a buggy-back ride?"

"Oh yes, ohyesohyes!" The angelic countenance whirled on her parents. "Maman?"

"I don't know . . ." The broad smile faded slightly, but did not disappear.

"It's perfectly safe, madam," Briann assured her. "Twikanrozex is quite used to humans. He's done this before. He enjoys it." That was only partially true, Briann knew, but Twikanrozex had offered. It was part of their calling. Briann was only sorry that he could not reciprocate, because thranx larvae had no arms or legs with which to hold on.

His reassurance was good enough for the girl. Without waiting for formal consent—or further objection—from her mother, the girl scrambled around to the back of the alien. Kneeling, Twikanrozex instructed her to climb up onto the upper part of his abdomen. Once she was seated comfortably on his upper wing cases, he told her to hold on by putting her arms around his thorax, but to be careful not to cover any of the eight breathing spicules located there. That led to a discussion of whether it was better to breathe through holes in one's face or at the base of one's neck. Confident the girl was secure, the thranx started off, utilizing all six legs to support her properly. Once, he stood back on his four trulegs only, rising a little higher and making her shriek with delight as she was forced to hang on to keep from sliding off his smooth back and wing cases. Twikanrozex's aquamarine backpack, b-thorax muffler, and leg warmers did not get tangled in her limbs.

Looking on, the husband murmured to Briann. "They really are remarkable creatures. I mean, once you get past their unsettling physical appearance, they're quite likeable."

"It depends on how badly you're afraid of insects." Briann stood watching with arms crossed. Choosing not to chat, the woman had eyes only for her daughter. The longer the interaction went on, the louder her daughter screamed with delight, the more she mellowed. "Some humans have no trouble with it at all. Others are . . . Well, there are xenophobes among most intelligent species. The important thing to always keep in mind is that the thranx are not Terran insects. They're not related to the much smaller arthropods that we've been battling since we came down out of the trees. Appearance-wise, it's a pure case of convergent evolution."

The husband nodded slowly. "Not to mention that they helped save our butts at Pitar."

"There is that, too. But they would rather be known for their art and philosophy than their military prowess. As would we. At least, as most of us would."

They were silent for a while, watching and delighting in the sight of human child and thranx adult gamboling freely in one corner of the expansive fairgrounds. Then the father indicated Briann's garb. "Interesting raiment you're wearing. I notice that it's the same color and shows the same symbols as that decorating your many-limbed companion. Is it significant of something more than friendship?"

The moment had arrived. As was proper, it was the attendee who had brought it up. As acolytes, Briann and Twikanrozex were discouraged from broaching the subject directly. "The United Church settled on aquamarine as its color designate because it is the predominant coloration among adult thranx as well as representing the bountiful and prominent oceans of Earth."

The man frowned. "United Church? Never heard of it." His expression mutated. "You're not going to ask me for money, are you?"

"No. We're not allowed to do that. One of the basic tenets of the church is that it never asks for donations. From the beginning, the idea was that it was to be entirely self-supporting."

The man relaxed, albeit not completely. "By charging for buggy-back rides?"

It was Briann's turn to smile. Not everyone he and Twikanrozex had encountered since arriving to work the fair had shown a sense of humor. "There is a set schedule of fees for services. You must request them. Nothing is proffered."

"Glad to hear it. If you're looking for converts, I'm afraid you're out of luck. I'm Catholic, and my wife is Fifth-Term Shiite Zoroastrian."

"We never look for converts. Though you could remain as you are and still enjoy the fruits of the Church."

The man was intrigued in spite of himself. "How can you belong to your church without converting?"

"It's simpler than you might think. The Church extends itself to everyone: other believers, atheists, agnostics, aliens. Everyone. One of the first things you learn is that to belong, you don't have to believe in anything. No deity, no special books, nothing. We minister to that part of sapience that is not entirely satisfied by logic and reason. It exists. We don't try to deny it."

"Sounds like a pretty weird outfit to me." When Briann did not reply or comment, the man continued. "Well? Aren't you going to offer me some free literature or something?"

The padre shook his head. "Reams of printout tend to intimidate people, or make them feel uncomfortable. The Church wants people to feel comfortable in its presence. We have a small display here—one among hundreds. If you're interested in learning more, or asking additional questions, you can find it on your fairgrounds readout. The display is unstaffed. Everything is automated. No one will try to talk your ear off."

"Even weirder. Not that Peal and I need anything like this. We're both perfectly happy the way we are. So is Iolette."

Briann nodded. "She seems a wonderfully well-adjusted child, with equally well-adjusted parents. I think you're right: You probably don't need any of the Church's services. But you might want to read more about it, just to satisfy the curiosity I see written on your face. You can have a good laugh about it with your friends when you get home. Another amusing anecdote from the fair on distant Dawn."

The husband eyed Briann uncertainly. "Are you serious about this Church business? This isn't some sort of wandering comedy routine sanctioned by the fair programmers? You're not a performer?"

"I am a true acolyte of the United Church. I can recite to you its founding principles as well as all the One Hundred and Five Maxims of Indifferent Contentment. I am qualified to minister in a number of specialties. But why should I bore you with that which you have not requested? Go and have a read about it if you're curious, or pull up the general literature on your personal communicator. Code MT-DF-186. You don't have to visit the display. You can also access the same information when you get home."

"So you're already on New Riviera, too?" The man was quietly impressed.

"The Church suffers from increasing popularity. We try to keep a low profile. Here comes your daughter."

"I hope she didn't wear your friend out." The man hesitated. "I've never heard of a Church that extends to all species. How do you manage it?"

Briann leaned close and whispered. "We proceed from the notion that good ideas know no shape. Then we're careful not to take any of it too seriously."

Uncertain whether to smile or not, the man settled on a half grin. Then he walked over to join his wife in assisting their daughter in her dismount.

"Careful of my spicules—that's it, there." As soon as the girl was off his back, Twikanrozex turned and preened an antenna. "Did you have fun, little one?"

"Ohyesohyesohyes! Let's do it again!"

Her mother bent to place a hand on the girl's shoulder. "Don't you think Mr. Twikel . . . Mr. Twiken . . ."

"Twikanrozex," the thranx said, enunciating it slowly for her.

She smiled gratefully at him. "Don't you think Mr. Twikanrozex might be a little tired? Maybe he needs to rest."

"For a little while, *crr!!ckk*." Briann could see that Twikanrozex was breathing hard but was far from exhausted. Clearly, the little girl would have been happy to bounce along on his back all day.

"Say thank you to Mr. Twikanrozex," her father ordered.

Walking up to the thranx, the girl extended a hand. Instead of proffering one of his own, Twikanrozex leaned forward and brushed her open palm with the tips of both antennae. She clutched at her hand, giggling.

"That tickles!"

"A last smile." The thranx stepped back. "Perhaps I'll see you again before the fair is over, little one."

"I hope so, Mr. Twikanrozex. Thank you for the buggy ride." Turning, she placed her right hand in her mother's and looked up. "Can we get ice cream now? I'm hungry!"

"I'm sure you are, after all that hopping around." The woman looked back at Twikanrozex and beamed. There was no trace of the uncertainty and hesitation that had marked her initial approach. It was utterly gone. "Thank you."

"You're welcome." Raising a truhand and a foothand, Twikanrozex imitated the simplistic human gesture of farewelling. "Another time." As soon as the couple and their daughter were out of earshot, he turned to his companion.

"How did it go?"

"The seed is well planted. Like most, he tried to affect disinterest. And like most who take the time to ask questions and to listen, he's interested. Maybe not today, or tomorrow, or even until he's back home months from now, but he'll definitely research the Church." Briann chuckled. "Nothing like telling them you don't want their money to pique their interest."

"That's good. The larv—the little girl was fun. Human children are so full of energy."

"That's a difference between us. Thranx larvae think before they act. Human children act before they think. Of course, being hatched with functional limbs has a lot to do with it."

"Yes." Twikanrozex sighed softly. "Many's the time I remember lying in the nursery longing for the day when I would be able to pupate and emerge with arms and legs. Your kind is fortunate in that fashion."

"It does make us more impulsive, though." Together, they resumed their walk. Briann badly wanted to see the demonstration of thranx acrobatic music, while Twikanrozex was fascinated by everything around them. Simply being on a human-colonized world was entertainment enough for him.

They had come prepared to deal with all manner of possible problems, of protests and objections. But the last thing they expected to have to deal with was competition.

They did not think of it that way, of course, but the cluster of well-dressed young humans who surrounded them in front of one of the numerous water sculptures contributed by the thranx hydrosculptors of Willow-Wane felt otherwise.

"We've been hearing about you." The young man who spoke was tall, slim, handsome, and syrupy of voice.

"Already?" Briann glanced at Twikanrozex, who could not disguise his apprehension at being surrounded by so many exceedingly intent, larger humans.

"And we decided we had to do something about it." The woman wore her hair cropped short, like her syllables. "Before it got out of hand."

Briann was not yet ready to begin looking for fair security personnel, but the idea that he might have to do so had crept rapidly to the forefront of his thoughts. "That sounds ominous. Who are you, and what do you want?"

Members of the enclosing circle looked at one another in apparent disbelief before their spokesman turned back to Briann. "You don't recognize our garments? The white suits and dresses, the decorations of virtuous gold?"

"I'm afraid we don't."

It was the woman's turn. "We represent the Unity of Traditional Religions, Dawn branch. We were informed that an odd pair, consisting of human and thranx, were proselytizing here at the fair on behalf of some new cult. As representatives of the old beliefs carried out from Earth, we felt it incumbent on us to seek you out, and to appraise your message."

Another woman spoke up. "You understand, there are a lot of children here."

"The United Church makes no distinction between children and adults," Briann explained. "Only between intelligence and nonintelligence. The two do not always evolve in parallel." It would have been an excellent moment to eye the young leader of the white-clad group meaningfully, but Church protocol strictly forbade the application of sarcasm at the personal level.

"Or between humans and aliens?" another woman wondered aloud.

Briann nodded in Twikanrozex's direction. "My thranx friend is not an alien; he is only nonhuman. Again, we clearly differ in some of our definitions."

"There's no provision in terrestrial theology for sentients that are not created in God's image," another man declared with complete conviction.

"Many of us feel similarly," Twikanrozex replied calmly.

That put a momentary halt to the questioning as the assembled devoted murmured among themselves. The two representatives of the United Church waited patiently. Patience was among the first qualities they were taught. It was becoming clear that these young folk meant no physical harm. They wanted only to assure themselves that the eccentric couple were not bent on seducing human children to the ways of evil. Briann and Twikanrozex could deal with that. The United Church had firm ideas of its own about evil: It was against it.

"How can you offer to minister to something that looks like that?" The woman who had first spoken stared unashamedly at Twikanrozex. "That aroma, though . . ."

"Shapeism is to be abhorred in all things," Briann pointed out. "Intelligence marked by understanding and compassion are the hallmarks of a spiritual being. We don't go into specifics. Every species seeks the answers to the ultimate questions in its own way. The Church doesn't attempt to define them, or to restrict them."

"Then how," another man wondered, "can you offer solace?" His friend tried to interrupt, but the younger man, now curious, shrugged him off.

Twikanrozex gestured with all four hands, wondering if any of the humans would respond in kind. They did not, but neither were they visibly repulsed. He was encouraged. "Sympathy does not demand to be underwritten by dogma. Pain is a universal constant that may be assuaged by any concern irrespective of source."

"We don't feel the need to speak a lot of mumbo jumbo to help someone feel better," Briann added.

Several among the white-clad looked upset. "You speak blasphemy," one insisted.

"Fluently," Briann assured her. "Our organization has no truck with archaic attempts to help people by filling them up with guilt. Ample guilt is acquired soon enough, through the mere process of living. The last thing any sentient needs is the unrequested addition of external culpability. How many of you feel guilty about something?"

The several expressions of concern that appeared in reaction to Briann's question were drowned out by the loud words of the young spokesman. "Look here, we're the ones asking the questions! We're the ones who'll determine whether you'll be allowed to continue to work this fair or not."

"Firstly, *ci!!llp*," Twikanrozex began, "we are not 'working' this fair. We confront no one, pressure no one, seek out neither individuals nor families nor groups. We only respond to questions freely directed at us. The UC does not seek converts. There is nothing to convert people to. We have nothing like official membership. The Church and its services are freely available to anyone who is interested."

"What happens," another woman demanded to know as she pushed her way forward, "if someone chooses to participate in your church? What happens to their former religion?"

"Annamarie," the man next to her began warningly. She ignored him.

"Whatever you wish to happen." Briann was warming to the discussion, now that it had turned into a discussion and away from unfounded accusations. "You may continue to practice as you did before encountering our organization. There are participants in the United Church who practice many religions, and participants who espouse none at all. We are very undemanding."

"How can someone belong to two churches and champion two different beliefs?" the woman persisted.

"Beliefs?" Twikanrozex waved his truhands in her direction. "We don't require that you believe in anything."

The spokesman's brows drew together. "What kind of a church is it that doesn't require belief?"

Briann smiled invitingly. "A new kind. Try it and see. You'll find it remarkably liberating. Most who come to us do."

The young man drew himself up. "I'm already liberated—by the knowledge that I am following the one true path."

"Of course you are!" Briann responded exuberantly. "All of you are, no matter what your particular individual belief. Realizing that allows you to participate freely in the UC."

One heavyset fellow on the edge of the group was nodding knowingly. "I understand now." He smiled at his associates. "We have nothing to fear from these people, or from their establishment—because they're crazy. They argue in circles."

"That is it!" Twikanrozex gestured vigorously. "We argue in circles, just like the universe. In the same fashion as a gravitational lens bends light so that you can see behind large stellar objects, the United Church bends reason so that you can see the truths that hide behind reality."

"We're wasting our time here." The spokesman, now satisfied that the two robed preachers, or whatever they were, represented no threat to the established theological order, turned away. "The girot mimes from Coolangatta are starting their show soon. We still have time to hop a transport and get there before the opening."

The white-clad gathering began to fall away—but not quite all of them. A pair lingered: the woman Annamarie and a male friend. Ignoring the admonishments of their companions, they remained behind. They were curious, which is the first step toward enlightenment. Briann and Twikanrozex were delighted to accommodate their many questions. The man went so far as to buy Briann a cup of mochoka and Twikanrozex a helix of *cherel!l* tea. The four of them sat sipping and chatting for several hours. When the conversation was finally brought to an end by the woman named Annamarie, the two priestly acolytes watched the young humans depart still deep in conversation.

"There are good folk here." Twikanrozex sucked the last liquid from the bottom of his nearly empty turbinate. "People willing to listen."

"Yes." Briann scanned the milling crowds. "I would have wished for more thranx, though."

"The larger contingents will not be arriving for a day or two yet," Twikanrozex pointed out. "All have to come from offworld, and only the boldest will consider attending a function on a human-settled colony. But they will come, rest assured. My people are irresistibly drawn to the neoteric."

"I hope I can meet some and convince them of the kindly nature of my species," Briann murmured. "I've lost weight specifically for that purpose."

"It was a good thing for you to do," Twikanrozex told him. "Too much jiggling of loose human flesh can nauseate even the most courteous and well-disposed thranx. It is a reaction as unfortunate as it is involuntary."

"Not to mention one that's likely to put a damper on casual conversation," Briann noted dryly.

From time to time they would wander back to the automated display that had been set up and activated on the first day of the fair, both to ensure that it was functioning properly and to deal with individuals and sometimes small groups that had gathered there. Accustomed after the first couple of days to all manner of reactions, they encountered an entirely new one when, on the third morning, they confronted a well-dressed man in his early forties who was viewing one of the tridee hover messages while chuckling constantly.

"Usually," Briann offered by way of greeting, "our presentation meets with skepticism, or open hostility, or indifference, or interest. You're the first person we've met whose primary reaction has been laughter."

"Oh, hello." Turning, the man grinned at Briann, eyed Twikanrozex with more than casual interest, and reached up to dab at his face with an absorptive pad. "I didn't mean any disrespect."

"None taken," Twikanrozex clicked. His response intrigued the man even more.

"So you're a thranx. I've seen a number wandering about the fair, but mostly they're working displays and performances. It's nice to finally meet one of you in person."

"The touch be mine." Twikanrozex extended a truhand, which gesture humans found less alien than the caress of feathery antennae. The man took it, was surprised to find his own gently shaken, and withdrew his fingers thoughtfully.

"The actual contact is warmer than I thought it would be. Not crustaceanlike at all. Do you see multiple images of me out of those compound eyes?"

"While multiple images are perceived," Twikanrozex replied, "they are linked in my mind to create a single image. Our eyes are more advanced than those of the terrestrial insects whom you are utilizing for reference."

"Not from Earth, myself." The man shrugged. "New Paris, actually." He indicated the lively display. "Your church sounds interesting. Complete waste of time, of course."

"In what way?" Briann was silently disconcerted by the casual dismissal from so obviously intelligent and interested an observer.

"Too many religions already. Humankind's got a house full of 'em. Always has. Every year, every month, it seems like a new fad pops up, attracts a horde of eager adherents, and then just as quickly fades away. At best, that's what you're looking at." He smiled approvingly at Twikanrozex. "Although with the thranx involved you certainly have real novelty value going for you."

Briann could tell from the man's tone and attitude that he was in no way trying to be offensive. He was simply stating his mind.

"We who believe think that you're wrong." Twikanrozex added a whistle of conviction.

"Well, without a doubt you would." The man's good nature continued to shine through his disparaging words. "But I've spent some years in the business of fads, done pretty well out of it, and I know whereof I speak. Just a friendly warning: Make sure you have some kind of professional position to fall back on when it all goes flat. How are you doing here, by the way?" Briann mentioned a number. The man was suitably impressed.

"You've been quiet about it, anyway."

"We don't believe in trumpeting our accomplishments."

Their visitor chuckled anew. "Believers in word-of-mouth, eh? Can't say as I blame you. It's the best advertising no matter what you're selling."

"We are not 'selling' anything," Twikanrozex corrected him. The thranx was growing irritated with this self-assured human.

"Sure, sure." The visitor spoke as if humoring a child. "That's the baseline every religion has used since the beginning of time. Well, how do I join?"

Briann frowned. They had finally encountered someone for whom their training had not prepared them. "You mean, after all that cynicism you're still interested in joining the Church?"

"Why not? I'm always in need of fresh amusement. In my work I have access to the latest stimsims, tridee plays, prose, you name it. So I'm highly cultured but easily bored. Your church will be a diversion, a lark, a fashionable fancy. My friends are very big on one-upmanship, but I don't know a single one who can claim to have worshiped alongside a bug. Your pardon, sir or whatever—a thranx. When I'm bored again, I'll move on to something else." He spread his arms wide. "Meanwhile, your organization will have gained another new, albeit transient, neophyte."

Recovering nicely, Briann extended a hand. Shaking it, the other man seemed to lose just a hint of his astonishing self-assurance. "You're going to accept me in spite of my avowed lack of expectation?"

"The United Church turns no one down. There is room within for all," Briann affirmed. "Even the incredulous."

"Well, that's mighty obliging of you! I look forward to reading your source materials, and to having a good laugh at their expense."

Twikanrozex saw to it that the visitor's communicator accepted the information transfer before congratulating him in turn. "If you gain a few days' amusement from all that we have given you, that will be reward enough. An amused species is a contented species."

"Glad to know that you bu—thranx have a sense of humor."

"You will learn more about us from the Church materials," Twikanrozex informed him. "The UC was formed by a human and a thranx working in concert. It is an entirely new idea in interspecies relations."

"And one that neatly sidesteps the current controversies raging between our respective governments." Exaggerating the gesture, the man put a finger to his lips. "You're very clever, you people are, but it won't make any difference in the end."

"We think it will," Briann replied. "Enjoy your literature."

"So I will; so I will. It'll give me something to wade through in space-plus, on the way back to New Paris." With that he departed, tucking his communicator back into his shirt pocket.

"What do you make of our chances with that one?" Twikanrozex tracked the human's progress across the strip of fairgrounds pavement, which looked and felt exactly like grass except that it was impervious to both footwear and the elements and needed neither light nor water to maintain its springiness and color.

"He's intelligent." Briann turned back to their display, wondering if he ought to switch the order of presentation to present a new field of images to first-time viewers who happened to be passing by. "But I have yet to meet the individual who was so smart they could keep from fooling themselves. If he reads, and doesn't just delete the load you gave him, I think he very well might choose to partake. I'd much rather try to convince an intelligent cynic than a willing ignoramus."

"Maxim forty-seven." Twikanrozex shuffled around to the back of the display tower. "Let's put the site selection first for a while. Looking at your equatorial lands helps to take the chill out of this air for me. Mentally, at least."

"Sorry you're cold. As soon as we're done here, we'll go spend some time in the Willow-Wane pavilion."

"*Srr!rrt*—ah, for the feel of real air in my lungs! You'll be all right there, Brother Briann?"

The human nodded. "I don't mind sweating in the service of the Church—or for my friends."

9

The more Pilwondepat thought about it in the days that followed, the more the affair nagged at him. Probably he was obsessing on nothing, haunted by matters of no real consequence, simply because he was personally irritated at what was happening on Comagrave. It detracted from his work, and he knew it. But he could not stop himself. He had always been afflicted with something of a suspicious nature, and as an exoarcheologist he was trained to draw substantiative conclusions from dozens, often hundreds, of miniscule, seemingly unrelated sources.

It wasn't just the circumstance of the unfortunate human who had been bitten by a native arthropod only to be saved by the extraordinarily fortuitous proximity of an AAnn mineralogical sampling team. That was what had sparked his imagination, true, but reports of other incidents had been festering in his mind for many weeks now. Festering, until the occasion of the arthropod bite had caused all of it to burst forth in the full flower of anxiety.

Too many bad things were happening. Surely, Comagrave was a dangerous place, newly discovered and barely explored. Trouble was to be expected, even the occasional disaster, but there were no hostile native sentients to fear, no overwhelming profligacy of inimical life-forms. Either the humans who had come to study and explore were an exceedingly inept bunch, or else too many of them had been born in the hive of the unlucky. From personal experience, Pilwondepat knew the former to be untrue, and he did not believe in the latter.

Therefore, something else was going on.

He was circumspect in his investigation. It was not his province to ask personal questions of individuals from various camps and outposts, though he had the means to do so. Drawing together individual recollections of seemingly unrelated incidents might have enabled him to come to a conclusion more swiftly. But it would also have drawn attention to him. He did not fear such attention from the humans themselves. It was the presence of so many AAnn "observers" on the planet that induced him to keep a low profile.

While he could only exchange communications with the occasional human, there was nothing to prevent him from examining the contents of every unrestricted report that was being filed or sent offworld. These were available to all at the touch of the right button. Electronic translation supplemented his growing knowledge of Terranglo, enabling him to inspect the relevant correspondence as rapidly as any other potential reader. And the more he read, the more convinced he became of the correctness of his suppositions.

They were very clever. Not every catastrophe was on the order of the complete destruction of the thermal supply depot and research station. The multitude of incidents varied in degree between that and the bite that had nearly killed a single researcher. Some of the details were almost amusing in their resourcefulness. A case of food poisoning at one paleontological camp, for example, resulted in not a single fatality. But once again, it was the AAnn who were conveniently positioned to provide the fresh fruit that cured the humans' digestive upsets. Studying the information, Pilwondepat stridulated involuntarily. Though they shared the omnivorous appetites of most intelligent species, AAnn appetites fell decidedly on the carnivorous side of the food spectrum. How convenient of them to have fresh fruit at their disposal! How implausible. And just the right sort of fruit to cure a digestive disorder within the human system, too.

An aircar carrying a quartet of avian researchers went down in a deep canyon. With human help already on the way, an AAnn craft in the vicinity arrived first to render assistance and effect the needed repairs. A lone prospector—half geologist, half entrepreneur—was found dead in the wildly eroded territory human cartographers had named the Bacunin Badlands. Cause of death: a bad fall. No AAnn available to recover the body, Pilwondepat read. He made a mental note to suggest that a larger, better equipped expedition explore the region. If the AAnn were responsible, as he was beginning to suspect they were in the majority of such unexplained incidences, it was because they wanted to prevent the humans, or in this case one solitary adventurer, from finding something. Pilwondepat was willing to bet a case of goldel *surr!onyy* from Trix that the Bacunin Badlands hid mineral deposits of some value.

Considered individually, the incidents he waded through would not have drawn more than passing commiserations from those who scrutinized them. Assessed together, they comprised a litany of AAnn involvement in human misery and misfortune on Comagrave that could hardly count as coincidence. But who could he lay his case before? The few other thranx on the planet were wholly immersed in their own activities. Sending his conclusions offworld might eventually bring a response, but without any hive authority on the human colony world, he would be left to implement any decision all by himself. And he was a scientist, not a soldier.

He was left to ponder who best among the human population to present with his findings. He knew none of the planetary authority personnel individually. Handing the information to a skeptical official might have any number of consequences, many of which could be bad. They might laugh at him or dismiss his allegations out of hand. Swamped by the difficulties of supervising the exploration and development of a complex new world, the authorities were likely to have little time to spare for the complaints of their own kind, much less for the wild inferences of a visiting alien. Worse yet, the AAnn might be monitoring, officially or otherwise, all such planetary transmissions. If he did not proceed with care and caution, he might well find himself the victim of still another of the inexplicable accidents that up to now had plagued only the resident humans.

Who could he talk to? Who could he converse with who would not treat him as a bug afflicted with paranoia? If it could not be an outsider, then it would have to be a colleague, and one with enough authority to make recommendations that would be listened to. His choices were very limited.

The following morning was bright and clear. The desiccating wind that perpetually scoured the crest of the escarpment was blissfully subdued, and there were even a few dark clouds marring the cerulean blue of the sky. His lungs sucked at the distant suggestions of humidity like a drowning man gasping for any hint of oxygen. Busy, energetic humans crawled over the excavation site, resembling more than they knew the terrestrial insects they professed to loathe.

He was pleased to find Cullen in his portable, prefab living chamber. Confronting him outside, where someone else might overhear, was best avoided. Not that Pilwondepat worried about the energetic bipeds who were laboring on the site, but there was always the possibility that anything said out in the open might get back to Riimadu. That was the one consequence Pilwondepat knew had to be avoided.

As soon as he descried his visitor, Cullen immediately shut off the chamber's air-conditioning. No thranx could take more than a few minutes of the dry, refrigerated air without passing out. Setting aside the viewer and spheres he was working with, he greeted the insectoid with a nod.

"Morning, Pilwondepat. You look tired."

"You've grown perceptive in my company." Unable to use any of the furniture in the chamber, Pilwondepat sagged into a six-legged stance opposite the desk. Thus positioned, he could barely see over it. "Most humans would not have noticed."

Putting his hands behind his head, Cullen leaned back in the chair. "I do occasionally look up instead of down." He gestured past his guest. "Work's going well. The clouds will cut the heat today."

"I welcome the clouds for the moisture they contain, but lament the lowering of the temperature. As your kind are wont to say, in this place I am climatologically damned if it does and damned if it doesn't." Edging forward, he reached up to grasp the edge of the lightweight desk with both truhands. His blue-green exoskeleton gleamed in the filtered light that poured through the integrated skylight. "If something isn't done, I think the human presence on Comagrave is damned as well."

Blinking, Cullen sat forward. "I thought you seemed awfully preoccupied these past couple of weeks, but I couldn't be sure." Reaching up, he tugged playfully at the corners of his mouth with both index fingers. "Your people are the original poker faces."

Pilwondepat gestured with a truhand. "I am not familiar with the reference."

"It means someone can't tell what you're thinking just by looking at your expression."

"Because we have no expressions, due to the inflexible nature of our countenances. Now I understand. A good joke. As I said before, you are perceptive. And correct. I have been very much preoccupied, to the detriment of my work here, I fear. But what I have learned is of far greater importance."

Cullen checked the chamber's climate control one more time to make certain the air-conditioning was off. "And what have you learned, my friend?"

Pilwondepat wished for a greater mastery of Terranglo: for the ability to speak smoothly as if burbling, for the talent to convey overtones of meaning without the use of moving limbs. "That the AAnn are working to actively eradicate the human presence on Vussussica, as they so indifferently call it."

"Everyone knows they'd like to have this world." Cullen was rocking gently back and forth in his chair. The silent floating support conformed to and tried to anticipate the twitching of his muscles. "It suits them perfectly. But it does just fine for us, too, and we were here first. As they have acknowledged—rather gracefully, some of my colleagues feel."

"AAnn 'grace' is a cover for their natural cunning. They are very shrewd, are the AAnn. They want you off this world, and they mean to have it." Pilwondepat was gesturing with all four hands now; he couldn't help it. "They are not so foolish as to challenge you openly, or to attempt to take Comagrave by force. Though they could do so easily, ever since the war with the Pitar they have a healthy respect for human military power. Overrunning this world with ships and soldiers would only bring inevitable retribution down upon them."

"Damn right it would." Cullen had work to do, but the thranx's energy was infectious, even if his message was nonsensical.

"So they work slowly, with great subtlety. Instead of attempting to throw you off this world, or negotiate you off, they are working hard to see to it that you choose to depart voluntarily. They don't want you to surrender Comagrave to them. They hope to induce you to cede it gladly." Reaching back into a thorax pouch, the exoarcheologist withdrew a small mollysphere.

"This is one of your storage devices. In the time I have spent among your kind, I have learned how to manipulate and make use of many such moderately ingenious devices. I used one of your own recording appliances instead of mine so that copies could be easily made, transshipped, or otherwise passed along." He laid the molly on Karasi's desk. "It contains exhaustive documentation of the kinds of incidents I have been examining."

For the first time, Cullen's curiosity surpassed his sense of courtesy. "What incidents?"

"Almost from the day humans claimed Comagrave and began to establish a presence here, there have been a disturbing number of fatal accidents and confrontations."

Cullen was solemn, but not particularly impressed. "Exploration and development of a new world invariably entails sacrifices. And Comagrave is no New Paris or New Riviera—or Willow-Wane, for that matter. If not unreservedly hostile, the environment here can be difficult. So can the flora and fauna."

Pilwondepat gestured impatiently, not even bothering to wonder if the human exoarcheologist understood any of the elaborate hand movements. "All that is true, but it does not explain the consistency of catastrophe you have been experiencing." He indicated the molly. "I have taken the liberty of putting together several mathematical models based on my studies that I think your people will find interesting."

"Why?" Cullen challenged him politely. "Because they'll show that Comagrave is a little more dangerous than most? We know that already."

Pilwondepat's frustration continued to grow. By now, his antennae were bobbing and weaving wildly. "It's not that! Far too many times, when misfortune has struck, the AAnn have been right there, either with assistance or advice."

Cullen pursed his lips. "Some people might think that was good of them."

"There is on Hivehom a class of scavengers who invariably materialize at the scene of a catastrophe, as if they can smell death. Unchallenged, they will immediately start to consume the dead. No one thinks that is especially good of them." He thrust the tips of both antennae in the human's direction. "The AAnn are too often present at the finish of assorted tragedies, like unsought punctuation at the end of a statement." A chitinous blue-green finger nudged the molly. "Go on, Cullen. See for yourself. Nearly every 'accident' reported therein coincides with a concurrent episode of AAnn 'helpfulness.' "

"I'm still not sure what you're trying to say," the exoarcheologist replied softly.

The thranx sat back on four trulegs. "That almost without exception, whenever some tragedy has befallen your people on this world, AAnn have followed close, too close, behind. That in these matters they are being proactive and not reactive."

Cullen's attention was now fully engaged. "You're trying to tell me that they're not responding to these mishaps, but that they're causing them?"

Taking no chances, Pilwondepat did not rely on strong gesticulations to convey his response. "That is exactly what I am saying."

"But . . . why?"

"To convince you that Comagrave is not worth the grief it can cause you. To persuade your government, or at the very least your public opinion, that human interests in this part of the Arm would be better served by turning administration and development of this particular planet over to the Empire. And they will accomplish this, I fear, if your people are not enlightened as to what is taking place under their very olfactory organs, and do not become alert to the scaled ones' calculating machinations."

The chief scientist was silent for a long moment. Rising from his contemplation, he regarded the gleaming being who waited patiently on the other side of the desk.

"That's quite an accusation, Pilwondepat."

"I assure you, my friend, that it is not made lightly."

Cullen nodded, more to himself than to the thranx. "I hardly know what to say. I'm an exoarcheologist. I'm someone who's at home below ground level, not in the rarified atmosphere of interstellar intrigue."

"Say that you'll study the recording device, and consider its contents." To his satisfaction, Pilwondepat saw that the biped was doing that already. "And you must not discuss this meeting with Riimadu, or let on in any way that we have talked about such things."

"I won't. I promise. Just for the sake of discussion, though—why not? You don't think he'd do anything, do you? He's an exoarcheologist, just like you and me. He's completely absorbed in the excavation we're undertaking here atop this escarpment."

"Riimadu is AAnn. He is absorbed in promoting himself foremost, yes, but he is also part of the web that his kind are attempting to weave around this world. Step lightly in his presence, and have a care you are not unwittingly caught in that snare." One more time, Pilwondepat indicated the sphere. "There are already enough unpleasant statistics recorded on that device. I would hate to see you, my friend, become another."

"Now you're being overly dramatic."

"Am I, *chirritt*? Peruse the molly. Then decide."

Cullen looked unhappy. "I'm not saying you're wrong, Pilwondepat. Not without having a look at that molly. But a conspiracy on that scale is hard to envision."

"The AAnn would not say conspiracy. They would say 'diplomacy.' Their definitions are somewhat rougher than yours or ours."

The exoarcheologist rose from behind his desk and began pacing parallel to the back wall of the room. "For the sake of discussion, let's say there's something to your assertions. What am I supposed to do with Riimadu? I can't just kick him off the dig. His government expects him to be here, recording and observing. He has authorization."

Pilwondepat gestured with both truhands. "You are in charge of the project. Exercise that authority. Find an excuse. Say that it's for his own benefit. Or propose that he enjoy the break from work that his hard labor has earned him. There are ways."

"I know; I know." Cullen's discomfort level was rising with every moment. "But it's going to be difficult. If not for his suggestions, we wouldn't even be digging here." He halted suddenly to stare down at the thranx. "How about that, Pilwondepat? If there's some widespread intrigue on the part of the AAnn, why would one of them point out what could prove to be an important archeological site? Why not direct us elsewhere and keep the site discovery quiet until they can excavate on their own?"

Air whistled softly through Pilwondepat's spicules. It was important to be patient with this human, he reminded himself. Sometimes they failed to make out certain aspects of the world around them until it landed on their heads. And they had experienced only a comparatively few years of contact with the AAnn, as opposed to the hundreds the thranx had been compelled to endure. They could not be expected to understand right away.

But somehow, he had to make at least one of them in a position of some importance learn to *see*. For a number of reasons, not least that he knew and worked with him, he had chosen the one called Cullen Karasi.

"Why not let you provide the muscle power and equipment and do the work for them? If their ultimate aim is to ease you off the planet, what you do here will not matter. It's not as if you are attempting to ascertain the existence of an enormous body of valuable ore. It's only pure science. From my studies, I believe that pure science does not command many votes on your world council."

"You're quite the cynic, Pilwondepat."

Antennae bobbed. "All thranx are realists, Cullen. When you come from a society where in primitive times every individual knew their entire life's work from birth, you have no choices."

The human nodded slowly, another gesture Pilwondepat recognized. Humans preferred broad, easy-to-read gestures that rarely displayed the subtlety of the AAnn. There was not much there to admire, but it made for ready understanding.

Ceasing his pacing, Cullen resumed his seat behind the field desk. "All right. Let's have a look at this accumulated 'evidence' of yours." Picking up the molly, he dropped it into the appropriate receptacle on top of his desk reader. Images appeared in the air in front of him.

Though he wanted to comment on every picture, every article, Pilwondepat forced himself to hold his peace. Interrupting the already skeptical Cullen would break the human's concentration and prevent him from absorbing the full impact of the thranx's research. It was important that the man not blindly accept Pilwondepat's accusations, but that he draw his own conclusions directly from the available evidence. So Pilwondepat sat in silence, not moving except for the familiar involuntary weaving of his antennae, and tried not to stare.

Half an hour later, Cullen switched off the viewer and sat back in his chair. "It's disturbing. I'll give you that. Some of it is unsettling, even. But it's not conclusive."

"Will you at least agree that it is worthy of further examination?"

Cullen might be skeptical, but he was not stupid. A trained scientist, he could not ignore evidence when it was laid out before him. "Yes, I'm afraid that it is. I just don't think I'm the one to pursue it." He indicated the viewer. "This sort of thing needs to be distributed to the supervising colonial authority, not somebody involved in research, like myself. Why did you show it to me instead of taking it directly to them?" he finished curiously.

"Because it will have more force coming from you," Pilwondepat explained. "Too many of your people shy away from contact with my kind. Others are instinctively suspicious, and there are also those who are openly hostile. Had I been the one to lay this evidence directly before the most relevant human authority, I might well have been dismissed without a hearing. Or I might have been received politely, only to have the data tossed into the nearest disposal as soon as I departed. But if you, a recognized figure of some stature within your chosen specialty, make a presentation on its behalf, you will be listened to; and the documentation, if not instantly acknowledged, will at least be discussed." He dropped to all sixes again. "You will make such a presentation, Cullen? I did not invent the collusions you just viewed. They are as real as the rock we are standing upon. As are the intentions of the AAnn."

The human scratched at the back of his head. "You're putting me in a very awkward position, Pilwondepat. Especially as regards Riimadu's continued presence on the site. There are a lot more AAnn on Comagrave than there are thranx."

"A consequence of an unfortunate climate, but I sympathize with your circumstances. Consider that being dead would put you in a much more difficult position."

"Regardless of what his Imperial brethren may be up to, I'm not sure I can accept your portrait of Riimadu. He's been nothing but helpful ever since he was attached to the project. We talk science all the time, and I really do see him as a kindred spirit, albeit one covered with scales. It's very hard for me to envision him participating in some kind of hostile activity, much less one that might prove antiscientific."

Pilwondepat executed a complicated gesture that Cullen did not understand, which was probably just as well. "Whatever you think, whatever occurs in his presence, all I ask is that you never forget that he is AAnn. *Yi!mt,* he is a scientist. *Yi!mt,* he has been helpful. But if the appropriate situation presents itself, I can assure you from the bottom of my individual and racial hearts that he will put a weapon to the side of your skull and without a second thought, blow your brains out through your opposite ear."

He'd gone a little too far, Pilwondepat saw. In his anxiety to persuade his friend of the danger he had uncovered, he had stepped beyond the bounds of courtesy and diplomacy that Cullen was willing to accept. It was as visible in the human's rubbery face as if it had been written there with an antique stylus.

"Do this, then," he added quickly. "Leave Riimadu alone. Let him do his work. I'll watch him myself. I do it anyway, out of a historical sense of self-preservation. But convey my findings to the appropriate planetary authority. Relate what I have concluded, give your own opinion, and let them view the facts that are known. If you will do that much, I will be able to sleep a little easier knowing that something is being done."

Cullen willingly agreed. "I'll send off a copy of the information together with my personal comments right away. Tonight, if you think it that important."

"No, no!" Four hands waved frantically at the taller human. "Nothing can be sent via the planetary communications net. I would bet my antennae that the AAnn have been intercepting and monitoring all such transmissions ever since their presence on the planet was allowed. I would not feel secure forwarding the data under anything less than military-level encryption."

Cullen shrugged apologetically. "This is only a scientific outpost. I don't have access to anything that hard."

"I understand. Therefore, in order to ensure not only the security of the findings but of your own self, you will have to deliver the information in person."

Cullen hesitated. For an awful moment Pilwondepat felt as if the human was going to dismiss the entire matter. Then the senior scientist nodded once, slowly. "All right, we'll do it your way. The next regular supply flight will be in nine days. I have a few things I'd like to do in town, and I'm overdue for a scheduled break. In addition to making the necessary rounds, and enjoying a little rest and relaxation, I'll make an appointment with the highest-level enforcement official who has time to spare, and I'll present your report. I'll also relay your conclusions. Myself, I'm not quite ready to draw any. No final ones, at least."

Pilwondepat would have heaved a sigh of relief, except that thranx do not heave. He did, however, exhale softly. "That will be most satisfactory, Cullen. Meanwhile, I will keep track of the activities, both formal and otherwise, of our mutual acquaintance Riimadu. The critical thing is not that action is taken immediately, but that your authorities are made aware of what the AAnn are doing. Alerted, they will be able to draw their own conclusions. Especially when further incidents of the type I have compiled continue to recur. Your people will then be able to view them with a different eye. I am satisfied."

Cullen was relieved. "Then we can get back to the business of science?"

The thranx gestured straightforward agreement. "It will be a comfort to me, though I will not be able to entirely relax until the last AAnn is expelled from this world. Politely and diplomatically, or otherwise."

Cullen tried to explain without dismissing. "You have to understand, Pilwondepat, that in the absence of direct evidence of wrongdoing, human authorities have a tendency to move with caution. Nothing's likely to happen right away."

"It will come." Pilwondepat was confident now. "The more unfortunate coincidences involving the AAnn that occur, the more likely your people will be to see that they are not coincidences at all. There will be an acceleration of awareness."

"Nine days." Cullen came around from behind the desk to place a reassuring hand on the thranx's b-thorax. "Think you can stand working in Riimadu's company that long?"

"As long as should prove necessary." The thranx swiveled his head almost 180 degrees. "It's easier for me to watch my back than it is for you to guard yours."

At that point Therese Holoness burst into the chamber, nearly beating the doorway's announcing buzz. Her face was flushed and her eyes wide open and alert. She glanced uncertainly at the thranx before settling her gaze on Cullen.

"Come quick, Mr. Karasi!"

Cullen's eyes flicked in Pilwondepat's direction before returning to the young woman. "What is it, Therese? What's wrong?"

She blinked in confusion. "Wrong? Nothing's wrong, sir. Please, come with me. You're not going to believe what we've found."

10

The humidity at Chitteranx Port hit Baron Preed NNXV like a grit-heavy sandstorm. Gasping, he hastened to activate the dehumidifier strapped to his snout. Immediately, air from which virtually every trace of moisture had been removed flowed down his nasal passages and into his lungs. Relieved, he stepped out into the otherwise amenable climate that filled the terminal. What he really needed, he reflected, was the visual equivalent of a dehumidifier for his eyes. Or more properly, a debugger.

The place was full of thranx. The insectoids were everywhere: operating greeting stations, food and drink facilities, rushing to and fro in hideous numbers. That was not surprising, since Chitteranx was a major port of arrival and embarkation on this continent, and Hivehom was their homeworld. That did not make the place any easier to tolerate. Like all his kind, Preed loathed the multilimbed, hard-shelled creatures. What he wanted to do was wade into the seething mass and start pulling off arms and legs and heads. Aside from the fact that he was more than slightly outnumbered and such action would result in his own expeditious demise, it would reflect badly on his mission.

Diplomats, he reminded himself, were to be discouraged from dismembering their hosts.

It was not the thranx he had come to see, however. Had that been the case, he would have landed at Daret and checked in with the official Imperial Embassy there. His mission was rather more circumspect. The thranx had been reluctant to allow it. But since no state of active hostilities existed between the Great Hive and the Empire, they were unable to find a good reason to refuse the official request. It was to be an informal visit, the AAnn officials in charge of making the arrangements had insisted. Nothing conclusive was on order. As a major power friendly to both sides, the AAnn simply wished to see how the humans who had located on Hivehom were doing. The thranx didn't like it, but could not find a legitimate way to refuse without giving unnecessary offense.

Preed had been chosen because of his mastery of the humans' language and a tolerance for difficult conditions. He was flattered by the endorsement and could not in any event have gracefully refused. So here he was, surrounded by bugs, on his way to see spongy, soft-skinned mammals. The familiar comforts of Blassussar seemed a very long way off indeed.

The heavy protective clothing he would need to tolerate the visit to the human outpost was packed securely in the satchel he carried slung over his right shoulder. Striding forward, the dehumidifier across his snout distorting his otherwise courtly profile, he searched in vain for the tube that would take him to the shuttle that would convey him to the Mediterranea Plateau, where the humans had their settlement. His flight connection was deliberately scheduled tight, so that he would not have to spend any more time in lowland Chitteranx than was absolutely necessary. A check of his chronometer showed that he had no time to linger. Growling deep in his throat, he realized that he was going to have to ask directions.

Steeling himself, he used the general terminal guide to locate an information kiosk. At least he would be spared direct contact with one of the bugs. The kiosk was designed to be utilized by offworlders. As such, its instrumentation was intuitive, and though it could not communicate in the Imperial Tongue, he soon had his directions. Striding off in the indicated direction, he had to struggle not to kick crowding thranx aside. Bipedal and as tall as the average human, he towered over the milling natives. With their compound eyes, you could not even tell if they were looking in your direction, but he knew that they were staring. The presence of an AAnn on Hivehom, outside the diplomatic mission located in the capital, was highly unusual. He fancied he could smell hatred and fear emanating from them. A good feeling, it made him smile inside.

The aircraft that would carry him to the high plateau was specially retrofitted to accommodate humans as well as thranx but was virtually empty. The few insectoids aboard crowded as far forward as they could, maintaining as much space as was practical between themselves and the unusual passenger. This suited Preed well. As for his own perch, the AAnn found that while his legs bent in places different from those of humans, he could still fit his backside into one of the flight chairs that had been designed for them. The only difficulty lay with his tail. While flexible, it still had to go somewhere. As there was no proper slot in the rear of the seat, he was reduced to thrusting it off to one side and over the rim of the chair for the duration of the flight. The resulting contortion was uncomfortable, but not impossible. At least, he reflected, he was not reduced to being strapped down like a piece of cargo.

The flight on the superswift craft carried him high above the clouds that swathed the jungles, rain forest, plantations, and conurbations below. Once they passed over the edge of the Hysingrausen Wall, the weather cleared above the plateau. It would be refreshingly drier in the human settlement, he knew, but also much colder. He would be compelled to swap the uncomfortable dehumidifier on his snout for a bulky set of cold-wear gear. Such were the travails a multispecies ambassador was expected to endure.

There were compensations. Preed's ability to deal with an assortment of sentients, plus his unusual linguistic gifts, had elevated him to rarified status. Actually, his rank should have guaranteed him a home posting in a comfortable villa, with perhaps a view of the Sandronds on Blassussar's southernmost continent. But his skills made him too valuable to keep at home. So he had become a rover in the service of the Empire. The lifestyle suited his temperament if not his liver.

From the air Azerick was unimpressive. He had not expected much. The human outpost was still of comparatively recent vintage, both physically and politically. It could not be allowed to grow rapidly for fear of unsettling the locals. This was too bad. There was nothing Preed, or any other AAnn, enjoyed more than seeing the multilimbed thranx unsettled.

Hence his visit.

His principal purpose was not to unnerve the thranx. That was only a side benefit. He was here to talk with the resident humans, to ascertain a number of possibilities, to formulate appraisals, and with luck to make more than mischief. His hopes were high. Despite all the lies the thranx had told humans about the AAnn, despite their unprecedented and unrepeated cooperation during the course of the Pitarian War, relations between the two powerful entities were still in a state of uneasy flux. Relations could evolve, or devolve, on the basis of very small developments. It was these that Preed was on Hivehom to influence. His energetic, mischief-making colleagues, he knew, were busy elsewhere.

The dryness of the air that assailed his nostrils when he emerged from the aircraft into the local terminal was a huge relief after trying to breathe the damp mud that passed for atmosphere in Chitteranx. He immediately removed the clumsy dehumidifier and stored it in his baggage. Finding a personal hygiene chamber, he attended to necessary ablutions while donning the lightweight but still unwieldy special garb that would keep the air next to his scales fifteen degrees warmer than the ambient temperature outside. Only his head, tail, and hands remained exposed to the chill air. When he emerged from the chamber, he felt refreshed and ready to begin work.

A voice in halting Imperial hailed him as soon as he stepped outside. "Envoy Preed! Over here, sir."

Espying the only human who was both staring and gesticulating in his direction, Preed approached the individual and replied in near-perfect Terranglo. The language was easier on his larynx than either High or Low Thranx. Something else, he mused, his people and these mammals had in common. Extending a hand, he noted the human's obvious surprise as the clawed fingers enveloped the mammal's soft skin and shook gently.

"You ssee?" the envoy informed his greeter. "No brushing of antennae. Your kind have one digit too many, and your clawss are exceedingly inadequate, but otherwisse there iss virtually no difference."

Pleased by the flattering comparison, the human stepped back. "I'll be your principal contact during your visit to Azerick, Envoy Preed. Members of our guest support staff will look after your daily needs. Whenever you are ready for formal talks, just let me know. I can say that I personally have been looking forward to them for some time."

"A chance to sspeak with ssomething bessidess a bug?" Preed ventured.

Gratifyingly, the human essayed a half smile. "I didn't say that."

An excellent beginning, Preed decided. This human, an important member of the local diplomatic staff, was already predisposed toward the AAnn and against his hosts. With more such benign developments, much might be accomplished in the coming days.

"May I carry your baggage, Envoy?" The human extended a helpful hand. To Preed, it looked as if the straps on his case would cut right through the soft, unprotected flesh. "By the way, my name is Jorge Sertoa."

"Yess. I wass informed it would be you who would be meeting me. No thank you, truly, Jorge. I prefer to carry my own gear. The exercisse iss a good thing for me."

Outside the little terminal, the all-pervasive green of the plateau forest made him wince slightly. He longed for familiar earth tones: for yellows and reds, burnished orange and fiery vermilion. Such hues were not to be found anywhere on Hivehom, and certainly not here in the place of the humans' choosing. Gasping as the chill air entered his lungs, he bundled his weather suit tighter around his neck, clasped his hands together, and paced the escorting human to the impressive little high-speed transport. Within moments, they were racing northward through the towering woods.

"This transport cabin is equipped with an individual climate control."

The human was at pains to be accommodating. "Would you like me to turn up the heat?"

Diplomacy be strangled, Preed decided. "I would like that very much, truly. My thankingss, Jorge."

Within minutes the temperature inside the cabin had risen to nearly thirty-three degrees. Though the human was starting to look uncomfortable, he did not ask to reduce the temperature, and Preed gladly took advantage of the other's obliging nature.

They bantered inconsequentialities all the way to the outpost. There, Preed was assigned quarters that had been hastily adapted for his arrival. There were chairs with slots in the back for his tail. The high bed had been replaced with a basin filled with sand, complete with a crude, hastily adapted, but functionally adequate warmer. As with the cabin aboard the high-speed transport, the room's temperature could be individually regulated to suit its occupant. Preed immediately pushed it to maximum without bothering to try to translate the digits on the readout and without worrying about the possible consequences to the room's contents.

He spent the rest of the day relaxing as best he could amid the alien surroundings and renewing his acquaintance with his recordings of human facial expressions, which AAnn xenopsychs had discovered early on in the course of formal exchanges were a vital key in understanding the mammals. Oftentimes they would say one thing while their countenances would convey something entirely different. The fact that the thranx were not yet very good at this business of interpreting facial muscle positioning only inspired Preed's people to try to master it. No one could claim that ability yet, but among those assigned to diplomatic posts especially, great progress had been made.

For example, his host, the human male Sertoa, had been politely neutral in his greeting and conversation. But the subcutaneous flexing of his facial muscles had suggested a warmer predisposition toward his AAnn guest. As time passed, if his interpretation was further confirmed, Preed could play on that. Much good could be done here. He reminded himself of that repeatedly, by way of compensating himself for having to endure the frigid conditions atop the plateau. At least the local humidity, while higher than any AAnn would choose, was tolerable, as opposed to the simmering soup of an atmosphere that prevailed in the bug-infested lowlands below.

"We have sso much more in common," he hissed to his host the following day, as Sertoa toured the visiting diplomat through the facility. "Physsically, we are infinitely more alike than either of our resspective sspeciess are to the bugss." By way of demonstration, he reached out and put a four-fingered hand, polished claws and all, on the human's shoulder.

The flesh was soft beneath the thin garment, but Preed had expected and prepared for that.

"You ssee? We are on average nearly the ssame height, though your kind runss to more extremess than mine. We are both bipedal, though you lack the counterbalance of a tail. Internally, we are both bissymmetrical. Your earss are rather prominently external, but our eyess are identically possitioned, though your pupilss are round and ourss vertical. Your facess are pusshed in—excusse my terminology, are flat—but when you look me in the eye and I look back, I see a being that iss not sso very different from mysself." He gestured southward, toward the teeming lowlands. "When I look at a thranx, I ssee ssomething that iss truly alien."

"The thranx are as intelligent as you or I, and as deserving of respect," the human responded.

"Truly." Had he overstepped his bounds? Preed wondered furiously. After all, the humans were on this planet by the grace of their insectoid hosts. Had he misread this mammal so badly? "I wass ssimply pointing out ssome interessting and unavoidable ssimilarities. I did not mean any dissresspect to thosse who, after all, are hosstss here to uss both." Disrespect, he mused silently, could come later.

"I understand." The human directed his guest down a footpath paved with round stepping-stones. Preed's sandals clicked softly on the artificial rock, his feet swathed in protective cold-resistant gear. Meanwhile, the human strolled about virtually naked in the chill air of afternoon.

"We musst all get along in thiss tiny corner of a vasst galaxy. You know that the emperor hass petitioned your government for the ssame ssettlement and ssharing rightss that are pressently enjoyed by thesse thranx?"

Sertoa's face revealed his surprise. "No, I didn't know that. In what way?"

The AAnn diplomat explained. "As the thranx have esstablished ssmall hivess in your Amazon and Congo Bassinss, and are consssidering another in your Ssepik River region, my government hass requesssted that we be allowed to conssstruct a tesst community in either the center of your Ssahara Desert or an alternate region called the Ssonoran."

"That's exciting news." Sertoa led the way into one of the complex's sealed structures. The air inside was slightly warmer than without, for which Preed was inordinately grateful. "I hope it comes to pass."

"You do?" Preed kept his tone subdued.

"Why, of course. I've always admired the accomplishments of the AAnn. At least, what we know of them. No one looks forward to closer relations between our two peoples more than I."

Breakthrough. Though his scale-covered snout and face were far less flexible than those of any human, they were still capable of movement. Lest the humans be studying the expressions of the AAnn as intensely as his kind were scrutinizing theirs, Preed struggled to hide the quiet exultation he felt at the human's response. This diplomat was not only friendly toward his kind: If his words could be believed, he was positively enthusiastic.

There were a number of ways of checking.

"If you are interessted, I might perhapss be able to arrange a reciprocal vissit to the Imperial capital at Blassussar, or at leasst to one of the principal Imperial worldss."

Sertoa's expression brightened. "That would be wonderful! I'd enjoy that very much."

Confirmation of a quickly formed opinion, however casual, was always welcome. Here, on the thranx homeworld, was a sympathetic if not openly biased human diplomat. This was in itself enough to justify the discomfort of his trip, and he had only just arrived.

"I have a surprise for you." A grin, an expression that Preed recalled indicated a combination of personal satisfaction and amusement, dominated the human's face. "I think you'll like it."

They entered a substantial edifice where Preed was startled to encounter humans in various states of undress. If anything their naked bodies were, while of scientific interest, more disconcerting than their clothed forms. Leading the way deeper into the complex, Sertoa guided his guest to a windowless chamber. The pair of humans there hurried their dressing when they discerned the nature of the alien visitor.

"If you would kindly disrobe, sir. I know that your people do not suffer from any nudity phobias." As he ventured the suggestion, Sertoa had already begun the process of removing his own clothing.

"That iss true, but I am not ssure thiss iss in accordance with proper diplomatic procedure, my friend." The AAnn eyed the human uncertainly.

"Trust me, Baron Preed." By this time the human diplomat was nearly naked.

We must all make sacrifices for the Empire, Preed told himself. He began to remove his decorative official garments.

When both were unclad, Sertoa led his guest to a smaller chamber. Preed did his best to avoid gawking at the jiggling, pulpy body of his host. Sertoa opened a door and stepped inside. Preed followed, only to find himself in—if not the fabled nirvanic sands of Ss'ra'oun, at least a place where he could feel comfortable. The small chamber was suffused, bathed, washed in perfectly dry heat. It was almost, but not quite, a slice of home.

"Tanning room." Sertoa sat down on a convenient bench. "To make sure we get our proper bimonthly dose of the right kind of sunlight. I thought you'd be more comfortable conversing here than anywhere else in the settlement."

Embracing the arid, humidityless heat, Preed almost unbent. "I am more grateful than I can ssay. Ssuch courtessy doess you proud, Jorge Ssertoa."

The human shrugged off the compliment. "Just doing my job." At his touch, a concealed wall alcove disgorged a thin-walled metal container containing a mix of both liquid and frozen water. Preed eyed it askance, hoping he would not be asked to partake of the frigid concoction. When he found out he could request uniced, room-temperature water, he relaxed once more.

"Now then." Sertoa smiled at his reptilian guest. "If you're reasonably at ease, what would you like to talk about? What exactly is the purpose of your visit here? Why aren't you at the AAnn diplomatic mission in Daret?"

By shifting his tail to one side, Preed found he could repose quite comfortably on the bench fashioned of native wooden slats. "There are a number of issuess involving the relationsship between your people and the thranx that intimately affect my kind. Given the natural biological ssimilaritiess between AAnn and human, my ssuperiorss felt that thiss outposst of yourss might be an appropriate place to broach them. Truly. Of coursse, we are alsso curiouss to ssee how you have progressed and what you have accomplisshed here. Though but recently arrived, I am already much impressed."

"I'm listening. Go on." Sertoa took a long swig of his water and Preed cringed internally as he heard cubes of frozen water actually clink against the human's teeth.

"My government feelss sstrongly that you are devoting far too many ressourcess to developing relationss with these bugss, when ssimilarr overturess between alike ssentientss ssuch as humankind and AAnn could be of infinitely greater benefit to both."

Sertoa nodded, an easy gesture to recognize and interpret. "First let me say that I couldn't agree with you more. I think trying to develop anything beyond standard diplomatic relations between humans and thranx, given the obvious profound differences between our respective species, is a waste of time and money. And I think the neglect of relations between your people and mine has been shameful. The thranx, of course, feel otherwise."

"That iss undersstandable." Preed started to gesture, then remembered to dip his head in the simple human nod. "As you may know, from the time of firsst contact, relationss between my people and the thranx have been . . . awkward. No amount of perssuassion and imploring on the part of my government hass ssucceeded in altering their beliefss." Luxuriating in the dry heat that saturated the chamber, he leaned forward. Not too far, aware that proximity to sharp, curved AAnn teeth had been known to unsettle an unwary human.

"Thiss need not affect in any way developing relationss between our resspective sspeciess. It iss good to have come all thiss way and know that we have at leasst one friend and ssympathizer among thosse of your kind empowered to make the decissions affecting thosse relationss."

Leaning back against the wall, his eyes half closed against the overhead tanning lights, Sertoa replied quietly. "There are others. Some feel even more strongly about this matter than I."

Preed considered. It was silent in the chamber for several moments before he made the decision to take a step that as recently as yesterday he had not believed would be possible. "How sstrongly, my friend?"

The human turned toward him. "More strongly than I am at liberty to say."

"That iss mosst encouraging. Truly. Perhapss before I depart I might be able to meet ssome of thesse like thinkerss?"

"Perhaps," Sertoa replied noncommittally. While willing to be obliging, Preed noted, the human remained cautious. "Meanwhile, I consider this a promising vein for further discussion, which I hope we may enlarge upon during the rest of your visit." He waved a hand, and Preed marveled at the sheer slackness of the gesture. "When we happen to find ourselves in appropriate surroundings, of course."

"Truly," Preed agreed. "Allow me, if you will, to detail ssome of the sspecific ssuggestionss I am authorized to make, and to elaborate upon how they might be implemented to our mutual advantage."

"I would enjoy hearing them." Smiling encouragingly, Sertoa turned fully toward his reptilian guest, admiring the play of the tanning lights on the AAnn's gleaming, iridescent scales.

When in the course of the next morning's casual conversation an acquaintance happened to mention that Jorge Sertoa had spent the entire previous morning and well on into the afternoon in the company of a visiting, high-ranking AAnn envoy, Fanielle Anjou began a frantic search of the compound for the pair. She was more than a little exhausted and out of breath when she was eventually directed to the diplomatic compound's gymnasium and health complex. At first thought, it seemed an unlikely venue in which to pursue diplomacy between differing species. It did have the virtue of comparative privacy, however. That in itself conjured unwelcome possibilities she tried but was unable to put out of her mind.

She thought about mentioning it to Toroni, but without anything more to go on than suspicions of suspicions, she could hardly go barging into his office with eyebrows raised and arms flailing. She would have to bring something more to such a confrontational meeting than a personal dislike of the reptilian bipeds.

It was midafternoon when she found herself peeling off her clothes as she strode determinedly through the changing room. A few users she knew spoke to her. She returned their hellos and greetings as amiably as she could, even though her mind was elsewhere.

It was almost worth forcing the encounter just to see the look on Sertoa's face when, as naked as anyone else in that end of the complex, she pushed her way into the otherwise deserted tanning room to confront him and the AAnn envoy. Ignoring her open-mouthed colleague, she directed her attention to the alien, whose shimmering, leathery scales served to frame an otherwise interesting if unremarkable anatomy.

"Fanielle . . ." More than a little nonplussed, the unabashedly uncomfortable Sertoa struggled to keep his eyes on her face. Though she paid little attention to him, his efforts to appear resolutely uninterested amused her. She was far more interested in the AAnn. Seated on one of the long wooden benches, his tail switching from floor to wall, the envoy regarded her with curiosity. That his slitted eyes roved freely over her nude form unsettled her not a bit. Being utterly nonhuman, there was nothing in his gaze to affect her.

Bypassing Sertoa, she approached the alien and extended a hand. Not as her colleague had done, but with fingers upraised, crooked at both joints and parted, nails pointing forward. The AAnn did not rise, but gracefully met her gesture with his left hand. Their fingers interlocked, her soft ones separating his tough, leathery digits. She felt the strength of the highly evolved carnivore held in reserve. Then he released his grip. The not-unpleasant sensation reminded her of letting go of the strap of a particularly well made leather handbag. As he leaned back against the molded wall, she introduced herself. Nearby, Sertoa was stammering something as he tried to regain control of the situation. AAnn and female ignored him. For a brief moment, he was unsure which of the two was the more alien.

"I am Fanielle Anjou, second assistant undersecretary for thranx affairs on Hivehom."

Slitted, reptilian eyes met her own. Neither pair fell; neither pair wavered. "I am Baron Preed NNXV, sspecial envoy at large for his Imperial Majessty Hezenezzk V. I greet you as an equal, and wissh you all the natural warmth that doess not exisst in thiss place." One clawed hand gestured second-degree irony. "Except in thiss peculiar but mosst welcome inner chamber. While my quarterss are ssatissfactory, if the facilitiess would allow it, I would gladly sspend the remainder of my sstay right here." Before Anjou could respond, he added, "Does not thiss sstrong light burn your pale, unprotected sskin?"

"If one spends much time in here, yes, it does," she admitted.

Double eyelids blinked. "But you come in here to do thiss voluntarily."

"I already told you; it's necessary for our health," an increasingly impatient Sertoa reminded his guest.

"Most remarkable." The AAnn's gaze traveled unapologetically up and down Anjou's nude form. Not only did it not trouble her, she found it instructive to reciprocate the action. "I was enjoying a usseful chat with your good friend and colleague here concerning the lamentable sstate of human-AAnn relationss, and how it would be agreeable if more attention could be devoted to improving the nasscent relationsship that pressently exisstss between our two peopless. But it sseemss that certain of your associatess feel ssuch time iss better sspent attempting to win over the affection of thesse reeking, sswarming bugss."

"The government of Earth and its colonies manages the development of all interspecies relationships with equal care and attention. I'm sorry if the AAnn feel neglected." Off to one side, Sertoa was looking unhappy.

Preed's jaws parted, showing very sharp theropod-like teeth. "It iss not that we feel neglected. Intersstellar, intersspeciess conssanguinity cannot be fasshioned overnight. It iss merely that ssome of uss feel your people are devoting overmuch in the way of diplomatic energiess to attempting to create ssome kind of association with thesse hard-sshelled creaturess that goess beyond the ussual diplomatic formalitiess. As you musst know, the Empire hass had ssome ssmall differencess with the bugss in the passt. Therefore, it iss only natural that we would pay sspecial attention to anything that would ssuggesst the bugss are attempting to misslead another, powerful sspeciess ssuch as yoursselves as to the true nature of our hisstorical relations."

"I can assure you that is not the case." Perspiration was beginning to pour in tiny rivulets down her body: her cheeks, her shoulders and breasts, down her belly and thighs and back. She ignored the damp stickiness. "My government respects all sentients, and treats equally with all. As to any quarrels you and the thranx may have had in the past, that is none of our business and does not affect our relations with them or with you."

Preed's hands wove patterns in the superheated air, indicating contentment and—something else she could not interpret. "It iss alwayss reassuring to hear ssuch words, particularly from ssomeone sso clearly verssed in the realitiess of intersstellar diplomacy as yoursself, Ms.

Anjou. While I have time left here, I would look forward to converssing with you at greater length on ssuch interessting matterss."

"So would I." She blinked sweat from one eye. "Unfortunately, I have to travel to Daret tomorrow."

Sertoa frowned. "I don't recall your being scheduled for a visit to the capital this week."

"You can't know everything, Jorge. You know how these things come up. I'm not happy about it myself." She returned her attention to the AAnn diplomat. "I regret that I will not be able to talk with you further, noble Preed."

He gestured his disappointment. "We musst each of uss follow our directivess. My own sschedule iss ssimilarly inflexible. I wissh you a ssafe journey. I undersstand there wass a ssorrowfully fatal accident recently in your local transsport ssystem that affected you perssonally."

She stiffened slightly. "Yes, it did."

He tilted his head to one side as he gestured balletically with his left hand. "I would disslike hearing that a ssimilar fate had befallen one sso charming and knowledgeable as yoursself."

"I'll be careful," she assured him evenly. "As for you, have a care with your room's climate control. It can sometimes get quite chilly up here at night. And chilly for us could mean forced enervation for you." Somewhat against her better judgment, she allowed herself a small smile. "I would dislike hearing that your stiffened form had to be shipped back to Blassussar in a crate because you forgot to check your room's temperature settings."

Again the AAnn's head and hands danced in concert. This time she could not tell what, if anything, he was gesturing. "I will remember your cautioning with thankss."

Turning, she exited purposefully from the tanning chamber. Sertoa watched her for longer than he intended before resuming his interrupted dialogue with the AAnn.

"I fear that where human-thranx versus human-AAnn relations are concerned, my colleague is of a different mind than you or I. She has developed not only a working relationship with the bugs, but something suspiciously like affection. I'm afraid she's allowed her admiration for the local culture to cloud her professional judgment." He resumed his seat on the wooden bench. "She and I often find ourselves on opposite sides of discussions. It's all very polite and professional, of course, but each of us knows where the other stands."

Swinging his long tail around, Preed used the tip to scratch under his left leg. "It iss of no import. My government undersstands that opinion among your kind iss sstrongly divided over how to proceed with human-thranx relationss. It iss my tassk, and that of my compeerss operating on other worldss, to enssure that human-AAnn relationss are not overlooked in thiss headlong russh that iss being advocated by ssome of your people to erect an unnecessarily intimate association with the bugss. In the coursse of normal negotiationss it would be unreassonable to expect that everyone in your diplomatic sservice would believe as ssenssibly as yoursself. But that iss all right; that iss acceptable. We musst ssimply work harder to convince Ms. Anjou of the right way of thinking."

Sertoa let out a derisive laugh. "You've only just met Fanielle. You might as well try to move the local star to another system as change her mind."

Preed gestured, expanding to soak up the wonderful parching heat of the chamber. "My people were engaged in the bussiness of intersstellar diplomacy long before your kind took itss firsst tentative sstepss into deep sspace. We have made it, if not a sscience, at leasst a very well honed tool. With great experience and patience, many thingss originally thought impossible have come to pass. Perhapss thesse achievementss might even extend to recruiting your redoubtable Ms. Anjou to our way of thinking." Lowering his spread arms and upraised tail, he settled himself as best he could on the bench opposite the human.

"Now let uss sspeak of comely thingss, of what pleasses you and what pleasses me, and for a while at leasst, talk no more of diplomacy and matterss portentouss."

But while Sertoa nattered on, a portion of the noble's thoughts were devoted to the female human who had so recently departed. She was bright, that one, and determined. An unhealthy combination. Despite what he had told Sertoa about the experience and expertise of the AAnn diplomatic service, and the skill of its operatives, she would be difficult to convince of the right way of seeing things. Procedures lined up in his mind like spikes in an advanced game of *jyss-ul-nacch*.

If she could not be convinced, she would have to be persuaded.

11

As the most populous of the thranx colonies and the first to be settled from Hivehom, the prideful inhabitants of Willow-Wane had worked to conceive and erect an exceptionally interesting pavilion for the fair on Dawn. Situated in the northern section of the grounds, on a slight rise, it offered much to interest both human and thranx visitors alike. Incidental to its design, its builders had created a place where members of both species could relax in one another's company in ways only the most dedicated adherents of closer ties could have envisioned years earlier.

The pavilion's purpose was entirely nonpolitical. Its exhibits were intended to entertain, amuse, and delight, not proselytize. That they had unintended effects on their audiences, both mammalian and insectoid, might have been predicted but was not considered. Certainly those families, groups, and individuals who found themselves wandering among the displays were not conscious of being bombarded with preconceived propaganda. Nevertheless, a number of innocuous messages managed to manifest themselves amid the more immediate.

We can enjoy one another's company, the several eating and drinking facilities declared wordlessly. *We can appreciate each other's art,* multiple slash sculptures and background music insisted. *We can band together to accomplish that which we cannot do by ourselves,* the build-and-climb exhibit demonstrated.

That there were differences could not be denied. For example, the pavilion contained no playground for children, because thranx larvae existed in a state of limbless attention. Their amusements were wholly nonphysical. As a result, there were dozens of visual and aural displays entirely controlled by voice. Larvae could speak, but were otherwise completely dependent on the resources of the modern nursery.

This realization and the accompanying demonstrations had an unintended effect: They generated immediate sympathy on the part of visiting human children for their temporal thranx counterparts. Those larvae who had been chosen to participate in the exhibition found themselves the recipients of sympathetic attention from sad-eyed young bipeds who were already fully capable of movement. Many of the subsequent discourses between the young of both species were recorded for later study and proved highly revealing in the understanding of future developments.

As for the incipient as well as the fully mature adults of both species, they were enthralled by the excellence of the elaborate displays. One of the more popular involved demonstrations of human martial arts and their thranx equivalents. Both species had evolved from warlike ancestors. Humans who were embarrassed by a past now seen to be irrational if inevitable were startled and often overcome by the history display that showed entire hives of ancestral thranx engaging in endless primitive warfare.

As for the martial artists, humans were larger and heavier, and faster over a short distance. But thranx had more endurance and eight limbs to utilize in fighting instead of four, although the delicate truhands were not of much use in hand-to-hand combat and were usually kept folded close to the body and out of the way. Still, clever and well-trained thranx could often hold their own against combative humans. Built closer to the ground, they were harder to get off their feet. A judo leg sweep was not of much use against an opponent who could stand on six legs, and the bodies of the chitinous insectoids offered few soft spots to attack.

Such demonstrations were carefully choreographed and all in good fun. At other exhibits, the individual inclinations of humans contrasted sharply with the thranx tendency to perform tasks through cooperation. Human gymnasts tended to flip and fly by themselves, while their thranx counterparts built astonishingly stable pyramids consisting of dozens of individuals interlocking their hands and feet. These latter edifices were judged not only by their size and by the number of thranx involved in each structure, but by the aesthetics of the completed design.

But it was at the food stations where inhibitions really dropped away, as thranx discovered numerous human foods they could consume and humans luxuriated in the literally hundreds of new juices and soups concocted by thranx food preparators. Great scientific discoveries interest people, as do entertaining new works of art or exceptional demonstrations of physical skill, or ways to improve an individual lifestyle. But nothing enthralls quite so homogeneously as a new flavor.

Briann and Twikanrozex wandered through the pavilion, drawing fewer and briefer stares than they had elsewhere. Everyone was too intent on the exhibits, or on trying new foods and drinks, or on laughing at the wandering thranx sniggle poets, to pay special attention to one roving human-thranx pair. As for the two padres, they did not comment on the obvious lack of attention being paid them. They were too used to each other's company.

But they did observe, with pleasure, the unconscious ease with which their respective species had begun to relax in one another's presence. Seduced by the exotic surroundings of the pavilion, by its engaging food and drink, marvelous exhibits, unusual demonstrations, and the multitude of singular diversions set before them, few visitors had any time left in which to remark unfavorably on the mere physical differences between them.

"Observe," Twikanrozex remarked, "how the essence of shapeism vanishes when everyone involved is having a good time."

Briann nodded. "It's hard to hate when one is laughing too hard. Barring a very few isolated incidents, everything I've seen so far at this fair bodes well for better relations between our species. Amid such good feelings, the Church should prosper."

Twikanrozex indicated second-degree concurrence. "*Criill,* we need to nurture these good feelings, and to be available to succor and assist those whose inner emotions are conflicted. There is still an enormous amount of work to be done."

They rounded a slowly rotating disc on which thranx body-poets were arranging themselves in ever-more-complex patterns. Ancient traditions that had once been employed in the service of constructing impressive underground chambers had been transformed into a wondrously intricate kind of performance art human acrobats could only hope to emulate, but never duplicate.

"Myself," Briann declared, "I'll know we've achieved our goals when I see a human outside the Church consent to be ministered to by a thranx."

With delicate movements of head and antennae as well as hands, Twikanrozex insinuated a fusion of understanding and general bemusement. "It is a puzzle to me how sentient beings can feel more relaxed in the presence of a hostile but similar shape than in the company of a sympathetic but differently constructed intelligence."

Using their rigid exoskeletons like pieces of sculpture, the body-poets had erected a complex geometric structure that reached almost to the polarized roof of the pavilion. A mixed audience of complimentary thranx and perspiring humans stridulated and cheered in unison. As always, the reaction of the human children was particularly heartening. To them—to those children whose minds had not yet been poisoned by prejudiced or chary parents, Briann reminded himself—the thranx were a beautiful mystery, aromatic and alien, like oversized toys that could talk back. As Twikanrozex had pointed out, there was much work to be done. The Church intended to be in the forefront of such work. There was no place in its self-deprecating structure or formal hierarchy for shapeism or any other kind of species bigotry—only for souls. And as far as anyone had yet been able to determine, scientifically or theologically, all souls had the same shape. Exactly what the "soul" consisted of was a question both humans and thranx had been dealing with for thousands of years. Despite enormous advances in the technology of quantification, it remained an abstract, something that still could not yet be measured or weighed. The taxonomy of metaphysics was still in its infancy. In that sense it was akin to the never-ending search for the ultimate building blocks of matter, which every fifty years or so seemed to shrink a little farther in the direction of infinite smallness.

Briann did not worry overmuch about such matters. Or nonmatters, depending on one's point of view. He had joined the Church to help people, no matter their shape. Thus far he had encountered nothing to make him second-guess his decision. His family remained puzzled, but supportive. Interestingly, Twikanrozex had encountered even more difficulty with his choice. Thranx society was not as fluid as that of the humans. Radical changes in lifestyle and direction were not as freely countenanced. Twikanrozex had been compelled to hoe a harder row than his human companion.

Still, even though both considered themselves more sophisticated in matters of interspecies relations and had prepared themselves for this occasion with much serious study and preparation, the fair had already shown itself capable of delivering an endless round of surprises. Presently, they were passing a lively display devoted to illustrating the history of agriculture on Willow-Wane. Virtual thranx drove virtual machines to the accompaniment of narration in both Low Thranx and Terranglo. Appropriate odors suffused the area immediately around the exhibition. Generating the story via tridee transducers allowed the thranx producers to incorporate huge mechanicals and hundreds of workers without overwhelming the individual display.

Passing by, a larger than usual human family paused briefly to gaze at the roof-high exhibit, whereupon the smallest child in the group raised a hand and pointed, yelling gleefully.

"Look, look—an ant farm!"

Briann felt his face flush slightly as he and Twikanrozex ambled on past the thoroughly enchanted family. His reaction was not in response to the child's comment, but because Twikanrozex, overhearing, requested an explanation of the term. When a slightly flustered Briann had finished elucidating, as diplomatically as he was able, the thranx gestured reassurance.

"There's no need to be embarrassed, my friend. Your native arthropods are not my ancestors. Actually, I find the concept rather endearing." Swiveling his head to look directly back over his shoulder at the gawking family, he gestured with both truhands. "Certainly it has proven useful, as the larvae in question show no fear of my kind. Perhaps a general distribution of the educational toys to which the youngest referred might be considered by the Church."

"There are other concerns," Briann endeavored to explain. "Although I have never owned such a bio-apparatus myself, I believe that the resourceful little arthropods in question have a tendency to escape their controlled environment, to the annoyance of any resident adults. I think the Church is better to stick with those visual aids that can provide instruction without the possibility of accompanying infestation."

Twikanrozex's antennae drew together, showing that he was deep in thought. Finally he responded. "Perhaps, *sellicc,* you are right. I don't think self-contained habitats holding miniature humans would be welcome in the private chambers of many hives, either." He glanced at his friend. "Assuming such a contrivance could be constructed."

"A people farm?" Briann pondered the notion. "I don't think so. Although if you offer humans enough monetary compensation, they'll do just about anything. In that respect, the thranx are more virtuous than my kind."

"Not at all," Twikanrozex demurred. "It is only that we are most of the time too busy to be corrupted. When time exists for contemplation of possibilities, we too can be persuaded to make fools of ourselves."

"Another vinculum between our peoples." Reassured by his friend's reiteration of the existence of mutual foolishness, Briann led the way out of the pavilion. All the walking, not to mention all the talking, was making him hungry.

He shared the state of his stomach with his companion, who allowed as how he, too, could stand some sustenance.

"What would you like?" Briann inquired. "We can go back inside, where the climate is more to your liking, or continue wandering until we come across something that appeals to both of us."

"Let us wander." Twikanrozex was enjoying himself hugely. "The air is a little dry today, but not entirely intolerable."

Briann hitched his sweat-dampened shirt higher on his shoulders and chose a pedestrian walkway at random. There was no need to consult a fair directory. The Church would guide them.

It did indeed, as they soon found themselves resting comfortably in an outdoor venue that was raised slightly above ground level, giving the patrons a pleasant view of the busy fairgrounds that stretched to the lake and the green-clad hills beyond. Not for the first time, Briann reflected on what an excellent choice Dawn had been for such an enterprise. The semitropical nature of the climate was bearable to the thranx while not unduly uncomfortable for humans. Locating the fair next to a large lake had the effect of injecting additional humidity into the local atmosphere, thus pleasing the insectoids even further.

At the moment, one of those aliens was finding exceptional pleasure in a mango-starfruit-guanabana crush, the terrestrial fruit juice drink being not only acceptable to his system, but avidly welcomed. The only difference between that and a similar beverage being enjoyed by Briann was that the thranx had ordered it made with tepid water instead of pulverized ice, a request that had left the perspiring human attendant shaking his head in silent disbelief. To the thranx, the notion of a "cold drink" was an oxymoron.

Twikanrozex admired the flexibility of his friend's prehensile lips as Briann sipped easily at his own libation. With four opposing mandibles, the thranx could make quicker work of solid food than any human, but liquids gave them problems. Fluids had to be poured directly into the open mouth, or inhaled via often elaborately swirled and decorated, narrow-spouted drinking utensils. Only by inserting the tip of such a siphon partway down the insectoid throat could a thranx generate enough esophageal vacuum to draw liquid from a container. In contrast, the malleability of human flesh allowed someone like Briann to form an airtight seal around the edge of an open container and pull fluids up and in. There were advantages to having a ductile epidermis.

Of course, Twikanrozex mused, such abilities were more than offset by the inherent aesthetic handicaps all humans suffered from. The thranx would not have exchanged his burnished, gleaming, blue-green exoskeleton for all the fluid-vacuuming abilities in the Arm. Slipping the drinking tip of his siphon-cup between his parted mandibles, he luxuriated in the slippery, sugary taste and feel of the exotic terrestrial refreshment as it coursed down his throat.

"Ah, there you are!"

Briann looked up from his chair to see two men advancing toward him. Both were older, one considerably so. Their eyes were intense, but not baleful. They were neatly dressed. Excessively so, given the ambient temperature and humidity within the pavilion.

"May we join you?" the younger of the two asked politely. "We've been searching for you two ever since we came across your display."

"We like to move around." Briann set his drink aside. "You know: meet folks, see the fair, try new experiences."

"Well, you two are certainly a new experience for us. We've read about you, and seen bits and pieces about your organization on the tridee. I am Father Joseph." He indicated the distinguished, white-haired senior who had settled into the chair alongside him. "This is Father Jenakis. I am Twelfth Baptist, and he is Orthodox Episcolic."

Briann explained to his watchful companion. "Traditional human churches."

Twikanrozex gestured welcome to the two men of the cloth. "I'm pleased to meet a pair of fellow theologians."

Joseph accepted the proffered chitinous hand tentatively. Making no move to emulate the gesture, Father Jenakis maintained a respectful distance to go with his thoughtful silence.

"We hadn't expected you to be so fluent in our language."

Twikanrozex dipped his antennae forward, keeping one truhand wrapped around his drinking utensil. "I am conversant in several languages, including one that involves only the use of gestures. If one has information to impart, one cannot expect the audience to go to the trouble of learning the imparter's tongue."

Briann smiled pleasantly. "Twikanrozex doesn't have a tongue, of course. The thranx modulate sounds deep within their throats, by means of mechanisms that would choke a human. That it comes out sounding so similar to us is as remarkable as it is advantageous. I am Padre Briann and this is Padre Twikanrozex."

Father Jenakis snorted curtly. His younger associate winced ever so slightly before resuming the conversation. "As you may know, a number of the established Terran religions are having some trouble with this United Church of yours."

"It's yours, too," Twikanrozex observed, managing to unsettle the earnest Father Joseph in as few words as possible.

"No, not mine, I'm afraid. Some of my colleagues and I are concerned. At first, no one paid much attention to your efforts."

"No one paid *any* attention to our efforts," Briann corrected him, still smiling.

Joseph had the grace to smile back. "But now your message, peculiar and unconventional as it is, appears to be having some small effect. In particular, you are making inroads among the young who dominate the upper intelligence percentiles. This is not only disturbing, it is unprecedented."

"Yes, we know." Briann sat back in his chair. Around them, crowd sounds rose and fell: laughter and squeals of delight and shouts of surprise. "Usually it's the other way around. It's those in the lower percentiles who tend to be persuaded first."

"Dangerous nonsense!" the older man huffed, deigning to speak for the first time.

"Not a bit of it." Briann had heard it all before, though not usually from official representatives of terrestrial churches. "We don't proselytize. We don't try to convert anyone. We just put our creed out where it can be examined by anyone who might be interested. We don't push it. It's a free society we live in, in these days of open communications and galactic colonization. Anyone is free to join any organization they wish, provided the tenets of that fraternity do not impinge on the rights of others." He spread his hands wide. "We don't even ask anyone who joins the UC to give up their previous religion, if they have one, or stop going to that particular church, if they wish to continue to do so."

"So how can we be dangerous?" Twikanrozex finished for his friend.

"Your doctrine is seductive," the older man growled, his true sentiments clearly held in check by the admonitions of his own. "Worse than seductive, it mocks all other religions. You worship nothing but irrelevancy!"

Twikanrozex motioned for understanding. "We don't worship irrelevancy: We simply recognize it. We *are* irrelevant. All of us. I, my colleague Briann, you, everyone in this pavilion, everyone on this planet. Our presence justifies nothing, and signifies only the accidental evolution of some exceptionally active amino acids. The results are admirable, even praiseworthy. But they are not relevant to the evolvement of the universe. One of the core beliefs of the United Church is that every sentient being should come to understand its place in the scheme of things."

"And what is that place?" Father Joseph ignored his senior's look of disapproval.

"A little to the left, we think." Briann's smile widened. "I'm sorry if that sounds too irrelevant. You see, we are a dogma that is founded on full comprehension of our own individual and collective insignificance. Having accepted that, we can mature in comfort. I am quite content with who I am and with my place in the cosmos. Likewise, Twikanrozex is content with his."

"What about eternal damnation and salvation?" Father Jenakis looked as if he wanted to thunder the question but, mindful of the many others seated nearby, restrained himself.

"Questions we can't answer," Briann replied. "If they exist, we can't do anything about them. And if they don't, why, we'd be wasting an awful lot of otherwise productive lifetime agonizing over them." He met the older man's gaze unflinchingly. "There are plenty of others willing to do the agonizing already, and we have no desire to intrude on their territory."

Joseph turned apologetic. "You know that there are proposals being put forth to limit your activities."

"Among my people, as well," Twikanrozex felt compelled to point out.

Briann shrugged. "We don't spill time worrying about that. It's a matter for the legal logisticians. Twikanrozex and I, we're just two among many who have chosen to help spread the message." He sat forward. "Having been by our display, you know that everything about the Church is available for the asking. Why don't you try reading the first forty maxims or so and their antecedents?"

Joseph replied with the confidence of the convicted. "I already have plenty to read, both religious and otherwise."

Briann sighed resignedly. "Too bad. They'd give you a couple of good laughs. What is it you want from us? If it's simply to discuss theology and the economics of organized religion, we're happy to oblige you. If there's something more . . ."

Father Jenakis looked as if he were about to rise from his seat. "We want you to shut down that infernal display of yours and stop trying to convert people! Especially young people."

"But we have told you." Twikanrozex responded with a four-handed gesture of some directness. "We are not trying to convert anyone—much less anyone of a particular age. I must add that in this respect I have already encountered such a request. The fanciful situation to which you allude arouses even greater passions among my people, since our children are incapable of moving about on their own. There is much unreasoning talk of what you call, I believe, 'captive audiences.'"

"Our display stays." Though still conventionally courteous, Briann's tone hardened slightly. "We have the permit, and as much right to exhibit as any other authorized vendor at this fair."

"Vendor!" Father Jenakis shook his head slowly. "If you are willing to denigrate your own beliefs so freely, how can you expect others to take them seriously?"

"We don't," Briann informed him. "That is, we don't expect others to do anything, except read what is on offer. And since we don't expect others to take us seriously, why should you? If we're going to, as you put it, denigrate our own beliefs, why should you take the trouble to do so when we're doing it for you?"

"We told you," Joseph declared softly. "Because it's that very irreverence that appeals to intelligent youngsters. It intrigues them."

"It also makes them laugh," Briann could not keep from pointing out.

"Nothing like a lack of seriousness, of preaching, and of regulations to puzzle a clever kid. Where is it writ that a religious organization can't consecrate fun?" He shook his head. "I won't tell you from what particular theology I came to the United Church, but suffice to say I never could understand how making you continually feel bad was supposed to ultimately make you feel good." He folded his arms and radiated quiet contentment. "We have the same eventual end in mind as do you. We've simply chosen to follow a path that cuts out all that conflicting, confusing first step. We proceed directly to making people feel good."

"You will be stopped." Father Jenakis was quite convinced. "Laws will be passed to prevent you from doing any more harm. Furthermore, people will soon begin to see through the insubstantialities of your clever but childish polemics. You are a fad, gentlemen. Nothing more. I feel sorry for you, and will pray for your souls."

Briann maintained his maddening air of self-assurance. "As to the possibility of restrictive laws being used against us, Father, only time will tell. I can tell you that we have very good lawyers. As to people seeing through what the Church propounds, we intend that they do so. That's why we abjure complex dogma, and try to keep things simple. When they see through our maxims, we hope that on the other side they will find truth. That is all that we seek: truth and happiness. The former to gratify the mind, the latter to satisfy the soul. And we thank you for your offer to pray for us. We of the Church would never turn down such a benevolent offer. 'In a Universe vast with uncertainties, never turn down an offer of expiation, no matter what the source.' Maxim number sixty-eight, part four."

The older man rose precipitously. "You people are impudent and shameless!"

"I know," Briann admitted, "but it keeps us smiling."

Jenakis looked like a man ready to begin a sermon. Thinking better of it, he reached down and put a hand on his younger associate's shoulder. "Come, Father Joseph. We can do nothing more here. One cannot reason with harlequins."

His expression rueful, the younger man rose. "I'm sorry. We can't help you if you won't let us. I will pray for you, too."

"That's very kind of you." Leaning forward, Briann whispered conspiratorially, "Remember—all our literature is easily mollyed right from our display tower!" As the younger man turned to depart in the wake of his senior, Briann placed a thumb in each ear, raised his hands, and wagged his fingers at the retreating figures while simultaneously sticking out his tongue.

Twikanrozex eyed him with interest. "That is a gesture I do not recognize from the Church canons."

Looking content, Briann dropped his hands. "It's decidedly nontheological in origin. Among my people, an ancient and traditional folkloric form of farewell."

"Very kinetic. Can you teach it to me?"

Briann considered. "You have no ears to stick thumbs into, but your ability to make use of an extra pair of hands more than compensates. I think you'll do well with it—but you have to pick the operative situations carefully."

"I know that you will instruct me properly." Twikanrozex shifted his lower abdomen on the padded straddle bench, eager to learn.

Padre Briann proceeded to enlighten him.

12

A breathless Therese Holoness led Cullen Karasi and Pilwondepat out of camp and down the walking track that led to the primary excavation. Along the way they passed the location of several other smaller digs begun in the hopes of finding something interred in the hard-packed earth of the escarpment. Every one of these was deserted; tools powered down, water bottles set aside, laser grids shining unimpeded in the morning sun. When Pilwondepat remarked on the absence of workers, Holoness pointed ahead.

"They're all down at the main site. Everyone's gathering there." She hopped over a narrow ravine. Cullen followed easily, while Pilwondepat had to pick his way. He did not fall behind, but neither did he hop. Thranx were not very good jumpers.

The truth of her words became clear as they neared the site. A large crowd had assembled. As they drew nearer, Cullen saw that not only the exoarcheological crew but a goodly portion of the camp's nonscientific staff was also congregating around the open pit. As he approached, he was recognized, and murmuring onlookers moved aside to make room for him and Holoness. A few less-than-friendly looks greeted the presence of the thranx in their midst, but he was granted passage, as well, and no one said anything. At least, nothing that could be overheard.

A number of Cullen's people were clustered around something at the bottom of the excavation, blocking it with their assembled bodies. Pilwondepat was inordinately displeased to see Riimadu among them. The AAnn was standing slightly to one side, tail switching back and forth in as transparent an indication of excitement as if he had been hissing wildly and throwing his arms in the air. Holoness led the way to the earthen staircase and then downward into the depths. Around the rim of the hole in the ground, the crowd continued to enlarge until it seemed to Pilwon-depat that every worker on the site was present.

Descending the steps cut into the hard-packed earth more slowly than his human companions, he waited for the cluster of diggers to part. He thought Riimadu might have glared once in his direction, but he could not be sure. In any event, it didn't matter, since he was soon as dumbstruck as everyone else by what the excavators had uncovered.

It was a vitreous dark brown surface with a meter-wide dimple in the center. That in itself was not especially striking, nor was the fact that they had certainly uncovered an artifact. What was of far greater import was the realization that the object was not made of stone, like the grand statues that dominated the far side of the valley opposite the escarpment.

"It's not metal." Holoness started talking before anyone asked. "Or plastic. As best we've been able to determine without knocking off a chunk for analysis, it's some kind of bonded ceramic." Crouching over the depression, she used one palm to brush at the sensuous alien curve. "See how it shines?"

Stepping forward, both Pilwondepat and Cullen made their own cursory examination of the phenomenon. The thranx did not have to bend to do so. The unusual material was slick to the touch and unexpectedly warm. He would have expected something that had been buried at the top of the escarpment for untold eons to be much colder, the temperature of the ground notwithstanding.

"Any ideas as to its function?" Straightening, Cullen kept his eyes on the article of all their fascination.

Holoness shook her head. "It's plenty solid, sir. Chenowitz took the liberty of tapping gently on it with a rock, then harder. It's not hollow."

"Well, whatever it is, it's different from anything anybody's found on Comagrave to date. We'll be able to get a better idea of its intended purpose when we've dug it out."

That was the signal for the diggers to go back to work. Pilwondepat waited and watched their laboring until the afternoon light began to wane. While the falling temperature had no effect on the much more heat-tolerant humans and the single AAnn in their midst, it soon drove him back to his quarters. There he performed his regular evening ablutions while waiting for the excited call that never came. Surely Cullen would not be so indifferent as to forget to notify him when they finally freed the object from its stony matrix.

He was right. It was still there when he emerged the following morning, after the sun was well up in the sky and the surrounding high desert had heated up enough to accommodate him without danger of hypothermic paralysis.

His fixed compound eyes could not widen, the multiple lenses could not expand, but his antennae stood straight up and his abdominal gaster contracted, letting out an involuntary stridulation of surprise, when next he cast his gaze down into the pit.

It had grown. Apparently, the humans had been sufficiently intrigued—or perhaps *astounded* was the better description—to work on the site all through the night. Holoness confirmed his supposition when he confronted her on the now rapidly expanding rim.

"We thought we'd have it out, even if it was pretty big, by dinnertime last night." She was perfectly polite, but he noticed she consciously avoided contact with him. As always, he let the implied slight pass without comment. "But the more dirt and rock we cut away, the bigger it got." She gestured into the hole. "As far as anyone can tell, we're still nowhere near reaching its limits."

The excavation was now some twenty meters on a side and still expanding. Every piece of heavy exhuming equipment in the camp had been brought into play within the depths of the widening cavity. As laser drills sliced rock into manageable chunks and sonic blasters shattered the larger boulders into powder that could be easily vacuumed, the exoarcheological staff employed finer tools around the edge of the artifact. Additional dimples had been revealed in the lustrous, gently undulating surface. More significantly still, the succession of concavities had given way on the eastern flank of the relic to a perfectly flat surface devoid of indentations or any other blemish. A team of workers was laboring relentlessly to extend this platform, or landing, or whatever it was, in Pilwondepat and Holoness's direction.

"If they don't come to the end of it soon," the female told him, "we're going to have to start thinking about moving camp."

He gestured understanding, then remembered to add the easily mimicked human head nod. "Has any further progress been made, *sir!ilp,* in identifying the material of which it is made?"

"Actually, yes. Mr. Karasi gave permission last night for a sample to be taken for analysis. It resisted like mad, until we finally got a laser tuned enough to cut away a tiny piece. It's a bonded ceramic, all right. Incredibly tough stuff. The internal crystal lattice is unique, and the molecular structure designed, if that's the right word, to last pretty close to forever. It has a beryllium base, and then it starts to get crazy with introduced metallic salts. Or so the chemistry people tell me. You can't get them to stop talking about it."

Pilwondepat did not inquire about the artifact's purpose. That was unlikely to be ascertained until they had all of it exposed. "One presumes it's of Sauun manufacture, but without proof . . ."

"Mr. Karasi thinks he has that." The admiration in her voice for the abilities of the project's leader bordered, Pilwondepat thought, on reverence. "There's a temple on the Coruumat Plain that has a couple of interior walls bearing the same alternating dome-and-depression pattern. The concavities are even the same size. But those on the plain are of stone." She gestured down into the excavation. "No one working on Comagrave has encountered anything like this material before now."

Pilwondepat watched the humans at work: energetic, capable, able to labor efficiently in a climate so dry the thranx's lungs would have shriveled to half their size after less than a couple of days of exposure to such a desiccating atmosphere. But they were not as precise in their movements as his kind. Still, they were not excavating a pin-sized structure. There was margin for error with hand pick or drill.

"What," he wondered aloud, "if there *is* no end to this expanding flat surface?"

"I don't follow you." She looked over at him curiously. "There has to be an end."

"Does there?" Seeking signs of an edge, a rim, to the steadily broadening artifact, he saw none. "What if this object, whatever it is, has been built on an order of magnitude comparable to the icons across the valley? What if it is even larger?"

It took her only a moment to formulate a reply. "Why then, it will take a long time to get there, but it will still have an end."

"I wonder. Perhaps instead of trying to expose it all, we should be trying to penetrate it."

Now she laughed. "A lot of good that will do, if it's as solid as a statue."

"I am not saying that it is. Only that in light of its size, seeking an interior or an underside is another option that should at least be considered."

She suppressed her amusement. "Talk to Supervisor Karasi. He would be the one to make that determination. If you'll excuse me?" In the brusque manner of humans, she started down into the pit without waiting to learn if he would.

Pilwondepat stood staring down into the rapidly expanding pit. Riimadu was there, as usual: chatting with individual humans, gesturing suggestions, frequently pausing to consult his communicator. Pilwondepat envied the AAnn researcher his easy camaraderie with the mammals. Not only was their stature similar; so were their movements. Upright bipeds, albeit one tailless, they shared physical commonalities he could not hope, despite his best efforts, to emulate. Certainly the reptiloids enjoyed advantages in establishing relations with the humans that immediately put any hopeful thranx at a disadvantage.

It frightened him. It was bad enough that no human could follow the threatening sequence of calamity that was being subtly propagated by the AAnn. That they should become friends with the very people who sought their ultimate ouster from Comagrave was worse than sinister: It was downright infuriating. He wanted to grab Cullen or someone of equal authority with all four hands and shake them until they began to molt. He did not only because he knew that they would react defensively, and with even less interest in what he had to say than before.

At least Cullen had promised to convey Pilwondepat's findings to the central colonial administration. Another few days, and he could rest a little easier knowing that his findings had been passed on to, hopefully, more perceptive authorities. Until then, and until a reply was forthcoming, he could only continue with his own research, while incidentally keeping a close watch on Riimadu. That the AAnn appeared wholly engrossed in his fieldwork might deceive the humans. It would never be so with a thranx. The two species knew each other too well.

Cullen gave up on the horizontal dig two days later. By that time, the excavation crew had exposed an area of glistening brown ceramic more than a hundred meters square, lying an average depth of twelve meters. Nowhere could the diggers discern an edge or a break in the material. Nor could they locate a single seam, joint, nail, bolt, clip, or path. The mysterious material appeared to have been poured whole and entire into a huge mold, like lava into a bowl. Of dimples and ripples, of small protuberances and extensive flat surfaces, there were plenty. Of indication as to dimensions, function, or age, there was none.

Brard Johannsen, the expedition's chief geologist, chipped in with a report stating that the location of the site, almost proximate to the rim of the escarpment, exposed it to howling winds heavily laden with particulate matter. As a consequence, erosion was considerably more active near the campsite than it was farther inland. Preliminary dating of the rock and the packed earth layer overlying the artifact suggested that it had originally been buried far deeper beneath the surface, which had been worn down and carried away by untold millennia of strong winds.

"There's no question that it's a significant relic, and not just because of its fascinating composition." Cullen had invited Pilwondepat to join him for midday meal. They were seated away from the now quiescent excavation, on a little ridge that provided a fine view over the great valley beyond. The human gnawed on a stratified pulpy compaction called a sandwich, while Pilwondepat chewed *jheru*-flavored food pellets and sipped from his turbinate juice bottle.

"That was suspected from the very beginning." In the absence of teeth or horn-covered maxilla, Pilwondepat's four opposing mandibles worked against one another to masticate his food. Since he breathed through the spicules on his thorax, he did not suffer from a fear of choking on his food, as humans were frequently wont to do. In a thranx, air and food took separate internal paths.

Raising a hand, Cullen pointed across the valley. There was no wind today, and the air was absolutely still. The vast wild panorama possessed an absolute clarity that stunned the eyes.

"It gains in significance every day. There's nothing of importance behind the Mountain of the Mourners. Similarly, only very minor discoveries have been made to its north and south. Yet here, we find this boundless brown ceramic enigma—right where the Mourners are staring."

"As Riimadu originally pointed out." Pilwondepat was surprised he could say it without stridulating. "But what can it be?"

Cullen shook his head and took another bite of his sandwich. Pilwondepat would have had no trouble digesting the human food, but the smell was not to his liking. Anyway, the supervisor had not offered.

"Nobody has any idea yet. I suppose you've heard that we're due to get the results of the combined surveys back some time this evening?"

The thranx's antennae twitched with agitation. "No, I had not."

Rising, Cullen mashed the wrapping that had contained and warmed his sandwich into a compact ball. Drawing back his arm, he flung it forward in a smooth, arcing motion no thranx could duplicate. The ball sailed out over the edge of the escarpment. By nightfall its transiently bonded organic components would have disintegrated.

"Come by the presentation tent. I'd be interested in your opinion."

"I would not miss it." Tucking his drinking bottle neatly into his thorax pack, Pilwondepat followed the human back toward the camp.

The double survey Cullen had authorized was intended to furnish some dimensions for the object the team had unearthed. Any additional information gleaned in the course of the survey would provide a welcome bonus. Riding in the camp's two aircars, separate teams had utilized a pair of sonic scanners to probe beneath the barren Comagravian surface. Reflected back to the scanners' receivers, measured and recorded, these sonic echoes could be instantly analyzed by onboard instruments to give a detailed picture of any buried artifact.

But not, it seemed, this one.

The inability of any of the scanners' sensors to penetrate the ceramic material was revealing in its inadequacy. It proved that the brown stratum was far thicker, and denser, than anyone had previously imagined. Whatever lay beneath the ceramic layer, it could not be perceived by the scanners. What the survey teams *were* able to do was to come up with an estimate of the layer's horizontal dimensions. These were sufficiently mind-boggling that both teams were compelled to return to base to have their equipment rechecked, and then checked again. Assured that everything was working properly, the team members returned to their task. By nightfall this had not yet been concluded. Even so, the occupants of both aircars voted to return to camp to present what findings they had managed to accumulate.

At the same time, a third team dropped over the edge of the escarpment and proceeded to perform a vertical scan, hovering above the valley floor while traveling slowly back and forth along the sheer rock wall. With their sensors aimed not down, but sideways, they hoped to obtain clues as to how deep the ceramic layer ran. Information they gathered in abundance: They simply refused to believe it.

Meanwhile, at Cullen's request, the orbit of a mapping and climate-monitoring satellite had been shifted slightly so it could take several high-resolution vits of the dig site and the region immediately surrounding it. These proved to be of little beyond aesthetic value. No underlying pattern of construction could be distinguished from overhead. Geology had not masked from above what lay hidden beneath the ground.

Following the informative presentation, Pilwondepat sought out Cullen. As soon as they saw the thranx approaching, the human couple who had been conversing with the supervisor found reasons to be elsewhere. Ordinarily, Pilwondepat might have been mildly miffed at the slight. Tonight, he did not care.

"Hello, Pilwondepat." A subdued Cullen peered down at the thranx. "What did you think of the presentation?" Around them, site workers and scientists were taking their flustered conversations and often wild suppositions out into the swiftly cooling night. Pilwondepat knew he was in danger of freezing on the way back to his chamber, but he didn't care.

"*Cwissk*—we're sitting atop a seamless layer of radical ceramic material that is, according to the reports handed in by the survey teams, hundreds if not thousands of square kilometers in area. One that also, according to the other team, is at least as high as the escarpment itself. It is surely the single largest artificial structure found to date on this world, easily dwarfing even the icons comprising the Mountain of the Mourners."

The human nodded. "Yet we're no nearer to knowing its function than we were when Verwoerd and Olsen exposed the first depression. If it is solid, then it is certainly the biggest enigma we've yet uncovered here. If it's hollow . . . If it's hollow, there's no telling what it might contain."

"Perhaps only dead air," Pilwondepat ventured.

Cullen responded with an emphatic denial. "Nobody, no sentient species, builds a box of these dimensions, if that is indeed what it is, to hold nothing."

"It could be that it was intended to accommodate certain contents that never arrived prior to the emptying of this world. It might also be designed not to store something, but to hide it. To seal it up."

The biped gazed back into enigmatic compound eyes. "Are all thranx as cheerfully optimistic and reassuring as you, Pilwondepat?"

"Most of the time we tend to be..." Examining the human's expressive face, the thranx researcher terminated his intended reply. "Oh, I see. You are being sarcastic. We regard ourselves as more than a little adept at the behavior ourselves, you know." He gestured repeatedly and eloquently with his truhands.

"I have been proposing for days that instead of expending time and resources in trying to seek out an external boundary, your people make an effort to search out an entrance to the hypothesized interior."

Cullen let out a derisive grunt. "There are no seams, no doorjambs, no rills or surface inclusions. Where do you propose that we start?"

Pilwondepat had prepared for the question. "At the bottom of one of the innumerable concavities that dot the otherwise smooth surface. With cutting lasers and other devices. Dampened shaped charges, if necessary."

"What if the material is combustible? The use of either lasers or charges could cause the entire structure to oxidize." He chuckled humorlessly. "That would make a fine headline in the *Journal of Interstellar Archeology*. 'Comagrave Dig Supervisor Discovers Greatest Single Artifact in North Arm. Promptly Burns It to a Crisp.' "

"You are being theatrical. Good material for ire-poetry; not for science. One sample of the ceramic has already been subjected to thorough analysis. Others can be taken from elsewhere and checked to ensure that such an explosive reaction will not take place."

"It's going to take time," Cullen warned him. "The stuff is incredibly tough."

"But not impenetrable," Pilwondepat reminded him.

"No," the supervisor was forced to concede. "Probably not impenetrable. The question remains, is there anything down there to penetrate?" Wearied from work and worry, he reached up to rub the base of his neck. "If it's an ancient floor, we're going to waste an awful lot of time digging our way through it just to find more rock on the underside."

"The alien ceramic protects the greatest treasure in the Arm," the thranx exoarcheologist countered. "All the knowledge and riches and wealth of the Sauun, just waiting for someone to uncover it."

Cullen's gaze narrowed, a peculiar ability of humans. The AAnn could not do it, Pilwondepat knew. "What evidence do you have to support such a claim?"

The thranx gestured elaborately. Sarcasm, indeed. "None whatsoever. But it is an inspirational notion, is it not? And what are your alternatives? To keep surveying and measuring, forever expanding the size of the mystery without ever making an effort to solve it." Stepping forward, he placed his left tru- and foothand on the human's lower arm.

"I know that your kind shares the same distinguishing characteristic of intense curiosity as those of us who have been born to the Great Hive. You want to know what lies beneath this outer layer of rigid matter as badly as do I."

"Probably more layers of rigid matter," Cullen muttered. "You're right, of course. We'll get started tomorrow. I'll authorize the necessary heavy equipment—and attitude."

"One more thing." Pilwondepat spoke as the human had turned to depart. "It would be salutary to keep the AAnn away from any discoveries that may appear. Can't you send him away somewhere while the penetration attempt is taking place? To confer with his own legation in Comabraeth, perhaps, or on some superficially significant field trip?"

Looking back, Cullen eyed the thranx pityingly. "You know I can't order him to do anything, unless it can be proven he has broken some colonial law, or flouted scientific convention in the course of his work, or otherwise made his presence here intolerable." A small smile creased the supervisor's face. "I'm afraid your enduring dislike of him doesn't qualify."

"Then at least set a watch on him while the work is being carried out," Pilwondepat begged with his four-fingered hands as well as with his words. "If something of real significance should be unearthed, he will report it to the AAnn delegation immediately." He hesitated, wondering how best to balance fact and supposition.

"Sorry, Pilwondepat. This is yet another occasion on which I can't indulge your personal paranoias. I have more pressing concerns—like whether I'm about to preside over the opening, or the destruction, of something of real importance." Turning on his sandaled foot, he exited from the large, seamless tent.

Pilwondepat stood, watching the human depart. Against his thorax, the backpack humidifier hummed softly as it extracted moisture from the arid atmosphere and supplied it to his lungs. Cullen Karasi, who had previously demonstrated at least mild interest in the thranx exoarcheologist's conclusions, was now consumed by the need to comprehend what might prove to be the most important find in the brief history of human exploration on Comagrave. He had no time to devote to the fears of a double-antennaed, eight-limbed alien, however insistent.

If humans knew the AAnn better, Pilwondepat brooded in frustration, he would not be having this problem. He forced himself to stay calm.

What mattered now was that the supervisor convey Pilwondepat's findings to the human authorities at the capital. Would Cullen be too preoccupied with the unfolding discovery to do so? Worse, would he postpone the journey altogether, perhaps assigning it to an underling with no understanding of or interest in the succession of inimical coincidences Pilwondepat had so painstakingly compiled?

He had no choice but to exercise patience. It was already apparent that if he tried to force the issue, the human would react defensively and the vital information would never reach the appropriate colonial authorities. Therefore Pilwondepat would have to keep silent on the matter, at least until it was time for the supervisor to make his excursion to the capital. Pilwondepat could corner him then and remind him of the matter as forcefully as discretion allowed.

Resigned but not content, he ambled out of the tent. He was as interested as anyone else on the project to see what tomorrow's digging might reveal. If only he could bury his fears as easily as the ancient Sauun had inurned their marvelous, enigmatic, sinuous layer of impermeable ceramic.

Asking for volunteers to run a night shift, Cullen had been overwhelmed with offers. Quickly setting up lights, workers and machines continued to probe the site all through the chill desert night and on into morning, when fresh laborers took over. By the time Pilwondepat emerged from his sealed environment to check on their progress, the sun was already high.

When next he strolled to the edge of the pit, he was astonished at the progress that had been made while he slept. Utilizing every bit of the precision cutting equipment at their disposal, the adrenaline-pumped staff had cut a circular shaft into the cinnamon-hued ceramic to a depth of nearly ten meters. If the extraordinary material was a foundation for a vanished building of some kind, the thranx exoarcheologist reflected, it must have been a mighty structure indeed. But why pour such a formidable base for so easily erodable an upper edifice? As the shaft continued to deepen, the likelihood of Cullen's comment about the tough ceramic forming some kind of ancient floor seemed less and less probable.

Then someone working in the depths of the excavation screamed, and Pilwondepat felt himself running forward and down as fast as all six legs could carry him.

Cullen was not there. Nor, thankfully, was Riimadu. The senior overseer on the site bridled slightly at Pilwondepat's arrival but did not try to prevent the thranx from advancing to the very edge of the excavation. Hearing the scream, every member of the staff within earshot had clustered around the rim of the opening. Anxious, sweaty humans pushed and shoved for the best view, unlike an equivalent group of thranx who would have assembled in an orderly manner.

Simple ladders made of artificial fiber with sturdy plastic steps dangled over the edge of the hole. Designed to accommodate human hands and feet as well as the upright human form, Pilwondepat could not have mounted any of them had he tried. To descend to the bottom of the shaft, he would have to use the single power lift that had been hastily attached to the far side. As he peered over and down, he had no fear of falling. Carrying the bulk of their bodies parallel to the earth and with six strong legs to grip the ground, he was in less likelihood of falling than any of the humans clustering around him.

Down at the bottom of the pit, two humans in shorts and shirts were beginning to rise from their crouching positions. Pilwondepat's interest, like those of the others gathered around him, was not on the extraordinary flexibility of the two men but on the figure they were slowly pulling upward. Ashen-faced, the young woman had apparently fallen into a smaller hole that had been started at the bottom of the main shaft.

As soon as they had the distraught woman safely clear, the site supervisor looked up. Studying the faces arranged around the rim of the excavation, she settled on the one Pilwondepat would have least expected: himself. Given that she had been noticeably cool to him during their previous encounters, the thranx was therefore surprised when Therese Holoness beckoned for him to come down.

A number of the assembled workers watched in surprise as he hurried to the power lift and descended to the bottom of the excavation. By this time the shaken young woman had been helped to the side of the dig. With her back against the smooth, gleaming ceramic, she sipped cold sweetened tea from a dispenser cradled in shaky hands.

"What happened?" Though she was addressing the three workers, Holoness's gaze was fixed on the central cavity that dominated the center of the main dig.

Looking up over her tea, the younger woman responded carefully. "I was working the drill over the center of the next start hole when I heard a funny cracking sound. It was different from the stuttering splits you get when you cut into the ceramic. Then the surface collapsed under my feet, and I felt myself falling." She struggled to bring the rim of the container to her lips. Her hands were shaking so badly that tea was flying out of the container. "I'm afraid I lost the laser."

"Never mind that." Holoness glanced at the larger of the two men. "You caught her."

His expression drawn, the man nodded slowly. "Just barely. When I heard Miranda scream, I was working a scooper. I dumped that and made a dive in the direction of the center hole. Caught her right arm and held on tight."

The other, smaller worker chimed in. "I managed to grab her left wrist. Together, we pulled her out."

The woman looked up again. "I don't know how deep the fissure is. My feet never touched bottom."

Holoness considered, then glanced over at Pilwondepat. "Like to have a look? Understand, I don't particularly like you, or your kind, but I think it's vital when something like this happens to have the advantage of a completely different point of view."

Without commenting on her opinion of him, Pilwondepat gestured acknowledgment. As the two men wrestled a pair of powerful lights toward the cavity, he walked gingerly toward the dark aperture. To put as little pressure on the now unpredictable surface as possible, Holoness approached from the other side.

The lights were gradually positioned until they were hanging directly over the opening, with their beams aimed straight down. Remembering that he was a guest, Pilwondepat gestured courteously in Holoness's direction. "You first, if you like," he said.

Nodding, she dropped to all fours and crept to the edge of the dark cavity. Pilwondepat was quietly amused at this human effort to imitate the more stable thranx stance. Peering into the darkness, she gazed downward. She stared for a long time, in fact, saying nothing. After several minutes of this Pilwondepat felt he would not be breaching either personal or professional etiquette if he joined her. Moving to the gap, secure in his six-footed stance, he tilted his head forward.

A constant breeze was pouring out of the opening. It was cold with the echo of ages past. Dipping his antennae into the hole, he tried to identify the strange smell that rose upward on the steady wind. It reminded him of something familiar. He pushed the thought aside. The eccentric efflux could be dealt with later. Of much more immediate importance was the identification of what they could not see, and why. Powerful as they were, the deeply penetrating survey lights that were shining directly down into the black void revealed nothing.

Not because there was necessarily nothing to reveal, but because despite the fact that their operators had them pushed to maximum, the powerful beams could not reach bottom.

13

It was not to be an official excursion. Mindful of what had happened to her late fiancé, and acutely conscious of the continued presence of the AAnn envoy Preed NNXV at Azerick, her trip back to Daret was officially listed as a "vacation." She had ample off-time coming to her, and while some might have remarked on her unusual choice of a destination at which to relax, there was nothing illicit about it.

Had Toroni or anyone else known the real purpose of her visit, they would at the least have been seriously upset. Technically, what she was about to do constituted a clear case of ignoring the diplomatic chain of command, if not directly undermining local authority. This was a risk she was prepared to take. Issues of far greater import were at stake.

Diplomats, too, could belong to secret organizations.

She was especially careful to avoid the inquisitive Sertoa as she slipped out of the settlement in the early hours of the morning. Always ready to disparage the thranx in conference, he had been positively enamored of the AAnn envoy ever since Preed had arrived at the settlement. She had no fear of her colleague, whom she regarded as too irresolute to cause real trouble. The AAnn, however, was another matter.

Acquiring a transfer from Chitteranx to Daret was no problem, but the comings and goings of every human from Azerick and its vicinity was carefully monitored by the settlement's transportation staff. Therefore she made no advance reservation, but instead appeared at the terminal hoping to secure a vacancy on the next air shuttle. There were usually a number of empty seats, and this morning was no exception. Unaccountably nervous during the tube journey from the settlement to the shuttleport, she did not relax until the aircraft was airborne and heading south toward the Hysingrausen Wall.

She was no longer surprised by how comfortable she felt in Daret. From the shuttleport, one of eight enormous facilities that surrounded and served the thranx capital, to the low-ceilinged transport shells that carried travelers deep into the sprawling underground metropolis, to the tens of thousands of crowded corridors packed with locals, she was utterly relaxed. There was crime in Daret, for no civilized species seemed to have completely solved the problem of how to wholly eliminate or integrate an antisocial underclass, but it was far less than what one might expect to encounter in a human conurbation of similar size and density. And as a human, she was virtually immune from such limited threats as did exist. Not only would assaulting her possibly result in an interstellar incident, she carried nothing the average thranx castoff would want to steal.

Since she was not in the capital on official business, there was no reason for her to revisit the burrow where the diplomatic service chambers were located. Instead, she took lodging in one of the two establishments within the city that specialized in catering to offworld travelers. Not only were individual quarters equipped with instrumentation for adjusting the proportion of nitrogen, oxygen, and trace gases within the sealed rooms, there were even provisions and facilities for methane breathers, and for those two sentient species who extracted their oxygen directly from liquid water. Light, temperature, and to a certain extent gravity could also be tailored to suit individual requirements.

Best of all, more than half the rooms were located above ground, with views of the domesticated jungle that grew atop the subterranean megalopolis like wild green hair on a multileveled head. Her fluency in Low Thranx helped her to secure lodgings on the top floor, with a superb view to the west. Native avians and other rain forest dwellers occasionally appeared before her window, indifferent to the presence just below the surface of some thirty-five million industrious thranx.

She spent the first day of her holiday enjoying the room and the services provided by the hotel, luxuriating in doing absolutely nothing, improving her language skills by monitoring the local tridee equivalent, and indulging in a positively hedonistic massage at the hands, or rather the tendrils, of an exceptionally cosmopolitan Nevonian masseur. Employing six sensitive tentacles, it somehow achieved the seemingly impossible task of relieving her of six months of accumulated tension. She'd heard stories of the legendary Nevonian nerve and muscle therapists, beings dedicated to mitigating the accrued stress of chaotic civilized galactic life, but this was the first time she had been able to experience their talents. Suffice to say that had she been a person of means, she would have hired the quasi-cephalopodian away from the hotel so it could attend to her on a daily basis.

It was thus relaxed in body if not entirely in mind that, by sheer designed coincidence, while strolling through the rooftop garden and observation deck the following morning, she encountered none other than Haflunormet. After exchanging greetings that would have piqued the interest of no one—and were intended to do precisely that—she agreed to accompany him to a place of exceptional natural beauty located on the northern outskirts of the urban dominion.

On the way there they intentionally confined their conversation to small talk; Anjou avowing as how she was doing as well as could be expected considering the unexpected passing of her fiancé, Haflunormet responding with the mundane details of the daily life of a minor thranx diplomat. She let him rest a truhand on her belly, which was only just beginning to show. This prompted him to observe that while the effort of passing objects through a pair of ovipositors was a strain on the thranx female, at least eggs did not move on the way out.

When they arrived at the preserve, they took a circuitous path to the destination Haflunormet had chosen. Despite her anxieties, Anjou could not help but be enchanted by the silvered streams of the twin waterfalls that spilled into a turquoise pool below, like rivers of mercury gushing from a gigantic stone bottle. Built up over the millennia by the accumulation of red- and yellow-tinted limestone, the rills that dammed the turquoise pool sparkled with pockets of embedded calcite and selenite crystals.

Swooping and diving at the twin cascades, the pools, and the small river these begat, hundreds of *pecrikks*, looking like faceless chameleons sporting the most marvelously stained butterfly wings, filled the heavy, humid air above the glistening water. A few other visitors, thranx all, lounged among the striking surroundings, boldly taking their ease above ground, away from the immense city whose farthest reaches extended even beneath the wholly natural preserve. It was doubtful that any of them had chosen to visit the place of exceptional beauty because the splash and crash of the twin cataracts conveniently combined to do an excellent job of masking their conversation.

"Has he arrived?" Calm and at ease as she was, Anjou could restrain herself no longer.

"Not yet." With multiple lenses, Haflunormet studied every tree and bush, every lounging thranx and proximate creature. Espying nothing unnatural or out of place, he continued. "His ship is due to arrive tomorrow, or possibly the following day. I cannot check too often without incurring suspicion, or at least questions I would rather not have to answer."

Nodding, she bent slightly to study something like an animated ruby necklace that was munching on a spatulate leaf. "I'm eager to hear the latest news. It's too bad we have to rely on couriers, but when you work for the government there's no such thing as a private space-minus communication."

He gestured agreement mixed with understanding. "It's always better to receive vital information in person, and far easier than trying to carry on a conversation between star systems. Not to mention infinitely less expensive."

"Do you anticipate any difficulty in arranging our meeting?"

Haflunormet's antennae had not stopped moving since they had arrived at the pool. No thranx went too close to the water, of course. While they could admire its beauty, they elected to keep well clear of its dangers. Had Anjou felt like a swim, she would have had the warm, crystalline lagoon all to herself, and would invariably have drawn an audience. Not only were the thranx prone to drowning because of the location of their breathing orifices, they swam like bricks.

"Everything is already in place. I will notify you with an invitation to attend a musical performance that will give both time and place. You are familiar with the applicable code. I also have, of course, the necessary means for contacting your personal communicator directly, via closed transmission. If there are any changes, rest assured you will be informed of them the instant they are confirmed." He touched one antenna to the skin of her right arm, bare below the short sleeve of her blouse. "At this point, I foresee no problems." Executing the thranx gesture indicative of wry amusement, he simultaneously whistled softly through his spicules. "After all, we are all three of us 'on vacation.' "

They wandered along the discreet path that bordered the turquoise pool, chatting for a while about personal matters, before retracing their steps to halt close by the base of the twin falls. Up close, the coupled cataracts were even more beautiful than they were from a distance. Their thundering roar would also serve to prevent anyone monitoring their stroll who happened to be equipped with sophisticated eavesdropping apparatus from picking up the threads of their conversation.

"Events are clearly moving toward a climax, though one whose eventual outcome none can foresee." With his superb natural peripheral vision, the thranx was able to keep a sweeping watch on their surroundings. "I can tell you that there is pressure within the Grand Council to do something definitive soon."

Anjou kicked at the colored pebbles that lined the pathway. Though her specially designed tropical clothing was not burdensome, she wanted to strip off every hi-tech stitch and run splashing into the cool, inviting, pale blue pool. She wanted to sink beneath the surface and let the pristine waters wash over her, obscuring the alien world above and all the apprehension, strain, and tension that seemed to control every one of her waking thoughts these days. But she could not, of course.

As far as the pressure was concerned, she had no one to blame but herself. She could have, she reflected, chosen a less stressful profession to enter. In fairness, when she had decided to enter the diplomatic service, she had never expected to find herself at the center of galactic politics, much less at a flash point where the profound interests of not one but three burgeoning civilizations were colliding. She had anticipated long days of shuffling information, attending dull meetings, and filling out boring forms. Certainly she had not foreseen her eventual membership on an "advisory" committee that was semilegal at best. If her participation was discovered, she would be searching for a new career soon enough. Haflunormet's situation was no less ticklish than her own.

"What *is* happening with the council?" she finally asked.

"Reactionary elements are working to abrogate many details of existing treaties, and to prevent consideration of new ones. They are pushing to formalize a much more conventional relationship between my people and yours. No more reciprocal settlements. A limiting of cultural exchanges. A ban on the informal contacts that are being instituted between individual organizations." He looked up at her. "There is talk of trying to halt any further expansion of Azerick, and the placing of a permanent ban on any more human outposts on any of the thranx worlds. All contact to be between formal diplomatic missions only, *seelliik.*"

Her lips tightened. "That's pretty much what the retrogressive fanatics among my kind are up to. Their first order of business is to shut down the hives in the Reserva Amazonia and the Congo." She allowed herself a small smile. "The success of both settlements, particularly the way in which they are successfully integrating themselves into the local culture and economies, is driving some of these regressives a little crazy. It's a beautiful thing to see—or at least, to hear about on the tridee." Reaching out with cupped hands, she caught water from a warbling rivulet and brought it to her lips. A taste of thranx homeworld, she mused, quietly astonished at how rapidly she had come to feel at home in the hothouse, alien civilization of Hivehom.

"They're still in the minority," she continued, "but like all radical minorities they're very vocal. They make irresistible media copy, especially on slow news days, so their message is extensively disseminated and widely seen. They have powerful friends whom members of our organization keep watch on, and more sympathy in the Terran Congress than actual votes." Splashing water on her face, she blinked and shook droplets from her fingers as she turned back to Haflunormet.

"The Pitarian War did more to mute their influence than all the logical and reasoned argument that had gone before it. But good feelings fade, memories slip into the past, and there is always a new generation of ignorant innocents determined to overturn the carefully considered judgments of their wiser elders."

Haflunormet gestured a mix of sympathy and understanding. "So it is among any sentients with typical life spans." He edged closer to her, mandibles in motion, unafraid of the water so long as there was solid ground underfoot. "There are rumors of great resolutions astirring. I have not been able to verify their nature. Presumably, they are among the details that our mutual friend is coming to speak to us about."

She nodded absently. "I hope so. I could use some good news." Glancing down at her belly, she wondered how much longer she would be able to devote her full attention to such matters.

Four blue-green, chitinous fingers, each roughly a third shorter than their human counterparts, rested lightly on her left forearm. Eyes composed of multiple golden mirrors stared up into her own.

"Be of good hearts, Fanielle. Not for such as you and I the contentment of a quiet burrow. We each of us do as we must, because we serve a higher cause."

Reaching down, she placed the soft fingers of her right hand over his sleek, harder ones. "Who would have thought that the forging of friendship among sentients of like mind would entail so much personal anxiety?"

Feathery antennae waved at her. "Not all are of like mind," he reminded her somberly. "In our mutual racial immaturity, there still exist those who seemingly employ no mind at all."

They were quiet for a while then, each lost in thought, contemplating a future neither of them could have anticipated when they were young. Around them, a few other individuals and couples strolled, enjoying the peace and tranquility of the park, the additional moisture diffused into the already saturated air by the twin falls, and the free-roaming native fauna. Below their feet, an immense, vibrant metropolis pulsed and surged with the activities of tens of millions of intelligent beings, very few of whom were aware of the issues of great import that were being decided by a comparatively small number of their own kind and a comparable group of soft-skinned, fleshy, flexible-skinned mammalian bipeds from a planet whose modest star was but one of thousands visible in the night sky.

"I am most concerned of all," Haflunormet finally murmured after the long silence, "about the possibility of violence."

Anjou sighed heavily. "I also. I don't know much about your radicals, but among my kind, both on Earth and at least two of her major colonies, there are known groups of hotheads who'll do anything to prevent a deeper, more singular relationship from developing between a 'blinded' humankind and a race of 'bugs.' We both know the specific incidents that have already occurred." Kneeling, she ran a hand through turquoise water, stirring memories of motherworld sky. "It's the groups we don't know about and therefore cannot keep track of that have me worried."

"It's easier for us." He crouched to join her, bending all four trulegs beneath him. "We are more organized than you, and so it is harder for splinter organizations to form. Nonconformist individuals, however, are another matter."

"If only they were all like Ryozenzuzex, or Desvendapur."

He whistled soft laughter. "You speak of exceptional thranx. I could as soon cite the intervention of noteworthy humans. Strange, is it not, how history imprints itself so similarly on different minds?"

She put a comforting arm around his b-thorax. They stared at the rippling waters together. " 'Intelligence and sentience share the same shape, and ignorance is its own reward.' "

His head swiveled to regard her thoughtfully. "I had not heard it put quite that way before."

She shrugged. "I'm quoting one of the wild new religious orders. This particular one is fond of propounding a lot of irreverent maxims. You know the type: They try to explain life and the meaning of everything in one sentence or less. It's almost frivolous, yet oddly engaging." She straightened. "An intellectual diversion. A friend back at Azerick passed the information on to me. This lot seems to be the spiritual flavor-of-the-moment."

"They seem to be well scribed. I would not mind skimming a little more of their oratory myself. I could use some fresh entertainment. Do you think it will last?"

"What, this 'United Church' bunch?" She replied with confidence and the knowledge that history was on her side. "They never do."

It was dark by the time she returned to her lodgings. Sealing the door behind her, she walked to the window and gazed out at the surrounding jungle. Transported directly to such a room without first transiting the city, no traveler eying the verdant panorama could imagine that a nonhuman megalopolis of tens of millions toiled and thrived beneath the surface. Like all other thranx hives, Daret never slept. Accustomed to and comfortable with life beneath the ground, day and night were discretional terms dictated only by classical thranx custom. As such, their internal biological clocks were far more flexible than those of humans, being unaffected by the presence or absence of daylight.

Fanielle was not thranx, however. Tired as she was, she was tempted to go down with the sun. Contemplating the view, she considered opening the window to let in fresh air and the night sounds of the alien rain forest. As that would have meant trading the delightfully cool, drier atmosphere maintained by the room for the hot, muggy air outside, she decided against it.

A bath, then, followed by perusal of her private notes, and a good night's rest. The meeting with Haflunormet had gone well. If their mutual friend arrived in good order and on time tomorrow, she would have accomplished all she had come for. Then she could embark sincerely upon the aboveboard portion of her vacation.

"Sso very green, thiss world. *Jississt,* I do find it sso."

She did not scream because her lungs were too busy sucking in her breath. By the time she had whirled and focused on her unexpected visitor, that instinctive urge had left her. Given her quarters' special sound-proofing attributes, characteristic of every individual room in the establishment, it was moot whether anyone would have heard her anyway.

Baron Preed NNXV made no attempt to conceal himself. He had been standing by the entrance to the hygienic facilities. Engrossed in the view beyond the plasticine transparency, she had walked right past him.

"I am ssorry." He took a stride toward her. "Did I sstartle you?"

She took an equivalent step back, acutely aware that if the tentative dance were to continue, she would be the one to eventually run out of maneuvering room. The AAnn was not between her and the door, nor did he give any indication of attempting to block her exit. But the reptiloids could move very fast. She decided to save the proverbial mad dash to safety for a last resort.

His tone, if not his presence, was apologetic. As apologetic as an AAnn could manage, she decided.

"What the hell are you doing here? How did you get into my room?"

She tracked him warily as he sidled slowly to his left—and sat down on the bed. The juxtaposition was openly ludicrous: Had he been a human male, her anxiety level would have gone up. The end of his tail flicked against one of the two pillows, which she then and there irrationally determined not to use for sleeping. The AAnn might be a pugnacious species, even as treacherous as Haflunormet and his hive mates claimed, but they were exceedingly clean in their personal habits.

"I have been unable to esscape the feeling that our previouss encounter went badly, and ever ssince have ssought a meanss by which I might redress any lingering awkwardnesses." Reaching up, he scratched at an exfoliating neck scale with the index claw of his right hand. "When I went looking for you to requesst a ssecond meeting, I learned that you had departed the compound at Azerick."

"Not through the usual channels, you didn't." Willing herself to relax, she found that her muscles remained tight. Her specialist training proved unequal to the task of countering the atavistic urge to retreat in the face of subdued lighting, sharp teeth, and long claws—even though the latter belonged to an educated, multilingual member of another species' diplomatic corps.

"Truly." The acknowledgment was accompanied by a second-degree indication of recognition tempered with irony. The subtleties of the gesture were lost on Fanielle. "It wass not difficult to learn where you had gone." He indicated her lodgings, a hand movement sufficiently obvious that it needed no translation.

"Or to bribe or force your way into my private quarters, evidently." Along with the fear, some of her initial fury was beginning to fade. That did not lead her to unbend, or to relax her vigilance for a moment. She could not see a weapon or other threatening device, but their visual absence was hardly conclusive. The diplomat wore a standard-issue vest replete with pockets over the usual loose-fitting swirls of feathery opaque material, sandals, and muted tail makeup. Small pockets could conceal large surprises.

"*Tsstt,*" he admonished her. "I did no more than bend a few housse ruless, not break them." There was nothing reassuring in the diplomat's expression. "That iss no more than the nature of our profession, iss it not?"

She strove to establish some sort of command of the situation. "Good old Jorge. I knew that he favored the AAnn above the thranx, but I never dreamed—"

"Do not be too hard on your colleague." The smile widened. Sophisticated and educated or not, the envoy's teeth were very pointed, and very sharp. "He iss compossed of lesser material than yoursself, and iss ssubject to flattery and manipulation."

"Don't think you're going to escape the consequences of this break-in with flattery," she warned him.

"I have already apologized." Preed hesitated and gestured simultaneously for emphasis. "For intruding upon your 'vacation.' " The gesticulation that accompanied his pronunciation of the last word was as sharp as it was unmistakable. "A relaxing few dayss in the ssuccoring ressort city of Daret. From what I know of your kind, thiss sstrikes me as a mosst peculiar choice of desstinationss for taking one'ss easse."

"I'm a peculiar sort of human," she shot back.

He indicated comprehension. "Peculiaritiess can have their virtuess. I admired your professional and intellectual qualitiess during our previouss meeting. I ssit in praisse of them now. They are why I have gone to ssome painss to meet with you in thiss fasshion."

She considered. The route to the door remained unbarred, and the envoy was seated with his legs facing in the opposite direction, watching her over his left shoulder. How high could a middle-aged AAnn leap? How fast? She took a couple of casual steps in the direction of the doorway. Preed did not move.

"All right. I won't call for Security—yet. You certainly have gone to a lot of trouble. Not to mention exposing yourself to possible prosecution, diplomatic immunity notwithstanding. Say what you have to say."

The AAnn responded with a gesture of unsurpassing elegance. "That iss very politic of you. As I ssaid, I have admired your sskillss from the sstart. It hass therefore been thrice disstressing to me that our earlier encounter ended sso poorly. Even sso, it wass clear to me at the time that you are perhapss immoderately fond of thesse thranx, and thuss inclined to take their sside in all matterss, be they large or small. I would be grateful of the opportunity to assk that you do no more than keep an open mind on the subject where my kind are concerned. Someone of your sself-evident erudition musst perforce be aware that a certain amount of hisstory exisstss between the bugss and my people, and that not all of it iss pleassant. Thiss undersstandably colorss their ssentimentss toward uss."

Haflunormet was right, she reflected. An accomplished AAnn could make gravel taste like butter. Preed was by far the suavest emissary she had ever encountered, either in person or via tridee.

"Alsso," he added while she mulled his words, "regardless of your perssonal feelingss toward my kind, or toward me, you should resst assured that I intend you no perssonal harm. Had that been my intention, I could have torn your unprotected flesshy form to sshredss while you sstood unawaress, contemplating the sstinking forest outsside."

"Or maybe not," she countered. "In tests comparing the respective physical abilities of different sentient species, humans consistently surpass AAnn in strength."

His gesture she could not interpret. His words were quietly chilling. "Truly, that iss sso. But the sscales comprissing your epidermal layer are ineffectual in combat, your clawss are frail even when not overly trimmed, and your teeth are dessigned for grinding and biting, not sshearing." He had the grace, she noted, not to smile when he said this.

"But why sspeak of unpleassantnesses that will not happen? Will you at leasst, in the sspirit of fairness, impart ssome value to my wordss?"

She ought to order him out, she knew—if only to test the veracity of his promise. She ought to make a break for the door, or shout aloud the personal lodging code she had been given at check-in. The room's sensors would pick it up, relay it to the appropriate station, and Security would arrive on the run. That she did not do this spoke more for an innate sense of tolerance than for any feeling that this emissary or any other could convince her to change her opinion of the thranx or the AAnn.

"All right. In the interests of impartiality, I promise to consider what you've said. And as long as you're here uninvited, why don't you tell me what else the emperor's manifold cheerful subjects want from me?"

Either Preed did not detect her sarcasm, or else he tactfully chose to ignore it. With an AAnn, it was always difficult to tell. She really did not expect the envoy to reply at length, much less to provide specifics.

"All the People of the Ssand wissh from humankind and itss coloniess iss a certain degree of resspect."

Professional interest was beginning to supplement, although it could not entirely replace, her initial fear. "You enjoy full diplomatic relations with us. The Empire is treated on an equal basis with the two other major interstellar powers we know: the thranx and the Quillp."

"Truly." Preed gestured acknowledgment. "Yet sstill we feel our petitioningss diminisshed in the ssight of the bugss. We are concerned, and have been from the time of firsst contactss, that your government continuess to favor them above uss."

For that complaint she had a ready rejoinder. "First of all, you're wrong. My government, and the average citizen of Earth and its colonies, does not prefer the thranx to the AAnn. Indeed, among many of my kind, the reverse is true. This despite the invaluable aid the thranx rendered to us in the Pitarian War." Slitted eyes blinked back at her, the double lids adding an oddly feminine fluttering to the action. "You are accorded equal treatment, both formally and otherwise."

One clawed hand described an intricate succession of curves in the air. She noted that the envoy was wearing no special supplemental attire. The air-conditioning that kept the muggy Hivehom night at bay must be chilling him to the bone. This realization did not upset her. Though she could have done so, she made no move to adjust the temperature.

"Why then have our propossalss to esstablissh reciprocal ssettlementss in your Ssonoran and Ssaharan desertss been refussed? You grant thiss intimate privilege to the thranx but deny it to uss."

"Truly," she told him, utilizing the soft AAnn word, "I don't know. Personally, it strikes me as unfair, and contrary to the spirit of the treaties that exist between our two peoples. But that is only my opinion. As a minor diplomat assigned to this world, I have no voice in the making of policy."

"But you would perssonally ssupport ssuch an exchange?" For a moment, his interest struck her as going beyond the professional. Here was a matter in which the AAnn envoy took a specific interest.

"Of course," she lied facilely. "Why not? The regions you refer to are to this day little utilized or visited. Why *shouldn't* the AAnn have the same rights of reciprocal settlement as the thranx?"

His tail switched from side to side. "It sshortenss my journey to hear you ssay that." Had he believed her? She couldn't tell. "Truly, if only your people would recognize what to uss is sso blatantly obviouss. That we have far more in common with one another, both in sshape and attitude, than your kind ever could with thesse pesstilential bugss. That we sshare sso very many ultimate aimss and interessts. That a closser alliance between our peopless would permit the resultant political force to permanently dominate this one modesst portion of the cossmoss, to our mutual benefit. Perhapss, with time, thiss may come to pass."

"Perhaps," she responded noncommittally. It was not a lie. Who knew what the future would bring? No one could predict the course of interstellar relations. The way contact between humankind and the thranx had developed—accidentally, unpredictably, and in defiance of careful diplomatic procedures—had already proven as much. That she intended to do everything in her power to prevent the scenario Preed had just laid before her from ever coming to fruition was something she kept wholly to herself.

His unannounced nocturnal visit only served to confirm everything she already knew or had ever heard about the AAnn. They were sly and cunning, skilled sycophants, adept students of other cultures. All of which made perfect sense. One did not have to be a professional diplomat to realize that if one species wished to dominate another, learning everything there was to know about one's quarry was a prerequisite for ultimate success.

The AAnn were devoted scholars of other cultures. She had no doubt that Preed was well versed in the fragmented, frequently unseemly history of humankind. Like others of his kind, he would employ that learning to exploit any discernible divisions within human government and society to the eventual benefit of the People of the Sand. She did not condemn him for this. It was his job as well as his nature. Feint and retreat, test and examine: That was how Haflunormet and the other thranx diplomats she had spent time with had told her the AAnn operated. That was the AAnn way. Avoid far-reaching, open confrontation. Poke and probe and wait for the victim to bleed to death.

That was not going to happen to humankind, she knew. Any chance of that, any naïveté on the scale of interstellar relations, had vanished in the macabre upheaval of the Pitarian War. What might have happened had her kind first encountered the subtle, duplicitous AAnn and not the Pitar, she did not know. The most dangerous, the most ominous explosives did not always produce large, easily visible fireballs in space.

He was playing to her, ever the urbane and accomplished diplomat despite his rather fearsome appearance. Gazing back at him, she did indeed see a being much closer to her in appearance than any thranx. Only when one looked deeper did one begin to discern the insidious nature and intent that lurked beneath every AAnn and that, insofar as she had been able to discover, was absent among the thranx. What was it the ancient writer Melville had written? "Better to sleep with a sober cannibal than a drunken Christian." In the context of future relations, of humankind's ultimate destiny, she had become convinced some time ago that the interests of her kind would be far better served by lying down with oversized, aromatic insectoids than upright, sharp-toothed reptiloids. If there was one lesson her people should have learned since venturing into deep space and making contact with other intelligent species, it was that physical appearance counted for nothing.

But all too many of her kith and kin had not yet mastered that lesson. Hence the continued need for diplomats, for subterfuges, and for the kinds of lies she was all too often forced to live.

"I wonder," he murmured, interrupting her thoughts. "I wonder truly how much of what you have jusst told me you believe, and how much you have sscribed for my benefit. Equivocation and invention iss, after all, your vocation."

"As it is yours—truly." She met his stare unwaveringly. Let him accuse her of lying if he wished. He could prove nothing. Her only real fear was that, having tracked her down with such apparent ease, he might somehow also have become aware of the meeting she was due to have tomorrow with Haflunormet and their arriving friend. Though he had given no indication of cognizance, she knew the possibility would trouble her until the meeting was concluded.

Concentrate on the moment, she told herself. One small galactic step at a time. For right now, it would be enough to get him out of her room.

"We undersstand one another, then." Gesticulating gracefully with both hands, he tilted his head down and slightly to one side. "As before, I sstand in admiration of your sskillss, and can only hope that all you have told me arisses from the inner depthss of your true sself." Straightening, he approached until he was standing closer to her than formal diplomatic protocol required. She held her ground. Easier to do in the room than elsewhere, she reflected nervously, since there was a wall not far behind her and she could not retreat anyway.

His bright yellow eyes with their vertical pupils peered down into her own. He was of average height and build for an AAnn, slightly taller than she but not proportionally as massive as a comparable human male. But there were those teeth, bequeathed from a wholly carnivorous ancestry, and those hooked, knifelike claws.

Reaching up, he let the sharp, pointed tip of one talon graze her right cheek. His hissing voice was a singular whisper. "Sso profoundly, abssurdly pliant. It is a curiossity to uss how your sspeciess ssurvived ssuch fragile integumentss long enough to develop intelligence. Truly, the universse iss full of wonderss." To her considerable relief, he let the clawed hand drop, holding it in front of his chest parallel to the other in the familiar resting position of his kind.

"I hope we can meet and talk like thiss again. I have already sspoken of you to otherss of like mind. Their interesst matchess mine."

"I have no objection to meeting with or talking to anyone," she admitted truthfully. "Provided that next time, certain minimal courtesies are observed."

He acknowledged her outrage without argument as he backed toward the door. "Truly. Until then, I wissh you, Fanielle Anjou of Earth and not of Hivehom, ssafe sstriding and ssmooth ssurfacess under your feet." As the door responded to the shrouded covert electronics that had gained him entrance, he added, "And may your pending offsspring emerge into the world sslick of sscale and free of blemissh."

He was out the door and gone before she could ask him how he knew of her pregnancy. But of course, she realized when he had left, he could have found that out from the garrulous Sertoa, or many others at Azerick Station. One hand dropped unconsciously to her upper belly as she saw the door shut. She resecured it as best she could. To her surprise, she found that her heart was racing and her lungs were pounding against her chest. All the tension, all the pent-up anxiety engendered by the AAnn's unexpected appearance, now raced to the fore.

Stumbling into the bathroom, she rummaged through her gear until she found the bottle she wanted. One—no, two—of the pills accompanied by hastily gulped water slid down her throat. Leaning back against the glassy wall, she wondered if she ought to change rooms. That would not be easy to do. Not in the middle of the night, on a thranx world, in an establishment dedicated to providing adequate accommodation not only to visiting humans but to representatives of many other species who frequently had very different lodging requirements. Besides, if Preed could gain entry to one room, there was no reason to assume entering another would present him with any insurmountable obstacles.

In the end she settled for the bath that had been her initial goal. After a while she managed to stop glancing in the direction of the outer room and the doorway beyond. She needed to be rested and alert for the meeting tomorrow. Haflunormet would want to know all about the intrusion, of course. Steps could be taken to prevent a recurrence.

Raising a hand, she touched her cheek where the diplomat's claw had lightly depressed the flesh. *Did rather well at that moment,* she complimented herself. *No shuddering, no trembling.* Toroni and the rest of her colleagues would have been proud of her, standing up to a carnivorous AAnn like that, alone and unarmed. She smiled hesitantly, relishing once more the memory of the small triumph.

Then it all hit her at once, and she finally began to shake.

14

"Don't tell me—it is not possible." The short, dark human was gazing at the two padres with eyes that were a little too wide and muscles that were taut to the point of twitching. His chest had begun to heave. "It is not bad enough to see untainted humans congregating in this place and mixing together with filthy bugs and dirty bug activities: Now you are trying to get people to worship with them! What will come next? Bugs teaching human children? Preparing our food? Sleeping in the same rooms with us?"

Briann listened in silence to the angry tirade, forbearing from interruption or reply. Twikanrozex did his best to memorize it all, down to the last sputtering slur. Neither man nor thranx was especially offended. They had heard it all before, though usually couched in flaccid overtones of false civility. Unusually, this human was unabashedly vociferous in his bigotry, not caring if anyone overheard. It was possible, Briann mooted, that he wanted to be overheard. Certainly those strollers within easy hearing distance, human and thranx alike, turned to stare in the direction of the diatribe. To their credit, most appeared embarrassed by the outburst of undisguised vitriol.

Her dark green hair cropped fashionably short, the ranter's taller female companion made an effort to calm her comrade. He would have none of it, disdaining her murmured words and twice shaking her hand off his shoulder. When neither of the targets of his interminable vehemence showed any signs of reacting, either to his tone or to his words, he began to advance in their direction.

"That's close enough." Briann's tone was decidedly sharp, sufficiently so to bring the man to a surprised halt. His countenance twisted into a perfect sneer.

"Why, Padre, or whatever it is you degenerates choose to call yourselves, that's hardly a spiritual attitude."

"You're wrong, visitor. The spirit takes many forms. Hallowed also is the spirit of defiance."

Looking decidedly uneasy, the woman continued to badger her companion from behind. "That's enough, Nevisrighne. We'll be late for our . . . appointment."

The man gestured in her direction, evidently enjoying himself. "No, no, Pierrot. We have time. Time enough to instruct the degraded." His attention shifted back to the quietly watching Briann. "Why, I do believe, Padre, that if I were to intrude too much on your personal space, you would physically push me away."

"I might." Briann's tone had not changed.

"You might even take a swing at me."

"In a universe of infinite possibilities, all things are possible," Briann admitted piously.

"In which case I would be forced to defend myself. While it is true that we stand equal here in the number of witnesses, mine is human, whereas yours is only a lowly bug."

"Enough of this. Come away from here, Nevisrighne!" The woman was not distraught, Briann noted, so much as she was enraged.

"Shut up, Pierrot." The dark man's sneer slipped smileward. "Just a quick lesson. In possibilities." His right hand slipped toward the inside of his open shirt—and froze before the first finger could edge inside. His rage vanished, subsumed by a look of total surprise. It was focused not on Briann, but behind him.

Twikanrozex held a gun in each gleaming, chitinous hand. All four of them. Faced with this entirely unexpected and formidable quadruple arsenal, the swarthy fanatic slowly drew his one hand away from his chest and let it fall back to his side. So shocked was he that it took him a moment to find his voice.

"Very spiritual," he finally muttered uneasily to Briann without taking his eyes off the unexpectedly heavily armed thranx. "Not only have you become personally debased, whoever you are: Your so-called holy organization is founded on hypocrisy."

"Wrong again. This must be your day to wallow in wrongness, my friend." Briann did not have to look behind him to know what Twikanrozex had done. The thranx's actions were reflected in the shorter man's reaction as clearly as if in a mirror. "We who serve the United Church believe very strongly in always maintaining a sound defense against any who would do us harm. It is one of the fundamental tenets of our belief."

"What about turning the other cheek?" The ranter had forgotten whatever lay hidden against his left armpit. And wisely so.

"We are always willing to do that. Twikanrozex, turn the other cheek for this man." Behind him, the thranx obediently turned his head to the right. His astonishing peripheral vision still allowed him to keep that now subdued individual in view. At the same time, the muzzles of the four pistols did not waver.

"An unsurpassed model of sarcastic religious miscegenation." Retreating, the speaker rejoined his plainly exasperated companion. "If the Fates so decree it, we may meet again some day, Padre. I would enjoy having the chance to resume your education."

"And I yours, my friend. Enjoy the fair."

"Indeed, I will. More than you can imagine." With that he turned and stomped off, making no effort to disguise his enduring furor, brushing aside the arm of his annoyed companion.

Briann followed the curious pair until they passed out of sight behind a cluster of bobbing, transparent spheres that periodically paused to engulf unsuspecting passersby in an assortment of cleverly preprogrammed advertisements.

"That was unpleasant," he observed.

"Yes." Twikanrozex had slipped his quartet of weapons back into their respective pouches. "I'm convinced that if I had not intervened, he might have tried to do you an injury. A disappointing first for us."

"Maybe more than that." Briann's thoughts were churning. "Unless you have a specific destination or prospect in mind, I think I'd like to follow those two for a while."

Twikanrozex moved forward to join his friend. "Follow them? To what end?"

"I don't know." The human half of the team rubbed the damp back of his neck. "That one was more than xenophobic. There was something in his gaze. Just a little wildness, maybe. Or perhaps a little something more."

"You are suggesting he is even more volatile than he appears?"

"I'm thinking that, at least when he was looking at you, he bordered on the homicidal. I may be imagining things, but it wasn't just him, either. The woman he was with? The longer he rambled on, the more agitated she became. And it wasn't the kind of nervousness that someone exhibits when their companion is making a fool of himself. It struck me as more profound than that."

Reaching up, Twikanrozex touched his friend's bare arm with a truhand. "Like you, I have no agenda for the remainder of this day other than to wander, to observe, to converse, and to learn."

"Then let's track those two for a while. If nothing else, it ought to be educational." He grinned over at his colleague. "While we're at it, you can still realize three out of four."

It was not difficult to do. Outside the fairgrounds, their pairing would have made them conspicuous. Strolling along the shore of the great lake would have seen them stand out against the flat, unsparing surface. But lost among the bustling crowds that had begun to swarm the exhibition in ever-increasing numbers, they were able to blend in without being noticed. Acolytes of the Church received training in how to be inconspicuous as well as obvious.

Though they spent some time wandering among the exhibits and made a show of feigning interest in several, it was evident to the pair of trailing Church representatives that neither the slim woman nor her excitable male companion were much interested in the components of the fair. They spent a lot of time looking around while expending a considerable effort not to be seen looking around. Once, they disappeared into a public rest room and did not reemerge for nearly thirty minutes, a visitation that suggested they were responding to a call that came from someone other than Nature. Not once did they pause to eat, drink, shop for souvenirs, ask questions, try out hands-on displays, participate in a virtual, or otherwise indicate that they were somewhere besides an ordinary city street.

"I can't figure them out." His face blocked by a large cerise blob of calorie-free sugared air puff, Briann watched the peculiar pair pause in front of an exhibit on the undersea life of Cachalot. They managed to look bored and apprehensive at the same time. "If these are your standard-issue xenophobes, then why are they spending any time at all in the thranx-built zones of the fair? We've followed them through three already. Are they just eccentric, or is there something to them we're not seeing?"

Twikanrozex idly groomed an antenna, bending it forward and down with a foothand until he could slide the plumed prominence between his mandibles. Unlike Briann, he did not try to conceal his presence from the couple they were following. There was no need. Except at the diplomatic and governmental level, contact between humans and thranx was sufficiently infrequent that the majority of humans were convinced that all thranx looked alike.

"I feel that I have spent enough time in the company of humans to know that the behavior of this pair is most unusual, *crr!ll*. Their actions do not strike me as those of a mated couple, yet that is the appearance they clearly are striving to convey. We have already observed several instances of interaction suggesting they do not especially even like one another."

Briann inhaled a portion of his air puff. "Among humans, that does not necessarily signify the absence of ceremonial union. But in this case, I happen to agree with you. None of their actions seem normal. Still, while interesting from an anthropological point of view, it's not grounds for alerting the authorities." He glanced surreptitiously in the couple's direction. They were arguing again.

"Let's give this another ten minutes or so. Then I suppose we should get back to the tower and check its condition."

Twikanrozex gestured agreement. Five minutes into Briann's proposed ten, something so extraordinary happened that all thoughts of abandoning the unobtrusive stalk were forgotten.

Both padres saw the approaching thranx. One was especially large, with prominent wing cases and a deep blue sheen to his exoskeleton. Except for a possible passing glance of disgust from the humans, there was no reason to suppose the two pairs would even acknowledge each other's presence. Absolutely the last thing Briann expected was for them to swerve toward one another. No, that was not quite right, he corrected himself. That was the second last thing. The first last thing occurred when they met in the middle of the busy pavilion walkway, pointedly inspected their immediate surroundings, and then fell into what could only be described even at a distance as casual conversation.

Not only was the rabid antithranx human male palavering with representatives of the species he had a little while earlier professed to loathe, he was doing so without any sign of distaste. His taller female companion likewise participated in the conversation enthusiastically.

"These are not strangers talking." Twikanrozex was as spellbound by the unexpected tableau as was his soft-skinned friend. "They know one another."

"Or of one another." Shielding his face as best he could, Briann watched the four-way conversation. "I am of the feeling that more than the preposterous domesticity of our couple is on view here. But what, I can't begin to imagine."

"Nor I." Twikanrozex inclined his antennae forward, but the voices of the nattering quartet were drowned out by the shifting, swirling babble of the crowd. "What can they possibly be talking about?"

"Whatever it is, they've finished." Briann pointed. "The party is breaking up."

As they looked on, the humans and thranx parted company. As if to cap the unreality of the encounter, they exchanged formal farewells before heading off in opposite directions. Twikanrozex started forward immediately.

"You want to keep following them?" Briann trailed his friend for a moment.

"Not them. It may be that we have, *kuiit,* learned all we can from the odd human pairing. I think we should follow these new thranx that they met for a while." He glanced over at his brother-in-the-Church. "For reasons too convoluted to explain in a short time, and because of regrettable omissions in your cultural education, I must tell you that the two representatives of my kind are acting in a manner as strange as the humans'. This bespeaks eccentricities that go beyond individual iconoclastics. I should very much like to be enlightened."

Of like mind even though he could not be sure of his colleague's analysis of the encounter they had just witnessed, Briann nodded and followed.

Since any meeting between a group of apprehensive humans and an equally large clutch of edgy thranx was bound to attract the attention of curious fair-goers, Skettle arranged to have only Martine accompany him to the final pre-Armageddon rendezvous. Having been guided to the place chosen for the final meeting by Skettle's followers Nevisrighne and Pierrot, Beskodnebwyl met them attended by, as agreed upon, one other single representative of his kind. On this, the fifth day of the fair, the two humans and two thranx drew hardly a glance as they convened in the farthest reaches of the joint human-thranx forestry pavilion.

Giant *tceri!xx* from Willow-Wane grew side by side with tall kauri from Earth. Twisted kokerbooms shared the magnified heat of the day with lush *gotulba* from Hivehom. There were sequoias and *serypta, volmats* and ginkgo, diterocarps and the famous flowering *eryouou* from Long Tunnel that grew only in perfect circles from a common root.

In nature, none of these formidable growths grew together in the same ecozone, and many of them came from different planets. As representative examples of their kind, they had been selected for individual elegance and overall appearance. Only through the application of advanced hydroponics could they share the same ground. Each had been carefully sterilized prior to transport to ensure that no unwanted fellow travelers accompanied them on their mission of education. Each had been rendered incapable of reproduction to make certain no seed or cone, no spore or shoot could take root in the untainted alien soil of Dawn.

Into this impossible artificial forest, Beskodnebwyl and his companion wandered. Near the back, in the farthest reaches of the soaring pavilion with its transparent divisions, they found Elkannah Skettle sharing a hot drink with his collaborator Martine. Thranx and humans greeted one another formally. While the two leaders conversed, Martine and her thranx counterpart took up positions between them and the pathway. Deep in apparent discourse, they were paying as little attention to each other as possible while keeping their eyes on the pavilion's transient visitors. Though expecting neither trouble nor interruption, they were fully prepared to deal with either.

"Interesting, isn't it?" Skettle ventured conversationally. "That in this time of instantaneous local and rapid interstellar communication we still find the best way to assure a private conversation is to meet in person?"

Beskodnebwyl gestured agreement mixed with contempt, confident his human counterpart was incompetent to detect the latter. It amused him to so denigrate the unwitting biped. "Electronics are too easily intercepted, and voices imitated. Better to meet face-to-face."

"Even if you don't have one." Skettle smiled thinly. He was wonderfully content, secure in the knowledge that by this same time tomorrow chaos would have paid its long-planned visit to the fair, leaving death, destruction, and ravening hatred for the thranx in its wake. No doubt this odoriferous pest with whom he had agreed to temporarily cooperate felt similarly.

"At least I know my face." Antennae and truhands waved in Skettle's direction. "It was thus when I was young, it will be the same tomorrow, and except for a darkening of color will be unchanged when I am old. Whereas yours will shrink and crumple like a fruit left too long in the sun, until it threatens to disintegrate from its own rotting loathsomeness."

Skettle's smile slipped away. "I'm certain this happy little tryst is as disagreeable to you as it is to me. Therefore let us do our business so we can both be spared any unnecessary additional contact." Glancing back the way he had come, he proceeded only when Martine acknowledged his wordless inquiry with a slight wave of one hand.

Clicking a button on his handheld, he projected into the air between himself and a nearby tree a perfect miniature replication of the fairgrounds. There was no one else around to see, the nearest tourists being some distance away from the two alert scouts. As Skettle manipulated the elementary controls on the handheld, portions of the projection lit up accordingly.

"My people will set to work where you see the red highlights." As his fingers moved, so did the responsive lights. "We'll be starting fires in the most vulnerable places. Each of my people has undergone extensive training and is dedicated to the cause. In the event of unforeseen interruption or capture, they are prepared to operate independently of one another. Their assignments are overlapping, so that if one or more are intercepted or otherwise detained, any other can strike their missed targets for them." Using the controls, he rotated the projection and expanded individual sections, finally settling on one bordering the lake.

"I myself will be seeing to the interfair communications facilities, and then sabotaging the relevant backup installation so that my original work will not be detected." His voice had taken on a biblical tone that was lost on the thranx.

"Deprived of a central command, the fair security personnel will be unable to properly coordinate any reaction with one another. Separated and assailed on all sides by both my people and yours, they will either flee in confusion or be cut down should they attempt to interfere with us. Long before reinforcements can be brought from Aurora, we will have completed our cycle of destruction." He offered the handheld to Beskodnebwyl, who took it in a truhand. Having paid careful attention to the human's hand movements, the thranx had no difficulty operating the straightforward device.

"My followers will spread out from this central point." Another bright light appeared in the air before the conversants. "Each will be carrying a small arsenal of compact high explosives as well as hand weapons with which to ward off the curious security personnel to whom you have already referred. As you have pointed out, by the time adequately armed forces can arrive from the city, my people will also have finished their work. Weapons and any other incriminating evidence will have been abandoned at preselected points, and my clan mates will have rejoined the pitiful surviving remnants of the panicked crowd. Any visiting thranx who happen to observe us at work will be killed. I am not worried about surviving humans identifying us, since it is well known the casual mammalian observer cannot tell individual thranx apart. In any event, the turmoil and disorder should be enough to blind even the most heedful of your kind."

Skettle was nodding appreciatively. "Once their work is done, my people will embark on a similar course of action, whereupon among the resulting turmoil and confusion we can all go our separate ways, having accomplished far more together than we ever could have hoped to working separately." Except, he added to himself, I'm going to try and kill you myself while Martine and Botha and Pierrot and the others dismember the rest of your revolting entourage. And if you and your disgusting fellows are entertaining similar thoughts in regard to us, you'll see why we humans didn't really need your help at Pitar.

"Then all is in readiness." Glistening compound eyes stared up at the tall human. "This time tomorrow will see us putting a glorious end to any thoughts of closer human-thranx contact while consigning them forever to the wholly conventional level where they belong."

Skettle voiced his agreement. He did not offer to shake hands with his many-limbed fellow terrorist, and Beskodnebwyl was careful to keep his delicate antennae as far from the foul-smelling human as possible. As soon as they had rejoined their respective lookouts, the four parted company, striding purposefully out of the pavilion.

Behind, they left only silent, imported trees to bear witness to the appalling plan of mass murder they had agreed upon. Trees, and as unlikely a pair of bystanders as were to be found promenading the fairgrounds.

As Briann helped his companion climb down out of the baobab, the padres considered what they had just seen. Not even Twikanrozex, with his sensitive antennae, could overhear conversation at such a distance. But he had been able to follow the complementing hand gestures of his fellow thranx, while Briann was an accomplished lip reader. Intervening vegetation and the need to avoid the attentions of the two lookouts had conspired to interfere with their observations, but they had seen and read enough to realize that something monstrous had been planned for the following day.

"It is so sad." Twikanrozex's antennae were weaving alternately back and forth. "To see humans and thranx working in concert together, only to discover that they are doing so for all the wrong reasons."

Briann let out a despondent sigh of resignation. "And to think I was worried that the humans we followed for a while might go so far as to insult someone else, or that the two thranx might be involved in creating an incident."

"And so they are." Truhands wove patterns in the air as the two padres exited the pavilion. "An incident that beggars the imagination."

"I wish we had been able to learn all the details of their plan."

A truhand reached up to touch his shoulder. "We did well enough, Brother, and a good thing we did, too, else thousands might have died."

"Some might yet." Briann raised his gaze. Around him music and gaiety, laughter and contented clicking filled the bright blue of afternoon like birdwing butterflies dancing above a tropical pool. "We don't know where they're staying, or what the rest of them look like."

"Steps can be taken. There may be some small disruption."

Briann lengthened his stride, trying not to look at the children or the young unmolted thranx among whom he and his friend were walking. "There will have to be. The authorities can't shut down the fair. If they do that, it will only help to frighten these people offworld, human and thranx alike. Based on our descriptions they might stop the four we saw at the shuttleport. Regardless, their associates will be alerted and take care to slip quietly offworld. The next time they strike, society might not be so fortunate. We have to catch them all, every one of them, here and now."

Twikanrozex whistled affirmation. "You're right, Brother. To accomplish everything, some risk will have to be taken. Some innocents may be hurt."

His friend nodded. "Fortunately, the Church understands the necessity of proportional sacrifice to achieve a greater goal. I hope the local authorities will see it that way."

"If not," Twikanrozex observed as they turned a corner, heading for the tasteful, sweeping structure that housed Fair Administration, "then we will have to convince them."

"It must be done the right way," Briann concurred, "though it will not be easy. The Church does not yet command immediate respect from secular authorities. It will fall upon you and me as individuals rather than as Church representatives to make the case for an immediate and discriminating response to this threat. We will have to be direct and convincing. In this the Maxims are not likely to be of much help to us. When it comes to matters of philosophical discourse, police are notoriously indifferent."

15

Due to the thickness and strength of the ceramic strata, it took several days to enlarge the opening through which the unfortunate digger had almost fallen to where it was wide enough to admit a small aircar. In that time, a laser rangefinder had been lowered into the fissure to measure the distance from the opening to the first surfaces below. The distances were not as great as first supposed. Still, had anyone fallen through the gap, they would have suffered a fatal plunge of several hundred feet into the lightless depths.

The laser and other scanning devices revealed the presence of nothing but empty space. The brown ceramic appeared to form a roof above an artificial void. No one in the camp accepted this conclusion. It would be a truly eccentric species indeed that would go to so much trouble and expense to seal such a vast volume of apparent nothingness away from the world. There had to be something more. Given the extent of the disclosed subterranean space, an aircar equipped with powerful lights and calibrating lasers would be the simplest, safest, and quickest means of exploring the mysterious alien emptiness. Hand weapons were also issued all around. On closer inspection, seemingly secure large underground spaces often were not as hermetically sealed as initially supposed. Local fauna might well have made use of so much protected, enclosed living space and needed to be guarded against accordingly.

Cullen and Pilwondepat were accompanied by Holoness and an air-car operator named Dik. To Pilwondepat's barely concealed delight and in spite of energetic protestations, Cullen insisted that Riimadu remain behind on the surface. The thranx made an effort not to gloat over this decision.

Their vehicle was the smallest available to the exploration team, one intended to be used for quick jaunts to outlying sites of interest. As Dik maneuvered it over the edge of the much enlarged and thoroughly shored excavation, a crowd of students and workers gathered to see the voyagers off. Pilwondepat forced himself not to search among the gathering for the scaled face of the frustrated AAnn representative.

Eager but restrained, Cullen was musing aloud as the craft began to descend slowly into the pit. "Usually, archeologists crawl into ancient monuments and mausoleums, or if they are lucky, walk. In all my experience I don't know of any expedition that uncovered an artifact large enough to fly into."

"Personally," Pilwondepat replied reflectively, "I happen to like crawling."

"If I had six legs, so might I." Cullen went quiet as the softly thrumming aircar approached the augmented cavity.

Their driver maneuvered the compact craft into the opening, fixed for vertical hover, and then dropped them through the cleft ceramic layer and down into the alien void itself. "Lights," an unintimidated Cullen snapped briskly. Instantly, their immediate surroundings were illuminated by the spray of high-intensity search beams that had been hastily attached to the vehicle. Recorders mounted within the body of the craft switched on. Around them, all was blackness save where the powerful beams penetrated.

Holoness activated the scanning laser. Utilizing its far greater throw range, she played it across the western wall, a task for which it was not designed. Beyond that bulwark of dark ceramic lay an unbroken rampart of metamorphic rock and eventually, the outer wall of the escarpment.

"Turn." Cullen was standing next to the driver. Everyone was too excited and nervous to make use of the aircar's available seats. Even had he wished to lie down, the design of the seats rendered them useless to Pilwondepat. "Let's have a look at the opposite wall." Dik complied, and the craft pivoted neatly on its axis. As they came about, Holoness kept the ranging laser aimed parallel to the vehicle's keel. The bright beam revealed—nothing. The opposite wall was so distant that even the laser's tuned coherent beam could not illuminate it.

There was, however, a floor. Dropping down, the driver tentatively tested its solidity. It appeared to be composed of the same cryptic ceramic material as the ceiling. Against all reason, the vast chamber, of still unknown dimensions, appeared to have been built to hold nothing but ancient air.

"This doesn't make any sense." So far apart were the walls that Cullen's voice produced no echo. The emptiness swallowed his emphasis. "There has to be something more to it than this. No species goes to this much trouble just to build an enormous empty box."

"Who can quantify alien intentions?" In the dim glow of the aircar's subdued internal lights, the multiple lenses of Pilwondepat's compound eyes sparkled like mirrors tinted gold. "There are still many things humans do that strike my people as having no basis in reason."

"Many humans would agree with you on that." Opening one of the two personnel hatches in the transparent cab, Holoness started down the integrated steps molded into the hull and put a tentative foot on the floor. It supported her weight easily. "It's solid enough."

"As solid as the ceiling?" Tilting back his head, Cullen was able to make out the narrow shaft of sunlight that marked the hole the digging team had drilled in the rugged material. "All right: We're in a big box with no visible internal landmarks. Where do we go from here?"

"Over there, perhaps?" Pilwondepat was pointing with all four hands. "*Creellt*—I think I see something."

Dik swung a search beam in the indicated direction. Sure enough, the glossy bulge of a small dome marred the otherwise perfect flatness of the floor. It was about four meters in diameter and completely isolated. "Looks a lot like all those decorative bulges we found on the outside of this roof." He grunted.

"So it does." Holoness was staring, shining her own hand beam in the direction of the unassuming protrusion. "But why only one?"

"Get back aboard and we'll go have a look," Cullen told her.

Smacking the ceramic underfoot with her heel, she shook him off. "It's solid as a rock here. I'm going to walk."

With the aircar paralleling her, she strolled over to the swelling protuberance. It was a dark brown, the exact color as the rest of the ceramic material. Its central apex rose no higher than her waist. Reaching down, she tapped it with her light beam. The muted plasticene-on-ceramic clacking that resulted was not nearly loud enough to produce an echo in the enormous chamber.

"Likewise solid." She straightened. "Maybe these isolated domes have some ceremonial significance. Let's see if we can find some more." She started to walk around the wide, low protrusion.

When she was halfway around, something hissed imperceptibly, and the entire dome began to slide in her direction.

Stumbling backward, she nearly fell as the massive convexity slid silently toward her. The blast of incredibly frigid air that erupted from the opening the dome had been covering might reasonably have been expected. The pale light that accompanied it could not.

"Therese, get back in here!" Cullen was shouting at her through the open hatch.

His anxious urging was superfluous. She all but flew back aboard. As soon as she was safely back inside, the exoarcheologist shut the hatch behind her. The icy atmospheric swirl that accompanied her retreat did little more than briefly chill the humans, but it threatened to freeze the moisture in Pilwondepat's less tolerant and unprotected lungs. Fortunately, the craft's heater quickly brought the internal temperature back up to human normal and thranx tolerable.

"What the hell happened there?" Cullen found himself gazing out through the transparent cowl at a perfectly circular opening in the ceramic floor. The dome that had blocked it lay to one side, apparently disinclined to move any farther.

"Maybe her walking on the floor has annoyed the gods." Dik kept his hands on the aircar's controls, ready to boost ceilingward and take them out of the murky chamber at an instant's notice.

"Very funny." As her breathing steadied, Holoness moved next to the cowl to stare out at the aperture. It was perfectly round, with walls as sleek as the floor beneath them. "Cold air I can understand—though maybe not *that* cold. But not light. Where can it be coming from, down here?"

"I expect," Cullen responded, "we'd better go and see. Dik? Take it slow."

The pilot nodded as he edged them toward the opening. The glow emerging from the passage Holoness had inadvertently brought to light was not intense. It dissipated long before reaching the ceiling of the vast, empty chamber. Gingerly, Dik eased the aircar forward, positioned it carefully over the opening, and then commenced a controlled descent.

The gap in the floor was wide enough to admit the craft, but with little margin for error on any side. They descended five meters, ten, thirty, with no sign of the walls surrounding them either opening up or contracting. As near as Cullen could tell, the perfectly vertical shaft had been formed to tolerances of less than a millimeter. Then, as abruptly as they had entered, they found themselves floating free in another open chamber. According to the console instrumentation, the temperature outside the aircar's canopy was well below freezing. No one paid much attention to the external temperature readout, or for that matter, any of the others. They were too entranced by the light.

Tinted a pale green, it seemed to emanate from the floor overhead that had now become another ceiling. Below, revealed by the ethereal yet extensive illumination, was . . .

Pilwondepat uttered something in High Thranx that was incomprehensible to his human companions. Dik cursed under his breath. Holoness just stared. Cullen, their leader, mouthed the inaudible human equivalent of Pilwondepat's whistling and clicking.

They were in another room. Except that *room* was so inadequate a designation to describe their surroundings that it did not bear audiblizing. Below them, rank on rank, tier on tier, row on row, were thousands upon thousands of teardrop-shaped cylinders. These stretched as far as the eye could see to north, to south, and to the east. Only to the west could the possibility of a boundary be faintly discerned. In that direction, Pilwondepat realized, lay the outside wall of the escarpment.

Below the hovering aircar, the endless tiers of cylinders dropped away to infinity. Searching for an end, for the bottom, brought only tears to the eyes of straining observers, and no closure. Lying between each level of cylinders were strips of gleaming metal and of plastic, and conduits of the ever-present ceramic. Only here, the latter was present in a veritable rainbow array of hues. The tiers were wrapped, crisscrossed, enveloped, in a web of lines and connectors and ducts that looked to have been spun by the mad mother of all spiders.

Gently swathing each cylinder, seemingly supported only by their flimsy, deceptively fragile selves, were halos of filaments and fibers that pulsed with a soft golden glow like the breath of babies become glass. So delicate were they that they might have been spun instead of wired. A narrow strip of some transparent substance ran the length of each cylinder, which themselves appeared to be fashioned from some dark purple metallic substructure.

"What can they be?" Holoness was standing as close to the canopy as possible, her nose pressed against the transparent plexalloy. "There must be *millions* of them." She waved a benumbed hand in the pilot's direction. "Dik, you've got to let them know about this up top!"

Emerging from the same daydream into which all of them had been plunged, the pilot nodded. After a couple of tries, he looked up and shook his head. "No can do. Something in this ceramic sucks up even long-wave transmissions like a sponge. I've lost the outpost's carrier wave, too."

Cullen swallowed hard, aware he was in the presence of something as exalted as it was alien. "Can you get us any closer? We can't go outside here without environment suits."

"No kidding." The pilot manipulated controls. "At these temperatures I'm surprised there's no frost on anything."

"No moisture." Everyone turned to look in Pilwondepat's direction.

"Hot desert above, cold desert below. No moisture. This place must be absolutely dry." He gesticulated irony seasoned with aversion even though he knew that his companions would not be able to properly interpret the entire gesture. "Temperature excepted, Riimadu would probably like it down here."

Under Dik's circumspect guidance, the aircar drifted over to the nearest rank of cylinders. In the process, it passed above a narrow strip of metal, one of uncounted thousands that crisscrossed the chamber like steel silk. They might be walkways, Cullen reflected. If so, they had been designed for beings with far more slender builds than humans or thranx. Beings who were also utterly unafraid of heights. Despite omnipresent drops that could only be measured in the hundreds of meters, there were no railings.

With practiced hands, Dik drew the skimmer closer to the uppermost row of cylinders than Pilwondepat would have thought possible. While the pilot remained in his seat and at the controls, everyone else moved to stand next to the portside. From there they could look out and down at the first cylinder in the row. It lay directly below the edge of their vehicle's hull. The vitreous band that ran down the center of the artifact was perfectly clear. Gazing through it, they could see the cylinder's contents clearly. These immediately and unexpectedly supplied the answer to the main question that had plagued exoarcheologists ever since they had first begun to explore the wilds of Comagrave.

What had happened to the Sauun?

They had not expired of loneliness due to a failure to achieve space travel. They had not perished of racial melancholia. They had not obliterated one another in some undetected, undeclared war for which no evidence had yet been found.

They were still here.

Cullen remembered to breathe. "Next cylinder," he ordered Dik. "We have to confirm similitude."

"Okay, but this isn't easy going. We're in pretty tight quarters here." As he adjusted the controls and the aircar began to move again, he indicated the pulsating nimbus that seemed to float just above each cylinder. "There's a hell of a lot of energy fluxing here, and I'd just as soon we don't make contact with any of these filaments, or whatever they are. Nonconductive hull notwithstanding."

"We just need to be able to look into a few more," Cullen assured him. "Then I think we can safely begin to hazard some preliminary extrapolations."

Each cylinder, or pod, held a single Sauun. They were instantly recognizable as such because their features were intimately familiar to the three awestruck exoarcheologists—familiar from the graven faces of the Mourners, visible to anyone who cared to gaze from the escarpment across the great valley. Here were their living likenesses, held immobile in some kind of deepsleep. The same narrowness of features, the same sorrowful countenance, the familiar long faces that had been cut out of an entire mountainside—all were replicated in multiples of individual detail within the cylindrical pods. Millions upon millions of pods.

Pilwondepat had tried to count, multiply, and estimate, and had quickly given up. Without knowing the dimensions of the chamber, any guess would invariably fall short of the far more majestic reality. How many of the Sauun had sought slumber in this place? A quarter of the planetary population? Half? All of it?

"This explains why they never expanded into space." Holoness was staring down at the dignified, composed alien visage sealed behind the transparency below. "They were too busy expanding into this plateau. It must have taken the combined energy and output of their entire civilization. But why?"

"Some kind of gel." Cullen seemed not to hear her. "Probably heavily oxygenated, temperature and greatly reduced nutrient level sustained by all this machinery, which in turn has to be able to maintain itself." He shook his head slowly. "Incredible, just incredible." Blinking, he summoned up a delayed reaction to her question. "Why indeed? Perhaps they retreated here to escape some incurable plague that was ravaging the surface. Or maybe this was once a much wetter world. A long-term planet-wide climate change could have threatened famine." He gestured at the row upon row of pods and their dreaming occupants. "Put everyone in stasis, program appropriate instrumentation to awaken everyone when the rains return, and sleep until the planet is receptive to large-scale agriculture again."

"No."

Cullen frowned as he turned to regard the thranx. "No? Why 'no'?"

Pilwondepat's head swiveled to meet the human's stare. "The technology we see here exceeds the difficulties you hypothesize." He gestured with both his right truhand and foothand. "Any civilization capable of constructing a sleeping sepulcher on this scale could surely have solved the problem of climate change and potential famine. Or of a devastating pandemic. The time and physical resources expended just do not resonate with your theorized causations."

Had not Cullen Karasi's skills as a scientist exceeded the demands of his ego, he would never have been given charge of an expedition on a plum outpost like Comagrave. "Granted, for the moment, your reasoning: What would you propose as a motive?"

"Some external threat. Something they could not have anticipated, and therefore not prepared for. Perhaps the spread and sweep of an interstellar conflict they wished to avoid. Not the AAnn. I am willing to venture that neither the AAnn nor for that matter the hives or your people had achieved even rudimentary space travel by the time this place was finished and sealed." He glanced upward. "The chamber above us may be an airspace, intended to provide insulation—or a decoy area, to distract any curiosity seekers. Or probers with less altruistic motives."

"You sound like a paranoid Quillp." Moving away from the canopy, Holoness turned her attention to the endless corridor that extended eastward into the unfathomable distance. "Still, any and all theories are open to investigation. What can't be denied is the reality of this place, and the extraordinary effort that went into its construction."

"Certainly," Cullen agreed, "something drove them to this. I find it hard to imagine that all this—" He gestured with one hand at the immense enclosed universe outside their craft. "—came about as the result of casual choice, or boredom, or a desire simply to pass a few eons without dying."

"Fear," Pilwondepat observed quietly, "can drive people to greater heights than aspiration."

"Easy enough to find out." Holoness turned to the senior scientist. "All we have to do is wake one of them up and put the question to it." She made no attempt to mask her eagerness.

"In good time, that is precisely what we will try to do." Cullen's tone was carefully neutral. "But killing a few of the Sauun would not be a good way to endear ourselves to the rest of the survivors. We must be sure of what we're doing before we commence. That means study, plenty of preliminary work." His voice softened as he moved closer to her. Not for the first time, Pilwondepat thought there might be something more to their relationship than supervisor to subordinate.

"There's work here for a thousand researchers for a dozen lifetimes. Much as I'd like to know the answers to all the big questions, this is still a traditional dig, and we have to proceed in accordance with traditional procedure. That means measure and record, record and measure. Extrapolation with models will follow. Only when we're sure we know what we're doing, or as sure as anyone can ever be when something like this is encountered, will we advance to more dramatic steps." He pondered a new thought.

"If Pilwondepat is right, or even half right, and these people with-drew to this place to escape some unknown threat, there might be more overt defenses in place to deal with intruders than simply an empty decoy of a room. Maybe we should count ourselves not only fortunate in mak-ing this discovery, but lucky that no such devices have taken an interest in us—yet." He turned back to the pilot.

"Dik, let's take a look around. Keep it straight and simple. We don't want to get lost down here."

Nodding, the pilot manipulated controls. Gingerly, he backed the craft away from the row of pods they had been examining, pivoted the air-car on its axis, and accelerated slowly, heading east and down. Pilwonde-pat stopped counting levels at four hundred. No one tried to count the number of pods. The actual figure was beyond casual estimation. Cullen had used the word *millions* when they had first dropped into the deep-sleep chamber. As they dove ever deeper into the dreaming vastness, that began to seem a quaint underassessment.

"I'd like to know where the power to sustain all this comes from." Away from the rows of closely ranked tiers, Dik had time for musings of his own. The open corridors between banks of pods were far more expansive than the narrow walkways that linked them would have sug-gested. Support vehicles larger than their aircar would have required access to every row, to each individual pod. "Sure as hell there's more than one central support facility. Wouldn't make sense to concentrate everything in one place. Me, I'd disperse backup capacity throughout the project."

Cullen was in agreement. "There are some clues in the abandoned Sauun cities on the surface. That's one of the reasons why nobody thus far has been able to explain their failure to achieve space travel. They appeared to have all the necessary technological capability. They simply chose not to develop it."

"Maybe Pilwondepat's right." Holoness glanced over at the awe-struck thranx. "Maybe they didn't have a choice."

"What would impel an entire species to burrow underground and place themselves in deepsleep, at the mercy of machines, to awaken at some far future time to unfamiliar surroundings and an unpredictable fate?" Pilwondepat gestured with both antennae. "With time to examine and reflect, we may find the answer." He looked back at her, his mandibles working. "Perhaps we may even be able to do so without hav-ing to wake the Sauun." Walking on only his four trulegs, he ambled over to stand alongside Dik. The vacant seat next to the pilot was useless to him. "We spoke earlier of defenses. Now I think there may be none."

"Why not?" Unlike some humans, the pilot did not shy away from proximity to the thranx.

"Any danger sufficiently profound to force the Sauun to resort to racial deepsleep as a means of avoiding it would likely not be discouraged or deflected by what weapons their technology suggests they were capable of constructing."

"Certainly wouldn't be of any use against plague or famine." Cullen refused to surrender so quickly his initial theses. "Take us back up, Dik. Everett, Bajji, and the others will be in an agony of impatience wondering what's happened to us. Besides—" He smiled. "—I think we've accomplished quite enough for one afternoon."

Obediently, the pilot pirouetted the craft and began to retrace their course. Endless rows of shimmering purple pods sped past on either side, rising to imposing heights above and majestic depths below. Millions upon millions of sentient beings, suspended in silence, each of them heir to a great and tantalizing secret, silently tracked their progress. And across the great valley, the statues of the Mourners stood gazing eternally in this direction, the reason for their melancholy expressions now perfectly clear.

Did the Sauun raise this immense mausoleum first and then surround it with masquerading stone, Pilwondepat wondered, or did they burrow into an already existing plateau? If the former, it would explain why the edge of the escarpment was so near to the entrance they had found. He tried to envision an entire race striving mightily to prepare a vault of almost incalculable proportions, to receive every one of them before something happened. Instead of choosing to fight whatever it was that threatened them, they had elected to go into hiding. Whatever that something might be, the Sauun had decided they could neither confront it, nor negotiate with it, nor appease it. They had fled into deepsleep, hoping to awaken to find that the threat, whatever it was, had gone, had passed them by.

Plague, Cullen had suggested. Famine. To Pilwondepat such explanations seemed wholly inadequate to the Sauun's response. Even his own hypothesis, that some as-yet-undocumented interstellar conflict had threatened them, was already beginning to sound incommensurate. Whatever had driven an accomplished, intelligent species to hide itself away like an estivating *hrulg* grub surely was of greater consequence than that.

While his human associates chattered around him, he tilted back his head to gaze up and out through the skimmer's transparent roof. Two hundred levels surpassed, two hundred more to go. He found himself suddenly longing to be out of that boundless, brooding place, away from those millions and millions of living corpses. Checking the ascending craft's chronometer, he saw that less time had passed since they'd left the surface than he thought. They would emerge into daylight. That meant he would not have to look up at the grim immensity of the night sky and wonder at what might lie in hiding behind the stars.

16

When she awoke the next morning, Fanielle saw that she had overslept. The last thing she wanted, after the menacing encounter of the night before, was to be late for the rendezvous with Haflunormet and their mutual friend. As she dressed, she found herself looking sharply in directions and at places that would never have previously engaged her attention. With each mercifully unrequited glance, she relaxed a little more. The Baron Preed NNXV was, as he might have put it, truly gone. From her lodgings, if not from her thoughts.

She waited for Haflunormet at an eating establishment he favored, resting her bifurcated behind on a padded bench designed for thranx to straddle. As the only human in the underground insectoid bistro, her presence drew stares and remarks. The looks were less direct than the comments, given the thranx mastery of peripheral vision. Other patrons were quite capable of staring *at* her without actually turning in her direction. After a while, the novelty of her silent presence wore off, and they returned to their own conversations. The air around her was filled with a harmonious cacophony of clicks, whistles, and words.

She was sucking on a domestic fruit juice blend that was more than palatable to her digestive system when Haflunormet arrived. A prearranged glance and gesture told her all she needed to know for the moment. "He's here." One of the few humans on Hivehom with access to local methods of reimbursement, she paid for her half-finished drink and followed the diplomat out into the bustling corridor.

Roof over a New New York street to a height of ten meters or so and you would have a good analog for the principal burrows of Daret. Still, it was not a place for the claustrophobic, or for those who were uncomfortable in crowds.

From the burrow, they took public transport to an outer suburb. Yet again, Fanielle was grateful for her petite frame. It allowed her to ride thranx transportation without having to bend uncomfortably at the waist. Twenty minutes later they exited the transport system and took a lift to the surface, where Haflunormet had a private vehicle waiting. Following a preprogrammed course, the small aircar rose and headed westward, flying above untouched savanna and low-lying jungle. Several hours later it slowed as it approached a clearing at the base of rolling, verdure-covered hills. Not far from this easily visible landing site, enormous bulk carriers wound in procession past triple loaders, grinding their ponderous way along the base of the nearest hill with cargoes of recently extracted ore.

"*Sat!wi!t* rare metals." Haflunormet took manual control of the aircar and directed it toward a covered parking area. "The mine's owners are sympathetic to our cause." Multiple-lensed eyes looked over at her. "A more difficult place to eavesdrop on a conversation I could not find. I was determined to arrange one where after the unfortunate encounter in your room you would feel comfortable about speaking freely."

She gestured understanding and thanks, her two hands having to do the work of four. That they would be rendezvousing in a mine did not trouble her. Its interior could be no more confining than the side streets of Daret.

After securing the aircar, Haflunormet led the way past busy workers and administrators. Fanielle drew more direct stares here than she had in the cosmopolitan capital. Not all of them bespoke affection. She might well, she reflected as she ignored some of the less-friendly gestures, be the first human to visit this place, the first one many of the miners had ever seen in the flesh.

At the entrance Haflunormet made contact with Security. Conversations were exchanged via communicator, subsequent to which the two visitors were allowed to enter. From time to time Haflunormet would pause to check directions on his recorder. Unlike in the city, internal transportation here operated on an irregular schedule. Twice, they had to wait for an automated conveyance to arrive. A tall human, Fanielle reflected as they zoomed along one subterranean track deep within the mountain, might easily have lost his head in such a place. Within the tunnels and shafts there was very little overhead clearance.

From time to time they passed a bore or passageway where active mining was in progress. Here was another justification for closer commercial, if not political, contact, Fanielle saw. No human miner could compete with an equally well-trained thranx, who was not only more comfortable beneath the surface than above it, but enjoyed a greater tolerance for the heat that often turned mine tunnels into sweltering saunas. A crew of these highly trained workers could find top-salaried gainful employment at any tunneling mine on Earth or any of its colonies.

The transport they were riding began to slow. As it did so, the narrow corridor opened up to reveal a spacious underground rest area. Here miners could relax in comfort, waiting for assignment to the far-flung reaches of the diggings. There was illumination, and refreshment, and vit-style entertainment.

Haflunormet led her to a distant corner, where a single middle-aged thranx was engrossed in the concealed readout of a personal recorder. Antennae rose in their direction as they approached. As Haflunormet made the introduction, the other thranx slid off the bench he had been straddling and dipped both antennae forward. Fanielle brushed the feathery extremities with her fingertips, a gesture that in the past couple of years had become more familiar to her than the shaking of hands.

"I am Lyrkenparmew. Before we begin, I would like to wish you painless deposition of your egg."

Taking a seat on an empty bench, Fanielle glanced wryly in Haflunormet's direction. "Does everyone on this planet know that I'm pregnant?"

Where a human might have responded with something like "Good news travels fast," her fellow diplomat did not comment verbally. In place of words, Haflunormet gestured ambiguousness leavened with gentle humor.

"Thank you," she replied dryly. "However, I still feel compelled to point out that we are not here to discuss my maternal condition." By now used to thranx benches that were devoid of back support, she found herself leaning forward automatically as she addressed the new arrival. "Haflunormet has apprised you of my recent difficulties here, and in Azerick?"

Lyrkenparmew gestured acknowledgment. "I've been briefed. I am sorry for the many inconveniences you have suffered. I myself lost a close clan member three years ago to the gentle ministrations of the AAnn." He added a series of rapid clicks that were shocking in their manifest obscenity. Fanielle decided she liked him right away.

"What results can you report from your recent informal sojourn on Earth?" Haflunormet's antennae were aquiver with eagerness. "Deliberation still burrows faithfully?"

"More than faithfully. Beneath the surface turmoil there is a newly dug tunnel that runs straight to the light, with walls that have been burnished to an unfolding glow by truth." He paused to check his own recorder, which at present was set not to record but to scan for others who might be recording. Assured that their conversation was being monitored neither in person nor electronically, he continued.

"It has been proposed, and preparations are being made to announce, a formal union between our two governments. The resulting Grand Hive is to be known as the Humanx Commonwealth. There is to be full integration of all administrative functions, first on the interstellar level, later on the local. This is not an alliance; it burrows far deeper." Having delivered himself of this extraordinary pronouncement, he took a sip of the sugary liquid that half filled the translucent green container standing by his side. "Nothing else like it exists in this part of the Arm. Once integration is complete, other species will be invited to join. An official Commission of Interest to the Quillp has already been drafted, though it is considered unlikely the ornithorps will wish to confederate. Nevertheless, it will be extended out of courtesy."

Haflunormet and Fanielle hardly knew how to react. Desiring to hear that relations between their respective species were on the upswing, Lyrkenparmew had unloaded on them the culmination of hopes that heretofore both diplomats had only dared to dream about. Until now, neither of them had ever heard of a proposed "Humanx Commonwealth." Haflunormet said as much.

Lyrkenparmew gestured apologies. "As you know, the friends of the committee have had to function on multiple levels in order to escape potentially injurious scrutiny on all those worlds where we are active. I assure you, this is not some wild rambling on the part of our mutual friends. It's quite real. The details have been carefully worked out, debated, refined, and prepared for general dissemination on all thranx- and human-occupied worlds. A small band of especially adept agents have been working on the minutiae ever since we entered the Pitarian War on the human side."

"I hardly know what to say." Haflunormet's antennae were waving about as if in a dream. "This is more than I, than any of us here on Hivehom, dared to hope for."

Fanielle scrutinized their surroundings. A few miners were staring in their direction. In her direction, she corrected herself. But they appeared to be no more than what they were, and after a while they departed aboard a battered transport. She was determined not to let paranoia get the best of her. Not now, after receiving news of such import.

"How is this proposal going to be presented to the public?" she finally managed to ask their guest.

Lyrkenparmew employed all four hands for emphasis. "If the proponents did not do it themselves, it would never be brought up for consider-

668 THE FOUNDING OF THE COMMONWEALTH

ation by our respective dominions. The intention is to spring it on both governments simultaneously, and bring it to a vote in yours and to a mass closing in ours as quickly as possible, thereby catching our xenophobic opponents by surprise. Continued secrecy is obviously therefore of utmost importance."

Haflunormet whistled for attention. "Presentation before council is one thing; adoption something else entirely. Does this astounding concept have any real chance of being affirmed?"

Now it was the otherwise academically inclined Lyrkenparmew's turn to manifest excitement. "In all seriousness, three cycles ago I would have laughed at such a notion. Two cycles and I would have responded to you with an unequivocal no. This last cycle past I might not have replied at all, foundering deep in contemplation of the previously unthinkable. Tomorrow . . ." He finished with an unexpectedly emphatic gesture and a particularly piercing click of his two vertical mandibles.

"There has been a recent and unexpected upsurge of support on both sides from a number of previously disinterested clans. Coupled with those important individuals who have already previously espoused these sentiments—influential politicians of Earth and tri-eints and others here on Hivehom—it is believed that there may exist on both capital worlds sufficient votes to just barely pass the proposal. I am also assured that we can count in council on the voting bloc that dislikes humans but desperately wishes for such an alliance."

Fanielle frowned. "Isn't that a contradiction?"

Lyrkenparmew gestured ironic amusement. "Indeed—a very useful one. Among the military, there are those who will agree to anything if it will secure the promise of human intervention against the AAnn. These high-ranking eints have a positive affection for humans as—what is your colorful term?—*cannon fodder*. They seek allies who can be placed between the hive worlds and the Empire. If humans desire to occupy such a position voluntarily, why, there are many semixenophobes among my kind who are ready to welcome them."

"Strange," Haflunormet mused aloud. "To think that those who may support this proposed Commonwealth the most enthusiastically may also intensely dislike the people to whom they are about to surrender a portion of their sovereignty."

"It's not important." Fanielle was confident in her reply. "All that matters is the final, irrevocable cementing of relations and melding of our two societies. In the service of that end, we'll take what help we can get."

"So we shall," Lyrkenparmew agreed readily. "Once it becomes clear that ratification is not only possible but probable, I have been assured that others who would like to declare for a Commonwealth but who for reasons of provincial politics or hive affiliation have not yet been able to do so will announce their support." He gesticulated urgency. "But the proposal must pass on the first inclusive stridulating. After that, our opponents will be able to muster their objections and quite likely defeat any reconsideration."

"This is grand news." Haflunormet was struggling to find something to do with all his hands. "When you return to Earth, you may inform our mutual acquaintances that their friends here in the capital will be ready to move the instant their support is required."

"I can't vouch for what will happen in the Terran Congress," Fanielle added, "but as you know, I am not alone in my sympathies at Azerick Outpost. We'll be ready to offer what help we can from here."

"As will your counterparts on your homeworld, in the Reserva Amazonia, and elsewhere." Having delivered himself of the most critical news, the envoy finally began to relax. His trulegs were no longer clasped tensely against the padded flanks of the bench he was straddling, and his antennae inclined forward in a more natural resting position instead of being held vertically by the muscles in his forehead.

"Everything—hopes, dreams, and much effort—is building to a peak. The timing has been very carefully worked out. The sometimes bumpy relations between our species are about to crest at a high point. There are at present no major disagreements in dispute. The controversy over exploration rights on Comagrave has been settled in return for reciprocal rights on Drax Four. Ongoing commercial disputes of note have at last found a home in the binary-staffed commission that has been designated to review and settle such matters. The intercultural fair on the human colony world of Dawn is, by all accounts, performing to large crowds and great acclaim among those of both our peoples who have attended. Unless some unforeseen catastrophe of major proportions occurs within the next several weeks, the relevant edicts should be presented and the appropriate votes called for." He took a long, throaty swig of his remaining drink.

"This is a most momentous time in the history of our respective species. It will go down as such in the history scrolls—or else be memorialized as one of the great lost opportunities in this sentient part of the galaxy. Though you and I are but insignificant players in the sublime drama, we must each of us strive at the moment of truth to maximize our whistling."

It was a fine sentiment, Fanielle felt. There was a nobility to it that calmed her anxieties. Very rarely are individuals actually aware of balancing on the crux of history. She hoped she would live long enough to see come to pass all that the glittering-eyed Lyrkenparmew had described. For that matter, painfully recalling what had happened to Jeremy, she hoped she would just live long enough to see the actual voting on the proposal take place.

Lyrkenparmew had set his drinking utensil aside. His manner had grown more somber. "There are other threats besides the declared intention of our opponents on both councils to vote no on any such proposition. While our people have been hard at work behind the scenes, lobbying human politicians and thranx eints alike, the AAnn have not rested. They are ever active, making mischief." He glanced in Fanielle's direction. "As I have been informed you know from more than merely speculative experience."

She nodded slowly, a gesture both thranx would recognize. "As you know, I lost . . . I lost the father of my child." She swallowed hard. Though she had been down this road many times since Jeremy's death, remembering was still agonizing. Only her work, into which she had thrown herself with more intensity than ever, kept her from seeing his face in familiar places and from crying uncontrollably.

Something hard and unyielding brushed softly against her right side. Eight of Haflunormet's fingers grazed her ribs in a particular ellipsoidal motion, a soothing motion designed to show sympathy for both egg-layer and prospective offspring. She sniffed only once as she returned his touch with a smile. Surrounded though she was at residence and on the job by fellow humans, it took a bug's caress to put her at ease.

"Surely," she observed, collecting herself, "the AAnn can't hope to match this flowering joint effort with one of their own?" Around them, clusters of miners came and went, toiling at flexible shifts. Whenever a new group lay down on benches nearby, the diplomats' conversation shifted to innocuous, generalized topics until the diggers departed. The information being discussed at the small table in the back was too sensitive for general dissemination. It would have to remain so until the grand proposition had been announced to the public.

Lyrkenparmew indicated mild distress. "They've been very busy, the scale-skinned ones. In the area of commercial treaty making they have been especially active. The accumulation of individual wealth occupies greater status among the AAnn and humankind than it does among my people. This similar outlook affords a kind of instant rapport among certain of your kind and many of the AAnn." His truhands were in constant motion, making it difficult for Fanielle to follow every subtle overtone of the conversation.

"Many covenants have been proposed between AAnn and human, and several adopted, but nothing like the Commonwealth. The AAnn would never contemplate such an intimate union with anyone." He let out a series of shrill clicks. "They are too enamored of their own imagined destiny as rulers of this part of the galaxy to ever surrender any real control to another species. But beyond that, they are quite willing to consider all manner of agreements."

"The problem," Haflunormet continued, "is that too many humans are easily blinded by promises of the riches to be gained from trade with the scaled ones, who are not above bribing your people to secure support, special treatment, and whatever other perks they believe they can so acquire."

Fanielle was embarrassed for people she did not know and would never meet. "My kind have come a long way from the time when we used to beat one another's heads in for the most insignificant reasons. But there still exist those who crawl through life as ethical hemophiliacs."

"What they don't realize," Lyrkenparmew went on solemnly, "is that opportunism is ingrained in the AAnn social structure. They will treat fairly when it best suits their needs, and break legs when it does not. The grief arises from their skill. They have made a science of duplicity. I am not saying that humans are naïve, but there is no sentient in the known universe as crafty, sly, and cunning as a mature, experienced AAnn." He gestured mild apology of oversight. "But then, there is no need for me to tell you this. You have already met one such."

She nodded. "The emissary in question could charm a *sifla* out of its *morgewout*. When not tearing out your throat."

Haflunormet whistle-clicked concurrence. "His reputation spreads wider than does his water."

"I know he charmed a colleague of mine back at the compound." She looked straight at Haflunormet. "Mind the name 'Jorge Sertoa.' He's a very clever fellow, but a bit of cold plasma. Has dark matter in place of a backbone." At the dual gestures of bemusement from her companions, she hurried to modify the simile. "Sorry—in place of his predominate dorsal chitin." At this clarification, they gesticulated knowingly.

"And he's not alone in his sympathies for the AAnn. There are others at the settlement who feel similarly, though I'm happy to say they're in the minority. When the proposal is announced, I think you'll be able to count on the support of the majority of the staff, diplomatic and support personnel alike, at Azerick." Her expression hardened. "I'll arrange to keep an eye on Jorge and the others so they don't cause any trouble."

Lyrkenparmew indicated understanding. "Everything is suddenly starting to move very rapidly. There is a sense of great events having been set inexorably in motion. I hardly need tell either of you that if this proposal goes down to defeat, it could be fifty or a hundred cycles before anyone dares to bring it up again. Failure carries with it the concurrent risk that the opponents of unification, alarmed by the boldness of the proposition, will unite in even more formidable leagues to oppose any reconsideration." His voice lowered as his clicking subsided to the intensity of pins landing on a metal sheet.

"I'm not trying to alarm you, but this is the way the gist is seen. Our first chance may very well prove to be our best chance, if not necessarily our last."

"I wonder if it's too soon." Fanielle almost leaned back on her bench before she remembered that it had no back. "I wonder if we're pushing too much too fast."

The genial twisting of Lyrkenparmew's truhands insinuated inevitability. "Those in charge of making such decisions feel they have no choice but to press for the establishment of the complete Commonwealth. Now that the concept has been brokered, it has gained a momentum all its own. It is like entering into a burrow that has been slimed. Once you've started downward, there's no stopping until you reach the bottom."

Haflunormet drained the last of his drink. It was nearing time to leave, lest they become too conspicuous. "This will be the cycle that the progeny of our clans will venerate forever."

"*If* our designs are fulfilled." Lyrkenparmew slipped sideways off his bench while Fanielle straightened and stretched. Her back was stiff from sitting so long in one place without any support.

"I suppose I'll be heading back to the plateau in a few days." She checked her comm unit. "They won't be expecting me so early, but no one will question the timing of my return." She smiled wryly. "After all, what right-minded human could stand more than a couple of days of vacation in a place like Daret?"

"We are all of us hoping," Lyrkenparmew commented quietly as they left the table behind and headed for the transport platform, "that it is individuals like yourself who are the right-minded humans."

Reaching out, she momentarily rested the flat of her hand against the back of the envoy's abdomen, feeling his upper set of wing cases vibrate against her palm. "I'm not alone in liking your kind, Lyrkenparmew, and not just for the ever-amazing variety of wonderful fragrances you emit, or for your aid in the Pitarian War. There are plenty of us who are fond of thranx culture, and philosophy, and your way of looking at the universe. It's minds we seek in common, not shapes."

"How fortunate." The widely spaced nerve endings in Lyrkenparmew's exoskeleton conveyed to him the warmth of the barely insulated mammalian flesh. Such a strange sensation it was, to be accompanied by a creature that was little more than a loose sack of fluids wrapped around a barely balanced upright bony framework held together by fragile bonds of stretched protein. That this female's often erratic kind might be the ones to at last put an end to centuries of AAnn depredations was scarce to be believed. Many thranx, in fact, would not believe it.

They would have to be convinced.

17

Conversation in the room was subdued. Skettle let them talk. It helped to relieve the tension. As Nevisrighne and Botha, Pierrot and Davies and the others chatted quietly, the old man looked on with pride. In a stern, paternal fashion he was as proud of them as if they were his real children. Very soon now they would join gloriously together, patriarch and progeny, to sow destruction in order to prevent an onslaught of racial commingling of a kind their virtuous ancestors could never in their wildest dreams have imagined.

Walking over to where Botha was seated poring one last time over his beloved charts, he put a hand on the other man's shoulder. "The special explosives are ready?"

The other man adjusted his multifunction lenses and nodded. "It's a shame we couldn't disguise them the way we did the smaller stuff and just bring them in with us. I'd feel better knowing the full provenance of the ingredients."

"I know. But even a couple of small tanks of highly sensitive reactant would have set off alarms in customs. How fortunate that you and our other equally brilliant technical people have been able to devise a liquid explosive that can be produced from widely available materials."

Botha allowed himself a rare grin. "Catalyzed right here in their own city, too. Anyone reviewing the purchases would think one group was going to mix up some lacquer to paint a house, and the other a few crates of home brew."

"Home brew it is," Skettle replied, "only this blend is not for drinking." He raised his gaze to the far corner of the hotel's reserved and shielded conference room. The pair of trivarium tanks standing upright on the floor near the window—through which they could be hastily chucked in the event of a lightning raid by the authorities—were small, light, exceptionally strong, resistant to the caustic liquids they were originally designed to hold, and of a familiar commercial design that would spark no alarms in the minds of anyone who happened to see them. For all anyone espying them might know, they could easily contain cold-drink concentrate destined for delivery to one of the fair's numerous food concessions.

Skettle would take charge of one, Martine the other, in the unlikely event either of them should be stopped and questioned. The volatile contents of one tank should be more than sufficient to blow the bulk of the fair's central communications facility halfway across City Lake. As a further security precaution, they would take separate routes to the complex. Meeting there, they would then make their way into the facility by a prearranged, rehearsed route. Any security or communications personnel unlucky enough to encounter and query them would be dealt with as necessary.

Once the explosives had been placed and set, the two would join their companions in creating general havoc. Skettle was a tower of tranquility among his associates, some of whom for the first time since they had arrived on Dawn were beginning to exhibit the first understandable symptoms of agitation. Even the righteous, he reflected calmly, could grow nervous on the eve of retribution.

He had boundless confidence in all of them. All of them, men and women alike, had dedicated themselves to the cause of the Preservers. They were here to buy time, to allow humankind to reflect upon the mad course of action a few species traitors were hell-bent on pursuing. By tomorrow evening, the festering pace of human-thranx relations would have come to a crashing halt. By the day after, he and his companions would be safely on their way home, on separate KK-drive ships, able to relax and reflect on the good work they had done.

Yes, some innocent humans would have to die. It was quite possible some of his own people would also perish, although every precaution had been taken to ensure their quiet and successful escape from the zone of carnage they intended to enkindle. These unwitting tourists and visitors would go down as martyrs to the cause of species purity. It would take time, but when humankind finally came to its senses and realized the absurdity as well as the danger of trying to merge with another species, the names of the dead would be remembered gratefully by many millions more than the few relatives who would grieve over their loss next week and next month.

When he raised his hands for quiet, the low buzz of conversation ceased. All eyes—some anxious, some expectant, others alive with the anticipation of the work to come—were on him.

"My friends, my good companions: We stand at the threshold of the greatest calamity mankind has ever experienced. The uneducated and ill-informed gather in mindless herds, ready to be pushed into oblivion by the traitorous politicians and philosophers among them. Shall we who have taken the name Preservers allow this to happen?"

The multitude of murmured "no"s that rose in response to his query were no less bone-chilling for the restraint with which they were ululated.

Skettle's jaws tightened. "Then let us go forth, comrades mine, and once and for all put a stop to this murderous collision course on which the betrayers of our own kind have set us." He smiled at them, and though he was quite unaware of it, it was a smile that would have set young children to running. "And while we are doing so, let us be sure to kill as many worthy people as possible while taking care to spare the visiting bugs."

This last bit of carefully concocted perfidy would serve to further heighten the suspicions of those humans who would rush to investigate the tragedy. There was delicious irony in the knowledge that the ones the Preservers most wanted to kill would, by surviving, serve to impair the cause of their own conciliators. Beskodnebwyl's coworkers would not be so lucky. Skettle had given his colleagues free rein to shoot down as many of them as they could as they made their way clear of the pandemonium. It was the ordinary, bewildered thranx they planned to spare—to suffer the suspicions and outrage of the surviving humans.

As his people began to file out of the room, individually and in pairs so as not to draw the attention of the hotel staff or anyone else to their departure, Skettle paused to glance out the window. Across the great lake, shimmering like a sheet of blue metal in the pellucid morning sunshine, the swooping, soaring structure of the fairgrounds could just be seen in the distance. By this evening, all of it would be in flames, cleansed and deserted, its name become tragedy spread by space-minus communications throughout the civilized portions of the Arm. Walking to the window, he picked up one of the two inauspicious-looking tanks of liquid explosive. Martine had already left with hers.

As the last one out of the conference room, he was careful to close the door behind him. He would make his own separate way to the fair. There he would pause for coffee and a quick meal, his attention on his own synchronized chronometer.

At exactly half past one, it would be time to start killing.

Nordelmatcen, one of the most able among the Bwyl, sidled up next to his clan leader and touched the latter's right antenna with one of his own. Beskodnebwyl turned immediately.

"I don't trust my own chronometer. How long until we induce permanent collapse into this vile burrow?"

Around them, blissfully ignorant humans and thranx alike promenaded to and fro throughout the fairgrounds. They had no reason to glance in the direction of the three thranx who were quietly scrutinizing an exhibition of art especially prepared for the fair by creative talents of both species working in tandem. Nordelmatcen had taken one look at the prancing abominations and dismissed them as obscene. Beskodnebwyl was too indifferent to be similarly enticed.

Had any curious passersby paused to stare in their direction, they might have wondered at the extra layers of external sheathing that enclosed the trio of insectoid males. Given the subtropical climate of the region in which Aurora had been founded, these wrappings might have struck even another thranx as excessive. Closer inspection, had it been allowed, would have revealed that the innermost layer of covering consisted not of finely machined fabric from Drax IV or special lightweight abdominal insulation from the *sythmills* of Amropolus, but of self-propelled explosives and kindred virulent mechanisms.

"Patience," Beskodnebwyl lectured his companions. "The time for dispensing annihilation will come soon enough."

Deimovjenbir whistled his displeasure. "I would have preferred that we proceed with our intended business on our own, without having to rely on, of all things, a group of contemptible if like-minded humans."

Beskodnebwyl gestured to emphasize lofty thoughts. "But it is the fact that they are like-minded that compels us to restrain ourselves. If we can make use of some of the soft ones to triple the amount of chaos we can create, should we not do so?"

"I did not say that." With a series of deep clicks, Deimovjenbir mimicked a disapproving human grumble.

"The humans of Skettle—I have still not been able to decide if that is properly a family or clan designation—are convinced they are making use of us. We feel the opposite is true. None of which matters. What is important is the result. It doesn't matter if the humans blame the thranx or the thranx blame the humans. What is meaningful is that blame is ascribed." He gestured with a truhand. "Are you ready to kill some artists?"

"I am ready to kill anything that thinks it controls the destiny of my hive. Artist, worker, prognosticator, musician, scientist—occupation is unimportant. What matters is that we stop this unclean mixing before it has a chance to fuse." Reaching back with a foothand, he caressed a brace of the self-propelled explosives that were bound to his abdomen. "I am anxious to spread the flowers of destruction."

"Soon." Beskodnebwyl checked his own chronometer. "Within the current major time-part." Slipping a foothand into a thorax pouch, he removed a communicator. Holding it in all four fingers, he used a truhand to activate the compact device. "Time to make certain everyone else is in position." Addressing the pickup softly, he called to the team of Vedburankex and Hynwupletmer.

There was no answer.

He tried again, with the same result. Nordelmatcen's attention was still concentrated on the swirling, cheerful crowd. "Trouble with their units. Perhaps they are in a location that restricts short-range, closed-beam communications. Try Yiwespembor and Cuwenarfot."

Beskodnebwyl did so, to another nonresponse. "Possibly there is something wrong with my unit." He extended a truhand. "Let me have yours."

Nordelmatcen obediently passed over his own communicator. Beskodnebwyl first tried Vedburankex and Hynwupletmur again, only to be rewarded with the same pensive electronic silence. It was the same for Yiwespembor and Cuwenarfot, who were supposed to be milling about among the largest of the eating pavilions that had been built out into the shallows of the lake. If they were in position, as they ought to already have been for several time-parts, there should be nothing around to interfere with the receptiveness of their communicators.

Growing increasingly concerned, Beskodnebwyl proceeded to try to contact every one of the widely scattered armed teams. It quickly became apparent that the rest of the Bwyl either could not or would not respond. As for the possibility that Nordelmatcen's as well as his own communicator was defective, that was a likelihood so unreasonable as to be beneath consideration. Designed to take a lot of mistreatment, field communicators simply did not fail. The thought that two could falter in such close proximity to one another was not to be believed. Beskodnebwyl did not even bother to try Deimovjenbir's unit.

They were standing on a raised platform that wound its way through the interspecies exhibition of art. While it was conceivable that some of the larger sculptures might block communication to and from the east, there was nothing to divert beams being broadcast in the other three directions. Searching for an explanation, Beskodnebwyl could conceive of none.

Then Nordelmatcen was striving to suppress an instinctive stridulation as he tapped his mentor on the thorax and pointed sharply.

Beskodnebwyl recognized the strike team that was walking rapidly toward the art exhibit. They had just appeared inside one of the entrances on the far side of the pavilion. Sujbirwencex and Waspulnatun were look-ing around more than was necessary, and their antennae were positively dancing. There appeared to be nothing wrong with them, either physically or mentally. For the first time since he had started scanning, Beskodneb-wyl received an acknowledgment in response to his query signal.

He was about to ask if the recently arrived team members were having similar difficulties contacting other members of the group when Sujbir-wencex and Waspulnatun were abruptly swarmed by a collapsing ring of humans and thranx. Shocked by the swiftness of the maneuver, Beskod-nebwyl could only stare, one finger still on the *send* contact of his commu-nicator. It was as if a portion of the milling crowd had collapsed on top of the stunned pair. Neither had a chance to fire a shot in their own defense, or even unlimber one of the many weapons they carried. One time-part frac-tion they had been making straight for Beskodnebwyl and Nordelmatcen; the next, both were in custody and in the process of being disarmed.

Deimovjenbir benefited from a slightly different perspective on the calamity. "Sujbirwencex and Waspulnatun have both been immobilized. Whether by fume, shock, or other means I cannot say, but both are now lying on their sides and offering no resistance."

Beskodnebwyl's colleague was not quite right. As the three dismayed thranx looked on, Sujbirwencex managed to wrest free a small hand weapon not yet confiscated by her attackers. She was immediately swarmed, but not before she succeeded in getting off at least one shot. A few nearby wanderers looked on in shock as the explosive shell blew one human patroller in half. In response, the downed Sujbirwencex received half a dozen blasts of varying intensity from at least three different kinds of weapons. The ferocious counterattack left little behind suitable for future identification.

From the brief but lethal confrontation nary a sound was heard.

"Silencing sphere," Nordelmatcen clicked unnecessarily. Whoever had ambushed the two Bwyl carried equipment to ensure that whatever else resulted from any confrontations and challenges, crowd panic would not be among them. The throng of sightseers had been effectively and efficiently shielded from the unsettling sounds of violent verbal and phys-ical combat. One human and one Bwyl lay dead on the pavilion floor, but only those visitors who had been close enough to observe the challenge directly had any inkling that anything untoward had taken place in their midst. It was all very slick and masterful. The actions of the ambushers smacked of extensive training and ample rehearsal.

They suggested, inescapably, the participation of skilled profes-sionals.

Deimovjenbir moved to discard his unnecessary outer garb, the better to access his firepower. "We have been betrayed! The burrow where we have stored our secrets has been breached!"

"No." Though he disagreed with his clan mate's appraisal of the situation, Beskodnebwyl was also scrambling to unlimber his weapons. "The Skettle folk would not do that. Revealing us would gain them nothing, since the first Bwyl to be captured would immediately expose them in turn."

Deimovjenbir almost had the streamlined launcher free and ready to lock in position on Nordelmatcen's back, where it could be clipped firmly to the other thranx's wing cases to provide an excellent mobile firing platform.

"But someone *has* delivered us up to the Dawn authorities. I cannot envision who. Somehow, somewhere, there must have been a fault in our planning. We will locate it, however."

"*Srrillp!* Yes we will!" Nordelmatcen avowed. He was fully alert now, alive with anticipation as he prepared to join his honored mentor in blowing the adulterated physical arts pavilion to splinters. "There is no reason to wait any longer to begin what we came for."

"No, *crr!!t!*" Deimovjenbir slipped a compressed charge into the launcher now resting securely on his colleague's back.

He was preparing to activate the firing sequence when a pair of very small shells composed almost entirely of radioactively neutral depleted uranium passed through his head, entering via the left compound eye and exiting at the back of the skull. Barely slowed by the organic contact, they continued onward to pierce the wall of the pavilion and eventually fall harmlessly into the lake. Slowly, the four trulegs of the Bwyl gave way in response to an absence of instructions from their controlling cerebrum, and the gleaming blue-green body slumped to the floor. The extended truhand never came closer than half a meter to the firing mechanism of the launcher fixed to Nordelmatcen's back.

Emitting the sharpest, most piercing whistle of which he was capable, Nordelmatcen sprang forward on all four trulegs, firing a pair of hand weapons as he leaped. Undeadened by a silencing sphere, the racket his firearms made was as loud as the death of his friend and colleague had been comparatively silent. Humans scattered and let out satisfying screams. Less prone to panic, adult and adolescent thranx nonetheless broke out in alarmed clicks and stridulations, adding to the general confusion. Meanwhile, Beskodnebwyl used the diversion to force his way in the opposite direction, finding a path through the forest of sculptures. Human, thranx, and jointly conceived alike, the towering works of art seemed to be leering down at him. Or worse, laughing.

The ensuing uproar lasted less than a couple of minutes. Firing madly, Nordelmatcen brought down one human and one thranx patroller before he was obliterated in a hail of gunfire as lethal as it was diverse. Alert for any surprises, such as booby-trapped internal organs, plain-clothes police surrounded the shattered remnants of the insectoid terror-ist. One kicked at the badly burned head, which had been separated from the rest of the body.

"Stupid bug—pardon, thranx—bastard. What are they trying to accomplish with all this?"

His female companion made a disgusted sound in her throat, behind her face shield. "We'll know when the psychs get to the live ones and their human cronies who've already been taken into custody." Raising her gaze, she stared hard at the raised walkway from which the dead thranx had leaped. "There's another dead one up there. I thought I saw three."

Her comrade pushed at the back of his slightly too-tight helmet. "Dunno. Must've just been the two. We've been mostly picking 'em up in twos."

"I guess you're right." It was her turn to nudge the black-streaked insectoid head with a booted foot. "Funny how the color drains out of the eyes when they die. Their equivalent of a human closing her lids, I guess."

Her fellow officer shrugged. "Dead is dead. Me, I leave the dirty details to the biologists." He brightened slightly. "Hey, you ought to join me and Vermenyarkex one night."

"Why? Is there such a thing as a thranx strip club?" she replied dryly.

"I wouldn't know." Her partner looked hurt. "He said something about sharing some special hi-ups that work equally well on both our metabolisms."

"Oh, that's different, then." Holstering her pistol in its hidden com-partment inside her casual tropical blouse, she turned to rejoin the rest of the covert patrol. "Let's make sure we've got the rest of this mess cleaned up, first."

Lawlor and Rabukanu were getting nervous. Everything had gone according to plan: their arrival at the fair, the gradual dispersal of the group, the casual stroll to their assigned position. No one had contested their entrance or challenged their presence. Uniformed security personnel had ignored them, treating them like any other visitors. They had fol-lowed a memorized, circuitous route to the Pavilion of Cooperative Sci-ence and remained there, wandering through and about the exhibits until they were as sick of each and every one as they were of the unrestrained fraternizing of thranx and human tourists. Still, they waited. And waited.

They continued to wait, but with a growing sense of unease long months of training could no longer dispel. Around them, the crowds thickened. There was no indication anything was amiss at the fair.

Then Rabukanu frowned and pointed. "Isn't that Botha and Marion?"

Lawlor strained to see past a drifting tactile holo that was entertaining a clutch of delighted, laughing children. A pair of adolescent thranx, their blue-green exoskeletons jewel-like with the freshness of recent emergence from pupahood, looked on in silence, striving to puzzle out the attraction the yellow-and-pink electronic apparition held for their human counterparts.

A well-dressed—indeed, overdressed—middle-aged couple had just entered the far side of this quadrant of the extensive pavilion. Their constant glancing to right and left betrayed no ulterior motives: Striving to see everything at once was a common affliction among fairgoers. Then Marion happened to meet Lawlor's distant glance. Despite the range, she stared fixedly in his direction, as if trying to impart a question through sheer force of expression.

"It's them, for sure." Lawlor blinked. "What are they doing in here? They're supposed to be working the health and gengineering displays."

"She looks confused." At a distance, Rabukanu's eyesight was slightly sharper than that of his companion. "Maybe you were right when you wondered a few minutes ago if something's gone wrong."

"What about Botha?" After Skettle, the engineer was the most admired member of the group.

Rabukanu fought to see through the noisy, milling throng. "Hard to say. He never looks confused."

"Well, something must be up for them to vacate their position." Lawlor checked his timer. "Elkannah's late."

The other man did not bother to corroborate. "There's still plenty of time. More accurate to say that he's not early. Maybe he and Martine had to take a more roundabout route to the communications center. Maybe they were delayed. It's plenty early. Relax."

"Yar, surely I'll relax." Beneath his lightweight tropical jacket, strips of explosive material vied for room with a brace of exceedingly stylized pistols. The pockets of his pants held handfuls of tacnites. He forbore from sarcastically pointing out to his companion that neither of them had come dressed for leisure. "What are they doing?"

"Still coming this way." The more laid-back Rabukanu shrugged. "Maybe they just want to kill a few minutes." He wore the unpleasant, sadistic smile of a schoolteacher who enjoys humiliating his students. "As opposed to bugs. Or maybe something's rendered their assigned position untenable. You know that if that happens we're supposed to join up and share locations. A number of possible developments might have forced them to make a move."

Lawlor scanned the eddying herd of sightseers. "Yar, you're right." He could not repress another quick glance at his timer. "I just wish Elkannah would do the communications facilities so we can get to work."

"Itchy to lay down a little arson?" Rabukanu's smile vanished. "Me, too. Know what a fried bug smells like?"

Lawlor did not reply. Rabukanu had an irritating tendency to repeat himself. It was an old joke among the group, and he didn't need any distractions right now. Instead, he focused on their approaching collaborators, still wondering what had driven them to abandon their assigned location. Rabukanu's appraisal of the situation had been reassuring, but a lingering concern continued to nag at him.

It all happened so fast he hardly had time to react. One minute, their compatriots were strolling toward them; the next, they had been smothered by more than a dozen tourists. Men, women, even a couple of teenage girls. Except they were not tourists. Coagulating restraints glued Marion's fingers together and her hands to her sides, rendering her immediately helpless. Botha managed to retreat a couple of steps before a shaped shot of soporific mist splashed his wide-eyed face. One sniff, and he collapsed like a broken doll. Moving with far more athletic grace and digital dexterity than any dozen tourists could muster, the party of plainclothes agents wrapped up the two terrorists as efficiently as a swarm of communal arachnids enwebbing a trapped moth.

Lawlor stood frozen where he had been standing. "How did they know? *How did they know?*"

Once more it was left to the sharp-eyed Rabukanu to explain what was happening. "Weapons sensors. I think I can see the bulge of one under one woman's jacket." He smiled faintly. "I thought she was awfully well equipped, but I had no clue. Funny—if we were all carrying nothing but the components of the explosives, the sensor probably wouldn't pick anything up. Elkannah erred on that one."

Lawlor found himself disagreeing as he reached inside his shirt and brought out the three-thirds of an explosive whole. "We can't wait for him and Martine anymore. We can't wait for anyone." His eyes were blazing in advance of the fires he was preparing to set.

His companion looked at him in alarm. "Hey, we can't start anything on our own! You know the rules. In the event of a general breakdown in planning, we're supposed to dispose of our materials and make our way out of here and offworld, so we can strike again later somewhere else."

"Distractions of evil. Suck bug blood!" Lawlor was backing away from his colleague. "I didn't spend a year busting my brain and my butt in training just to walk away from this." Pressing the three sections of the explosive components together, he slapped the resultant compaction against a nearby pillar and doused it with catalytic fluid. The three-centimeter square instantly began emitting smoke. Reaching inside his jacket, he used one hand to draw a pistol while the other fumbled frantically for more squares. While his words had been frenzied, his expression fully reflected his inner zealotry. Catching sight of the pistol, nearby visitors screamed and ducked or ran for cover.

With a curse, Rabukanu saw that several of the agents who had taken Botha and Marion down were now looking in his direction, pointing and jabbering excitedly. They'd probably already recorded his image, he thought helplessly. For better or worse, the decision to *act* had been made. He hoped Skettle would not be too upset. Maybe it would turn out to be a good thing. Time *was* running.

As the wild-eyed Lawlor stumbled away from him, Rabukanu started digging for his own carefully stored essentials. If they could just set off one or more detonations, they might have a chance to slip away unscathed in the ensuing turmoil. Already, there were indications of general panic among those tourists who were close enough to see what was happening.

The catalyst would take several minutes to fully bind the tripartite ingredients into an explosive whole. The delay was intended to allow those planting the devices enough time to escape the blast zone, but not enough for possible searchers to find the weapon.

If only, Rabukanu thought as he prepared a second explosive patch, Skettle could take out the central communications facilities, the general chaos and destruction they had come to Dawn to wreak would manifest itself fully, to the greater glory and preservation of an unadulterated humankind. Fired with the devotion that had led him to give his life to Elkannah Skettle and to the Preservers, he prepared to apply the explosive patch to an exterior wall of the pavilion. Around him, humans and a few thranx continued to scatter. Their screams and stridulations melted together into a dull ache at the back of his mind.

As if from far away, he heard Lawlor alternately howling defiance at the onrushing agents and spewing frantic warnings into his communicator. Probably trying to alert the others, Rabukanu knew. The crisp electric *spang* of the other man's pistol going off penetrated the general tumult like a sore-throated trumpet criticizing a balm of violins. Then he smelled something sweet as chocolate and stifling as a pillow. Reaching for a single tacnite, he managed to drag a stiffening thumb down the short length of the electronic trigger.

The powerful little grenade was still clutched firmly in his fingers when it went off.

As Lawlor's crazed, bloodthirsty alert was received by those of his fellow Preservers who were still at large, they quickly came to the shocked realization that their purpose and presence had somehow been exposed to the authorities. One couple was taken into custody even as they were preoccupied with listening to the broadcast. Another pair were debating whether to try to flee the grounds or proceed with their assignment when they were enveloped by a sphere of silence and a strong dose of the same immobilizing gas that had toppled their comrade Rabukanu.

Several, however, were able to set in motion fire and destruction, albeit on a greatly degraded scale. Having heavily infiltrated the fairgrounds in response to the padres' advance warning, well-prepared local police equipped with sensitive weapons sensors were able to pounce on the perpetrators even before they could reveal themselves. Those few disturbances that did occur were localized, explosive appliqués that were neutralized before they could go off, and there was no widespread panic among the fair-goers. In the midst of rounding up the last of the terrorists and their even more baffled thranx counterparts the Bwyl, fair business proceeded as usual.

Beskodnebwyl's two companions had reacted sharply to the approach of the human and thranx agents. In the ensuing firefight, both had been slain before they could make use of the heavy explosives they were carrying. The consequent confusion had opened an almost imperceptible escape route for Beskodnebwyl, who had seized upon it the instant it had revealed itself.

Now he found himself staggering through a service corridor, surrounded by the portentous hum of machinery, bleeding green from one side. Both his left truarm and foothand had been shot off, and he had only barely been able to slap a brace of traumagulents over the gushing injuries, followed by strips of self-adhering surgical chitin. Much more running threatened to reopen the life-threatening wounds. If he was not to bleed to death, he needed to seek medical attention soon.

Not a problem, he told himself sardonically as he skittered along down the dark, conduit-strewn tunnel. He found comfort in its shadowy confines, a reminder of more congenial burrows back home. All he had to do was present himself at the nearest medical facility in Dawn, and they would fix him up. Him, a thranx, obviously damaged by weaponry, on a day when the most important public activity on the planet had been rent by a fusillade of gunfire. Not a problem at all.

It was over, all over. Everything he and the rest of the Bwyl had worked so long and hard to achieve. Finished. When the mostly human authorities had begun taking his compeers into custody, he had at first been bewildered, then frustrated. That had long since given way to anger. Though the Bwyl's human counterparts were also being killed or captured, it was clear that somehow, the local authorities had been alerted to their mutual presence and intent. Who would do such a thing, and why? Not one of the Bwyl. There were no traitors among his dedicated, adoptive clan.

No, *crr!!k,* it had to be someone with a thorough knowledge of the overall strategy, someone who had access to both the Preservers and the Protectors as well as the authorities. Someone who could be sure of a favorable, even laudatory reception among the species traitors on both sides. Who? Who had not yet been slain, or captured? Who had the wherewithal to call forth such a general alert, and to possibly profit from it?

Skettle.

His now-deceased companions had been right to challenge his initial disbelief. Weakened but resolved, Beskodnebwyl of the Bwyl knew he had one last duty to carry out before he could begin to devote any time to the admittedly increasingly remote possibility of preserving his own life.

18

In the short time people had spent on Comagrave, much progress had been made in deciphering the elegant, elaborately ideographic Sauun script, though much remained to be done before complex thoughts could be translated in detail. The discovery of the gigantic mausoleum offered up thousands of new inscriptions for study. Meanwhile, researchers utilizing the camp's two smallest aircars undertook to carry out a preliminary census of the silent sleepers. Preparing a simple mathematical model based on dimensions and density observed within one sizable portion of the crypt, they came up with an initial figure of between two and five billions. If not the entire planetary population at the time of final suspension, it was certainly a substantial portion of the total. And over every new discovery, over each new revelation, hung one single foreboding, dominating question.

Why?

Though he had been nominated to lead the expedition and oversee the excavation because of his organizational and leadership skills, Cullen Karasi was also a formidable analyst. Poring over raw data, dissecting and repositioning with the aid of several exoarcheoanalytical programs he had helped develop himself, he felt the key to the mystery of the mass Sauun deepsleep was not nearly as problematic as initially believed. Given sufficient time in which to work, he was confident he would have solved it already. But the need to supervise everyone else's labor slowed his own efforts significantly. He felt like a sprinter forced to muddle along in the middle of the pack during an especially dull marathon.

Even so, he was close to the answer. He knew it.

So when Riimadu volunteered the unpaid assistance of a professional, well-trained crew of excavators, Cullen jumped at the offer.

Though some of his own people expressed hesitation at allowing the AAnn an intimate look at the work in progress, Riimadu assured them that the crew would operate entirely under human supervision and would strictly follow camp regulations. Furthermore, they would do no work on their own or without first obtaining human authorization. Besides which, there were only four of them. Eager to make as much progress as possible as quickly as possible, the humans' initial uncertainty quickly vanished when they had the chance to observe the AAnn team in operation.

As for Pilwondepat's vociferous objections to the presence of still more AAnn at the site, these were dismissed as without foundation. "I'd be just as happy to have four, or forty, trained thranx assisting here, if they were made available and were willing to work under the same guidelines," Cullen told him. Needless to say, the thranx exoarcheologist was less than delighted with this response, but there was nothing more he could do.

With the aid of the skilled AAnn, exploration proceeded apace. Results were passed along on a regular schedule to planetary administrative headquarters. There they were compiled for forwarding to the specific Terran institutions that were supporting the dig. Everything was going so smoothly that when Cullen's people began to fall sick around him, coughing and breaking out in red blotches on their faces and upper bodies, he was particularly anguished. The more everyone else's work suffered, the more it slowed his own.

Bhasiram, the camp physician, diagnosed the rapidly spreading contagion as an upper respiratory disease caused by exceedingly fine spores arising from the excavation. Dust masks were of no use. Nothing in her arsenal of antibiotics had any effect on the condition, which one camp wag christened "Sauunusitus." While not fatal, it was exceedingly debilitating and beyond the frustrated Bhasiram's ability to cure. Hospitalization was required to restore the strength of the afflicted. Pilwondepat and the AAnn were not affected.

It was clear that work at the dig could not go on until a cure, or at least a suitable prophylactic, was found for the spores. Working in sealed masks and breathing canned air was a possibility, but the necessary equipment was not available on Comagrave and would have to be imported. Neither solution was satisfactory. It was therefore proposed that the AAnn, who were by now familiar with the site, would remain to maintain it without in any way advancing the work until their human supervisors could safely return. Though they expressed sorrow at the need for the humans to temporarily leave the dig, the AAnn agreed to care for it in their transitory absence. Riimadu CRRYNN would stay behind to oversee. In the absence of any immediate availability of human vehicles, the AAnn also thoughtfully offered to bring in several of their largest cargo carriers to ferry the afflicted and their as-yet-uninfected companions on the long journey back to Comabraeth.

As soon as he got wind of the proposal, Pilwondepat stormed into Cullen's quarters. It required a considerable effort on the thranx's part not to stridulate wildly as he entered. Even so, with antennae waving and mandibles clacking, he still presented a highly agitated figure. An insectophobe would have been intimidated. The head of the excavation team was not.

"Something I can do for you, Pilwondepat?" Cullen inquired pleasantly. Though he had not yet succumbed to the insidious spores, the noticeable splotch of scarlet that marred his left cheek was not a blush.

"Do for me? Do for me! *Crllhht!*" The need to speak in Terranglo forced the insectoid exoarcheologist to keep his thoughts as well as his words under control. "I can't believe you are going to turn this unprecedented scientific discovery over to the AAnn!"

"We are not turning over anything to the AAnn." Having previously experienced the thranx's ire, Cullen was not disturbed by Pilwondepat's latest outburst. The supervisor knew it was merely the latest in a long series of attempts to freeze Riimadu out of the ongoing research. "Since arriving to assist us, they have conducted themselves in an exemplary manner. They've done exactly as they were told, and no more. Would that I had another dozen humans on staff who took instructions as well."

"That is precisely my point." Antennae whipped forward. "Don't you remember any of our discussions? Have you forgotten all that I've told you about AAnn methodology and technique? They rely foremost on cunning, and deception." Both antennae straightened. "It's patent they have certainly deceived you."

Cullen's civility gave way to annoyance. "Until and unless they act in a nonprofessional manner, neither I nor any of my people have any quarrel with them." He continued packing away his personal effects. These would remain behind until he returned from Comabraeth, properly equipped to work among the drifting spores. "Other than academically, I'm not interested in the personal animosities that endure between your people and Riimadu's. You're both of you here thanks to the magnanimity of the local government." Setting aside a container of clothing, he added pointedly, "That permission can be withdrawn at any time."

Pilwondepat brushed off the quiet threat. "Would you say that infecting you and every member of your team with imported bacteria designed to drive you away from the site constituted acting in a nonprofessional manner?"

Cullen gaped. "You're joking, aren't you?"

"Do I sound like I am jesting? Do I look like I am jesting?"

"I wouldn't know, not being versed in the more subtle overtones of thranx enunciation and gesture. You can't be serious, Pilwondepat."

The thranx exoarcheologist raised all four of his vestigial wing cases. Another thranx would have recognized the action as expressive of the absolute utmost seriousness. To Cullen, it was unfortunately only interesting from a morphological point of view.

"Do you really think I would joke about such a thing? What has happened here, to this expedition, fits with all that I have been telling you for many time-parts. The AAnn want your kind off this world. To accomplish that they are willing to do anything and everything to obstruct, inhibit, and damage your efforts here. Even, should it prove necessary, to kill. These incidents are disguised, with typical AAnn cunning and thoroughness, as accidents. When they occur, the AAnn are always right there ready to assist in any way they can." He paused, clicking all four mandibles for effect.

"Consider, Cullen: You make a great discovery here. Word of what you have found begins to leak out. Following the breakthrough and initial follow-up, your crew begins to come down with a previously undetected ailment. Only nonhumans are resistant. How convenient for the AAnn."

"We're not abandoning the site," the human reminded his visitor. "Our departure is only temporary, until suitable protection can be secured against the vector of infection." He continued with his packing, wishing the thranx would leave but unwilling to order him out. Let him rant, the exoarcheologist mused. Soon enough he'll run down and depart of his own accord.

" 'Temporary,' *z!!lnn!* While you are absent from this place, the AAnn will go through it with an intensity they have so far barely managed to hold in check. Anything of significance that they find, they will keep to themselves. Most likely they have prepared other surprises, to keep you away from specific areas below or even from the surface itself, until they have accomplished all that they wish. Leave now, and your absence from the site will be as 'temporary' as the AAnn desire."

Unable to stand it any longer, Cullen put his packing aside and turned to confront the agitated thranx. "Look, you've been bugging me"—the choice of verb was inadvertent on the exoarcheologist's part—"with your AAnn conspiracy theories for weeks now. I said I would convey your concerns and your 'findings' to the proper authorities for further study, and that I'll do. But as for myself, I'm sick and tired of it, understand? From now on, you keep your suspicions and your racial enmity to yourself." He grunted testily. "As if I didn't have enough to worry about."

"They'll drive you off the planet." Pilwondepat gestured desperately with all four hands. "This is only one more in a long succession of incidents cleverly designed by them with that end in mind. You must resist! And you must not give them free and unsupervised access to this site. It is simply too significant."

"And you are simply too paranoid." Fed up, Cullen turned his back on the distraught alien. Among the thranx, he knew, the gesture was even more final a form of dismissal than it was among humans.

Remarkably, Pilwondepat persisted. "Then you will not order an end to the evacuation, or at least assign a few of your healthiest people to remain until the rest can return?"

"Absolutely not." Resuming his packing, Cullen did not look back at the thranx. "I won't trifle with the health of my staff, and I have confidence in Riimadu. You forget that I've worked with him even longer than I have worked with you."

"Very well. I understand your position. I will trouble you about this matter no more."

When he finally looked around, Cullen saw that the thranx had left. It was sad, he reflected, that two such admirable species as the thranx and the AAnn could not settle such long-standing differences. That could not be allowed to affect either human-thranx or human-AAnn relations, he knew. " 'Drive humans off the planet.' " The exoarcheologist might not be politically sophisticated, but he could recognize blatant propaganda when he heard it. He also knew what the insectoid's most recent visit was really all about.

Pilwondepat was afraid to remain behind in the company of five AAnn. That fear, at least, was one that Cullen could accept. The thranx was welcome to join the humans in their evacuation to Comabraeth. It would give the insectoid exoarcheologist time to collate his own research.

All the rest of that day and into the night, Pilwondepat agonized over how to proceed. The AAnn and their transports would arrive tomorrow morning. What, after all, could he do to affect things in the limited time that remained? He was but one of the family Won set down among many humans and AAnn. If the leader of the humans would not listen to him, it did not matter if anyone else did. He could envision Riimadu, grinning contentedly, his sharp carnivore's teeth glinting in the bright light of his quarters as he finalized strategy with his quartet of "well-trained" colleagues. Who among them had brought along and introduced the carefully cultivated spores into the excavation, there to fester and multiply and spread until the unsuspecting mammals were infected? What vital, important secrets had Riimadu inventoried that were to be accrued to the

AAnn alone as soon as the overseeing humans had been evacuated? Isolated in his quarters, Pilwondepat sensed threat and smelled danger.

Very well—he was alone. Like a solitary male of ancient days, soaring high on his single glorious but brief mating flight, he would have to act. If he did not, others would, and his flight would be wasted. In response to a muted mandibular click, a chronometer appeared briefly before him in the hot, humid air of the room. He considered his options.

There was still time.

Along with everyone else in the camp except the seriously ailing, he was up early the following morning. Despite a lack of sleep due to undertaking the task he had set himself, he was alert and observant. He would sleep later, he knew. Sleep soundly.

Activity was picking up throughout the site as the evacuation gathered steam. Those too ill to walk were being assembled beneath a temporary field canopy that had been erected to protect them from the wind and the sun. Nonmedical personnel not assisting with the infirm were stacking individual baggage next to the landing area's service shed. These were minimal, since everyone fully expected to return to work as soon as an appropriate treatment for the mysterious ailment was devised. No one would bother personal effects left in the camp. Not out in the middle of a place that ranked as nowhere even for a world as sparsely populated as Comagrave.

Pilwondepat took in all the activity, occasionally pausing to converse briefly with members of the staff he knew. He tried not to envision the dig where he and everyone else had worked so hard to make the great discovery overrun with gimlet-eyed AAnn.

He found Cullen Karasi in his quarters, packing a small travel bag with the trivialities that humans seemed to deem necessary for even short-term travel. Idly, he wasted a couple of moments attempting to identify the unfamiliar. The function of many of the devices was known to him by now. His time spent among the mammals had expanded his education.

"I came to ask you one last time to change your mind, *cirraat*."

The supervisor glanced back and down at the hovering thranx. "Listen, I'm sorry about the tone I used with you yesterday, Pilwondepat. I was tired, and frustrated, and yes, angry. But not at you. At having to leave this place just when I feel I'm on the verge of answering the biggest question of them all."

"Why the Sauun sealed themselves away the way they did."

Cullen nodded. "I'll lay out my hypothesis for you when we're back in Comabraeth. I think you'll find it interesting." His thoughts wandered to distant visions of academic glory and professional acclaim. "I promise that everyone will find it interesting. But there's no time now. According to Riimadu, the AAnn transports will be here any minute."

" 'According to Riimadu.' I'm not going back to Comabraeth, Cullen."

Curious, the senior exoarcheologist frowned at his visitor. "You're not? I know that, to all intents and purposes and everything the medical people have been able to determine, your kind is immune to this infection. And I can understand your not wanting to leave your work if you don't have to. But I don't see you being very comfortable staying here among Riimadu and the rest of the AAnn conservation staff."

"You're correct. I would not be comfortable. But neither am I going to the settlement." Without hurry, he reached back into the pouch slung against his abdomen. "Nor are you."

Cullen Karasi was not a man easily startled. He had spent too much time on other worlds, working and surviving in alien environments, to be surprised by much of anything. The gun that had appeared in the thranx exoarcheologist's right truhand surprised him. No, he corrected himself. It astonished him.

He was too dumbfounded to be frightened. "So that is what happens when a thranx loses its mind. Very interesting. My first observation is that your people go about slipping into the pool of insanity more peacefully than do mine."

"I am not psychotic. I was awake all last night, and though tired, I assure you I am in complete command of my mental and physical faculties. Would, *sevvakk,* that it were otherwise."

Placing his hands on his hips and tilting his head slightly to one side, the unruffled scientist regarded his weapon-wielding caller. "What do you intend to do with that firearm? It is a firearm, I presume, and not an ingredient in some eccentric thranx ritual of which I am unaware?"

A steady thrumming noise was now audible off to the east. It grew steadily louder, heralding its approach with a deep, mechanical hum. Gazing past his deranged visitant, Cullen tried to see out the partially open doorway to the distant landing site.

"That's our transportation arriving. Go or stay, I don't care, but make up your mind. And put down that silly gun. I know everyone carries something when they travel outside camp boundaries to protect themselves in the unlikely but possible event of attack by one of the local inimical life-forms, but it hardly becomes your academic standing."

"I'm staying." Mandibles closed, and a soft whistle emerged from between flinty insectoid jaws. "So are you. Everyone is staying."

Cullen inhaled deeply. "You realize that after this, there's no way I can in good conscience recommend extending your permit to work here?"

"Of course I understand. If our situations were reversed, I should act in exactly the same fashion." The thrum of heavy transports now permeated the walls and floor of the prefabricated structure. "The point is, as you humans are fond of saying, moot." He repeated the word, savoring it. "Moot." With a small *c!k* on the end, it could almost be a word in Low Thranx. "It is moot because of the pending AAnn attack on your camp here."

Cullen's pitying aloofness quickly gave ground to sudden anxiety. "What kind of nonsense are you talking? What AAnn attack? The AAnn are here to help us travel to Comabraeth. Why on Earth or any other world of your choosing would they want to attack an inoffensive, non-strategic scientific site?"

Pilwondepat waved the gun with disarming indifference as to his surroundings. "Why indeed? I am certain that very question is going to puzzle many who will try to rationalize what is going to happen here. It would be interesting to be able to examine some of the explanations. Unfortunately, that will in all likelihood not be possible."

The senior exoarcheologist's gaze narrowed sharply. "What do you mean, 'what *is* going to happen here'? What do you know?" Dawning realization began to transform his expression. Color drained from his face. "Good God, Pilwondepat—*what have you done?*"

The thranx gestured a first-degree expression of regret. It was heartfelt, and very lissomely executed. "I believe too strongly in the importance of this discovery to allow it to be turned over to the AAnn. I am convinced, without having to hear your nascent theory, that something on this world holds the key to matters of very great consequence. Too consequential to leave to the discretion of the scaled ones. Casting about for a means with which to ensure the continuation of the human presence on Comagrave and the possible expulsion of the AAnn, I find myself caught in a noteworthy irony: To secure both, I must make use of the techniques of the latter."

The explosion that punctuated the thranx scientist's somewhat cryptic explanation caused the shelter to shudder on its foundation. Cullen had to catch himself on a nearby cabinet to keep from stumbling as the earth heaved beneath him. Standing firm and foursquare on his quartet of trulegs, Pilwondepat experienced no such unsteadiness.

"That was satisfyingly loud," he murmured softly. "More substantial than I had hoped."

"What? What are you jabbering about?"

"The first AAnn cargo carrier attempting to set down at the camp's landing site has been fired upon by the site's occupants. A shocking and unprovoked attack. The AAnn will react instinctively. Among the AAnn, this takes the form not of query or discussion, but of returning fire immediately. Having been attacked in turn, your people will struggle as best they can to defend themselves. They will fail, of course." He spoke so casually, so diffidently, that he might have been relating a minor point of relic dating taken from a recent learned journal.

"The AAnn are used to and expect conflict. Your staff here is drawn from scholars and students, not soldiers. They will all be killed. The only chance the AAnn will have to explain away the frightful misadventure depends on there being no human survivors to contradict whatever feeble story they will strive to contrive." He gestured again with the gun, making Cullen flinch. "It doesn't matter. Whatever fiction they fabricate will not be believed by your people."

"How . . . ?" Cullen was struggling desperately to understand what was happening around him. The first explosion had been followed by a second of lesser magnitude, then a third. Shouts and screams in abundance could be heard echoing throughout the camp. "How can you be so sure of that? If we all die . . ."

"I programmed my own communications unit to transmit an alert via the camp's automatic relay. It contains a full explanation of the treacherous assault by the AAnn, which they have carried out under cover of evacuating innocent personnel to Comabraeth."

"What if they intercept it?" By now Cullen was too dazed to question anything but the abject reality he was experiencing.

"They can't intercept. The alert was programmed to send as soon as the AAnn transports were detected approaching. It has already gone out."

"Those explosions—can they really be firing on us?" Once more, the exoarcheologist tried to see out the door. Cries of confusion and despair filled the air outside with a general disharmony of desperation.

Pilwondepat's sensitive antennae had twisted about to focus directly behind him. "Not at first. They are now. I told you I did not sleep last night. The last two detonations you heard were simple excavation charges, creatively positioned and designed to go off subsequent to the first. That one required a good deal more effort to get right. Shaped disinterring charges are not intended to be retrofitted with proximity programming. It took several time-parts to modify the instrumentation to where I was reasonably certain it would operate properly.

"The first vehicle attempting to set down at the landing site activated the sensor attached to the charge. Though not as suitable as military munitions, I suspect that the ensuing blast destroyed or damaged the alighting AAnn cargo carrier and killed or seriously injured many if not all of its occupants. *Triillc,* I certainly hope so."

Wide-eyed now, but no longer with disbelief, Cullen started to push past his former colleague. "You *are* insane. You'd have everyone murdered, people you've come to know, people who have learned to trust and even like you, just because you want the AAnn off this world!"

"And humans to remain on it. Yes, that's the intention. There are matters of significance at stake here, Cullen."

"Well, it won't work." The furious supervisor was almost to the doorway. "There's still time to put a stop to this madness. I'm going to find Riimadu. Together, we'll get on the camp communicator and issue a statement on all frequencies explaining what has happened. With Riimadu translating, I'm sure we can make the rest of the AAnn understand."

"No, you won't." The muzzle of the gun in Pilwondepat's truhand shifted slightly to the right.

Cullen glared pityingly back at the ludicrous insectoid. "What are you going to do, Pilwondepat? Shoot me in the back?" He turned to exit the shelter.

"I could not do that. It goes against everything my hive stands for," the sorrowful scientist confessed. "But an AAnn would."

The very tiny shell made a very loud noise and a very large hole in the middle of the stunned supervisor's dorsal side, blowing a majority of his internal organs out through his flaring ribs. Pilwondepat did not have the opportunity to appraise the exoarcheologist's final expression because the biped toppled forward onto his front, facedown on the packed earth. No doubt his countenance was as fully convulsed as the wonderfully expressive human face could manage.

"Primitive things, explosives." Pilwondepat ambled past the wide splotch of spreading redness as he exited the shelter. "They have the useful virtue of being entirely non–species specific. As long as no identifying residue is left behind, it is credible that any idiot intelligence can assume responsibility for them going boom." In Low Thranx, this concluding sentiment emerged as a long, drawn-out whistle marked by a single intermediary sharp click.

"The AAnn are not the only sentients capable of cunning, Cullen. I did like you. Very much. You forgot that for my kind, the safety and security of the hive comes first. Even if it is not our hive, but one that is of potential importance to us. Say for example, *sr!iik,* the human hive." Dolefully, he ululated a final, forlorn whistle of farewell. "You might be willing to relinquish Comagrave to the care of the AAnn. We will not, I will not, the Great Hive will not let you. Not even at the cost of all our lives." Clutching the tiny but lethal firearm in both truhands, he inclined forward to place his foothands on the ground. Supported now by all six lower limbs, he exited the edifice and surveyed the rising panic outside. He did not look back at the body lying on the ground behind him. Unfortunately, the proper expiration formalities could not be observed on behalf of his late colleague. There was simply no time for lengthy lamentations. He regretted that, but knew he had no choice.

Not when there was an efficacious chaos in need of stoking.

For once, he was hardly noticed. Flames and smoke rose from the direction of the landing site. In crashing, the AAnn cargo carrier had evidently sparked fires among the assembled baggage and modest temporary buildings. Intended to advance the cause of science, the explosives he had spent the night modifying and setting into position had apparently performed better than expected in the service of conspiracy.

Nearby, the crashed and burning transport's two sister craft hovered ten meters off the ground. A few desultory bursts of gunfire issued from one, while the other was quiet. That would not do. Firing his weapon, he raced through the encampment yelling at the top of his voice. It was weak compared to the deeper intonations of humans. Clicks and whistles and stridulating would have reached much farther, but were incomprehensible to the bewildered mammals stumbling all around him.

"Defend yourselves! Shoot back—don't let them kill you all!" All the long hours practicing the difficult vowel sounds, the endless evenings spent listening to human conversation, now paid off in what ironically was likely to prove to be an elaborate and unrecognized epitaph. He could even manage the correct inflections, as was shown by the alacrity with which the humans he encountered responded to his shouts of alarm.

A number of those emerging from the camp's shelters were doing as he hoped without having to be prompted. As more and more small arms were brought into play, their combined firepower began to inflict real damage on the nearer of the two AAnn transports. Fired upon for what must have seemed to them to be no reason, the AAnn finally responded in traditional fashion. One after another, every camp structure was obliterated, though without the usual reptilian efficiency. They were still confused.

Then someone aboard one of the surviving transports, probably a senior military advisor, realized that the abrupt and unanticipated confrontation had passed a political point of no return. Humans had been slain, in numbers too large to explain away as the result of an accident. Having plunged too deeply into slaughter, the visitors now had no choice, as Pilwondepat had surmised, but to eliminate any possibility of contradiction in the hopes that a suitable postmortem explanation could be concocted by their military psych specialists.

The much-vaunted AAnn martial methodology was applied to the scientific camp. Moving off in different directions both to make a more difficult target for the humans below and to enhance their operative efficiency, the two transports positioned themselves to flank the camp and trap the remaining humans between their combined fire. Pilwondepat agonized as he watched one dazed but defiant human after another go down beneath the heavier firepower of the two cargo carriers. It was doubly hard for him to look on knowing that those who were sacrificing themselves for a greater cause had no inkling that they were doing so.

He continued to take cover where possible and fire his own weapon. The handgun could not bring down a vehicle as substantial as a cargo carrier, but with luck he might penetrate its lateral edge and kill an AAnn or two. Sprinting on all six legs from a large rounded boulder toward the still-standing communal eating building, he found himself suddenly face-to-face with one figure that was neither trying to flee nor fighting back. He slowed.

Slitted eyes flicked sideways in his direction, and the silky voice that had been hissing harshly into a handheld communicator turned on him. "You. *Fssst!* You have ssomething to do with thiss, thiss outrageouss happening. Thiss iss no accident, inssect!"

"We are all of us accidents in the sight of the cosmos, scaled one," Pilwondepat declared humbly as he raised his gun and shot the surprised AAnn exoarcheologist square between his glaring, accusing eyes. Peaceable soul that he was, the action gave Pilwondepat more satisfaction than anything else he had done that day. He did not wait for the body to hit the ground, but instead rushed toward the still-standing structure to further incite those inside.

Battles that begin in confusion often end the same way. So it was with the massacre at the camp. Without knowing exactly what had happened, the AAnn found themselves presiding over a scene of complete devastation. One of their own craft had been destroyed, and many of its crew killed or seriously injured. A second transport was severely damaged but still capable of flight, albeit at a greatly reduced speed. The deceitful humans had perished to the last, males and females alike. So had the Empire's sole representative in the camp, who had he survived might have been able to shed some light on what was becoming an increasingly disturbing and impenetrable conundrum. There was also one dead bug, to whom the AAnn paid no attention.

Precisely why this had all taken place, in the space of less than an hour, no one on the surviving AAnn craft could say. Hasty tight-beam communications were exchanged with the AAnn consulate in

Comabraeth. A frantic exchange of appalled questions and choleric recriminations followed. Presented with a horrific fait accompli, the ranking AAnn determined to contrive an elaborate explanation for the tragedy that had devastated the human scientific outpost. This involved the rapidly spreading disease to which many of the humans had previously succumbed, consequent nervous disorders, a few cases of isolated madness and paranoia, followed by something akin to mass hysteria.

Intruding with the best of intentions onto this psychochaos, the neighborly AAnn had found many humans already dead at the hands of their fellows. Coming under relentless and inexplicable attack, they had been forced to defend themselves with no more than a minimal amount of firepower. Meanwhile, the crazed humans had continued to go on about killing one another, much to the anguish of the observing AAnn, who were powerless to stop the disease-induced madness.

An improbable story, it was the best the AAnn tacticians could devise while operating under the press of time. It was not, however, inconceivable. Lending support to the elaborate fabrication was the self-evident fact that there was no reason, no reason whatsoever, for the AAnn to attack and annihilate a peaceful, harmless scientific campsite. In the absence of motive, it was hard to see how the humans could accuse the AAnn of anything more than a serious but not malevolent lapse in judgment.

Therefore, Vaarbayel CCVT, senior consul for the Empire on Comagrave, was feeling hopeful if not completely confident as she was admitted to the office of Malor Narzaltan. The old human was disgustingly wrinkled and shamelessly exhibited an unrepentant mane of white keratin that spilled down the back of his head and neck. His eyes were small, sharp, blue, and seemed to take in tiny bits of airborne debris the way a magnet attracts iron filings. Vaarbayel tried to look at him without staring. Her tail switched lazily back and forth behind her, a sign of patience.

"You requessted that I appear before you. I assume thiss iss not an informal vissit."

"It never is with your kind, is it?" Narzaltan was standing, not sitting, behind his desk. It was a simple artifact, as were the remainder of the complementary furnishings that filled the office. As an outpost world, Comagrave made do with the hand-me-downs and leftovers of government.

She chose to ignore the query, which insofar as she could judge carried with it some small suspicion of sarcasm. "Then everything will be recorded by mysself as well, sso that there can be in the future no missundersstandings as to what wass ssaid or disscussed."

"No," the human administrator agreed quietly, "we certainly wouldn't want there to be any misunderstandings. Not like the one that led to yesterday's tragedy near the Mountain of the Mourners." Aged though they were, those tiny blue eyes seemed lit from within. "I was hoping you could shed some light on the matter."

"Having recently been given the opportunity to fully perusse the official report on the distressing and tragic incident, I assure you I can do precissely that." She proceeded to give the AAnn version of the "grim misadventure," concluding that the eventual devastation was the result of terrible conditions on the ground and consequent grave miscommunication between the humans at the site and the AAnn who had been sent to ferry them back to the capital. This was followed by a formal apology— even though, given the circumstances, one was technically not required—and a conjoined offer to pay reparations. Within reason, of course.

She concluded by adding her personal, as opposed to official, condolences, taking care to remind the furrow-faced old human with both word and gesture that more than a few of her own kind had perished in the course of the incident. Despite this, the AAnn took no offense. Such calamities were bound to occur in the course of exploring unknown alien worlds. But among those who understood such things, who were mature explorers of a threatening and oftentimes bewildering firmament, they need not impair relations.

She felt she had done as best she could given the material the psychticians had prepared for her. Now she stood in silence, only her tail moving metronomically from side to side, waiting for the shriveled mammal to respond. After a long pause he finally did, in language that was somewhat less than tastefully diplomatic.

"You're a liar."

She blanched as much as an AAnn could. Anger rose in her throat. "You are inssulting."

"The truth is never insulting. You're a big-mouthed, carrion-eating, earless, bloodthirsty liar who probably shits where she eats. I'm starting to think that's true of all your kind. Like the rest of my people, I've been inclined to usually give you the benefit of the doubt here on Comagrave, even if you persist in your communications in referring to it as Vussussica. A recently viewed vit changed my mind. It's changed a lot of minds here. I expect that after it receives wider dissemination, its mind-altering potential will expand exponentially. Would you care to see it?"

Stunned beyond outrage, the AAnn representative could barely choke out a terse affirmative. "I sshould like to ssee what hass prompted thiss unprecedented outbursst of sslander, truly."

Without replying, Narzaltan waved a hand over a proximity control. A holo image appeared above his plain, unadorned desk. Vaarbayel recognized the restraining boundaries of a satellite scan. Without input from the human, the view plunged surfaceward until the slightly flickering but otherwise quite viewable image froze at a high magnification.

She had only read the hastily compiled formal report and seen the follow-up. Looked down on from above, the carnage took on a detached yet oddly individualistic horror. There were the two surviving AAnn transports, systematically sweeping the blazing encampment, the AAnn aboard utilizing their aerial platforms to methodically shoot down every last remaining human. Afterward, landing parties examined the camp, going through those structures that were still standing—making sure of possible survivors. There were too many details of the sweeping vit, too many peculiarly bloody episodes, that could not be faked. She could not question what she was seeing.

The image evaporated like a bad dream in a sandstorm. "I do not know how to properly resspond other than as I already have," she finally hissed. "I wass not there. I can only reference what I wass told, and explicate from thosse materialss that I have been given."

Narzaltan was nodding, a typically unsophisticated human gesture she readily recognized. "I understand that. In retrospect, if not now, maybe you will understand my bitterness. Not that I really care if you do. We're both vessels, you and I. Vessels and vassals, administrators and diplomats. We're supposed to transmit and forward, not think or feel. Right now I'm afraid I and everyone on my staff is failing that mandate.

"You're probably wondering how we came by that satellite imagery. Turns out the local thranx consulate here in Comabraeth received a request to run a high-magnification check on the campsite just as your people arrived. Standard procedure. Our technicians complied. When they saw what was happening in real time, they locked the satellite's orbit to keep the high-def scanners on location." He gestured at the empty air above his desk. "You just saw the result. If that particular request hadn't arrived when it did, I might, just might, have been willing to withhold judgment on your official story." He smiled, and although a human could not begin to match an AAnn for expanse of exposed teeth, it was threatening enough. "Now you've gone and contradicted that stinking small slice of reality. There will be consequences."

The thranx! Vaarbayel thought ferociously. Whenever something untoward happened, the *gssrsst* bugs seemed always to be found at the bottom of the contaminated dune. "I am ssure that upon further reflection, the incidentss ssurrounding thiss regrettable missundersstanding can be explained."

Once more the human administrator responded with little more than that terse and by now infuriating nod. "Until further notice, all AAnn on Comagrave are to consider themselves under detention. No vehicles or other craft are to travel beyond Comabraeth without permission from this office. Stellar proximity to the Empire notwithstanding, this is an officially recognized colony of Earth. Your people remain on this world on sufferance of my government and its colonies."

"This is outrageouss. I musst regisster an official protesst."

"You do that. You relay everything to Blassussar. I've already been in contact with Earth via the space-minus bore. My actions have been cleared, and I've been granted authority to augment however I see fit— short of shooting people. Further communications between your government and mine are in the process of being formulated." He crossed his slim but wiry arms in front of his unimpressive chest. As a gesture of dismissal and finality, it was oddly convincing.

"One last thing. If I were you, I'd start packing."

19

Like everyone else in the vast underground burrow that contained the diplomatic division serving the Great Hive, Haflunormet encountered the report from the human outpost world of Comagrave in advance of the general populace. That he was not the only one to respond with an involuntary stridulation of shock was shown by the number of abrasive chirrups that echoed in close succession through the various individual workstations. Staff rose from their positions to engage in intense informal discussions of the report's potential impact.

Haflunormet did not join them. While he was as stunned by the details as the rest of his colleagues, they did not sit quite right in either of his guts. Perhaps it was due to the increasing amount of contact he had been having with humans themselves, and with one individual in particular. Whatever the reason, he found himself impelled to dig deeper into the body of general information contained in the horrific account.

These personal preoccupations in no way mitigated his sympathy for the doomed humans of Comagrave or his outrage at the manner of their death. One could expect no less from the deceitful AAnn. Here at last was proof of their persistent perfidy so overwhelming that even those humans most favorably disposed toward them could not ignore it. That the incident would give at least a temporary, and perhaps a permanent, boost to the furthering of thranx-human relations could not be denied. In the Pitarian War the collected hives had shown themselves to be reliable allies. Now the AAnn had revealed the true nature of their innate treachery. Among those members of the diplomatic staff who had labored long and hard, suffering criticism and cynicism in tandem for their efforts to bring the two species closer together, there was quiet jubilation. The cautious and the outright dissenters were reduced to skritching their mandibles in quiet frustration.

And yet—and yet . . . certain facts, assuming they had been correctly recorded, continued to nag at him like the aggravating *sqik* parasites that could infect an ungroomed adult's exfoliating integuments.

The deeper he probed, the more convinced he became that he was on the track of uncomfortable truths. His colleagues in the section appeared to accept the report and its attendant conclusions without question. A perfectly normal reaction—but not for one who had spent time among humans. A little of their tendency to question everything seemed to have rubbed off on him. Of course, they also tended to suspect the obvious and the self-evident. This led to a widespread wasting of time the thranx could not stomach. Somewhere in between the two extremes, Haflunormet suspected, might lie the eventual path to a new way of looking at the universe.

His present interests, however, were not half so exalted. Details, details—so much of diplomacy was often in the details. When he finally stumbled over the one he was looking for, self-congratulation escaped him. He was too shocked.

It was plain enough for anyone who knew the ways of the hive to see—if one had the desire and determination to look for it. The contradictions lay in the timing. How had this scientist managed to send a warning that the human exoarcheological site was under attack several time-parts before the surveying satellite provided the first confirmation that an attack was actually under way? Haflunormet checked and rechecked the relevant chronologs. There was no mistake.

The warning had arrived *before* the attack.

Then there were the many protests, all ignored, that had been raised by the AAnn. That they had journeyed to the site with the declared intent of rescuing, not exterminating, its occupants. That upon preparing to touch down, one of their transports had been fired upon without warning and for no apparent reason. That its destruction had been followed by an outbreak of small-arms fire from the encampment, whereupon they had then, and only then, responded in kind. This last assertion had been met with the contempt it deserved. By no method of accounting could a defensive reaction "in kind" justify the complete annihilation of all the camp's inhabitants.

Delving ever deeper, Haflunormet noted that the initial blast that had crippled the AAnn transport could not be explained in light of the encampment's professed lack of heavy weapons. If the humans on Comagrave were lying and the occupants of the scientific camp *had* possessed such devices, why did they not use them on the other two AAnn transports? Someone in the report had hypothesized about the possibility of unstable explosives used for purposes of excavation having been stored at the landing site. This conjecture was quickly dismissed. Scientific teams did not make use of the risky or unstable. And why would humans fire on supposedly friendly AAnn if they did not feel directly threatened?

Haflunormet focused every one of his lenses on the series of high-res satellite images. Easy enough to see the AAnn transport crashing at the landing pad, vomiting flames. Then the flare-up of small-arms fire. How ultimately detailed was the imagery? He enhanced, zoomed, and enhanced again. At the maximum augmented magnification possible, a single figure could be observed firing at the incoming AAnn craft. A number of humans could be seen running, a couple cowering together behind a temporary shelter, but none of them shooting at the AAnn. Not yet. Haflunormet's wing cases quivered.

There had been exactly one thranx working on the site at the time of the tragedy. It was a thranx who had transmitted the very possibly premature report of the AAnn attack. Now, in imagery freshly augmented, it was a thranx who could be seen firing on the AAnn in advance of anyone else. Taken together, the evidence seemed to point to more than mere reaction, more than just coincidence.

It was entirely possible, a stunned Haflunormet realized, that the respected thranx exoarcheologist in question, a certain Pilwondepat, had not been reacting to an AAnn attack, but had been working to provoke one.

The potential ramifications were explosive. Throughout the human sphere of influence, outrage against the AAnn over the atrocity that had occurred on Comagrave was spreading like an unstoppable contagion. If it was disclosed that on this one exceptional occasion the AAnn were actually innocent, and that the massacre had in fact been initiated by a thranx, the shift in human public opinion could be devastating. What had possessed a respected scientist of the hive to do such a thing Haflunormet could not begin to imagine. Certainly the initial consequences were salutary, but the risk . . . !

He lay unmoving at his position, sprawled on his bench, until a neighboring coworker thought to inquire after his health. Responding positively, and as calmly as he could, Haflunormet realized that his long moments of contemplation had led him to a decision. Whatever justification might have been claimed by the perpetrator for provoking such a heinous incident had already been subsumed in matters of far greater import. Though every particle of his being screamed at Haflunormet to reveal the truth, he knew that he could not. To do so would be to set thranx-human relations back to a point where even formal diplomatic relations might be placed in jeopardy. As for any thought of forging stronger, deeper bonds between the two species, they would evaporate like dripping water on a hot rock.

But he could not keep the secret to himself. Others needed to know, deserved to know, so that in the event someone besides himself happened to chance upon the same conclusions, beings of like mind could be ready and prepared to deal with the potentially damaging revelation.

First, he erased every trace of his activity. What he could not erase because it had already been entered into general storage he buried as deeply and innocuously as he could. Satisfied at last that someone would have to be either very determined or very lucky to retrace his work, or to find the paths of inquiry he had taken, he steeled himself to confide his findings in the one other person he felt he could trust with so virulent a discovery.

But first he would have to find out where the human Fanielle Anjou was spending the remainder of her actual vacation.

The thranx liked mountains, but only from the inside. Mountains tended to be cold, or at least cool, dry places. Neither characteristic appealed to the heat- and humidity-loving insectoids. So the resting place where Fanielle had chosen to spend the remainder of her time away from Azerick lay at the upper limit of the thranx comfort zone.

Overlooking the undulating jungle-carpeted plains, beneath which lay the outermost suburbs of the city, the exclusive Retreat of Xer!kex featured individual burrows with spectacular vistas. The contradiction inherent in spending most of one's leisure time ignoring the view outside in favor of activities occurring deep within the mountainside was not lost on Fanielle. On the contrary, she was delighted by this wholly thranxish choice. It left her free to dawdle in the peculiar low-lying thranx version of a hammock, swinging outside above an exposed slope, sipping chilled fruit juice while gazing sleepily at the vast green panorama spread out before her.

Cool enough in its hillside location so that she felt comfortable in long pants and long-sleeved shirt, her communal refuge received occasional visits from other occupants of the retreat. They would click and whistle and chatter, pointing out this or that distant landmark, before retiring to their assigned burrows and away from the, to them, mountainside chill.

In the distance, the sporadic howl of a shuttle climbing heavenward rolled across the plains. Not even the distant Xer!kex could entirely escape the industrial-strength rumble and roar of the capital's major shuttleports. Relaxed and at ease, Fanielle viewed these isolated auditory interruptions with tolerant indifference. So content was she with the amenities of the retreat that neither shuttle yowls nor choruses of curious clicking could trouble her.

Among all the auditory distractions, the last thing she expected to hear was a familiar voice.

"Found you at last, *shleeck*! With only a handful of humans authorized to be in Daret, one would think it would not have taken so long."

Startled, she started to sit up, forgot where she was, and nearly ended as tightly wrapped up in the exotic hammock as a fly in a spider's shroud. Clearly ill at ease so close to an exposed cliff face, Haflunormet was nonetheless unabashedly pleased to see her.

"What are you doing here?" Carefully extracting herself from the hammocklike contrivance lest it try to ambush her dignity again, Fanielle sat on the edge of the low retaining wall that separated the scenic overlook from the jungle directly below. "I thought we had concluded all the necessary business between ourselves and our mutual friend."

Twisting an antenna around to make sure no one was standing behind him and listening, Haflunormet explained. "I came across a recent incident that in the course of further investigation has given birth to some disquieting conclusions." He indicated their surroundings. "You've been out of touch, and I presume you do not watch the local equivalent of your tridee broadcasts."

"No," she confessed. "I came up here looking for peace and quiet."

"I am sorry to intrude, but this matter cannot wait. I must tell someone I can trust, or I feel I will break into a premature molt. You've heard of Comagrave?"

She frowned, then brightened slightly. "Distant outpost world. Class X, I think. I remember reading something about a long-extinct but quite advanced native race. It's close, in galactic terms, to the AAnn Empire. What about it?"

Haflunormet proceeded to enlighten her as to the recent tragic developments on that world. When he had finished, she sat very still, digesting the scope of the disaster—and its diplomatic import.

"This will make the AAnn look bad. Very bad. A terrible thing to have happen—but perversely, it serves our ends."

Haflunormet gestured second-degree concurrence displaced by distress. "All true—except for my disquieting conclusions. They involve a respected exoarcheologist of the hive Pat, clan De. In the course of my investigation I researched this individual's background thoroughly. There is nothing in it to suggest a tendency to madness."

"I don't follow you, Haflunormet."

"This Pilwondepat filed a thick report detailing a list of incidents on Comagrave that he felt pointed to a methodical attempt on the part of the AAnn to drive your people off the planet, despite the official recognition of your suzerainty by the Empire. This report was filed the night before the event I have alluded to previously." He stridulated softly to emphasize his words. "That shocking incident would seem to provide final proof of his thesis, except for certain ambiguities that I have subsequently discovered." He proceeded to detail them for his friend.

She waited quietly until he was finished. "That's monstrous!" She hardly knew what to say to the quiet, expectant diplomat standing before her. "You're telling me that in order to back up his claims, this scientist provoked the AAnn into attacking and slaughtering everyone at the archeological site where he had been working?"

"Not sparing himself," Haflunormet reminded her solemnly.

"If word of this got out to the media . . ." Her voice trailed away, lost in hurried thought. "It would have exactly the opposite effect from what its perpetrator intended." She stared hard into those golden compound eyes. "You're *certain* of your findings?"

He gestured elaborately. "I wish it were otherwise. There are simply too many coincidences that cannot be rationalized away. And there is sufficient visual documentation to back up my conclusions, for any who happen to look in the right places. As far as I know, I am the only one to have done so." Both antennae had been pointing in her direction for some minutes now. The diplomat did not want to risk missing any critical nuances. "What do you think we should do?"

She started to reply. Before she could do so, they were interrupted by the sudden appearance from the mouth of the access passageway of three thranx: two males, and one female with particularly tightly coiled ovipositors. The younger male and female deferred noticeably to the older male in their midst.

"You don't have to decide." Though not especially elderly in thranx terms, the senior favored a noticeably gimpy right front truleg. "We will make the decision on your behalf."

Taken by surprise, Haflunormet whirled to confront the newcomers. Still seated on the stone retaining wall, Fanielle tensed. "You were listening to us," the thranx diplomat asserted accusingly.

"Most certainly we were." From a thorax pouch, the female removed a compact weapon. She held it casually in a truhand, not aiming it in any particular direction. Fanielle looked past the trio. In spreading out, they effectively blocked the way back to the tunnel. She and Haflunormet were alone on the outlook with the confrontational strangers. The female's tone, insofar as Fanielle could follow the stream of Low Thranx, was laced with contempt. "We have been listening in on you for a long time while following your deviant attempts to force thranx and humans obscenely closer together. To strive so hard to achieve secretiveness and to fail so miserably gains you little merit."

The elder in the middle spoke up, directing his words to Haflunormet. "The solution to your dilemma is simple, diplomat of the hive. You are going to tell the truth, difficult as that may be for one of your ilk. So . . . the AAnn are not responsible for what happened on Comagrave. It was the work of a brave and resourceful thranx determined to eliminate as many humans as possible. That, at least, will be how our organization will tell it."

Haflunormet's valentine-shaped blue-green head swiveled to appraise each of the intruders in turn. A sweeping gesture performed by both truhands underlined his pithy response. "You three are crazier than the suicidal exoarcheologist was."

"Who are you?" Handicapped by a lack of the requisite number of limbs, Fanielle tried her best to underline her queries with the appropriate hand gestures. "Why have you been following and listening to us?"

"We belong to a noble hiveless clan called the Bwyl," the oldest one told her. "We call ourselves the Protectors, and we work to preserve the purity of the Great Hive, to keep it free from outside corruption and defilement."

"Never heard of you." Haflunormet's words were cold, the verbal equivalent of blocking off a burrow to visitors.

"You will," the female assured him, waving her weapon around with blatant disregard for everyone's safety, including her own. "Very soon. Within a few time-parts." She whistled a terse tune of ironic humor. "A major element of our group is even as we speak working hard to pull down this false bridge of unwelcome conviviality that has been erected between the Great Hive and the filthy soft-bodied bipeds." Fanielle tensed, but said nothing.

"You are going to release your findings and all the evidence necessary to support your clever and correct deductions as to the truth of what happened on Comagrave." The elder spoke with the confidence of one who is convinced of his righteousness. "Both thranx and humans must know what happened on that world, and why. It is knowledge that will serve to drive a most satisfactory wedge between those misguided representatives of both species who seek a deeper and unnatural degree of harmonization." A soft whistle indicated a different kind of humor.

"Imagine it, diplomat. A chance to tell the truth of a matter instead of having to invent clever lies. Think of it as a novelty." His younger companions whistled and clicked approvingly.

"You can't do this," Haflunormet protested. "It will set back the course of thranx-human relations for an untold number of birth cycles."

"At the very least, one hopes," the speaker declared with satisfaction. "We don't need you to do this, *wirri!t*. Though we don't have access to your materials, they can be tracked down and recovered readily enough. We could make the announcement ourselves, but it will carry more weight if it comes from a representative of the diplomatic section." The confident male performed a hand gesture Fanielle did not recognize, but it was sufficient to cause Haflunormet to draw back slightly.

"If you refuse, you will be caught smothering the truth with the lie of omission. Your career will be ruined, and you will be consigned to simple information gathering and processing. Your family and clan will lose merit, and your disgrace will be substantial. We are offering you the opportunity to avoid all that. Indeed, by allowing you to reveal your discovery we give to you the chance to enhance your reputation."

"At the expense of seriously damaging thranx-human relations," Haflunormet responded.

Gesturing indifference, the younger male spoke for the first time. "We waste burrow-time here. Get the apostate to commit, or to decline. I am anxious to know of the success of Beskodnebwyl's enterprise."

"As are we all," the elder agreed, by his gestures counseling patience. "Beskodnebwyl works what he must, and we work what we do. No living chamber of significance is completed in a single birth cycle." He returned his attention to Haflunormet. "In keeping with the great traditions, we give you this choice. Make it now. By either means, the truth will become known."

Feeling completely left out, Fanielle sat stiffly on the barrier as she struggled to follow the conversation between the four thranx. The finely worked black schist was warm against her legs and backside. Haflunormet could not agree, of course. At the same time, how could he not? In her entire professional life, she had never felt so helpless, so completely at a loss for options. She was still agonizing over possibilities when Haflunormet stepped forward and extended both foothands.

"Very well, *sriippk*. I disagree with you completely, but it is better to dig through soft earth in the wrong direction than to break one's digits against solid rock in another." Reaching out, he took the senior Bwyl's

foothands in his own. "Let this grasping of work digits serve to emphasize the new bond between us."

The elder gestured gratification. "I am not surprised by your decision.
Most diplomats act in a sensible fashion when presented with clearly
defined parameters." He grasped Haflunormet's eight digits in his own.

Whereupon the diplomat bent and twisted with unexpected speed.
The thranx equivalent of jujitsu, involving as it did a maximum possible
eight limbs, was something to behold. The surprised Bwyl flew up and
over Haflunormet's abdomen, past a shocked Fanielle—and over the
retaining wall.

The dull *thump* humans make when they take a hard fall was in startling contrast to the loud *crack* of the thranx's exoskeleton shattering as it
struck the rocks below.

Before the elder's stunned companions could react, Haflunormet was
on top of and locked in a seemingly inextricable clinch with the younger
male. Superior knowledge and experience was matched against greater
strength. The former was, tragically, of no use whatsoever against even a
very small gun.

Discharged by the female, it replaced the struggling diplomat's left
eye with a large hole. Haflunormet's limbs went limp, his antennae collapsed atop his head, and the bright golden sheen of life began to fade
almost immediately from his remaining oculus. As the surviving male
strove to shove the now slack body away from his own, the female swung
the deadly little weapon in Fanielle's direction.

There is a time for diplomacy, and then there is a time for reverting to
the doctrines that have always preceded hopeless confrontations. Bringing her knees up toward her chest, Fanielle spun on her tail end; swung
her legs wide, high, and wild to her right; and dropped over the outside of
the overlook's stone wall. Faced with the gun, her reaction had been
entirely instinctive. Several thoughts collided for attention as she fell,
with one uppermost in her mind.

Dear God, please—not my baby.

She landed in untouched jungle some five meters below, the thick
undergrowth helping to cushion her fall. Pain shot up her right leg, lingered for a terrifying moment, and then began to diminish as rapidly as it
had arrived. Her hand went immediately to her slightly protruding belly.
Everything felt normal, unchanged. Healthy. Immensely relieved that her
body had handled the drop so well, she straightened, her mind taking
inventory of her condition before she had time to feel fear: She was not
crippled; nothing was broken, maybe a slight sprain. She could still walk,
but could she run? Could she run for two? She had no choice but to try.

As she started to push herself erect, her hand slipped against something thick and wet. Less than a meter from her eyes, the broken face of the elder Bwyl stared lifelessly back into her own. The stiff-limbed, stiff-bodied thranx had not taken the fall half as well as the more flexible human.

Something burned the foliage to her left, and she immediately stumbled off in the opposite direction, wiping her bloodstained hand against a leg of her pants. Surely the surviving Bwyl could not see her, concealed as she was by the thick rain forest vegetation. They were firing blindly, hoping to hit her. She had no doubt that they would pursue. With her witness to them having killed Haflunormet, they now had no choice. Despite their six legs, the thranx were not good leapers. They would have to find another way down. That would buy her some time.

She fought to remember everything she knew of thranx physiology. Over a short sprint, a human's longer legs would quickly outdistance them. But they had great endurance. If she couldn't lose them quickly in the forest, they would eventually run her to ground. If only there were a river to cross, or a lake to swim, she would be safe from them. But the steep hillside did not allow for the deep pooling of water. There was something else, something more useful still . . .

It flashed hot and bright in her mind. In addition to being weak jumpers, the thranx were poor climbers. They would expect a fugitive to go downward in any case. Angling more to her right, she struck off parallel to the slope. When she felt she had traveled far enough to be beyond the farthest extent of the retreat, she turned sharply and started upslope.

The grade was steep and the permanently damp ground underfoot slippery and uncertain. She had been wearing air sandals while relaxing in the pseudohammock—hardly the most appropriate gear for rain forest hiking. Their feet naturally shod in tough chitin, the thranx needed no footwear. Nor would the precipitous incline slow them down.

She found what she was looking for a short while later. The cliff face was dizzying, but fractured with plenty of handholds. Taking care to avoid a slip on the moist surface, a determined human would have no difficulty ascending. But the vertical rock face would stop a thranx cold. The exposed granite extended as far as she could see to right and left. With luck, her pursuers would give up the chase, or at least lose track of her at the base of the moderate precipice. At the very least, it would give her a chance to put some serious space between herself and her pursuers.

Once, she lost her grip and nearly fell. Though in good physical shape and something of an amateur athlete, she was no mountaineer. But by choosing her route of ascent carefully and taking her time, she found herself sitting at the top well before evening. That was important. Having evolved in a subterranean civilization, the thranx possessed far better night vision than the average human. It behooved her to find sanctuary, in one form or another, before nightfall, when she would be at a disadvantage.

Which way to go? The unspoiled rain forest was still home to dangerous as well as engaging creatures, the majority of which she had never encountered and knew absolutely nothing about—another reason for avoiding any nocturnal rambling. If the Bwyl were still on her trail, she might do well to try to circle back to the retreat. Once back inside, she felt sure she could rely on the well-trained staff to protect her until her pursuers gave up and departed.

Another, less acute slope lay before her. She would scale this final, foliage-choked obstacle and then try to descend down to the retreat without being observed. The last step up proving to be a bit of a reach for her, she sought support from a nearby tree, taking a firm grip on the blue-barked bole with her right hand. One strong pull, and she was up, gazing through an opening in the bushes and trees that promised a few moments of easier hiking before she had to start looking for a sheltered route across and down.

A quick glance behind showed no signs of pursuit. Either she had lost them, or the Bwyl were struggling to find a way around the bluff she had surmounted. She was breathing hard, but she was not exhausted. The knowledge that she had no more climbing ahead of her gave strength to tired leg muscles and invigorated her spirits. Thus renewed, and a little more confident of her chances, she started down the irregular path through the trees.

The gun that appeared in front of her face was held tightly in the grasp of not two, but four hands. Sixteen digits covered every possible switch and button, slide and trigger. Downy antennae and bulging eyes swung immediately in her direction as the muzzle of the rifle started to come around.

Of course. Her thoughts were oddly peaceful, and she found she was no longer tired. How stupid of me. Naïve and stupid. Forward thinkers like the Bwyl would be likely to bring backup along to any potential confrontation. The rifle and its handler both looked very efficient.

None of the armed patrollers who had been called out by the alarmed operators of the retreat to search for the missing human had ever encountered one in person, though they were familiar with the bipeds' appearance from the numerous visual displays that had played regularly ever since early contact. As to the murderous intruders, the surviving pair had already been apprehended. The patroller who encountered the human had, upon doing so, turned promptly to reassure her.

So, even though many aspects of human behavior were reputed to be strange and incomprehensible, he was still taken aback when the hunted one's single-lensed eyes appeared to perform the astonishing feat of rolling back inside her skull; her long, fleshy legs gave way; and without a word or gesture in his direction she crumpled unconscious to the damp earth.

20

Monitoring his tracker while listening to the reports filtering in from the other plainclothes police who had spread out to cover the fairgrounds, the supervising officer managed to spare a moment or two to contemplate the pair of peculiar padres chatting nearby. Though the purpose of the fair was to expose humans to thranx culture and, to a lesser degree, thranx to human culture, this association was sufficiently unusual to pique his normally pedestrian curiosity. That they had also saved hundreds, perhaps thousands of lives rendered them that much more interesting.

Representatives of something they called "the United Church," they were. Lieutenant Romero had never heard of it. His openly professed ignorance had sparked a quiet but eager interest on their part to resolve it, to a degree that had involved him in their disquisition despite his usual disdain for matters theological.

Time enough for that later, after this unpleasant business of die-hard terrorists had been concluded. Given the number of infiltrators, the police had been unable to round them all up in time. A few small fires were burning around the fairgrounds, but nothing, he had been assured by the relevant authorities, that the on-grounds facilities could not handle. The most stubborn blazes were already succumbing to flows of suppressant being pumped from the fair's central fire-control facility. Following a few anxious moments when the intruders' strength was still uncertain, everything was now under control. It was merely a matter of picking up those few remnant infiltrators who were still at large.

And best of all, he knew, it had not been necessary to close down or evacuate the fair. The majority of attendees would never know how close they had come to perishing in an orgy of deliberate, preconceived destruction.

For that, he, his department, and the people of Dawn had this oddly matched pair of proselytizers to thank. Looking up from his tracker, he was reminded to do so. It was the tenth or maybe the twelfth time he had given voice to his gratitude.

Briann was not counting, but he was embarrassed. Incapable of blushing, Twikanrozex was reduced to gesturing his discomfiture. "You have already thanked us enough, Lieutenant." As always, Romero was amazed at the thranx's fluency in Terranglo. There were a few words he did not recognize that the human padre had identified as belonging to a new class of informal communication street folk were calling symbospeech, but his unfamiliarity did not hinder his understanding.

"I've already been told by the Auroran city council that you two are to have the run of the city as well as the fair. Anything you want will be provided."

Briann smiled graciously. "Our needs are simple. We ask only to be allowed to continue in our work." He glanced in the direction of his companion, presently standing tall on four trulegs. "Our intentions in coming here were to operate only during the fair, but since your superiors have extended so gracious a welcome, it would be churlish of us to leave early."

"We only did what anyone would have done," Twikanrozex added.

Romero grunted softly. "Followed heavily armed outsiders to learn what they were up to? I don't think so." A voice yammered in his cochlear implant, bringing a taut look of satisfaction to his deeply tanned face. "Two more picked up. Thranx this time. They don't seem to be coordinating very well, these rogue antisocial elements of respective species."

Twikanrozex gestured with all four arms. While Romero had not a clue as to the meaning of the complex hand movements, they were fascinating to watch. Graceful creatures, these thranx, he thought. Wonder why I hadn't noticed that before?

A different voice in his ear caused him to glance once again at his companions. "They've located another weapons source." He nodded to his right. "Not far from here. Would you like to witness the arrest? Unless more of these fools are still outside waiting to enter the fair, we're running out of targets to pick up. My people will wait for us before moving in to make the seizure."

Briann responded for the both of them. "We might as well. If possible, Twikanrozex and I would like to question one or two of the arraigned. There are moral ambiguities in question we would like to establish, and perhaps help to correct."

Romero was firm in his reply. "That's not up to me. The invaluable aid you've rendered aside, you're not law enforcement or legal. Your official status is as ambiguous as those morals you'd like to investigate. But I'll see what I can do." Following the directions displayed on his tracker, he led them in the general direction of the lake. A red light blinked on the small readout, indicating the location of an unauthorized weapon.

As the officer led the way, the two padres conversed energetically in his wake. He wished he could make sense of what they were saying. What, for example, did immortality have to do with the story of the baker's wife and the two dwarves?

A most peculiar theology, indeed.

Elkannah Skettle was beyond apoplexy. The pressure of trying to keep calm and inconspicuous while running from the law threatened to burst a blood vessel in his forehead. Slipping out from behind one of several brightly colored pylons supporting a children's play area, he walked as rapidly as he dared toward the pavilion exit. Would he be more or less vulnerable to detection outside than within? Even that fragment of knowledge was denied him.

What had gone wrong? How had the authorities learned of the presence and plans of the Preservers and their thranx comrades, the Bwyl? Every few moments for the past hour, his communicator had informed him of the arrest of another one or two of his people. Attempts to contact the thranx had been met with streams of abuse in the coarse alien language, interspersed with a few crude bursts of Terranglo that were enough to tell him that his insectoid counterparts were also suffering the remorseless attentions of the authorities.

A year's planning, a year of dreaming and working and rehearsing, was falling apart all around him. A few fires had been set, a few bombs had been detonated, shots had been fired, but for the most part, the fair continued to function as smoothly and impassively as if Preserver and Bwyl had never set foot within its expansive boundaries. Some of his best people, dedicated individuals he had worked with for years and knew intimately, were dead or in custody. Botha and Lawlor, gone. Nevisrighne and Stephens, gone. The damage to the movement was so severe that it would take years to recover. Years during which, if something was not done, the unclean bond between human and bug might be cemented beyond sundering.

That could not be allowed to happen. Whatever happened to him now, or to any of his followers, paled into insignificance. Those few explosions that his fellows had succeeded in setting off held the key. If he could only follow through on destroying the fair's central communications facility, the consequences might be sufficiently distracting and damaging to allow him and his surviving collaborators to carry out at least a portion of what they had planned to do.

No one intercepted him as he strolled briskly, eyes darting constantly from left to right, across the fake Dawnic turf toward the fair maintenance facilities. Once, a child caught his eye, and he had to remind himself that police authorities rarely employed children of such a tender age. Still, he was relieved when the child's parents finally hauled it from view.

Behind the gaily decorated fencing lay support facilities for much of the fair. Food service, water, hygienics machinery, power distribution, communications—much of it specially modified to serve thranx as well as human needs. He did not need to check his communicator for the location of the communications center, having memorized the entire layout of the fairgrounds several months earlier.

Unusually, there was a live guard at the entrance. Short and burly, he looked ineffably bored. As Skettle approached, the man barely bothered to look up. The warm sun of Dawn was in his face, and he had to blink.

"Morning, visitor. Can I help you?"

"Yes, you can. Here is my identification." Reaching into a pocket, Skettle drew the compact pistol lying holstered and shoved it roughly against the other man's neck. With his free hand, he spun the startled attendant around. "I require admittance to the maintenance area."

Give the fellow credit; he tried. "You—you're not authorized, whoever you are. What is this?"

Skettle's voice was strained, but as controlled as ever. "Epiphany, my friend. Let us in, or I swear by every uncontaminated gene in your body, I'll blow your head right off its shoulders."

With the muzzle of the pistol dimpling his neck, the guard hastened to comply. "You won't get away with this, you know."

"Get away with what?" Skettle smiled humorlessly. "You have no idea what I'm doing here. Maybe I just need to use a bathroom."

The gate hummed to itself as it drew back. A second barrier lay beyond, which the guard also activated. Standing among muted machinery and functional buildings, unpolluted blue sky still visible overhead, Skettle felt he was at last approaching a small part of the triumph he sought.

"Thank you for your help," he told the guard as he fired. Contrary to his threat, the shot did not blow the unfortunate man's head off his shoulders. Skettle disliked a mess that could be difficult to conceal. Gripping the body by its sandaled feet, he dragged it behind a large pulsating tank and covered it with one of several sheets of green patching fabric he found there. A quick check to ensure that his actions had not been observed, and he resumed his advance. With no one to witness his progress, he broke into a run.

Minutes later he found himself standing across a walkway from the central communications facility. There were no guards here, deep within the restricted area. It would be assumed that anyone present inside the fenced perimeter had a reason to be where they were. Should he encounter any active personnel, he would be able to rely on that assumption.

The tall double doors that led into the building were unlocked. Inside, automated electronics and photonic circuitry filled the modest edifice with a compact network of switching and transmission instrumentation. Loud humming indicated that the facility was operating on a level higher than standby. That was hardly surprising, given the volume of communications that were doubtless flying not only at the fair but between the fairgrounds and the city.

With the internal schematic of the facility imprinted deeply on his memory, he hurried down several passageways until he found himself standing before the nexus he sought. Instrumentation mounted on a panel monitored the operational status of this small but critical portion of the complex. In a pants pocket lay the special key Botha had programmed to allow him to access the protected, lightly armored panel. All he had to do was pop the seal, affix the cylinder snugged against his chest to the internal components, activate the timer, and get clear.

He envisioned the consequences: confident police unable to contact one another; hasty attempts to relay all communications through distant city facilities; fair workers incapable of coordinating fire-fighting efforts; medics cut off in the process of receiving diagnostic and treatment information. Communicationswise, the entire fair should be shut down for a minimum of several hours—long enough for his surviving acolytes to wreak at least a portion of the havoc they had planned. He wished he could be there to see it, but knew he would have to wait to view the resultant catastrophe on the tridee. Human terrorists! the media would scream. No, thranx saboteurs! another would cry. He smiled to himself. Let the media apportion the responsibility however they wished. The resulting death and destruction would give pause to anyone inclined to think that the two species could enjoy closer relations than they did at present.

From his pocket he withdrew the key, then slapped the flexible circle of integrated circuitry over the sealed lock. He was preparing to activate the device and pop the covering panel when a voice commanded him to halt what he was doing, put his hands over his head, and lie down on the floor. It did not, he sensed despairingly, sound like the voice of a maintenance attendant, bored or otherwise.

With the two padres looking on, Romero nodded to his people. Holding a brace of body seals, one patroller advanced on the stunned Skettle while his two flanking companions kept the muzzles of their handguns aimed unwaveringly at the Preserver's torso. There was nothing Skettle could do, not a thing. Even if he disobeyed the command and activated Botha's key, it would only open the panel. The prospect that he would then have enough time to remove the key, detach the still-concealed cylinder of explosive, affix it to the instrumentation, and activate the trigger was nonexistent. It was all over. The traitors had won. The contamination of human society by the intrusive, alien bugs would continue unimpeded.

Something loud, threatening, and unseen resounded through the still air of the facility. The sonic burst struck the nearest patroller in the back of his head. Briann saw the man topple, the back of his skull caved in by the concussion. His comrades tried to react, but they were caught out in the open while their unknown assailants were firing from cover. Both Romero and the female officer went down in quick succession. The lieutenant managed to get off one shot before he, too, was felled. Whoever the attackers might be, Briann reflected tensely, they were excellent shots. As a consequence, he kept his hands out in plain sight, where they could be seen from a distance.

Both he and Twikanrozex were more than a little surprised when only a single injured thranx hobbled out from behind a dividing wall. Unwilling to grant that the assassin had acted by himself, Briann searched the shadows for others of his kind.

"You are alone," Twikanrozex declared in Low Thranx.

"It was not always so." The wounded sharpshooter stood halfway between the two padres and the perplexed Skettle. "I have been isolated by conspiracies, by failings, and by circumstance."

Skettle finally recognized the intruder. "Beskodnebwyl! Then not all of you bugs have been taken by the authorities."

"No," the leader of the Bwyl replied in Terranglo. "Not all of us bugs."

The Preserver promptly turned back to his work. As the key popped the seal on the panel, he reached inside his shirt and pulled out the cylinder of volatile solution. "We can still accomplish much of what we came for. Shoot these two and come and help me."

Twikanrozex performed a half bow in concert with a series of hand movements too rapid for Briann to follow. "We are spiritual advisors. We carry no weapons."

"That is unfortunate for you," Beskodnebwyl declared, "since it prevents you from defending yourselves." The muzzle of his sonic projector came up. Briann tensed.

"Come on; come on!" Skettle was struggling to affix the cylinder to the now open, blinking interior. "Let's do this and get out of here." On the floor nearby, the injured female officer moaned as she struggled to crawl toward the exit. He ignored her.

Beskodnebwyl turned slowly. The great golden eyes were as expressionless as ever, but the clipped thranx voice was not. "Are you giving me orders, you sickening sack of slack slush?"

Skettle barely looked over from his efforts. "Not now, bug. We can discuss species primacy another time. Come and help me."

"*Crr!!k*, I will help you." Whereupon he proceeded to shoot the leader of the Preservers in his left thigh. The blast of highly focused sound waves smashed into the thick quadriceps muscle and broke the bone within. Letting out a cry of anguish, Skettle collapsed to the floor clutching at his crushed leg.

Advancing with deliberation, the Bwyl approached him. As the thranx changed his focus, Briann considered reaching into his shirt's inner pocket. A glance in Twikanrozex's direction showed that his companion felt this would be, at least for the moment, a bad idea. Taking into consideration the Bwyl's phenomenal marksmanship with his frightening weapon, together with the usual exceptional thranx peripheral vision, Briann kept his hands out in front of him. Alert but cautious, the two padres waited to see what the other thranx would do.

"You cretinous insect!" Wincing in pain, Skettle was clutching his smashed leg. "What did you do that for?" Indicating the cylinder of liquid explosive, which was now securely fastened to the sensitive instrumentation and needed only to be activated to disrupt communications throughout the fair, the Preserver tried to pull himself back to the open panel, dragging his unusable leg behind him.

Beskodnebwyl calmly shot him in the other leg—the calf, this time.

Elkannah Skettle had been toughened, by work in the field and by philosophy both, but this time he screamed. Very little blood leaked from his ruined limbs, since the condensed burst of sound had compressed veins and arteries without cutting them. Designed to shatter the resistive chitinous material that comprised the thranx exoskeleton, the gun's output passed comparatively harmlessly through soft, spongy human flesh but was highly effective at breaking human bones.

As the two padres looked on, the leader of the hiveless clan Bwyl stood staring down at his whimpering human counterpart. "This is all your fault. If you people had not come here, all would have gone as planned. Everything would have transpired as set down in the burrow layout."

"You're out of your deranged bug mind!" Skettle tried to stand on his broken right leg, only to have it collapse beneath him.

"You betrayed us." Beskodnebwyl was quietly implacable. "Your clumsiness revealed our presence to the local authorities."

"Us!" Unable to walk or even to rise, Skettle was reduced to glaring murderously at his tormentor. "Our security was airtight! My people were, to an individual, highly trained and motivated. There were no breaches of security on our part. Somehow, someone from outside must have learned of our presence here. I am not accusing your kind directly, but—" He broke off unexpectedly.

An impatient Beskodnebwyl prodded the severely injured human with a foothand. "What now, *srrlkpp*? Finish your thought before I kill you."

Skettle said nothing, but instead continued to stare. He was looking not at his antagonist, but past him. Following his gaze—a simpler matter with humans than with thranx, Beskodnebwyl reflected—the Bwyl turned his head in the same direction to find himself gazing at the two beings who were still standing, hands held inoffensively in front of them. At the two padres. Theologians, by their dress and demeanor. Upholders of misplaced virtue and the wrong right. That by itself was not enough to condemn them.

Their presence among the dead and wounded police, however, was rather more suggestive.

"Yes, I will kill them," the Bwyl finally declared. "It may be that they are not responsible for this failure. But I am no longer willing to take chances, and what compassion remained within my upper gut has died along with my friends and companions."

Skettle spoke through pain-clenched teeth. "About time you came to your senses. We can still activate the explosive, still reduce this squalid convocation to pandemonium. Still accomplish many if not all of our goals here." He extended a hand upward. "Help me to finish this."

"I surely will do that," Beskodnebwyl agreed. Raising the muzzle of his pistol, he placed it against the top of the injured human's skull. Briann flinched inwardly, having already seen what the weapon could do to solid bone.

Screaming at the top of her lungs, Martine burst from the corridor behind the two padres, rushed past them, and brought the cylinder of explosive she had been carrying down with great force. The police trackers had never singled her out since she was carrying only the cylinder and not a weapon. Espying her charge without having to turn, Beskodnebwyl calmly fired in the wildly onrushing biped's direction.

The sonic burst struck the curved cylinder and glanced off, causing her to stumble but not to slow her mad charge. Before the startled Bwyl could get off a second shot, she brought the cylinder down on his V-shaped head as hard as she could. There was a loud, sickening sound as the insectoid skull was split. Blood and internal fluids gushed forth in a green fountain as the open circulatory system was ruptured. Falling sideways, Beskodnebwyl fired one last time. Too close to dodge, the woman caught the burst square in her chest. Fragments of shattered sternum were blown into her lungs and heart.

Briann immediately started to reach for his own concealed handgun, only to find himself restrained by his companion. Turning, he saw that Twikanrozex was pointing with both truhands.

Using both arms, a determined Skettle had levered himself into position to reach for and activate the cylinder of explosive. Neither padre knew what the slim bottle contained, but if it was worth this many lives to attach it to the appropriate instrumentation, then its contents would surely do the crowds of unsuspecting visitors who were presently thronging the fair no good.

Nor was there time to call in a warning. As Twikanrozex let go of his friend's arm and rushed forward, Briann was right behind him. The biped's greater speed over a short distance enabled the human to reach Skettle and the open panel at exactly the same time as his multilimbed companion.

Cursing defiance, Skettle mustered one last supreme effort. Pulling his useless lower body upright, he threw himself forward. Both hands latched onto the cylinder, one gripping it for support while the other stabbed at the softly blinking contact that would activate its contents. At almost the same instant, the leaping, stridulating Twikanrozex struck the larger biped with all six feet, knocking him away from the exposed instrumentation. Briann launched himself at the cylinder, grabbed hold, and twisted, throwing his whole body into the maneuver. The tough sealant that had been incorporated by the deceased engineer Botha to hold the cylinder against the panel's interior snapped beneath the padre's weight an instant after the desperate Skettle succeeded in activating it.

There was supposed to be a delay of several minutes between activation and detonation to allow the bearer enough time to escape the blast perimeter. Perspicacious terrorist that he was, however, the recently demised Botha had assumed that once the cylinders of liquid explosive were emplaced, the only individuals interested in removing them would be representatives of the unwelcome authorities. He had therefore rigged the cylinders' triggers to bypass the programmed time lapse in the event of early dislodging.

A frantic Skettle was in the process of trying to deliver himself of this explanation when the cylinder Briann and Twikanrozex were conveying as rapidly as possible toward the exit supplied its own clarification.

Explosively.

21

It was a locality Lyrkenparmew never expected to have to visit. It was not necessary that he do so now. Through the highly covert channels that were open to him, he could have requested that the individual in question return to meet with him, instead of him going to see her. But upon learning the details of what had happened, and knowing the suffering she had already endured on behalf of their mutual interests, he felt it was incumbent upon him to repay the honors.

Which was why he found himself, bundled and shivering beneath an overcast sky, walking slowly through an open, neatly tended garden asprout with vegetables so alien in shape and coloring he felt he might have fallen into the proverbial pupae land of psychedelic metamorphosis. At the moment, there was only one biped tending to the fantastic, exotic growths. She did so for purposes of therapy, he had been informed. What benefit there was to be gained from attending to an excrescence the shade and shape of a *gorn!eyak* he could not imagine. Just looking at it threatened to upset both his stomachs.

Fanielle glanced up at his approach. Rising, she wiped sweat from her forehead and dirt from her gloved hands. It was a pleasant, cool day, but the thranx envoy was obviously uncomfortable.

"No, *yrr!kk*," he replied when she suggested they go inside. "It is cold out here, but private. Let your friends think we are discussing the merits of rehabilitative agriculture." He searched her face, trying to apply what knowledge he had acquired of the multiple meanings conveyable by the wonderfully flexible human countenance. Insofar as he could tell, he detected there neither fear nor permanent damage. "I have seen the official report dealing with your unfortunate encounter. While vacationing outside Daret you were accosted by fanatical adherents of a xenophobically antihuman sect called the Bwyl. You fled, were chased, and were rescued by local peace patrollers called by the staff of the retreat, whereupon you lapsed into unconsciousness." His tone was candidly solicitous. "You suffered no permanent scarring, physical or psychological?"

She managed a thin smile. "I retain my fondness for your people, if that's what you mean. Physically, I'm fine." Her expression shifted as unpredictably as the low clouds overhead. A captivated Lyrkenparmew looked closer.

"Fascinating. There appears to be saline fluid leaking from the sockets in which your optics reside."

Reaching up, she wiped at her eyes with the back of one hand. The gesture rubbed a few grains of Hivehom soil into one eye, which resulted in an increased flow of the liquid to which her visitor referred. While the agent looked on, she fought to regain control of her emotions.

"It's an involuntary expression of remorse," she explained, seeking refuge in biology. "Analogous to certain of your sorrowing gestures. We call it *crying*. I'm crying for Haflunormet."

"A credit to his hive, his clan, and his family." Lyrkenparmew gestured appropriate melancholy. "Much merit did he bring to them."

"You have no idea." Putting down the nitrogen fixer, she settled herself into a sitting position alongside the cucumbers. They thrived in the clean air and fine soil of the Mediterranea Plateau, hundreds of parsecs from home. Responding to her action, Lyrkenparmew folded his legs beneath him and settled on the ventral side of his abdomen. She gazed evenly at her visitor.

"What do you know about a human outpost world called Comagrave?"

The agent gestured emphatically. "Until just recently, *viyyrp,* very little. A small outpost world undergoing exploration by your kind. Apparently, some serious unpleasantness occurred there recently that resulted in the expulsion of all transient AAnn on the planet." His next gesture probably should not have been translated, but Fanielle recognized it anyway. "I can't say that I, or anyone else in my section, is disappointed by the news. There was talk of a massacre perpetrated by the AAnn at a scientific site of considerable importance."

She nodded slowly, enveloped by the atavistic, loamy musk of freshly turned earth. Something black and slinky slithered through the dirt by her legs. Convergent evolution in earthworms, she thought as she watched its oily progress: refuge for a mind overwhelmed by clashes on a galactic scale. Nematodes crawling near her toes.

I'm getting silly, she told herself firmly, and this visit is serious.

"There's more to it than that. Much more." A glance showed that they were alone, and the device she was wearing beneath her gardening dress would ensure their privacy from any stray electronic pickups. "Haflunormet found out about it. In a way, that information contributed to his death. He had just finished telling me the details when we were attacked."

Lyrkenparmew gestured second-degree empathy swirled with intense curiosity. "Details of the incident were even then common knowledge. What about it was there that could prompt a violent assault on your persons, even by extreme xenophobes?"

She considered how best to tell him. "Insofar as Haflunormet was able to determine from the available records, the AAnn on Comagrave had no intention of attacking the archeological dig. Haflunormet became convinced they were provoked into doing so."

Unlike humans, Lyrkenparmew could not frown. But at the moment, he wished he could. It was so much more economical than waving one's limbs about. "Provoked? By whom?"

"By a resident thranx exoarcheologist named Pilwondepat." At the agent's gesture of disbelief, she added, "Haflunormet found proof. Enough to convince the skeptical. I don't know where it is now, or how he stored it, but without the requisite commands I'm sure it would be extremely difficult to recover." She put her fixer aside and pushed back the brim of her shade hat. "However, from the details he gave me, I'm sure that *I* could reconstruct the necessary evidence."

Lyrkenparmew was silent for a while, trying to comprehend the magnitude of what the human female had told him. If true in all details, it was an exceedingly dangerous bundle of knowledge. He eyed the biped closely. He liked a majority of humans, and this one more than most. Besides, she was *Bryn'ji!*. All of which, notwithstanding, did not prevent him from contemplating how best he might execute her and still slip away from the human outpost unnoticed.

No, that would not be necessary, he told himself. If she had intended to release the information, she would already have done so. And, she certainly wouldn't be sitting there in the dirt, relating it to someone she knew was likely to kill her to prevent its release. It was sufficient to reaffirm what he already knew: They were of different body, but like mind.

"If the substance of Haflunormet's report was to achieve general dissemination, it would rejuvenate human-AAnn relations while severely impacting those between your kind and mine." Feathery antennae waved gently. "I need not tell you that those are presently entering a most sensitive stage."

"No, you need not." Idly, she contemplated an incipient radish. "We want the same thing, Lyrkenparmew. You, I, poor Haflunormet, everyone who has worked so hard and for so long to achieve our final goal." Picking up a handful of alien earth, she let it trickle out between her dirt-smudged fingers. "But we might not have any choice. We may have to release the information and try to spin it as best we can."

"Why in the name of the Eight Original Great Hives would we want to do that?" Lyrkenparmew's disbelief was plain to see in his flowing gestures.

She swallowed hard. "Because others besides myself know the truth of what happened on Comagrave. Those xenophobes who attacked me and Haflunormet, who call themselves the hiveless clan Bwyl, are still in custody. I know—I've checked. But they have been allowed outside communication. I don't think there's any question but that they've passed the general thrust of Haflunormet's story, which they overheard that day on the lookout at the retreat, along to others of their kind." Her expression was stricken. "It's too late, Lyrkenparmew. Too late. By now the Bwyl have spread it to all their branches, possibly even off Hivehom. So you see, we can't bury it. All we can do is try to preempt their disclosure."

Lyrkenparmew considered a moment before gesturing with both right hands. "Is that what is worrying you so? Let them disclose all they want. Their story will not be believed."

"You don't understand." Full of regret for the consequences she knew would ensue the instant the story reached the unrestricted media, she looked at him intently. "Details can be researched, traced, unearthed. The truth can be reconstructed. Slowly, perhaps, but when the Bwyl release their version of what happened on Comagrave, some dedicated pundit oblivious to the consequences will find it intriguing enough to pursue."

"*Girritt,* that might have been the case a month or two ago, but no longer." The four delicate manipulative digits of a truhand reached out to brush against her forearm. "You haven't heard about what happened yesterday on Dawn?"

"Dawn?" Her expression twisted. "What has that colony got to do with what happened on Comagrave?"

"Directly, nothing. Coincidentally, perhaps quite a good deal." He gestured meaningful apology. "The details will not arrive through regular diplomatic channels until tomorrow morning, but I could not be certain of what you knew and what you did not without asking." He gestured meaningfully. "Our mutual confidants have their own sources. Because of what happened on Dawn, the Bwyl can now spew any tales they like. Whatever their superficial veracity, they will not be believed. Dawn has destroyed their credibility as a responsible clan. Anything they choose to say from now on will be regarded as a fabrication."

Fanielle mined her memory. "I remember reading something about

Dawn recently. The usual mundane fodder that those of us in the diplomatic service are expected to assimilate. Wasn't some kind of elaborate seminar or multispecies conclave going to be held there?"

"You are scurrying down the right burrow, but to the wrong destination," he corrected her with utmost finesse. "The term you are seeking in Low Thranx is *drim!!ata.*"

"Oh, that's right." She remembered now. "A fair. Something to promote interspecies harmony and understanding while hopefully making a little money on the side. It was to be quite a production, I recall now. The locals were putting everything they could muster into the effort, hoping it would raise their profile on the colonial scene. Planetary promotion, investment opportunities, tourism—that sort of thing."

Lyrkenparmew gesticulated sharp irony. "If it was attention they were seeking, they more than achieved their objective. But not for the reasons you might think." Emphasizing the importance of what he was about to say, he switched seamlessly to speaking in High Thranx. "Fan'l Anju, this has been an eventful succession of correlative time-parts. It seems that elements of the very same renegade clan that attacked you and Haflunormet at the Retreat of Xer!kex planned to disrupt this fair, setting off bombs and shooting visitors indiscriminately. By coincidence, the identical notion appears to have appealed to a group of similarly xenophobic humans who call themselves *the Preservers.*" He gestured confusion. "I am always astonished at the organizations and individuals formed to promote destruction who identify themselves with names like *Preserver*, or *Savior*, or *Rescuer*, and the like.

"Unaware at first of each other's existence and aims, these two groups apparently learned of their parallel intentions and presence sometime before attempting to carry them out. The scheme propounded by the human group was particularly insidious." He leaned toward her, bowing slightly from his thorax.

"That both of these antisocial organizations were found out and reported just in time for the domestic patrollers to prevent widespread disaster was due to the good work and intervention of a pair of theologians, or padres as they call themselves, who notified the local authorities. As a consequence, many hundreds of lives were saved and a diplomatic disaster was averted." Lyrkenparmew executed a gesture involving his entire upper body that Fanielle recognized as indicative of extreme regret. "Unfortunately, both of these heroic ecclesiastics perished in the course of the operation."

"That's too bad," she remarked sincerely.

"For them, yes. And personally, I would prefer they had survived." He straightened. "But since they did not, their unintentional sacrifice, combined with the debacle on Comagrave that has been ascribed to the AAnn, presents us with an exceptional opportunity."

She rested her hands in her lap. "I don't follow you, Lyrkenparmew."

Compound eyes glittered in the sun as the envoy drew his protective warming garments tighter around him. "One of these ill-starred padres was thranx. His companion was human. Don't you see? Thranx and human give their lives to save humans and thranx." He gestured first-degree significance. "The cause of unification has, inadvertently, acquired its first martyrs."

She considered the possibilities. They were striking. "Did they intend to become martyrs, these two?"

"Most probably not, but it will not matter to the general media that serve both our kind. Among humans, they will be remembered as having given their lives to save babies and innocents. Among my people, they will be thought of as two brave soldiers who sacrificed their bodies to seal a critical opening into a vulnerable burrow. It comes to the same thing. A report filed by two human patrollers who barely survived the final encounter corroborates the details of the matter." He gestured diffidently.

"The fringe belief system to which this pair belonged calls itself the United Church. A grandiose appellation, *crrk!k,* for so modest an organization—though I am told it is gaining adherents at a surprisingly rapid rate. Despite the fact that the sacrifice of their two disciples on Dawn will bring them a considerable amount of beneficial publicity, the leaders of this religious order interestingly want nothing to do with the promoting of it. They are sorry for the death of two of their own, but their doctrine apparently does not believe in or sanction the concept of martyrdom. They say there is no future in it.

"As long as they don't directly oppose our efforts to promote or make use of this sacrifice, be it intentional or otherwise, their indifference won't affect the results." Much intrigued by everything Lyrkenparmew had told her, Fanielle's active brain was starting to rev with possibilities. "And with the Bwyl utterly discredited, as you point out, by their actions, Haflunormet's investigation of the events on Comagrave becomes just one more apocryphal rant against closer cooperation." For the first time in many days, a smile began to spread across her suntanned countenance. "This is wonderful!"

"Yes, *ri!t,* wonderful it is, Fan'l." Moving closer, he extended his b-thorax in order to be able to reach and caress her forehead with both antennae. The touch was so light as to be nearly imperceptible. "I have been in frantic consultation with our supporters inside the Great Hive. They agree that now is the time to make an all-out push for amalgamation. Our supporters on Earth concur. A formal recommendation based on our earlier proposals is to be made in your government sometime during the Second Season of Gathering, when the publicity from the incidents on Dawn and Comagrave is predicted to have achieved maximum visibility. Both political efforts will be closely coordinated."

She was nodding understandingly, her face lit by rising excitement. "I'll do everything I can to help from my circumscribed position, of course."

"It may not be so circumscribed as you think. You are to be elevated in status. Raised to a higher level of significance within your profession."

She eyed the insectoid uncertainly. "I've heard nothing about a promotion."

"Sources," the thranx explained with admirable tact. "Do not reject the advancement. It will be useful to our mutual interests."

"Of course," she told him. Reaching over, she plucked a carrot from a row of green sprouts and showed it to the agent. "You can digest some of our food just as we can eat some of yours, so long as it's plant-derived. Have you ever had a carrot? Fresh grown. From my own little patch here." She extended the vegetable.

Taking it in his truhands, Lyrkenparmew inspected the yellow spike uncertainly. "How does one eat it?"

"Raw or cooked. Your mandibles will have no trouble with it. Go on," she urged him. "Try it. I know its composition lies well within the tolerances of your internal chemistry. I wouldn't offer it to you otherwise. Break off the root first and eat it from the bottom."

Hesitantly, the agent followed her instructions. Placing the end of the carrot between his mandibles, he bit down with all four, snapping off a piece between them. Having nothing to chew with, he had to wait for it to make the journey to his upper, grinding gut. The release of exotic, alien juices followed.

"That is . . . delightful," he finally was able to tell her. "A c'rt, you called it?"

"Carrot," she corrected him. If she could learn the two principal thranx dialects, then the agent could master Terranglo. Although *c'rt* had a nice, succinct ring to it. Perhaps the word could be compromised. Another addition to that strange multispecies patois its adherents were calling symbospeech, she decided absently.

"Whether it wants to or not, this United Church is going to gain a number of new followers as a result of all the fanfare. I suppose I'm going to have to study up on it further in case I'm asked to comment." She let out a resigned sigh. "These faddish creeds come and go, especially in an era of galactic exploration."

"Yes," Lyrkenparmew agreed. "Such caprices are common among

the thranx as well. The great majority are inevitably defined by their transitory nature. I'm sure that when the incident on Dawn becomes part of the public memory as opposed to an item of current interest, the same fate will befall this sect as well."

She nodded as she fondly surveyed the rest of the garden. "It certainly sounds like an eccentric little philosophy. Maybe there will at least be a laugh or two to be had from looking into it."

"Hopefully," Lyrkenparmew added. "For professional reasons only, of course."

"Of course," she agreed. "What else?"

From above, the benign sun of Hivehom shone down on their friendship, on the little garden in the diplomat compound, on the rest of the human settlement called Azerick, and on the dawning of a great many unknown but exhilarating possibilities that were fraught with promise.

22

Lord Naasab IV was brooding in the gallery when Eiipul II approached him. Below, the magnificent Great Hall of the People, the center of Blassussar and the locus of the Empire, was clearing out, the crowd of notables apportioning a babble of hissing conversation in their wake. The emperor himself had long since departed, leaving his constituents in the form of their representative nobles to debate and discuss any remaining business. It was the business that was not resolved, that could not be resolved, that troubled Naasab and left him pensive and ill at ease in mind and belly.

A gesture of greeting from Eiipul indicated that his fellow peer felt similarly. As if to further confirm his visitor's mind-set, one pair of eyelids remained half closed as he spoke.

"I fear, *rssst*, that regarding a certain matter too many of our colleaguess refusse to pull their headss out of the ssand."

Naasab was glad to see that, if nothing else, he was not alone in his concern. "We sspeak of the ssame certain matter, I am ssure."

Eiipul gestured second-degree concurrence. "Many feel there iss nothing more we can do, yet we cannot jusst ssprawl idly asside and concede to the inexorable. My family did not reach itss pinnacle of prominence by ssquatting alongsside the water hollowss and watching otherss catch the swimmerss."

His counterpart gestured almost impertinently. Eiipul forgave the discourtesy because he understood Naasab's distress. It was no less than his own.

"Let the otherss vacillate and fight with wordss if that iss all they can do. The emperor iss no fool. If we can proposse a coursse of action, he will ssee that it iss implemented. What ideass have you?"

Eiipul slapped his stomach with the tip of his tail, a sharp, smacking sound that did not travel far in the enormous, gold-toned gathering chamber. "Nothing sspecific, *gtssk*. As you know, I am on the committee that iss trying to undersstand what happened on Vussissica. We have yet to ressolve the many contradicting reportss. Thuss far the one point that everyone can agree upon iss that it hass been a complete and utter diplomatic dissaster. Chasstissement sshould already have been meted out, but no one can agree on who iss ressponssible for what. In every asspect, a truly unssettling epissode."

Naasab gestured agreement, rapidly blinking both sets of double eyelids. "My concern liess more with our notable failure on the disstant human world they call Dawn. A continuing run of bad luck. If not for the intervention of the two sstupid sspiritualisstss, all might have gone as planned. Now, that enterprisse alsso liess in ruinss." In his anger, he parted his jaws to show his tongue as well as all his teeth. "The combined effect of thesse two recent dissasters hass been to bring the bugss and the ssoftsskinss much closser together insstead of driving them apart, as we dessired."

Moving to the edge of the overlook, Eiipul gazed down at the now nearly empty gathering chamber. Glorious episodes from the history of the AAnn—from the race's humble beginnings as barely organized bands fighting for control of herds in the plains of Blassussar, to the wars of unification eventually won by Keisscha the First, to the rapid rise of technology and the eventual expansion of the Empire to other worlds—lined the walls in the form of mosaics fashioned from gemstones and rare metals. Strong light illuminated every corner of the impressive hall, and the sand that formed the floor was fashioned of specially ground synthetic corundum that gave it the appearance of a single multifaceted jewel. The dais where the emperor sat was as empty as the rows of individual reporting stations, and no informative holos floated free in the dry, heated air.

"Doess a closser union of the two lesser sspeciess really pose ssuch a threat? Are we perhapss not overreacting, my friend, and thosse of our compeerss who have jusst departed are the oness in the right?"

Naasab gestured his unhappiness. Was he about to lose his strongest ally among the members of the Imperial Gathering? "No one sshould forget what happened to the Pitar."

"That sspeciess received what they desserved. I wass never comfortable conssidering them as alliess. An unsstable race."

"Agreed. And now they are no more—thankss to the effortss of humanss and thranx fighting together. My greatesst fear, my friend, iss that thesse two sspeciess cojoined may ressult in ssomething far more powerful than the ssum of their individual partss."

"I, too, am concerned, as you know. But it may be that this proposed union of theirss, thiss Commonwealth, will be like a human mating: the living together more contentiouss than the courtsship."

Naasab gestured admiration for his counterpart's knowledge. He would not have suspected that the quiet Eiipul might be the master of arcane alien erudition. It was often the quiet ones, he reflected, who hid in the sand to spring on the unwary from behind. Henceforth, he would measure his comments with more care lest he reveal something that in the future might prove personally damaging. Eiipul would do no less, he knew. By such means did the ever-competitive AAnn acquire status and gain advancement. For the moment, however, the truce relationship between them was sound. As lords of the Empire, they could advance no farther—at least until the emperor began to show signs of mental or physical weakness.

"What of our dissappointing ssupporterss among the humanss?" Eiipul was asking.

Naasab hissed resignedly. "Many dead or captured on thiss Dawn world. Not all, I am told, but enough to prevent them from attempting anything ssimilar in the immediate future. I have taken sstepss to ssee to it that their organization continuess to receive the necessary funds to susstain them. They will go to ground until the furor over the incident on Dawn hass died down, then attempt to ressume their activitiess on our behalf. As for their thranx equivalentss, you know that we have no influence among them. No bug will accept assistance from an AAnn. That doess not mean they will not be usseful to uss in the future; only that we will, as alwayss, have no control over their actions."

Eiipul gestured understanding. Though he had much work to do, he continued to linger. Naasab always had interesting information to impart, and it was always good to know what so resourceful a rival was up to. Besides which, they shared many similar interests.

"If thiss union comess about, we will ssimply have to deal with it. It doess not pressage the end of our expanssion. Nothing can prevent that."

"Truly," Naasab agreed, adding a gesture of first-degree assent. "But it could make eassy thingss difficult, and ssimple undertakingss complex. Better to avoid complication where possible. It certainly would make harder bringing the obsstinate bugss to heel."

"You will ssee." Eiipul wished to depart on a positive note. "The bugss and the humanss will not get along. They are too different, far more sso than the humanss and oursselvess. Even if it should come to pass, this Commonwealth will collapsse of itss own inherent contradictionss. I am confident in that."

Wellness for you, Naasab thought. He wondered if he would live long enough to see Eiipul's prediction come to pass. He hoped so, because he sincerely feared the consequences for the Empire if it did not.

Truly, *fsssst . . .*

There was so much to do. Integrating colonies was one thing. Merging two entirely different political and social systems developed over thousands of years by two very different species reduced the complexities of the former task to insignificance.

Ordinary folk on both sides would notice no change for some time. Average citizens did not travel between worlds, did not participate in interstellar commerce or politics, and cared little for anything beyond the realm of their daily lives that did not impact on them directly. Politicians would be affected, and business folk, and of course the military. The latter would have perhaps the easiest time of it. Not only did warriors of different species possess an innate understanding of a profession whose basic tenets did not vary widely because of mere shape, but they had already cooperated closely with one another during the Pitarian War.

Changes would first manifest themselves in the largest, most cosmicpolitan cities. Humans would be able to move freely through the teeming thranx burrows, while their eight-limbed counterparts would no longer be restricted to a few specific locations on Earth and a couple of its more populous colonies. Without endless inspections and dozens of restrictions, trade would expand exponentially. Cultural exchanges of the kind that had taken place on the world of Dawn could proceed without reams of government paperwork, on scales both larger and more intimate. Integration did not happen overnight, but happen it would.

The announcement of the impending unification was greeted, except by those who had opposed it for so long, with a mixture of excitement, anticipation, and uncertainty. Since nothing like it had ever been tried before, no one was quite sure how it was going to work, or what would happen from day to day. But both sides went at it with a will.

The Terran government proceeded to orchestrate a number of grandiose celebrations, with the largest taking place in or near the most impressive cities; more modest festivities were contrived for smaller conurbations, and local demonstrations occupied the time and attention of towns and country. Among the thranx, the occasion was marked by congratulations on a much more individual and personal level, following which everyone went back to work. Above it all hovered a feeling of general satisfaction: The thranx had gotten what they wanted, and the humans what they needed.

After weeks of speeches, parades, demonstrations, fireworks, feasts, gatherings in stellar locations both astonishing and ordinary by the starships of both civilizations, hours of reciprocal programming by the media of both species, endlessly repetitive programs of the Why This Is Good For You kind, debates both tumultuous and politic, and a good deal of soul-searching among ordinary citizens, the public at large of both species discovered something else they had in common: the ability to rapidly get fed up with self-appointed experts and so-called specialists and zealous politicians who were determined to tell them what they should be doing and why. So when the time arrived to actually formalize the unification instead of simply praise or weigh it, the actual event came as something of a blissful anticlimax that was ignored by most folk, who were busy getting on with their lives.

The site chosen for the signing of the Articles of Amalgamation was as grand as the canyon after which it was named. Not far from the small amphitheater chosen for the official ceremony, moving walkways suspended from spidery supports carried a steady stream of tourists from the rim and its spectacular perspective to the surging, ice-cold river at the bottom. Most were intent on the scenery and took no notice of the cluster of diplomats and media reporters milling about nearby. A few thranx, Fanielle noted with satisfaction, were among the continuous stream of gawkers descending into the ancient depths carved by the river. In the heat of midafternoon they needed no supplemental attire, though each wore a compact humidifier over their breathing spicules. Of such incremental developments as mutual enjoyment of time's wonders were unbreakable bonds forged.

Stuck near the back of the gathering, but fortunate to have acquired an invitation at that, she listened with interest to the speeches whose brevity belied their significance. One by one, the various human and thranx dignitaries mounted the temporary dais, their physiques if not their words much reduced in perspective by the immense red rock panorama that filled the horizon behind them. The ritual could as well have taken place on Hivehom, she knew, or some neutral world, but the thranx had deferred to the wishes of their new human consociates. Though equally as fond of pomp and ritual as the bipeds, albeit on a much reduced scale, they were understanding when their mammalian counterparts asked if the first signing could be held on Earth. A second, equivalent ceremony would take place later in the high ceremonial burrows of Hivehom.

That kind of understanding, she reflected, was not only what was going to go a long way toward making the new union work, it was something the pysch techs insisted humankind had lacked, and had been looking for, ever since the species had first come down from the trees millennia ago.

Eventually the speech making, with its simultaneous translation, lurched to an end. Formal documents were signed, and initialed, and signed again, until there was no more room on paper or plastic for markings of the duly appointed representatives of either species. As each was completed, holos of the actual documents appeared in the air before the audience. These were broadcast to watchers whose distance from the site could sometimes be measured in kilometers and sometimes in parsecs. As each instrument was completed, it was simultaneously rendered in blocks of polished marble and sheets of anodized titanium that would more readily memorialize the gravity of the occasion.

When it was over, there was much gratified shaking of hands and touching of antennae. Fanielle was particularly struck by the moment when the current head of the United Church, the Fourth Last Resort David Malkezinski, grasped a truhand of the venerable Tri-eint Arlenduva while her antennae dipped forward to make contact with his forehead. Far from vanishing as she had once imagined it would, the still-evolving creed founded by a human minister and his thranx counterpart had continued to expand, swiftly gaining new adherents among human and thranx alike. If anything, its overall influence with the public at large had expanded even faster.

Counted among its followers was the diplomat Fanielle Anjou, recently promoted to assistant councilor for human affairs on Hivehom. It was about as significant a post as there was to be had in the rapidly reorganizing and consolidating governments.

As she stood chatting with friends and associates, doing her best to avoid the media, a small hand tugged at her arm. Eric Haf-Lyr Anjou looked up at her out of alert, anxious eyes that were largely indifferent to the import of the ceremony that had just concluded.

"Mom, Mom—Barehtezen and Jacque want to hike down to Indian Gardens. Can I go? Can I? Hey, did you know she smells like apple blossoms?"

She smiled down at him. "Of course you can go, Eric. Just make sure you and Jacque keep a close eye on Bar. There are plenty of fountains along the trail, and she'll adore the fact that it gets hotter the deeper you descend, but you know how quickly thranx can parch in this climate." She indicated the high, dry mountain country where they were standing.

"Aw, she'll be all right. She's wearing her humidifier, and she promised to use all six legs at all times, even on the easy parts."

"Make sure she keeps hydrated. Have a good time, and be back up here before six." She checked her chronometer. "We have to get up early tomorrow to catch the transit to the shuttleport."

He nodded, his words lost in the crowd as he yelled back at her while racing off in the opposite direction. "I know. I can't wait to get back to the burrow!"

Kids, she thought. Progeny. Offspring, with the emphasis on *spring*. Waking up to a new universe every day. Only tomorrow, it would be more than an aphorism. It would be for real. She wondered how it would all work out: the amalgamating of two radically different species, an unprecedented fusion of arthropod and anthropoid. Nothing like it had ever been attempted in the portion of the galaxy humankind had come to know. Just how close, how intimate could it become? Would the old adage "Don't let the bedbugs bite" come to take on an entirely new meaning? Or would it lead to, if not a golden age for humankind, at least a more settled and confident one?

She was wandering, she knew, and when she let her mind wander, her thoughts inevitably degenerated into flippancy. She wished she could live another couple of hundred years or so, long enough for any lasting doubts to be resolved. That was not possible. She let out a regretful sigh. We're too transitory, she mused. We don't live long enough to really learn anything. I need another five centuries.

It was not to be. Flesh is not so accommodating, and we all of us die just when we've acquired the minimum necessary wisdom to graduate the first grade. The universe belonged to her son now. To him, and to his new friends, even if they did have two extra sets of limbs, bulging eyes, and feathery stalks growing out of their foreheads.

To the universe of the Commonwealth.

ABOUT THE AUTHOR

ALAN DEAN FOSTER has written in a variety of genres, including hard science fiction, fantasy, horror, detective, western, historical, and contemporary fiction. He is also the author of numerous nonfiction articles on film, science, and scuba diving, as well as novel versions of several films, including *Star Wars*, the first three *Alien* films, and *Alien Nation*. His novel *Cyber Way* won the Southwest Book Award for Fiction in 1990, the first science fiction work ever to do so.

Foster's love of the far-away and exotic has led him to travel extensively. He's lived in Tahiti and French Polynesia, traveled to Europe, Asia, and throughout the Pacific, and has explored the back roads of Tanzania and Kenya. He has rappelled into New Mexico's fabled Lechugilla Cave, panfried piranha (lots of bones, tastes a lot like trout) in Peru, white-water rafted the length of the Zambezi's Batoka Gorge, and driven solo the length and breadth of Namibia.

Foster and his wife, JoAnn Oxley, reside in Prescott, Arizona, in a house built of brick that was salvaged from a turn-of-the-century miners' brothel. He is presently at work on several new novels and media projects.

For further information on the Commonwealth and other worlds of Alan Dean Foster, try this Web site: www.alandeanfoster.com.